# SCRIBBLENAUTS™
## UNMASKED

### A DC COMICS ADVENTURE

**JOSH ELDER**
writer

**ADAM ARCHER**
artist & collection cover artist

**IAN HERRING**
colorist

**SAIDA TEMOFONTE**
letterer

special thanks to **5TH CELL**

SUPERMAN created by **JERRY SIEGEL** and **JOE SHUSTER**
by special arrangement with the **JERRY SIEGEL FAMILY**

**ALEX ANTONE** Editor – Original Series
**RACHEL PINNELAS** Editor
**ROBBIN BROSTERMAN** Design Director – Books
**SARABETH KETT** Publication Design

**HANK KANALZ** Senior VP – Vertigo & Integrated Publishing

**AMIT DESAI** Senior VP – Marketing and Franchise Management
**AMY GENKINS** Senior VP – Business and Legal Affairs
**NAIRI GARDINER** Senior VP – Finance
**JEFF BOISON** VP – Publishing Planning
**MARK CHIARELLO** VP – Art Direction and Design
**JOHN CUNNINGHAM** VP – Marketing
**TERRI CUNNINGHAM** VP – Editorial Administration
**LARRY GANEM** VP – Talent Relations and Services
**ALISON GILL** Senior VP – Manufacturing and Operations
**JAY KOGAN** VP – Business and Legal Affairs, Publishing
**JACK MAHAN** VP – Business Affairs, Talent
**NICK NAPOLITANO** VP – Manufacturing Administration
**SUE POHJA** VP – Book Sales
**FRED RUIZ** VP – Manufacturing Operations
**COURTNEY SIMMONS** Senior VP – Publicity
**BOB WAYNE** Senior VP – Sales

SCRIBBLENAUTS UNMASKED: A DC COMICS ADVENTURE

J-GN
SCRIBBLENAUTS
441-5520

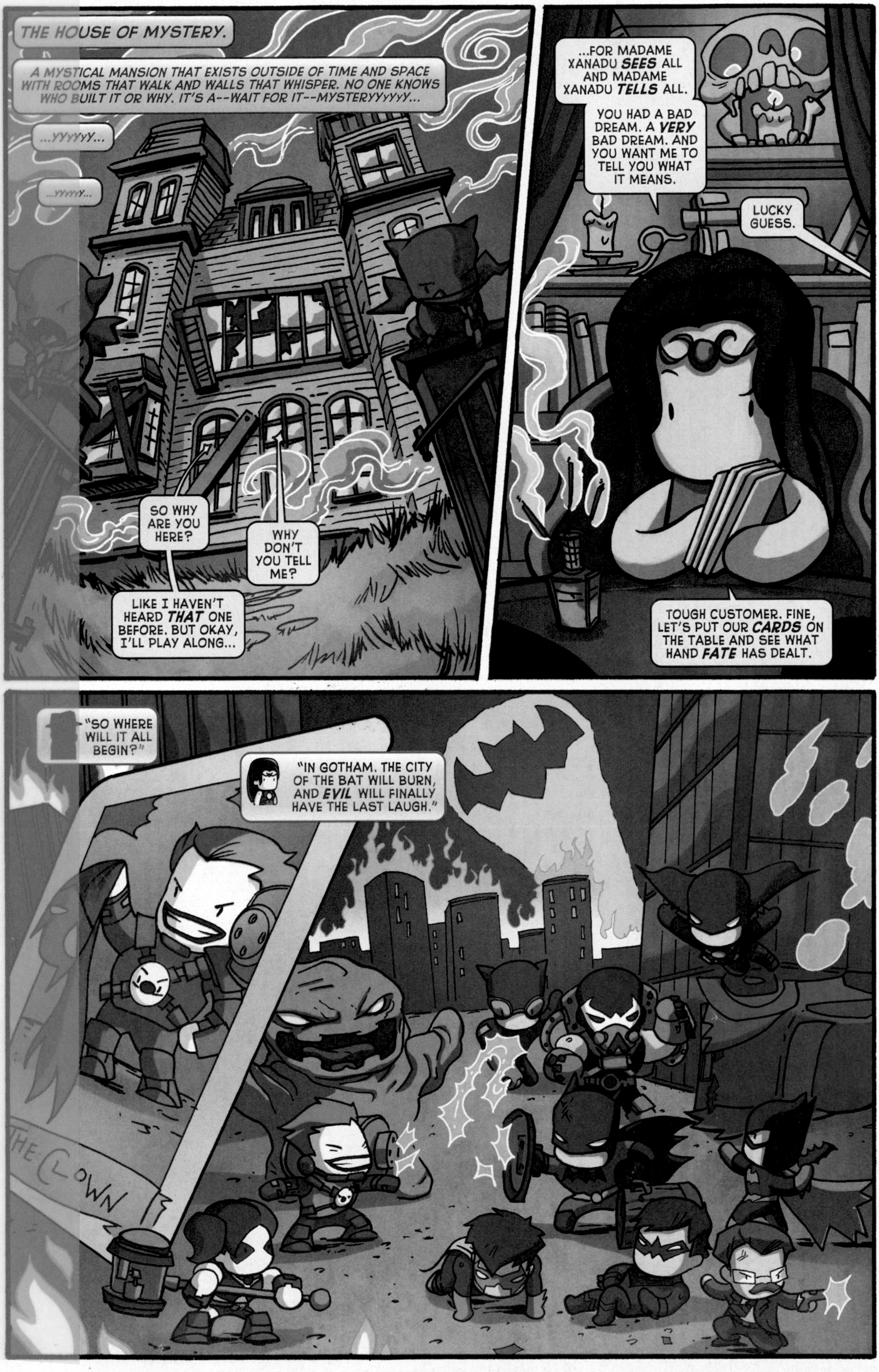

THE HOUSE OF MYSTERY.
A MYSTICAL MANSION THAT EXISTS OUTSIDE OF TIME AND SPACE WITH ROOMS THAT WALK AND WALLS THAT WHISPER. NO ONE KNOWS WHO BUILT IT OR WHY. IT'S A--WAIT FOR IT--MYSTERYYYYYY...
...YYYYYY...
...YYYYY...
SO WHY ARE YOU HERE?
WHY DON'T YOU TELL ME?
LIKE I HAVEN'T HEARD THAT ONE BEFORE. BUT OKAY, I'LL PLAY ALONG...
...FOR MADAME XANADU SEES ALL AND MADAME XANADU TELLS ALL.
YOU HAD A BAD DREAM. A VERY BAD DREAM. AND YOU WANT ME TO TELL YOU WHAT IT MEANS.
LUCKY GUESS.
TOUGH CUSTOMER. FINE, LET'S PUT OUR CARDS ON THE TABLE AND SEE WHAT HAND FATE HAS DEALT.
"SO WHERE WILL IT ALL BEGIN?"
"IN GOTHAM. THE CITY OF THE BAT WILL BURN, AND EVIL WILL FINALLY HAVE THE LAST LAUGH."
THE CLOWN

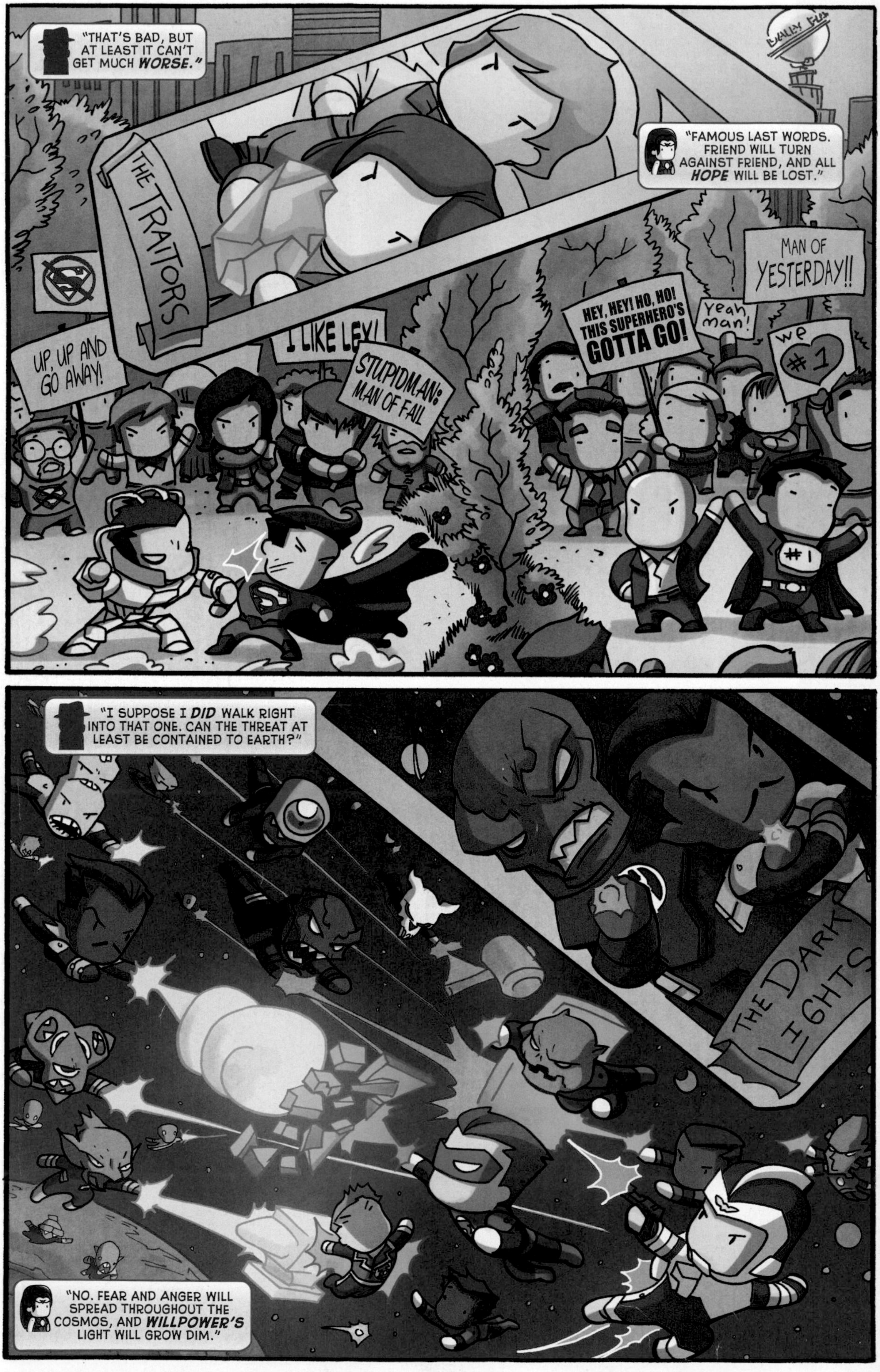
"THAT'S BAD, BUT AT LEAST IT CAN'T GET MUCH WORSE."
THE TRAITORS
"FAMOUS LAST WORDS. FRIEND WILL TURN AGAINST FRIEND, AND ALL HOPE WILL BE LOST."
MAN OF YESTERDAY!!
UP, UP AND GO AWAY!
I LIKE LEX!
STUPIDMAN: MAN OF FAIL
HEY, HEY! HO, HO! THIS SUPERHERO'S GOTTA GO!
Yeah man!
we #1
#1
"I SUPPOSE I DID WALK RIGHT INTO THAT ONE. CAN THE THREAT AT LEAST BE CONTAINED TO EARTH?"
THE DARK LIGHTS
"NO. FEAR AND ANGER WILL SPREAD THROUGHOUT THE COSMOS, AND WILLPOWER'S LIGHT WILL GROW DIM."

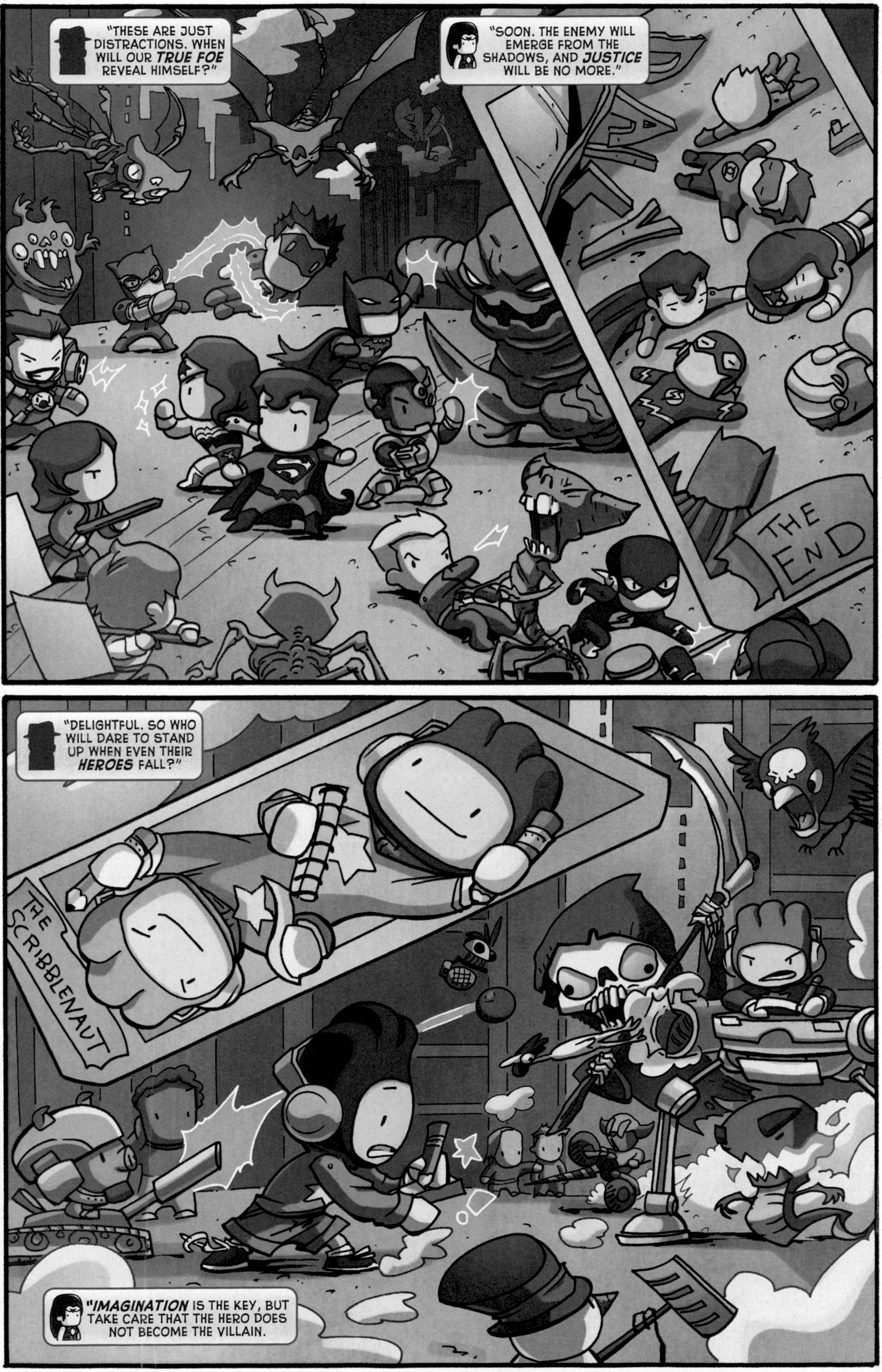
"THESE ARE JUST DISTRACTIONS. WHEN WILL OUR ***TRUE FOE*** REVEAL HIMSELF?"
"SOON. THE ENEMY WILL EMERGE FROM THE SHADOWS, AND ***JUSTICE*** WILL BE NO MORE."
THE END
"DELIGHTFUL. SO WHO WILL DARE TO STAND UP WHEN EVEN THEIR ***HEROES*** FALL?"
THE SCRIBBLENAUT
"***IMAGINATION*** IS THE KEY, BUT TAKE CARE THAT THE HERO DOES NOT BECOME THE VILLAIN.

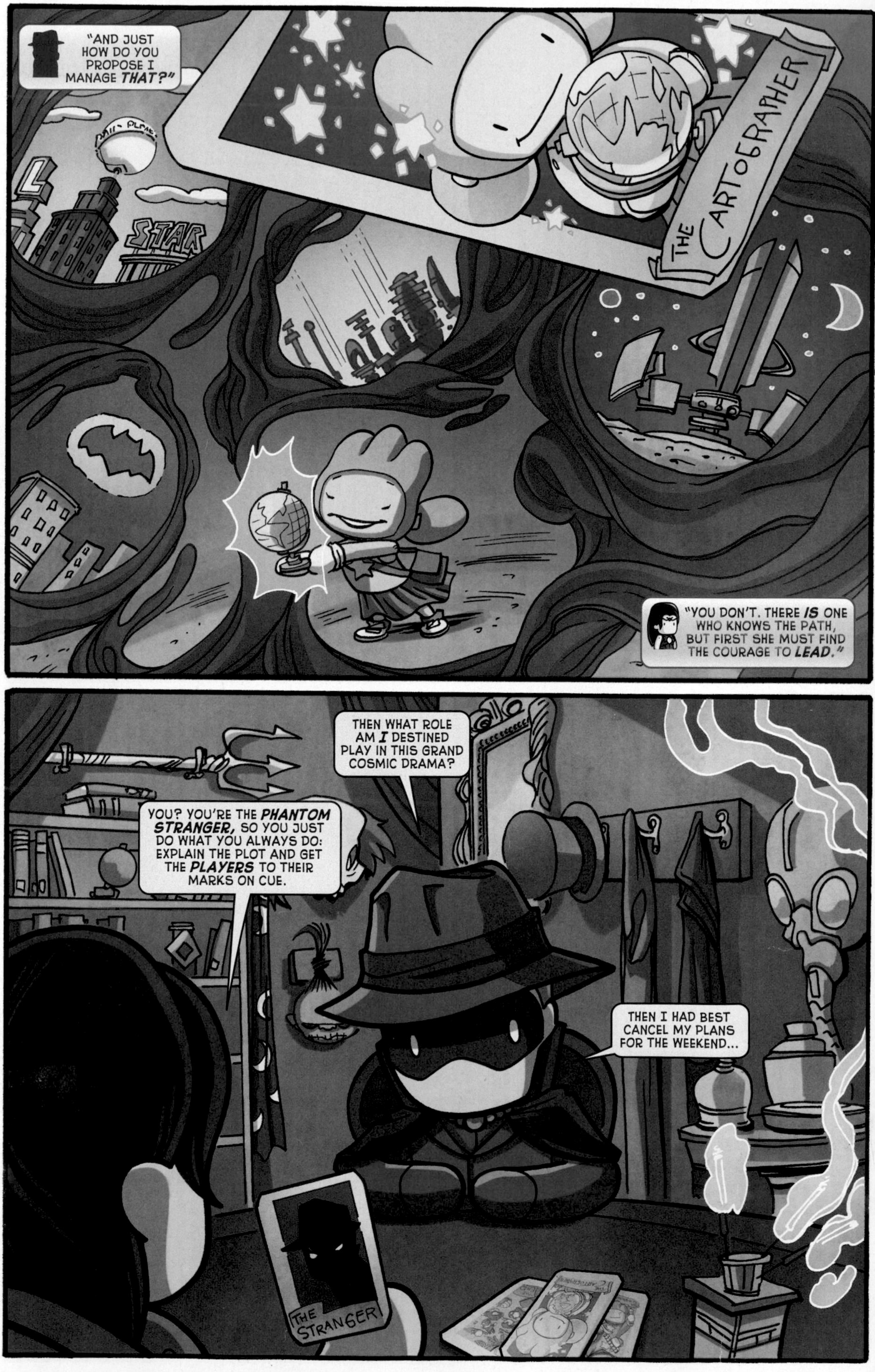
"AND JUST HOW DO YOU PROPOSE I MANAGE THAT?"
STAR
THE CARTOGRAPHER
"YOU DON'T. THERE IS ONE WHO KNOWS THE PATH, BUT FIRST SHE MUST FIND THE COURAGE TO LEAD."
THEN WHAT ROLE AM I DESTINED PLAY IN THIS GRAND COSMIC DRAMA?
YOU? YOU'RE THE PHANTOM STRANGER, SO YOU JUST DO WHAT YOU ALWAYS DO: EXPLAIN THE PLOT AND GET THE PLAYERS TO THEIR MARKS ON CUE.
THEN I HAD BEST CANCEL MY PLANS FOR THE WEEKEND...
THE STRANGER

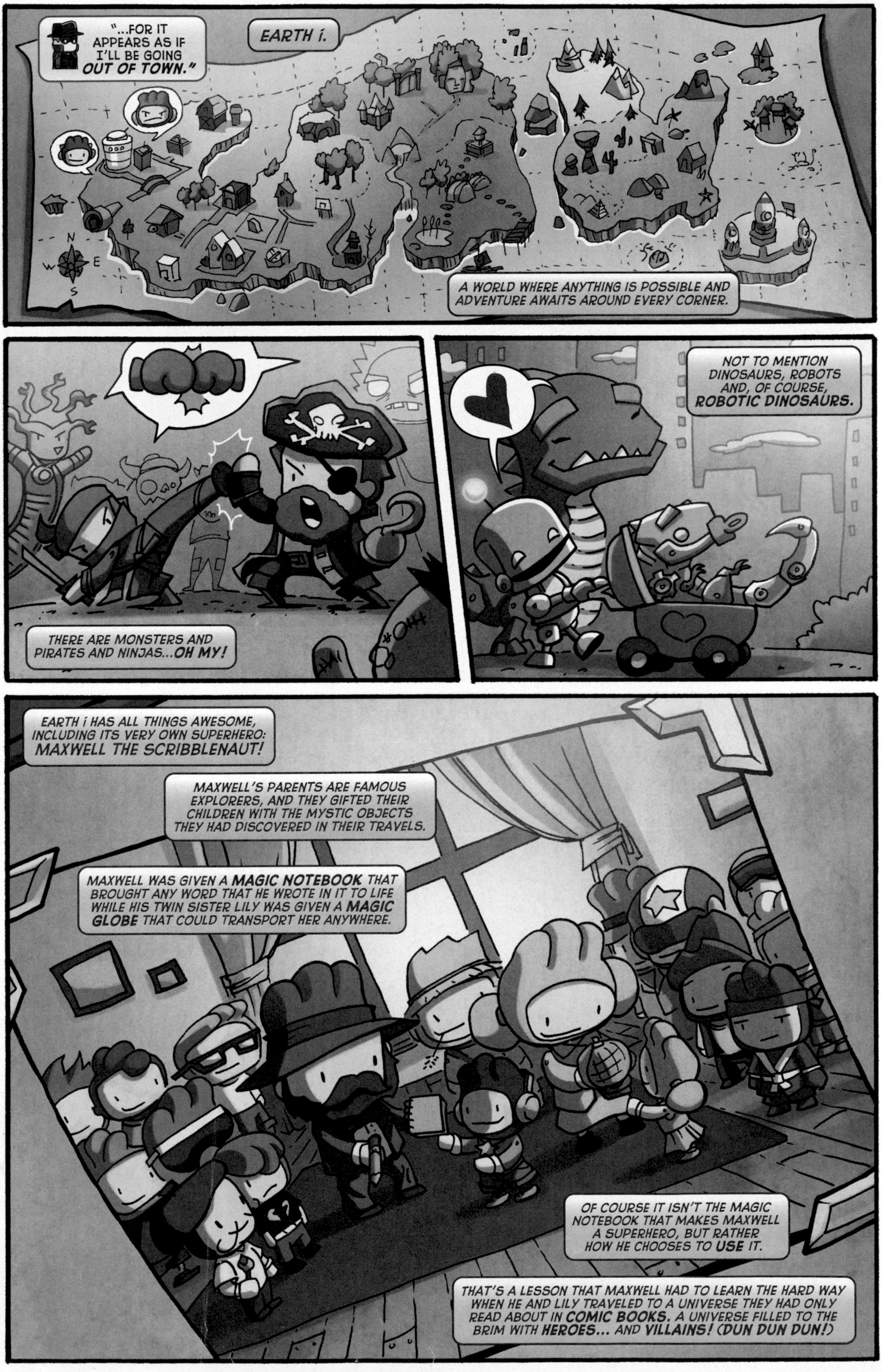
"...FOR IT APPEARS AS IF I'LL BE GOING OUT OF TOWN."
EARTH i.
N
W
E
S
A WORLD WHERE ANYTHING IS POSSIBLE AND ADVENTURE AWAITS AROUND EVERY CORNER.
THERE ARE MONSTERS AND PIRATES AND NINJAS...OH MY!
NOT TO MENTION DINOSAURS, ROBOTS AND, OF COURSE, ROBOTIC DINOSAURS.
EARTH i HAS ALL THINGS AWESOME, INCLUDING ITS VERY OWN SUPERHERO: MAXWELL THE SCRIBBLENAUT!
MAXWELL'S PARENTS ARE FAMOUS EXPLORERS, AND THEY GIFTED THEIR CHILDREN WITH THE MYSTIC OBJECTS THEY HAD DISCOVERED IN THEIR TRAVELS.
MAXWELL WAS GIVEN A MAGIC NOTEBOOK THAT BROUGHT ANY WORD THAT HE WROTE IN IT TO LIFE WHILE HIS TWIN SISTER LILY WAS GIVEN A MAGIC GLOBE THAT COULD TRANSPORT HER ANYWHERE.
OF COURSE IT ISN'T THE MAGIC NOTEBOOK THAT MAKES MAXWELL A SUPERHERO, BUT RATHER HOW HE CHOOSES TO USE IT.
THAT'S A LESSON THAT MAXWELL HAD TO LEARN THE HARD WAY WHEN HE AND LILY TRAVELED TO A UNIVERSE THEY HAD ONLY READ ABOUT IN COMIC BOOKS. A UNIVERSE FILLED TO THE BRIM WITH HEROES... AND VILLAINS! (DUN DUN DUN!)

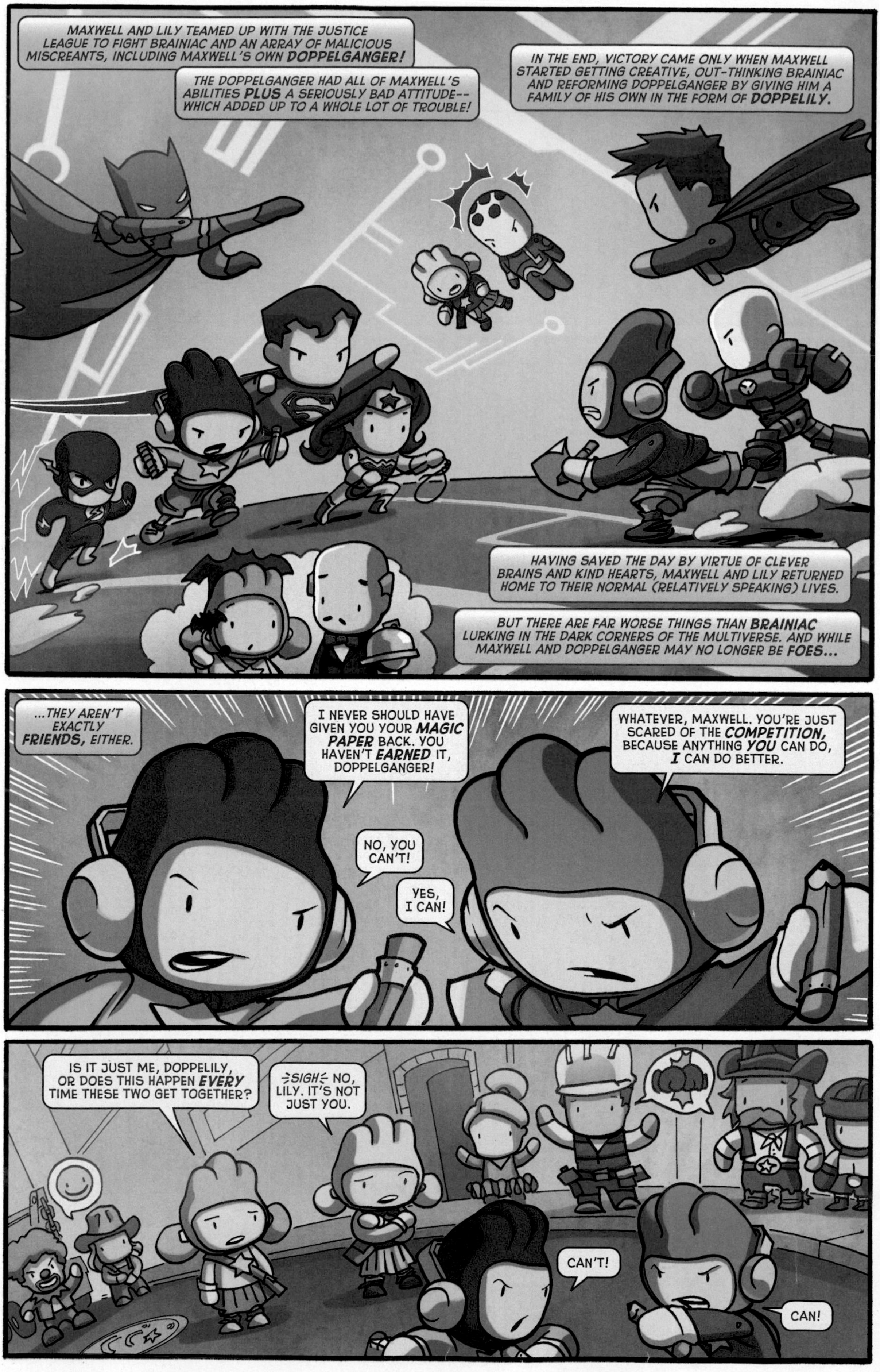
MAXWELL AND LILY TEAMED UP WITH THE JUSTICE LEAGUE TO FIGHT BRAINIAC AND AN ARRAY OF MALICIOUS MISCREANTS, INCLUDING MAXWELL'S OWN DOPPELGANGER!
THE DOPPELGANGER HAD ALL OF MAXWELL'S ABILITIES PLUS A SERIOUSLY BAD ATTITUDE-- WHICH ADDED UP TO A WHOLE LOT OF TROUBLE!
IN THE END, VICTORY CAME ONLY WHEN MAXWELL STARTED GETTING CREATIVE, OUT-THINKING BRAINIAC AND REFORMING DOPPELGANGER BY GIVING HIM A FAMILY OF HIS OWN IN THE FORM OF DOPPELILY.
HAVING SAVED THE DAY BY VIRTUE OF CLEVER BRAINS AND KIND HEARTS, MAXWELL AND LILY RETURNED HOME TO THEIR NORMAL (RELATIVELY SPEAKING) LIVES.
BUT THERE ARE FAR WORSE THINGS THAN BRAINIAC LURKING IN THE DARK CORNERS OF THE MULTIVERSE. AND WHILE MAXWELL AND DOPPELGANGER MAY NO LONGER BE FOES...
...THEY AREN'T EXACTLY FRIENDS, EITHER.
I NEVER SHOULD HAVE GIVEN YOU YOUR MAGIC PAPER BACK. YOU HAVEN'T EARNED IT, DOPPELGANGER!
WHATEVER, MAXWELL. YOU'RE JUST SCARED OF THE COMPETITION, BECAUSE ANYTHING YOU CAN DO, I CAN DO BETTER.
NO, YOU CAN'T!
YES, I CAN!
IS IT JUST ME, DOPPELILY, OR DOES THIS HAPPEN EVERY TIME THESE TWO GET TOGETHER?
SIGH NO, LILY. IT'S NOT JUST YOU.
CAN'T!
CAN!

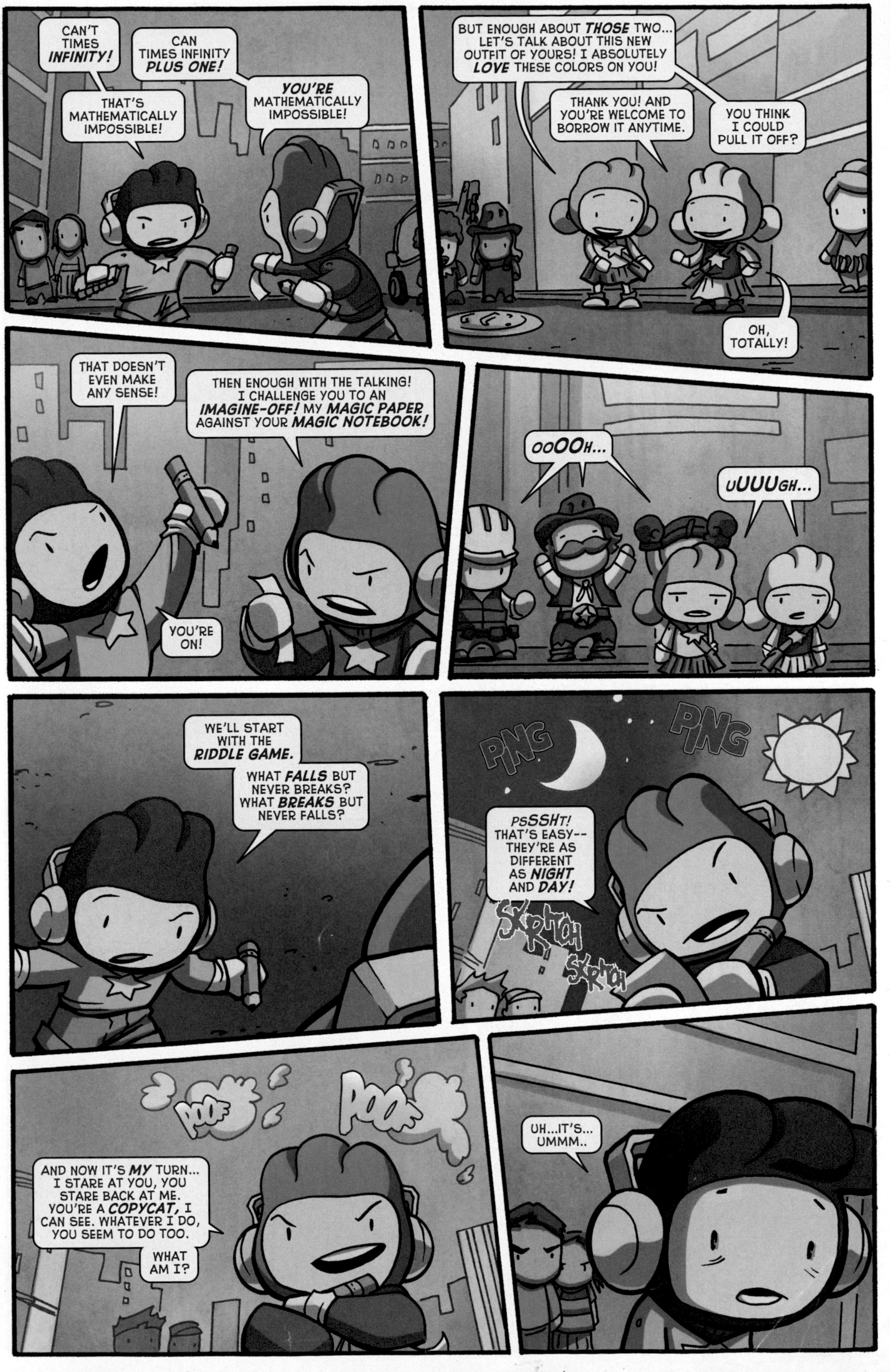
CAN'T TIMES INFINITY!
CAN TIMES INFINITY PLUS ONE!
THAT'S MATHEMATICALLY IMPOSSIBLE!
YOU'RE MATHEMATICALLY IMPOSSIBLE!
BUT ENOUGH ABOUT THOSE TWO... LET'S TALK ABOUT THIS NEW OUTFIT OF YOURS! I ABSOLUTELY LOVE THESE COLORS ON YOU!
THANK YOU! AND YOU'RE WELCOME TO BORROW IT ANYTIME.
YOU THINK I COULD PULL IT OFF?
OH, TOTALLY!
THAT DOESN'T EVEN MAKE ANY SENSE!
THEN ENOUGH WITH THE TALKING! I CHALLENGE YOU TO AN IMAGINE-OFF! MY MAGIC PAPER AGAINST YOUR MAGIC NOTEBOOK!
YOU'RE ON!
OOOOH...
UUUUGH...
WE'LL START WITH THE RIDDLE GAME.
WHAT FALLS BUT NEVER BREAKS? WHAT BREAKS BUT NEVER FALLS?
PING
PING
PSSSHT! THAT'S EASY-- THEY'RE AS DIFFERENT AS NIGHT AND DAY!
SKRITCH
SKRITCH
POOF
POOF
AND NOW IT'S MY TURN... I STARE AT YOU, YOU STARE BACK AT ME. YOU'RE A COPYCAT, I CAN SEE. WHATEVER I DO, YOU SEEM TO DO TOO.
WHAT AM I?
UH...IT'S... UMMM..

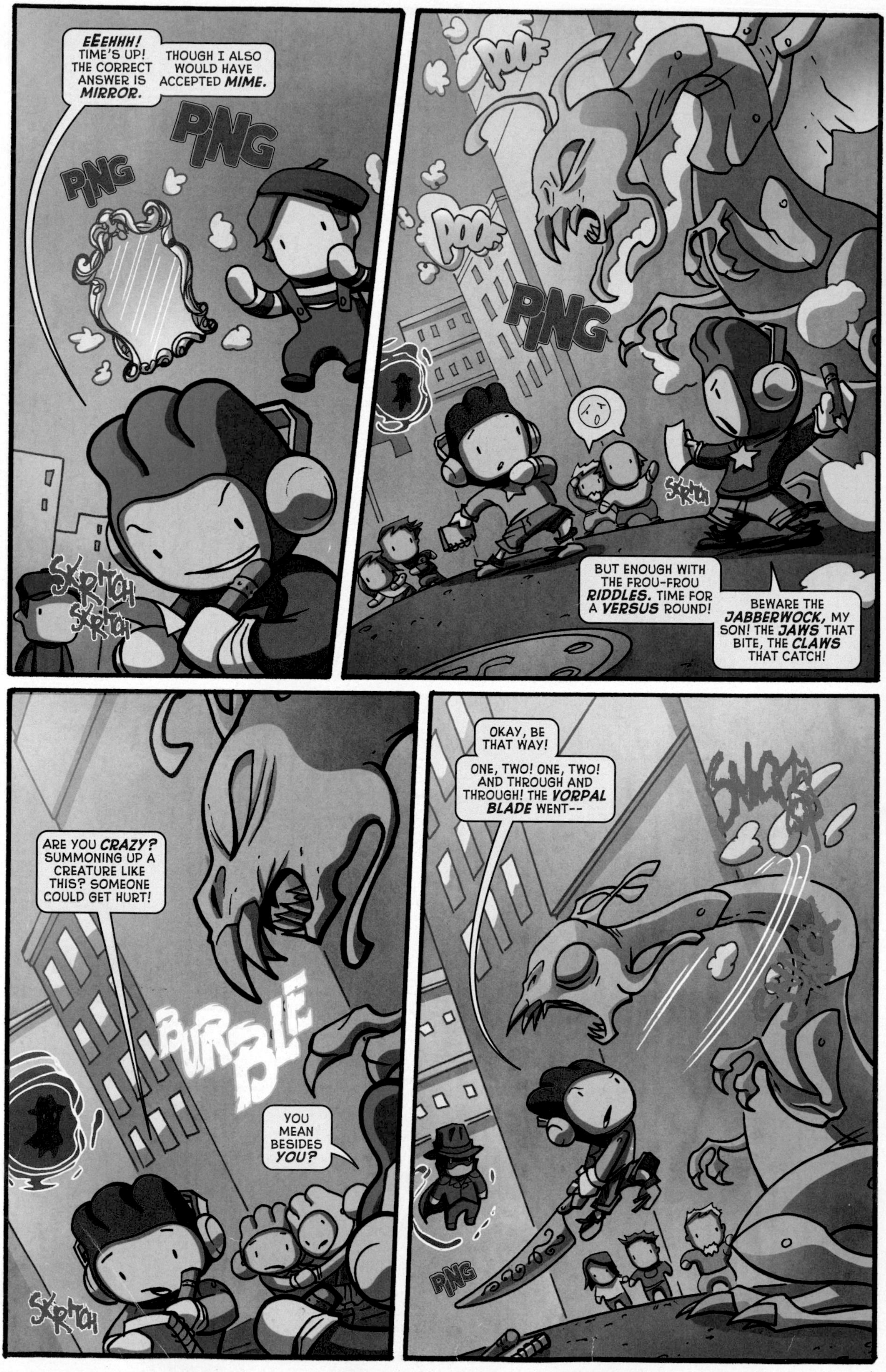
EEEHHH! TIME'S UP! THE CORRECT ANSWER IS MIRROR.
THOUGH I ALSO WOULD HAVE ACCEPTED MIME.
PING
PING
SKRITCH
SKRITCH
POOF
POOF
PING
SKRITCH
BUT ENOUGH WITH THE FROU-FROU RIDDLES. TIME FOR A VERSUS ROUND!
BEWARE THE JABBERWOCK, MY SON! THE JAWS THAT BITE, THE CLAWS THAT CATCH!
ARE YOU CRAZY? SUMMONING UP A CREATURE LIKE THIS? SOMEONE COULD GET HURT!
BURBLE
YOU MEAN BESIDES YOU?
SKRITCH
OKAY, BE THAT WAY!
ONE, TWO! ONE, TWO! AND THROUGH AND THROUGH! THE VORPAL BLADE WENT--
PING

POOF POOF

HOLD UP... WHO'S *THIS* GUY?

YOU MEAN HE'S NOT ONE OF YOURS?

I SERVE NO MAN. I AM--AND SHALL FOREVER BE-- A *STRANGER*.

THE KIND WE'RE NOT SUPPOSED TO TAKE CANDY FROM?

NO, HE'S THE *PHANTOM* STRANGER. THAT'S HIS *NAME*. I LOOKED HIM UP IN MR. BATMAN'S COMPUTER BACK WHEN WE WERE IN THEIR UNIVERSE.

YEAH, HE NEVER AGES, HE CAN WALK ACROSS DIMENSIONS AND DO *ALL SORTS* OF MAGIC-Y STUFF.

BUT WHAT'S HE DOING *HERE*?

I COME SEEKING *HEROES* TO STAND BESIDE THE *JUSTICE LEAGUE* AGAINST A GREAT EVIL THAT THREATENS OUR WORLD.

THE JUSTICE LEAGUE NEEDS *US*? THAT'S ALL YOU HAD TO SAY!

YEAH! WE'LL DO ANYTHING WE CAN!

FOR SURE!

SPEAK FOR *YOURSELVES*. I'M NOT PUTTING MYSELF OUT FOR SOME RANDOM *WEIRDO* IN A NECK CHAIN.

SKETCH

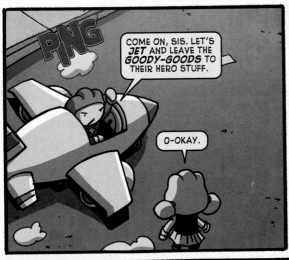

PNG

COME ON, SIS. LET'S *JET* AND LEAVE THE *GOODY-GOODS* TO THEIR HERO STUFF.

O-OKAY.

GOOD LUCK SAVING THE *UNIVERSE* AND STUFF.

GOODBYE.

THIS IS...*UNFORTUNATE.* WE COULD HAVE USED YOUR DOPPELGANGER'S POWERS IN THE BATTLE AHEAD.

WE'LL BE BETTER OFF *WITHOUT* HIM, BELIEVE ME.

THEN WE SHOULD TAKE OUR LEAVE, FOR TIME IS OF THE ESSENCE. LILY, WE WILL NEED TO USE YOUR *MAGIC GLOBE* TO TRANSPORT US ACROSS THE DIMENSIONS.

I CAN MAKE THE JOURNEY MYSELF, BUT I CAN'T TAKE ANYONE WITH ME.

OKAY. BUT EVERYONE BETTER HOLD TIGHT.

BECAUSE IT'S GOING TO BE A *BUMPY RIDE!*

VORP

GOTHAM CITY, HERE WE...

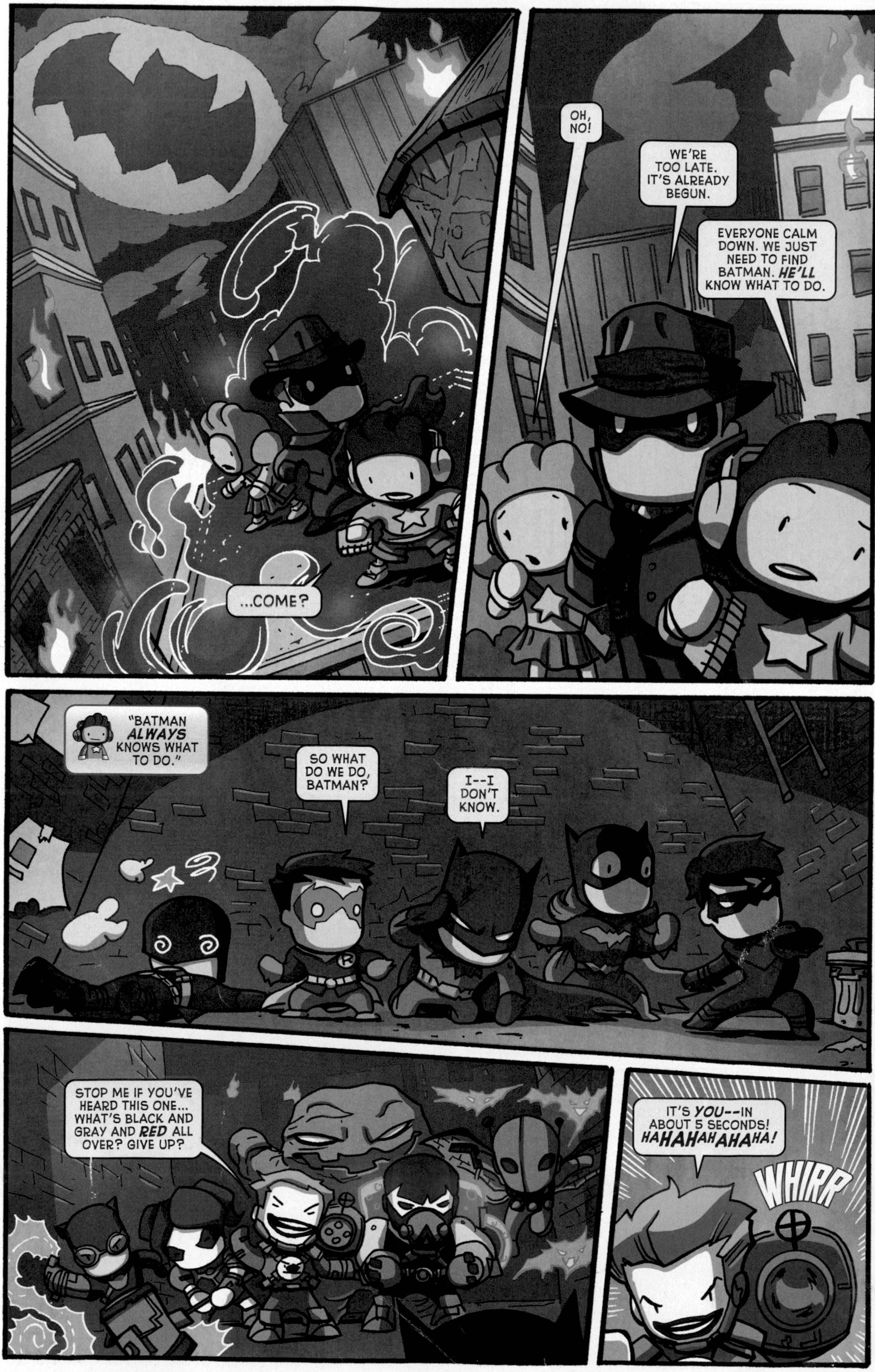
...COME?
OH, NO!
WE'RE TOO LATE. IT'S ALREADY BEGUN.
EVERYONE CALM DOWN. WE JUST NEED TO FIND BATMAN. HE'LL KNOW WHAT TO DO.
"BATMAN ALWAYS KNOWS WHAT TO DO."
SO WHAT DO WE DO, BATMAN?
I--I DON'T KNOW.
STOP ME IF YOU'VE HEARD THIS ONE... WHAT'S BLACK AND GRAY AND RED ALL OVER? GIVE UP?
IT'S YOU--IN ABOUT 5 SECONDS! HAHAHAHAHAHA!
WHIRR

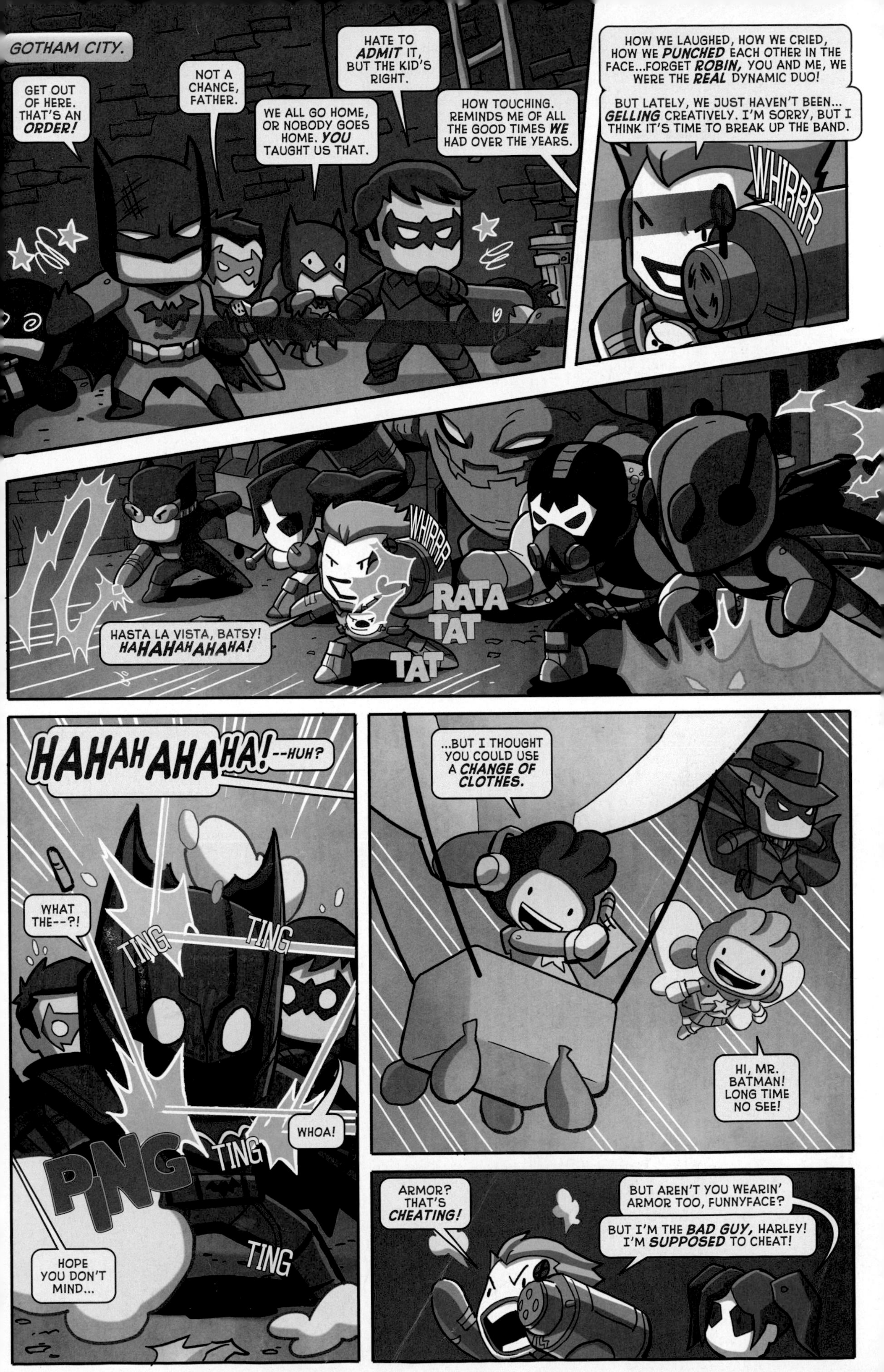

GOTHAM CITY.
GET OUT OF HERE. THAT'S AN ORDER!
NOT A CHANCE, FATHER.
WE ALL GO HOME, OR NOBODY GOES HOME. YOU TAUGHT US THAT.
HATE TO ADMIT IT, BUT THE KID'S RIGHT.
HOW TOUCHING. REMINDS ME OF ALL THE GOOD TIMES WE HAD OVER THE YEARS.
HOW WE LAUGHED, HOW WE CRIED, HOW WE PUNCHED EACH OTHER IN THE FACE...FORGET ROBIN, YOU AND ME, WE WERE THE REAL DYNAMIC DUO!
BUT LATELY, WE JUST HAVEN'T BEEN... GELLING CREATIVELY. I'M SORRY, BUT I THINK IT'S TIME TO BREAK UP THE BAND.
WHIRRR
WHIRRR
HASTA LA VISTA, BATSY! HAHAHAHAHAHA!
RATA TAT TAT
HAHAHAHAHA!--HUH?
WHAT THE--?!
TING
TING
WHOA!
PING
TING
TING
HOPE YOU DON'T MIND...
...BUT I THOUGHT YOU COULD USE A CHANGE OF CLOTHES.
HI, MR. BATMAN! LONG TIME NO SEE!
ARMOR? THAT'S CHEATING!
BUT AREN'T YOU WEARIN' ARMOR TOO, FUNNYFACE?
BUT I'M THE BAD GUY, HARLEY! I'M SUPPOSED TO CHEAT!

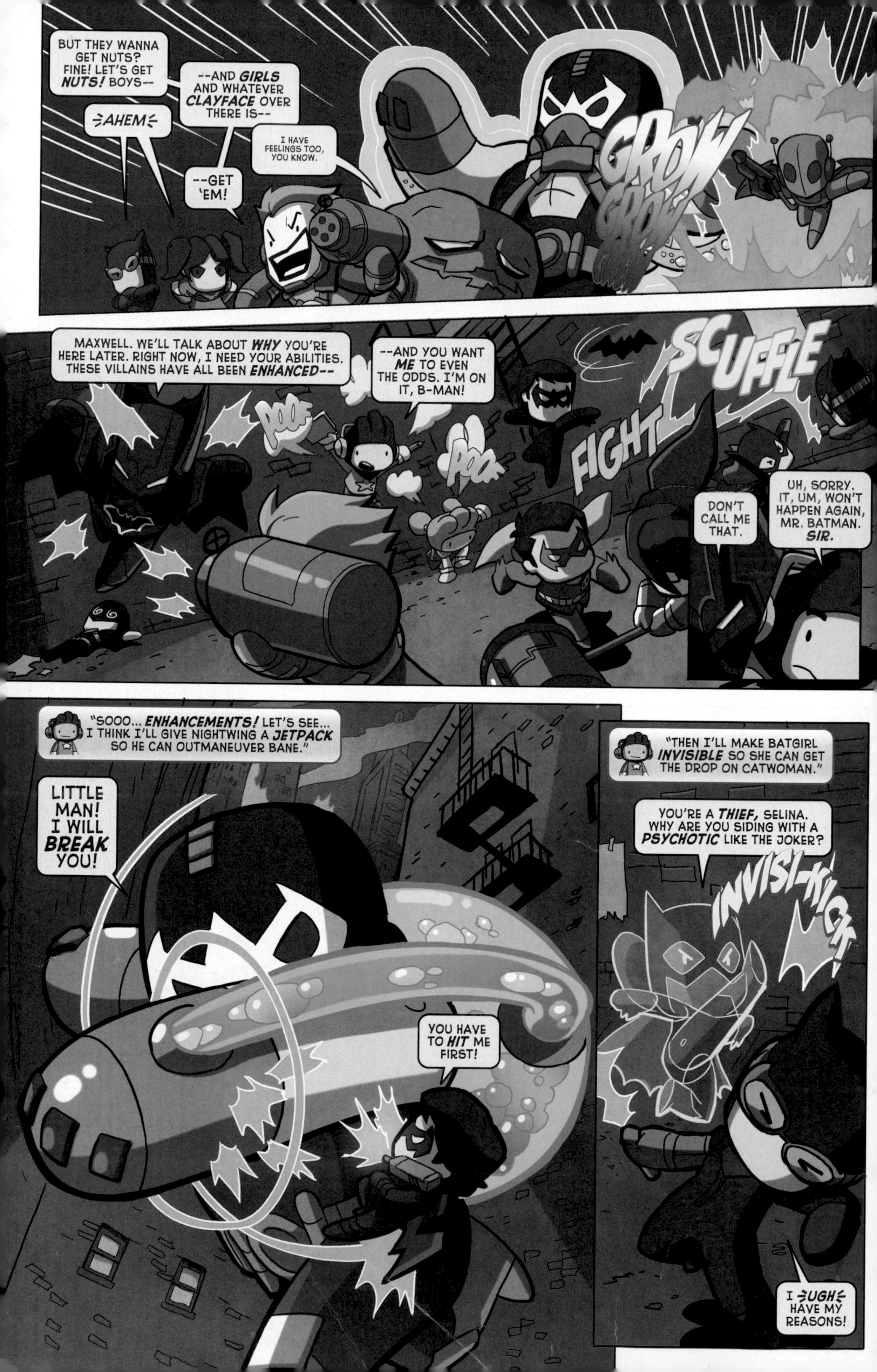

BUT THEY WANNA GET NUTS? FINE! LET'S GET NUTS! BOYS--
AHEM
--AND GIRLS AND WHATEVER CLAYFACE OVER THERE IS--
I HAVE FEELINGS TOO, YOU KNOW.
--GET 'EM!
GROW GROW
MAXWELL. WE'LL TALK ABOUT WHY YOU'RE HERE LATER. RIGHT NOW, I NEED YOUR ABILITIES. THESE VILLAINS HAVE ALL BEEN ENHANCED--
--AND YOU WANT ME TO EVEN THE ODDS. I'M ON IT, B-MAN!
POOF
POOF
SCUFFLE
FIGHT
DON'T CALL ME THAT.
UH, SORRY. IT, UM, WON'T HAPPEN AGAIN, MR. BATMAN. SIR.
"SOOO... ENHANCEMENTS! LET'S SEE... I THINK I'LL GIVE NIGHTWING A JETPACK SO HE CAN OUTMANEUVER BANE."
LITTLE MAN! I WILL BREAK YOU!
YOU HAVE TO HIT ME FIRST!
"THEN I'LL MAKE BATGIRL INVISIBLE SO SHE CAN GET THE DROP ON CATWOMAN."
YOU'RE A THIEF, SELINA. WHY ARE YOU SIDING WITH A PSYCHOTIC LIKE THE JOKER?
INVISI-KICK!
I UGH HAVE MY REASONS!

"AND SOMETIMES THE ONLY WAY TO *BEAT* ABSURDITY IS *WITH* ABSURDITY, SO TO TAKE ON HARLEY QUINN..."

"...I'LL PAIR ROBIN WITH *BAT-COW!*"

MOOOO!

PREPARE TO BE TRAMPLED BY THE *HOOVES OF JUSTICE!*

OKAY, THIS IS JUST WEIRD. EVEN FOR *ME.*

"YOU KNOW, 'HOOVES OF JUSTICE' WOULD MAKE A *GREAT* BAND NAME."

"I KNOW, RIGHT?"

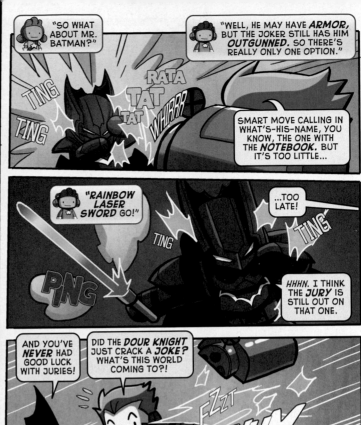

"SO WHAT ABOUT MR. BATMAN?"

"WELL, HE MAY HAVE *ARMOR,* BUT THE JOKER STILL HAS HIM *OUTGUNNED.* SO THERE'S REALLY ONLY ONE OPTION."

TING TING RATA TAT TAT WHIRRR

SMART MOVE CALLING IN WHAT'S-HIS-NAME, YOU KNOW, THE ONE WITH THE *NOTEBOOK.* BUT IT'S TOO LITTLE...

"*RAINBOW LASER SWORD* GO!"

...TOO LATE!

TING TING

PING

HHHN. I THINK THE *JURY* IS STILL OUT ON THAT ONE.

AND YOU'VE *NEVER* HAD GOOD LUCK WITH JURIES!

DID THE *DOUR KNIGHT* JUST CRACK A *JOKE?* WHAT'S THIS WORLD COMING TO?!

FZZT ZUUM

"REAL CUTE, KID."

BUT WHAT ARE YOU GOING TO DO WHEN *FIREFLY* TURNS THAT *NOTEBOOK* OF YOURS INTO A PILE OF *ASH?*

I'LL PROBABLY JUST GIVE MY SISTER HERE A *FIREHOSE.*

HI THERE, MR. FIREFLY! YOU LOOK LIKE YOU NEED TO *COOL OFF!*

WATER! ⇒BLUB⇒ MY ONE ⇒GURGLE⇒ WEAKNESS! ⇒CHOKE⇒

SKRITCH SKRITCH PING PSSHT

THUD

MAXWELL! LOOK OUT!

OH, NO... THERE'S SOMETHING *BEHIND* ME, ISN'T THERE?

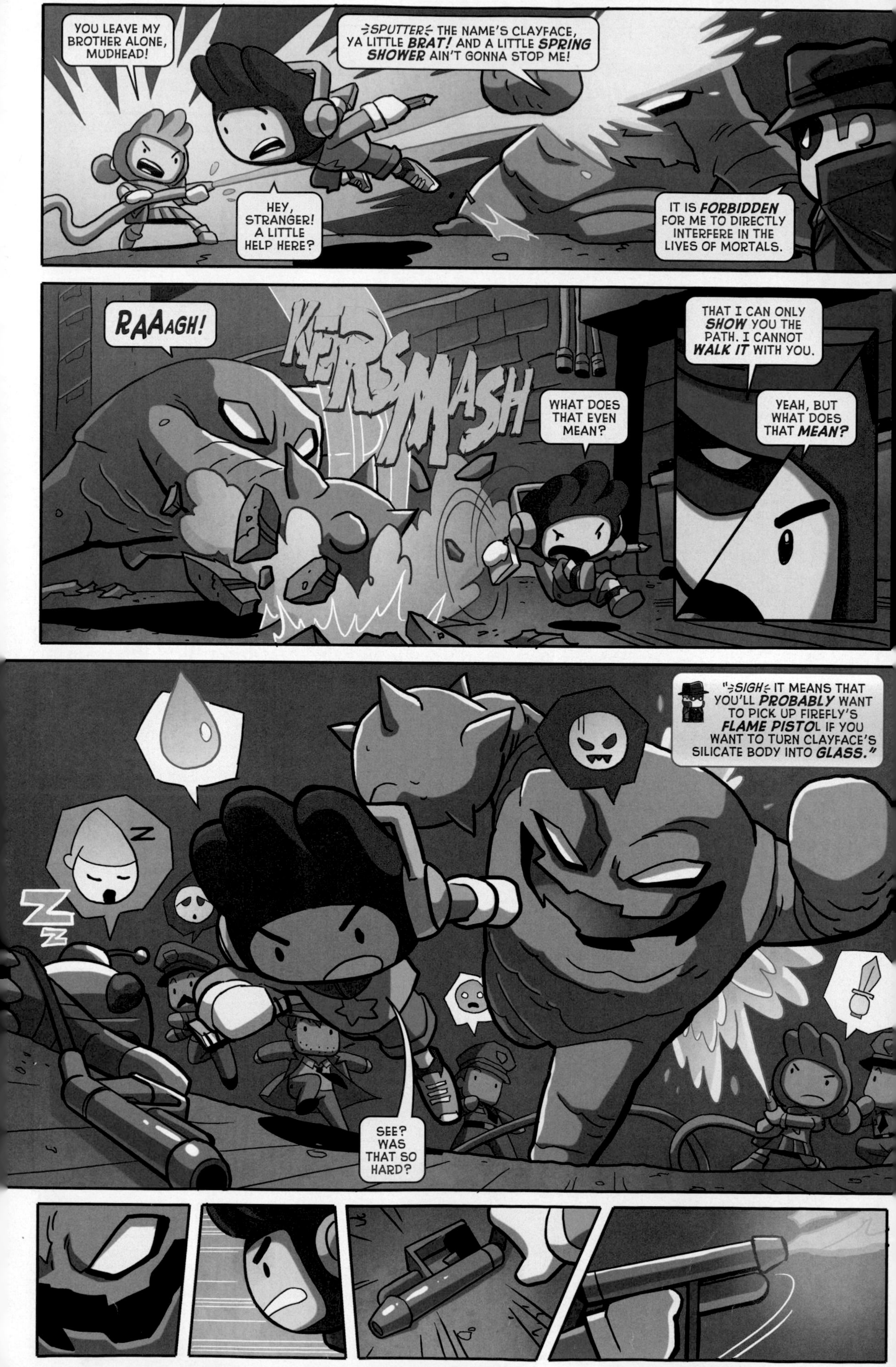
YOU LEAVE MY BROTHER ALONE, MUDHEAD!
⊰SPUTTER⊱ THE NAME'S CLAYFACE, YA LITTLE BRAT! AND A LITTLE SPRING SHOWER AIN'T GONNA STOP ME!
HEY, STRANGER! A LITTLE HELP HERE?
IT IS FORBIDDEN FOR ME TO DIRECTLY INTERFERE IN THE LIVES OF MORTALS.
RAAAGH!
KERSMASH
THAT I CAN ONLY SHOW YOU THE PATH. I CANNOT WALK IT WITH YOU.
WHAT DOES THAT EVEN MEAN?
YEAH, BUT WHAT DOES THAT MEAN?
"⊰SIGH⊱ IT MEANS THAT YOU'LL PROBABLY WANT TO PICK UP FIREFLY'S FLAME PISTOL IF YOU WANT TO TURN CLAYFACE'S SILICATE BODY INTO GLASS."
Z
ZZ
SEE? WAS THAT SO HARD?

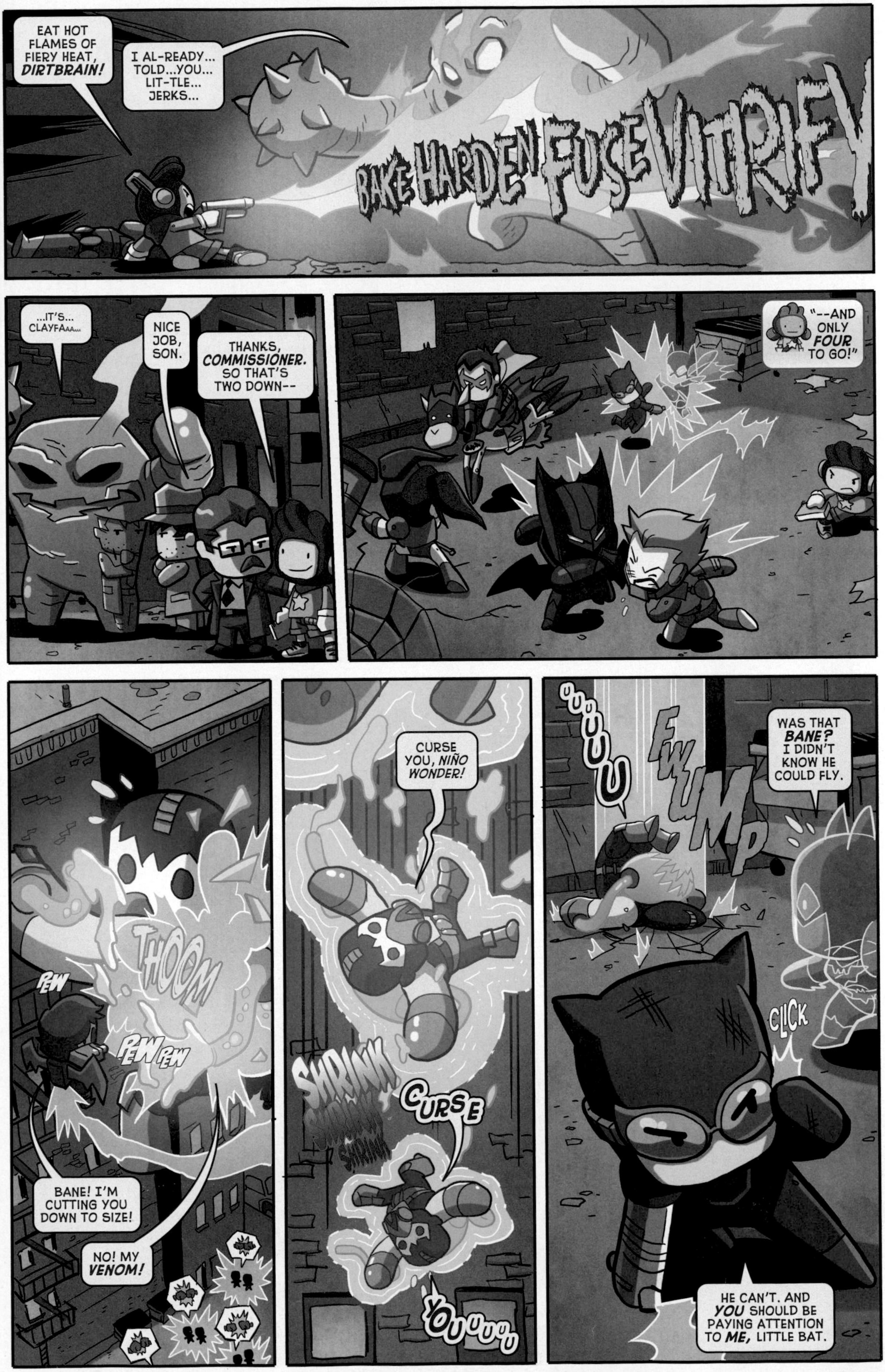
EAT HOT FLAMES OF FIERY HEAT, DIRTBRAIN!
I AL-READY... TOLD...YOU... LIT-TLE... JERKS...
BAKE HARDEN FUSE VITRIFY
...IT'S... CLAYFAAAA...
NICE JOB, SON.
THANKS, COMMISSIONER. SO THAT'S TWO DOWN--
"--AND ONLY FOUR TO GO!"
THOOM
PEW
PEW PEW PEW
BANE! I'M CUTTING YOU DOWN TO SIZE!
NO! MY VENOM!
CURSE YOU, NIÑO WONDER!
SHRINK
CURSE
YOUUUUU
UUUUUU
FWUMP
WAS THAT BANE? I DIDN'T KNOW HE COULD FLY.
CLICK
HE CAN'T. AND YOU SHOULD BE PAYING ATTENTION TO ME, LITTLE BAT.

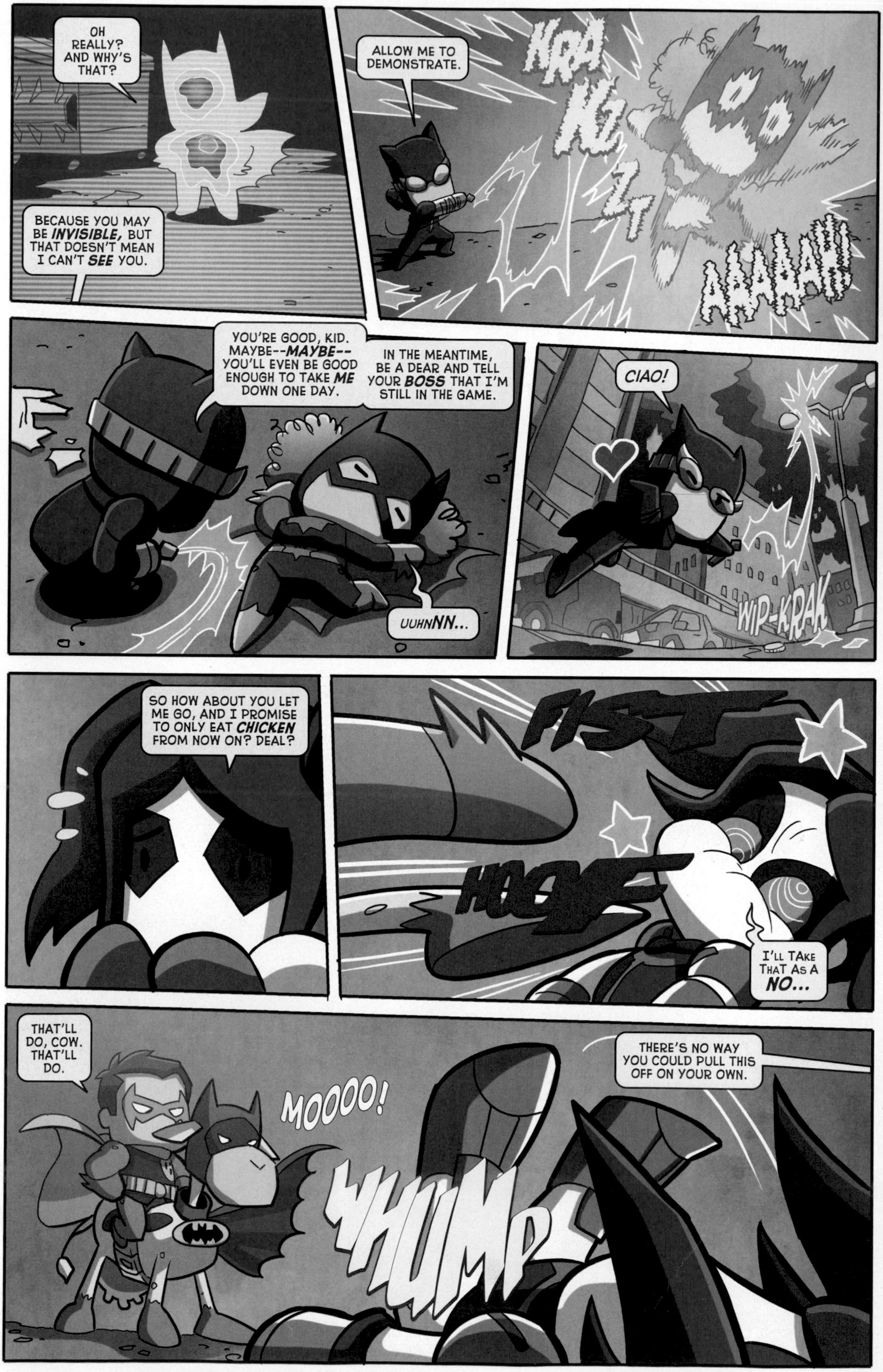
OH REALLY? AND WHY'S THAT?
BECAUSE YOU MAY BE INVISIBLE, BUT THAT DOESN'T MEAN I CAN'T SEE YOU.
ALLOW ME TO DEMONSTRATE.
KRA KZZZT
AAAAAH!
YOU'RE GOOD, KID. MAYBE--MAYBE--YOU'LL EVEN BE GOOD ENOUGH TO TAKE ME DOWN ONE DAY.
IN THE MEANTIME, BE A DEAR AND TELL YOUR BOSS THAT I'M STILL IN THE GAME.
UUHNNN...
CIAO!
WIP-KRAK
SO HOW ABOUT YOU LET ME GO, AND I PROMISE TO ONLY EAT CHICKEN FROM NOW ON? DEAL?
FIST
HOOF
I'LL TAKE THAT AS A NO...
THAT'LL DO, COW. THAT'LL DO.
MOOOO!
THERE'S NO WAY YOU COULD PULL THIS OFF ON YOUR OWN.
WHUMP!

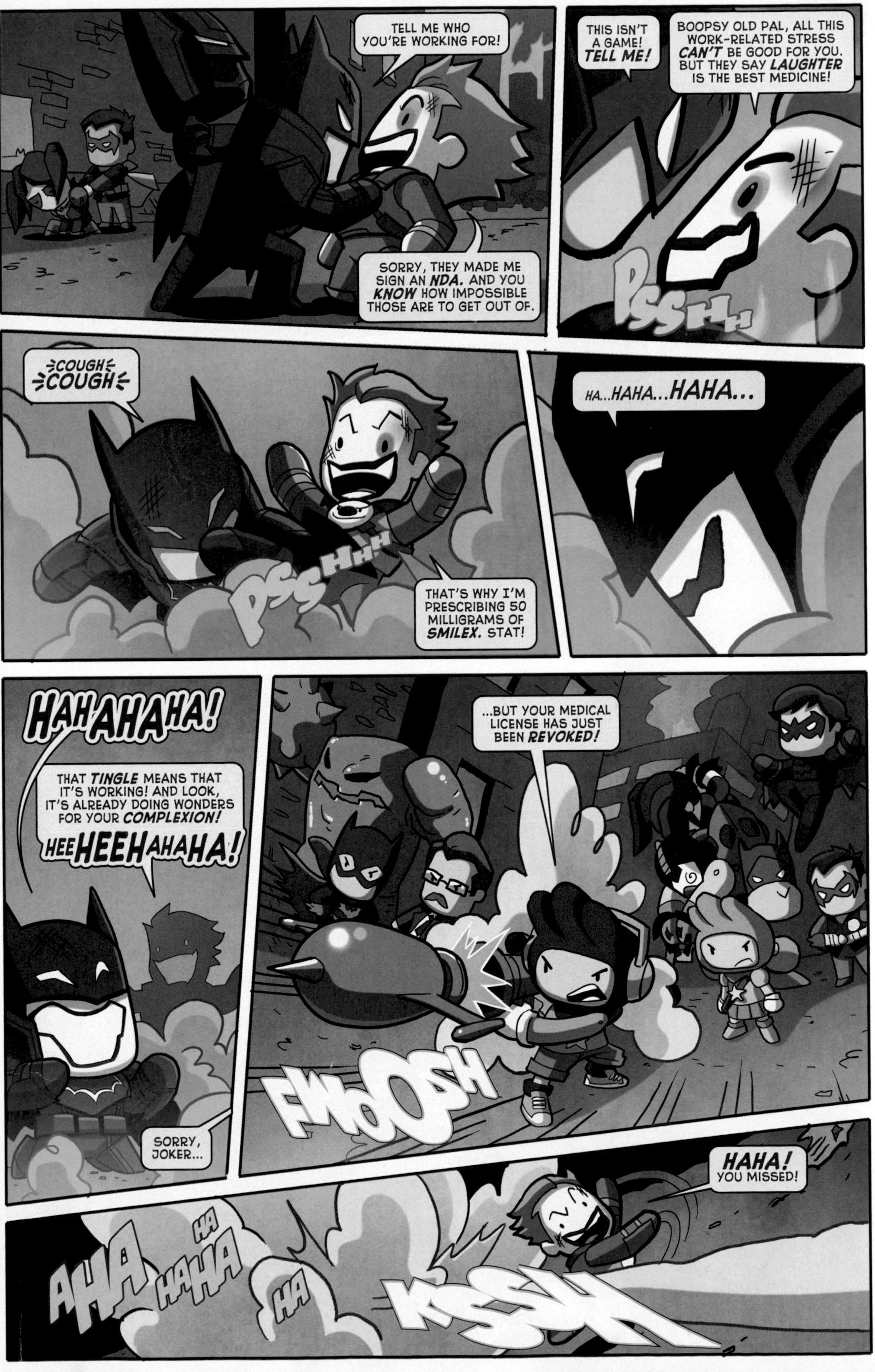

TELL ME WHO YOU'RE WORKING FOR!
SORRY, THEY MADE ME SIGN AN NDA. AND YOU KNOW HOW IMPOSSIBLE THOSE ARE TO GET OUT OF.
THIS ISN'T A GAME! TELL ME!
BOOPSY OLD PAL, ALL THIS WORK-RELATED STRESS CAN'T BE GOOD FOR YOU. BUT THEY SAY LAUGHTER IS THE BEST MEDICINE!
PSSHHH
COUGH COUGH
PSSHHH
THAT'S WHY I'M PRESCRIBING 50 MILLIGRAMS OF SMILEX. STAT!
HA...HAHA...HAHA...
HAHAHAHA!
THAT TINGLE MEANS THAT IT'S WORKING! AND LOOK, IT'S ALREADY DOING WONDERS FOR YOUR COMPLEXION!
HEEHEEHAHAHA!
SORRY, JOKER...
...BUT YOUR MEDICAL LICENSE HAS JUST BEEN REVOKED!
FWOOSH
HAHA! YOU MISSED!
AHA HA HAHA HA
KSSH

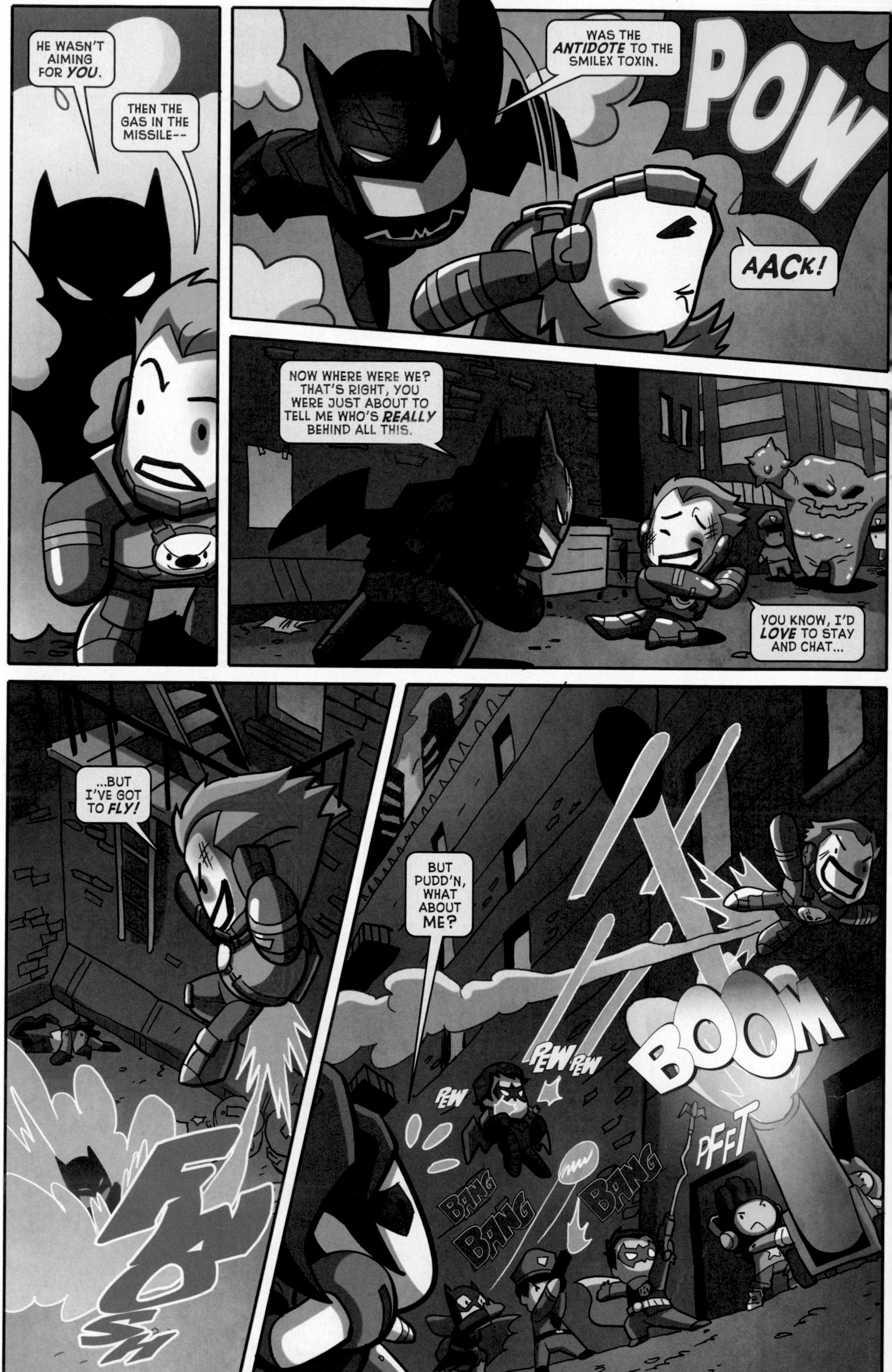
HE WASN'T AIMING FOR YOU.
THEN THE GAS IN THE MISSILE--
WAS THE ANTIDOTE TO THE SMILEX TOXIN.
POW
AACK!
NOW WHERE WERE WE? THAT'S RIGHT, YOU WERE JUST ABOUT TO TELL ME WHO'S REALLY BEHIND ALL THIS.
YOU KNOW, I'D LOVE TO STAY AND CHAT...
...BUT I'VE GOT TO FLY!
BUT PUDD'N, WHAT ABOUT ME?
BOOM
PEW PEW
PEW
BANG
BANG
BANG
PFFT

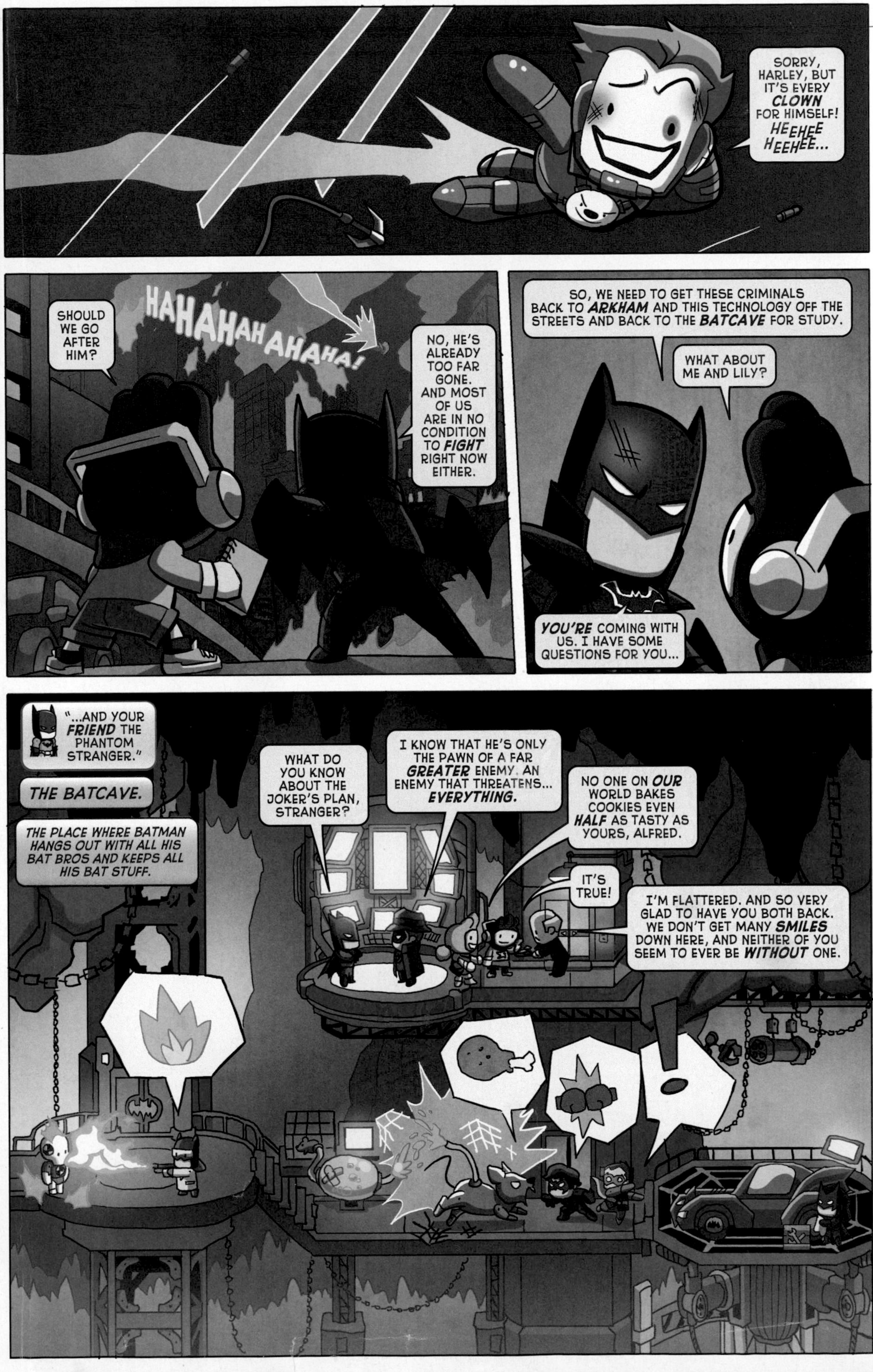
SORRY, HARLEY, BUT IT'S EVERY CLOWN FOR HIMSELF! HEEHEE HEEHEE...
SHOULD WE GO AFTER HIM?
HAHAHAHAHAHAHA!
NO, HE'S ALREADY TOO FAR GONE. AND MOST OF US ARE IN NO CONDITION TO FIGHT RIGHT NOW EITHER.
SO, WE NEED TO GET THESE CRIMINALS BACK TO ARKHAM AND THIS TECHNOLOGY OFF THE STREETS AND BACK TO THE BATCAVE FOR STUDY.
WHAT ABOUT ME AND LILY?
YOU'RE COMING WITH US. I HAVE SOME QUESTIONS FOR YOU...
"...AND YOUR FRIEND THE PHANTOM STRANGER."
THE BATCAVE.
THE PLACE WHERE BATMAN HANGS OUT WITH ALL HIS BAT BROS AND KEEPS ALL HIS BAT STUFF.
WHAT DO YOU KNOW ABOUT THE JOKER'S PLAN, STRANGER?
I KNOW THAT HE'S ONLY THE PAWN OF A FAR GREATER ENEMY. AN ENEMY THAT THREATENS... EVERYTHING.
NO ONE ON OUR WORLD BAKES COOKIES EVEN HALF AS TASTY AS YOURS, ALFRED.
IT'S TRUE!
I'M FLATTERED. AND SO VERY GLAD TO HAVE YOU BOTH BACK. WE DON'T GET MANY SMILES DOWN HERE, AND NEITHER OF YOU SEEM TO EVER BE WITHOUT ONE.
!

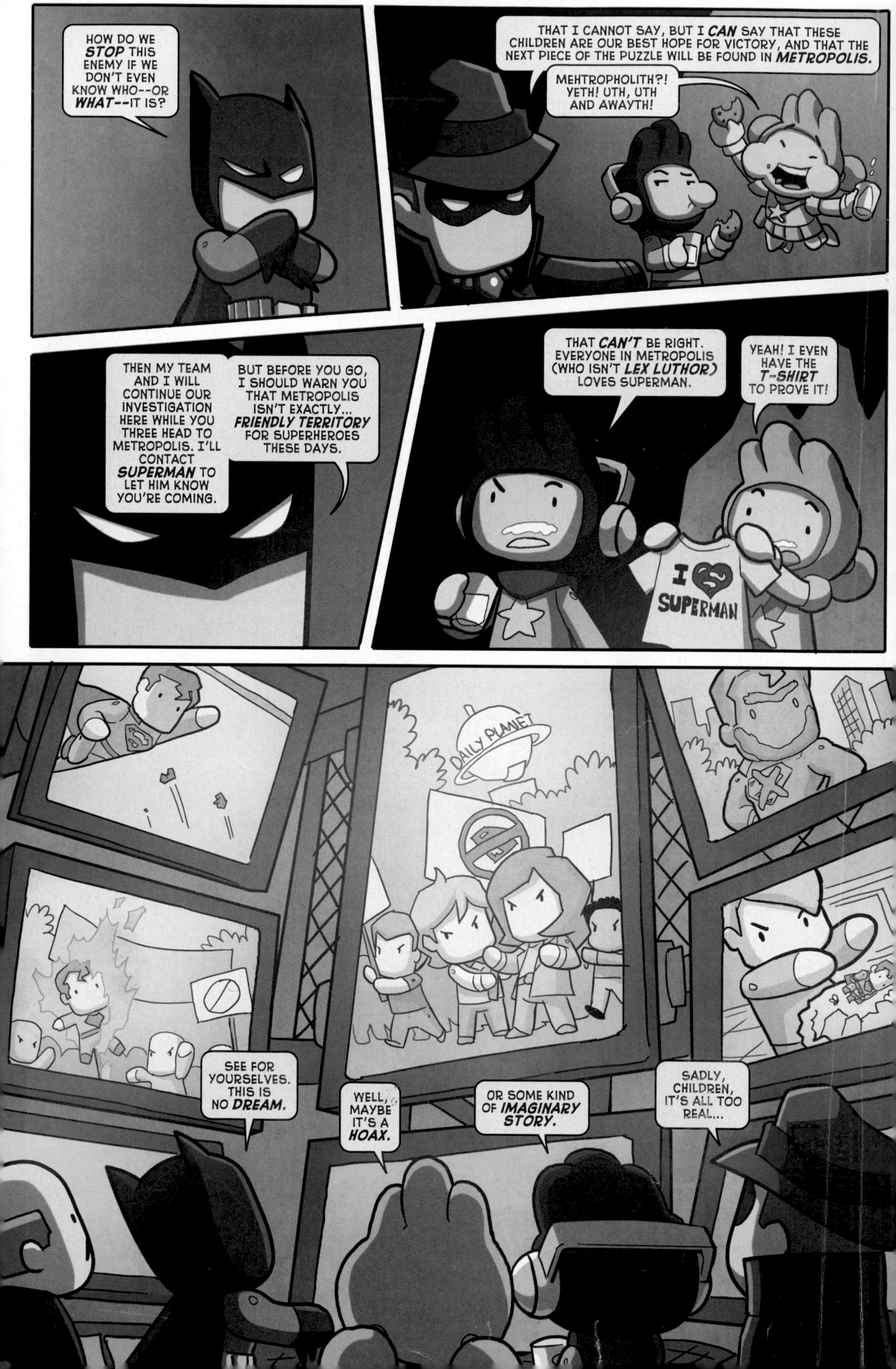
HOW DO WE STOP THIS ENEMY IF WE DON'T EVEN KNOW WHO--OR WHAT--IT IS?
THAT I CANNOT SAY, BUT I CAN SAY THAT THESE CHILDREN ARE OUR BEST HOPE FOR VICTORY, AND THAT THE NEXT PIECE OF THE PUZZLE WILL BE FOUND IN METROPOLIS.
MEHTROPHOLITH?! YETH! UTH, UTH AND AWAYTH!
THEN MY TEAM AND I WILL CONTINUE OUR INVESTIGATION HERE WHILE YOU THREE HEAD TO METROPOLIS. I'LL CONTACT SUPERMAN TO LET HIM KNOW YOU'RE COMING.
BUT BEFORE YOU GO, I SHOULD WARN YOU THAT METROPOLIS ISN'T EXACTLY... FRIENDLY TERRITORY FOR SUPERHEROES THESE DAYS.
THAT CAN'T BE RIGHT. EVERYONE IN METROPOLIS (WHO ISN'T LEX LUTHOR) LOVES SUPERMAN.
YEAH! I EVEN HAVE THE T-SHIRT TO PROVE IT!
I ♥ SUPERMAN
DAILY PLANET
SEE FOR YOURSELVES. THIS IS NO DREAM.
WELL, MAYBE IT'S A HOAX.
OR SOME KIND OF IMAGINARY STORY.
SADLY, CHILDREN, IT'S ALL TOO REAL...

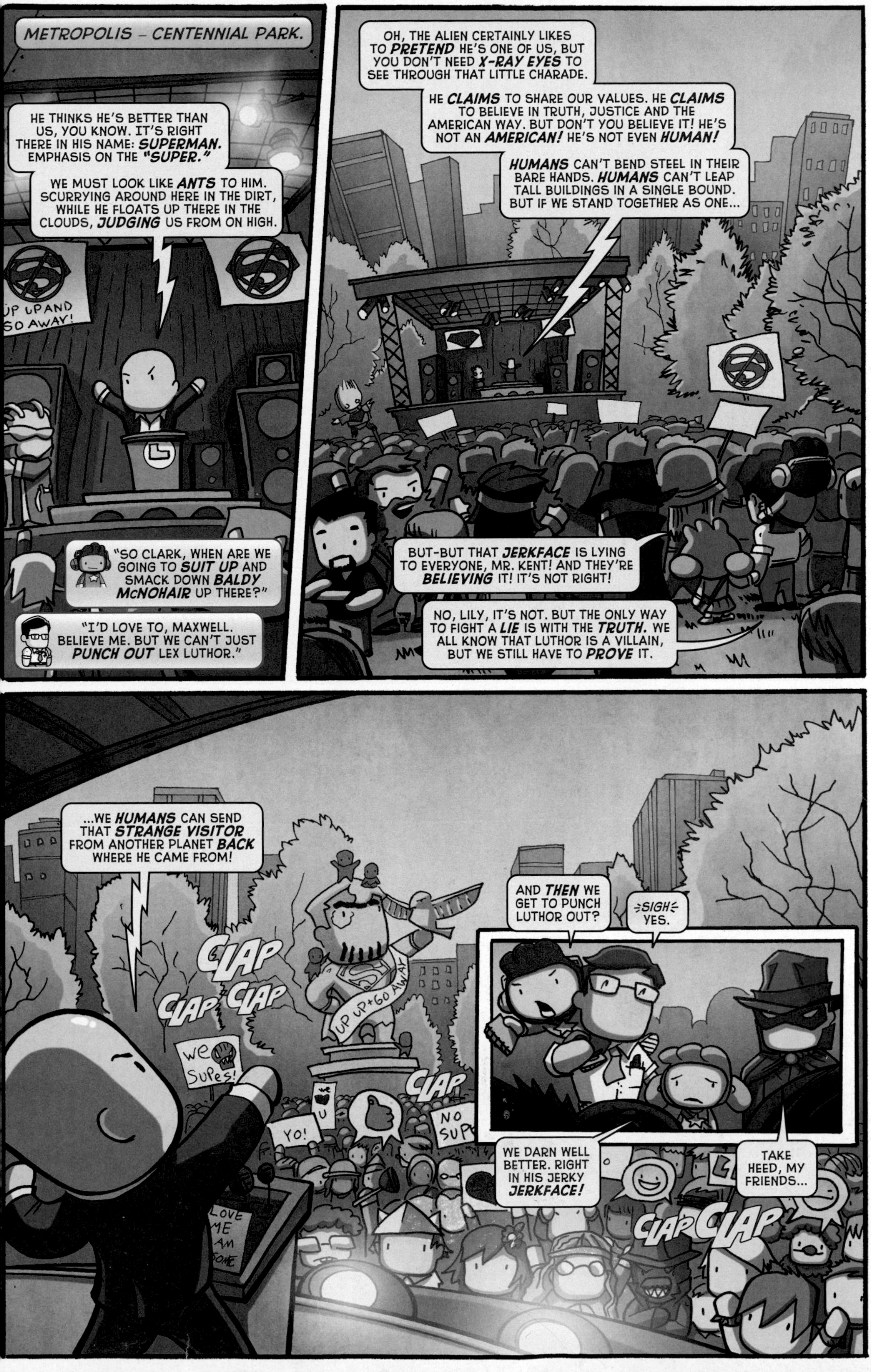
METROPOLIS – CENTENNIAL PARK.
HE THINKS HE'S BETTER THAN US, YOU KNOW. IT'S RIGHT THERE IN HIS NAME: SUPERMAN. EMPHASIS ON THE "SUPER."
WE MUST LOOK LIKE ANTS TO HIM. SCURRYING AROUND HERE IN THE DIRT, WHILE HE FLOATS UP THERE IN THE CLOUDS, JUDGING US FROM ON HIGH.
UP UP AND SO AWAY!
"SO CLARK, WHEN ARE WE GOING TO SUIT UP AND SMACK DOWN BALDY McNOHAIR UP THERE?"
"I'D LOVE TO, MAXWELL. BELIEVE ME. BUT WE CAN'T JUST PUNCH OUT LEX LUTHOR."
OH, THE ALIEN CERTAINLY LIKES TO PRETEND HE'S ONE OF US, BUT YOU DON'T NEED X-RAY EYES TO SEE THROUGH THAT LITTLE CHARADE.
HE CLAIMS TO SHARE OUR VALUES. HE CLAIMS TO BELIEVE IN TRUTH, JUSTICE AND THE AMERICAN WAY. BUT DON'T YOU BELIEVE IT! HE'S NOT AN AMERICAN! HE'S NOT EVEN HUMAN!
HUMANS CAN'T BEND STEEL IN THEIR BARE HANDS. HUMANS CAN'T LEAP TALL BUILDINGS IN A SINGLE BOUND. BUT IF WE STAND TOGETHER AS ONE...
BUT-BUT THAT JERKFACE IS LYING TO EVERYONE, MR. KENT! AND THEY'RE BELIEVING IT! IT'S NOT RIGHT!
NO, LILY, IT'S NOT. BUT THE ONLY WAY TO FIGHT A LIE IS WITH THE TRUTH. WE ALL KNOW THAT LUTHOR IS A VILLAIN, BUT WE STILL HAVE TO PROVE IT.
...WE HUMANS CAN SEND THAT STRANGE VISITOR FROM ANOTHER PLANET BACK WHERE HE CAME FROM!
CLAP
CLAP CLAP
UP UP + GO AWAY
CLAP
YO!
AND THEN WE GET TO PUNCH LUTHOR OUT?
SIGH YES.
WE DARN WELL BETTER. RIGHT IN HIS JERKY JERKFACE!
TAKE HEED, MY FRIENDS...
CLAP CLAP

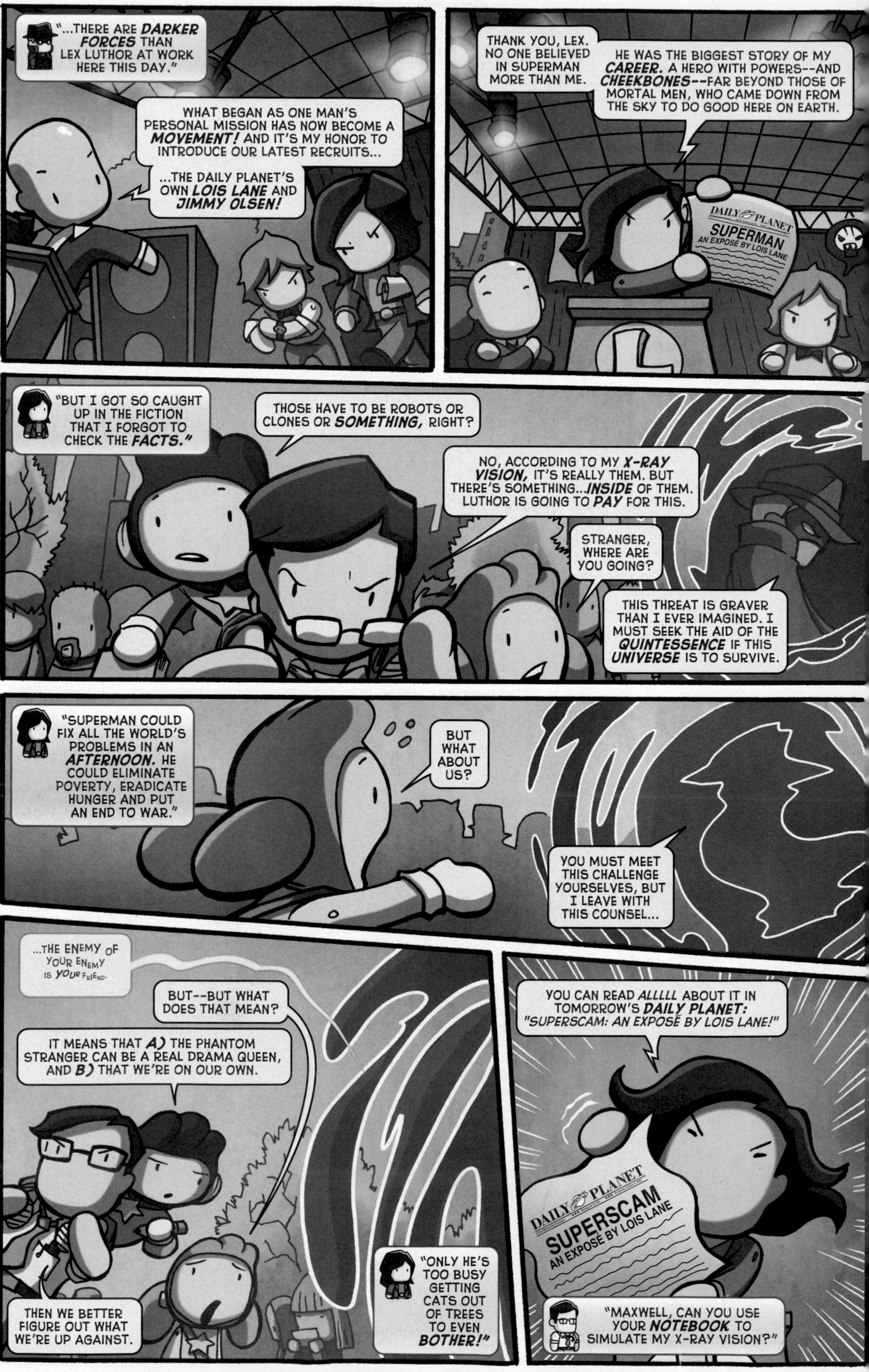
"...THERE ARE DARKER FORCES THAN LEX LUTHOR AT WORK HERE THIS DAY."
WHAT BEGAN AS ONE MAN'S PERSONAL MISSION HAS NOW BECOME A MOVEMENT! AND IT'S MY HONOR TO INTRODUCE OUR LATEST RECRUITS...
...THE DAILY PLANET'S OWN LOIS LANE AND JIMMY OLSEN!
THANK YOU, LEX. NO ONE BELIEVED IN SUPERMAN MORE THAN ME.
HE WAS THE BIGGEST STORY OF MY CAREER. A HERO WITH POWERS--AND CHEEKBONES--FAR BEYOND THOSE OF MORTAL MEN, WHO CAME DOWN FROM THE SKY TO DO GOOD HERE ON EARTH.
DAILY PLANET
SUPERMAN
AN EXPOSÉ BY LOIS LANE
"BUT I GOT SO CAUGHT UP IN THE FICTION THAT I FORGOT TO CHECK THE FACTS."
THOSE HAVE TO BE ROBOTS OR CLONES OR SOMETHING, RIGHT?
NO, ACCORDING TO MY X-RAY VISION, IT'S REALLY THEM. BUT THERE'S SOMETHING...INSIDE OF THEM. LUTHOR IS GOING TO PAY FOR THIS.
STRANGER, WHERE ARE YOU GOING?
THIS THREAT IS GRAVER THAN I EVER IMAGINED. I MUST SEEK THE AID OF THE QUINTESSENCE IF THIS UNIVERSE IS TO SURVIVE.
"SUPERMAN COULD FIX ALL THE WORLD'S PROBLEMS IN AN AFTERNOON. HE COULD ELIMINATE POVERTY, ERADICATE HUNGER AND PUT AN END TO WAR."
BUT WHAT ABOUT US?
YOU MUST MEET THIS CHALLENGE YOURSELVES, BUT I LEAVE WITH THIS COUNSEL...
...THE ENEMY OF YOUR ENEMY IS YOUR FRIEND.
BUT--BUT WHAT DOES THAT MEAN?
IT MEANS THAT A) THE PHANTOM STRANGER CAN BE A REAL DRAMA QUEEN, AND B) THAT WE'RE ON OUR OWN.
THEN WE BETTER FIGURE OUT WHAT WE'RE UP AGAINST.
"ONLY HE'S TOO BUSY GETTING CATS OUT OF TREES TO EVEN BOTHER!"
YOU CAN READ ALLLLL ABOUT IT IN TOMORROW'S DAILY PLANET: "SUPERSCAM: AN EXPOSÉ BY LOIS LANE!"
DAILY PLANET
SUPERSCAM
AN EXPOSÉ BY LOIS LANE
"MAXWELL, CAN YOU USE YOUR NOTEBOOK TO SIMULATE MY X-RAY VISION?"

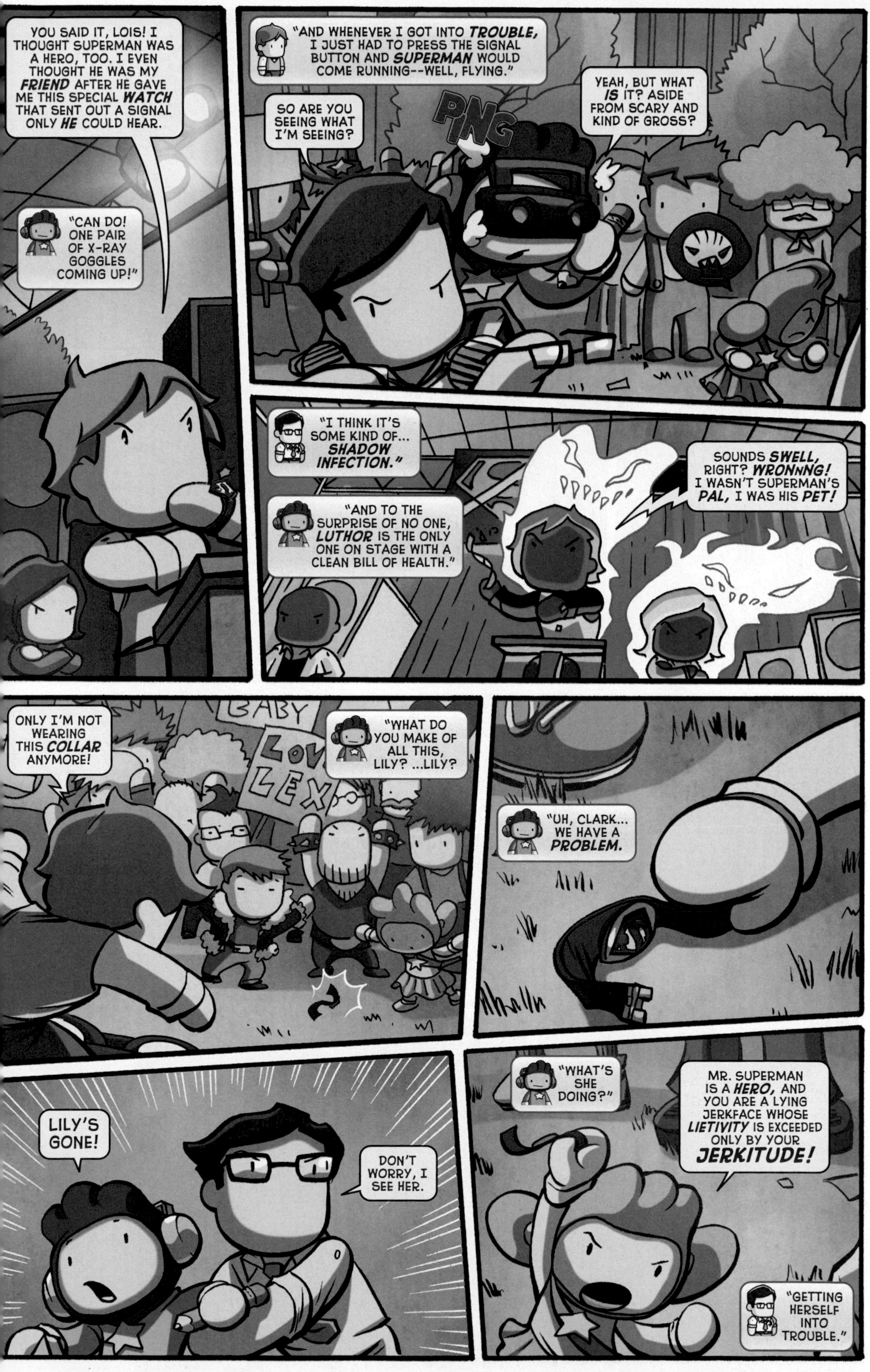

YOU SAID IT, LOIS! I THOUGHT SUPERMAN WAS A HERO, TOO. I EVEN THOUGHT HE WAS MY FRIEND AFTER HE GAVE ME THIS SPECIAL WATCH THAT SENT OUT A SIGNAL ONLY HE COULD HEAR.
"CAN DO! ONE PAIR OF X-RAY GOGGLES COMING UP!"
"AND WHENEVER I GOT INTO TROUBLE, I JUST HAD TO PRESS THE SIGNAL BUTTON AND SUPERMAN WOULD COME RUNNING--WELL, FLYING."
SO ARE YOU SEEING WHAT I'M SEEING?
PING
YEAH, BUT WHAT IS IT? ASIDE FROM SCARY AND KIND OF GROSS?
"I THINK IT'S SOME KIND OF... SHADOW INFECTION."
"AND TO THE SURPRISE OF NO ONE, LUTHOR IS THE ONLY ONE ON STAGE WITH A CLEAN BILL OF HEALTH."
SOUNDS SWELL, RIGHT? WRONNNG! I WASN'T SUPERMAN'S PAL, I WAS HIS PET!
ONLY I'M NOT WEARING THIS COLLAR ANYMORE!
BABY
LOVE LEX
"WHAT DO YOU MAKE OF ALL THIS, LILY? ...LILY?
"UH, CLARK... WE HAVE A PROBLEM.
LILY'S GONE!
DON'T WORRY, I SEE HER.
"WHAT'S SHE DOING?"
MR. SUPERMAN IS A HERO, AND YOU ARE A LYING JERKFACE WHOSE LIETIVITY IS EXCEEDED ONLY BY YOUR JERKITUDE!
"GETTING HERSELF INTO TROUBLE."

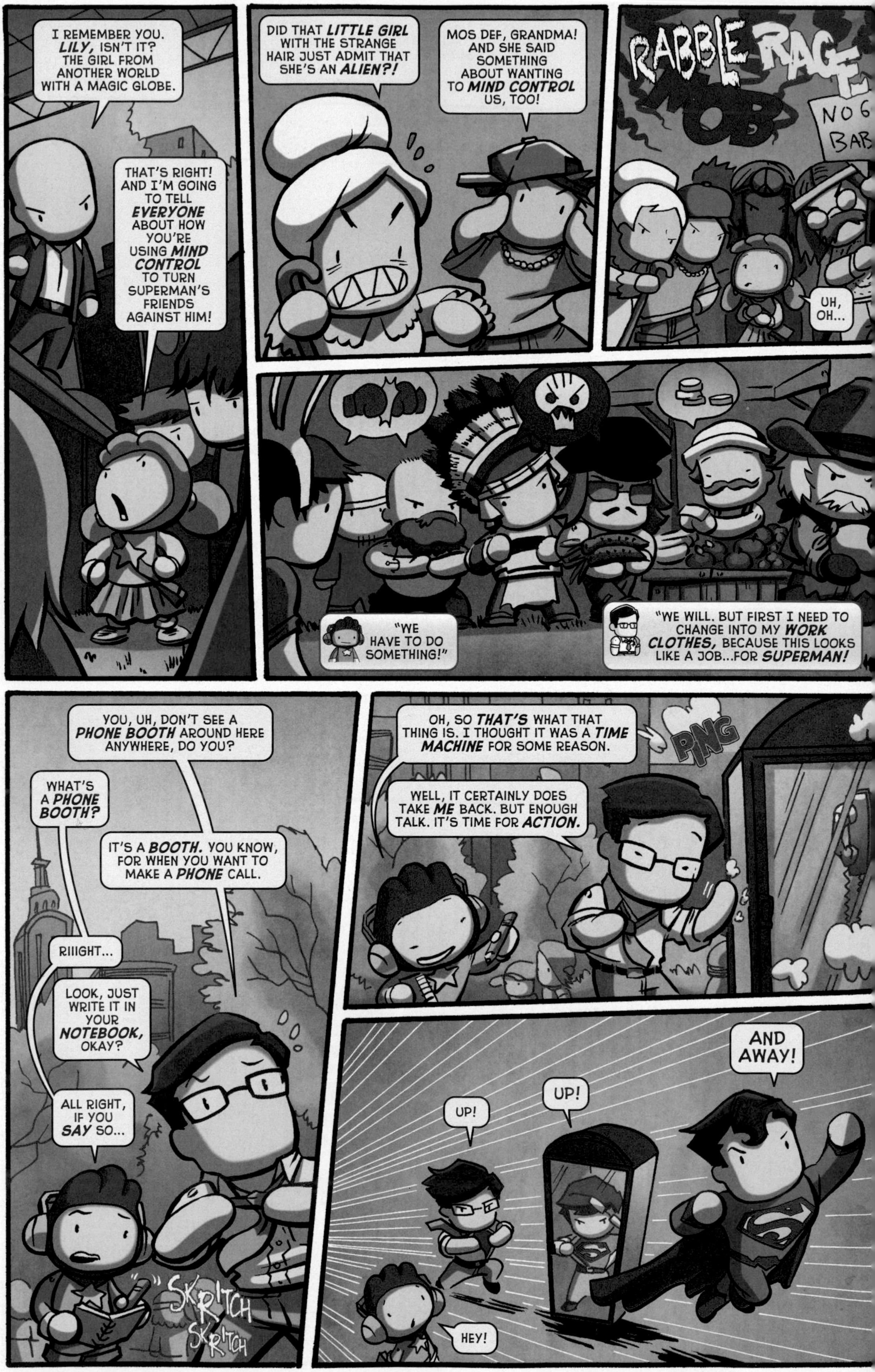
I REMEMBER YOU. LILY, ISN'T IT? THE GIRL FROM ANOTHER WORLD WITH A MAGIC GLOBE.
THAT'S RIGHT! AND I'M GOING TO TELL EVERYONE ABOUT HOW YOU'RE USING MIND CONTROL TO TURN SUPERMAN'S FRIENDS AGAINST HIM!
DID THAT LITTLE GIRL WITH THE STRANGE HAIR JUST ADMIT THAT SHE'S AN ALIEN?!
MOS DEF, GRANDMA! AND SHE SAID SOMETHING ABOUT WANTING TO MIND CONTROL US, TOO!
RABBLE RAGE MOB
UH, OH...
"WE HAVE TO DO SOMETHING!"
"WE WILL. BUT FIRST I NEED TO CHANGE INTO MY WORK CLOTHES, BECAUSE THIS LOOKS LIKE A JOB...FOR SUPERMAN!"
YOU, UH, DON'T SEE A PHONE BOOTH AROUND HERE ANYWHERE, DO YOU?
WHAT'S A PHONE BOOTH?
IT'S A BOOTH. YOU KNOW, FOR WHEN YOU WANT TO MAKE A PHONE CALL.
RIIIGHT...
LOOK, JUST WRITE IT IN YOUR NOTEBOOK, OKAY?
ALL RIGHT, IF YOU SAY SO...
SKRITCH SKRITCH
OH, SO THAT'S WHAT THAT THING IS. I THOUGHT IT WAS A TIME MACHINE FOR SOME REASON.
PING
WELL, IT CERTAINLY DOES TAKE ME BACK. BUT ENOUGH TALK. IT'S TIME FOR ACTION.
UP!
UP!
AND AWAY!
HEY!

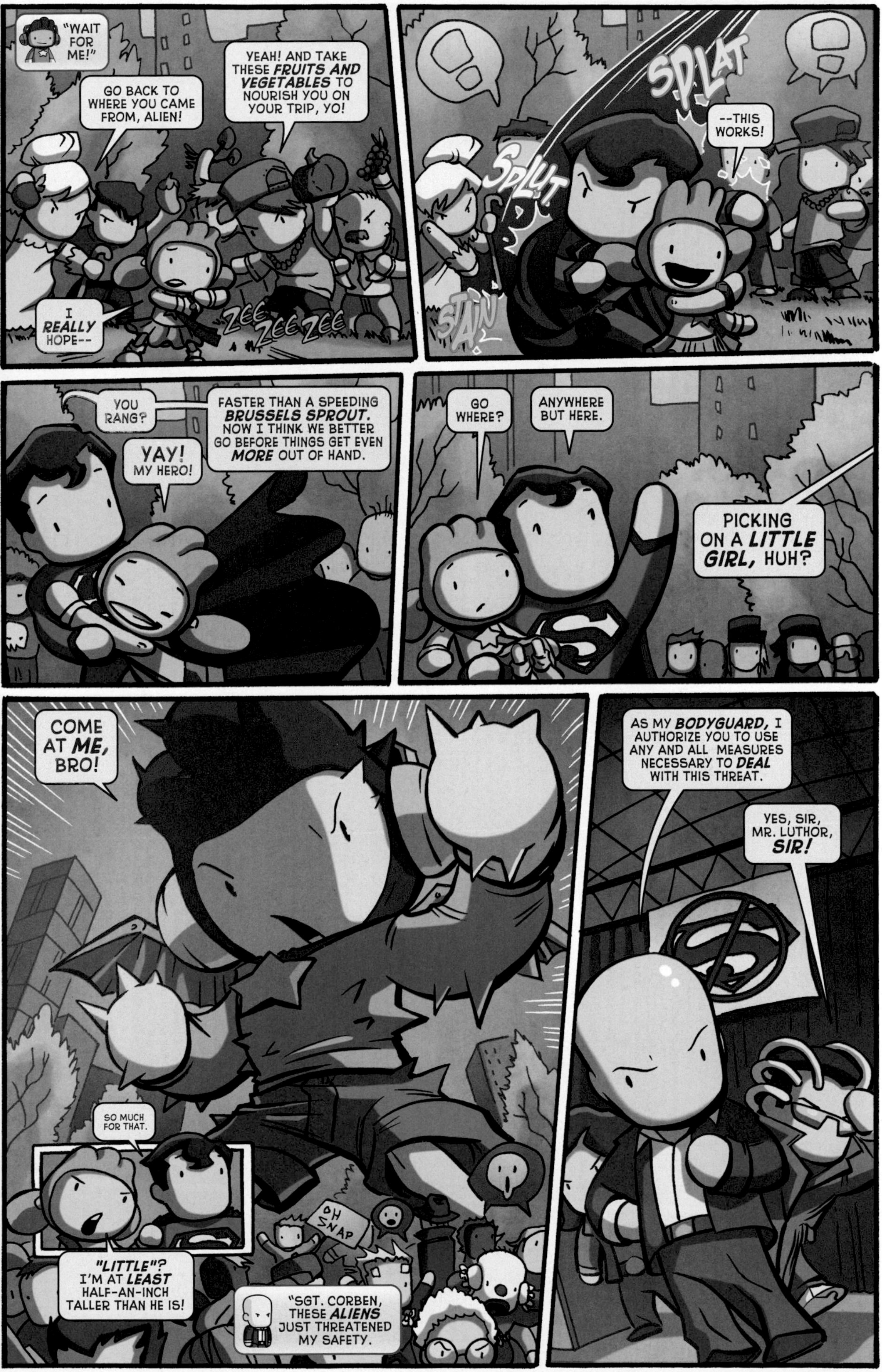

"WAIT FOR ME!"
GO BACK TO WHERE YOU CAME FROM, ALIEN!
YEAH! AND TAKE THESE FRUITS AND VEGETABLES TO NOURISH YOU ON YOUR TRIP, YO!
I REALLY HOPE--
ZEE ZEE ZEE
SPLAT
SPLUT
STAIN
--THIS WORKS!
YOU RANG?
FASTER THAN A SPEEDING BRUSSELS SPROUT. NOW I THINK WE BETTER GO BEFORE THINGS GET EVEN MORE OUT OF HAND.
YAY! MY HERO!
GO WHERE?
ANYWHERE BUT HERE.
PICKING ON A LITTLE GIRL, HUH?
COME AT ME, BRO!
SO MUCH FOR THAT.
"LITTLE"? I'M AT LEAST HALF-AN-INCH TALLER THAN HE IS!
OH SNAP
"SGT. CORBEN, THESE ALIENS JUST THREATENED MY SAFETY.
AS MY BODYGUARD, I AUTHORIZE YOU TO USE ANY AND ALL MEASURES NECESSARY TO DEAL WITH THIS THREAT.
YES, SIR, MR. LUTHOR, SIR!

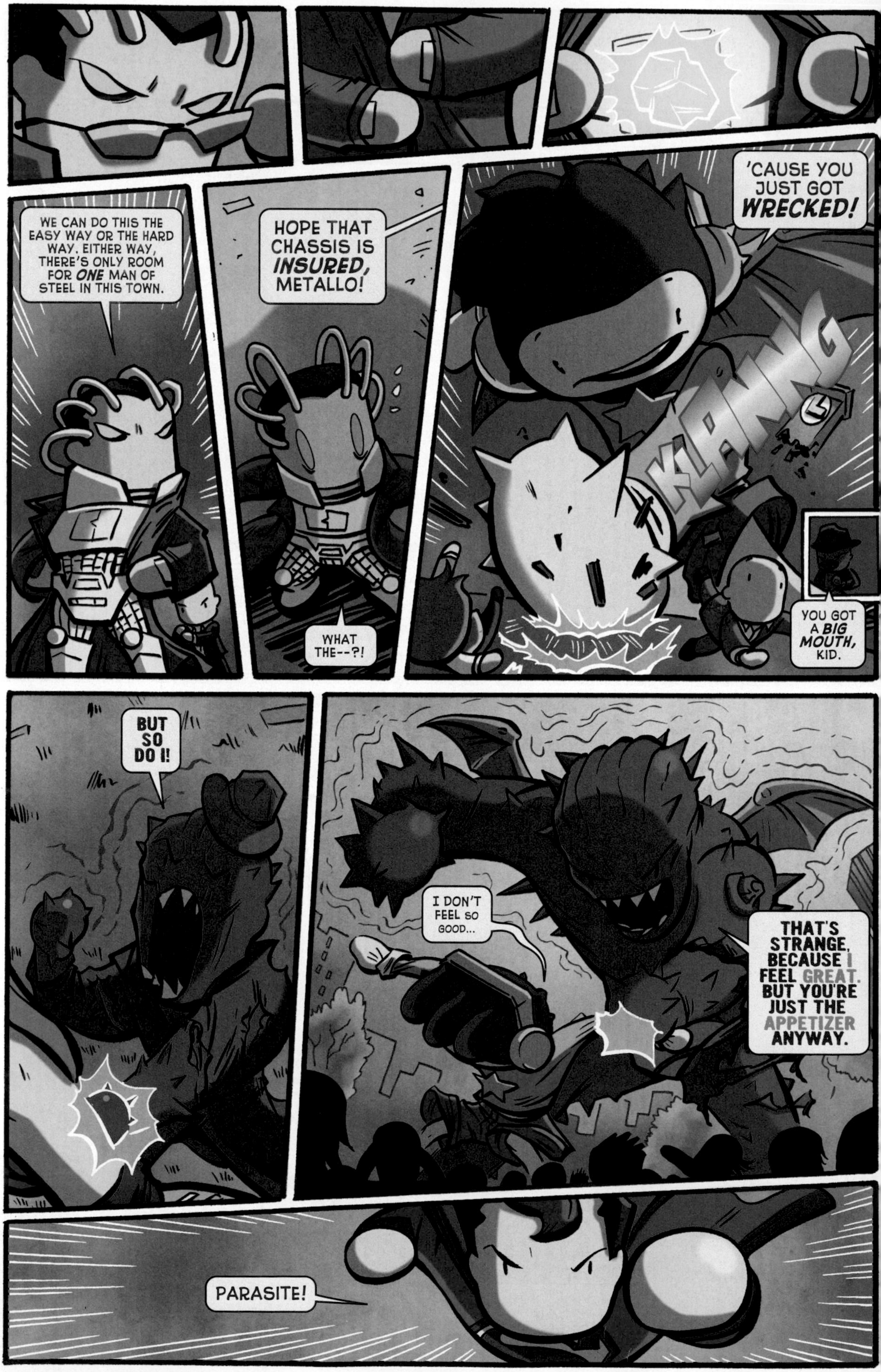
WE CAN DO THIS THE EASY WAY OR THE HARD WAY. EITHER WAY, THERE'S ONLY ROOM FOR ONE MAN OF STEEL IN THIS TOWN.
HOPE THAT CHASSIS IS INSURED, METALLO!
WHAT THE--?!
'CAUSE YOU JUST GOT WRECKED!
KLANNG
YOU GOT A BIG MOUTH, KID.
BUT SO DO I!
I DON'T FEEL SO GOOD...
THAT'S STRANGE, BECAUSE I FEEL GREAT. BUT YOU'RE JUST THE APPETIZER ANYWAY.
PARASITE!

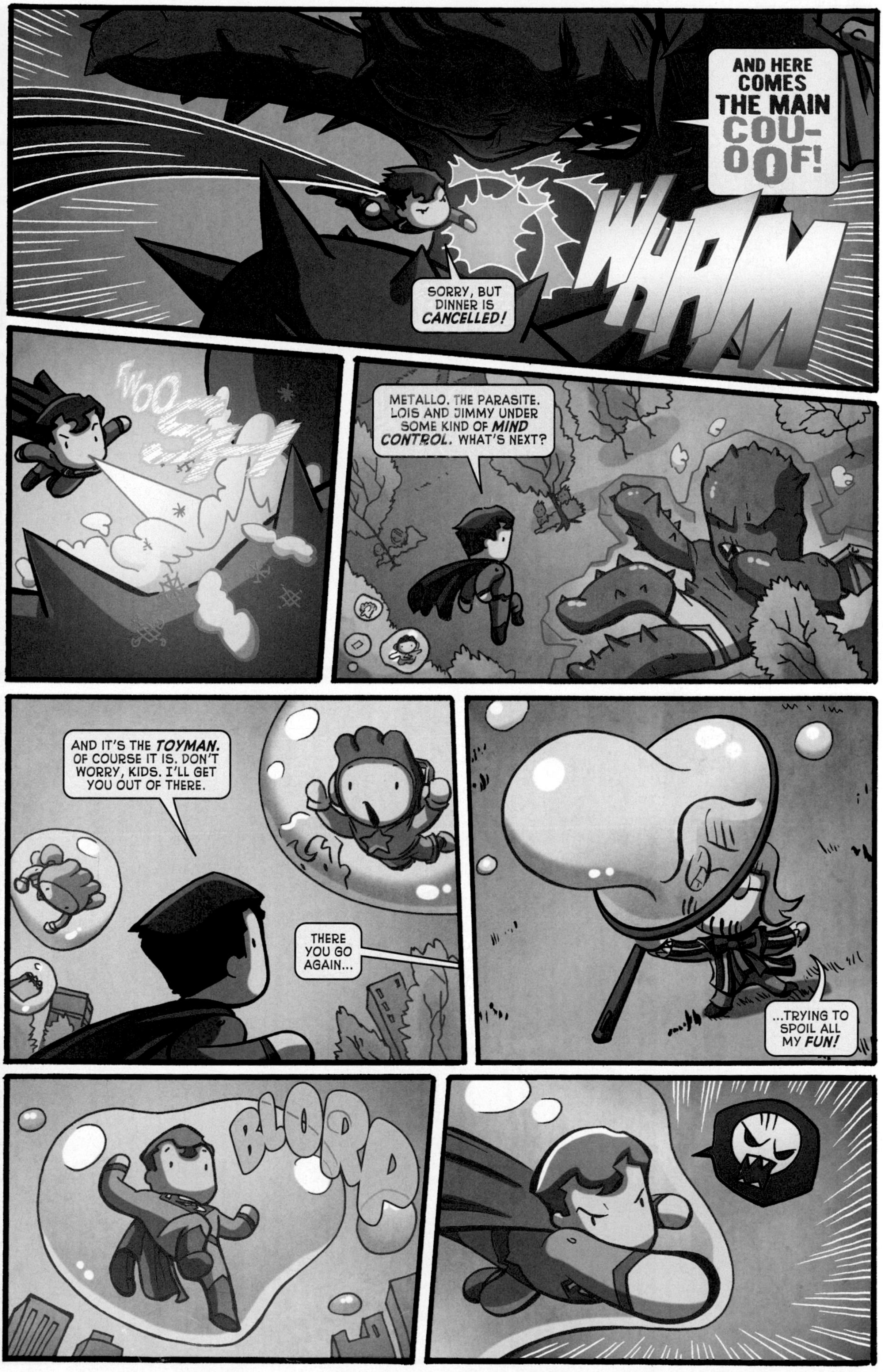
AND HERE COMES THE MAIN COU-OOF!
WHAM
SORRY, BUT DINNER IS CANCELLED!
FWOOSH
METALLO. THE PARASITE. LOIS AND JIMMY UNDER SOME KIND OF MIND CONTROL. WHAT'S NEXT?
AND IT'S THE TOYMAN. OF COURSE IT IS. DON'T WORRY, KIDS. I'LL GET YOU OUT OF THERE.
THERE YOU GO AGAIN...
...TRYING TO SPOIL ALL MY FUN!
BLORP

IT SEEMS NO ONE TOLD OUR ALIEN FRIEND THAT *MEGA-BUBBLES* REACT *VIOLENTLY* TO HEAT.

AN EXPLOSION LIKE *THAT* WILL SLOW SUPERMAN DOWN FOR A FEW SECONDS... IF YOU'RE LUCKY.

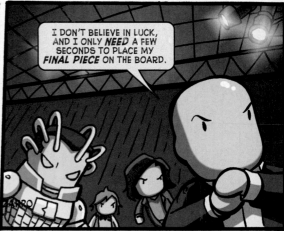

I DON'T BELIEVE IN LUCK, AND I ONLY *NEED* A FEW SECONDS TO PLACE MY *FINAL PIECE* ON THE BOARD.

BECAUSE YOUNG MR. OLSEN ISN'T THE *ONLY* ONE WITH A *SIGNAL WATCH.*

ZEE ZEE ZEE

LISTEN! DOWN IN OCEAN!

OH NO. NOT *HIM...*

IT AM FISH! IT AM SUBMARINE! NO, IT AM *BIZARRO!*

GOODBYE!

KWOOOM

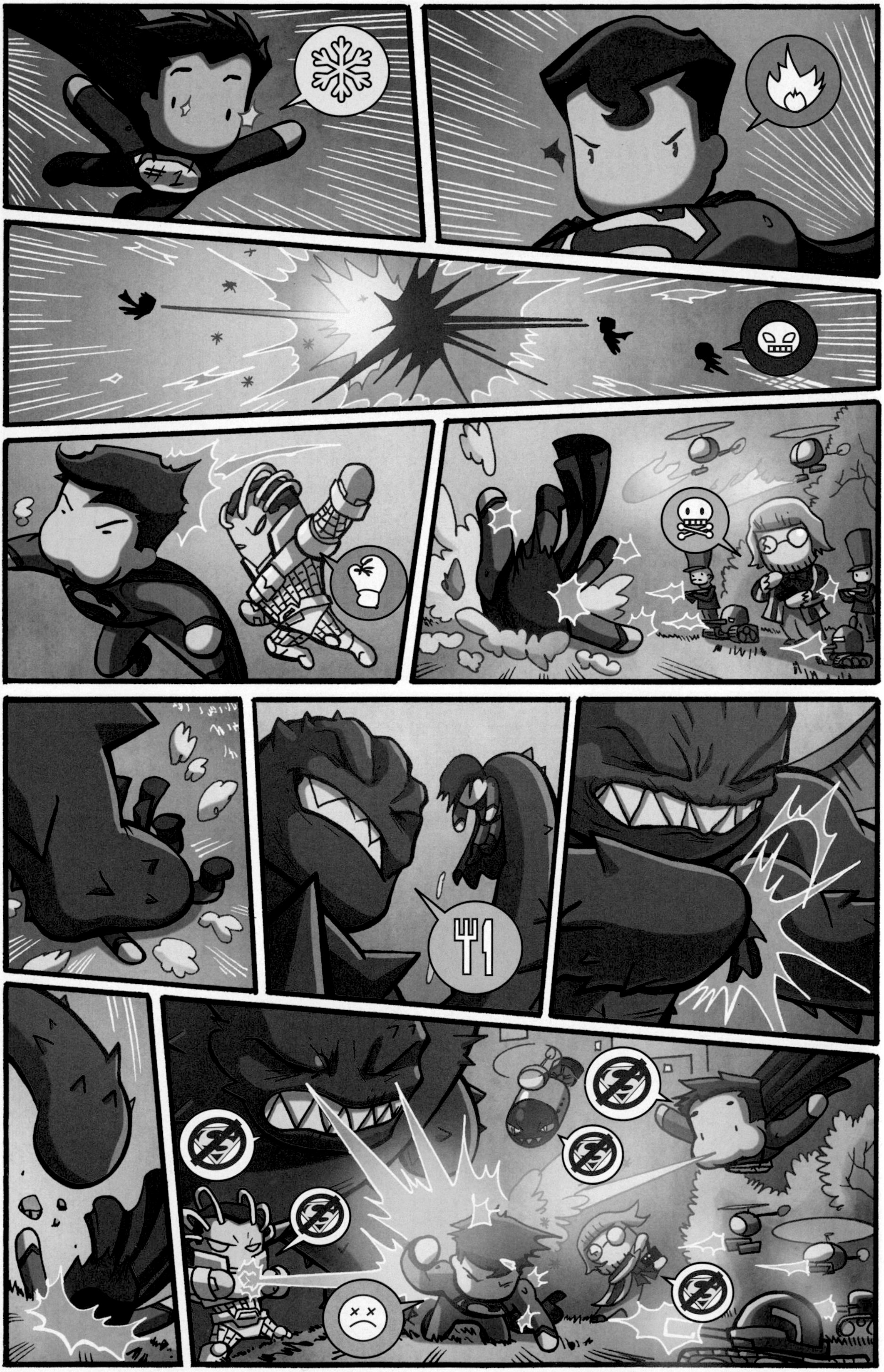
#1

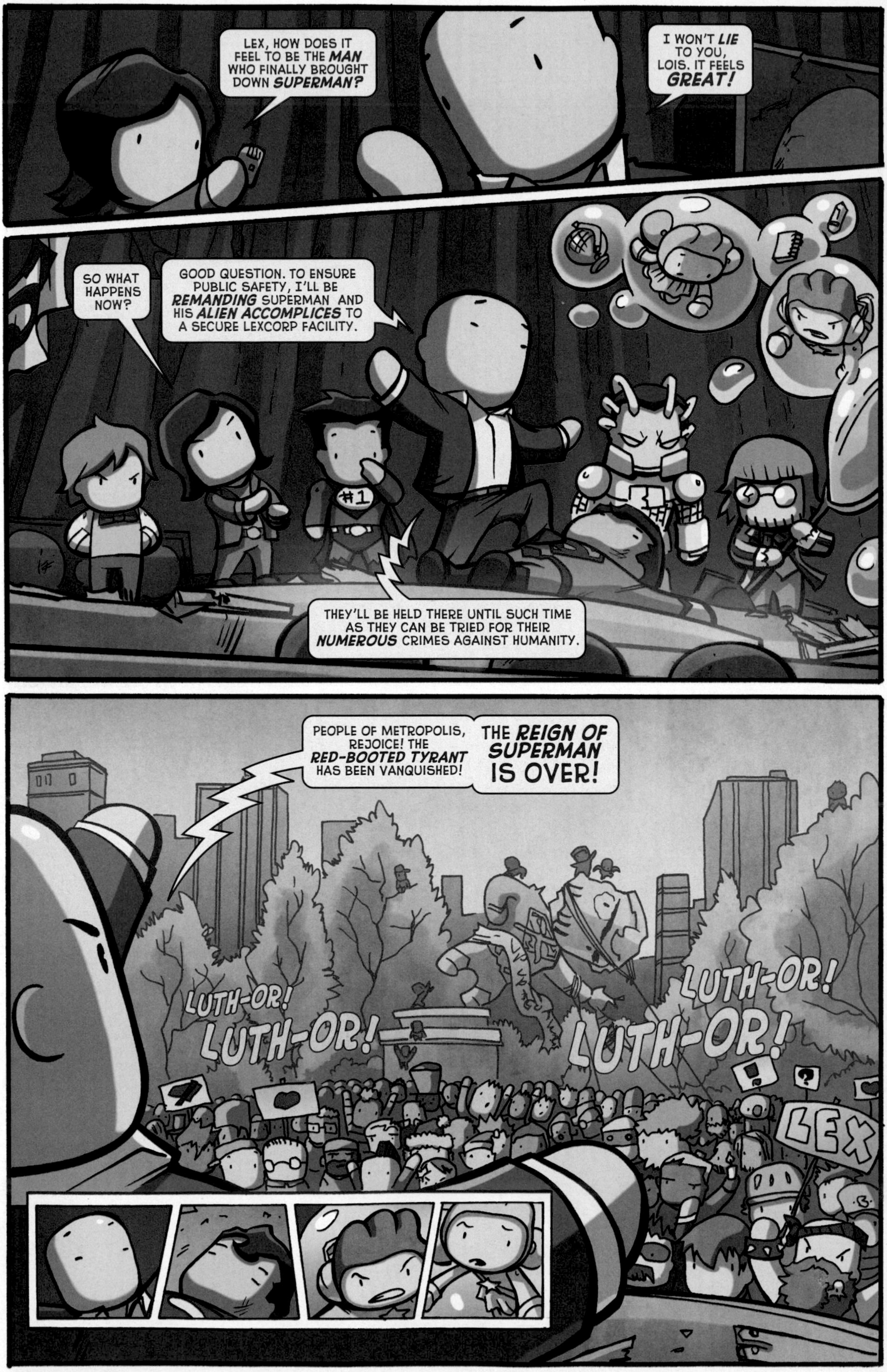
LEX, HOW DOES IT FEEL TO BE THE MAN WHO FINALLY BROUGHT DOWN SUPERMAN?
I WON'T LIE TO YOU, LOIS. IT FEELS GREAT!
SO WHAT HAPPENS NOW?
GOOD QUESTION. TO ENSURE PUBLIC SAFETY, I'LL BE REMANDING SUPERMAN AND HIS ALIEN ACCOMPLICES TO A SECURE LEXCORP FACILITY.
#1
THEY'LL BE HELD THERE UNTIL SUCH TIME AS THEY CAN BE TRIED FOR THEIR NUMEROUS CRIMES AGAINST HUMANITY.
PEOPLE OF METROPOLIS, REJOICE! THE RED-BOOTED TYRANT HAS BEEN VANQUISHED!
THE REIGN OF SUPERMAN IS OVER!
LUTH-OR!
LUTH-OR!
LUTH-OR!
LUTH-OR!
LEX

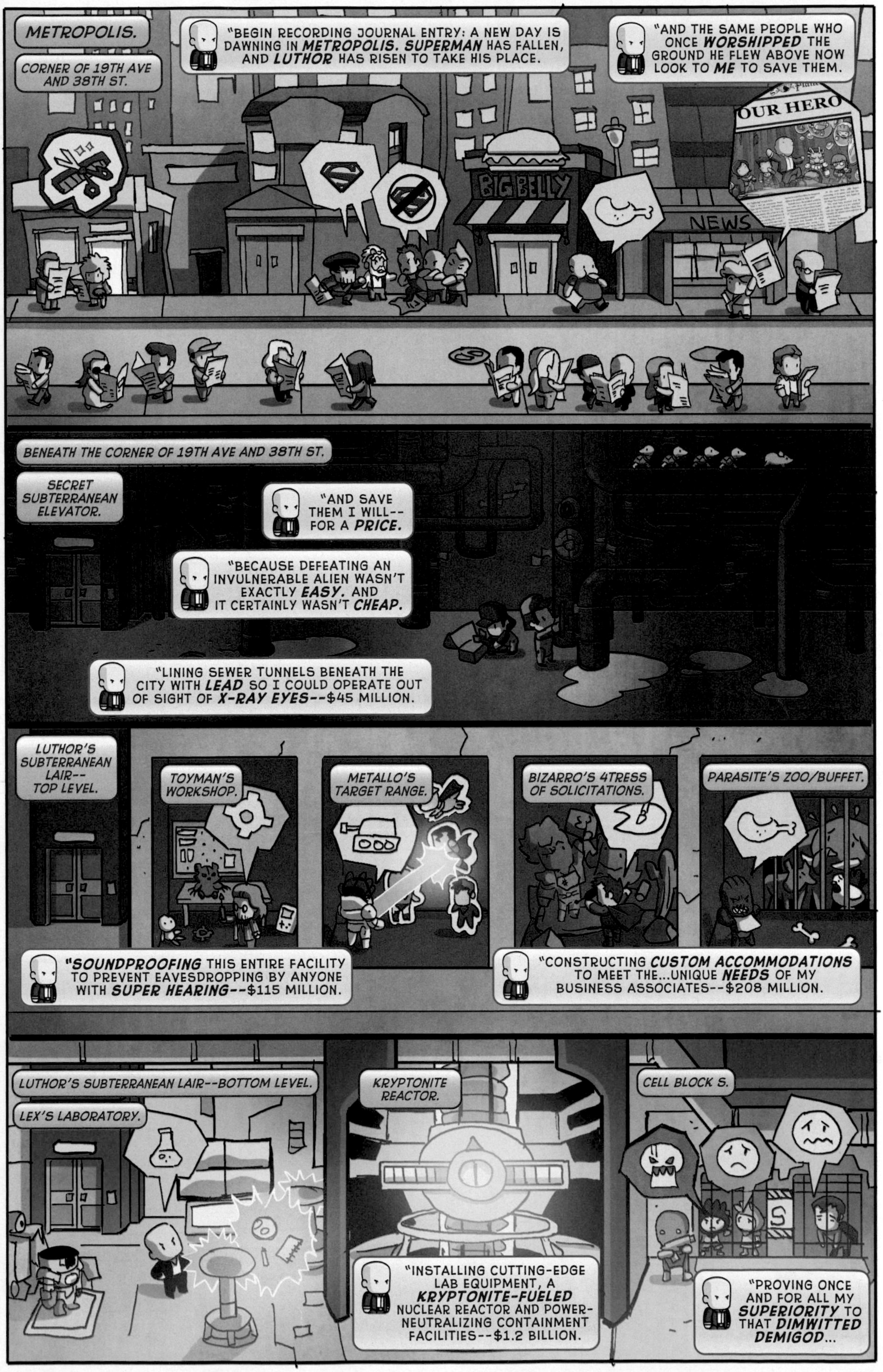
METROPOLIS.
CORNER OF 19TH AVE AND 38TH ST.
"BEGIN RECORDING JOURNAL ENTRY: A NEW DAY IS DAWNING IN METROPOLIS. SUPERMAN HAS FALLEN, AND LUTHOR HAS RISEN TO TAKE HIS PLACE.
"AND THE SAME PEOPLE WHO ONCE WORSHIPPED THE GROUND HE FLEW ABOVE NOW LOOK TO ME TO SAVE THEM.
OUR HERO
BIG BELLY
NEWS
BENEATH THE CORNER OF 19TH AVE AND 38TH ST.
SECRET SUBTERRANEAN ELEVATOR.
"AND SAVE THEM I WILL-- FOR A PRICE.
"BECAUSE DEFEATING AN INVULNERABLE ALIEN WASN'T EXACTLY EASY. AND IT CERTAINLY WASN'T CHEAP.
"LINING SEWER TUNNELS BENEATH THE CITY WITH LEAD SO I COULD OPERATE OUT OF SIGHT OF X-RAY EYES--$45 MILLION.
LUTHOR'S SUBTERRANEAN LAIR-- TOP LEVEL.
TOYMAN'S WORKSHOP.
METALLO'S TARGET RANGE.
BIZARRO'S 4TRESS OF SOLICITATIONS.
PARASITE'S ZOO/BUFFET.
"SOUNDPROOFING THIS ENTIRE FACILITY TO PREVENT EAVESDROPPING BY ANYONE WITH SUPER HEARING--$115 MILLION.
"CONSTRUCTING CUSTOM ACCOMMODATIONS TO MEET THE...UNIQUE NEEDS OF MY BUSINESS ASSOCIATES--$208 MILLION.
LUTHOR'S SUBTERRANEAN LAIR--BOTTOM LEVEL.
LEX'S LABORATORY.
KRYPTONITE REACTOR.
CELL BLOCK S.
S
"INSTALLING CUTTING-EDGE LAB EQUIPMENT, A KRYPTONITE-FUELED NUCLEAR REACTOR AND POWER-NEUTRALIZING CONTAINMENT FACILITIES--$1.2 BILLION.
"PROVING ONCE AND FOR ALL MY SUPERIORITY TO THAT DIMWITTED DEMIGOD...

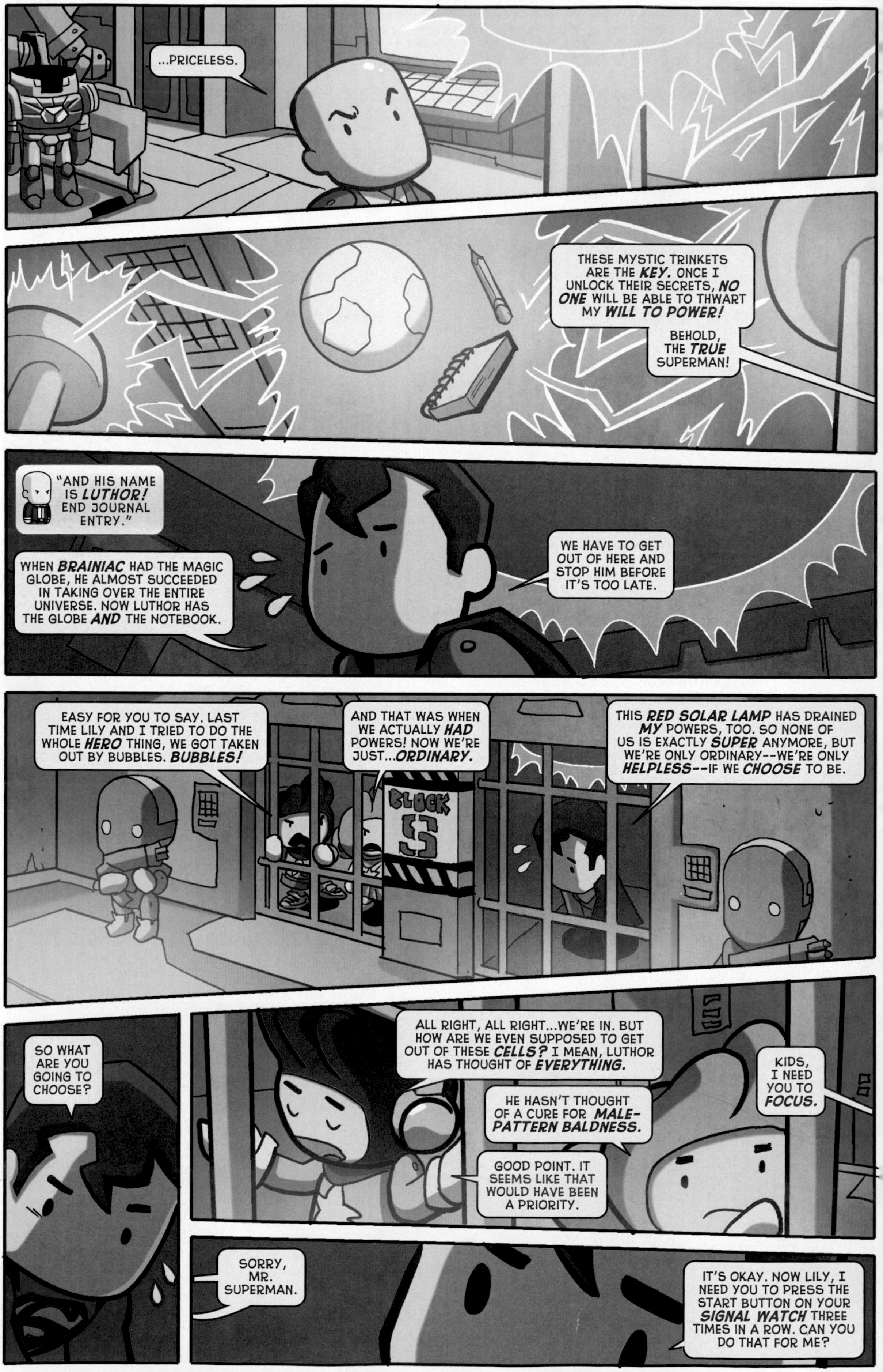

...PRICELESS.
THESE MYSTIC TRINKETS ARE THE KEY. ONCE I UNLOCK THEIR SECRETS, NO ONE WILL BE ABLE TO THWART MY WILL TO POWER!
BEHOLD, THE TRUE SUPERMAN!
"AND HIS NAME IS LUTHOR! END JOURNAL ENTRY."
WHEN BRAINIAC HAD THE MAGIC GLOBE, HE ALMOST SUCCEEDED IN TAKING OVER THE ENTIRE UNIVERSE. NOW LUTHOR HAS THE GLOBE AND THE NOTEBOOK.
WE HAVE TO GET OUT OF HERE AND STOP HIM BEFORE IT'S TOO LATE.
EASY FOR YOU TO SAY. LAST TIME LILY AND I TRIED TO DO THE WHOLE HERO THING, WE GOT TAKEN OUT BY BUBBLES. BUBBLES!
AND THAT WAS WHEN WE ACTUALLY HAD POWERS! NOW WE'RE JUST...ORDINARY.
BLOCK S
THIS RED SOLAR LAMP HAS DRAINED MY POWERS, TOO. SO NONE OF US IS EXACTLY SUPER ANYMORE, BUT WE'RE ONLY ORDINARY--WE'RE ONLY HELPLESS--IF WE CHOOSE TO BE.
SO WHAT ARE YOU GOING TO CHOOSE?
ALL RIGHT, ALL RIGHT...WE'RE IN. BUT HOW ARE WE EVEN SUPPOSED TO GET OUT OF THESE CELLS? I MEAN, LUTHOR HAS THOUGHT OF EVERYTHING.
HE HASN'T THOUGHT OF A CURE FOR MALE-PATTERN BALDNESS.
GOOD POINT. IT SEEMS LIKE THAT WOULD HAVE BEEN A PRIORITY.
KIDS, I NEED YOU TO FOCUS.
SORRY, MR. SUPERMAN.
IT'S OKAY. NOW LILY, I NEED YOU TO PRESS THE START BUTTON ON YOUR SIGNAL WATCH THREE TIMES IN A ROW. CAN YOU DO THAT FOR ME?

YEAH... BUT THE WALLS ARE TOO THICK--
--FOR A SIGNAL TO GET THROUGH TO ANYONE OUTSIDE. I KNOW, AND SO DOES LEX. THAT'S WHY HE LET YOU KEEP IT--TO MOCK YOU BECAUSE HE KNEW IT WOULD BE USELESS.
BEEPBEEP
?
ZEE
BUT WHILE LEX MAY BE A CERTIFIED GENIUS, HE'S STILL NOT HALF AS SMART AS HE THINKS HE IS.
!
AND THAT EGO HAS ALWAYS BEEN HIS DOWNFALL.
BLOCK S
KRIK
!
BECAUSE THE SIGNAL WATCH CAN ALSO BE TURNED INTO AN ULTRASONIC TRANSDUCER THAT GENERATES A STREAM OF POWERFUL, HIGH-FREQUENCY SOUNDWAVES.
THE KIND THAT CAN SHAKE WALLS AND SHATTER GLASS!
WHOA.
OF COURSE IT ONLY HAS A FEW SECONDS WORTH OF BATTERY POWER, BUT THAT'S ENOUGH TO DO THE JOB.
BECAUSE NOW THAT THE RED SUN RADIATION IS GONE, I'M ALREADY STARTING TO FEEL MY POWERS COMING BACK.
I JUST HOPE THE GUARDS DON'T COME IN HERE BEFORE I'M FULLY CHARGED.
BLOCK S
SURRENDER IMMEDIATELY, OR YOU WILL BE SUBDUED BY FORCE.
RESISTANCE IS FUTILE.

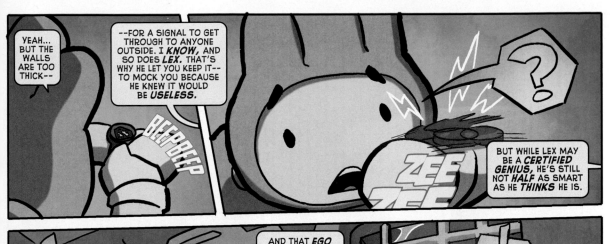

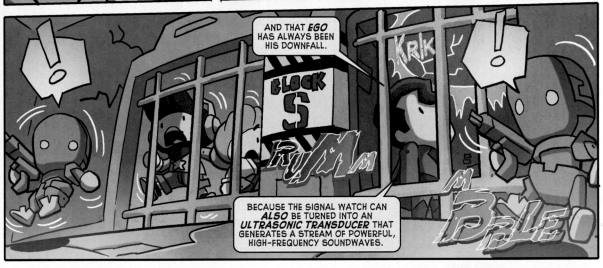

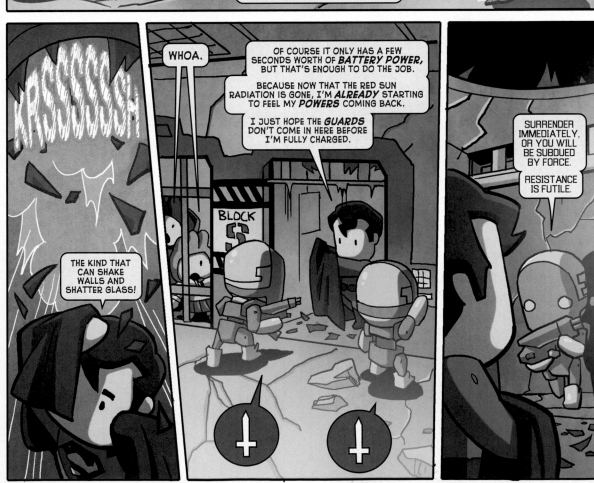

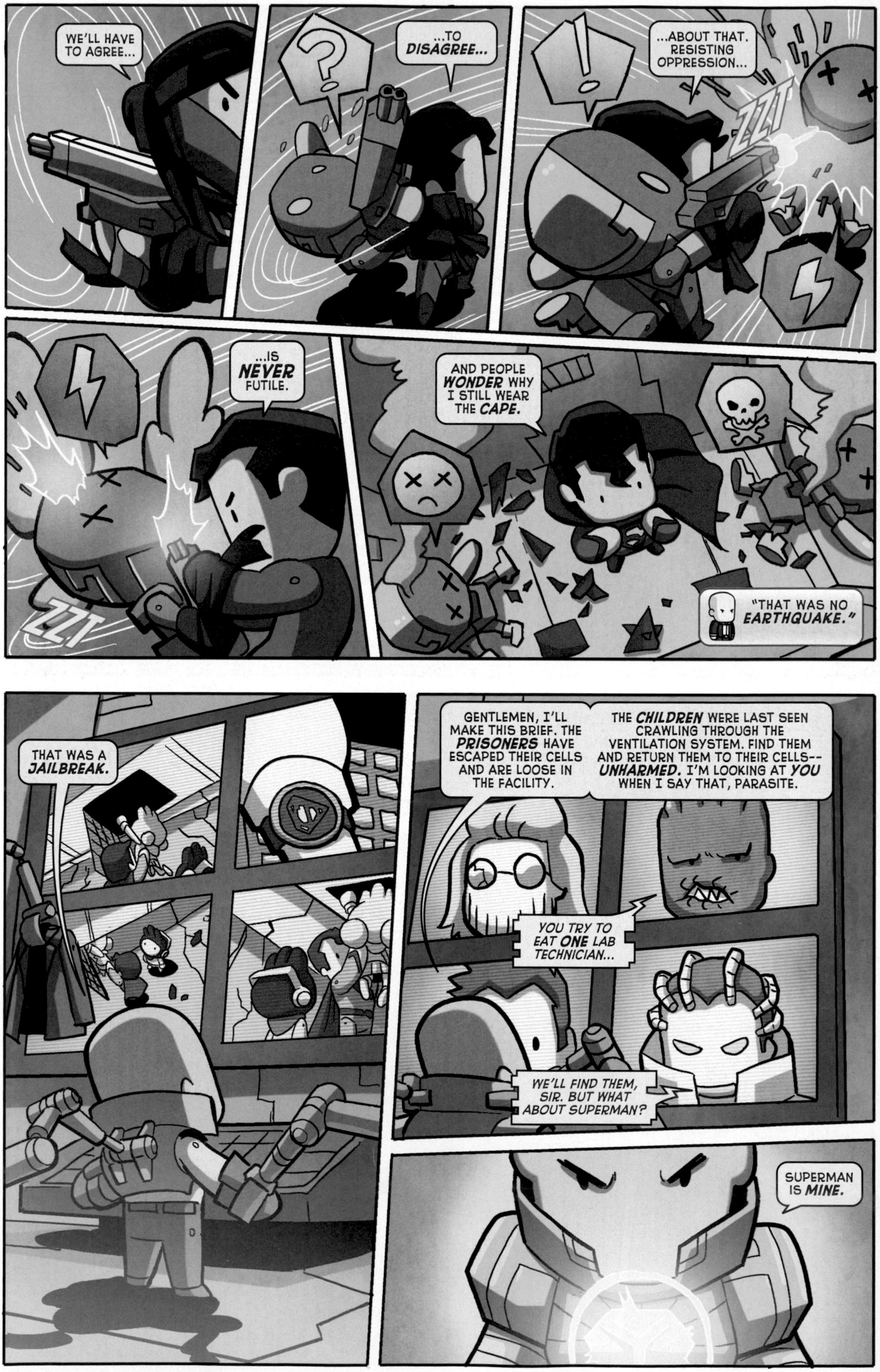
WE'LL HAVE TO AGREE...
?
...TO DISAGREE...
!
...ABOUT THAT. RESISTING OPPRESSION...
ZZT
...IS NEVER FUTILE.
ZZT
AND PEOPLE WONDER WHY I STILL WEAR THE CAPE.
"THAT WAS NO EARTHQUAKE."
THAT WAS A JAILBREAK.
GENTLEMEN, I'LL MAKE THIS BRIEF. THE PRISONERS HAVE ESCAPED THEIR CELLS AND ARE LOOSE IN THE FACILITY.
THE CHILDREN WERE LAST SEEN CRAWLING THROUGH THE VENTILATION SYSTEM. FIND THEM AND RETURN THEM TO THEIR CELLS-- UNHARMED. I'M LOOKING AT YOU WHEN I SAY THAT, PARASITE.
YOU TRY TO EAT ONE LAB TECHNICIAN...
WE'LL FIND THEM, SIR. BUT WHAT ABOUT SUPERMAN?
SUPERMAN IS MINE.

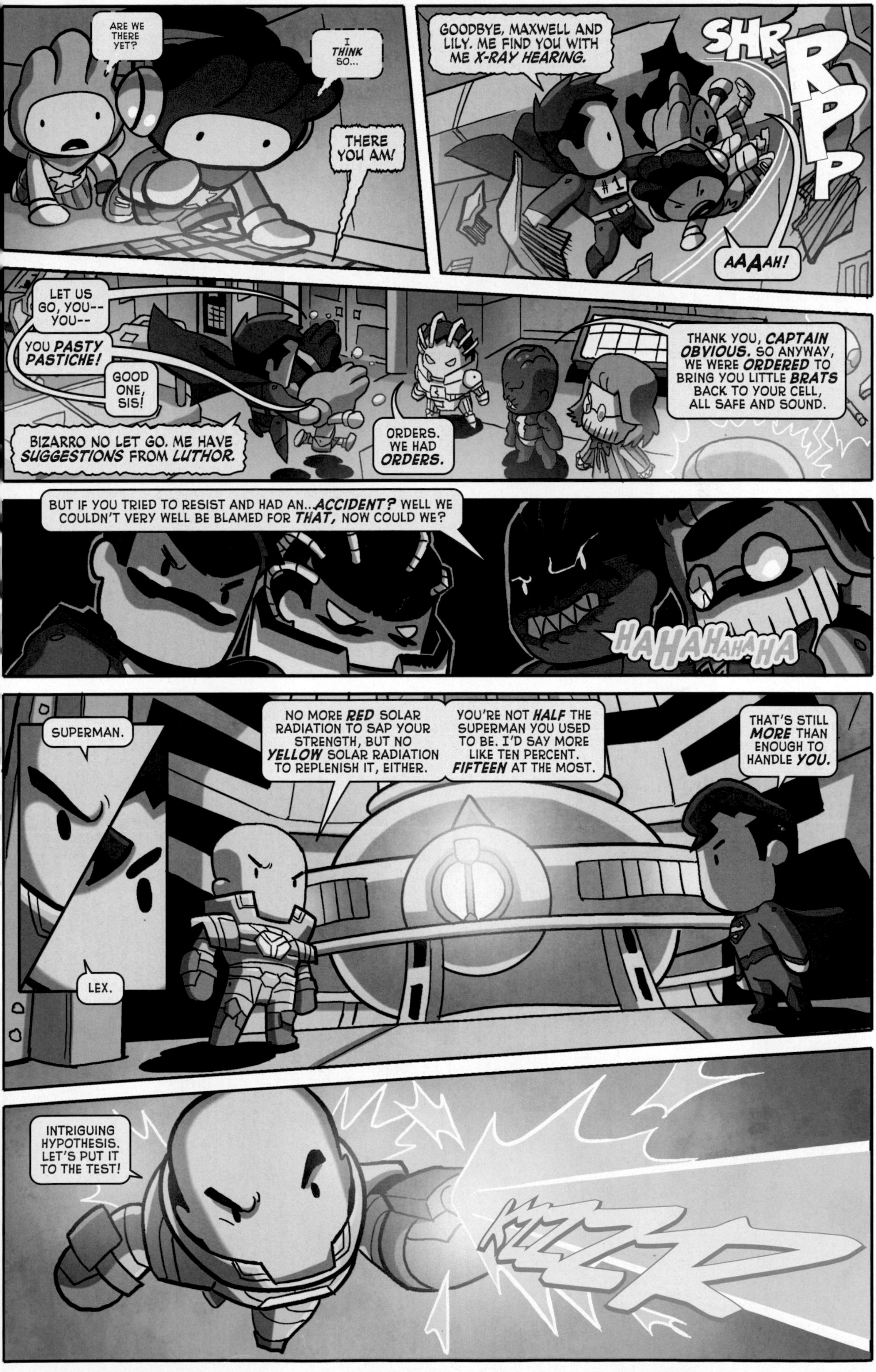
ARE WE THERE YET?
I THINK SO...
THERE YOU AM!
GOODBYE, MAXWELL AND LILY. ME FIND YOU WITH ME X-RAY HEARING.
SHRRPP
AAAAH!
#1
LET US GO, YOU-- YOU--
YOU PASTY PASTICHE!
GOOD ONE, SIS!
BIZARRO NO LET GO. ME HAVE SUGGESTIONS FROM LUTHOR.
ORDERS. WE HAD ORDERS.
THANK YOU, CAPTAIN OBVIOUS. SO ANYWAY, WE WERE ORDERED TO BRING YOU LITTLE BRATS BACK TO YOUR CELL, ALL SAFE AND SOUND.
BUT IF YOU TRIED TO RESIST AND HAD AN...ACCIDENT? WELL WE COULDN'T VERY WELL BE BLAMED FOR THAT, NOW COULD WE?
HAHAHAHAHAHA
SUPERMAN.
LEX.
NO MORE RED SOLAR RADIATION TO SAP YOUR STRENGTH, BUT NO YELLOW SOLAR RADIATION TO REPLENISH IT, EITHER.
YOU'RE NOT HALF THE SUPERMAN YOU USED TO BE. I'D SAY MORE LIKE TEN PERCENT. FIFTEEN AT THE MOST.
THAT'S STILL MORE THAN ENOUGH TO HANDLE YOU.
INTRIGUING HYPOTHESIS. LET'S PUT IT TO THE TEST!
KZZZR

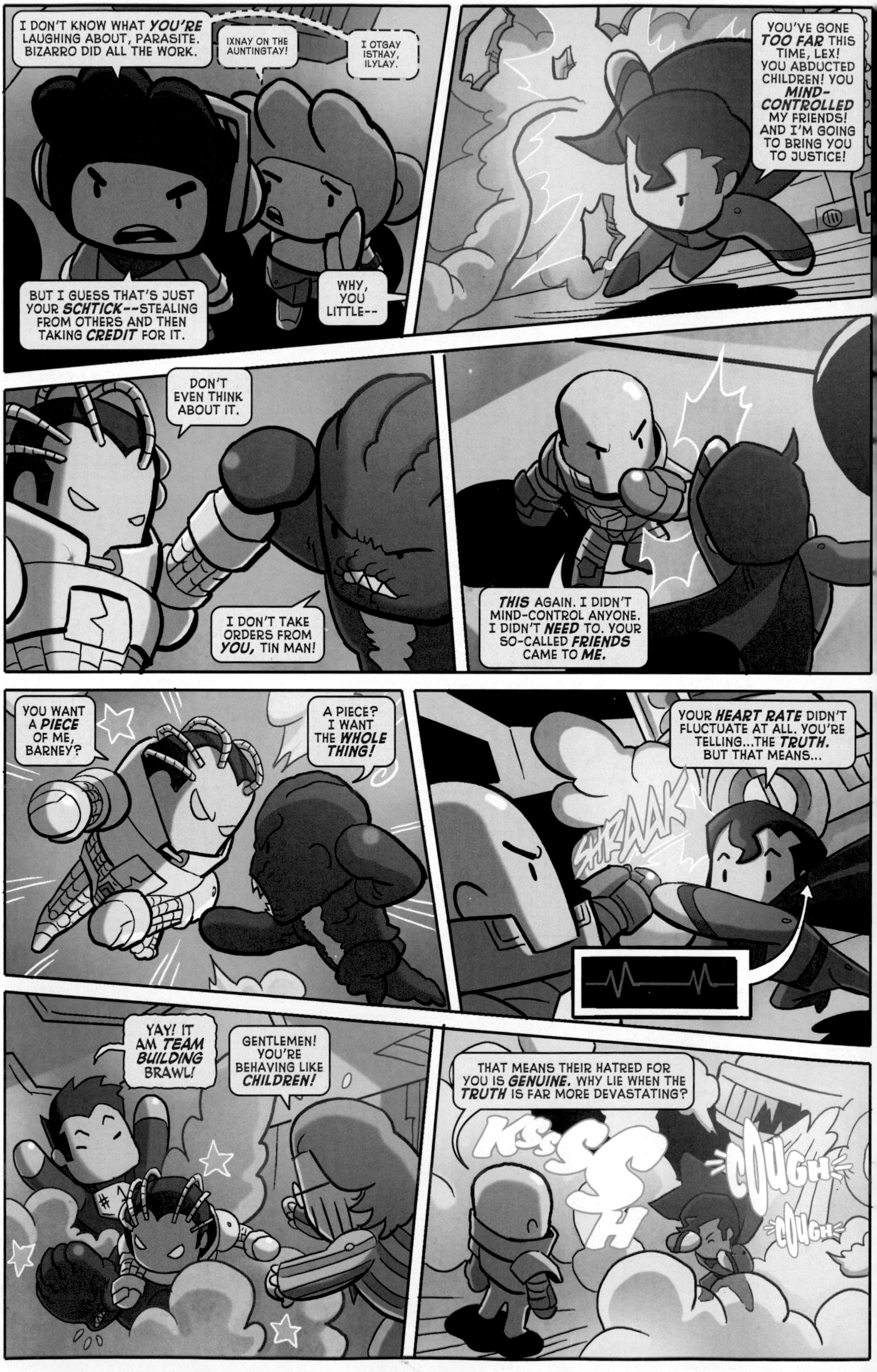
I DON'T KNOW WHAT YOU'RE LAUGHING ABOUT, PARASITE. BIZARRO DID ALL THE WORK.
IXNAY ON THE AUNTINGTAY!
I OTGAY ISTHAY, ILYLAY.
BUT I GUESS THAT'S JUST YOUR SCHTICK--STEALING FROM OTHERS AND THEN TAKING CREDIT FOR IT.
WHY, YOU LITTLE--
YOU'VE GONE TOO FAR THIS TIME, LEX! YOU ABDUCTED CHILDREN! YOU MIND-CONTROLLED MY FRIENDS! AND I'M GOING TO BRING YOU TO JUSTICE!
DON'T EVEN THINK ABOUT IT.
I DON'T TAKE ORDERS FROM YOU, TIN MAN!
THIS AGAIN. I DIDN'T MIND-CONTROL ANYONE. I DIDN'T NEED TO. YOUR SO-CALLED FRIENDS CAME TO ME.
YOU WANT A PIECE OF ME, BARNEY?
A PIECE? I WANT THE WHOLE THING!
YOUR HEART RATE DIDN'T FLUCTUATE AT ALL. YOU'RE TELLING...THE TRUTH. BUT THAT MEANS...
SHRAAK
YAY! IT AM TEAM BUILDING BRAWL!
GENTLEMEN! YOU'RE BEHAVING LIKE CHILDREN!
THAT MEANS THEIR HATRED FOR YOU IS GENUINE. WHY LIE WHEN THE TRUTH IS FAR MORE DEVASTATING?
KSSSSH
COUGH
COUGH

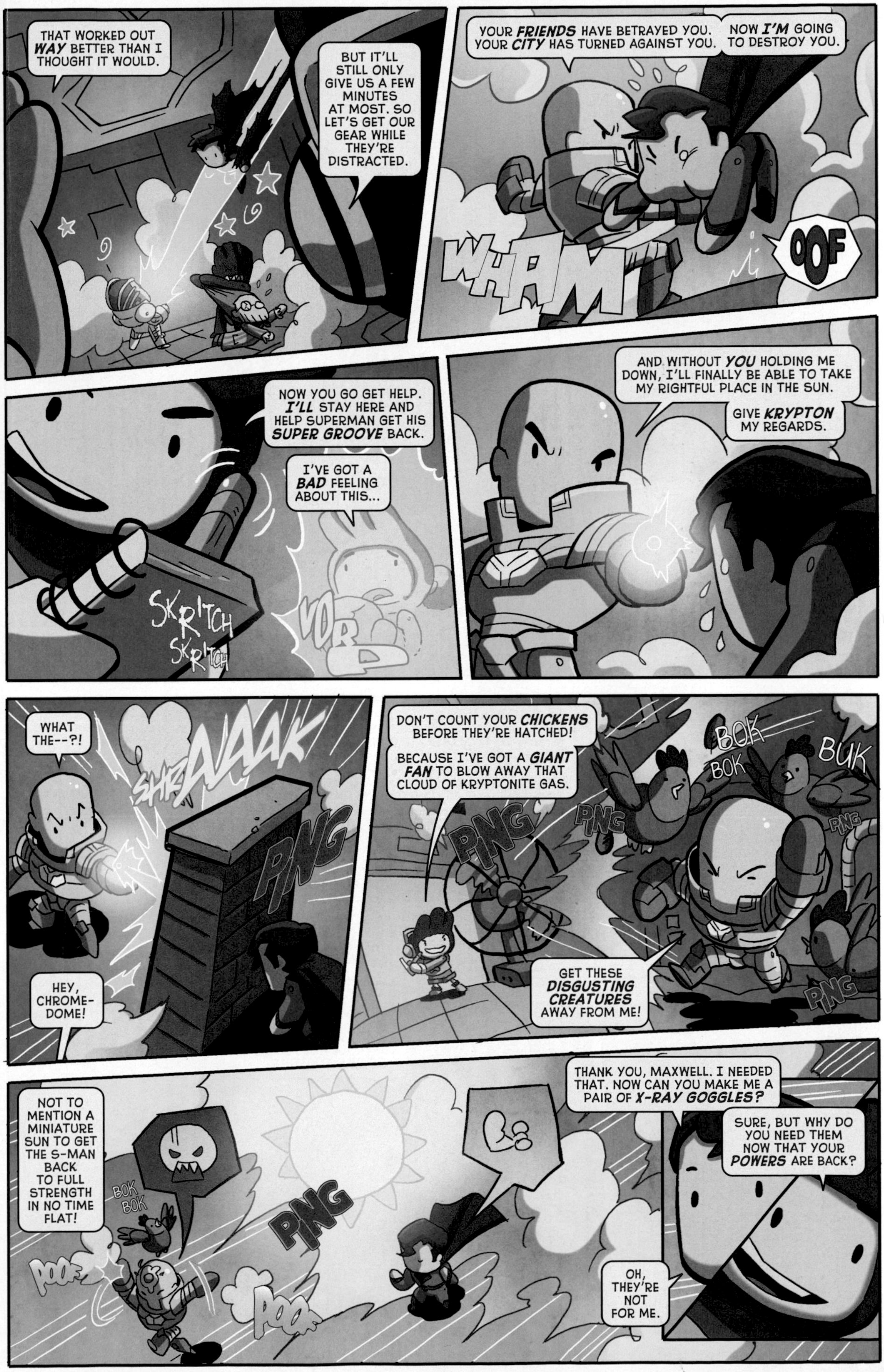
THAT WORKED OUT WAY BETTER THAN I THOUGHT IT WOULD.
BUT IT'LL STILL ONLY GIVE US A FEW MINUTES AT MOST. SO LET'S GET OUR GEAR WHILE THEY'RE DISTRACTED.
YOUR FRIENDS HAVE BETRAYED YOU. YOUR CITY HAS TURNED AGAINST YOU.
NOW I'M GOING TO DESTROY YOU.
WHAM
OOF
NOW YOU GO GET HELP. I'LL STAY HERE AND HELP SUPERMAN GET HIS SUPER GROOVE BACK.
I'VE GOT A BAD FEELING ABOUT THIS...
SKRITCH SKRITCH
VORP
AND WITHOUT YOU HOLDING ME DOWN, I'LL FINALLY BE ABLE TO TAKE MY RIGHTFUL PLACE IN THE SUN.
GIVE KRYPTON MY REGARDS.
WHAT THE--?!
SHRAAAK
PING
HEY, CHROME-DOME!
DON'T COUNT YOUR CHICKENS BEFORE THEY'RE HATCHED!
BECAUSE I'VE GOT A GIANT FAN TO BLOW AWAY THAT CLOUD OF KRYPTONITE GAS.
BOK BOK
BUK
PING
GET THESE DISGUSTING CREATURES AWAY FROM ME!
NOT TO MENTION A MINIATURE SUN TO GET THE S-MAN BACK TO FULL STRENGTH IN NO TIME FLAT!
BOK BOK
PING
POOF
POOF
THANK YOU, MAXWELL. I NEEDED THAT. NOW CAN YOU MAKE ME A PAIR OF X-RAY GOGGLES?
SURE, BUT WHY DO YOU NEED THEM NOW THAT YOUR POWERS ARE BACK?
OH, THEY'RE NOT FOR ME.

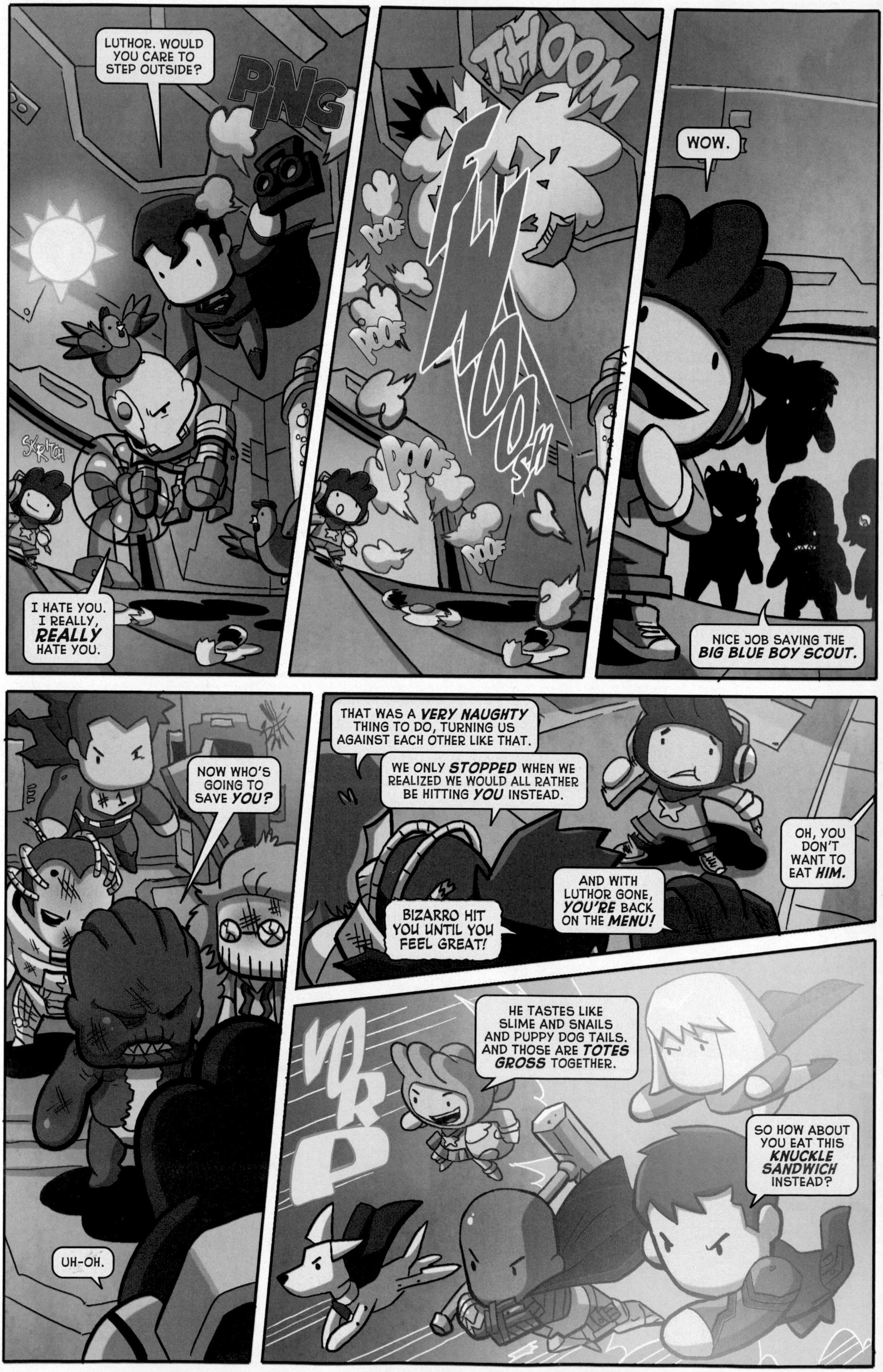

LUTHOR. WOULD YOU CARE TO STEP OUTSIDE?
PING
SKRITCH
I HATE YOU. I REALLY, *REALLY* HATE YOU.
THOOM
FWOOSH
POOF
POOF
POOF
POOF
WOW.
NICE JOB SAVING THE *BIG BLUE BOY SCOUT.*
NOW WHO'S GOING TO SAVE *YOU?*
UH-OH.
THAT WAS A *VERY NAUGHTY* THING TO DO, TURNING US AGAINST EACH OTHER LIKE THAT.
WE ONLY *STOPPED* WHEN WE REALIZED WE WOULD ALL RATHER BE HITTING *YOU* INSTEAD.
BIZARRO HIT YOU UNTIL YOU FEEL GREAT!
AND WITH LUTHOR GONE, *YOU'RE* BACK ON THE *MENU!*
OH, YOU DON'T WANT TO EAT *HIM.*
VORP
HE TASTES LIKE SLIME AND SNAILS AND PUPPY DOG TAILS. AND THOSE ARE *TOTES GROSS* TOGETHER.
SO HOW ABOUT YOU EAT THIS *KNUCKLE SANDWICH* INSTEAD?

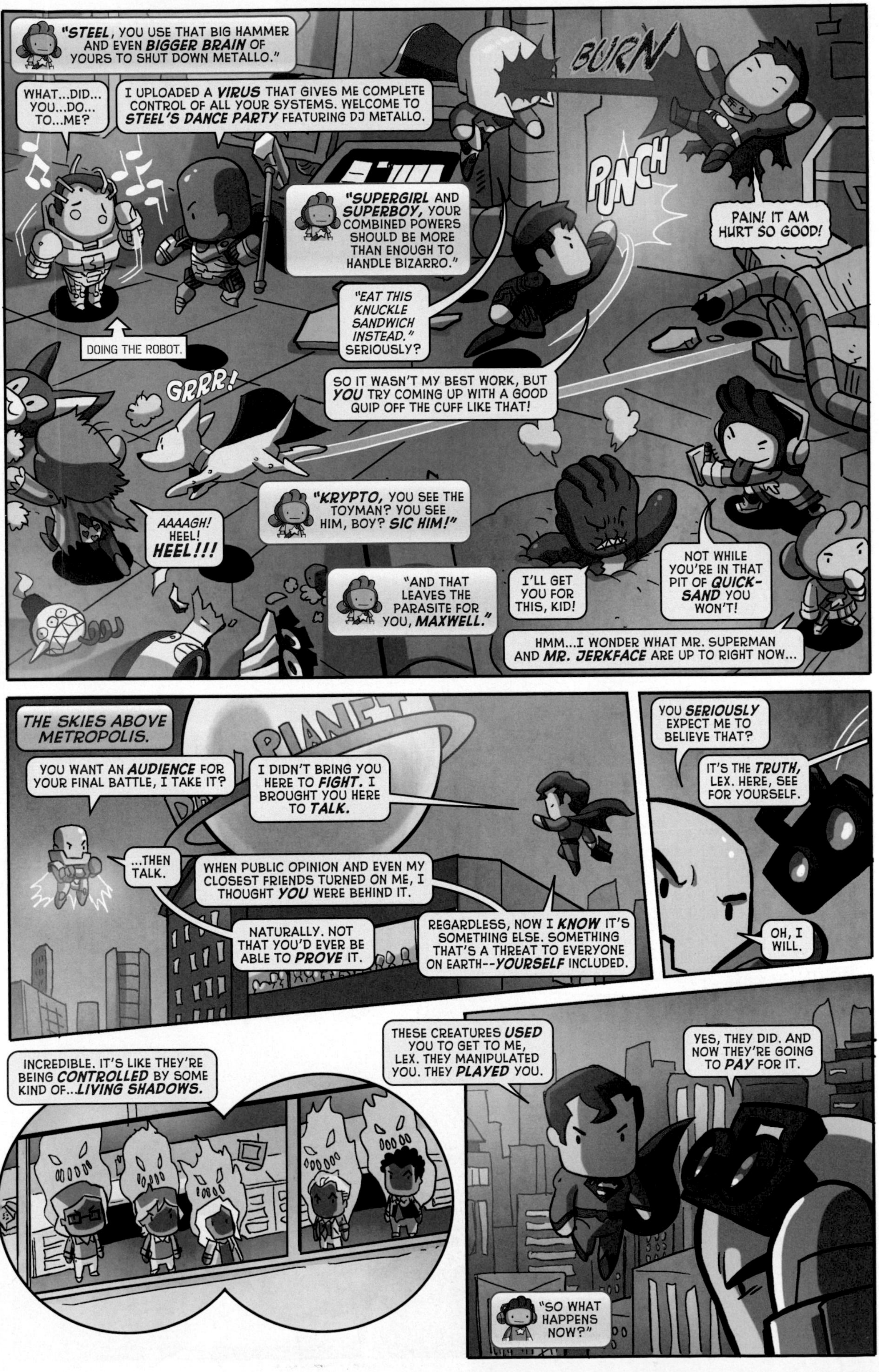
"STEEL, YOU USE THAT BIG HAMMER AND EVEN BIGGER BRAIN OF YOURS TO SHUT DOWN METALLO."
BURN
WHAT...DID... YOU...DO... TO...ME?
I UPLOADED A VIRUS THAT GIVES ME COMPLETE CONTROL OF ALL YOUR SYSTEMS. WELCOME TO STEEL'S DANCE PARTY FEATURING DJ METALLO.
PUNCH
"SUPERGIRL AND SUPERBOY, YOUR COMBINED POWERS SHOULD BE MORE THAN ENOUGH TO HANDLE BIZARRO."
PAIN! IT AM HURT SO GOOD!
"EAT THIS KNUCKLE SANDWICH INSTEAD." SERIOUSLY?
DOING THE ROBOT.
SO IT WASN'T MY BEST WORK, BUT YOU TRY COMING UP WITH A GOOD QUIP OFF THE CUFF LIKE THAT!
GRRR!
"KRYPTO, YOU SEE THE TOYMAN? YOU SEE HIM, BOY? SIC HIM!"
AAAAGH! HEEL! HEEL!!!
"AND THAT LEAVES THE PARASITE FOR YOU, MAXWELL."
I'LL GET YOU FOR THIS, KID!
NOT WHILE YOU'RE IN THAT PIT OF QUICK-SAND YOU WON'T!
HMM...I WONDER WHAT MR. SUPERMAN AND MR. JERKFACE ARE UP TO RIGHT NOW...
THE SKIES ABOVE METROPOLIS.
YOU WANT AN AUDIENCE FOR YOUR FINAL BATTLE, I TAKE IT?
I DIDN'T BRING YOU HERE TO FIGHT. I BROUGHT YOU HERE TO TALK.
...THEN TALK.
WHEN PUBLIC OPINION AND EVEN MY CLOSEST FRIENDS TURNED ON ME, I THOUGHT YOU WERE BEHIND IT.
NATURALLY. NOT THAT YOU'D EVER BE ABLE TO PROVE IT.
REGARDLESS, NOW I KNOW IT'S SOMETHING ELSE. SOMETHING THAT'S A THREAT TO EVERYONE ON EARTH--YOURSELF INCLUDED.
YOU SERIOUSLY EXPECT ME TO BELIEVE THAT?
IT'S THE TRUTH, LEX. HERE, SEE FOR YOURSELF.
OH, I WILL.
INCREDIBLE. IT'S LIKE THEY'RE BEING CONTROLLED BY SOME KIND OF...LIVING SHADOWS.
THESE CREATURES USED YOU TO GET TO ME, LEX. THEY MANIPULATED YOU. THEY PLAYED YOU.
YES, THEY DID. AND NOW THEY'RE GOING TO PAY FOR IT.
"SO WHAT HAPPENS NOW?"

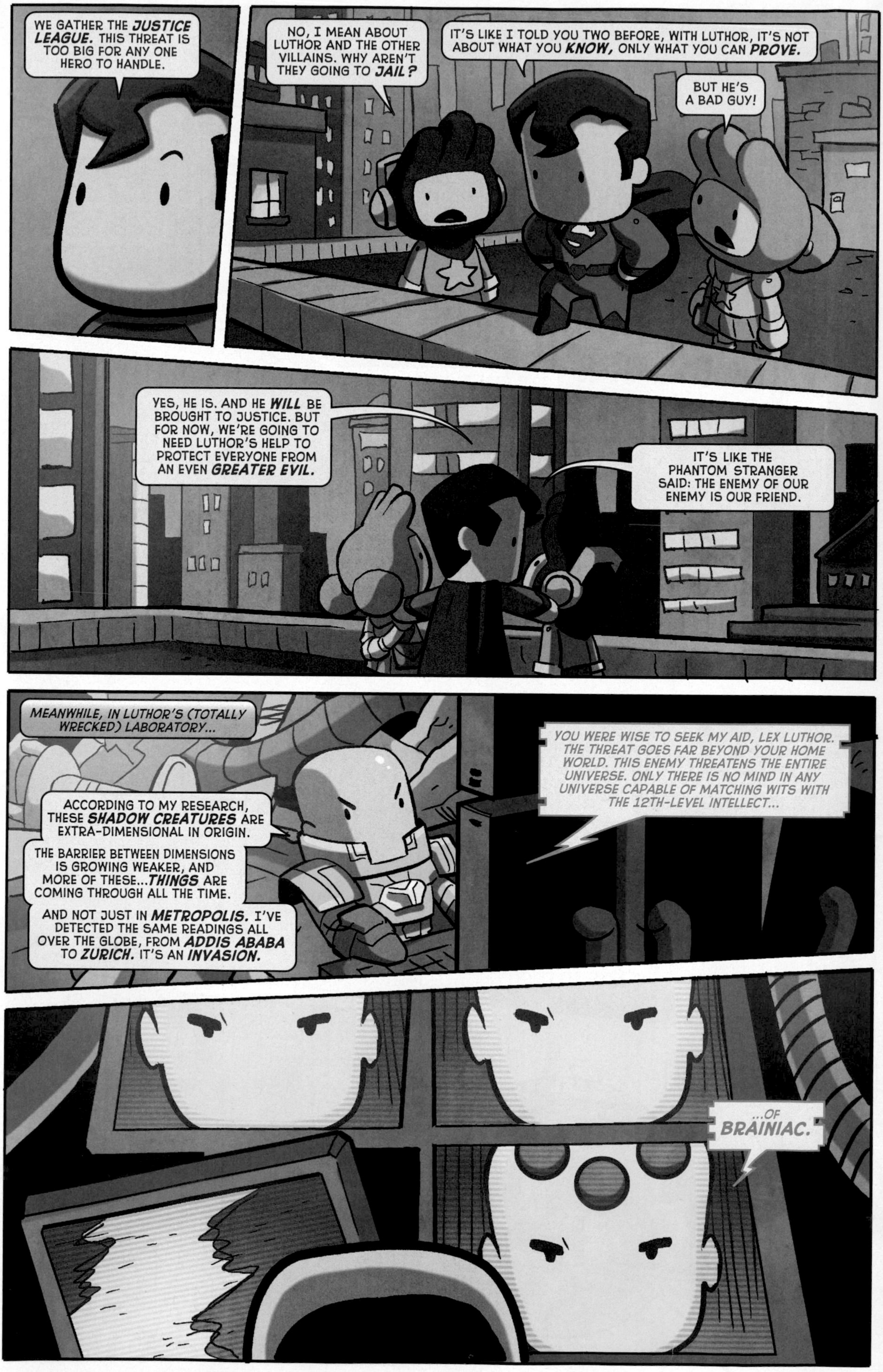
WE GATHER THE JUSTICE LEAGUE. THIS THREAT IS TOO BIG FOR ANY ONE HERO TO HANDLE.
NO, I MEAN ABOUT LUTHOR AND THE OTHER VILLAINS. WHY AREN'T THEY GOING TO JAIL?
IT'S LIKE I TOLD YOU TWO BEFORE, WITH LUTHOR, IT'S NOT ABOUT WHAT YOU KNOW, ONLY WHAT YOU CAN PROVE.
BUT HE'S A BAD GUY!
YES, HE IS. AND HE WILL BE BROUGHT TO JUSTICE. BUT FOR NOW, WE'RE GOING TO NEED LUTHOR'S HELP TO PROTECT EVERYONE FROM AN EVEN GREATER EVIL.
IT'S LIKE THE PHANTOM STRANGER SAID: THE ENEMY OF OUR ENEMY IS OUR FRIEND.
MEANWHILE, IN LUTHOR'S (TOTALLY WRECKED) LABORATORY...
ACCORDING TO MY RESEARCH, THESE SHADOW CREATURES ARE EXTRA-DIMENSIONAL IN ORIGIN.
THE BARRIER BETWEEN DIMENSIONS IS GROWING WEAKER, AND MORE OF THESE...THINGS ARE COMING THROUGH ALL THE TIME.
AND NOT JUST IN METROPOLIS. I'VE DETECTED THE SAME READINGS ALL OVER THE GLOBE, FROM ADDIS ABABA TO ZURICH. IT'S AN INVASION.
YOU WERE WISE TO SEEK MY AID, LEX LUTHOR. THE THREAT GOES FAR BEYOND YOUR HOME WORLD. THIS ENEMY THREATENS THE ENTIRE UNIVERSE. ONLY THERE IS NO MIND IN ANY UNIVERSE CAPABLE OF MATCHING WITS WITH THE 12TH-LEVEL INTELLECT...
...OF BRAINIAC.

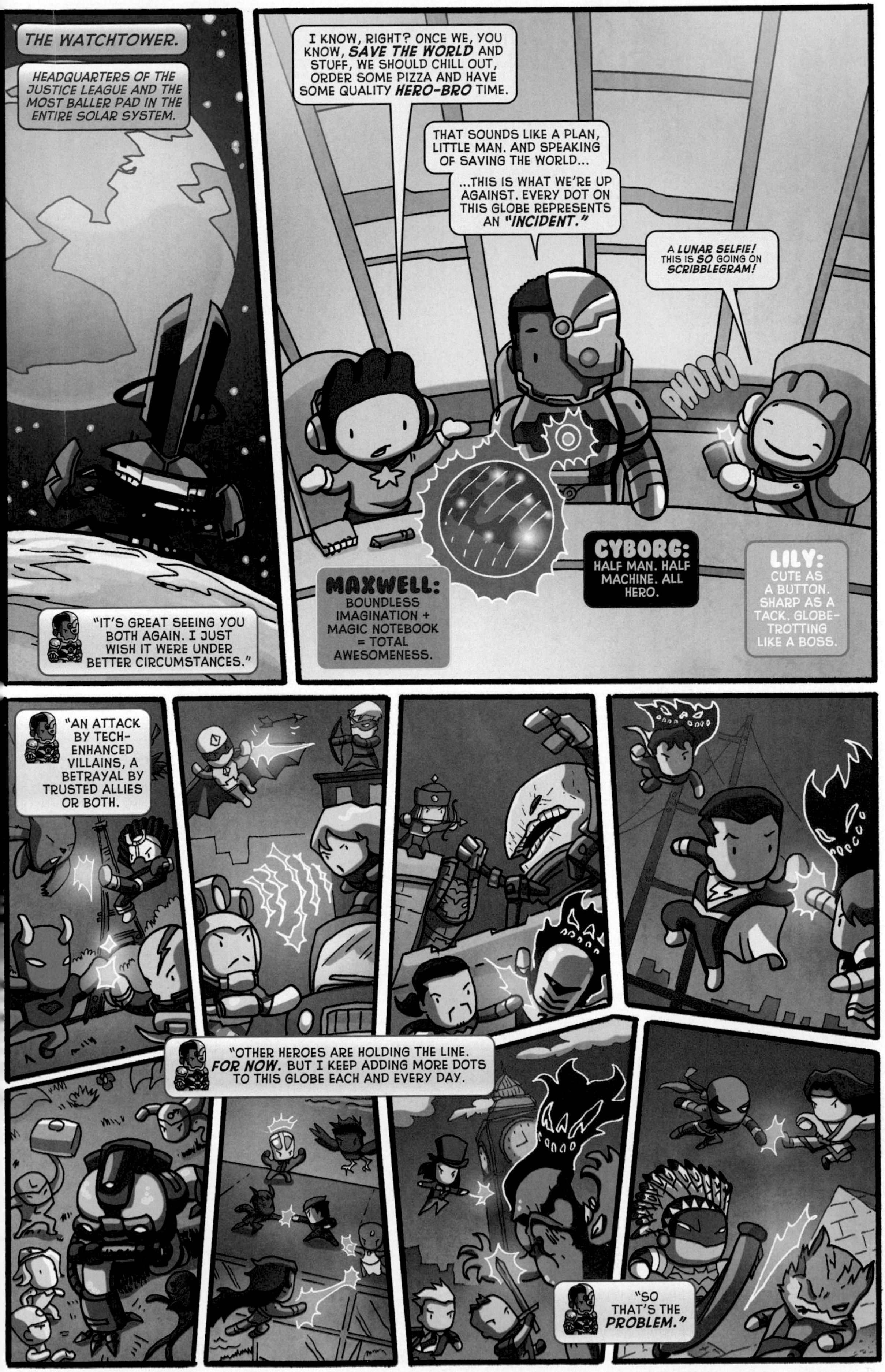
THE WATCHTOWER.
HEADQUARTERS OF THE JUSTICE LEAGUE AND THE MOST BALLER PAD IN THE ENTIRE SOLAR SYSTEM.
"IT'S GREAT SEEING YOU BOTH AGAIN. I JUST WISH IT WERE UNDER BETTER CIRCUMSTANCES."
I KNOW, RIGHT? ONCE WE, YOU KNOW, SAVE THE WORLD AND STUFF, WE SHOULD CHILL OUT, ORDER SOME PIZZA AND HAVE SOME QUALITY HERO-BRO TIME.
THAT SOUNDS LIKE A PLAN, LITTLE MAN. AND SPEAKING OF SAVING THE WORLD...
...THIS IS WHAT WE'RE UP AGAINST. EVERY DOT ON THIS GLOBE REPRESENTS AN "INCIDENT."
A LUNAR SELFIE! THIS IS SO GOING ON SCRIBBLEGRAM!
PHOTO
MAXWELL: BOUNDLESS IMAGINATION + MAGIC NOTEBOOK = TOTAL AWESOMENESS.
CYBORG: HALF MAN. HALF MACHINE. ALL HERO.
LILY: CUTE AS A BUTTON. SHARP AS A TACK. GLOBE-TROTTING LIKE A BOSS.
"AN ATTACK BY TECH-ENHANCED VILLAINS, A BETRAYAL BY TRUSTED ALLIES OR BOTH.
"OTHER HEROES ARE HOLDING THE LINE. FOR NOW. BUT I KEEP ADDING MORE DOTS TO THIS GLOBE EACH AND EVERY DAY.
"SO THAT'S THE PROBLEM."

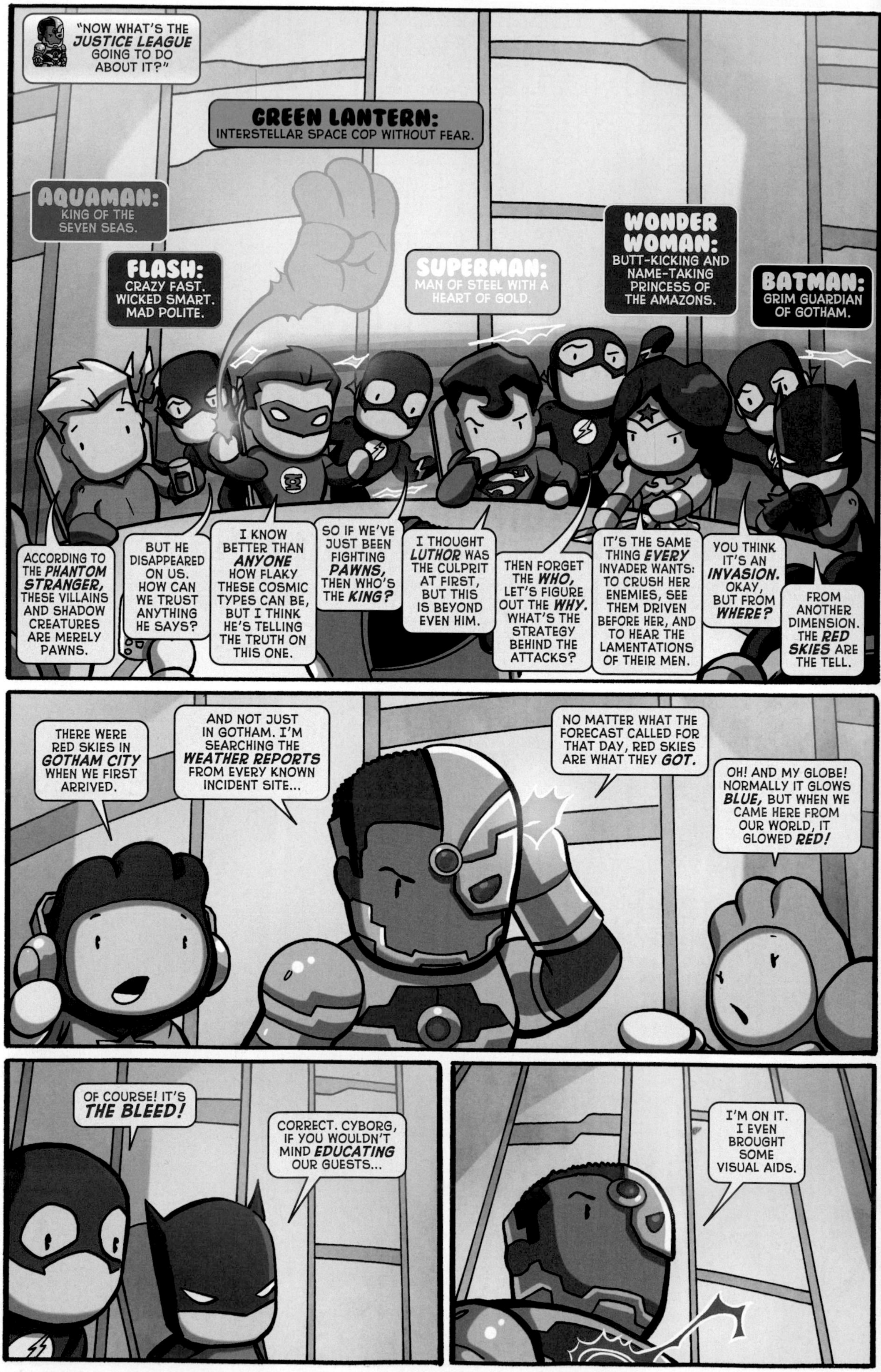
"NOW WHAT'S THE JUSTICE LEAGUE GOING TO DO ABOUT IT?"
GREEN LANTERN: INTERSTELLAR SPACE COP WITHOUT FEAR.
AQUAMAN: KING OF THE SEVEN SEAS.
FLASH: CRAZY FAST. WICKED SMART. MAD POLITE.
SUPERMAN: MAN OF STEEL WITH A HEART OF GOLD.
WONDER WOMAN: BUTT-KICKING AND NAME-TAKING PRINCESS OF THE AMAZONS.
BATMAN: GRIM GUARDIAN OF GOTHAM.
ACCORDING TO THE PHANTOM STRANGER, THESE VILLAINS AND SHADOW CREATURES ARE MERELY PAWNS.
BUT HE DISAPPEARED ON US. HOW CAN WE TRUST ANYTHING HE SAYS?
I KNOW BETTER THAN ANYONE HOW FLAKY THESE COSMIC TYPES CAN BE, BUT I THINK HE'S TELLING THE TRUTH ON THIS ONE.
SO IF WE'VE JUST BEEN FIGHTING PAWNS, THEN WHO'S THE KING?
I THOUGHT LUTHOR WAS THE CULPRIT AT FIRST, BUT THIS IS BEYOND EVEN HIM.
THEN FORGET THE WHO, LET'S FIGURE OUT THE WHY. WHAT'S THE STRATEGY BEHIND THE ATTACKS?
IT'S THE SAME THING EVERY INVADER WANTS: TO CRUSH HER ENEMIES, SEE THEM DRIVEN BEFORE HER, AND TO HEAR THE LAMENTATIONS OF THEIR MEN.
YOU THINK IT'S AN INVASION. OKAY, BUT FROM WHERE?
FROM ANOTHER DIMENSION. THE RED SKIES ARE THE TELL.
THERE WERE RED SKIES IN GOTHAM CITY WHEN WE FIRST ARRIVED.
AND NOT JUST IN GOTHAM. I'M SEARCHING THE WEATHER REPORTS FROM EVERY KNOWN INCIDENT SITE...
NO MATTER WHAT THE FORECAST CALLED FOR THAT DAY, RED SKIES ARE WHAT THEY GOT.
OH! AND MY GLOBE! NORMALLY IT GLOWS BLUE, BUT WHEN WE CAME HERE FROM OUR WORLD, IT GLOWED RED!
OF COURSE! IT'S THE BLEED!
CORRECT. CYBORG, IF YOU WOULDN'T MIND EDUCATING OUR GUESTS...
I'M ON IT. I EVEN BROUGHT SOME VISUAL AIDS.

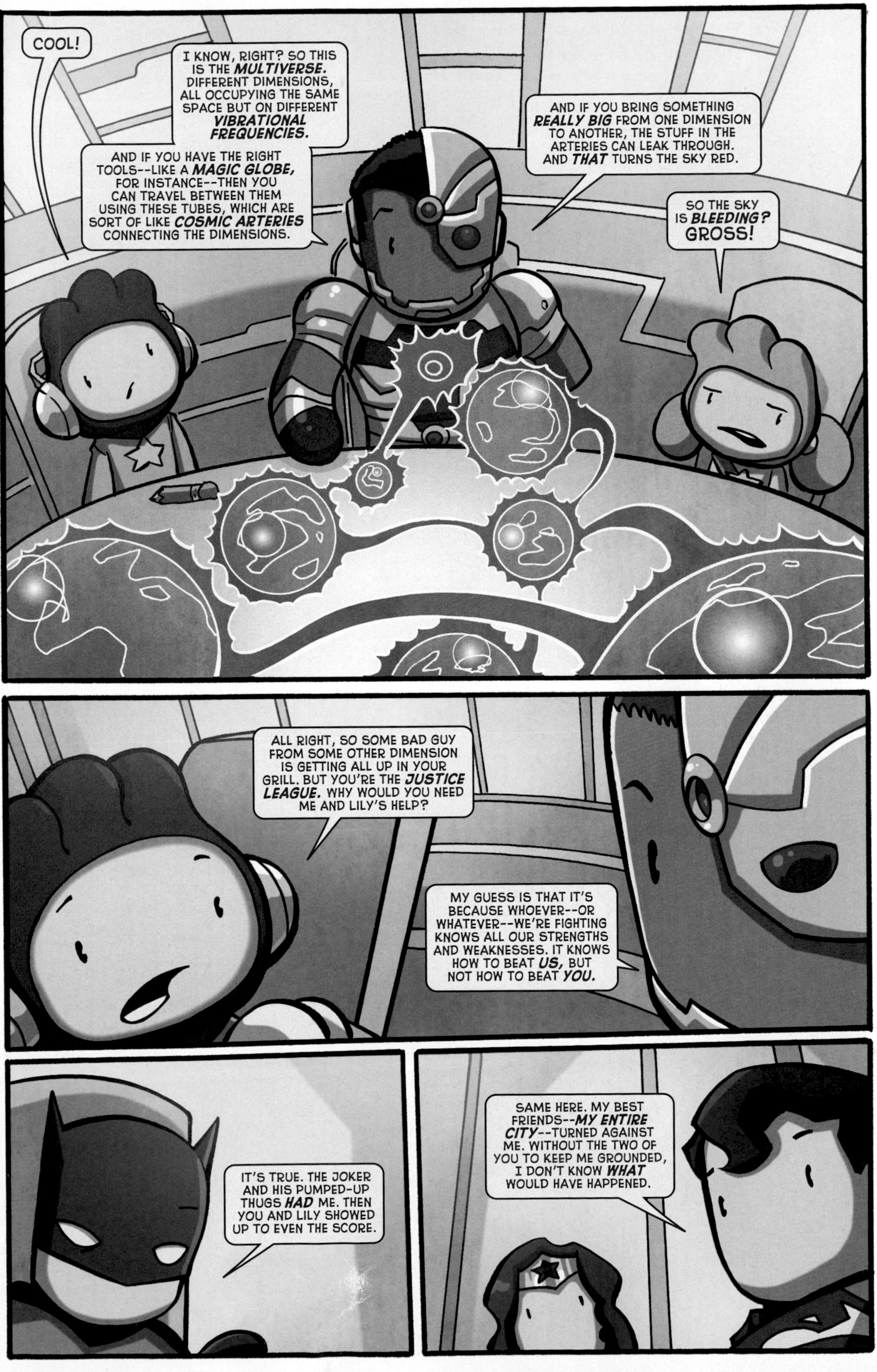
COOL!
I KNOW, RIGHT? SO THIS IS THE MULTIVERSE. DIFFERENT DIMENSIONS, ALL OCCUPYING THE SAME SPACE BUT ON DIFFERENT VIBRATIONAL FREQUENCIES.
AND IF YOU HAVE THE RIGHT TOOLS--LIKE A MAGIC GLOBE, FOR INSTANCE--THEN YOU CAN TRAVEL BETWEEN THEM USING THESE TUBES, WHICH ARE SORT OF LIKE COSMIC ARTERIES CONNECTING THE DIMENSIONS.
AND IF YOU BRING SOMETHING REALLY BIG FROM ONE DIMENSION TO ANOTHER, THE STUFF IN THE ARTERIES CAN LEAK THROUGH. AND THAT TURNS THE SKY RED.
SO THE SKY IS BLEEDING? GROSS!
ALL RIGHT, SO SOME BAD GUY FROM SOME OTHER DIMENSION IS GETTING ALL UP IN YOUR GRILL. BUT YOU'RE THE JUSTICE LEAGUE. WHY WOULD YOU NEED ME AND LILY'S HELP?
MY GUESS IS THAT IT'S BECAUSE WHOEVER--OR WHATEVER--WE'RE FIGHTING KNOWS ALL OUR STRENGTHS AND WEAKNESSES. IT KNOWS HOW TO BEAT US, BUT NOT HOW TO BEAT YOU.
IT'S TRUE. THE JOKER AND HIS PUMPED-UP THUGS HAD ME. THEN YOU AND LILY SHOWED UP TO EVEN THE SCORE.
SAME HERE. MY BEST FRIENDS--MY ENTIRE CITY--TURNED AGAINST ME. WITHOUT THE TWO OF YOU TO KEEP ME GROUNDED, I DON'T KNOW WHAT WOULD HAVE HAPPENED.

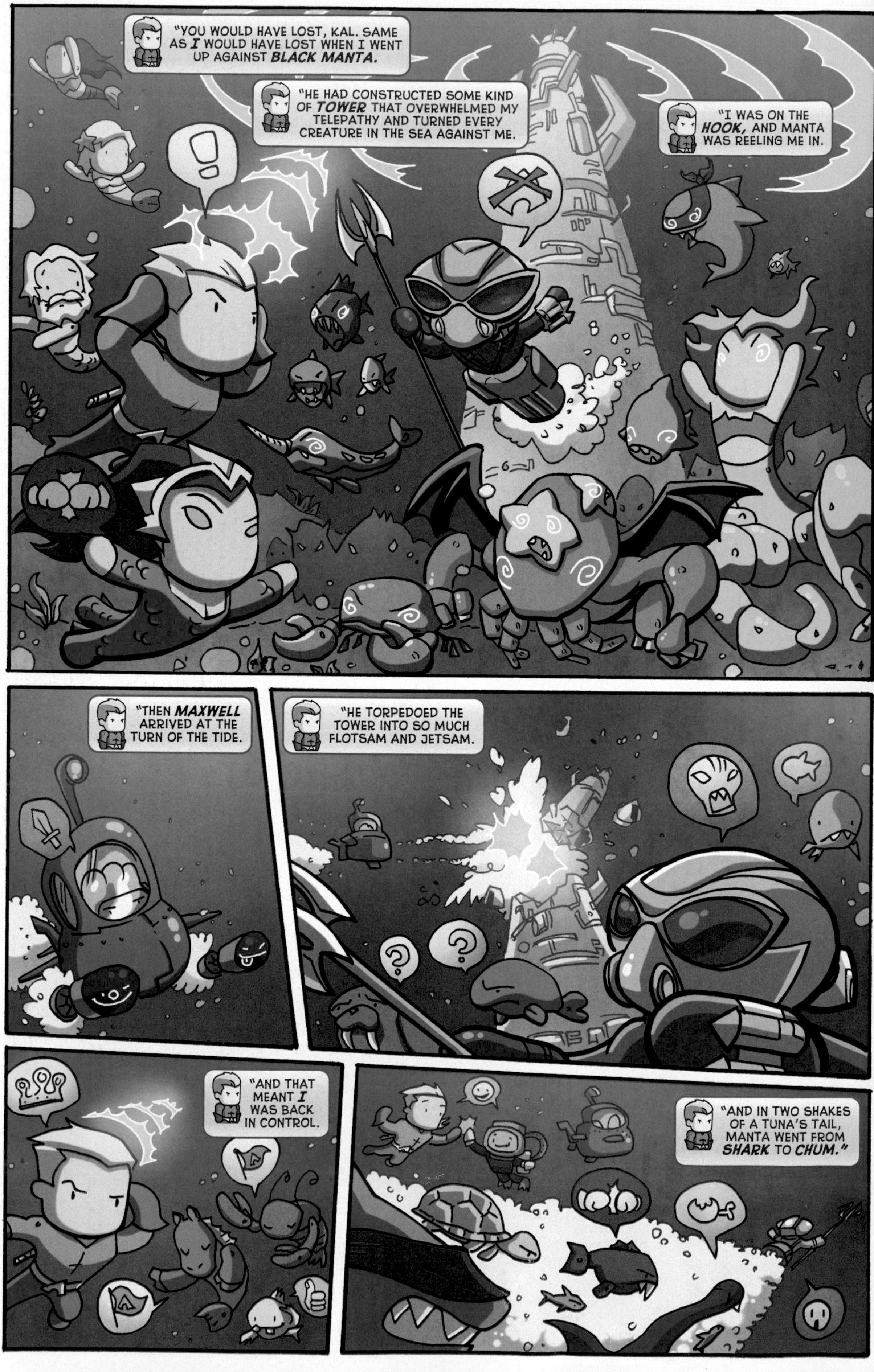
"YOU WOULD HAVE LOST, KAL. SAME AS I WOULD HAVE LOST WHEN I WENT UP AGAINST BLACK MANTA.
"HE HAD CONSTRUCTED SOME KIND OF TOWER THAT OVERWHELMED MY TELEPATHY AND TURNED EVERY CREATURE IN THE SEA AGAINST ME.
"I WAS ON THE HOOK, AND MANTA WAS REELING ME IN.
"THEN MAXWELL ARRIVED AT THE TURN OF THE TIDE.
"HE TORPEDOED THE TOWER INTO SO MUCH FLOTSAM AND JETSAM.
"AND THAT MEANT I WAS BACK IN CONTROL.
"AND IN TWO SHAKES OF A TUNA'S TAIL, MANTA WENT FROM SHARK TO CHUM."

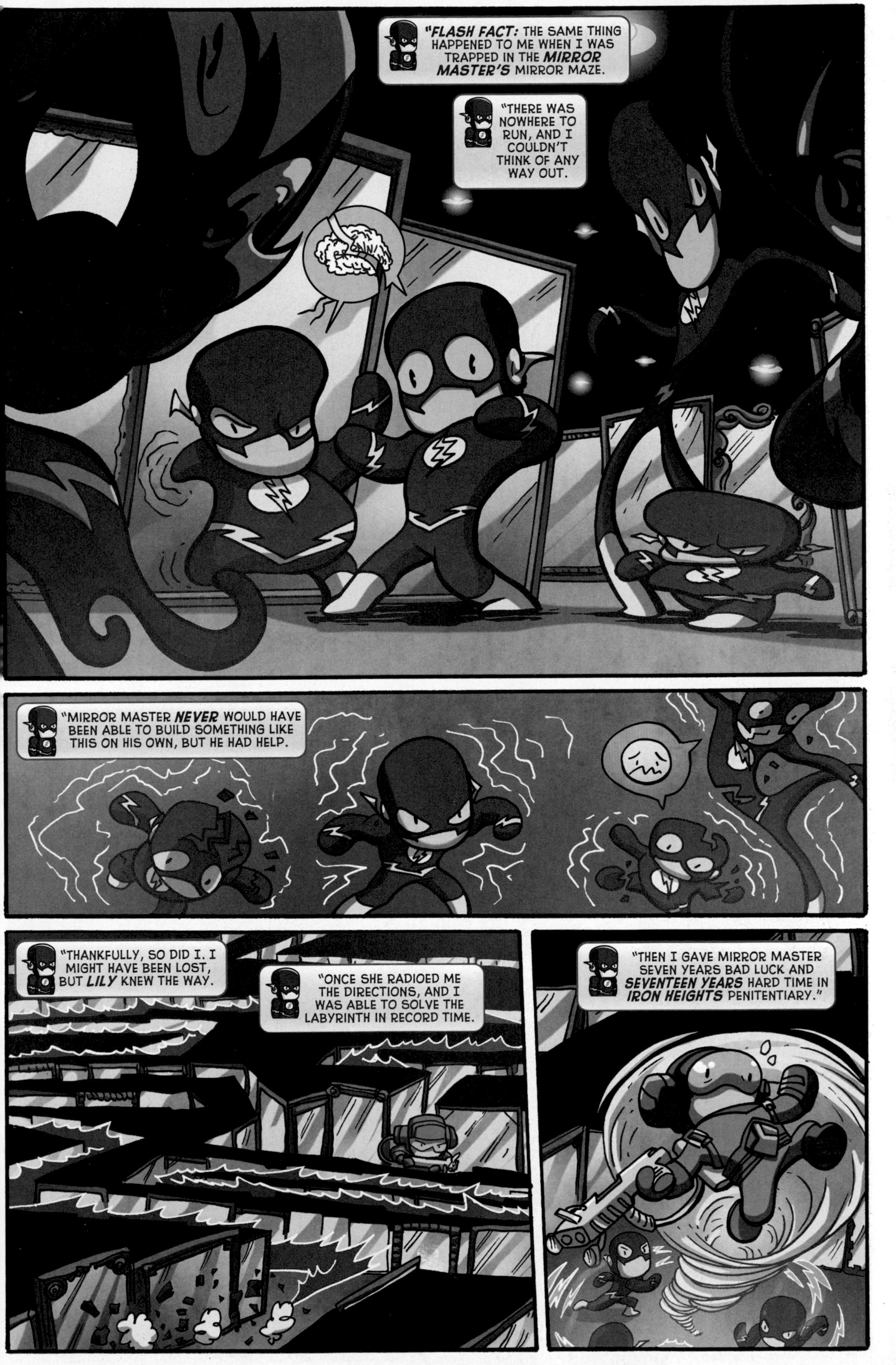
"FLASH FACT: THE SAME THING HAPPENED TO ME WHEN I WAS TRAPPED IN THE MIRROR MASTER'S MIRROR MAZE.
"THERE WAS NOWHERE TO RUN, AND I COULDN'T THINK OF ANY WAY OUT.
"MIRROR MASTER NEVER WOULD HAVE BEEN ABLE TO BUILD SOMETHING LIKE THIS ON HIS OWN, BUT HE HAD HELP.
"THANKFULLY, SO DID I. I MIGHT HAVE BEEN LOST, BUT LILY KNEW THE WAY.
"ONCE SHE RADIOED ME THE DIRECTIONS, AND I WAS ABLE TO SOLVE THE LABYRINTH IN RECORD TIME.
"THEN I GAVE MIRROR MASTER SEVEN YEARS BAD LUCK AND SEVENTEEN YEARS HARD TIME IN IRON HEIGHTS PENITENTIARY."

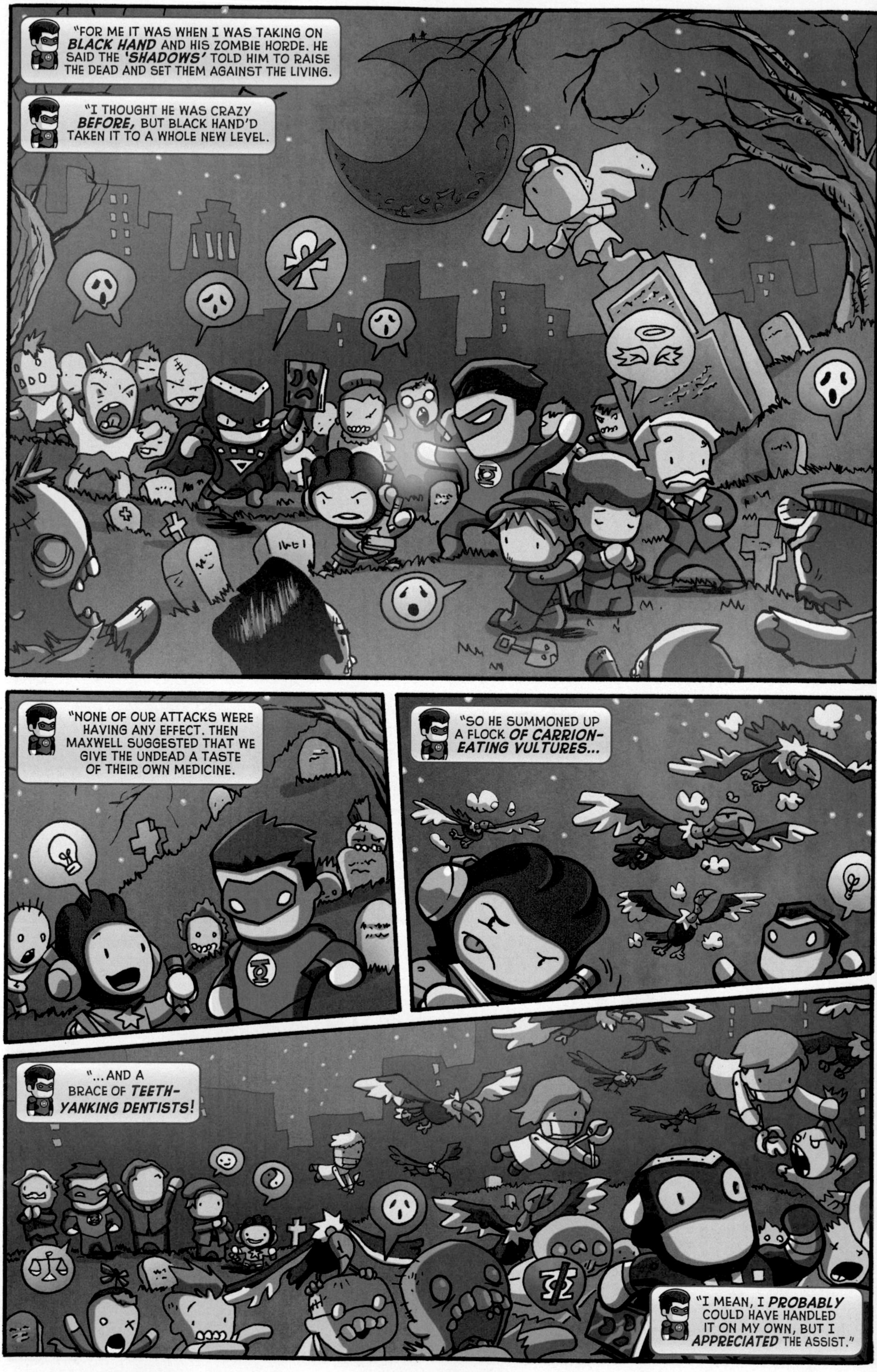
"FOR ME IT WAS WHEN I WAS TAKING ON BLACK HAND AND HIS ZOMBIE HORDE. HE SAID THE 'SHADOWS' TOLD HIM TO RAISE THE DEAD AND SET THEM AGAINST THE LIVING.
"I THOUGHT HE WAS CRAZY BEFORE, BUT BLACK HAND'D TAKEN IT TO A WHOLE NEW LEVEL.
"NONE OF OUR ATTACKS WERE HAVING ANY EFFECT. THEN MAXWELL SUGGESTED THAT WE GIVE THE UNDEAD A TASTE OF THEIR OWN MEDICINE.
"SO HE SUMMONED UP A FLOCK OF CARRION-EATING VULTURES...
"...AND A BRACE OF TEETH-YANKING DENTISTS!
"I MEAN, I PROBABLY COULD HAVE HANDLED IT ON MY OWN, BUT I APPRECIATED THE ASSIST."

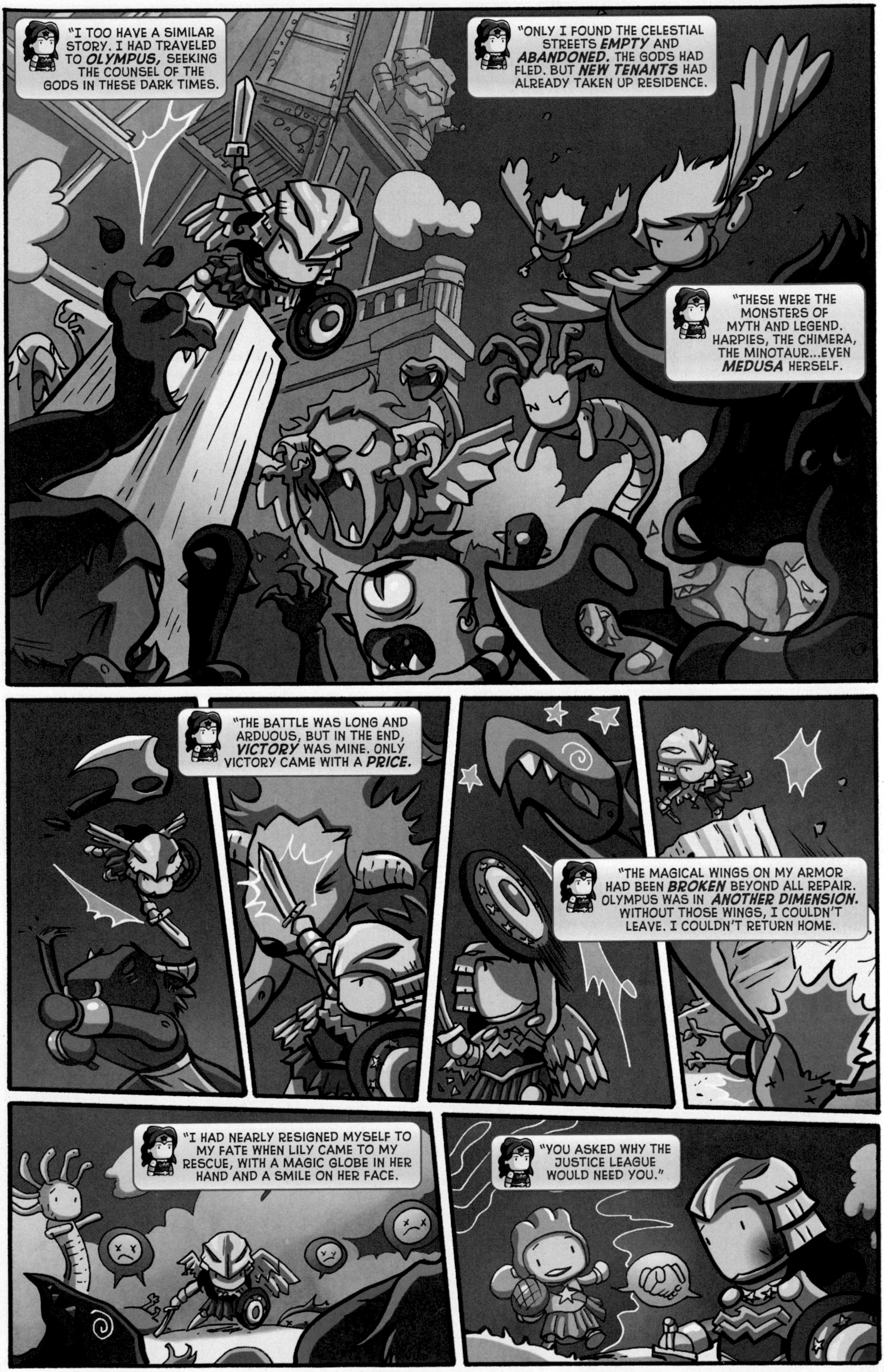
"I TOO HAVE A SIMILAR STORY. I HAD TRAVELED TO OLYMPUS, SEEKING THE COUNSEL OF THE GODS IN THESE DARK TIMES.
"ONLY I FOUND THE CELESTIAL STREETS EMPTY AND ABANDONED. THE GODS HAD FLED. BUT NEW TENANTS HAD ALREADY TAKEN UP RESIDENCE.
"THESE WERE THE MONSTERS OF MYTH AND LEGEND. HARPIES, THE CHIMERA, THE MINOTAUR...EVEN MEDUSA HERSELF.
"THE BATTLE WAS LONG AND ARDUOUS, BUT IN THE END, VICTORY WAS MINE. ONLY VICTORY CAME WITH A PRICE.
"THE MAGICAL WINGS ON MY ARMOR HAD BEEN BROKEN BEYOND ALL REPAIR. OLYMPUS WAS IN ANOTHER DIMENSION. WITHOUT THOSE WINGS, I COULDN'T LEAVE. I COULDN'T RETURN HOME.
"I HAD NEARLY RESIGNED MYSELF TO MY FATE WHEN LILY CAME TO MY RESCUE, WITH A MAGIC GLOBE IN HER HAND AND A SMILE ON HER FACE.
"YOU ASKED WHY THE JUSTICE LEAGUE WOULD NEED YOU."

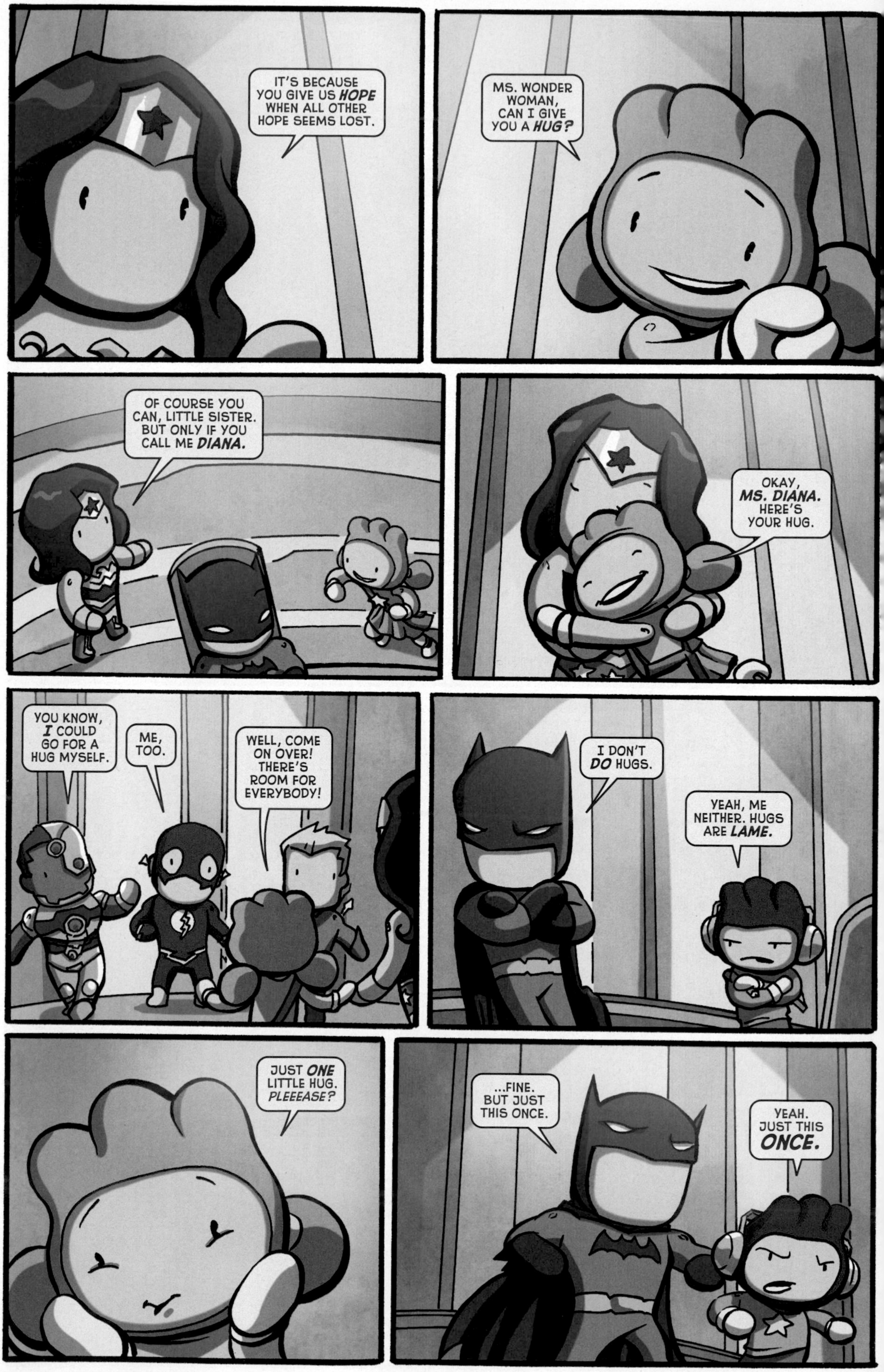
IT'S BECAUSE YOU GIVE US HOPE WHEN ALL OTHER HOPE SEEMS LOST.
MS. WONDER WOMAN, CAN I GIVE YOU A HUG?
OF COURSE YOU CAN, LITTLE SISTER. BUT ONLY IF YOU CALL ME DIANA.
OKAY, MS. DIANA. HERE'S YOUR HUG.
YOU KNOW, I COULD GO FOR A HUG MYSELF.
ME, TOO.
WELL, COME ON OVER! THERE'S ROOM FOR EVERYBODY!
I DON'T DO HUGS.
YEAH, ME NEITHER. HUGS ARE LAME.
JUST ONE LITTLE HUG. PLEEEASE?
...FINE. BUT JUST THIS ONCE.
YEAH. JUST THIS ONCE.

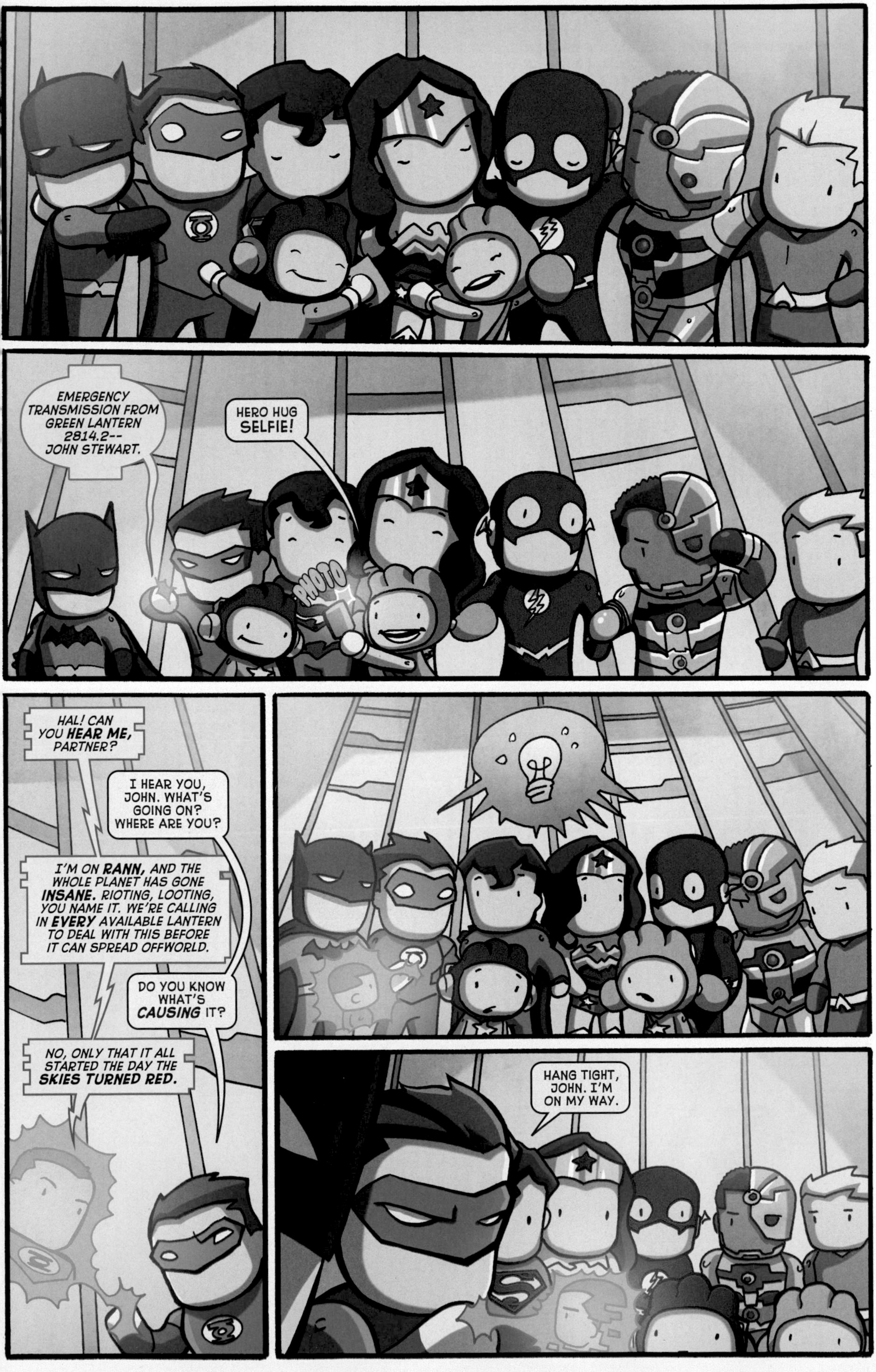
EMERGENCY TRANSMISSION FROM GREEN LANTERN 2814.2-- JOHN STEWART.
HERO HUG SELFIE!
PHOTO
HAL! CAN YOU HEAR ME, PARTNER?
I HEAR YOU, JOHN. WHAT'S GOING ON? WHERE ARE YOU?
I'M ON RANN, AND THE WHOLE PLANET HAS GONE INSANE. RIOTING, LOOTING, YOU NAME IT. WE'RE CALLING IN EVERY AVAILABLE LANTERN TO DEAL WITH THIS BEFORE IT CAN SPREAD OFFWORLD.
DO YOU KNOW WHAT'S CAUSING IT?
NO, ONLY THAT IT ALL STARTED THE DAY THE SKIES TURNED RED.
HANG TIGHT, JOHN. I'M ON MY WAY.

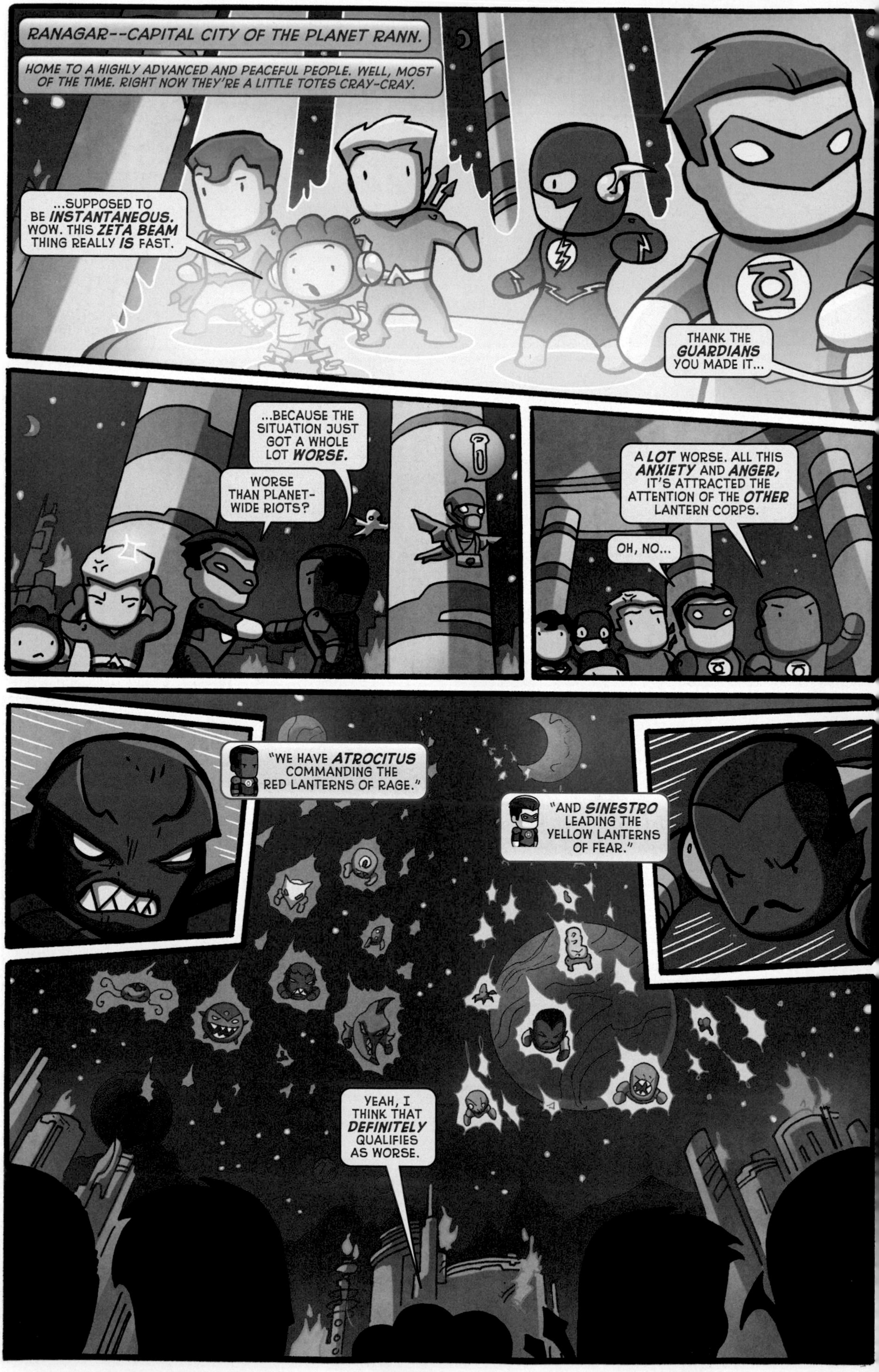
RANAGAR--CAPITAL CITY OF THE PLANET RANN.
HOME TO A HIGHLY ADVANCED AND PEACEFUL PEOPLE. WELL, MOST OF THE TIME. RIGHT NOW THEY'RE A LITTLE TOTES CRAY-CRAY.
...SUPPOSED TO BE INSTANTANEOUS. WOW. THIS ZETA BEAM THING REALLY IS FAST.
THANK THE GUARDIANS YOU MADE IT...
...BECAUSE THE SITUATION JUST GOT A WHOLE LOT WORSE.
WORSE THAN PLANET-WIDE RIOTS?
A LOT WORSE. ALL THIS ANXIETY AND ANGER, IT'S ATTRACTED THE ATTENTION OF THE OTHER LANTERN CORPS.
OH, NO...
"WE HAVE ATROCITUS COMMANDING THE RED LANTERNS OF RAGE."
"AND SINESTRO LEADING THE YELLOW LANTERNS OF FEAR."
YEAH, I THINK THAT DEFINITELY QUALIFIES AS WORSE.

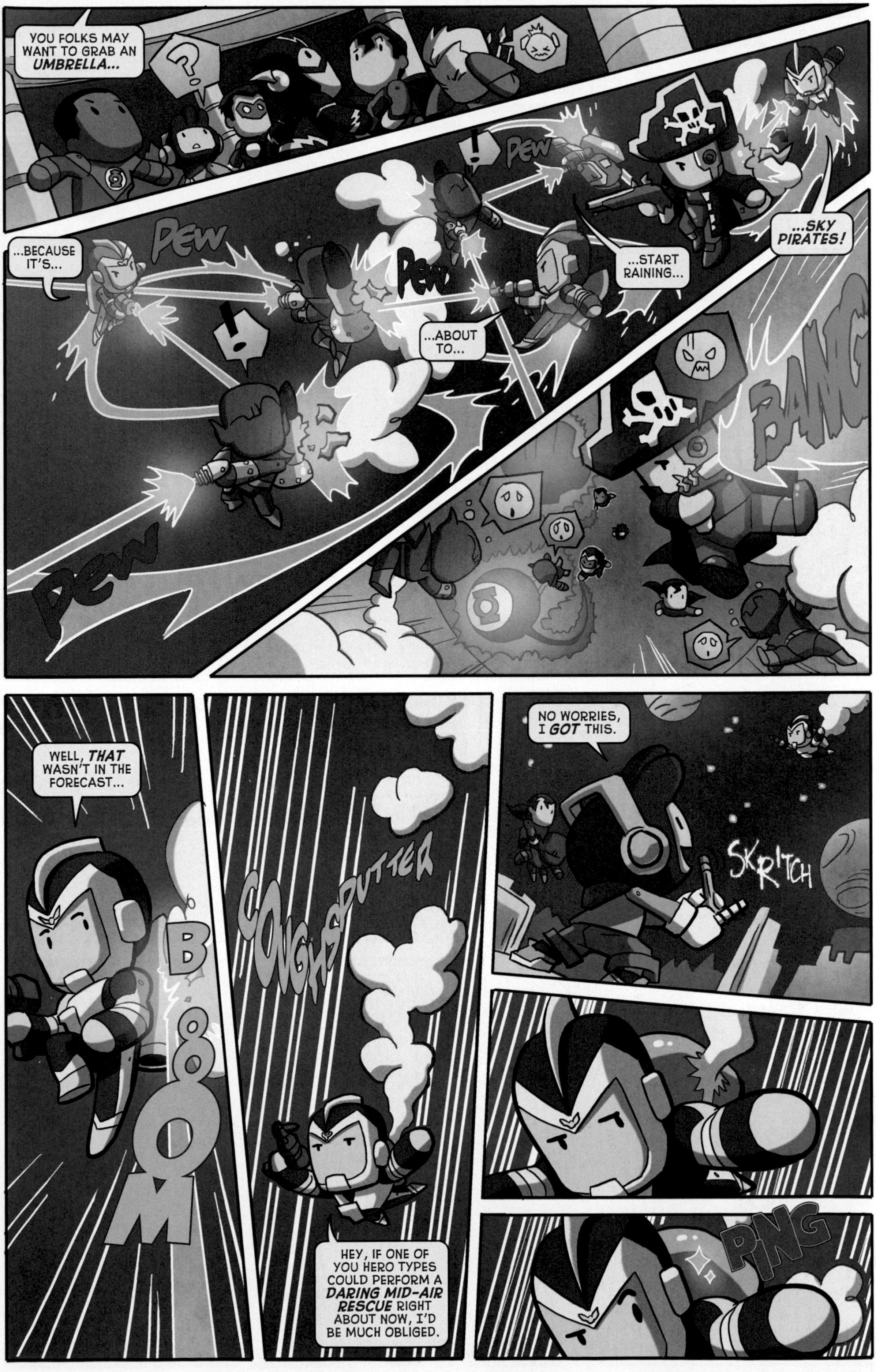

YOU FOLKS MAY WANT TO GRAB AN *UMBRELLA*...
?
!
PEW
...BECAUSE IT'S...
PEW
PEW
!
...ABOUT TO...
...START RAINING...
...SKY PIRATES!
PEW
BANG
WELL, *THAT* WASN'T IN THE FORECAST...
BOOOM
COUGHSPUTTER
HEY, IF ONE OF YOU HERO TYPES COULD PERFORM A *DARING MID-AIR RESCUE* RIGHT ABOUT NOW, I'D BE MUCH OBLIGED.
NO WORRIES, I *GOT* THIS.
SKRITCH
PING

WHOA! NICE **ABSOLUTELY LAST MINUTE** SAVE, KID. SO HOW'D YOU PULL IT OFF?

I JUST WROTE **"PRISTINE JETPACK"** IN MY NOTEBOOK, AND ANYTHING I WRITE IN MY NOTEBOOK BECOMES REAL. IT'S KIND OF MY THING.

REALLY? I OUGHTA GET ME ONE OF THOSE.

SORRY, IT'S **ONE OF A KIND.**

THEN I'M GLAD YOU'RE ON OUR SIDE. THE NAME'S **ADAM STRANGE,** DEFENDER OF RANN.

NICE TO MEETCHA! I'M **MAXWELL UNUSUAL,** SCRIBBLENAUT OF EARTH 1.

NOW THAT'S EVERYONE'S BEEN **PROPERLY INTRODUCED...**

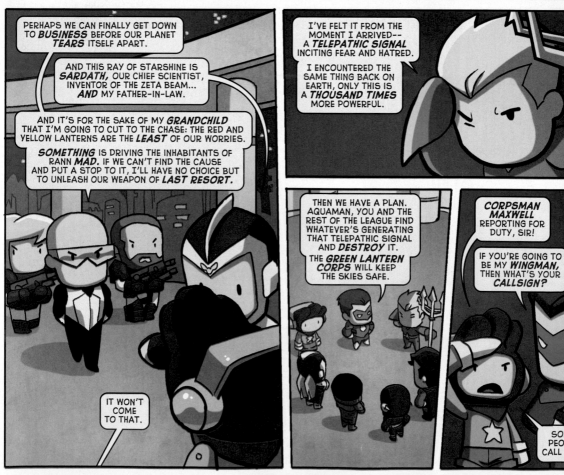

PERHAPS WE CAN FINALLY GET DOWN TO **BUSINESS** BEFORE OUR PLANET **TEARS** ITSELF APART.

AND THIS RAY OF STARSHINE IS **SARDATH,** OUR CHIEF SCIENTIST, INVENTOR OF THE ZETA BEAM... **AND** MY FATHER-IN-LAW.

AND IT'S FOR THE SAKE OF MY **GRANDCHILD** THAT I'M GOING TO CUT TO THE CHASE: THE RED AND YELLOW LANTERNS ARE THE **LEAST** OF OUR WORRIES.

**SOMETHING** IS DRIVING THE INHABITANTS OF RANN **MAD.** IF WE CAN'T FIND THE CAUSE AND PUT A STOP TO IT, I'LL HAVE NO CHOICE BUT TO UNLEASH OUR WEAPON OF **LAST RESORT.**

I'VE FELT IT FROM THE MOMENT I ARRIVED-- A **TELEPATHIC SIGNAL** INCITING FEAR AND HATRED.

I ENCOUNTERED THE SAME THING BACK ON EARTH, ONLY THIS IS **A THOUSAND TIMES** MORE POWERFUL.

THEN WE HAVE A PLAN. AQUAMAN, YOU AND THE REST OF THE LEAGUE FIND WHATEVER'S GENERATING THAT TELEPATHIC SIGNAL AND **DESTROY** IT. THE **GREEN LANTERN CORPS** WILL KEEP THE SKIES SAFE.

**CORPSMAN MAXWELL** REPORTING FOR DUTY, SIR!

IF YOU'RE GOING TO BE MY **WINGMAN,** THEN WHAT'S YOUR **CALLSIGN?**

IT WON'T COME TO THAT.

SOME PEOPLE CALL ME...

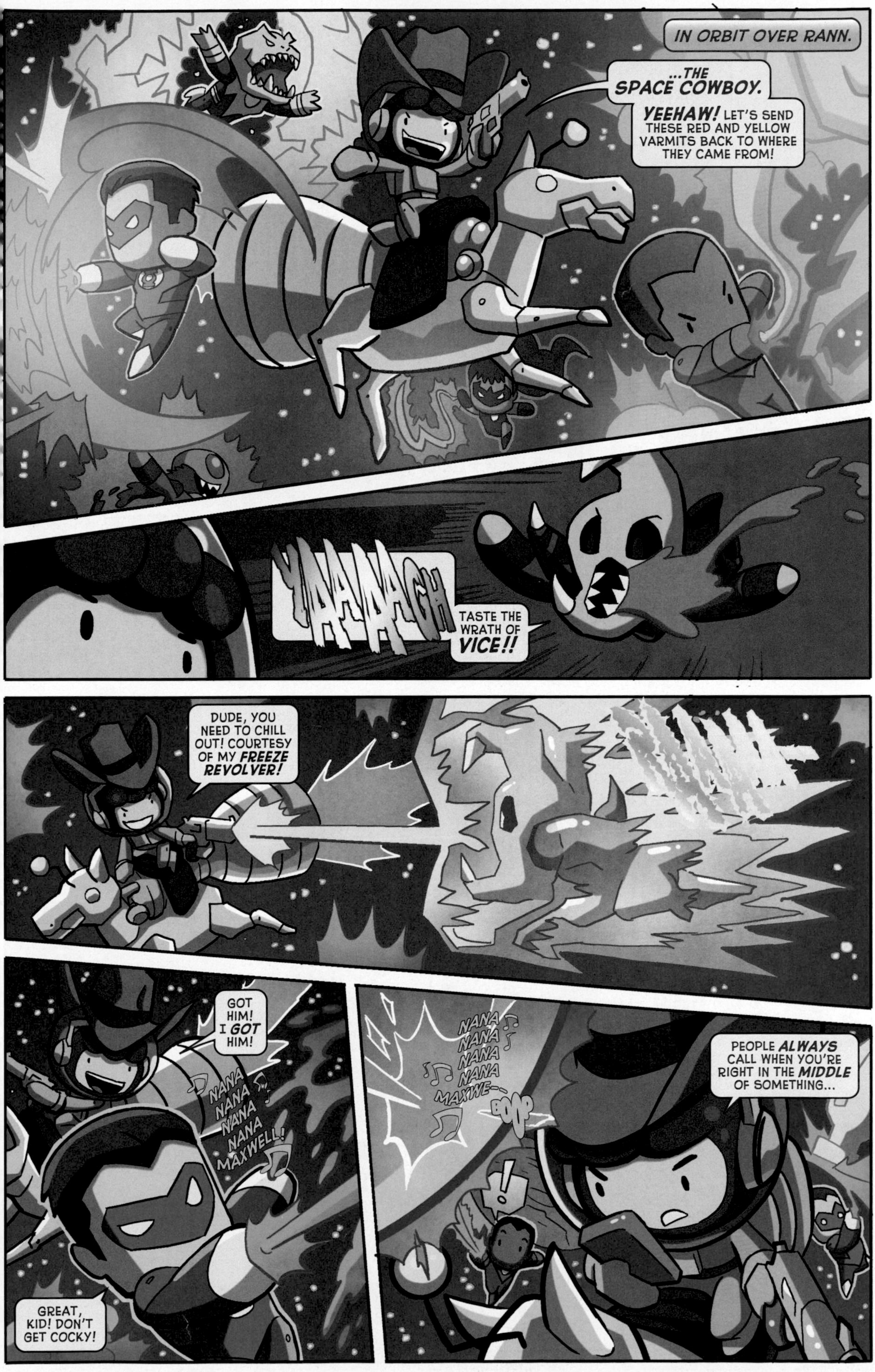
IN ORBIT OVER RANN.
...THE SPACE COWBOY.
YEEHAW! LET'S SEND THESE RED AND YELLOW VARMITS BACK TO WHERE THEY CAME FROM!
YAAAAAGH
TASTE THE WRATH OF VICE!!
DUDE, YOU NEED TO CHILL OUT! COURTESY OF MY FREEZE REVOLVER!
GOT HIM! I GOT HIM!
NANA NANA NANA NANA MAXWELL!
GREAT, KID! DON'T GET COCKY!
NANA NANA NANA NANA MAXWE--
BOOP
PEOPLE ALWAYS CALL WHEN YOU'RE RIGHT IN THE MIDDLE OF SOMETHING...
!

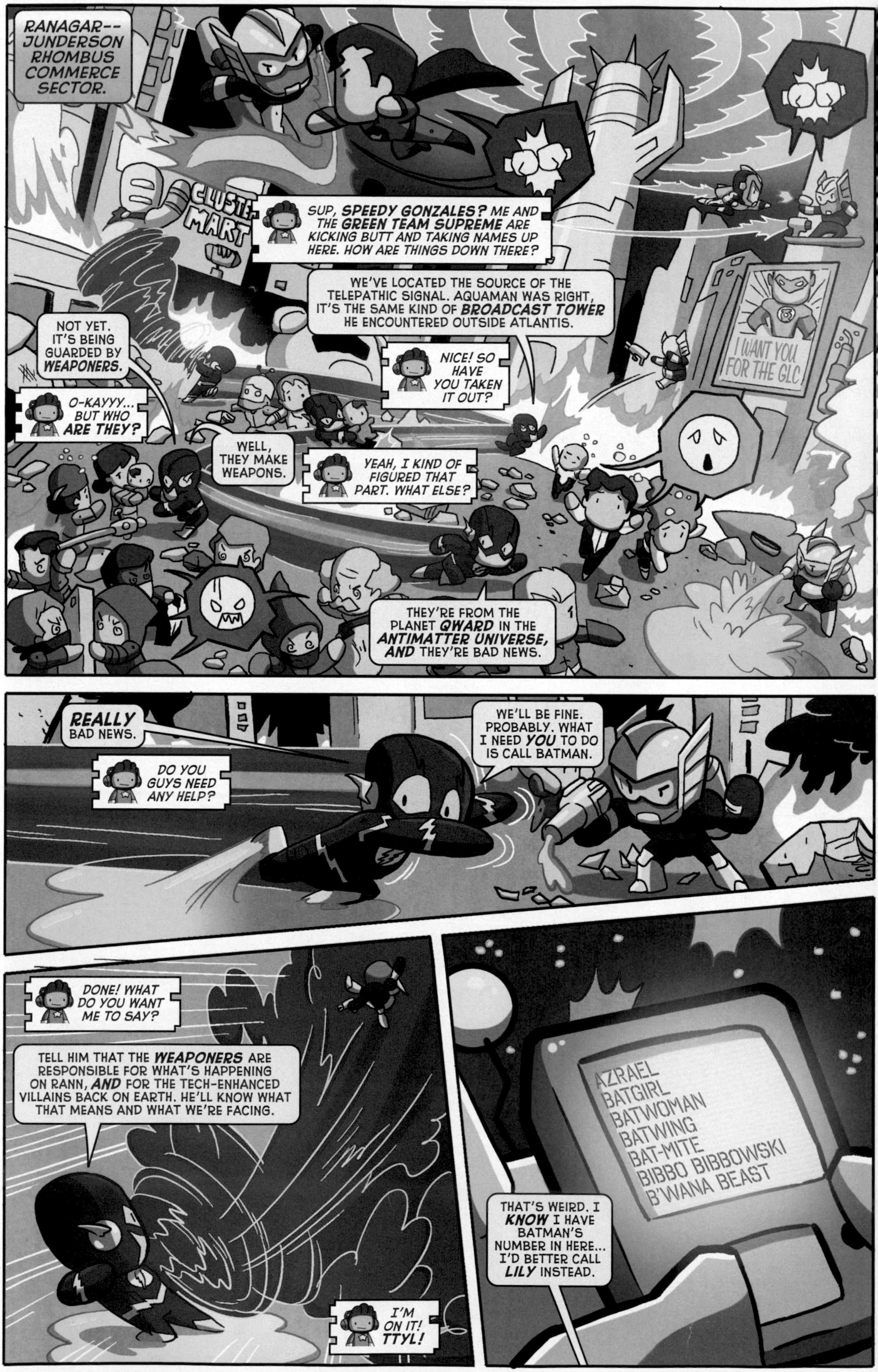
RANAGAR--
JUNDERSON RHOMBUS COMMERCE SECTOR.
CLUSTER MART
SUP, SPEEDY GONZALES? ME AND THE GREEN TEAM SUPREME ARE KICKING BUTT AND TAKING NAMES UP HERE. HOW ARE THINGS DOWN THERE?
WE'VE LOCATED THE SOURCE OF THE TELEPATHIC SIGNAL. AQUAMAN WAS RIGHT, IT'S THE SAME KIND OF BROADCAST TOWER HE ENCOUNTERED OUTSIDE ATLANTIS.
I WANT YOU FOR THE GLC
NICE! SO HAVE YOU TAKEN IT OUT?
NOT YET. IT'S BEING GUARDED BY WEAPONERS.
O-KAYYY... BUT WHO ARE THEY?
WELL, THEY MAKE WEAPONS.
YEAH, I KIND OF FIGURED THAT PART. WHAT ELSE?
THEY'RE FROM THE PLANET QWARD IN THE ANTIMATTER UNIVERSE, AND THEY'RE BAD NEWS.
REALLY BAD NEWS.
DO YOU GUYS NEED ANY HELP?
WE'LL BE FINE. PROBABLY. WHAT I NEED YOU TO DO IS CALL BATMAN.
DONE! WHAT DO YOU WANT ME TO SAY?
TELL HIM THAT THE WEAPONERS ARE RESPONSIBLE FOR WHAT'S HAPPENING ON RANN, AND FOR THE TECH-ENHANCED VILLAINS BACK ON EARTH. HE'LL KNOW WHAT THAT MEANS AND WHAT WE'RE FACING.
I'M ON IT! TTYL!
AZRAEL
BATGIRL
BATWOMAN
BATWING
BAT-MITE
BIBBO BIBBOWSKI
B'WANA BEAST
THAT'S WEIRD. I KNOW I HAVE BATMAN'S NUMBER IN HERE... I'D BETTER CALL LILY INSTEAD.

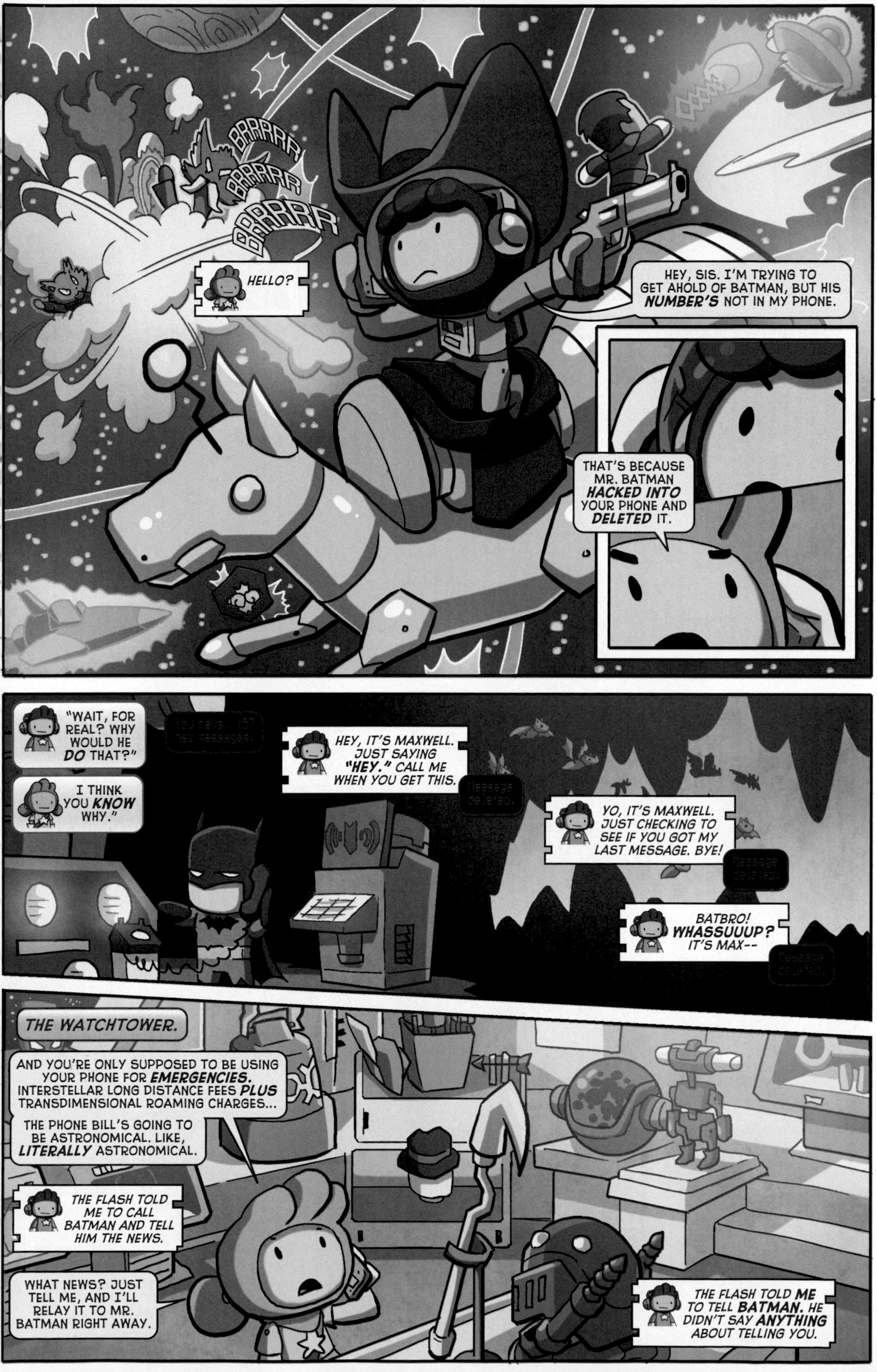
BRRRRRR
BRRRRRR
BRRRRRR
HELLO?
HEY, SIS. I'M TRYING TO GET AHOLD OF BATMAN, BUT HIS **NUMBER'S** NOT IN MY PHONE.
THAT'S BECAUSE MR. BATMAN **HACKED INTO** YOUR PHONE AND **DELETED** IT.
"WAIT, FOR REAL? WHY WOULD HE **DO** THAT?"
"I THINK YOU **KNOW** WHY."
You have... 157 new messages.
HEY, IT'S MAXWELL. JUST SAYING **"HEY."** CALL ME WHEN YOU GET THIS.
Message deleted.
YO, IT'S MAXWELL. JUST CHECKING TO SEE IF YOU GOT MY LAST MESSAGE. BYE!
Message deleted.
BATBRO! **WHASSUUUP?** IT'S MAX--
Message deleted.
THE WATCHTOWER.
AND YOU'RE ONLY SUPPOSED TO BE USING YOUR PHONE FOR **EMERGENCIES.** INTERSTELLAR LONG DISTANCE FEES **PLUS** TRANSDIMENSIONAL ROAMING CHARGES...
THE PHONE BILL'S GOING TO BE ASTRONOMICAL. LIKE, **LITERALLY** ASTRONOMICAL.
THE FLASH TOLD ME TO CALL BATMAN AND TELL HIM THE NEWS.
WHAT NEWS? JUST TELL ME, AND I'LL RELAY IT TO MR. BATMAN RIGHT AWAY.
THE FLASH TOLD **ME** TO TELL **BATMAN.** HE DIDN'T SAY **ANYTHING** ABOUT TELLING YOU.

YOU JUST WANT TO TALK TO MR. BATMAN, DON'T YOU?

...MAYBE.

≥SIGH≤ I'LL BRING HIM THE PHONE.

WOOHOO! BEST SISTER *EVER!*

SO HOW'S *RANN?*

IT'S GREAT! THERE ARE *SKY PIRATES* AND *EPIC SPACE BATTLES*...

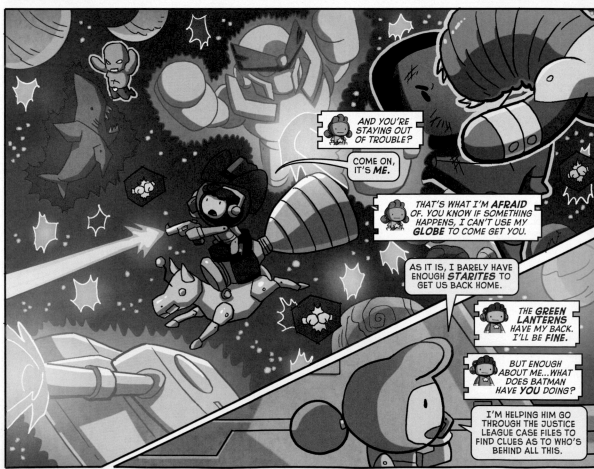

AND YOU'RE STAYING OUT OF TROUBLE?

COME ON, IT'S *ME.*

THAT'S WHAT I'M *AFRAID* OF. YOU KNOW IF SOMETHING HAPPENS, I CAN'T USE MY *GLOBE* TO COME GET YOU.

AS IT IS, I BARELY HAVE ENOUGH *STARITES* TO GET US BACK HOME.

THE *GREEN LANTERNS* HAVE MY BACK. I'LL BE *FINE.*

BUT ENOUGH ABOUT ME...WHAT DOES BATMAN HAVE *YOU* DOING?

I'M HELPING HIM GO THROUGH THE JUSTICE LEAGUE CASE FILES TO FIND CLUES AS TO WHO'S BEHIND ALL THIS.

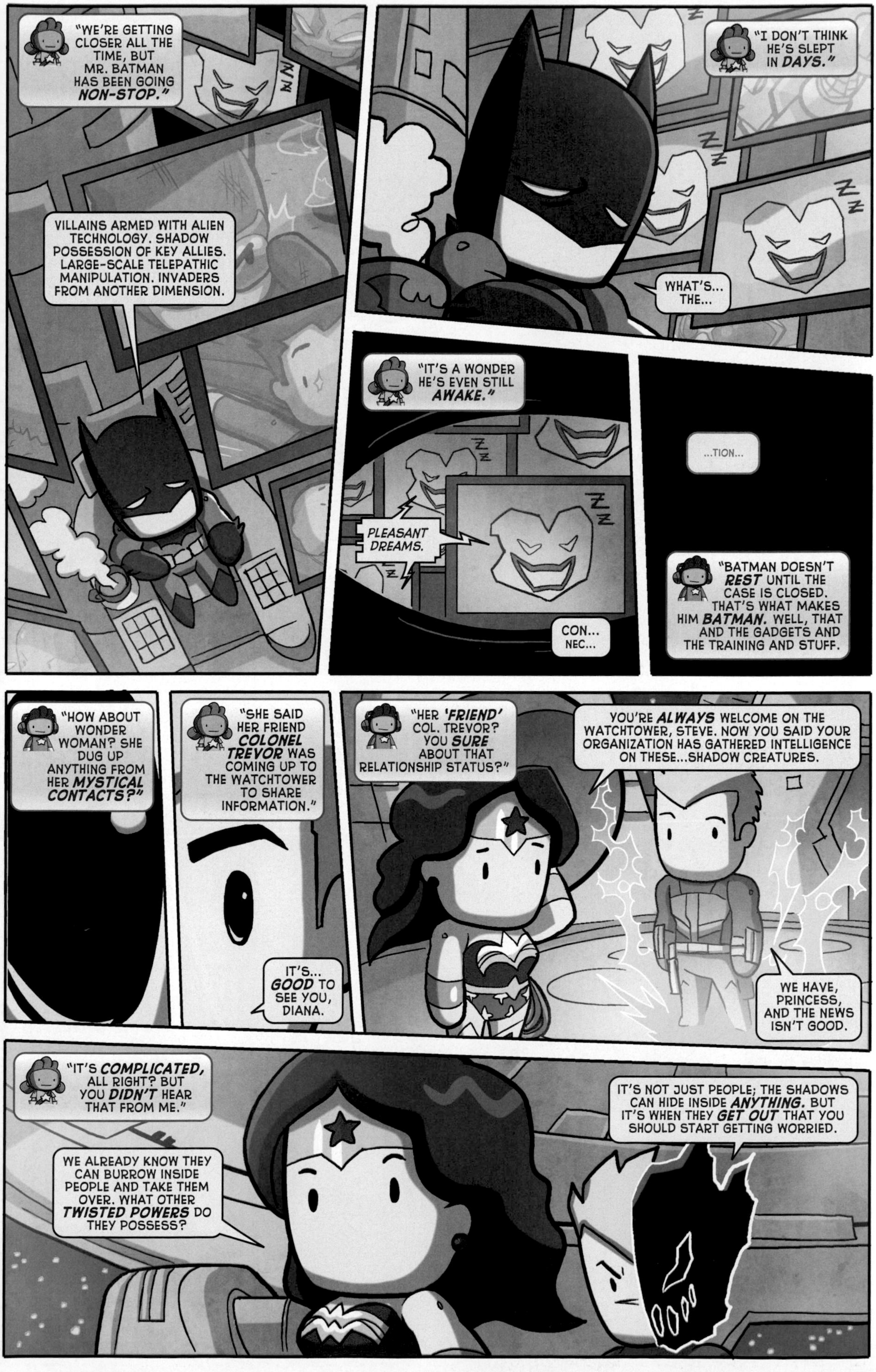
"WE'RE GETTING CLOSER ALL THE TIME, BUT MR. BATMAN HAS BEEN GOING NON-STOP."
VILLAINS ARMED WITH ALIEN TECHNOLOGY. SHADOW POSSESSION OF KEY ALLIES. LARGE-SCALE TELEPATHIC MANIPULATION. INVADERS FROM ANOTHER DIMENSION.
"I DON'T THINK HE'S SLEPT IN DAYS."
WHAT'S... THE...
"IT'S A WONDER HE'S EVEN STILL AWAKE."
PLEASANT DREAMS.
CON... NEC...
...TION...
"BATMAN DOESN'T REST UNTIL THE CASE IS CLOSED. THAT'S WHAT MAKES HIM BATMAN. WELL, THAT AND THE GADGETS AND THE TRAINING AND STUFF.
"HOW ABOUT WONDER WOMAN? SHE DUG UP ANYTHING FROM HER MYSTICAL CONTACTS?"
"SHE SAID HER FRIEND COLONEL TREVOR WAS COMING UP TO THE WATCHTOWER TO SHARE INFORMATION."
IT'S... GOOD TO SEE YOU, DIANA.
"HER 'FRIEND' COL. TREVOR? YOU SURE ABOUT THAT RELATIONSHIP STATUS?"
YOU'RE ALWAYS WELCOME ON THE WATCHTOWER, STEVE. NOW YOU SAID YOUR ORGANIZATION HAS GATHERED INTELLIGENCE ON THESE...SHADOW CREATURES.
WE HAVE, PRINCESS, AND THE NEWS ISN'T GOOD.
"IT'S COMPLICATED, ALL RIGHT? BUT YOU DIDN'T HEAR THAT FROM ME."
WE ALREADY KNOW THEY CAN BURROW INSIDE PEOPLE AND TAKE THEM OVER. WHAT OTHER TWISTED POWERS DO THEY POSSESS?
IT'S NOT JUST PEOPLE; THE SHADOWS CAN HIDE INSIDE ANYTHING. BUT IT'S WHEN THEY GET OUT THAT YOU SHOULD START GETTING WORRIED.

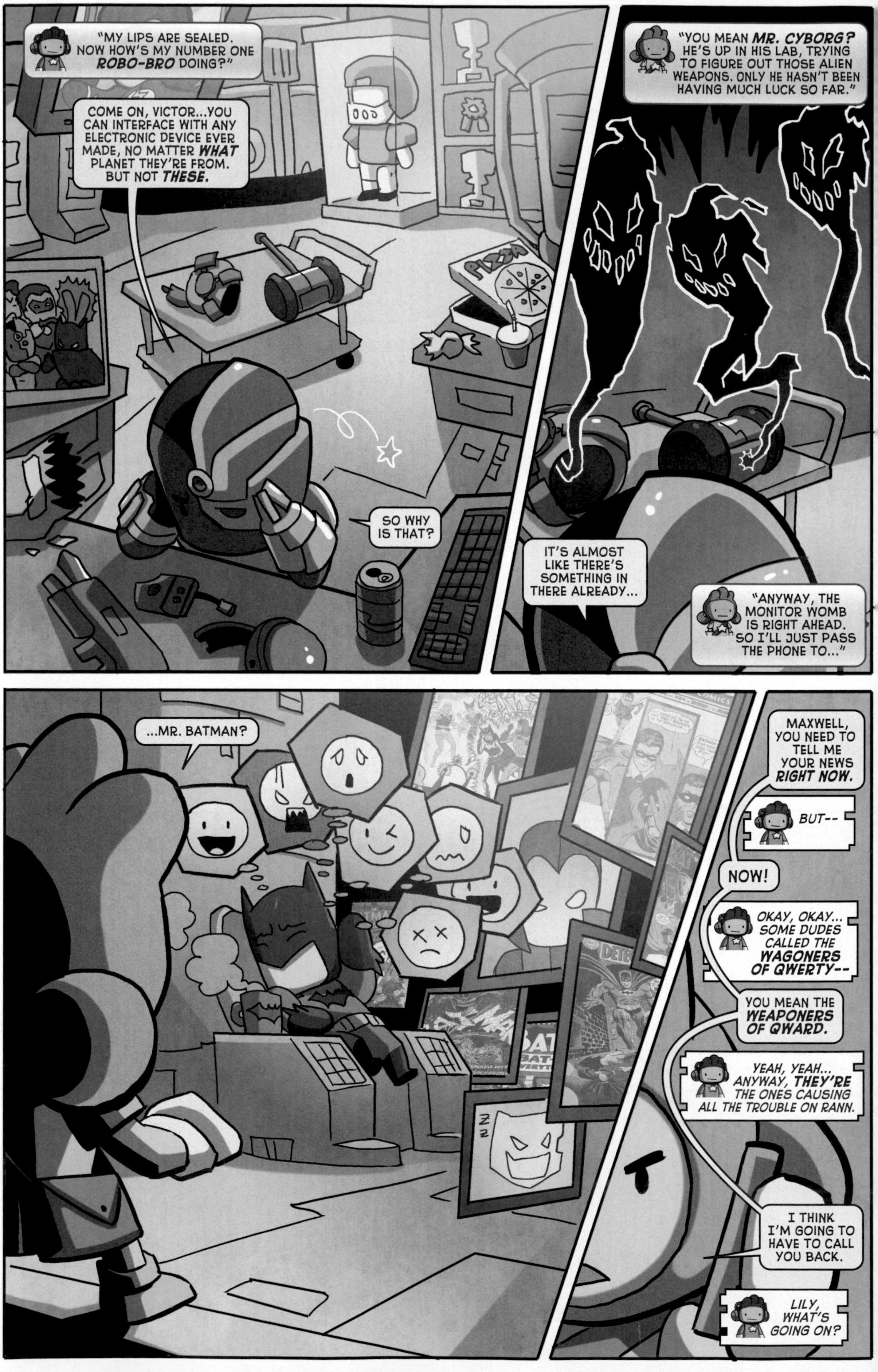
"MY LIPS ARE SEALED. NOW HOW'S MY NUMBER ONE ROBO-BRO DOING?"
COME ON, VICTOR...YOU CAN INTERFACE WITH ANY ELECTRONIC DEVICE EVER MADE, NO MATTER WHAT PLANET THEY'RE FROM. BUT NOT THESE.
SO WHY IS THAT?
"YOU MEAN MR. CYBORG? HE'S UP IN HIS LAB, TRYING TO FIGURE OUT THOSE ALIEN WEAPONS. ONLY HE HASN'T BEEN HAVING MUCH LUCK SO FAR."
IT'S ALMOST LIKE THERE'S SOMETHING IN THERE ALREADY...
"ANYWAY, THE MONITOR WOMB IS RIGHT AHEAD. SO I'LL JUST PASS THE PHONE TO..."
...MR. BATMAN?
MAXWELL, YOU NEED TO TELL ME YOUR NEWS RIGHT NOW.
BUT--
NOW!
OKAY, OKAY... SOME DUDES CALLED THE WAGONERS OF QWERTY--
YOU MEAN THE WEAPONERS OF QWARD.
YEAH, YEAH... ANYWAY, THEY'RE THE ONES CAUSING ALL THE TROUBLE ON RANN.
I THINK I'M GOING TO HAVE TO CALL YOU BACK.
LILY, WHAT'S GOING ON?

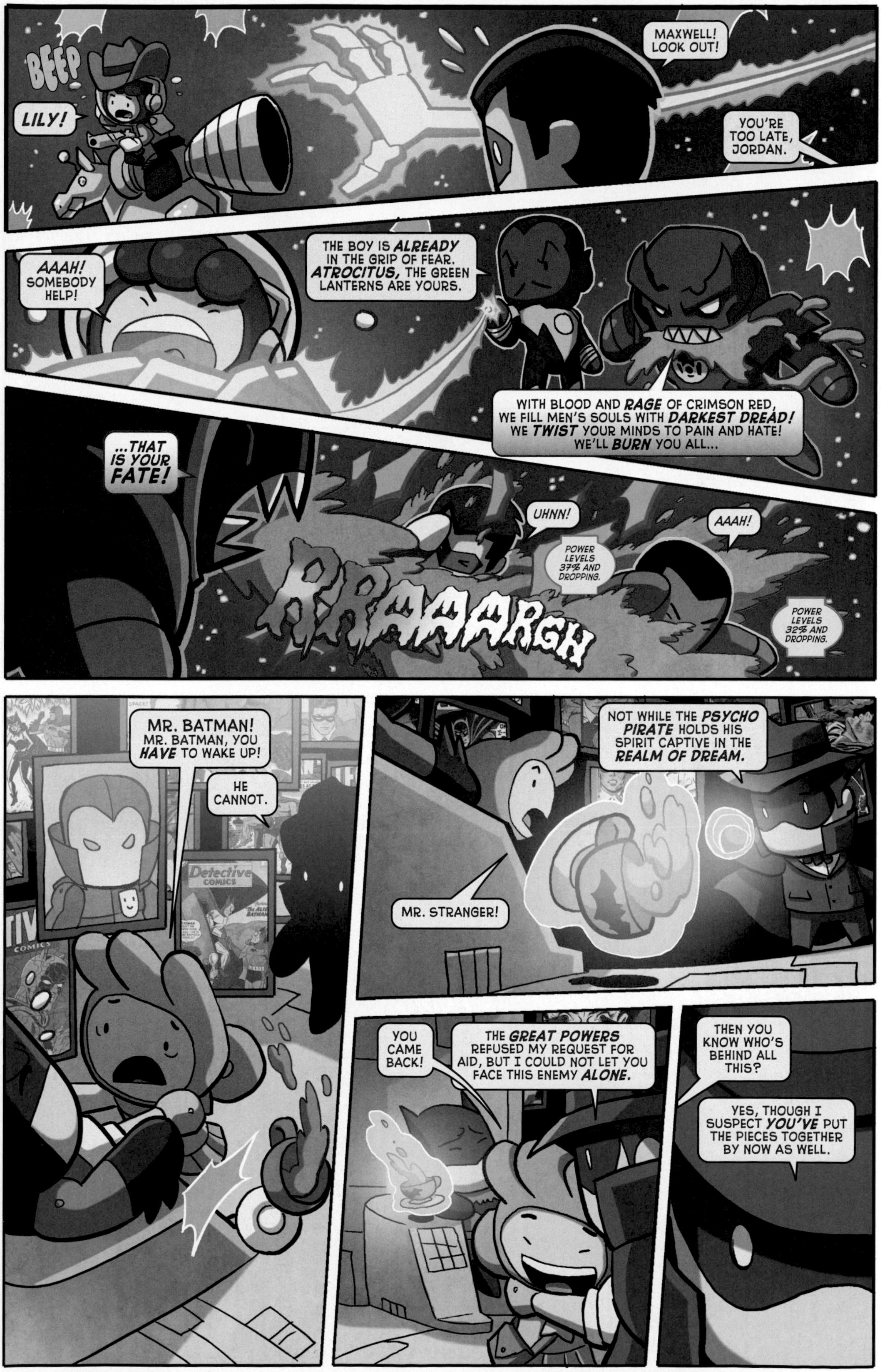
BEEP
LILY!
MAXWELL! LOOK OUT!
YOU'RE TOO LATE, JORDAN.
AAAH! SOMEBODY HELP!
THE BOY IS ALREADY IN THE GRIP OF FEAR. ATROCITUS, THE GREEN LANTERNS ARE YOURS.
WITH BLOOD AND RAGE OF CRIMSON RED, WE FILL MEN'S SOULS WITH DARKEST DREAD! WE TWIST YOUR MINDS TO PAIN AND HATE! WE'LL BURN YOU ALL...
...THAT IS YOUR FATE!
RRAAAARGH
UHNN!
POWER LEVELS 37% AND DROPPING.
AAAH!
POWER LEVELS 32% AND DROPPING.
MR. BATMAN! MR. BATMAN, YOU HAVE TO WAKE UP!
HE CANNOT.
NOT WHILE THE PSYCHO PIRATE HOLDS HIS SPIRIT CAPTIVE IN THE REALM OF DREAM.
MR. STRANGER!
YOU CAME BACK!
THE GREAT POWERS REFUSED MY REQUEST FOR AID, BUT I COULD NOT LET YOU FACE THIS ENEMY ALONE.
THEN YOU KNOW WHO'S BEHIND ALL THIS?
YES, THOUGH I SUSPECT YOU'VE PUT THE PIECES TOGETHER BY NOW AS WELL.

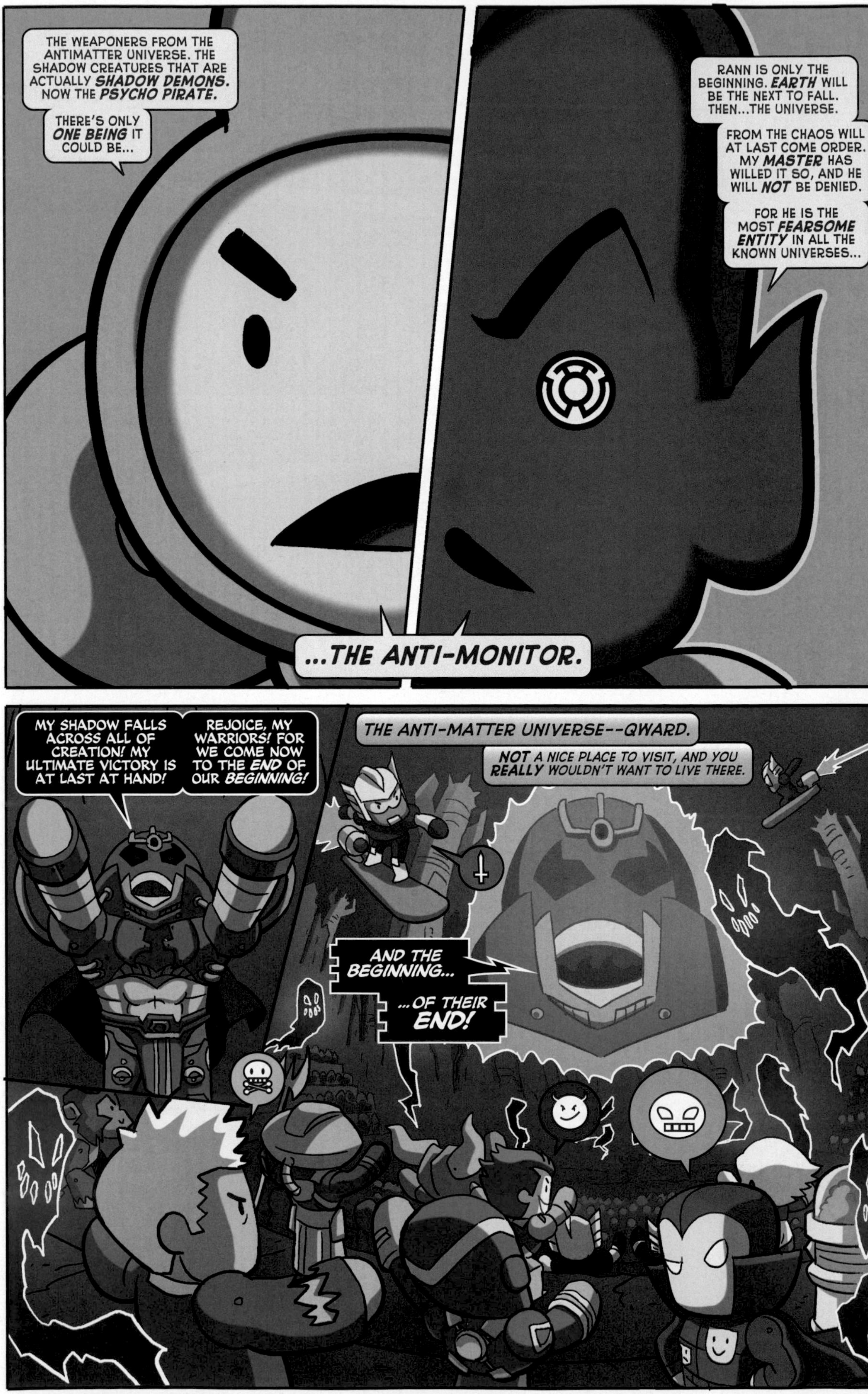

THE WEAPONERS FROM THE ANTIMATTER UNIVERSE. THE SHADOW CREATURES THAT ARE ACTUALLY SHADOW DEMONS. NOW THE PSYCHO PIRATE.
THERE'S ONLY ONE BEING IT COULD BE...
RANN IS ONLY THE BEGINNING. EARTH WILL BE THE NEXT TO FALL. THEN...THE UNIVERSE.
FROM THE CHAOS WILL AT LAST COME ORDER. MY MASTER HAS WILLED IT SO, AND HE WILL NOT BE DENIED.
FOR HE IS THE MOST FEARSOME ENTITY IN ALL THE KNOWN UNIVERSES...
...THE ANTI-MONITOR.
MY SHADOW FALLS ACROSS ALL OF CREATION! MY ULTIMATE VICTORY IS AT LAST AT HAND!
REJOICE, MY WARRIORS! FOR WE COME NOW TO THE END OF OUR BEGINNING!
THE ANTI-MATTER UNIVERSE--QWARD.
NOT A NICE PLACE TO VISIT, AND YOU REALLY WOULDN'T WANT TO LIVE THERE.
AND THE BEGINNING...
...OF THEIR END!

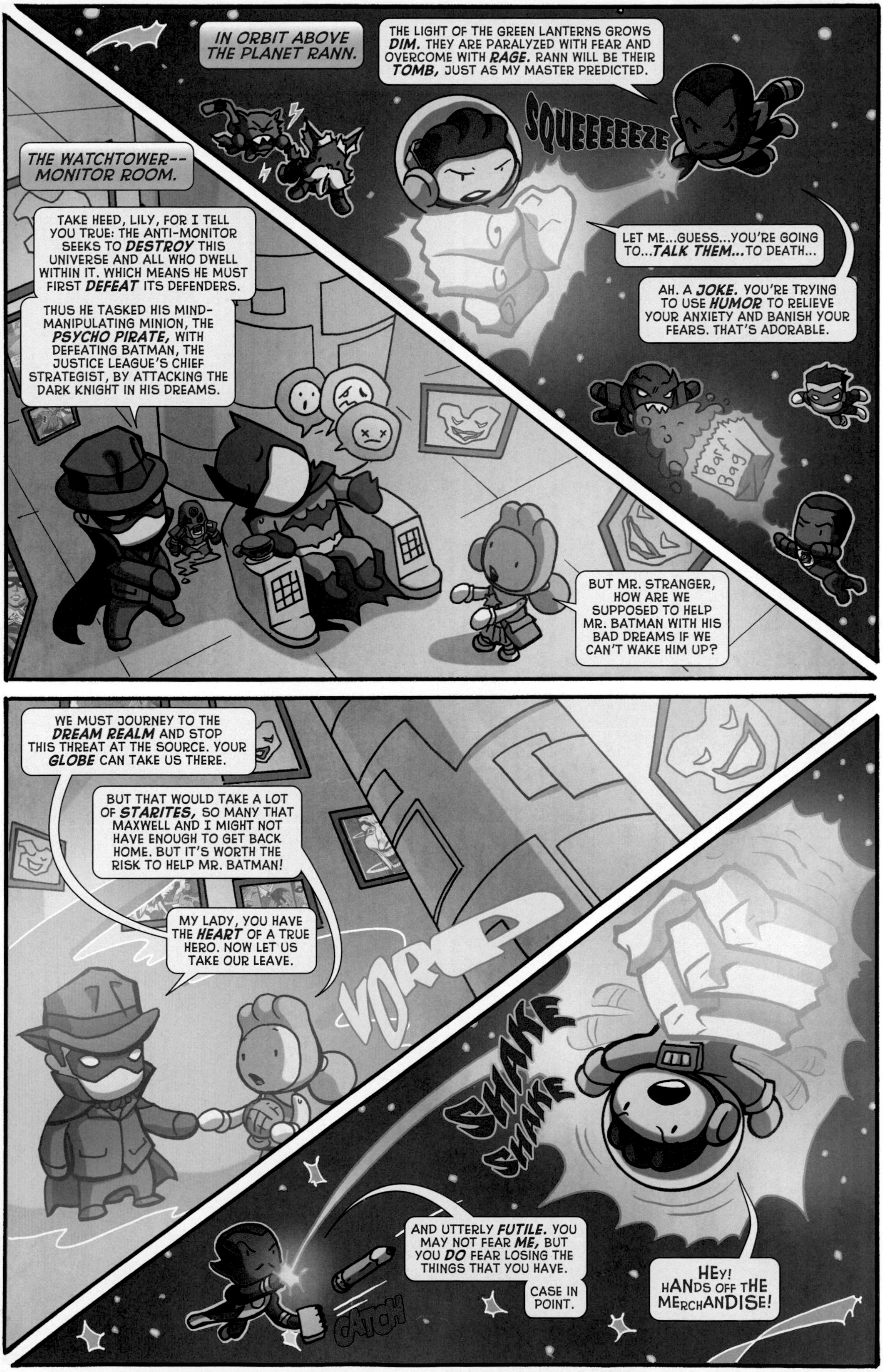

IN ORBIT ABOVE THE PLANET RANN.
THE LIGHT OF THE GREEN LANTERNS GROWS DIM. THEY ARE PARALYZED WITH FEAR AND OVERCOME WITH RAGE. RANN WILL BE THEIR TOMB, JUST AS MY MASTER PREDICTED.
SQUEEEEEEZE
LET ME...GUESS...YOU'RE GOING TO...TALK THEM...TO DEATH...
AH. A JOKE. YOU'RE TRYING TO USE HUMOR TO RELIEVE YOUR ANXIETY AND BANISH YOUR FEARS. THAT'S ADORABLE.
Barf Bag
THE WATCHTOWER-- MONITOR ROOM.
TAKE HEED, LILY, FOR I TELL YOU TRUE: THE ANTI-MONITOR SEEKS TO DESTROY THIS UNIVERSE AND ALL WHO DWELL WITHIN IT. WHICH MEANS HE MUST FIRST DEFEAT ITS DEFENDERS.
THUS HE TASKED HIS MIND-MANIPULATING MINION, THE PSYCHO PIRATE, WITH DEFEATING BATMAN, THE JUSTICE LEAGUE'S CHIEF STRATEGIST, BY ATTACKING THE DARK KNIGHT IN HIS DREAMS.
BUT MR. STRANGER, HOW ARE WE SUPPOSED TO HELP MR. BATMAN WITH HIS BAD DREAMS IF WE CAN'T WAKE HIM UP?
WE MUST JOURNEY TO THE DREAM REALM AND STOP THIS THREAT AT THE SOURCE. YOUR GLOBE CAN TAKE US THERE.
BUT THAT WOULD TAKE A LOT OF STARITES, SO MANY THAT MAXWELL AND I MIGHT NOT HAVE ENOUGH TO GET BACK HOME. BUT IT'S WORTH THE RISK TO HELP MR. BATMAN!
MY LADY, YOU HAVE THE HEART OF A TRUE HERO. NOW LET US TAKE OUR LEAVE.
VORP
SHAKE
SHAKE
AND UTTERLY FUTILE. YOU MAY NOT FEAR ME, BUT YOU DO FEAR LOSING THE THINGS THAT YOU HAVE.
CASE IN POINT.
HEY! HANDS OFF THE MERCHANDISE!
CATCH

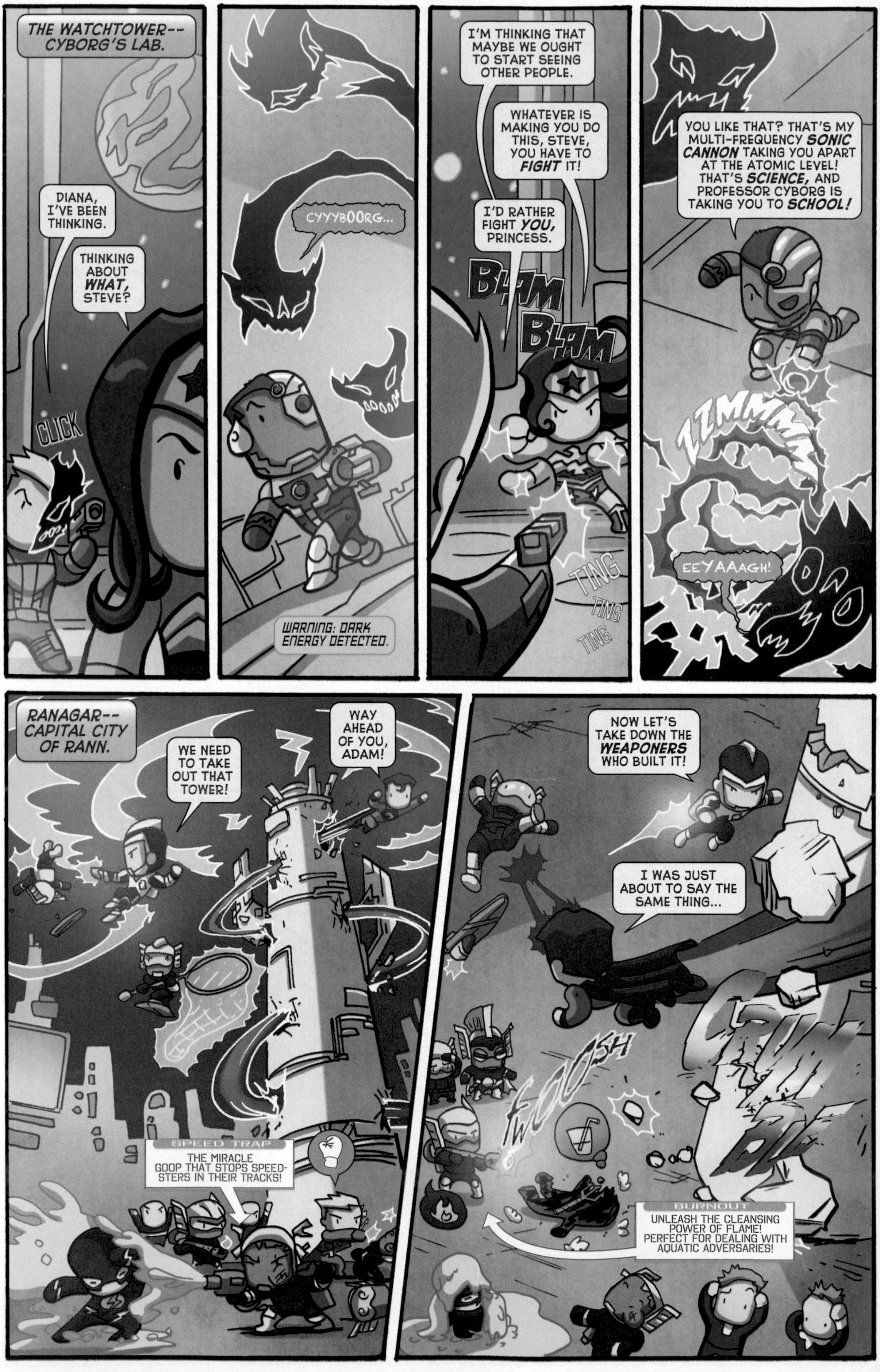
THE WATCHTOWER-- CYBORG'S LAB.
DIANA, I'VE BEEN THINKING.
THINKING ABOUT WHAT, STEVE?
CLICK
CYYYBOORG...
WARNING: DARK ENERGY DETECTED.
I'M THINKING THAT MAYBE WE OUGHT TO START SEEING OTHER PEOPLE.
WHATEVER IS MAKING YOU DO THIS, STEVE, YOU HAVE TO FIGHT IT!
I'D RATHER FIGHT YOU, PRINCESS.
BLAM
BLAM
TING
TING
TING
YOU LIKE THAT? THAT'S MY MULTI-FREQUENCY SONIC CANNON TAKING YOU APART AT THE ATOMIC LEVEL! THAT'S SCIENCE, AND PROFESSOR CYBORG IS TAKING YOU TO SCHOOL!
ZZMMMM
EEYAAAGH!
RANAGAR-- CAPITAL CITY OF RANN.
WE NEED TO TAKE OUT THAT TOWER!
WAY AHEAD OF YOU, ADAM!
SPEED TRAP
THE MIRACLE GOOP THAT STOPS SPEEDSTERS IN THEIR TRACKS!
NOW LET'S TAKE DOWN THE WEAPONERS WHO BUILT IT!
I WAS JUST ABOUT TO SAY THE SAME THING...
FWOOSH
BURNOUT
UNLEASH THE CLEANSING POWER OF FLAME! PERFECT FOR DEALING WITH AQUATIC ADVERSARIES!

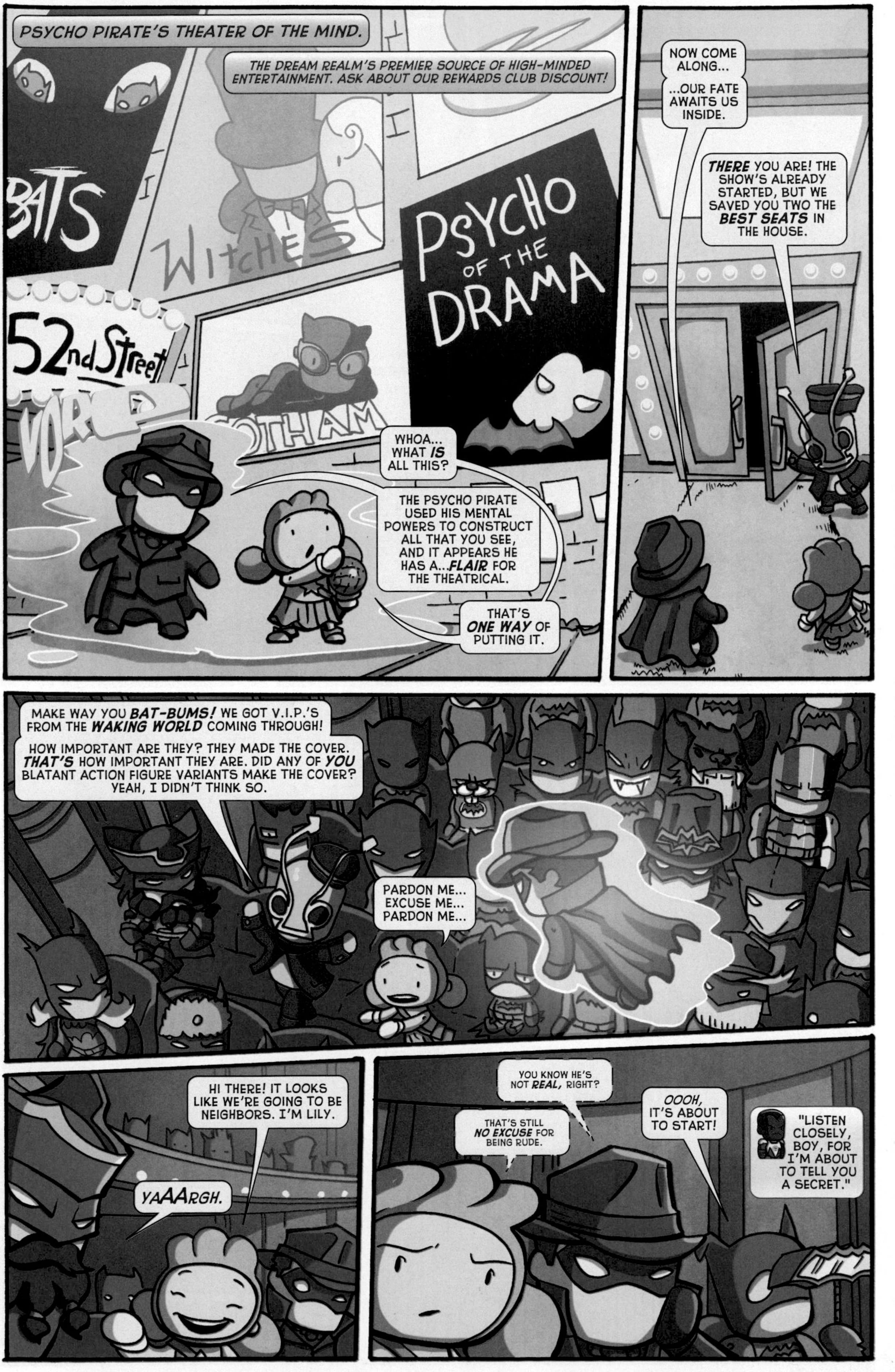
PSYCHO PIRATE'S THEATER OF THE MIND.
THE DREAM REALM'S PREMIER SOURCE OF HIGH-MINDED ENTERTAINMENT. ASK ABOUT OUR REWARDS CLUB DISCOUNT!
BATS
WITCHES
PSYCHO OF THE DRAMA
52nd Street
VORP
GOTHAM
WHOA... WHAT IS ALL THIS?
THE PSYCHO PIRATE USED HIS MENTAL POWERS TO CONSTRUCT ALL THAT YOU SEE, AND IT APPEARS HE HAS A...FLAIR FOR THE THEATRICAL.
THAT'S ONE WAY OF PUTTING IT.
NOW COME ALONG...
...OUR FATE AWAITS US INSIDE.
THERE YOU ARE! THE SHOW'S ALREADY STARTED, BUT WE SAVED YOU TWO THE BEST SEATS IN THE HOUSE.
MAKE WAY YOU BAT-BUMS! WE GOT V.I.P.'S FROM THE WAKING WORLD COMING THROUGH!
HOW IMPORTANT ARE THEY? THEY MADE THE COVER. THAT'S HOW IMPORTANT THEY ARE. DID ANY OF YOU BLATANT ACTION FIGURE VARIANTS MAKE THE COVER? YEAH, I DIDN'T THINK SO.
PARDON ME... EXCUSE ME... PARDON ME...
HI THERE! IT LOOKS LIKE WE'RE GOING TO BE NEIGHBORS. I'M LILY.
YAAARGH.
YOU KNOW HE'S NOT REAL, RIGHT?
THAT'S STILL NO EXCUSE FOR BEING RUDE.
OOOH, IT'S ABOUT TO START!
"LISTEN CLOSELY, BOY, FOR I'M ABOUT TO TELL YOU A SECRET."

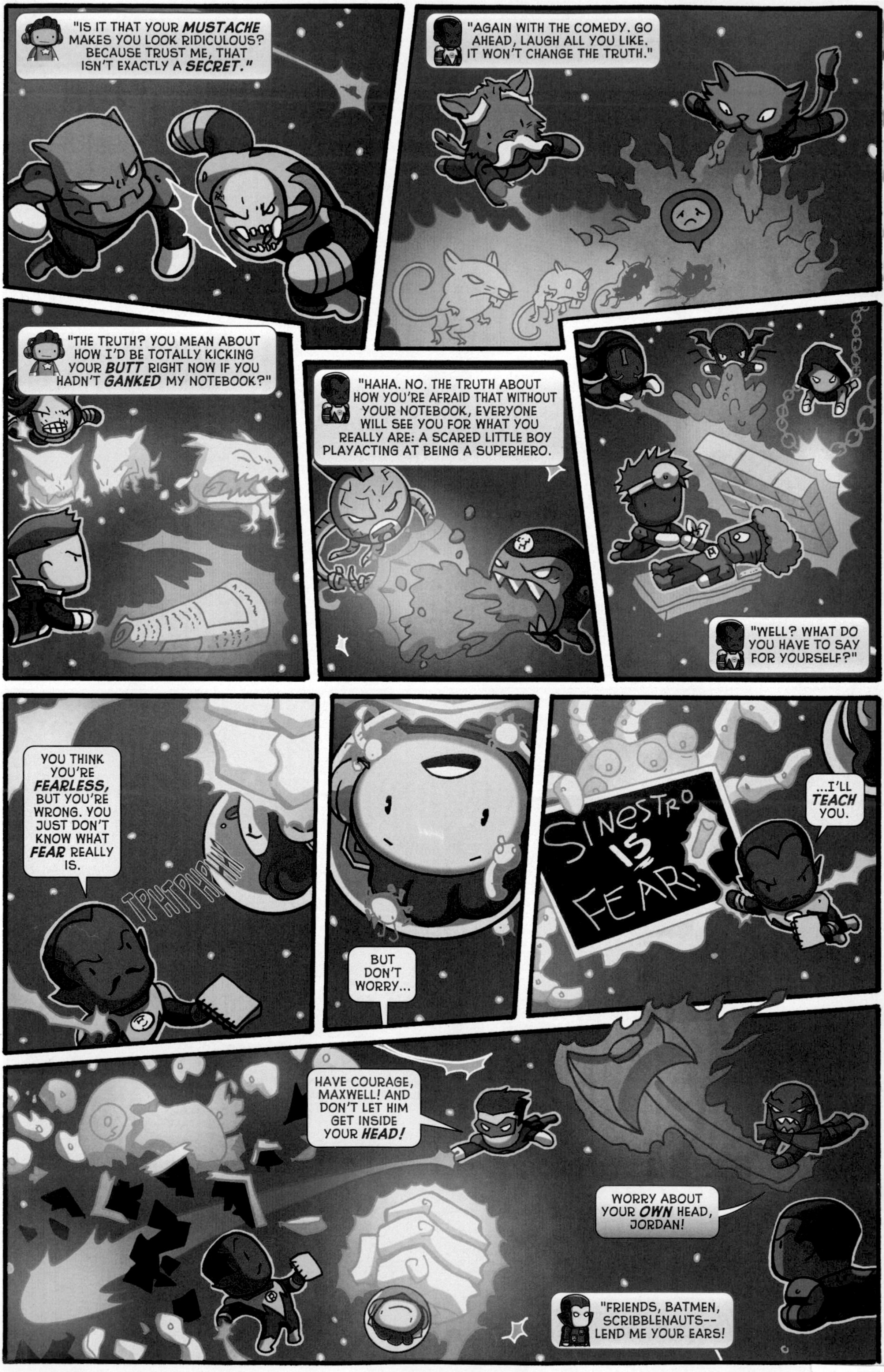
"IS IT THAT YOUR MUSTACHE MAKES YOU LOOK RIDICULOUS? BECAUSE TRUST ME, THAT ISN'T EXACTLY A SECRET."
"AGAIN WITH THE COMEDY. GO AHEAD, LAUGH ALL YOU LIKE. IT WON'T CHANGE THE TRUTH."
"THE TRUTH? YOU MEAN ABOUT HOW I'D BE TOTALLY KICKING YOUR BUTT RIGHT NOW IF YOU HADN'T GANKED MY NOTEBOOK?"
"HAHA. NO. THE TRUTH ABOUT HOW YOU'RE AFRAID THAT WITHOUT YOUR NOTEBOOK, EVERYONE WILL SEE YOU FOR WHAT YOU REALLY ARE: A SCARED LITTLE BOY PLAYACTING AT BEING A SUPERHERO.
"WELL? WHAT DO YOU HAVE TO SAY FOR YOURSELF?"
YOU THINK YOU'RE FEARLESS, BUT YOU'RE WRONG. YOU JUST DON'T KNOW WHAT FEAR REALLY IS.
TPHTPHHH
BUT DON'T WORRY...
SINESTRO IS FEAR!
...I'LL TEACH YOU.
HAVE COURAGE, MAXWELL! AND DON'T LET HIM GET INSIDE YOUR HEAD!
WORRY ABOUT YOUR OWN HEAD, JORDAN!
"FRIENDS, BATMEN, SCRIBBLENAUTS-- LEND ME YOUR EARS!

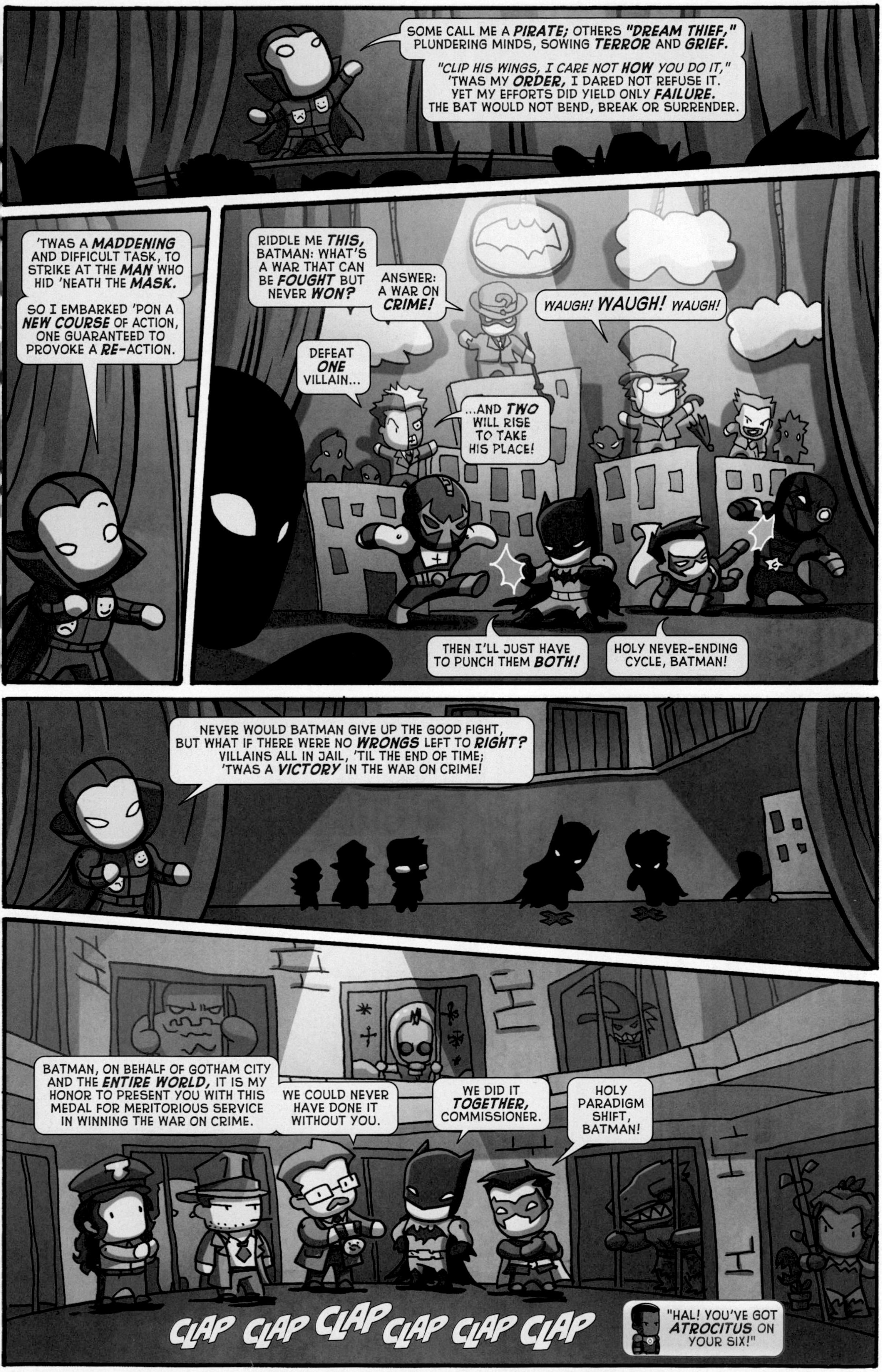
SOME CALL ME A PIRATE; OTHERS "DREAM THIEF," PLUNDERING MINDS, SOWING TERROR AND GRIEF.
"CLIP HIS WINGS, I CARE NOT HOW YOU DO IT," 'TWAS MY ORDER, I DARED NOT REFUSE IT. YET MY EFFORTS DID YIELD ONLY FAILURE. THE BAT WOULD NOT BEND, BREAK OR SURRENDER.
'TWAS A MADDENING AND DIFFICULT TASK, TO STRIKE AT THE MAN WHO HID 'NEATH THE MASK.
SO I EMBARKED 'PON A NEW COURSE OF ACTION, ONE GUARANTEED TO PROVOKE A RE-ACTION.
RIDDLE ME THIS, BATMAN: WHAT'S A WAR THAT CAN BE FOUGHT BUT NEVER WON?
ANSWER: A WAR ON CRIME!
WAUGH! WAUGH! WAUGH!
DEFEAT ONE VILLAIN...
...AND TWO WILL RISE TO TAKE HIS PLACE!
THEN I'LL JUST HAVE TO PUNCH THEM BOTH!
HOLY NEVER-ENDING CYCLE, BATMAN!
NEVER WOULD BATMAN GIVE UP THE GOOD FIGHT, BUT WHAT IF THERE WERE NO WRONGS LEFT TO RIGHT? VILLAINS ALL IN JAIL, 'TIL THE END OF TIME; 'TWAS A VICTORY IN THE WAR ON CRIME!
BATMAN, ON BEHALF OF GOTHAM CITY AND THE ENTIRE WORLD, IT IS MY HONOR TO PRESENT YOU WITH THIS MEDAL FOR MERITORIOUS SERVICE IN WINNING THE WAR ON CRIME.
WE COULD NEVER HAVE DONE IT WITHOUT YOU.
WE DID IT TOGETHER, COMMISSIONER.
HOLY PARADIGM SHIFT, BATMAN!
CLAP CLAP CLAP CLAP CLAP CLAP
"HAL! YOU'VE GOT ATROCITUS ON YOUR SIX!"

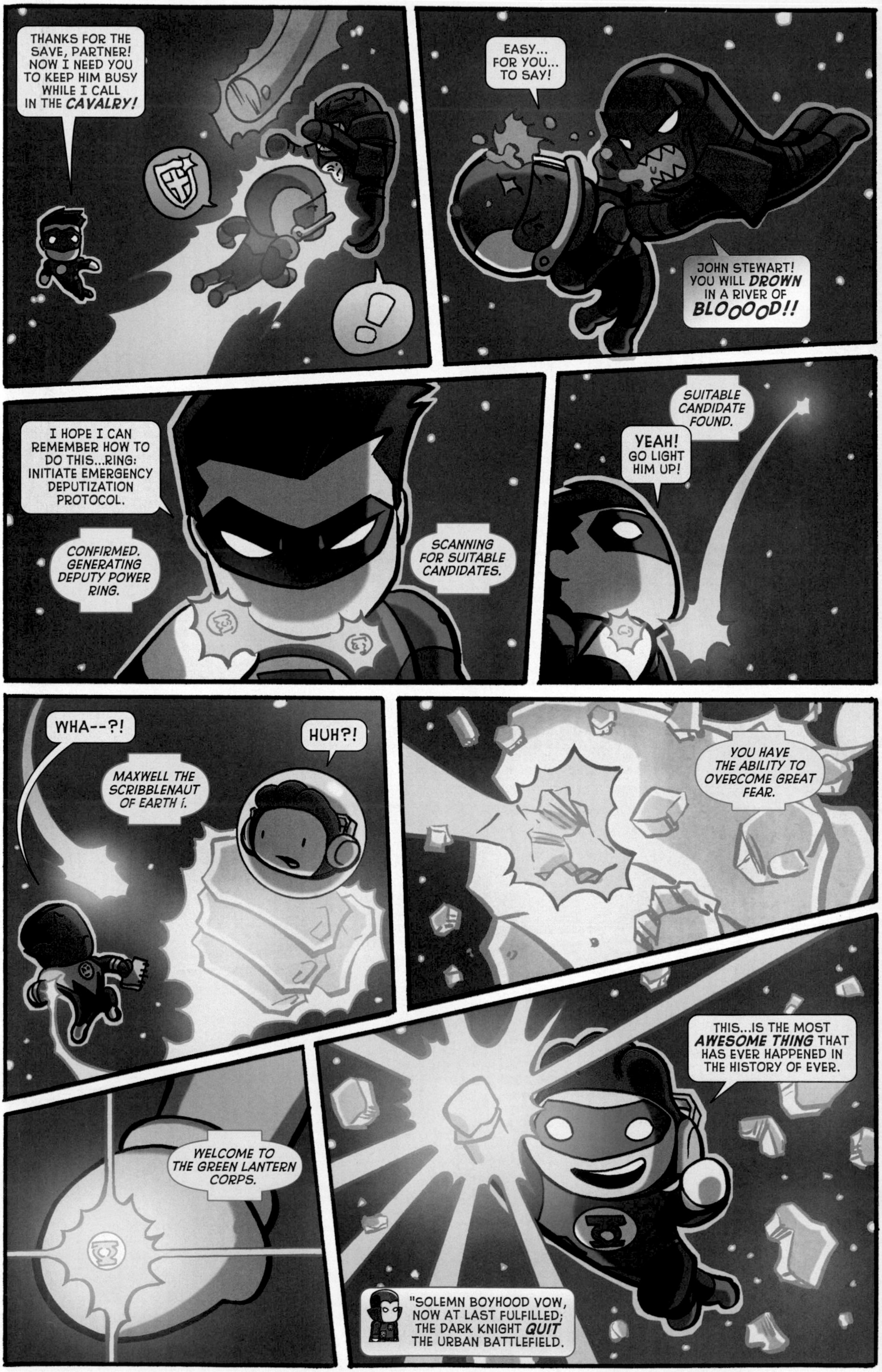
THANKS FOR THE SAVE, PARTNER! NOW I NEED YOU TO KEEP HIM BUSY WHILE I CALL IN THE CAVALRY!
!
EASY... FOR YOU... TO SAY!
JOHN STEWART! YOU WILL DROWN IN A RIVER OF BLOOOOOD!!
I HOPE I CAN REMEMBER HOW TO DO THIS...RING: INITIATE EMERGENCY DEPUTIZATION PROTOCOL.
CONFIRMED. GENERATING DEPUTY POWER RING.
SCANNING FOR SUITABLE CANDIDATES.
SUITABLE CANDIDATE FOUND.
YEAH! GO LIGHT HIM UP!
WHA--?!
HUH?!
MAXWELL THE SCRIBBLENAUT OF EARTH í.
YOU HAVE THE ABILITY TO OVERCOME GREAT FEAR.
WELCOME TO THE GREEN LANTERN CORPS.
THIS...IS THE MOST AWESOME THING THAT HAS EVER HAPPENED IN THE HISTORY OF EVER.
"SOLEMN BOYHOOD VOW, NOW AT LAST FULFILLED; THE DARK KNIGHT QUIT THE URBAN BATTLEFIELD.

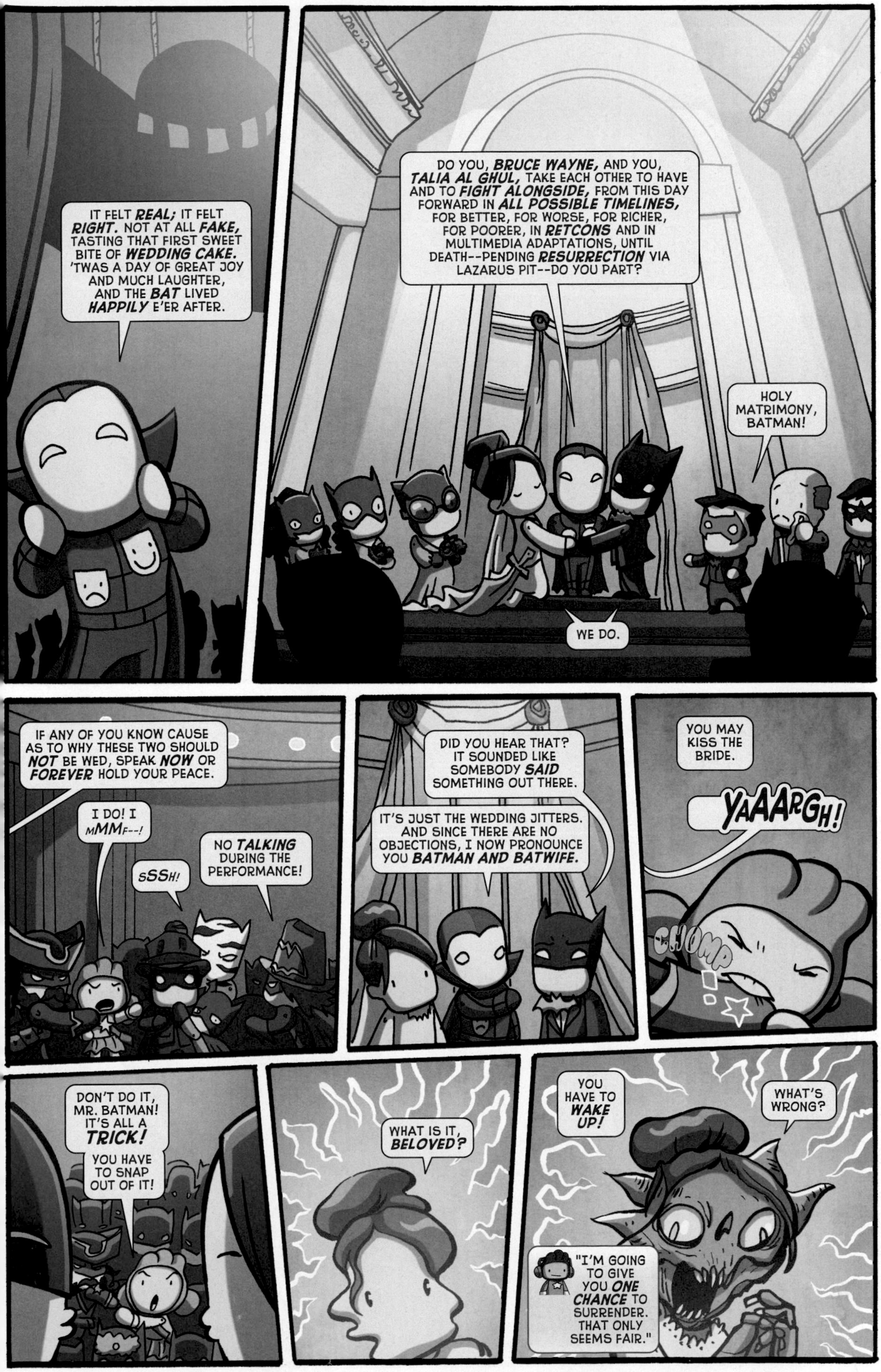
IT FELT REAL; IT FELT RIGHT. NOT AT ALL FAKE, TASTING THAT FIRST SWEET BITE OF WEDDING CAKE. 'TWAS A DAY OF GREAT JOY AND MUCH LAUGHTER, AND THE BAT LIVED HAPPILY E'ER AFTER.
DO YOU, BRUCE WAYNE, AND YOU, TALIA AL GHUL, TAKE EACH OTHER TO HAVE AND TO FIGHT ALONGSIDE, FROM THIS DAY FORWARD IN ALL POSSIBLE TIMELINES, FOR BETTER, FOR WORSE, FOR RICHER, FOR POORER, IN RETCONS AND IN MULTIMEDIA ADAPTATIONS, UNTIL DEATH--PENDING RESURRECTION VIA LAZARUS PIT--DO YOU PART?
HOLY MATRIMONY, BATMAN!
WE DO.
IF ANY OF YOU KNOW CAUSE AS TO WHY THESE TWO SHOULD NOT BE WED, SPEAK NOW OR FOREVER HOLD YOUR PEACE.
I DO! I mMMf--!
sSSH!
NO TALKING DURING THE PERFORMANCE!
DID YOU HEAR THAT? IT SOUNDED LIKE SOMEBODY SAID SOMETHING OUT THERE.
IT'S JUST THE WEDDING JITTERS. AND SINCE THERE ARE NO OBJECTIONS, I NOW PRONOUNCE YOU BATMAN AND BATWIFE.
YOU MAY KISS THE BRIDE.
YAAARGH!
CHOMP
DON'T DO IT, MR. BATMAN! IT'S ALL A TRICK!
YOU HAVE TO SNAP OUT OF IT!
WHAT IS IT, BELOVED?
YOU HAVE TO WAKE UP!
WHAT'S WRONG?
"I'M GOING TO GIVE YOU ONE CHANCE TO SURRENDER. THAT ONLY SEEMS FAIR."

AM I SUPPOSED TO BE INTIMIDATED BY A CHILD WIELDING A KNOCK-OFF POWER RING?
BECAUSE I ASSURE YOU, I AM NOT.
I MAY BE A ROOKIE...
...BUT AS THIS CHART CLEARLY SHOWS, I'M WAY MORE AWESOME THAN YOU.
Awesomeness
Maxwell
Sinestro
AND HE DIDN'T EXACTLY COME ALONE.
CHECK YOUR MATH, JORDAN. YOU'RE STILL OUTNUMBERED TWO CORPS TO ONE.
THAT IS WHERE YOU ARE MISTAKEN, THAAL SINESTRO.

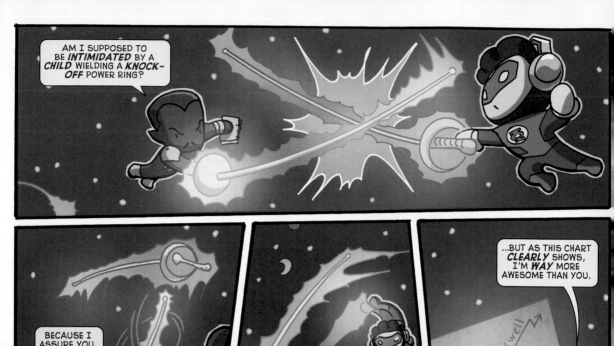

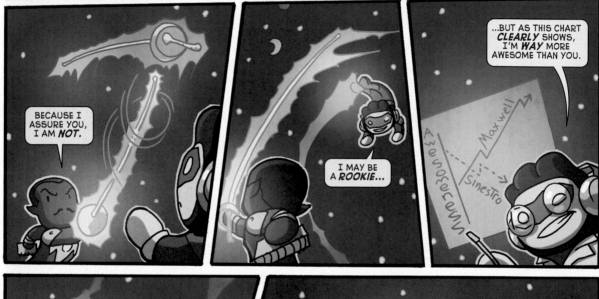

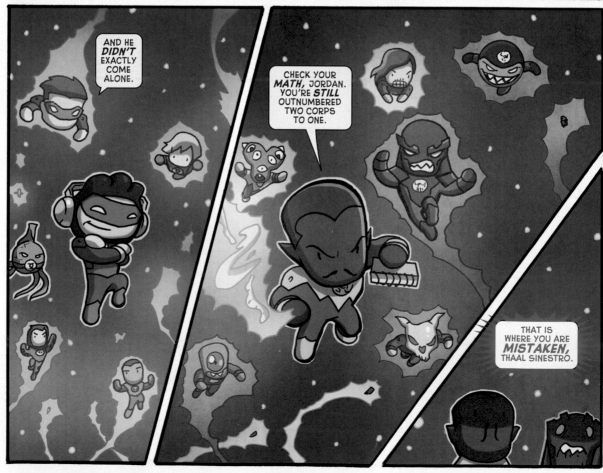

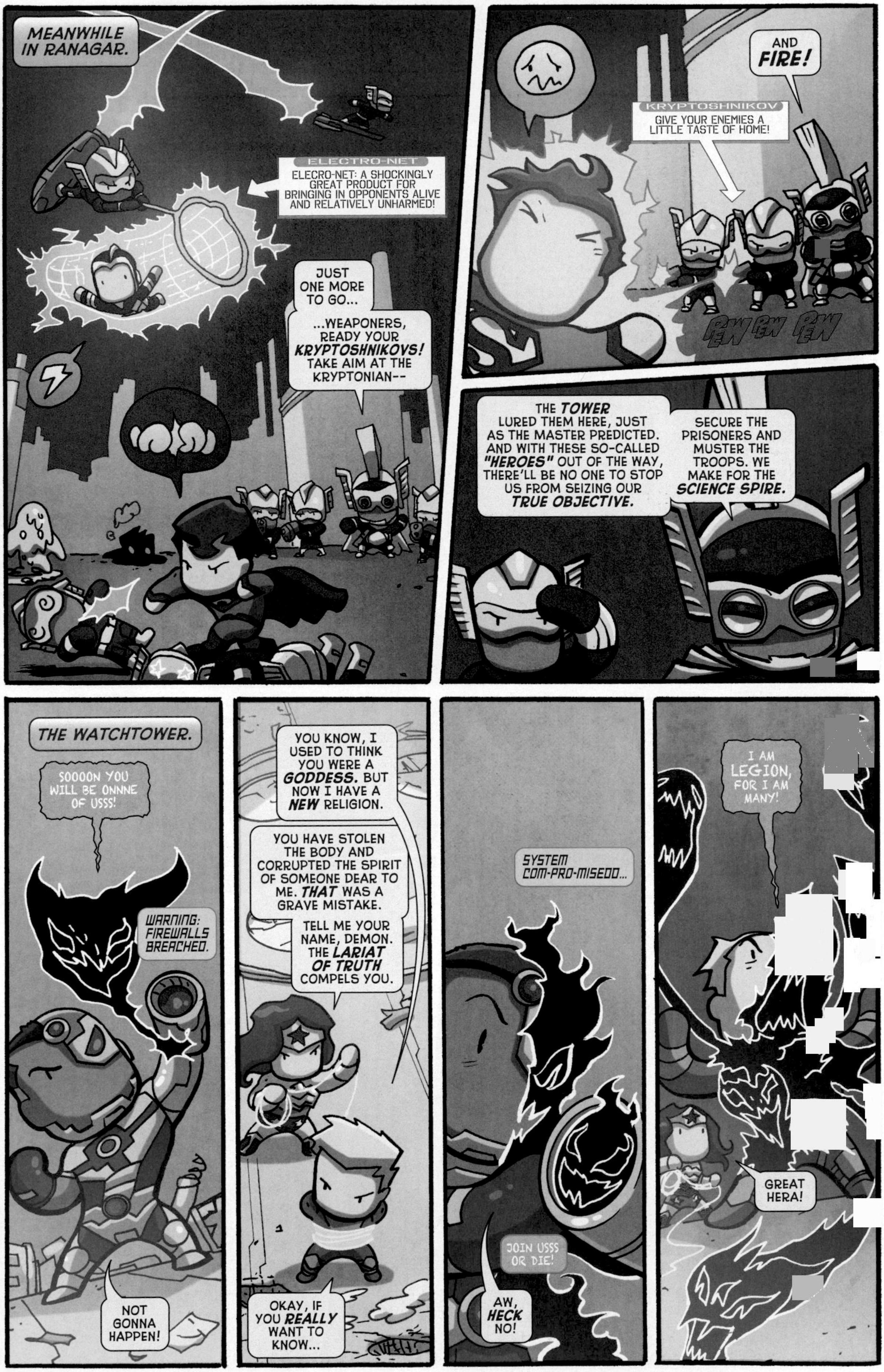
MEANWHILE IN RANAGAR.
ELECTRO-NET
ELECRO-NET: A SHOCKINGLY GREAT PRODUCT FOR BRINGING IN OPPONENTS ALIVE AND RELATIVELY UNHARMED!
JUST ONE MORE TO GO...
...WEAPONERS, READY YOUR KRYPTOSHNIKOVS! TAKE AIM AT THE KRYPTONIAN--
AND FIRE!
KRYPTOSHNIKOV
GIVE YOUR ENEMIES A LITTLE TASTE OF HOME!
PEW PEW PEW
THE TOWER LURED THEM HERE, JUST AS THE MASTER PREDICTED. AND WITH THESE SO-CALLED "HEROES" OUT OF THE WAY, THERE'LL BE NO ONE TO STOP US FROM SEIZING OUR TRUE OBJECTIVE.
SECURE THE PRISONERS AND MUSTER THE TROOPS. WE MAKE FOR THE SCIENCE SPIRE.
THE WATCHTOWER.
SOOOON YOU WILL BE ONNNE OF USSS!
WARNING: FIREWALLS BREACHED.
NOT GONNA HAPPEN!
YOU KNOW, I USED TO THINK YOU WERE A GODDESS. BUT NOW I HAVE A NEW RELIGION.
YOU HAVE STOLEN THE BODY AND CORRUPTED THE SPIRIT OF SOMEONE DEAR TO ME. THAT WAS A GRAVE MISTAKE.
TELL ME YOUR NAME, DEMON. THE LARIAT OF TRUTH COMPELS YOU.
OKAY, IF YOU REALLY WANT TO KNOW...
SYSTEM COM-PRO-MISEDD...
JOIN USSS OR DIE!
AW, HECK NO!
I AM LEGION, FOR I AM MANY!
GREAT HERA!

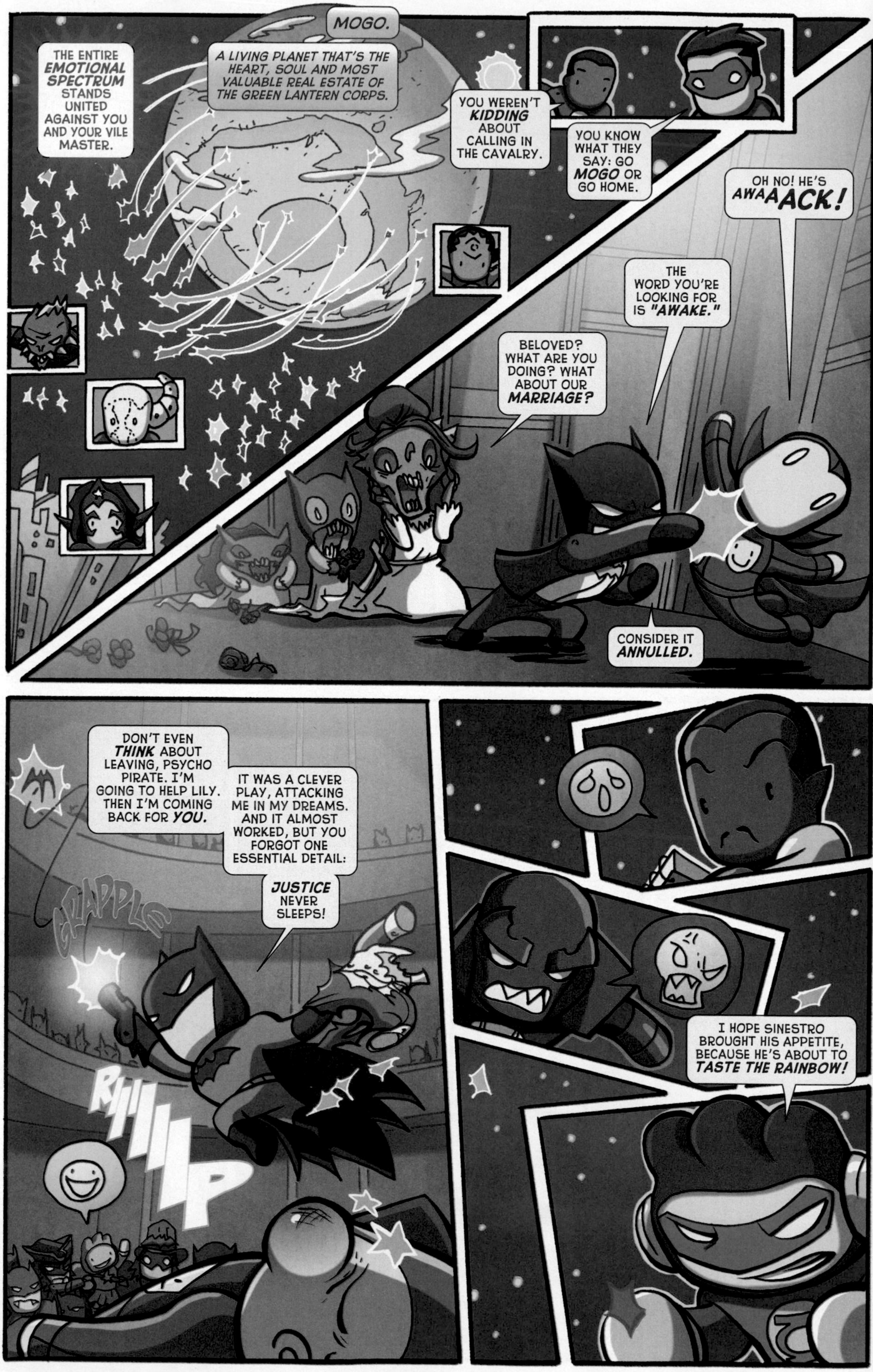
MOGO.
THE ENTIRE EMOTIONAL SPECTRUM STANDS UNITED AGAINST YOU AND YOUR VILE MASTER.
A LIVING PLANET THAT'S THE HEART, SOUL AND MOST VALUABLE REAL ESTATE OF THE GREEN LANTERN CORPS.
YOU WEREN'T KIDDING ABOUT CALLING IN THE CAVALRY.
YOU KNOW WHAT THEY SAY: GO MOGO OR GO HOME.
OH NO! HE'S AWAAAACK!
THE WORD YOU'RE LOOKING FOR IS "AWAKE."
BELOVED? WHAT ARE YOU DOING? WHAT ABOUT OUR MARRIAGE?
CONSIDER IT ANNULLED.
DON'T EVEN THINK ABOUT LEAVING, PSYCHO PIRATE. I'M GOING TO HELP LILY. THEN I'M COMING BACK FOR YOU.
IT WAS A CLEVER PLAY, ATTACKING ME IN MY DREAMS. AND IT ALMOST WORKED, BUT YOU FORGOT ONE ESSENTIAL DETAIL:
JUSTICE NEVER SLEEPS!
GRAPPLE
RIIIIIIP
I HOPE SINESTRO BROUGHT HIS APPETITE, BECAUSE HE'S ABOUT TO TASTE THE RAINBOW!

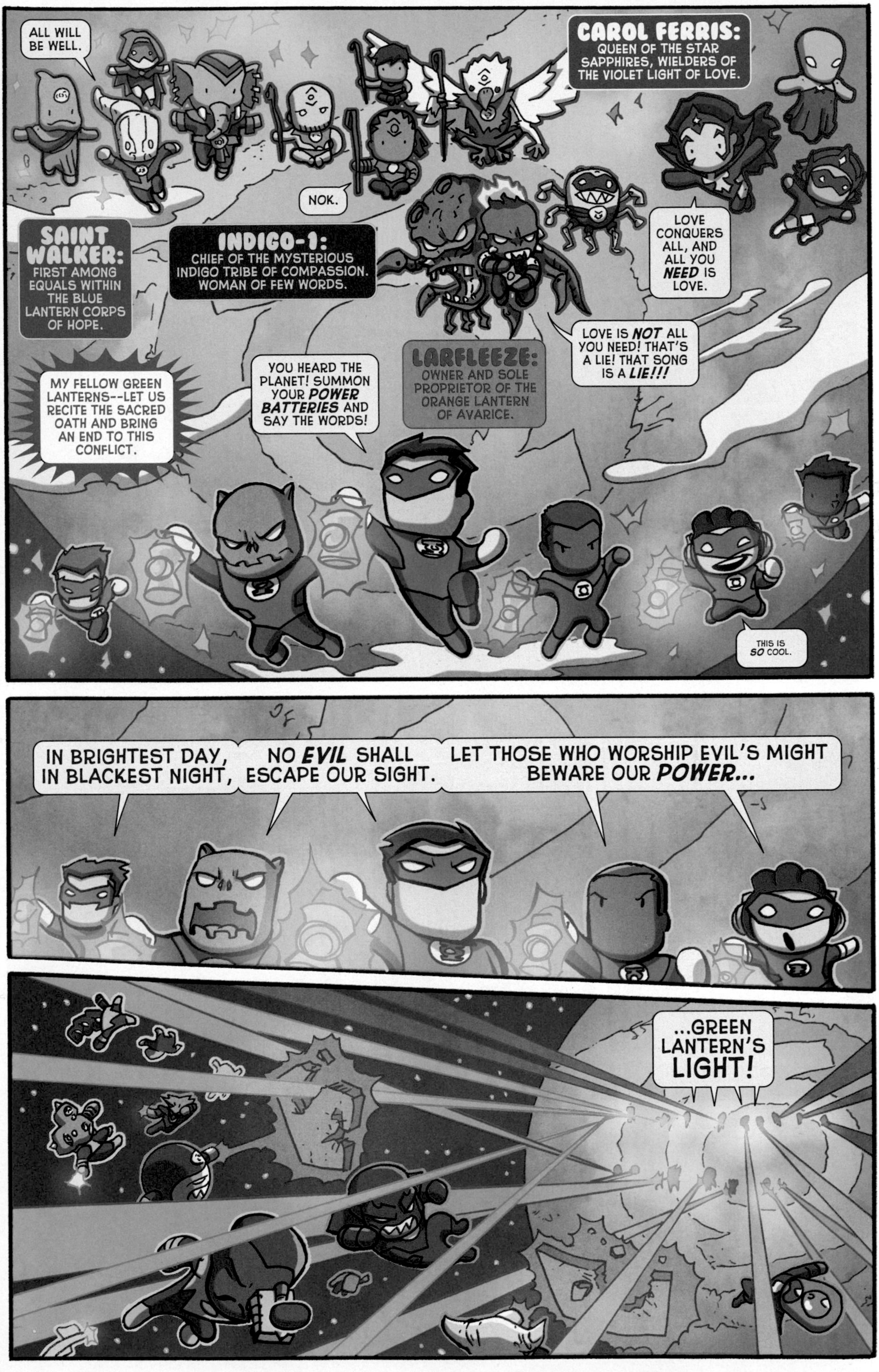

ALL WILL BE WELL.
CAROL FERRIS: QUEEN OF THE STAR SAPPHIRES, WIELDERS OF THE VIOLET LIGHT OF LOVE.
NOK.
SAINT WALKER: FIRST AMONG EQUALS WITHIN THE BLUE LANTERN CORPS OF HOPE.
INDIGO-1: CHIEF OF THE MYSTERIOUS INDIGO TRIBE OF COMPASSION. WOMAN OF FEW WORDS.
LOVE CONQUERS ALL, AND ALL YOU NEED IS LOVE.
LOVE IS NOT ALL YOU NEED! THAT'S A LIE! THAT SONG IS A LIE!!!
LARFLEEZE: OWNER AND SOLE PROPRIETOR OF THE ORANGE LANTERN OF AVARICE.
MY FELLOW GREEN LANTERNS--LET US RECITE THE SACRED OATH AND BRING AN END TO THIS CONFLICT.
YOU HEARD THE PLANET! SUMMON YOUR POWER BATTERIES AND SAY THE WORDS!
THIS IS SO COOL.
IN BRIGHTEST DAY, IN BLACKEST NIGHT,
NO EVIL SHALL ESCAPE OUR SIGHT.
LET THOSE WHO WORSHIP EVIL'S MIGHT BEWARE OUR POWER...
...GREEN LANTERN'S LIGHT!

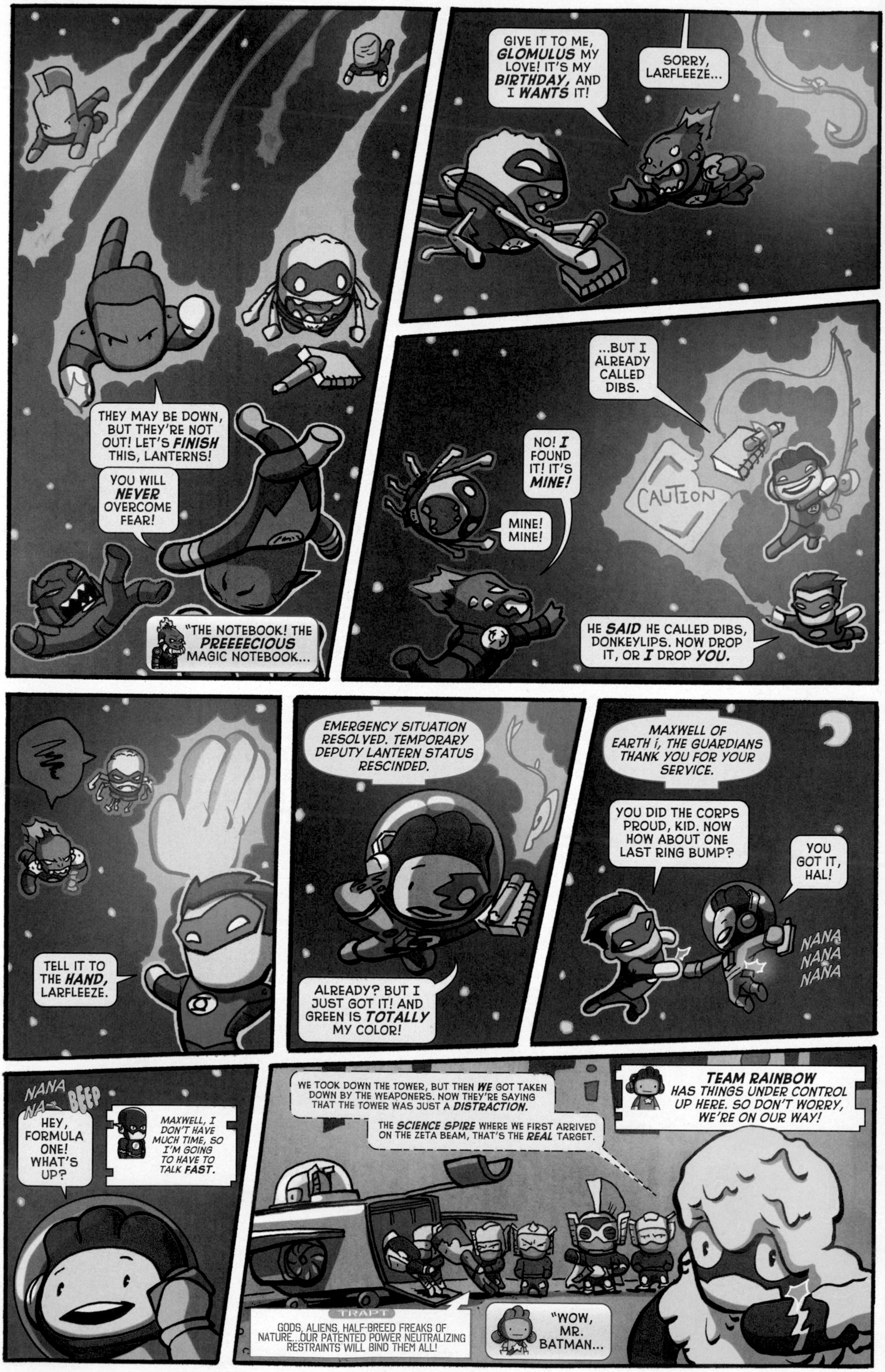
THEY MAY BE DOWN, BUT THEY'RE NOT OUT! LET'S FINISH THIS, LANTERNS!
YOU WILL NEVER OVERCOME FEAR!
"THE NOTEBOOK! THE PREEEECIOUS MAGIC NOTEBOOK...
GIVE IT TO ME, GLOMULUS MY LOVE! IT'S MY BIRTHDAY, AND I WANTS IT!
SORRY, LARFLEEZE...
...BUT I ALREADY CALLED DIBS.
NO! I FOUND IT! IT'S MINE!
MINE! MINE!
CAUTION
HE SAID HE CALLED DIBS, DONKEYLIPS. NOW DROP IT, OR I DROP YOU.
TELL IT TO THE HAND, LARFLEEZE.
EMERGENCY SITUATION RESOLVED. TEMPORARY DEPUTY LANTERN STATUS RESCINDED.
ALREADY? BUT I JUST GOT IT! AND GREEN IS TOTALLY MY COLOR!
MAXWELL OF EARTH i, THE GUARDIANS THANK YOU FOR YOUR SERVICE.
YOU DID THE CORPS PROUD, KID. NOW HOW ABOUT ONE LAST RING BUMP?
YOU GOT IT, HAL!
NANA NANA NANA
NANA NA-
BEEP
HEY, FORMULA ONE! WHAT'S UP?
MAXWELL, I DON'T HAVE MUCH TIME, SO I'M GOING TO HAVE TO TALK FAST.
WE TOOK DOWN THE TOWER, BUT THEN WE GOT TAKEN DOWN BY THE WEAPONERS. NOW THEY'RE SAYING THAT THE TOWER WAS JUST A DISTRACTION.
THE SCIENCE SPIRE WHERE WE FIRST ARRIVED ON THE ZETA BEAM, THAT'S THE REAL TARGET.
TEAM RAINBOW HAS THINGS UNDER CONTROL UP HERE. SO DON'T WORRY, WE'RE ON OUR WAY!
TRAPT
GODS, ALIENS, HALF-BREED FREAKS OF NATURE...OUR PATENTED POWER NEUTRALIZING RESTRAINTS WILL BIND THEM ALL!
"WOW, MR. BATMAN...

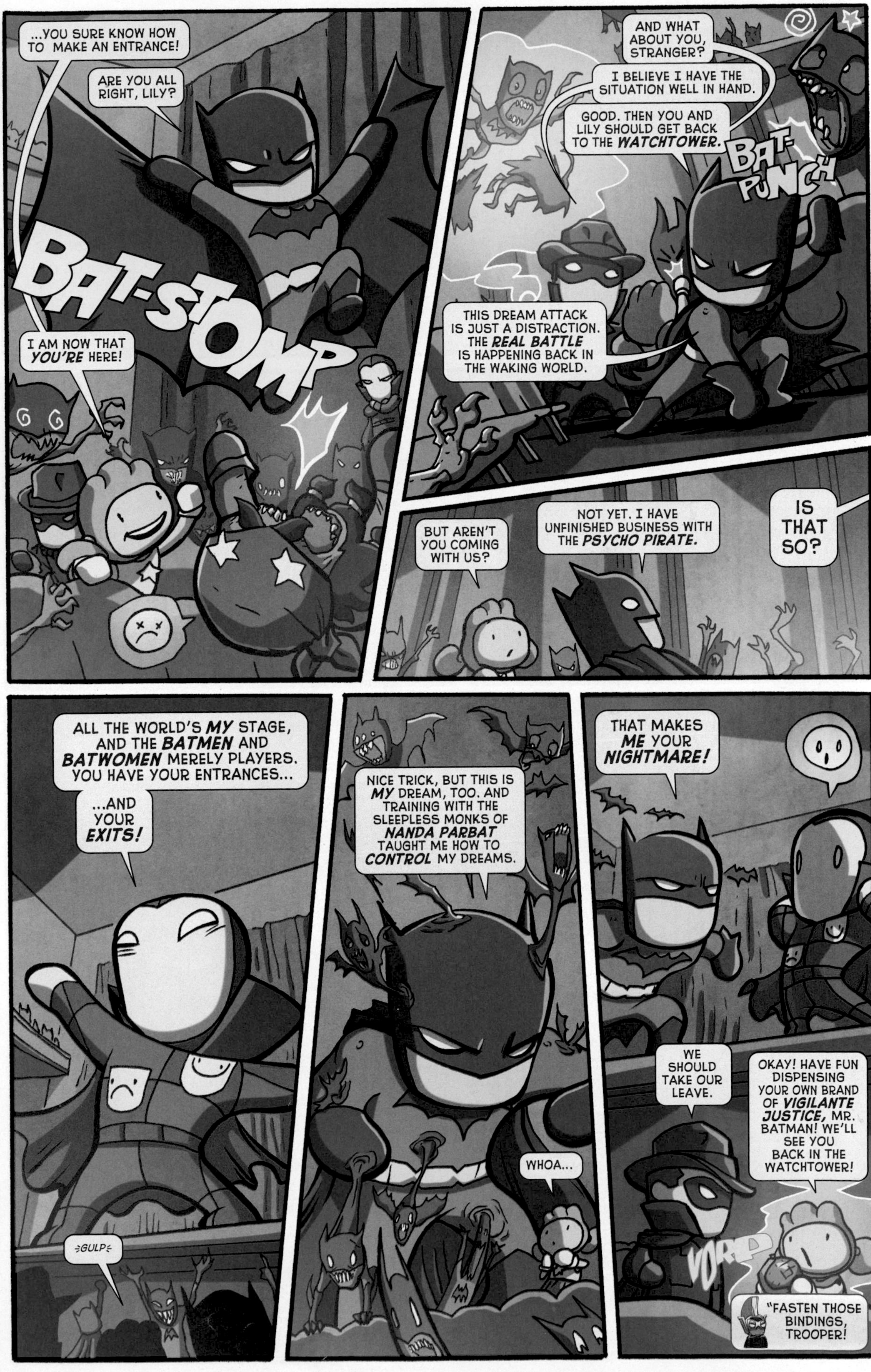
...YOU SURE KNOW HOW TO MAKE AN ENTRANCE!
ARE YOU ALL RIGHT, LILY?
BAT-STOMP
I AM NOW THAT *YOU'RE* HERE!
AND WHAT ABOUT YOU, STRANGER?
I BELIEVE I HAVE THE SITUATION WELL IN HAND.
GOOD. THEN YOU AND LILY SHOULD GET BACK TO THE ***WATCHTOWER.***
BAT-PUNCH
THIS DREAM ATTACK IS JUST A DISTRACTION. THE ***REAL BATTLE*** IS HAPPENING BACK IN THE WAKING WORLD.
BUT AREN'T YOU COMING WITH US?
NOT YET. I HAVE UNFINISHED BUSINESS WITH THE ***PSYCHO PIRATE.***
IS THAT SO?
ALL THE WORLD'S ***MY*** STAGE, AND THE ***BATMEN*** AND ***BATWOMEN*** MERELY PLAYERS. YOU HAVE YOUR ENTRANCES...
...AND YOUR ***EXITS!***
GULP
NICE TRICK, BUT THIS IS ***MY*** DREAM, TOO. AND TRAINING WITH THE SLEEPLESS MONKS OF ***NANDA PARBAT*** TAUGHT ME HOW TO ***CONTROL*** MY DREAMS.
WHOA...
THAT MAKES ***ME*** YOUR ***NIGHTMARE!***
WE SHOULD TAKE OUR LEAVE.
OKAY! HAVE FUN DISPENSING YOUR OWN BRAND OF ***VIGILANTE JUSTICE,*** MR. BATMAN! WE'LL SEE YOU BACK IN THE WATCHTOWER!
VORP
"FASTEN THOSE BINDINGS, TROOPER!

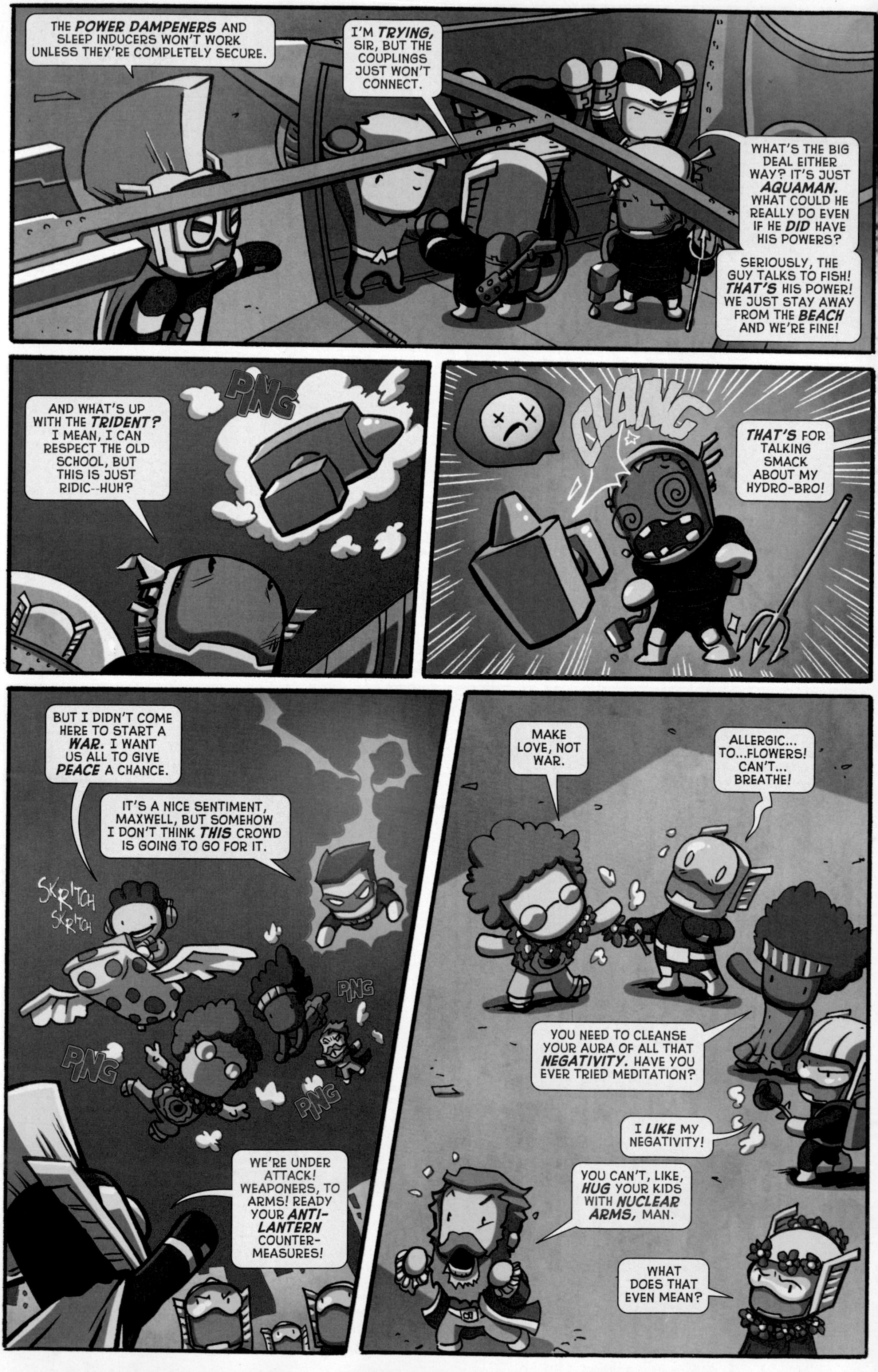

THE POWER DAMPENERS AND SLEEP INDUCERS WON'T WORK UNLESS THEY'RE COMPLETELY SECURE.
I'M TRYING, SIR, BUT THE COUPLINGS JUST WON'T CONNECT.
WHAT'S THE BIG DEAL EITHER WAY? IT'S JUST AQUAMAN. WHAT COULD HE REALLY DO EVEN IF HE DID HAVE HIS POWERS?
SERIOUSLY, THE GUY TALKS TO FISH! THAT'S HIS POWER! WE JUST STAY AWAY FROM THE BEACH AND WE'RE FINE!
AND WHAT'S UP WITH THE TRIDENT? I MEAN, I CAN RESPECT THE OLD SCHOOL, BUT THIS IS JUST RIDIC--HUH?
PING
CLANG
THAT'S FOR TALKING SMACK ABOUT MY HYDRO-BRO!
BUT I DIDN'T COME HERE TO START A WAR. I WANT US ALL TO GIVE PEACE A CHANCE.
IT'S A NICE SENTIMENT, MAXWELL, BUT SOMEHOW I DON'T THINK THIS CROWD IS GOING TO GO FOR IT.
SKRITCH SKRITCH
PING
PING
PING
WE'RE UNDER ATTACK! WEAPONERS, TO ARMS! READY YOUR ANTI-LANTERN COUNTER-MEASURES!
MAKE LOVE, NOT WAR.
ALLERGIC... TO...FLOWERS! CAN'T... BREATHE!
YOU NEED TO CLEANSE YOUR AURA OF ALL THAT NEGATIVITY. HAVE YOU EVER TRIED MEDITATION?
I LIKE MY NEGATIVITY!
YOU CAN'T, LIKE, HUG YOUR KIDS WITH NUCLEAR ARMS, MAN.
WHAT DOES THAT EVEN MEAN?

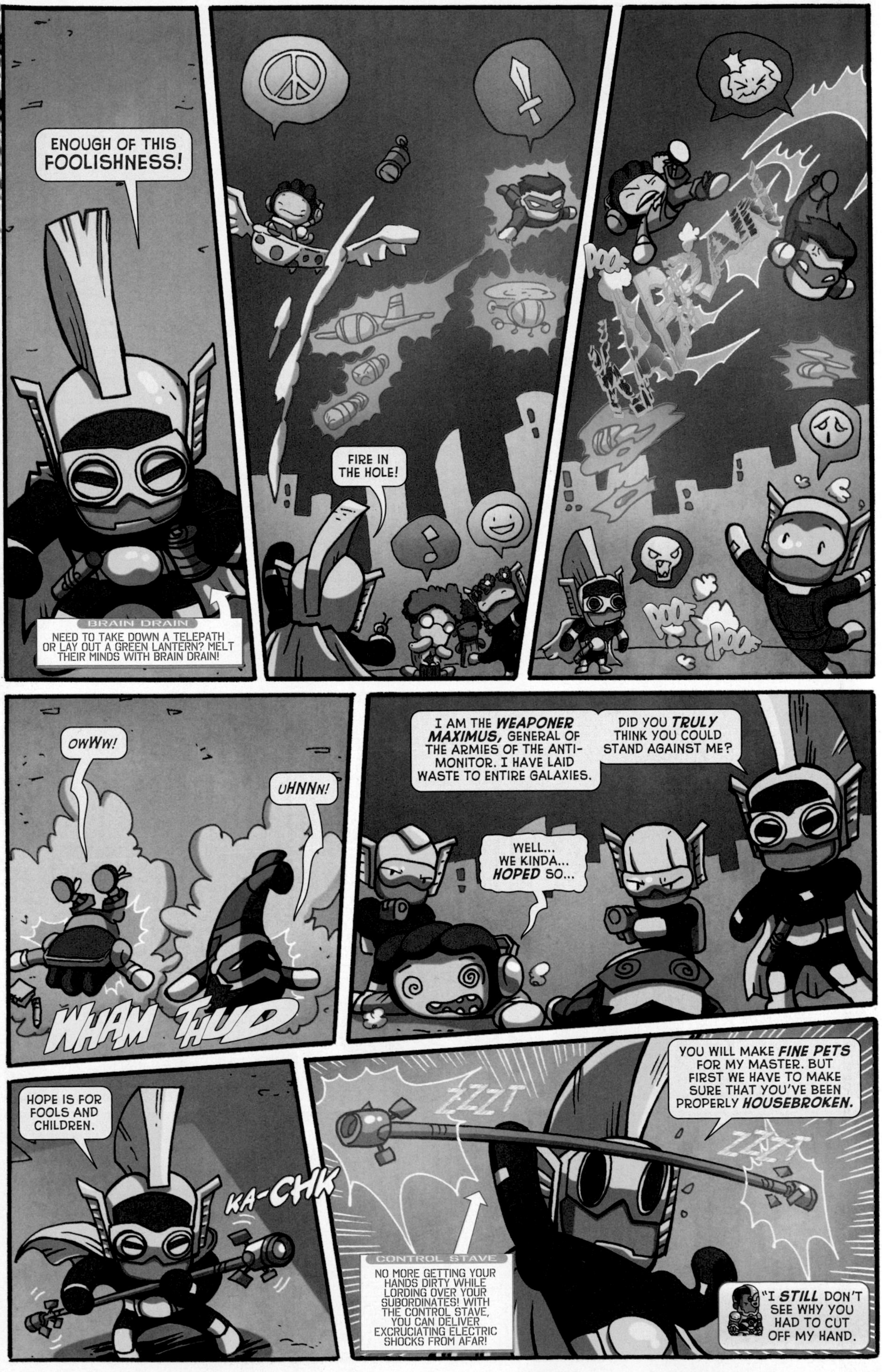
ENOUGH OF THIS FOOLISHNESS!
BRAIN DRAIN
NEED TO TAKE DOWN A TELEPATH OR LAY OUT A GREEN LANTERN? MELT THEIR MINDS WITH BRAIN DRAIN!
FIRE IN THE HOLE!
POOF
POOF
POOF
OWWW!
UHNNN!
WHAM
THUD
I AM THE WEAPONER MAXIMUS, GENERAL OF THE ARMIES OF THE ANTI-MONITOR. I HAVE LAID WASTE TO ENTIRE GALAXIES.
DID YOU TRULY THINK YOU COULD STAND AGAINST ME?
WELL... WE KINDA... HOPED SO...
HOPE IS FOR FOOLS AND CHILDREN.
KA-CHK
ZZZT
YOU WILL MAKE FINE PETS FOR MY MASTER. BUT FIRST WE HAVE TO MAKE SURE THAT YOU'VE BEEN PROPERLY HOUSEBROKEN.
ZZZT
CONTROL STAVE
NO MORE GETTING YOUR HANDS DIRTY WHILE LORDING OVER YOUR SUBORDINATES! WITH THE CONTROL STAVE, YOU CAN DELIVER EXCRUCIATING ELECTRIC SHOCKS FROM AFAR!
"I STILL DON'T SEE WHY YOU HAD TO CUT OFF MY HAND.

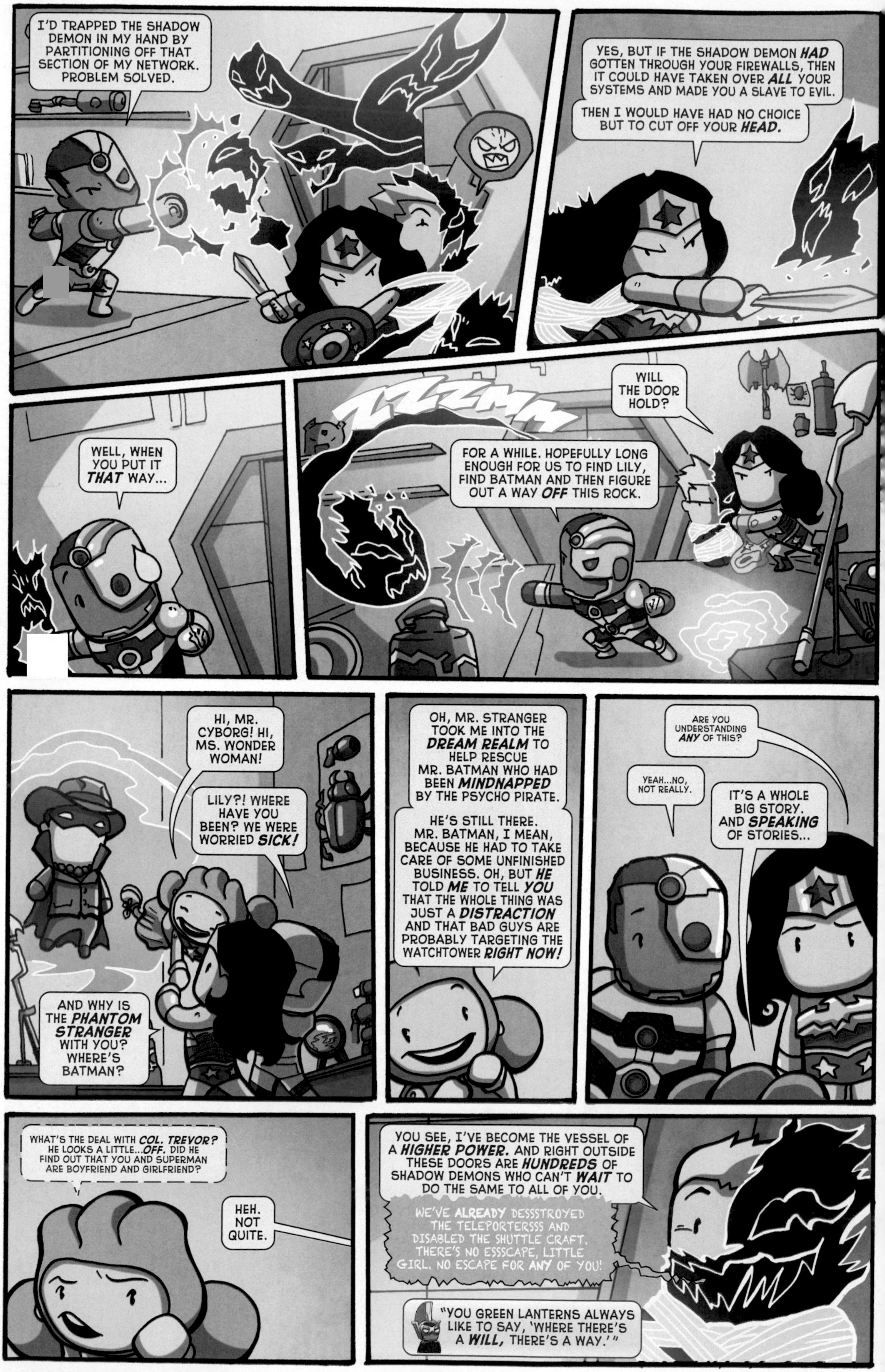

I'D TRAPPED THE SHADOW DEMON IN MY HAND BY PARTITIONING OFF THAT SECTION OF MY NETWORK. PROBLEM SOLVED.
YES, BUT IF THE SHADOW DEMON HAD GOTTEN THROUGH YOUR FIREWALLS, THEN IT COULD HAVE TAKEN OVER ALL YOUR SYSTEMS AND MADE YOU A SLAVE TO EVIL.
THEN I WOULD HAVE HAD NO CHOICE BUT TO CUT OFF YOUR HEAD.
WELL, WHEN YOU PUT IT THAT WAY...
ZZZMM
WILL THE DOOR HOLD?
FOR A WHILE. HOPEFULLY LONG ENOUGH FOR US TO FIND LILY, FIND BATMAN AND THEN FIGURE OUT A WAY OFF THIS ROCK.
HI, MR. CYBORG! HI, MS. WONDER WOMAN!
LILY?! WHERE HAVE YOU BEEN? WE WERE WORRIED SICK!
AND WHY IS THE PHANTOM STRANGER WITH YOU? WHERE'S BATMAN?
OH, MR. STRANGER TOOK ME INTO THE DREAM REALM TO HELP RESCUE MR. BATMAN WHO HAD BEEN MINDNAPPED BY THE PSYCHO PIRATE.
HE'S STILL THERE. MR. BATMAN, I MEAN, BECAUSE HE HAD TO TAKE CARE OF SOME UNFINISHED BUSINESS. OH, BUT HE TOLD ME TO TELL YOU THAT THE WHOLE THING WAS JUST A DISTRACTION AND THAT BAD GUYS ARE PROBABLY TARGETING THE WATCHTOWER RIGHT NOW!
ARE YOU UNDERSTANDING ANY OF THIS?
YEAH...NO, NOT REALLY.
IT'S A WHOLE BIG STORY. AND SPEAKING OF STORIES...
WHAT'S THE DEAL WITH COL. TREVOR? HE LOOKS A LITTLE...OFF. DID HE FIND OUT THAT YOU AND SUPERMAN ARE BOYFRIEND AND GIRLFRIEND?
HEH. NOT QUITE.
YOU SEE, I'VE BECOME THE VESSEL OF A HIGHER POWER. AND RIGHT OUTSIDE THESE DOORS ARE HUNDREDS OF SHADOW DEMONS WHO CAN'T WAIT TO DO THE SAME TO ALL OF YOU.
WE'VE ALREADY DESSSTROYED THE TELEPORTERSSS AND DISABLED THE SHUTTLE CRAFT. THERE'S NO ESSSCAPE, LITTLE GIRL. NO ESCAPE FOR ANY OF YOU!
"YOU GREEN LANTERNS ALWAYS LIKE TO SAY, 'WHERE THERE'S A WILL, THERE'S A WAY.'"

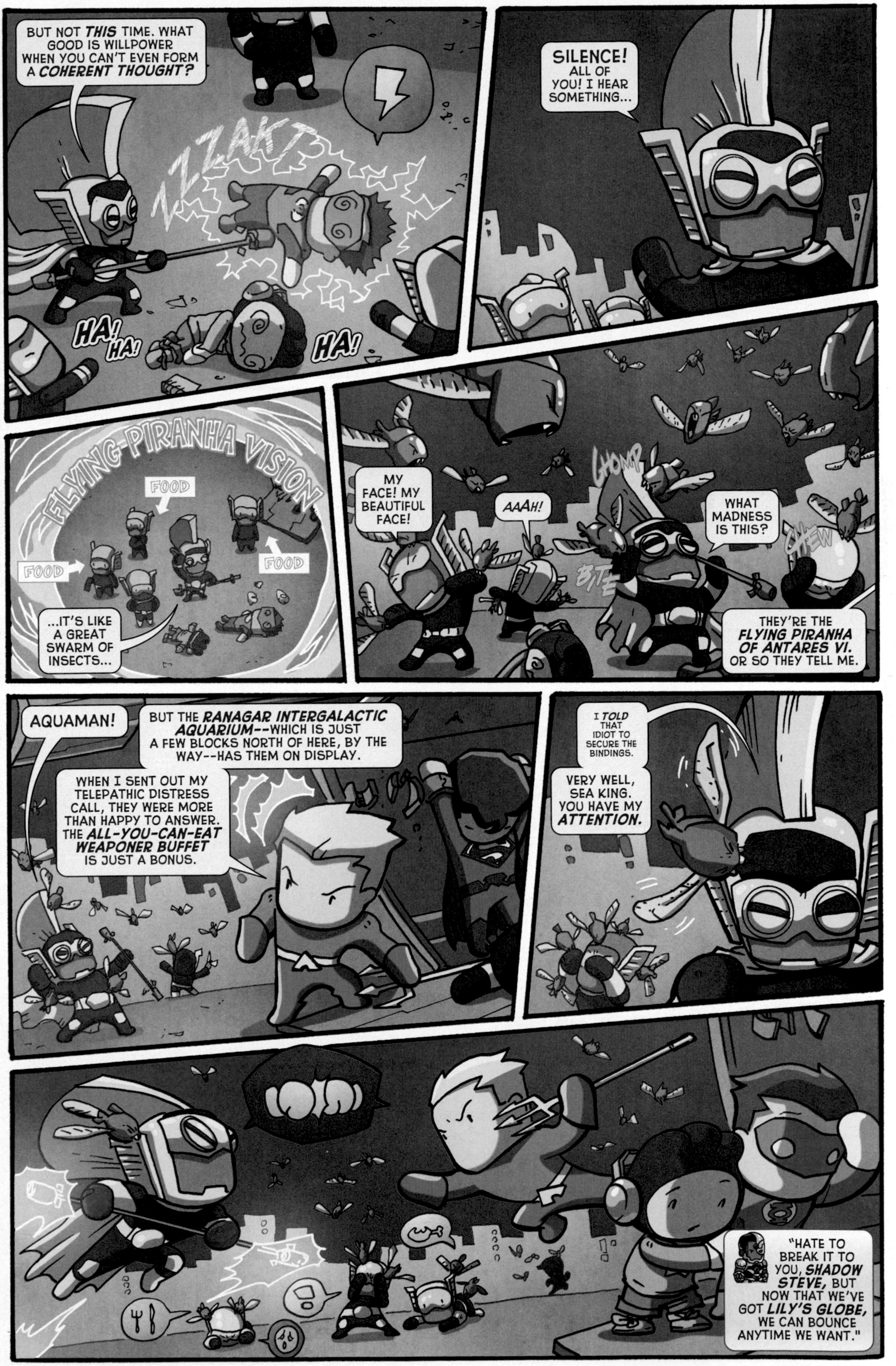
BUT NOT THIS TIME. WHAT GOOD IS WILLPOWER WHEN YOU CAN'T EVEN FORM A COHERENT THOUGHT?
ZZZAKT
HA! HA! HA!
SILENCE! ALL OF YOU! I HEAR SOMETHING...
FLYING-PIRANHA VISION
FOOD
FOOD
FOOD
...IT'S LIKE A GREAT SWARM OF INSECTS...
MY FACE! MY BEAUTIFUL FACE!
AAAH!
CHOMP
WHAT MADNESS IS THIS?
CHEW
BITE
THEY'RE THE FLYING PIRANHA OF ANTARES VI. OR SO THEY TELL ME.
AQUAMAN!
BUT THE RANAGAR INTERGALACTIC AQUARIUM--WHICH IS JUST A FEW BLOCKS NORTH OF HERE, BY THE WAY--HAS THEM ON DISPLAY.
WHEN I SENT OUT MY TELEPATHIC DISTRESS CALL, THEY WERE MORE THAN HAPPY TO ANSWER. THE ALL-YOU-CAN-EAT WEAPONER BUFFET IS JUST A BONUS.
I TOLD THAT IDIOT TO SECURE THE BINDINGS.
VERY WELL, SEA KING. YOU HAVE MY ATTENTION.
"HATE TO BREAK IT TO YOU, SHADOW STEVE, BUT NOW THAT WE'VE GOT LILY'S GLOBE, WE CAN BOUNCE ANYTIME WE WANT."

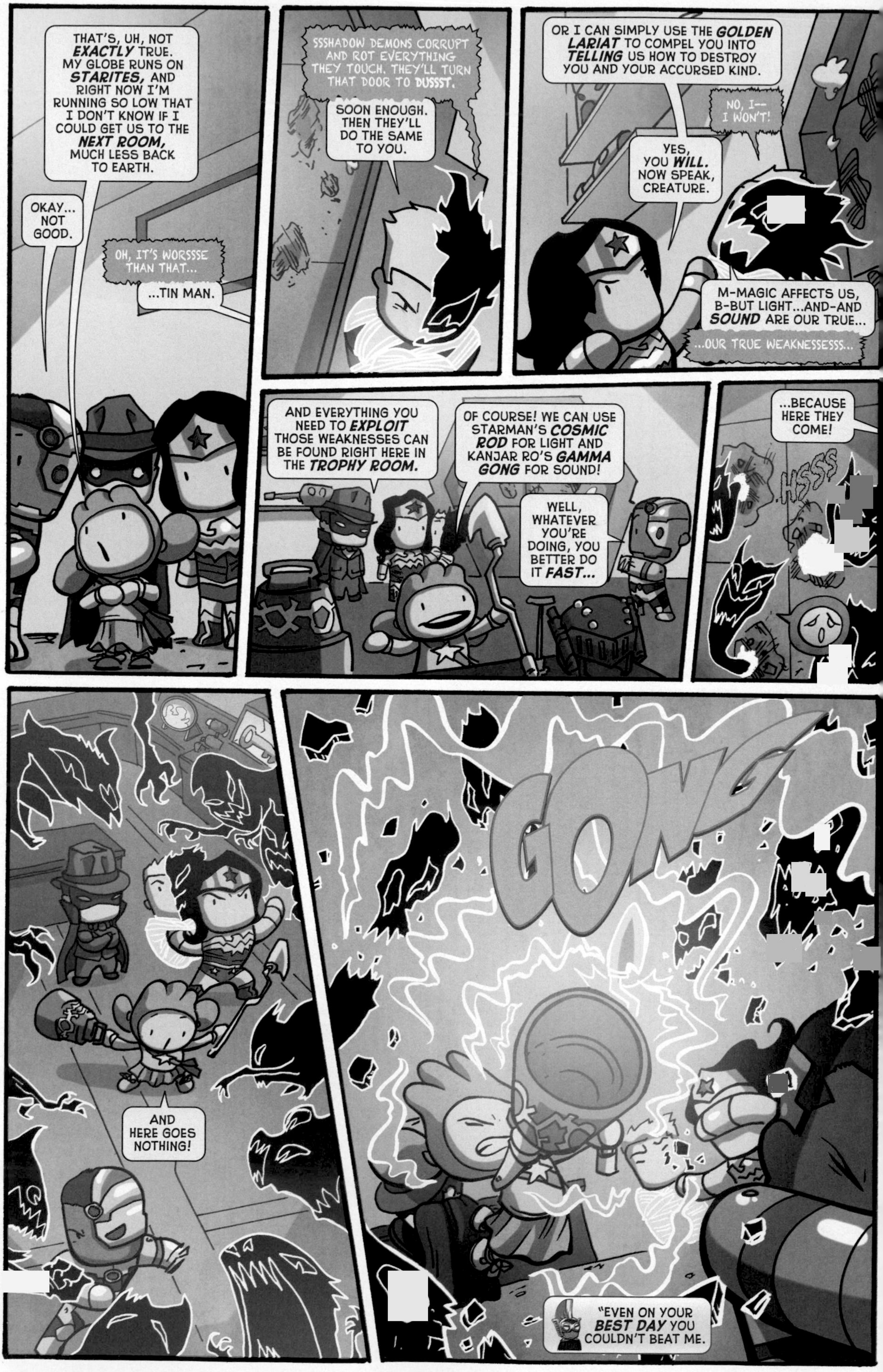
THAT'S, UH, NOT *EXACTLY* TRUE. MY GLOBE RUNS ON *STARITES,* AND RIGHT NOW I'M RUNNING SO LOW THAT I DON'T KNOW IF I COULD GET US TO THE *NEXT ROOM,* MUCH LESS BACK TO EARTH.
OKAY... NOT GOOD.
OH, IT'S WORSSSE THAN THAT...
...TIN MAN.
SSSHADOW DEMONS CORRUPT AND ROT EVERYTHING THEY TOUCH. THEY'LL TURN THAT DOOR TO DUSSST.
SOON ENOUGH. THEN THEY'LL DO THE SAME TO YOU.
OR I CAN SIMPLY USE THE *GOLDEN LARIAT* TO COMPEL YOU INTO *TELLING* US HOW TO DESTROY YOU AND YOUR ACCURSED KIND.
NO, I-- I WON'T!
YES, YOU *WILL.* NOW SPEAK, CREATURE.
M-MAGIC AFFECTS US, B-BUT LIGHT...AND-AND *SOUND* ARE OUR TRUE...
...OUR TRUE WEAKNESSESSS...
AND EVERYTHING YOU NEED TO *EXPLOIT* THOSE WEAKNESSES CAN BE FOUND RIGHT HERE IN THE *TROPHY ROOM.*
OF COURSE! WE CAN USE STARMAN'S *COSMIC ROD* FOR LIGHT AND KANJAR RO'S *GAMMA GONG* FOR SOUND!
WELL, WHATEVER YOU'RE DOING, YOU BETTER DO IT *FAST...*
...BECAUSE HERE THEY COME!
HSSS
AND HERE GOES NOTHING!
GONG
"EVEN ON YOUR *BEST DAY* YOU COULDN'T BEAT ME.

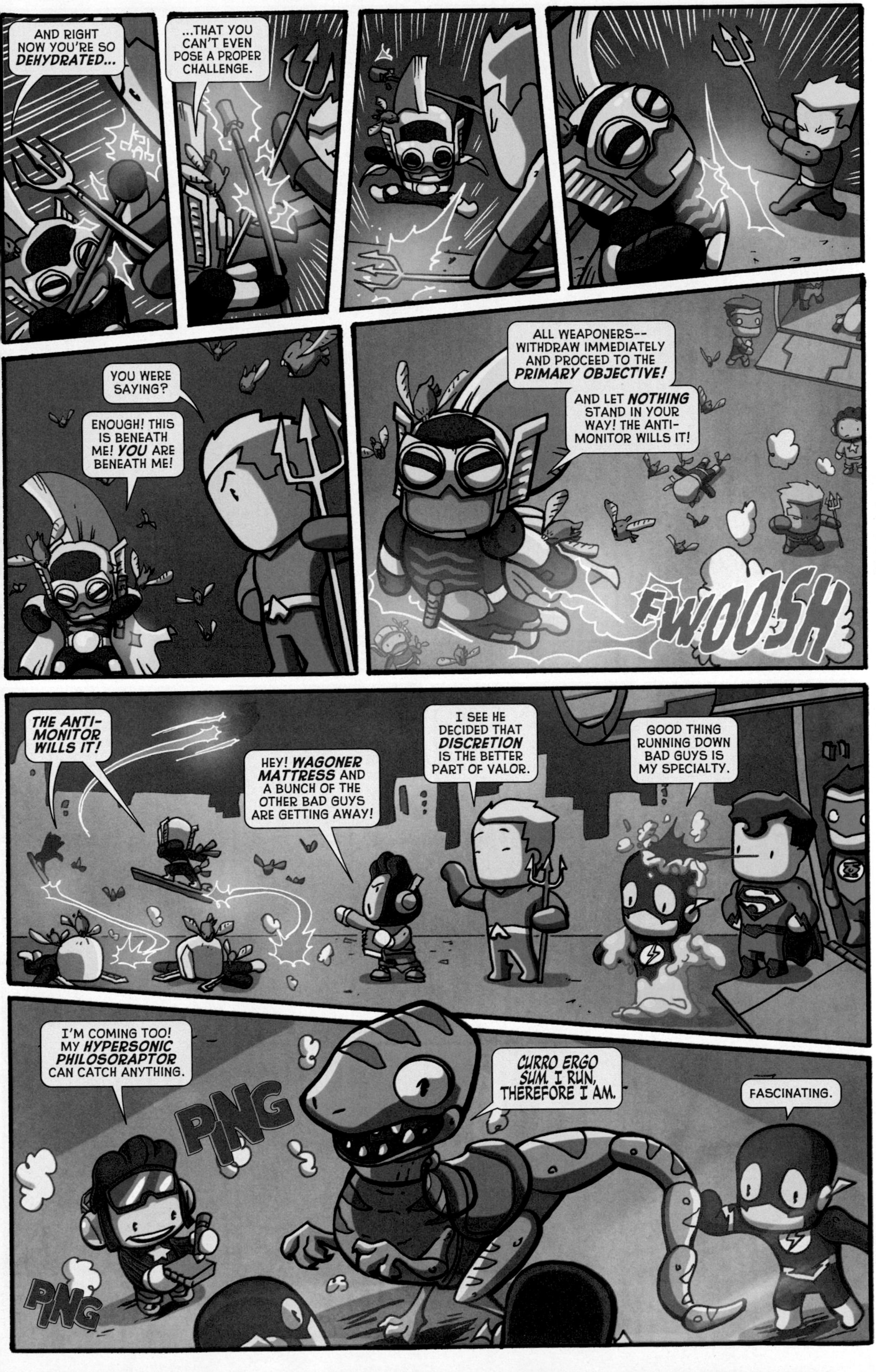
AND RIGHT NOW YOU'RE SO DEHYDRATED...
...THAT YOU CAN'T EVEN POSE A PROPER CHALLENGE.
YOU WERE SAYING?
ENOUGH! THIS IS BENEATH ME! YOU ARE BENEATH ME!
ALL WEAPONERS-- WITHDRAW IMMEDIATELY AND PROCEED TO THE PRIMARY OBJECTIVE!
AND LET NOTHING STAND IN YOUR WAY! THE ANTI-MONITOR WILLS IT!
FWOOSH
THE ANTI-MONITOR WILLS IT!
HEY! WAGONER MATTRESS AND A BUNCH OF THE OTHER BAD GUYS ARE GETTING AWAY!
I SEE HE DECIDED THAT DISCRETION IS THE BETTER PART OF VALOR.
GOOD THING RUNNING DOWN BAD GUYS IS MY SPECIALTY.
I'M COMING TOO! MY HYPERSONIC PHILOSORAPTOR CAN CATCH ANYTHING.
PING
CURRO ERGO SUM. I RUN, THEREFORE I AM.
FASCINATING.
PING

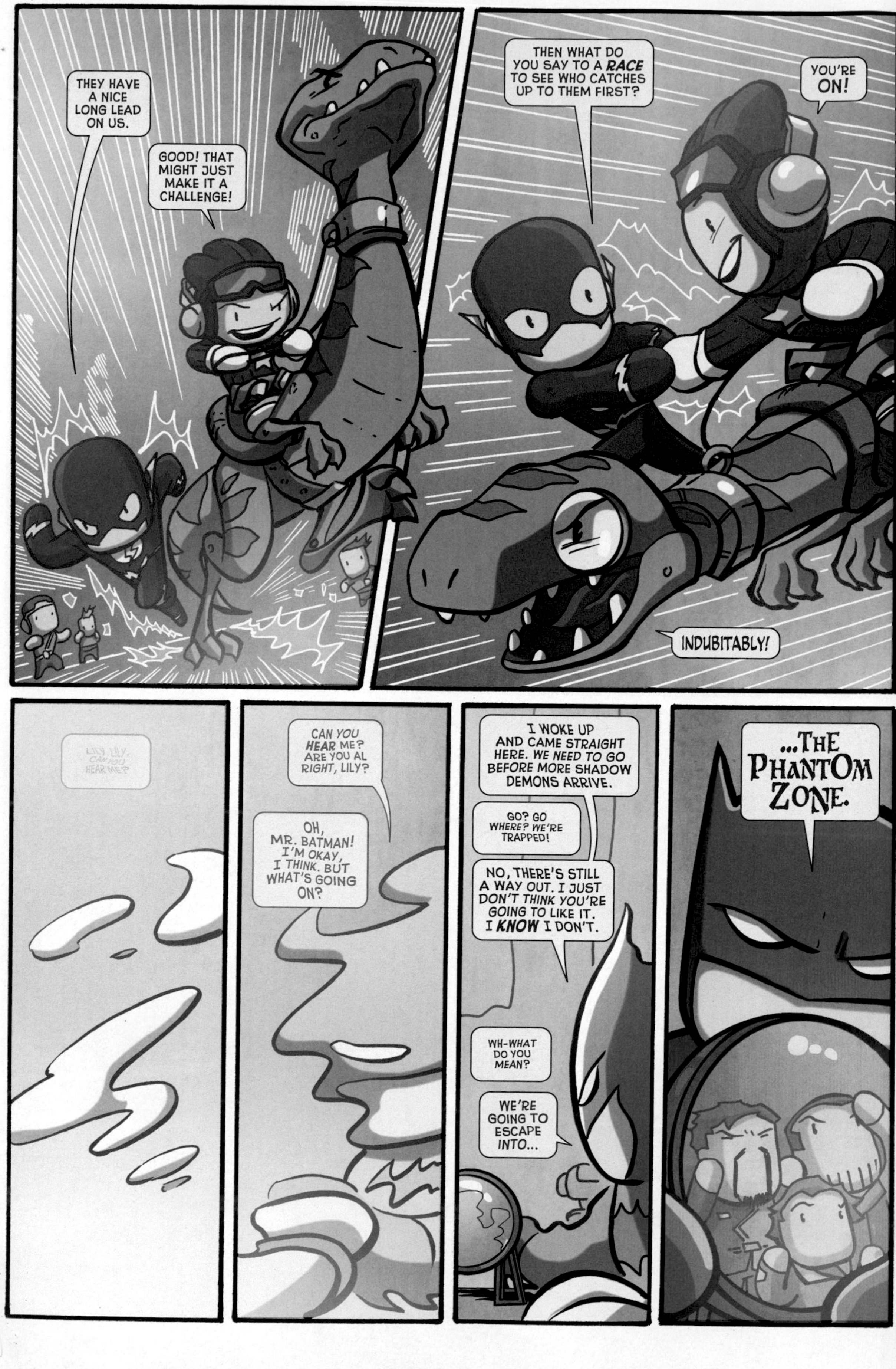
THEY HAVE A NICE LONG LEAD ON US.
GOOD! THAT MIGHT JUST MAKE IT A CHALLENGE!
THEN WHAT DO YOU SAY TO A RACE TO SEE WHO CATCHES UP TO THEM FIRST?
YOU'RE ON!
INDUBITABLY!
LILY, LILY, CAN YOU HEAR ME?
CAN YOU HEAR ME? ARE YOU AL RIGHT, LILY?
OH, MR. BATMAN! I'M OKAY, I THINK. BUT WHAT'S GOING ON?
I WOKE UP AND CAME STRAIGHT HERE. WE NEED TO GO BEFORE MORE SHADOW DEMONS ARRIVE.
GO? GO WHERE? WE'RE TRAPPED!
NO, THERE'S STILL A WAY OUT. I JUST DON'T THINK YOU'RE GOING TO LIKE IT. I KNOW I DON'T.
WH-WHAT DO YOU MEAN?
WE'RE GOING TO ESCAPE INTO...
...THE PHANTOM ZONE.

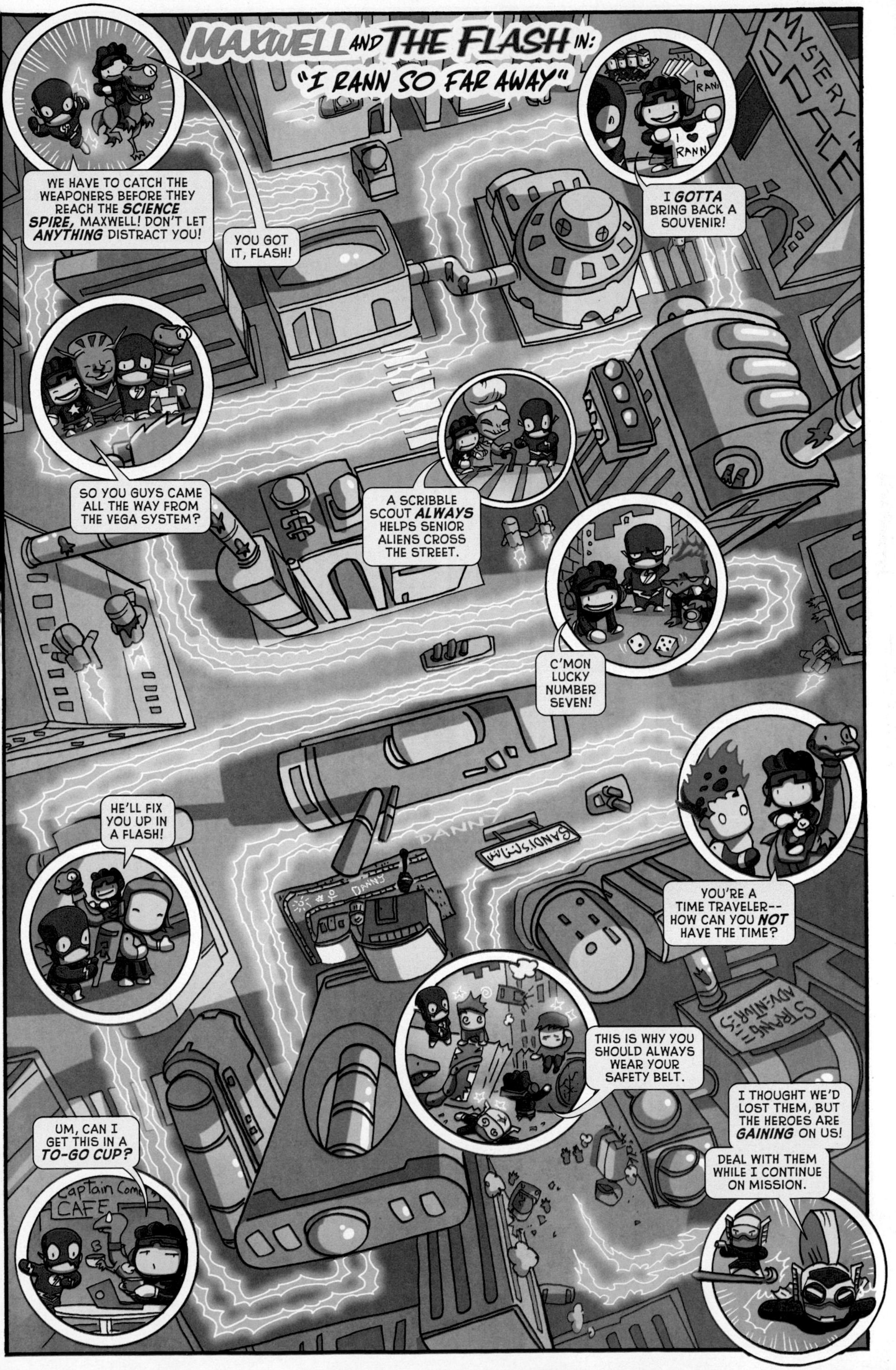

MAXWELL AND THE FLASH IN:
"I RANN SO FAR AWAY"
WE HAVE TO CATCH THE WEAPONERS BEFORE THEY REACH THE SCIENCE SPIRE, MAXWELL! DON'T LET ANYTHING DISTRACT YOU!
YOU GOT IT, FLASH!
I ♥ RANN
I GOTTA BRING BACK A SOUVENIR!
MYSTERY IN SPACE
SO YOU GUYS CAME ALL THE WAY FROM THE VEGA SYSTEM?
A SCRIBBLE SCOUT ALWAYS HELPS SENIOR ALIENS CROSS THE STREET.
C'MON LUCKY NUMBER SEVEN!
HE'LL FIX YOU UP IN A FLASH!
DANNY
YOU'RE A TIME TRAVELER-- HOW CAN YOU NOT HAVE THE TIME?
STRANGE ADVENTURES
THIS IS WHY YOU SHOULD ALWAYS WEAR YOUR SAFETY BELT.
UM, CAN I GET THIS IN A TO-GO CUP?
CAFE
I THOUGHT WE'D LOST THEM, BUT THE HEROES ARE GAINING ON US!
DEAL WITH THEM WHILE I CONTINUE ON MISSION.

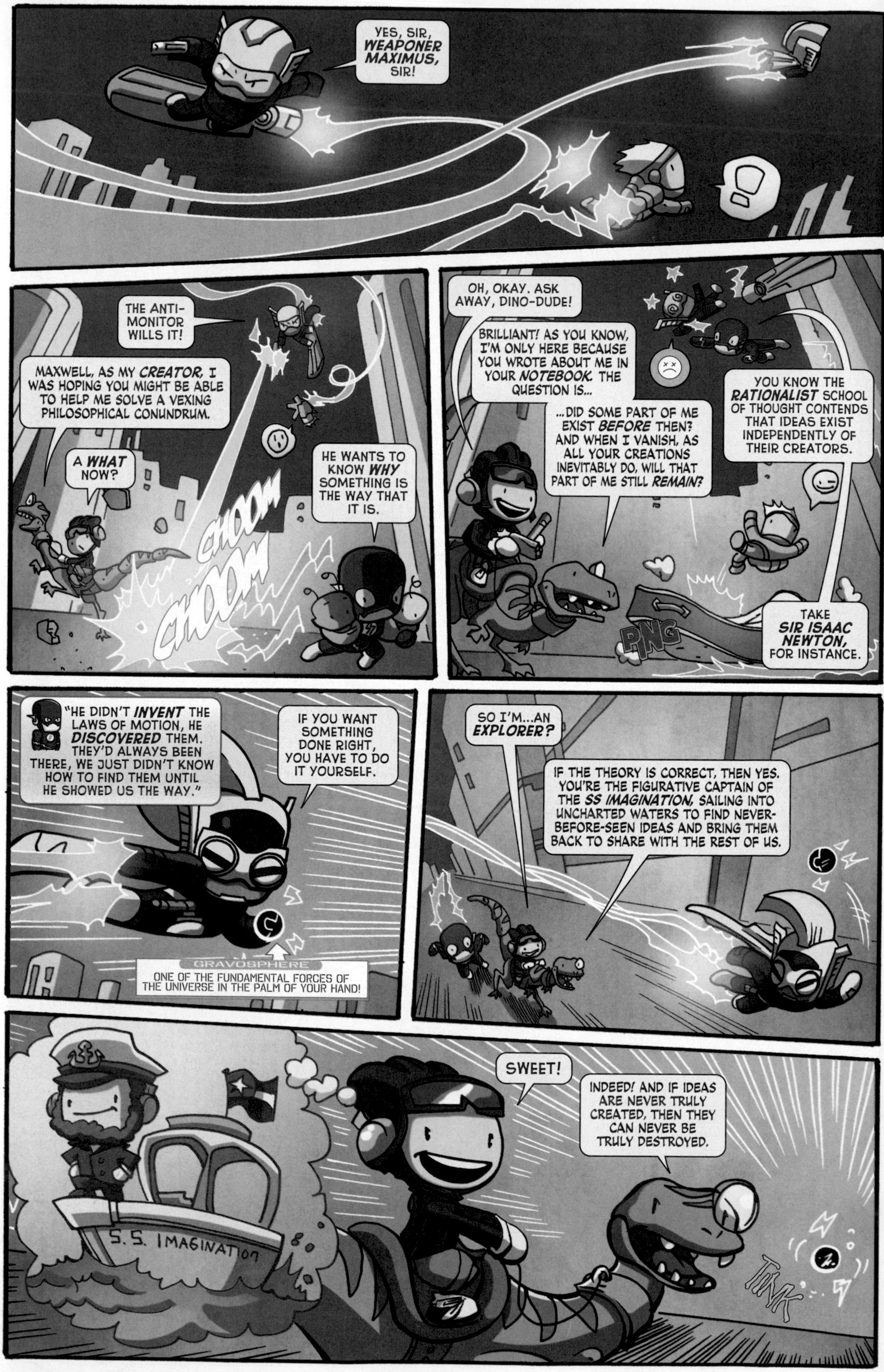

YES, SIR, WEAPONER MAXIMUS, SIR!
THE ANTI-MONITOR WILLS IT!
MAXWELL, AS MY CREATOR, I WAS HOPING YOU MIGHT BE ABLE TO HELP ME SOLVE A VEXING PHILOSOPHICAL CONUNDRUM.
A WHAT NOW?
HE WANTS TO KNOW WHY SOMETHING IS THE WAY THAT IT IS.
CHOOM
CHOOM
OH, OKAY. ASK AWAY, DINO-DUDE!
BRILLIANT! AS YOU KNOW, I'M ONLY HERE BECAUSE YOU WROTE ABOUT ME IN YOUR NOTEBOOK. THE QUESTION IS...
...DID SOME PART OF ME EXIST BEFORE THEN? AND WHEN I VANISH, AS ALL YOUR CREATIONS INEVITABLY DO, WILL THAT PART OF ME STILL REMAIN?
YOU KNOW THE RATIONALIST SCHOOL OF THOUGHT CONTENDS THAT IDEAS EXIST INDEPENDENTLY OF THEIR CREATORS.
PING
TAKE SIR ISAAC NEWTON, FOR INSTANCE.
"HE DIDN'T INVENT THE LAWS OF MOTION, HE DISCOVERED THEM. THEY'D ALWAYS BEEN THERE, WE JUST DIDN'T KNOW HOW TO FIND THEM UNTIL HE SHOWED US THE WAY."
IF YOU WANT SOMETHING DONE RIGHT, YOU HAVE TO DO IT YOURSELF.
GRAVOSPHERE
ONE OF THE FUNDAMENTAL FORCES OF THE UNIVERSE IN THE PALM OF YOUR HAND!
SO I'M...AN EXPLORER?
IF THE THEORY IS CORRECT, THEN YES. YOU'RE THE FIGURATIVE CAPTAIN OF THE SS IMAGINATION, SAILING INTO UNCHARTED WATERS TO FIND NEVER-BEFORE-SEEN IDEAS AND BRING THEM BACK TO SHARE WITH THE REST OF US.
S.S. IMAGINATION
SWEET!
INDEED! AND IF IDEAS ARE NEVER TRULY CREATED, THEN THEY CAN NEVER BE TRULY DESTROYED.
TINK

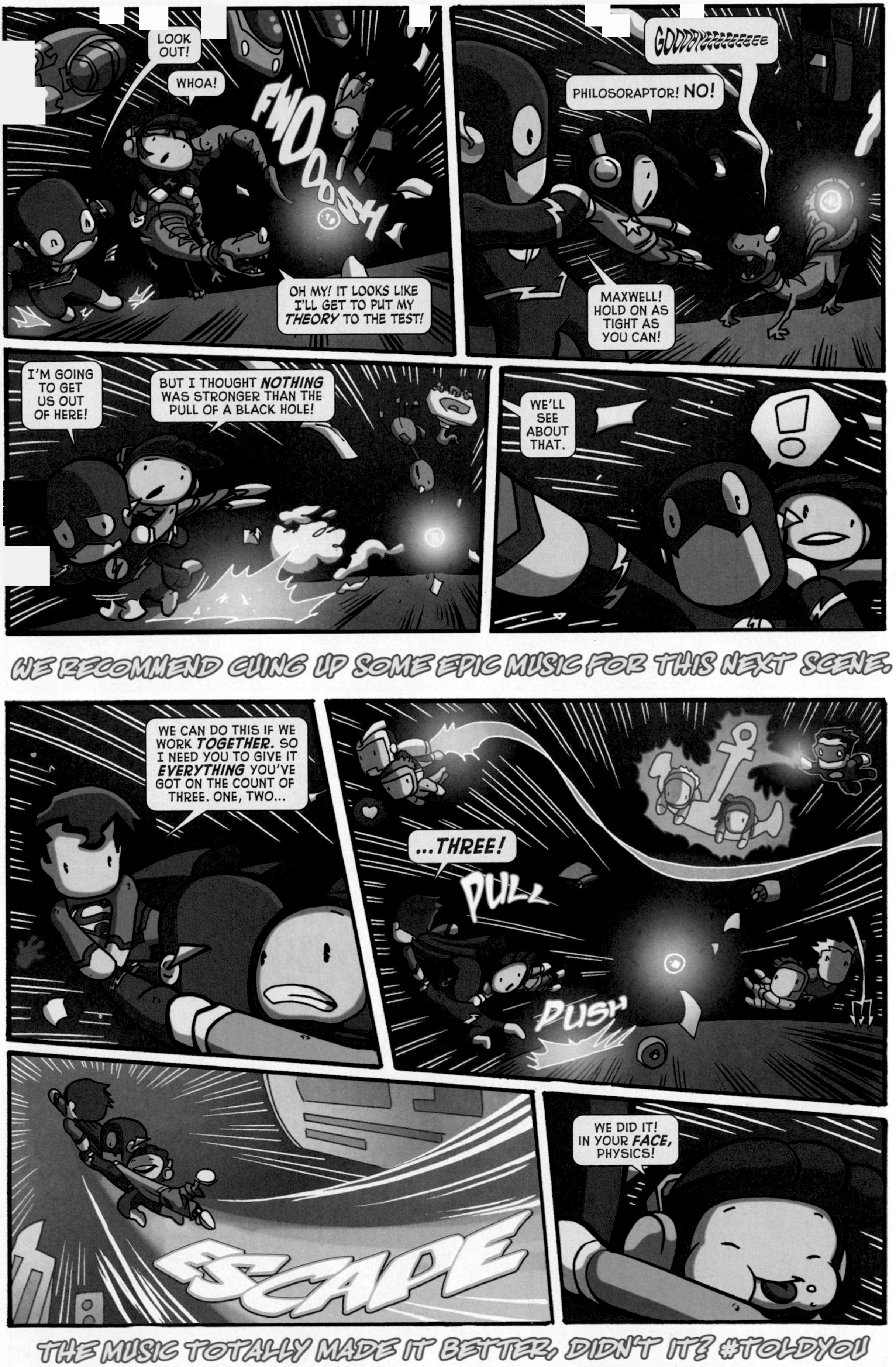
LOOK OUT!
WHOA!
FWOOOSH
OH MY! IT LOOKS LIKE I'LL GET TO PUT MY THEORY TO THE TEST!
GOODBYEEEEEEEEEE
PHILOSORAPTOR! NO!
MAXWELL! HOLD ON AS TIGHT AS YOU CAN!
I'M GOING TO GET US OUT OF HERE!
BUT I THOUGHT NOTHING WAS STRONGER THAN THE PULL OF A BLACK HOLE!
WE'LL SEE ABOUT THAT.
!
WE RECOMMEND CUING UP SOME EPIC MUSIC FOR THIS NEXT SCENE.
WE CAN DO THIS IF WE WORK TOGETHER. SO I NEED YOU TO GIVE IT EVERYTHING YOU'VE GOT ON THE COUNT OF THREE. ONE, TWO...
...THREE!
PULL
PUSH
ESCAPE
WE DID IT! IN YOUR FACE, PHYSICS!
THE MUSIC TOTALLY MADE IT BETTER, DIDN'T IT? #TOLDYOU

WHAT HAPPENED TO THE BLACK HOLE?

IT COLLAPSED IN ON ITSELF. IT'S OVER.

THEN IT LOOKS LIKE I CAUGHT UP TO YOU TWO JUST IN TIME. IS EVERYONE OKAY?

YEAH...BUT PHILOSORAPTOR... DIDN'T MAKE IT.

I'M SORRY, MAXWELL. BUT IF THE PHILOSORAPTOR'S THEORY IS TRUE, THEN HE'S NOT *GONE.* HE'S JUST NOT *HERE* ANYMORE.

I KNOW THIS ISN'T A GOOD TIME, BUT WE STILL HAVE A *VILLAIN* TO DEFEAT.

NO, ADAM, YOU'RE RIGHT, *LEAGUERS,* IT'S TIME TO FLY.

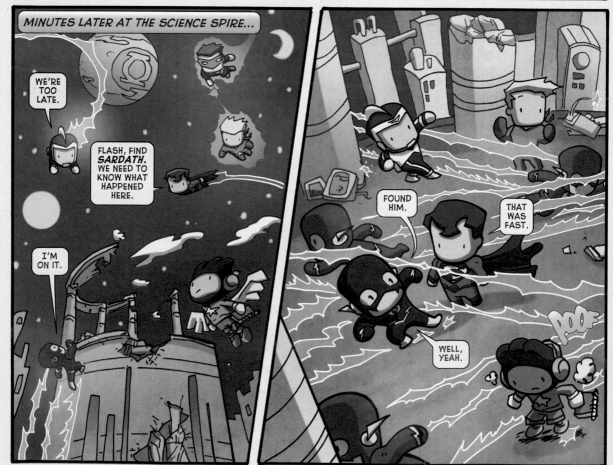

MINUTES LATER AT THE SCIENCE SPIRE...

WE'RE TOO LATE.

FLASH, FIND *SARDATH.* WE NEED TO KNOW WHAT HAPPENED HERE.

I'M ON IT.

FOUND HIM.

THAT WAS FAST.

WELL, YEAH.

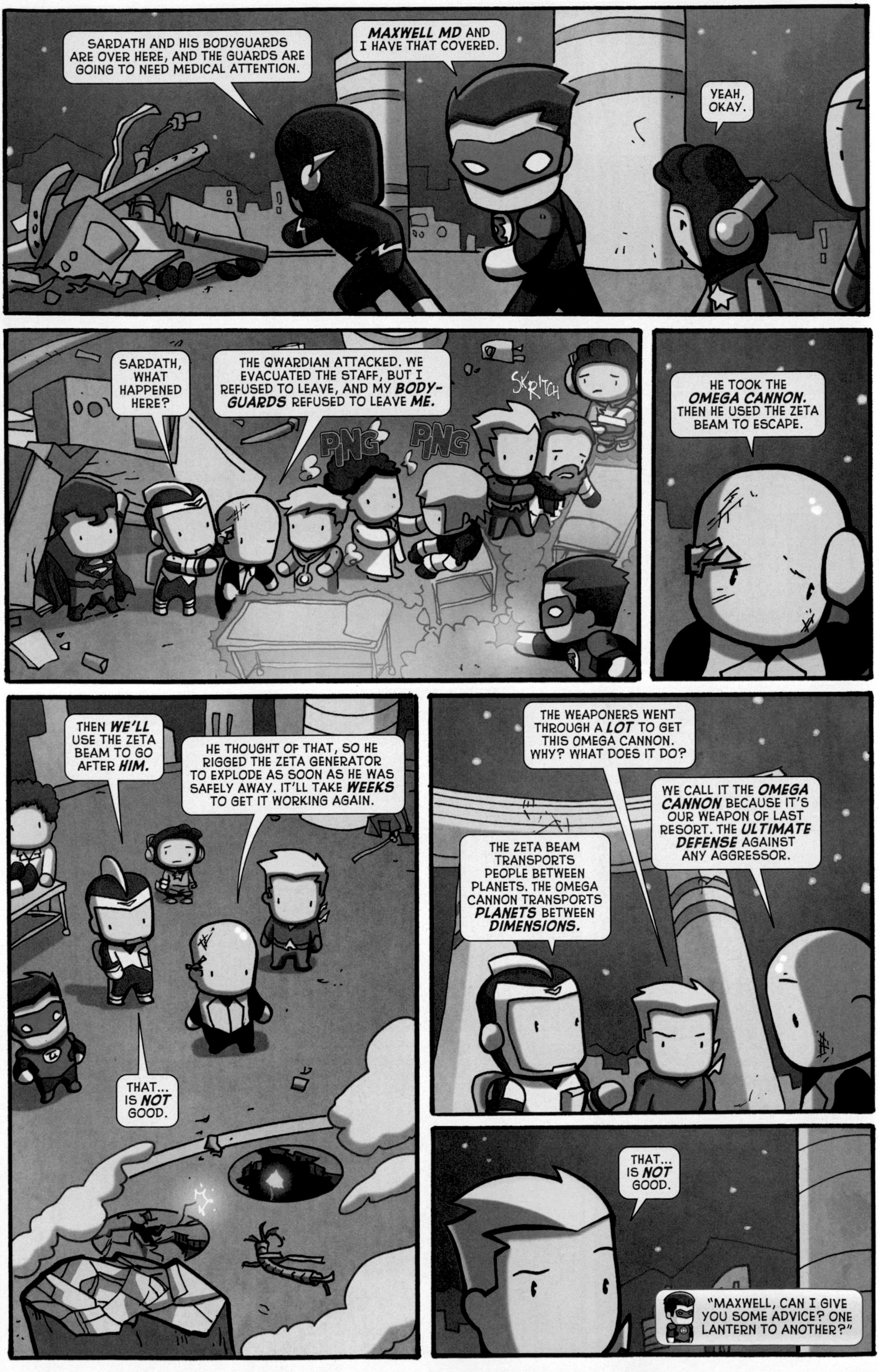
SARDATH AND HIS BODYGUARDS ARE OVER HERE, AND THE GUARDS ARE GOING TO NEED MEDICAL ATTENTION.
MAXWELL MD AND I HAVE THAT COVERED.
YEAH, OKAY.
SARDATH, WHAT HAPPENED HERE?
THE QWARDIAN ATTACKED. WE EVACUATED THE STAFF, BUT I REFUSED TO LEAVE, AND MY BODY-GUARDS REFUSED TO LEAVE ME.
PING
PING
SKRITCH
HE TOOK THE OMEGA CANNON. THEN HE USED THE ZETA BEAM TO ESCAPE.
THEN WE'LL USE THE ZETA BEAM TO GO AFTER HIM.
HE THOUGHT OF THAT, SO HE RIGGED THE ZETA GENERATOR TO EXPLODE AS SOON AS HE WAS SAFELY AWAY. IT'LL TAKE WEEKS TO GET IT WORKING AGAIN.
THAT... IS NOT GOOD.
THE WEAPONERS WENT THROUGH A LOT TO GET THIS OMEGA CANNON. WHY? WHAT DOES IT DO?
WE CALL IT THE OMEGA CANNON BECAUSE IT'S OUR WEAPON OF LAST RESORT. THE ULTIMATE DEFENSE AGAINST ANY AGGRESSOR.
THE ZETA BEAM TRANSPORTS PEOPLE BETWEEN PLANETS. THE OMEGA CANNON TRANSPORTS PLANETS BETWEEN DIMENSIONS.
THAT... IS NOT GOOD.
"MAXWELL, CAN I GIVE YOU SOME ADVICE? ONE LANTERN TO ANOTHER?"

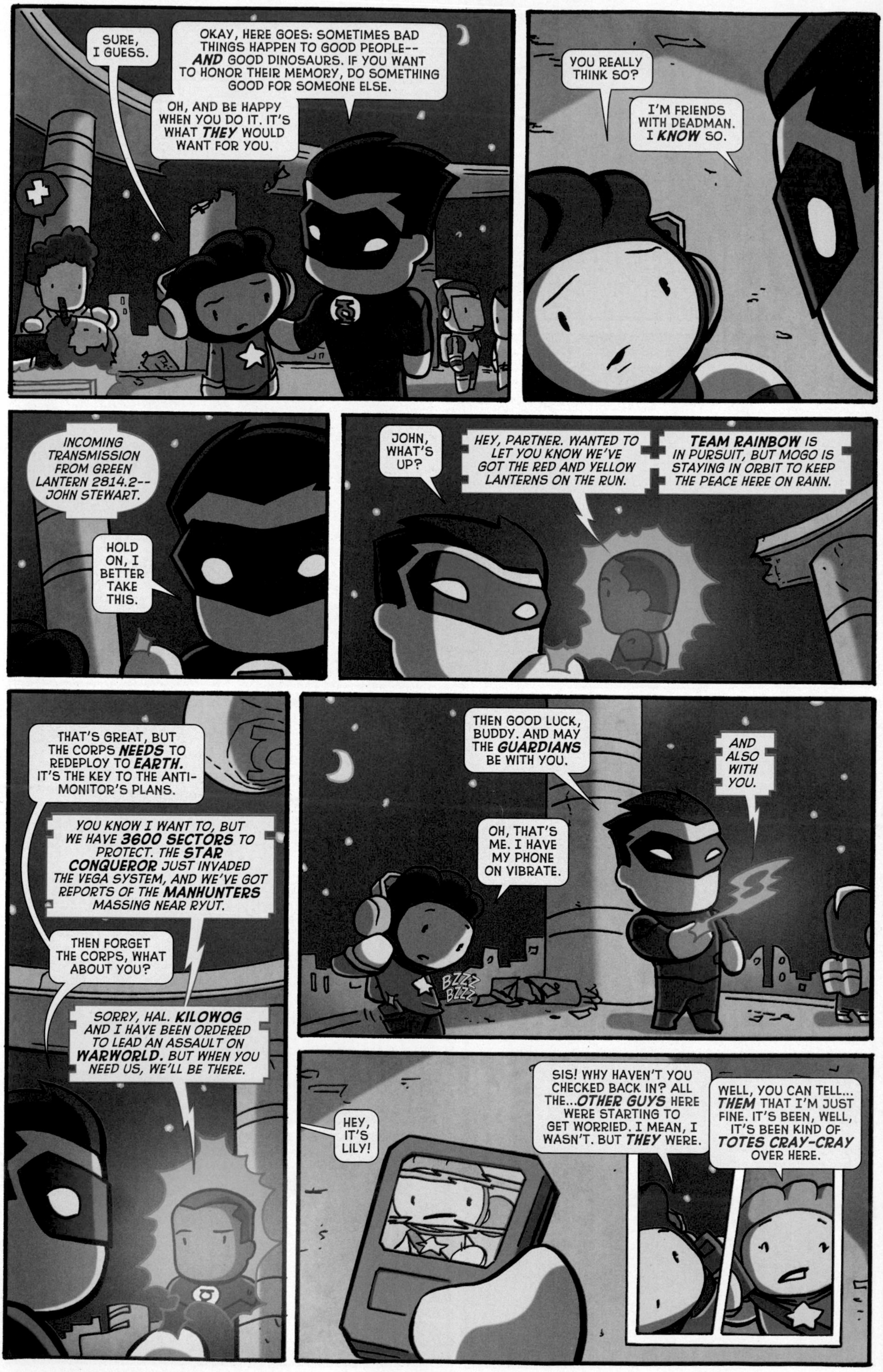
SURE, I GUESS.
OKAY, HERE GOES: SOMETIMES BAD THINGS HAPPEN TO GOOD PEOPLE-- AND GOOD DINOSAURS. IF YOU WANT TO HONOR THEIR MEMORY, DO SOMETHING GOOD FOR SOMEONE ELSE.
OH, AND BE HAPPY WHEN YOU DO IT. IT'S WHAT THEY WOULD WANT FOR YOU.
YOU REALLY THINK SO?
I'M FRIENDS WITH DEADMAN. I KNOW SO.
INCOMING TRANSMISSION FROM GREEN LANTERN 2814.2-- JOHN STEWART.
HOLD ON, I BETTER TAKE THIS.
JOHN, WHAT'S UP?
HEY, PARTNER. WANTED TO LET YOU KNOW WE'VE GOT THE RED AND YELLOW LANTERNS ON THE RUN.
TEAM RAINBOW IS IN PURSUIT, BUT MOGO IS STAYING IN ORBIT TO KEEP THE PEACE HERE ON RANN.
THAT'S GREAT, BUT THE CORPS NEEDS TO REDEPLOY TO EARTH. IT'S THE KEY TO THE ANTI-MONITOR'S PLANS.
YOU KNOW I WANT TO, BUT WE HAVE 3600 SECTORS TO PROTECT. THE STAR CONQUEROR JUST INVADED THE VEGA SYSTEM, AND WE'VE GOT REPORTS OF THE MANHUNTERS MASSING NEAR RYUT.
THEN FORGET THE CORPS, WHAT ABOUT YOU?
SORRY, HAL. KILOWOG AND I HAVE BEEN ORDERED TO LEAD AN ASSAULT ON WARWORLD. BUT WHEN YOU NEED US, WE'LL BE THERE.
THEN GOOD LUCK, BUDDY. AND MAY THE GUARDIANS BE WITH YOU.
AND ALSO WITH YOU.
OH, THAT'S ME. I HAVE MY PHONE ON VIBRATE.
BZZZ BZZZ
HEY, IT'S LILY!
SIS! WHY HAVEN'T YOU CHECKED BACK IN? ALL THE...OTHER GUYS HERE WERE STARTING TO GET WORRIED. I MEAN, I WASN'T. BUT THEY WERE.
WELL, YOU CAN TELL... THEM THAT I'M JUST FINE. IT'S BEEN, WELL, IT'S BEEN KIND OF TOTES CRAY-CRAY OVER HERE.

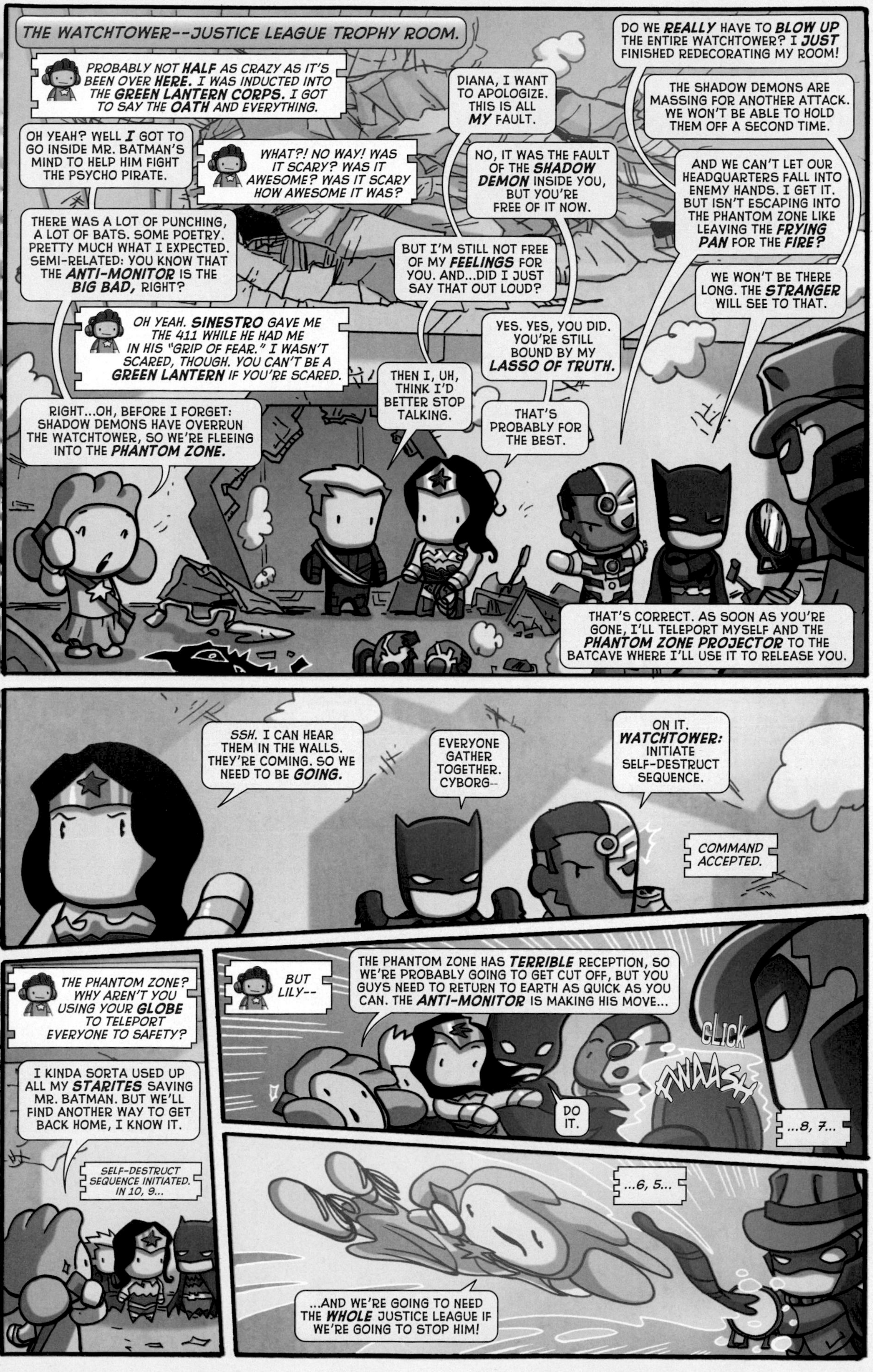

THE WATCHTOWER--JUSTICE LEAGUE TROPHY ROOM.
PROBABLY NOT HALF AS CRAZY AS IT'S BEEN OVER HERE. I WAS INDUCTED INTO THE GREEN LANTERN CORPS. I GOT TO SAY THE OATH AND EVERYTHING.
OH YEAH? WELL I GOT TO GO INSIDE MR. BATMAN'S MIND TO HELP HIM FIGHT THE PSYCHO PIRATE.
WHAT?! NO WAY! WAS IT SCARY? WAS IT AWESOME? WAS IT SCARY HOW AWESOME IT WAS?
THERE WAS A LOT OF PUNCHING, A LOT OF BATS. SOME POETRY. PRETTY MUCH WHAT I EXPECTED. SEMI-RELATED: YOU KNOW THAT THE ANTI-MONITOR IS THE BIG BAD, RIGHT?
OH YEAH. SINESTRO GAVE ME THE 411 WHILE HE HAD ME IN HIS "GRIP OF FEAR." I WASN'T SCARED, THOUGH. YOU CAN'T BE A GREEN LANTERN IF YOU'RE SCARED.
RIGHT...OH, BEFORE I FORGET: SHADOW DEMONS HAVE OVERRUN THE WATCHTOWER, SO WE'RE FLEEING INTO THE PHANTOM ZONE.
DIANA, I WANT TO APOLOGIZE. THIS IS ALL MY FAULT.
NO, IT WAS THE FAULT OF THE SHADOW DEMON INSIDE YOU, BUT YOU'RE FREE OF IT NOW.
BUT I'M STILL NOT FREE OF MY FEELINGS FOR YOU. AND...DID I JUST SAY THAT OUT LOUD?
YES. YES, YOU DID. YOU'RE STILL BOUND BY MY LASSO OF TRUTH.
THEN I, UH, THINK I'D BETTER STOP TALKING.
THAT'S PROBABLY FOR THE BEST.
DO WE REALLY HAVE TO BLOW UP THE ENTIRE WATCHTOWER? I JUST FINISHED REDECORATING MY ROOM!
THE SHADOW DEMONS ARE MASSING FOR ANOTHER ATTACK. WE WON'T BE ABLE TO HOLD THEM OFF A SECOND TIME.
AND WE CAN'T LET OUR HEADQUARTERS FALL INTO ENEMY HANDS. I GET IT. BUT ISN'T ESCAPING INTO THE PHANTOM ZONE LIKE LEAVING THE FRYING PAN FOR THE FIRE?
WE WON'T BE THERE LONG. THE STRANGER WILL SEE TO THAT.
THAT'S CORRECT. AS SOON AS YOU'RE GONE, I'LL TELEPORT MYSELF AND THE PHANTOM ZONE PROJECTOR TO THE BATCAVE WHERE I'LL USE IT TO RELEASE YOU.
SSH. I CAN HEAR THEM IN THE WALLS. THEY'RE COMING. SO WE NEED TO BE GOING.
EVERYONE GATHER TOGETHER. CYBORG--
ON IT. WATCHTOWER: INITIATE SELF-DESTRUCT SEQUENCE.
COMMAND ACCEPTED.
THE PHANTOM ZONE? WHY AREN'T YOU USING YOUR GLOBE TO TELEPORT EVERYONE TO SAFETY?
I KINDA SORTA USED UP ALL MY STARITES SAVING MR. BATMAN. BUT WE'LL FIND ANOTHER WAY TO GET BACK HOME, I KNOW IT.
SELF-DESTRUCT SEQUENCE INITIATED. IN 10, 9...
BUT LILY--
THE PHANTOM ZONE HAS TERRIBLE RECEPTION, SO WE'RE PROBABLY GOING TO GET CUT OFF, BUT YOU GUYS NEED TO RETURN TO EARTH AS QUICK AS YOU CAN. THE ANTI-MONITOR IS MAKING HIS MOVE...
DO IT.
CLICK
FWAASH
...8, 7...
...6, 5...
...AND WE'RE GOING TO NEED THE WHOLE JUSTICE LEAGUE IF WE'RE GOING TO STOP HIM!

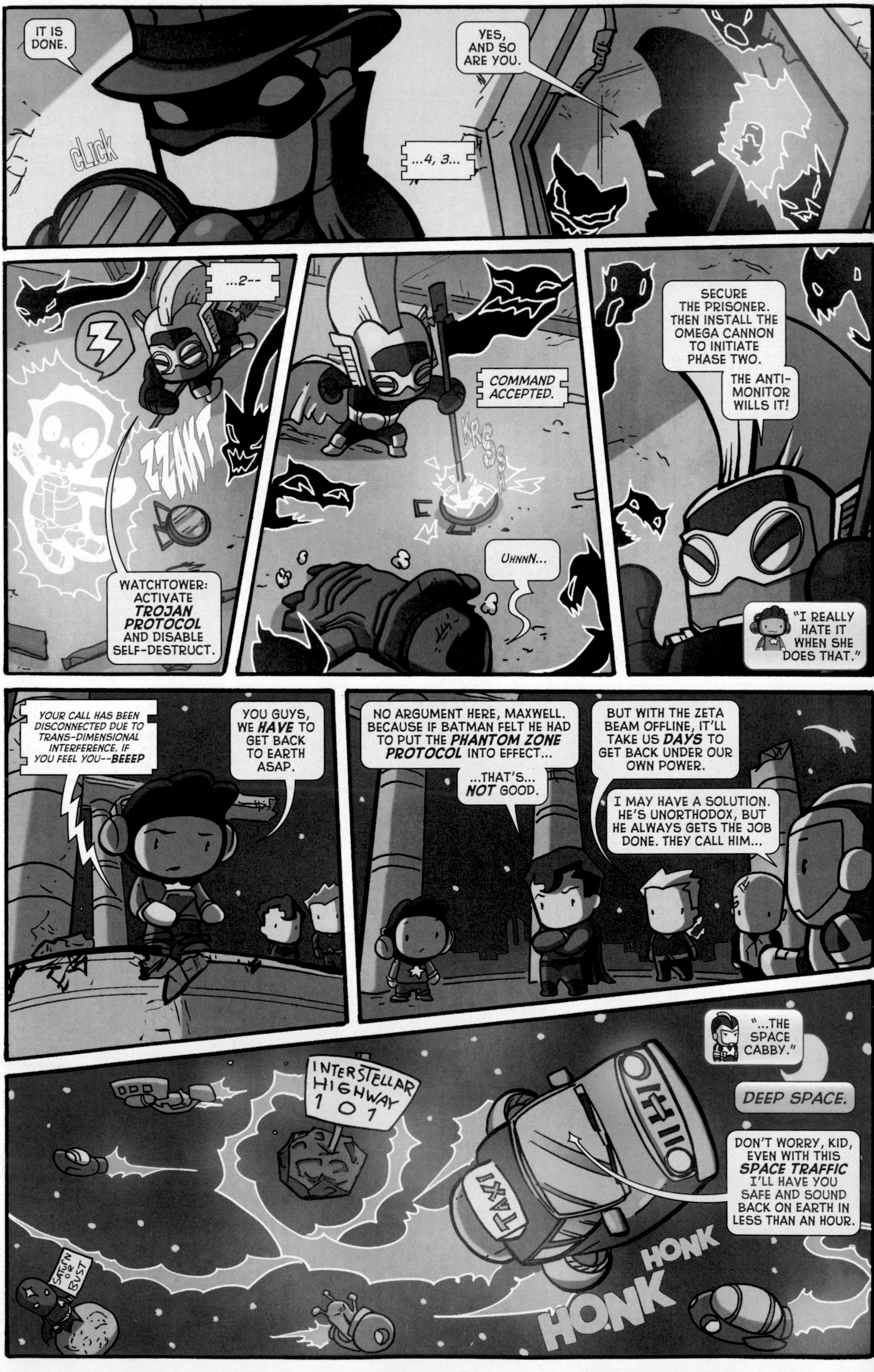
IT IS DONE.
YES, AND SO ARE YOU.
CLICK
...4, 3...
...2--
ZZAKT
WATCHTOWER: ACTIVATE TROJAN PROTOCOL AND DISABLE SELF-DESTRUCT.
COMMAND ACCEPTED.
KRSSSH
UHNNN...
SECURE THE PRISONER. THEN INSTALL THE OMEGA CANNON TO INITIATE PHASE TWO.
THE ANTI-MONITOR WILLS IT!
"I REALLY HATE IT WHEN SHE DOES THAT."
YOUR CALL HAS BEEN DISCONNECTED DUE TO TRANS-DIMENSIONAL INTERFERENCE. IF YOU FEEL YOU--BEEEP
YOU GUYS, WE HAVE TO GET BACK TO EARTH ASAP.
NO ARGUMENT HERE, MAXWELL. BECAUSE IF BATMAN FELT HE HAD TO PUT THE PHANTOM ZONE PROTOCOL INTO EFFECT...
...THAT'S... NOT GOOD.
BUT WITH THE ZETA BEAM OFFLINE, IT'LL TAKE US DAYS TO GET BACK UNDER OUR OWN POWER.
I MAY HAVE A SOLUTION. HE'S UNORTHODOX, BUT HE ALWAYS GETS THE JOB DONE. THEY CALL HIM...
"...THE SPACE CABBY."
DEEP SPACE.
INTERSTELLAR HIGHWAY 101
TAXI
DON'T WORRY, KID, EVEN WITH THIS SPACE TRAFFIC I'LL HAVE YOU SAFE AND SOUND BACK ON EARTH IN LESS THAN AN HOUR.
SATURN OR BUST
HONK
HONK

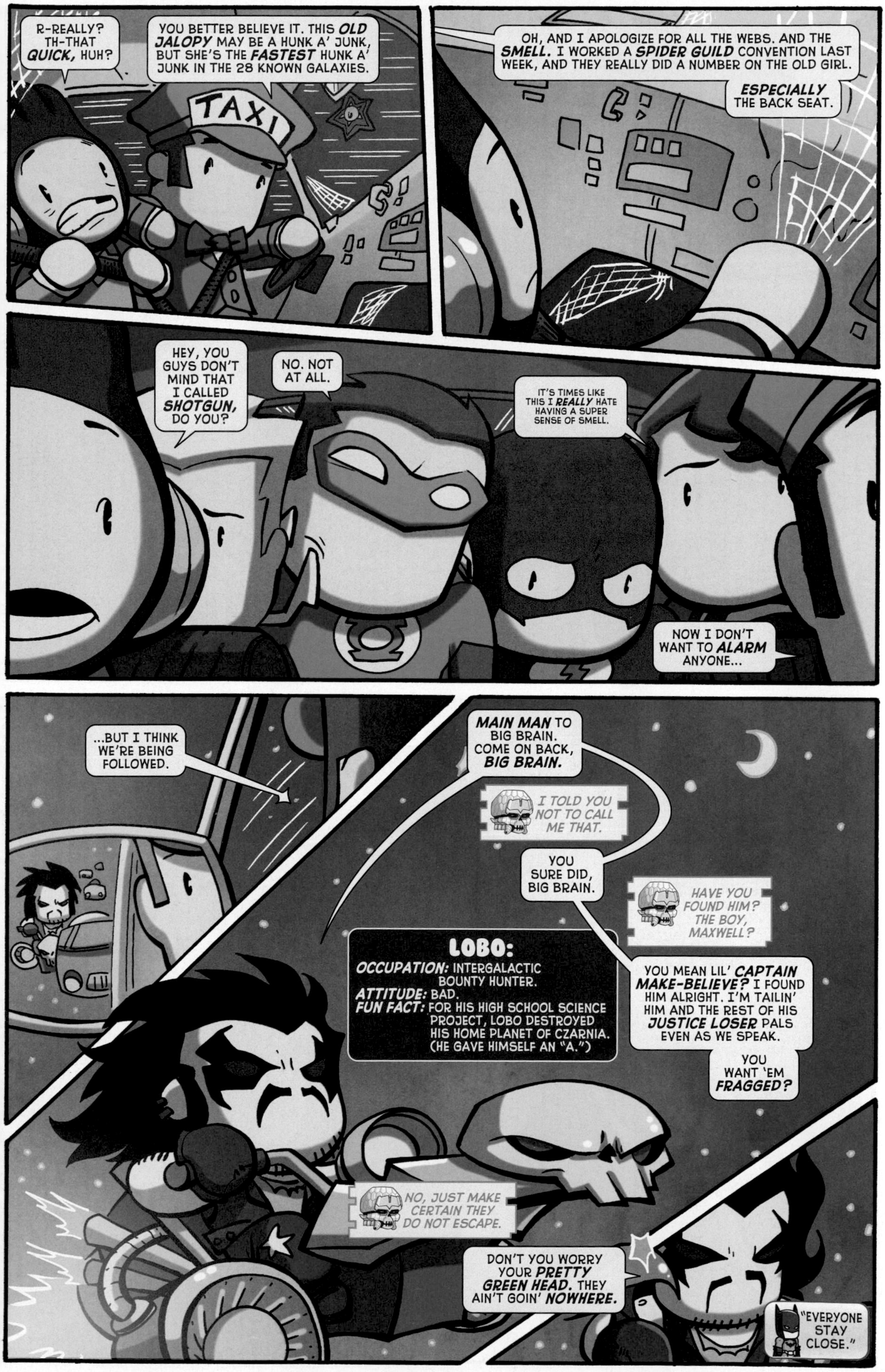
R-REALLY? TH-THAT QUICK, HUH?
YOU BETTER BELIEVE IT. THIS OLD JALOPY MAY BE A HUNK A' JUNK, BUT SHE'S THE FASTEST HUNK A' JUNK IN THE 28 KNOWN GALAXIES.
TAXI
OH, AND I APOLOGIZE FOR ALL THE WEBS. AND THE SMELL. I WORKED A SPIDER GUILD CONVENTION LAST WEEK, AND THEY REALLY DID A NUMBER ON THE OLD GIRL.
ESPECIALLY THE BACK SEAT.
HEY, YOU GUYS DON'T MIND THAT I CALLED SHOTGUN, DO YOU?
NO. NOT AT ALL.
IT'S TIMES LIKE THIS I REALLY HATE HAVING A SUPER SENSE OF SMELL.
NOW I DON'T WANT TO ALARM ANYONE...
...BUT I THINK WE'RE BEING FOLLOWED.
MAIN MAN TO BIG BRAIN. COME ON BACK, BIG BRAIN.
I TOLD YOU NOT TO CALL ME THAT.
YOU SURE DID, BIG BRAIN.
HAVE YOU FOUND HIM? THE BOY, MAXWELL?
LOBO:
OCCUPATION: INTERGALACTIC BOUNTY HUNTER.
ATTITUDE: BAD.
FUN FACT: FOR HIS HIGH SCHOOL SCIENCE PROJECT, LOBO DESTROYED HIS HOME PLANET OF CZARNIA. (HE GAVE HIMSELF AN "A.")
YOU MEAN LIL' CAPTAIN MAKE-BELIEVE? I FOUND HIM ALRIGHT. I'M TAILIN' HIM AND THE REST OF HIS JUSTICE LOSER PALS EVEN AS WE SPEAK.
YOU WANT 'EM FRAGGED?
NO, JUST MAKE CERTAIN THEY DO NOT ESCAPE.
DON'T YOU WORRY YOUR PRETTY GREEN HEAD. THEY AIN'T GOIN' NOWHERE.
"EVERYONE STAY CLOSE."

THE PHANTOM ZONE.
IF YOU GET LOST HERE, YOU MAY NEVER BE FOUND.
WHAT'S WRONG WITH ALL THESE PEOPLE, MR. BATMAN?
"THEY'RE NOT PEOPLE ANYMORE, LILY. THEY'RE PHANTOMS. THIS PLACE, IT MAKES YOU FORGET WHO YOU ARE UNTIL ALL THAT'S LEFT...IS THAT."
"TH-THAT WON'T HAPPEN TO ME, WILL IT?"
NO, LITTLE SISTER.
WE WON'T BE HERE LONG ENOUGH FOR IT TO HAPPEN.
AND EVEN IF WE WERE, WE WOULDN'T LET IT HAPPEN!
YOU'RE GOING TO BE SAFE, LILY. I PROMISE.
THANKS, EVERYONE. BUT YOU KNOW WHAT WOULD REALLY MAKE ME FEEL BETTER?
PHANTOM ZONE GROUP SELFIE! EVERYBODY SMILE! YOU TOO, MR. BATMAN!
THESE HUMANS SHOULDN'T BE MAKING PROMISES THEY CAN'T KEEP. DON'T YOU AGREE, MY GENERAL?
OH, I DO, URSA. KAL-EL'S COMPANIONS--HIS JUSTICE LEAGUE--WE WILL USE THEM TO ESCAPE. THEN WE WILL LEAVE THEM TRAPPED HERE IN THIS WAKING NIGHTMARE FOR ALL ETERNITY. BUT FIRST...
...THEY WILL KNEEL BEFORE ZOD!

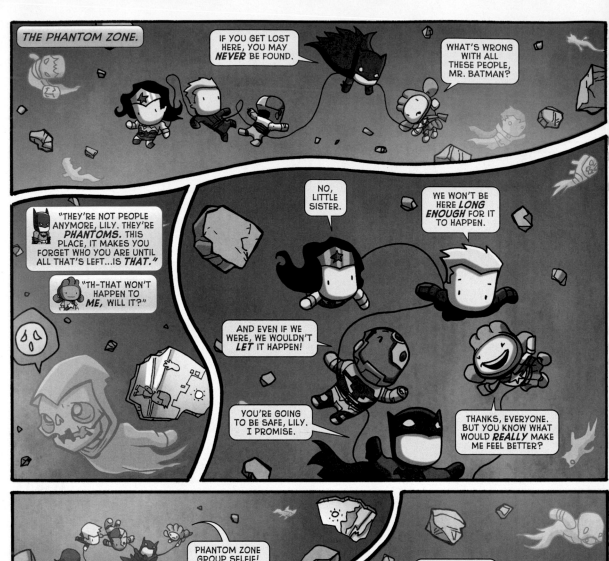

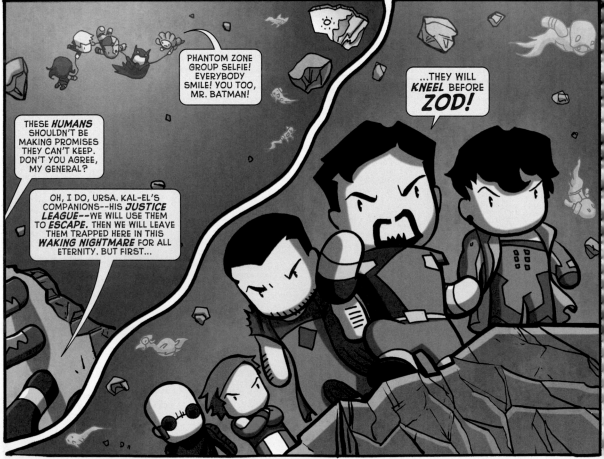

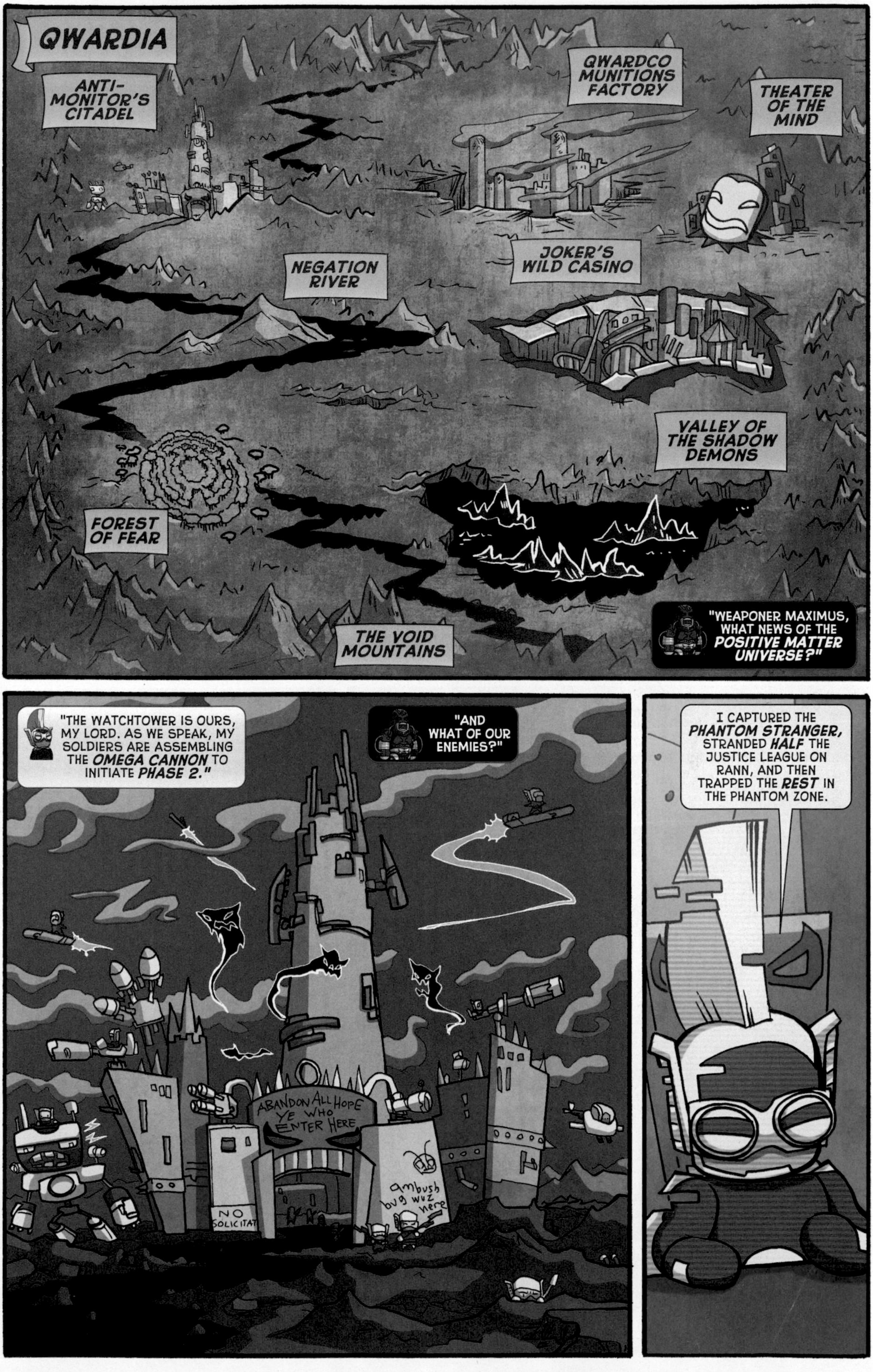
QWARDIA
ANTI-MONITOR'S CITADEL
QWARDCO MUNITIONS FACTORY
THEATER OF THE MIND
JOKER'S WILD CASINO
NEGATION RIVER
VALLEY OF THE SHADOW DEMONS
FOREST OF FEAR
THE VOID MOUNTAINS
"WEAPONER MAXIMUS, WHAT NEWS OF THE POSITIVE MATTER UNIVERSE?"
"THE WATCHTOWER IS OURS, MY LORD. AS WE SPEAK, MY SOLDIERS ARE ASSEMBLING THE OMEGA CANNON TO INITIATE PHASE 2."
"AND WHAT OF OUR ENEMIES?"
ABANDON ALL HOPE YE WHO ENTER HERE
ambush bug wuz here
NO SOLICITAT
I CAPTURED THE PHANTOM STRANGER, STRANDED HALF THE JUSTICE LEAGUE ON RANN, AND THEN TRAPPED THE REST IN THE PHANTOM ZONE.

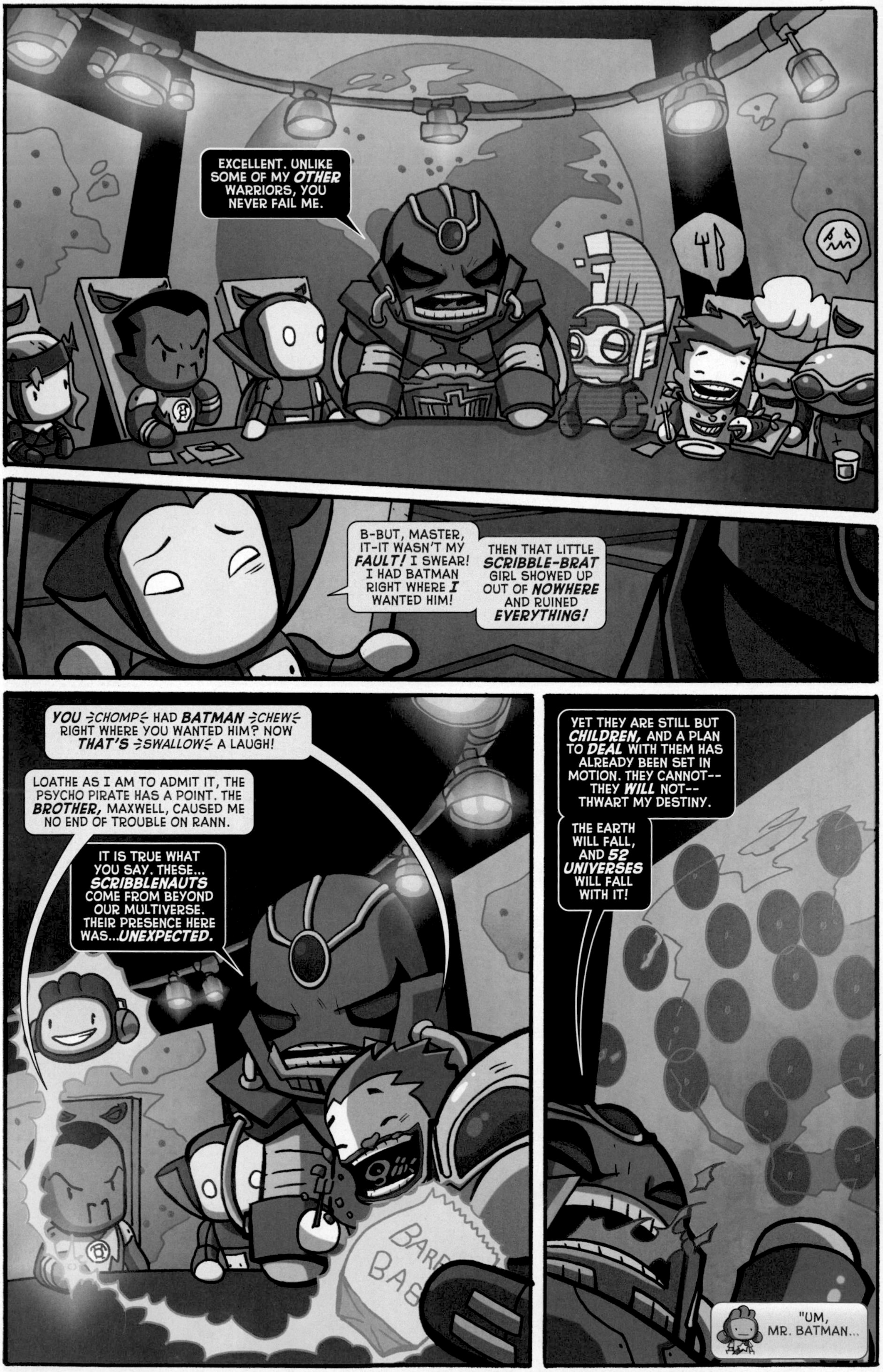
EXCELLENT. UNLIKE SOME OF MY OTHER WARRIORS, YOU NEVER FAIL ME.
B-BUT, MASTER, IT-IT WASN'T MY FAULT! I SWEAR! I HAD BATMAN RIGHT WHERE I WANTED HIM!
THEN THAT LITTLE SCRIBBLE-BRAT GIRL SHOWED UP OUT OF NOWHERE AND RUINED EVERYTHING!
YOU ⋺CHOMP⋲ HAD BATMAN ⋺CHEW⋲ RIGHT WHERE YOU WANTED HIM? NOW THAT'S ⋺SWALLOW⋲ A LAUGH!
LOATHE AS I AM TO ADMIT IT, THE PSYCHO PIRATE HAS A POINT. THE BROTHER, MAXWELL, CAUSED ME NO END OF TROUBLE ON RANN.
IT IS TRUE WHAT YOU SAY. THESE... SCRIBBLENAUTS COME FROM BEYOND OUR MULTIVERSE. THEIR PRESENCE HERE WAS...UNEXPECTED.
YET THEY ARE STILL BUT CHILDREN, AND A PLAN TO DEAL WITH THEM HAS ALREADY BEEN SET IN MOTION. THEY CANNOT-- THEY WILL NOT-- THWART MY DESTINY.
THE EARTH WILL FALL, AND 52 UNIVERSES WILL FALL WITH IT!
"UM, MR. BATMAN...

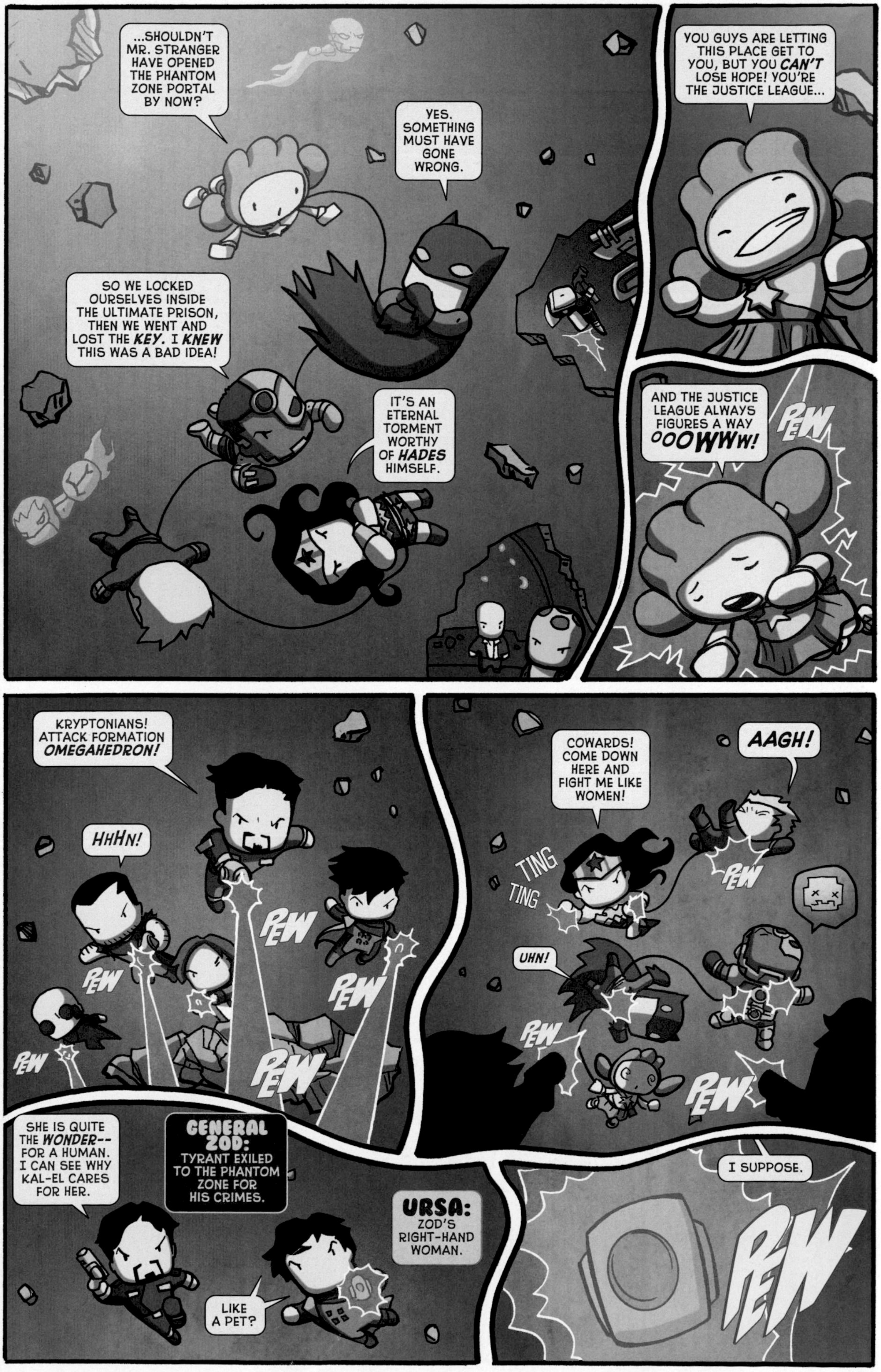
...SHOULDN'T MR. STRANGER HAVE OPENED THE PHANTOM ZONE PORTAL BY NOW?
YES. SOMETHING MUST HAVE GONE WRONG.
SO WE LOCKED OURSELVES INSIDE THE ULTIMATE PRISON, THEN WE WENT AND LOST THE KEY. I KNEW THIS WAS A BAD IDEA!
IT'S AN ETERNAL TORMENT WORTHY OF HADES HIMSELF.
YOU GUYS ARE LETTING THIS PLACE GET TO YOU, BUT YOU CAN'T LOSE HOPE! YOU'RE THE JUSTICE LEAGUE...
AND THE JUSTICE LEAGUE ALWAYS FIGURES A WAY OOOWWW!
PEW
KRYPTONIANS! ATTACK FORMATION OMEGAHEDRON!
HHHN!
PEW
PEW
PEW
PEW
PEW
COWARDS! COME DOWN HERE AND FIGHT ME LIKE WOMEN!
AAGH!
TING
TING
PEW
UHN!
PEW
PEW
SHE IS QUITE THE WONDER-- FOR A HUMAN. I CAN SEE WHY KAL-EL CARES FOR HER.
GENERAL ZOD: TYRANT EXILED TO THE PHANTOM ZONE FOR HIS CRIMES.
URSA: ZOD'S RIGHT-HAND WOMAN.
LIKE A PET?
I SUPPOSE.
PEW

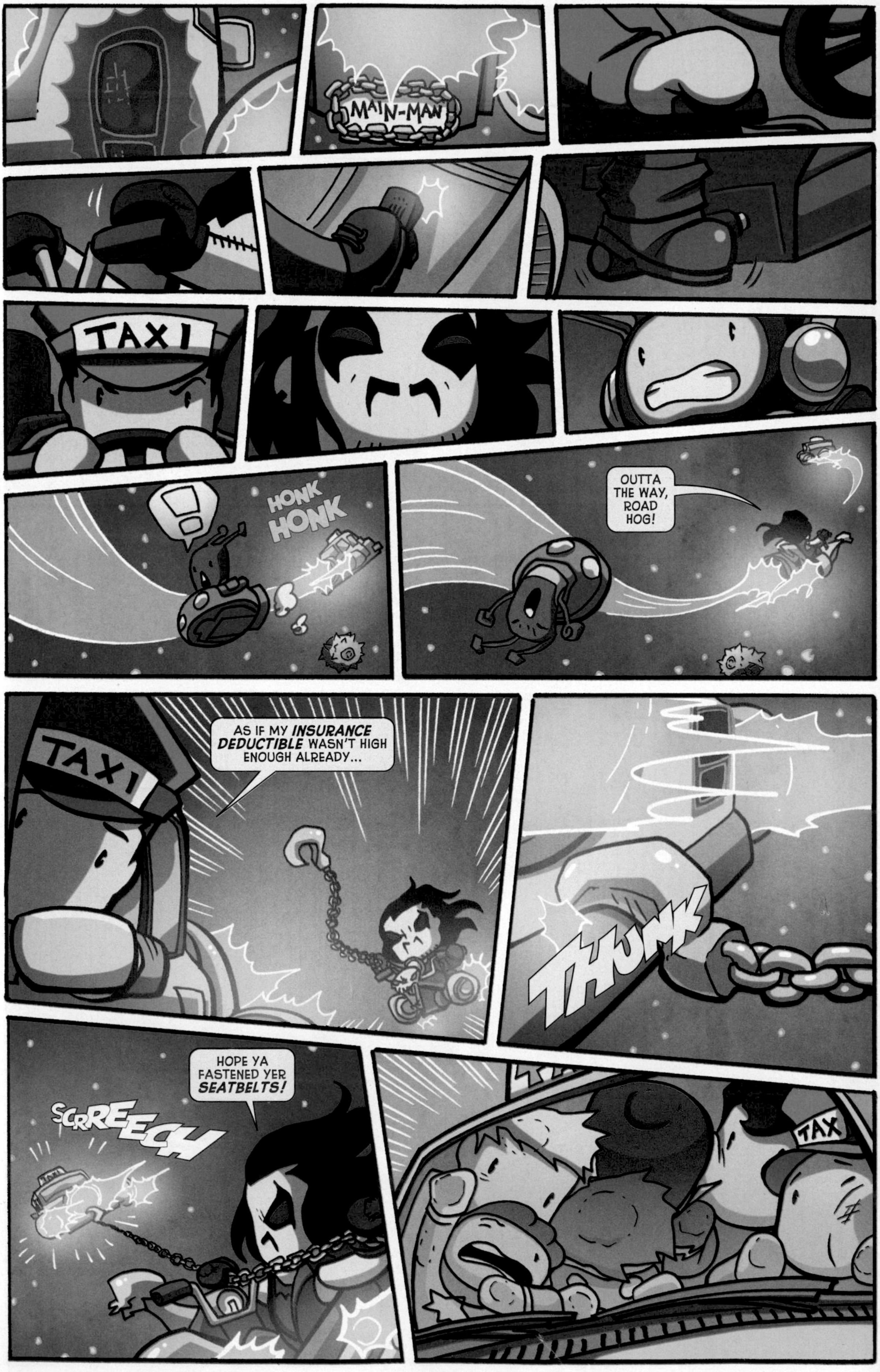
MAIN-MAN
TAXI
HONK HONK
OUTTA THE WAY, ROAD HOG!
TAXI
AS IF MY INSURANCE DEDUCTIBLE WASN'T HIGH ENOUGH ALREADY...
THUNK
HOPE YA FASTENED YER SEATBELTS!
SCRREECH
TAX

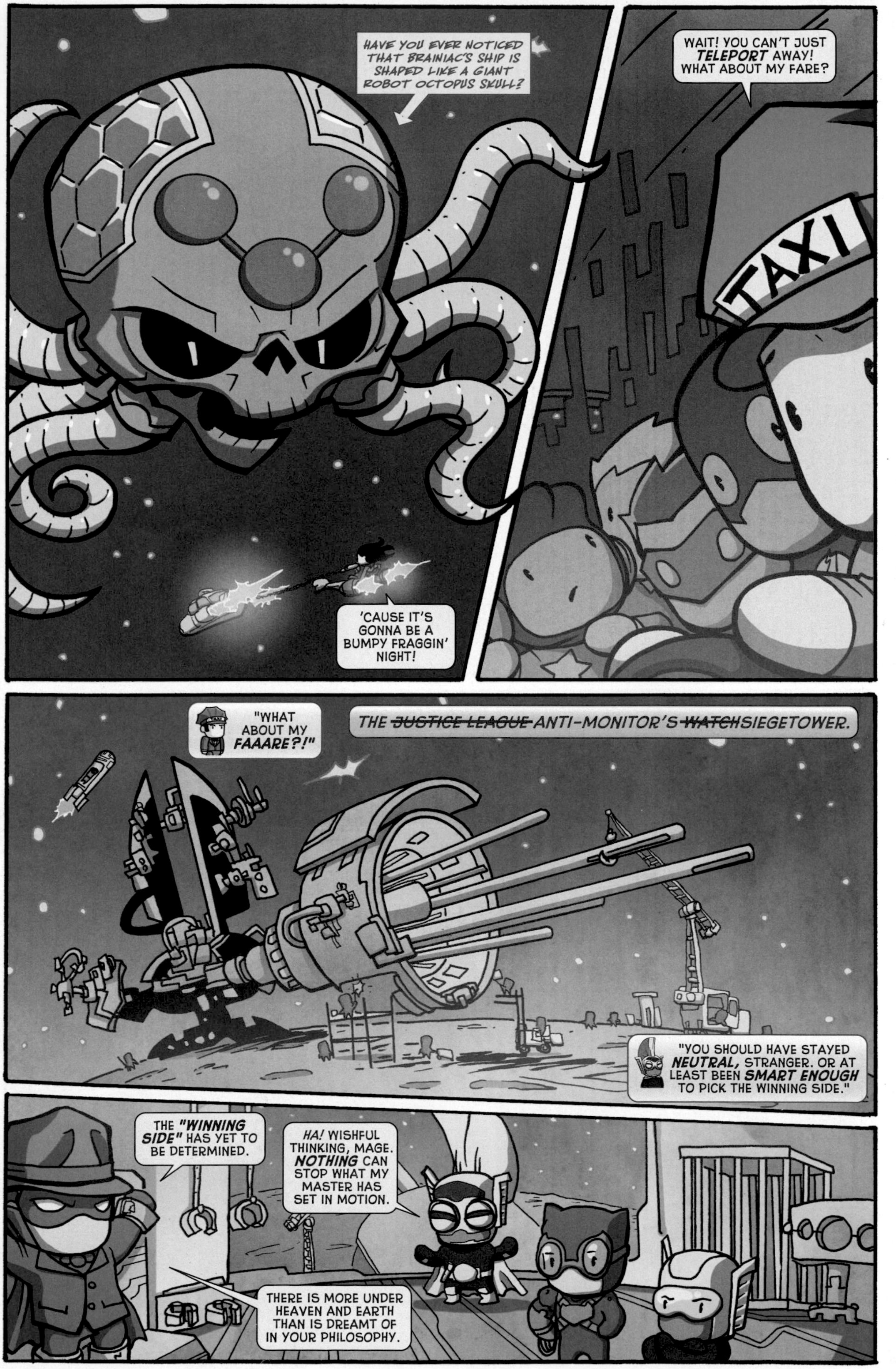
HAVE YOU EVER NOTICED THAT BRAINIAC'S SHIP IS SHAPED LIKE A GIANT ROBOT OCTOPUS SKULL?
'CAUSE IT'S GONNA BE A BUMPY FRAGGIN' NIGHT!
WAIT! YOU CAN'T JUST TELEPORT AWAY! WHAT ABOUT MY FARE?
TAXI
"WHAT ABOUT MY FAAARE?!"
THE ~~JUSTICE LEAGUE~~ ANTI-MONITOR'S ~~WATCH~~SIEGETOWER.
"YOU SHOULD HAVE STAYED NEUTRAL, STRANGER. OR AT LEAST BEEN SMART ENOUGH TO PICK THE WINNING SIDE."
THE "WINNING SIDE" HAS YET TO BE DETERMINED.
HA! WISHFUL THINKING, MAGE. NOTHING CAN STOP WHAT MY MASTER HAS SET IN MOTION.
THERE IS MORE UNDER HEAVEN AND EARTH THAN IS DREAMT OF IN YOUR PHILOSOPHY.

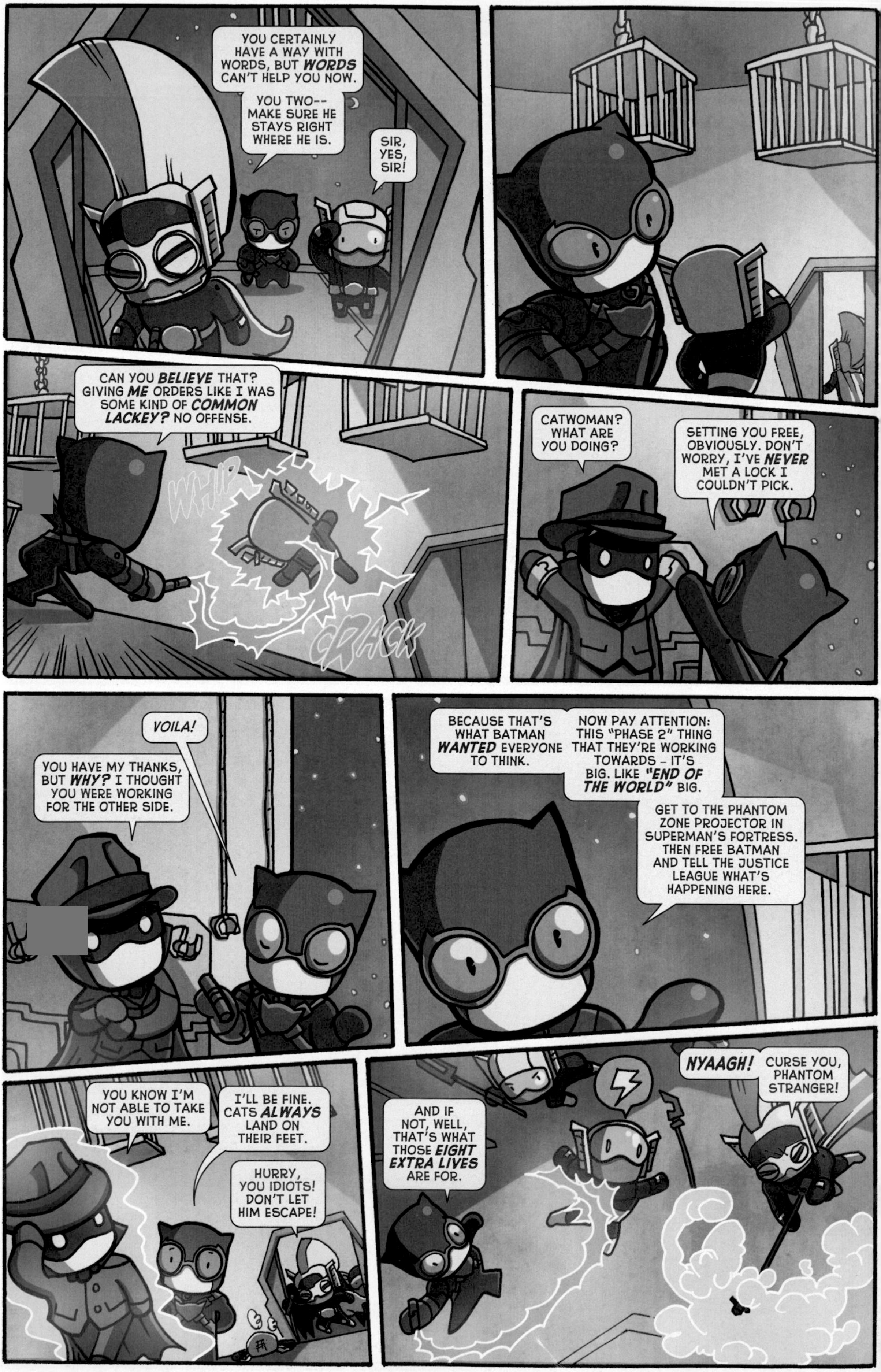
YOU CERTAINLY HAVE A WAY WITH WORDS, BUT WORDS CAN'T HELP YOU NOW.
YOU TWO-- MAKE SURE HE STAYS RIGHT WHERE HE IS.
SIR, YES, SIR!
CAN YOU BELIEVE THAT? GIVING ME ORDERS LIKE I WAS SOME KIND OF COMMON LACKEY? NO OFFENSE.
WHIP
CRACK
CATWOMAN? WHAT ARE YOU DOING?
SETTING YOU FREE, OBVIOUSLY. DON'T WORRY, I'VE NEVER MET A LOCK I COULDN'T PICK.
VOILA!
YOU HAVE MY THANKS, BUT WHY? I THOUGHT YOU WERE WORKING FOR THE OTHER SIDE.
BECAUSE THAT'S WHAT BATMAN WANTED EVERYONE TO THINK.
NOW PAY ATTENTION: THIS "PHASE 2" THING THAT THEY'RE WORKING TOWARDS - IT'S BIG. LIKE "END OF THE WORLD" BIG.
GET TO THE PHANTOM ZONE PROJECTOR IN SUPERMAN'S FORTRESS. THEN FREE BATMAN AND TELL THE JUSTICE LEAGUE WHAT'S HAPPENING HERE.
YOU KNOW I'M NOT ABLE TO TAKE YOU WITH ME.
I'LL BE FINE. CATS ALWAYS LAND ON THEIR FEET.
HURRY, YOU IDIOTS! DON'T LET HIM ESCAPE!
AND IF NOT, WELL, THAT'S WHAT THOSE EIGHT EXTRA LIVES ARE FOR.
NYAAGH!
CURSE YOU, PHANTOM STRANGER!

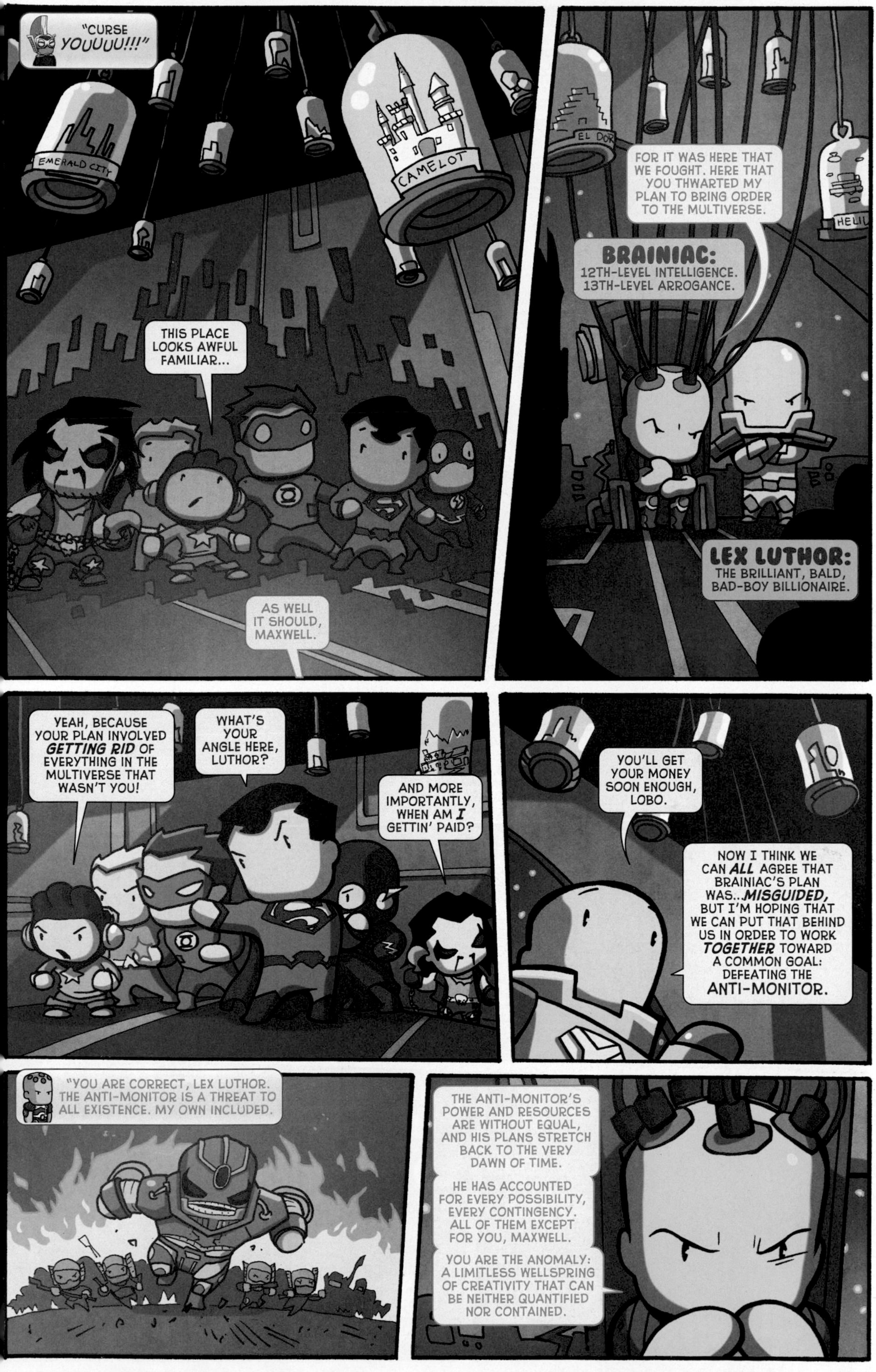

"CURSE YOUUUU!!!"
EMERALD CITY
CAMELOT
THIS PLACE LOOKS AWFUL FAMILIAR...
AS WELL IT SHOULD, MAXWELL.
EL DOR
FOR IT WAS HERE THAT WE FOUGHT. HERE THAT YOU THWARTED MY PLAN TO BRING ORDER TO THE MULTIVERSE.
BRAINIAC: 12TH-LEVEL INTELLIGENCE. 13TH-LEVEL ARROGANCE.
LEX LUTHOR: THE BRILLIANT, BALD, BAD-BOY BILLIONAIRE.
YEAH, BECAUSE YOUR PLAN INVOLVED GETTING RID OF EVERYTHING IN THE MULTIVERSE THAT WASN'T YOU!
WHAT'S YOUR ANGLE HERE, LUTHOR?
AND MORE IMPORTANTLY, WHEN AM I GETTIN' PAID?
YOU'LL GET YOUR MONEY SOON ENOUGH, LOBO.
NOW I THINK WE CAN ALL AGREE THAT BRAINIAC'S PLAN WAS...MISGUIDED, BUT I'M HOPING THAT WE CAN PUT THAT BEHIND US IN ORDER TO WORK TOGETHER TOWARD A COMMON GOAL: DEFEATING THE ANTI-MONITOR.
"YOU ARE CORRECT, LEX LUTHOR. THE ANTI-MONITOR IS A THREAT TO ALL EXISTENCE. MY OWN INCLUDED.
THE ANTI-MONITOR'S POWER AND RESOURCES ARE WITHOUT EQUAL, AND HIS PLANS STRETCH BACK TO THE VERY DAWN OF TIME.
HE HAS ACCOUNTED FOR EVERY POSSIBILITY, EVERY CONTINGENCY. ALL OF THEM EXCEPT FOR YOU, MAXWELL.
YOU ARE THE ANOMALY: A LIMITLESS WELLSPRING OF CREATIVITY THAT CAN BE NEITHER QUANTIFIED NOR CONTAINED.

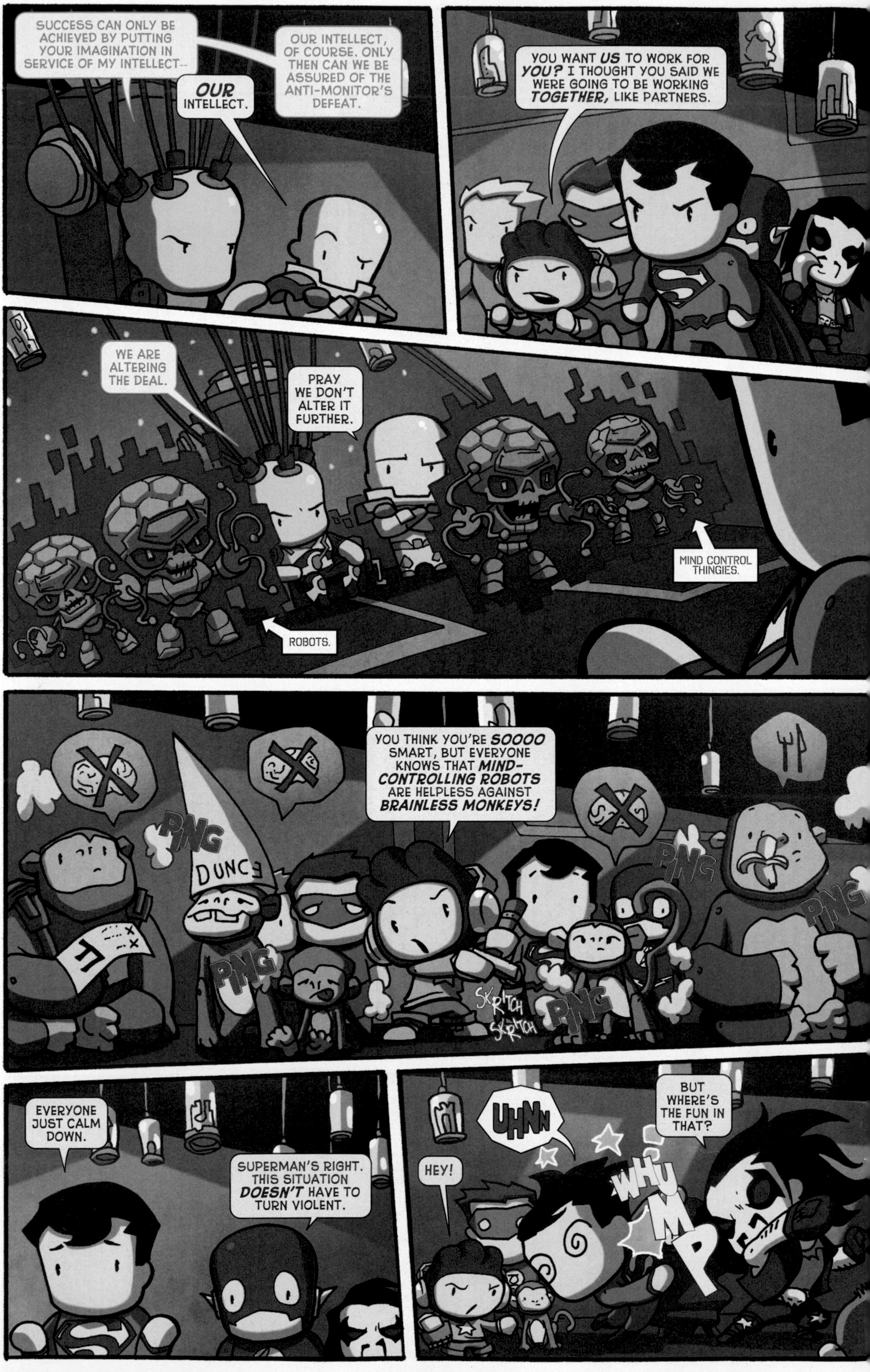

SUCCESS CAN ONLY BE ACHIEVED BY PUTTING YOUR IMAGINATION IN SERVICE OF MY INTELLECT--
OUR INTELLECT.
OUR INTELLECT, OF COURSE. ONLY THEN CAN WE BE ASSURED OF THE ANTI-MONITOR'S DEFEAT.
YOU WANT US TO WORK FOR YOU? I THOUGHT YOU SAID WE WERE GOING TO BE WORKING TOGETHER, LIKE PARTNERS.
WE ARE ALTERING THE DEAL.
PRAY WE DON'T ALTER IT FURTHER.
MIND CONTROL THINGIES.
ROBOTS.
YOU THINK YOU'RE SOOOO SMART, BUT EVERYONE KNOWS THAT MIND-CONTROLLING ROBOTS ARE HELPLESS AGAINST BRAINLESS MONKEYS!
PING
DUNCE
PING
SKRITCH SKRITCH
PING
PING
PING
EVERYONE JUST CALM DOWN.
SUPERMAN'S RIGHT. THIS SITUATION DOESN'T HAVE TO TURN VIOLENT.
UHNN
HEY!
BUT WHERE'S THE FUN IN THAT?
WHUMP

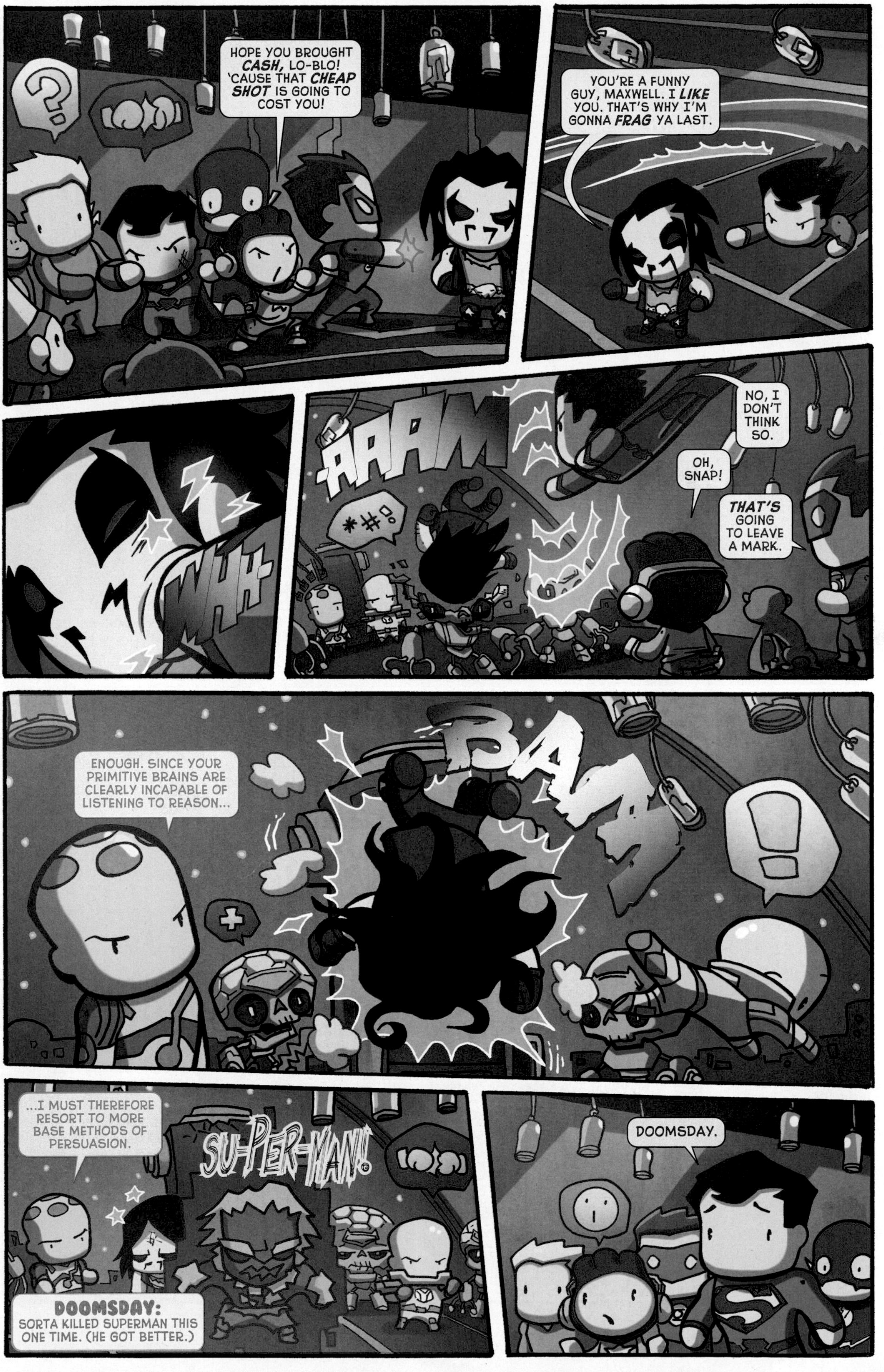
HOPE YOU BROUGHT CASH, LO-BLO! 'CAUSE THAT CHEAP SHOT IS GOING TO COST YOU!
YOU'RE A FUNNY GUY, MAXWELL. I LIKE YOU. THAT'S WHY I'M GONNA FRAG YA LAST.
WHH-
-AAAM
NO, I DON'T THINK SO.
OH, SNAP!
THAT'S GOING TO LEAVE A MARK.
ENOUGH. SINCE YOUR PRIMITIVE BRAINS ARE CLEARLY INCAPABLE OF LISTENING TO REASON...
BAM
...I MUST THEREFORE RESORT TO MORE BASE METHODS OF PERSUASION.
SU-PER-MAN!
DOOMSDAY:
SORTA KILLED SUPERMAN THIS ONE TIME. (HE GOT BETTER.)
DOOMSDAY.

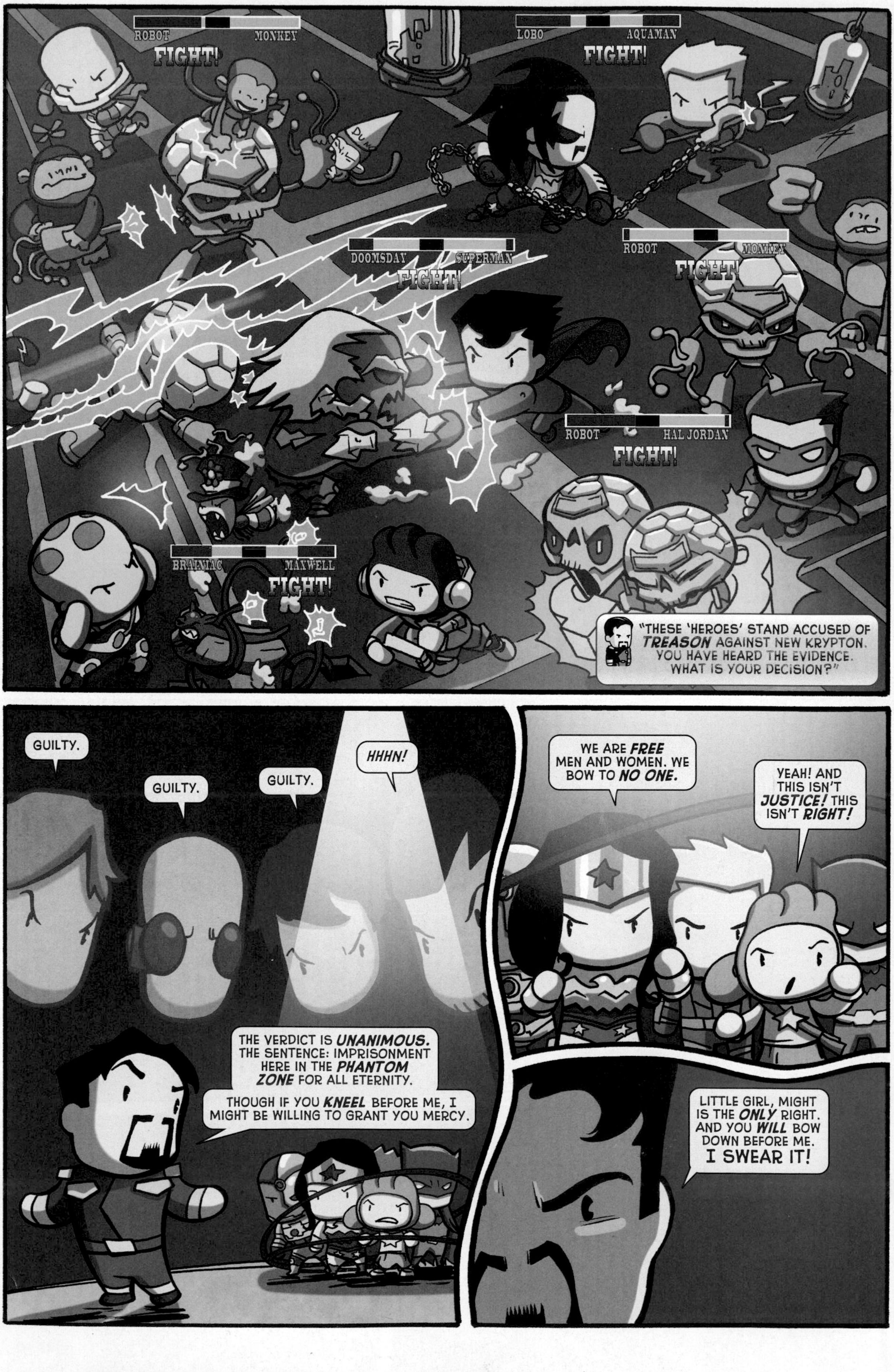

ROBOT
MONKEY
FIGHT!
LOBO
AQUAMAN
FIGHT!
DOOMSDAY
SUPERMAN
FIGHT!
ROBOT
MONKEY
FIGHT!
ROBOT
HAL JORDAN
FIGHT!
BRAINIAC
MAXWELL
FIGHT!
"THESE 'HEROES' STAND ACCUSED OF TREASON AGAINST NEW KRYPTON. YOU HAVE HEARD THE EVIDENCE. WHAT IS YOUR DECISION?"
GUILTY.
GUILTY.
GUILTY.
HHHN!
THE VERDICT IS UNANIMOUS. THE SENTENCE: IMPRISONMENT HERE IN THE PHANTOM ZONE FOR ALL ETERNITY.
THOUGH IF YOU KNEEL BEFORE ME, I MIGHT BE WILLING TO GRANT YOU MERCY.
WE ARE FREE MEN AND WOMEN. WE BOW TO NO ONE.
YEAH! AND THIS ISN'T JUSTICE! THIS ISN'T RIGHT!
LITTLE GIRL, MIGHT IS THE ONLY RIGHT. AND YOU WILL BOW DOWN BEFORE ME. I SWEAR IT!

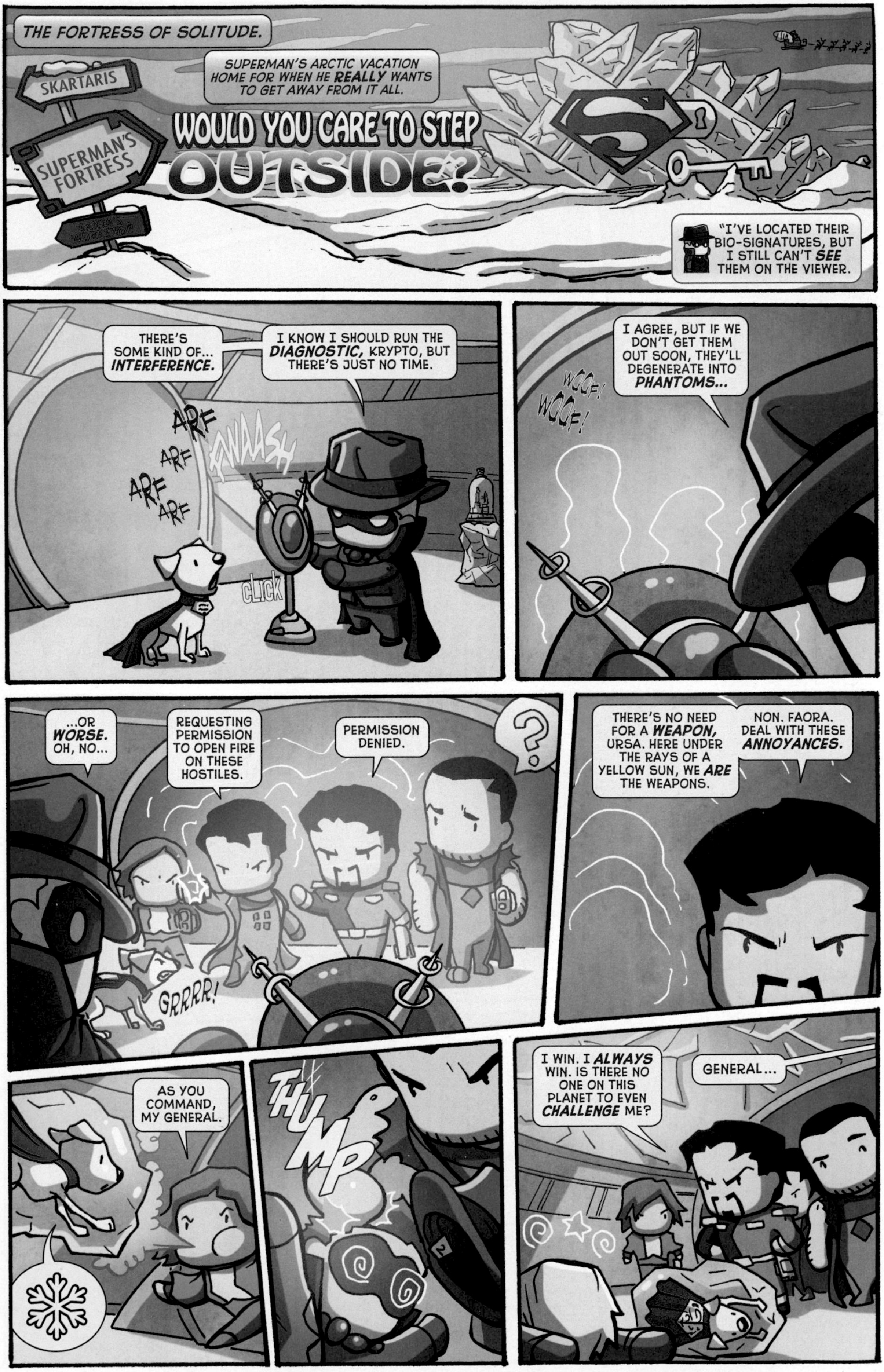
THE FORTRESS OF SOLITUDE.
SKARTARIS
SUPERMAN'S FORTRESS
SUPERMAN'S ARCTIC VACATION HOME FOR WHEN HE REALLY WANTS TO GET AWAY FROM IT ALL.
WOULD YOU CARE TO STEP OUTSIDE?
"I'VE LOCATED THEIR BIO-SIGNATURES, BUT I STILL CAN'T SEE THEM ON THE VIEWER.
THERE'S SOME KIND OF... INTERFERENCE.
I KNOW I SHOULD RUN THE DIAGNOSTIC, KRYPTO, BUT THERE'S JUST NO TIME.
ARF ARF ARF ARF
AWAASH
CLICK
I AGREE, BUT IF WE DON'T GET THEM OUT SOON, THEY'LL DEGENERATE INTO PHANTOMS...
WOOF! WOOF!
...OR WORSE. OH, NO...
REQUESTING PERMISSION TO OPEN FIRE ON THESE HOSTILES.
PERMISSION DENIED.
?
GRRRR!
THERE'S NO NEED FOR A WEAPON, URSA. HERE UNDER THE RAYS OF A YELLOW SUN, WE ARE THE WEAPONS.
NON. FAORA. DEAL WITH THESE ANNOYANCES.
AS YOU COMMAND, MY GENERAL.
THUMP
I WIN. I ALWAYS WIN. IS THERE NO ONE ON THIS PLANET TO EVEN CHALLENGE ME?
GENERAL...

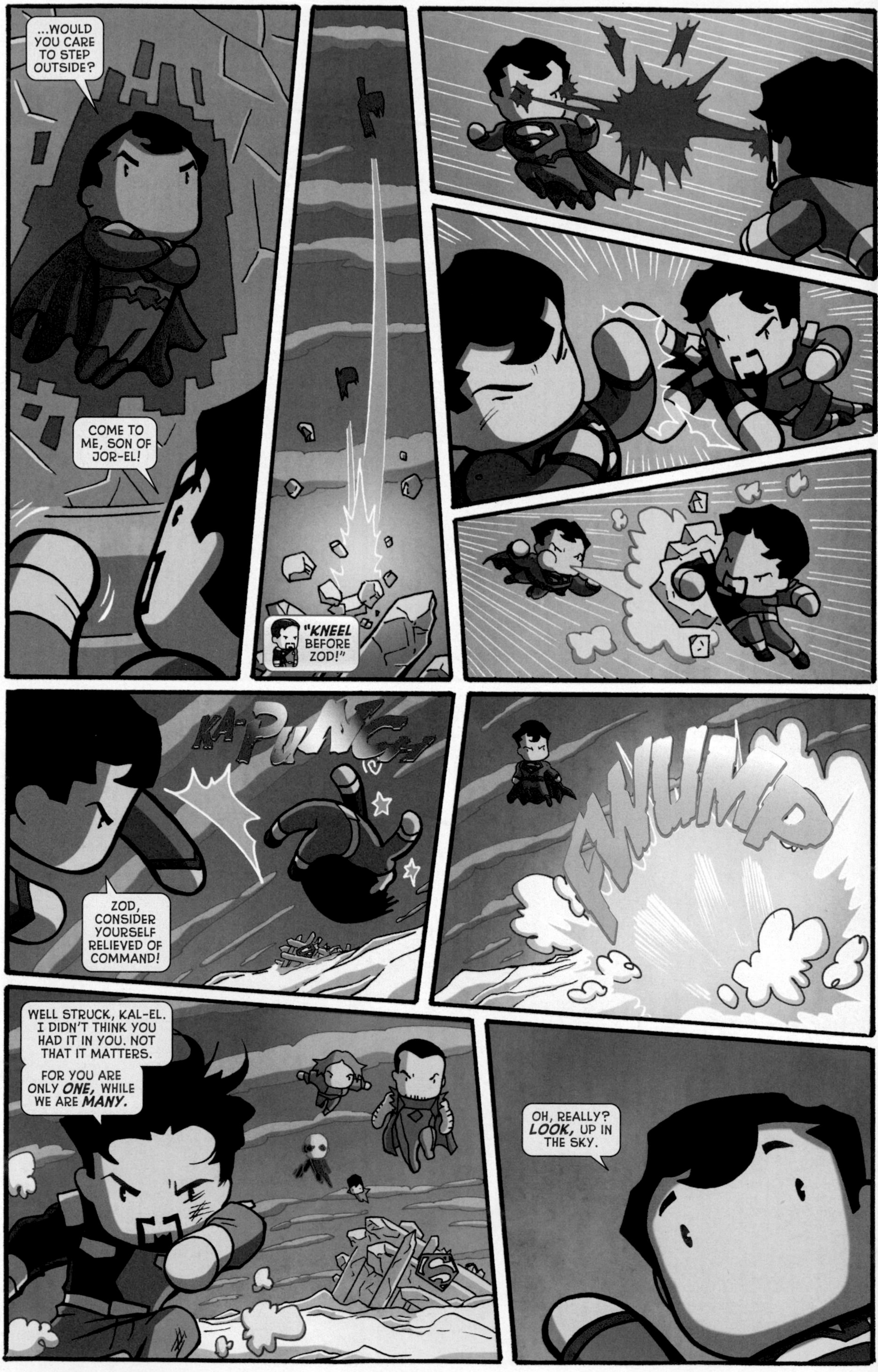
...WOULD YOU CARE TO STEP OUTSIDE?
COME TO ME, SON OF JOR-EL!
"KNEEL BEFORE ZOD!"
KA-PUNCH
ZOD, CONSIDER YOURSELF RELIEVED OF COMMAND!
FWUMP
WELL STRUCK, KAL-EL. I DIDN'T THINK YOU HAD IT IN YOU. NOT THAT IT MATTERS.
FOR YOU ARE ONLY ONE, WHILE WE ARE MANY.
OH, REALLY? LOOK, UP IN THE SKY.

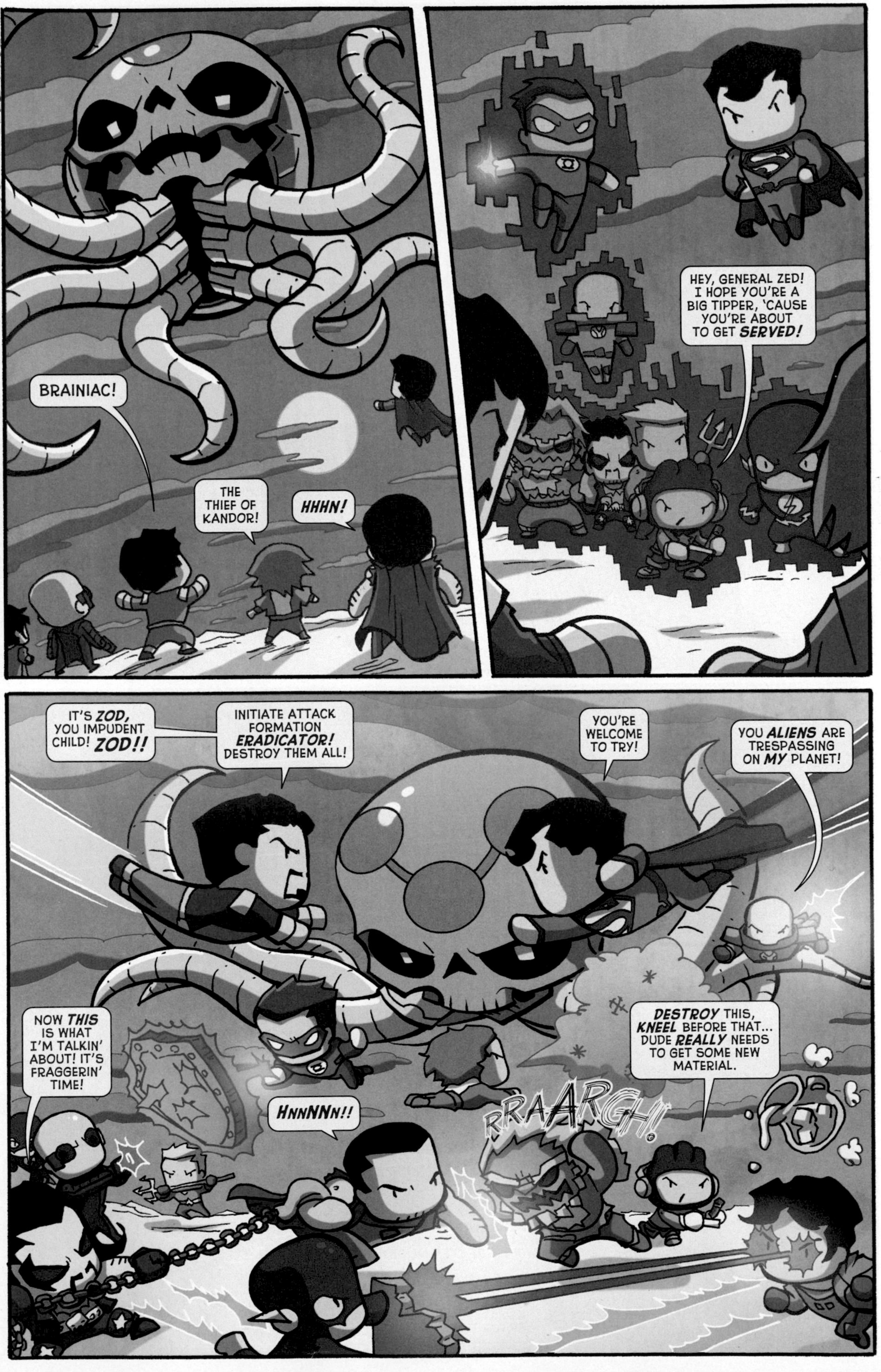
BRAINIAC!
THE THIEF OF KANDOR!
HHHN!
HEY, GENERAL ZED! I HOPE YOU'RE A BIG TIPPER, 'CAUSE YOU'RE ABOUT TO GET SERVED!
IT'S ZOD, YOU IMPUDENT CHILD! ZOD!!
INITIATE ATTACK FORMATION ERADICATOR! DESTROY THEM ALL!
YOU'RE WELCOME TO TRY!
YOU ALIENS ARE TRESPASSING ON MY PLANET!
NOW THIS IS WHAT I'M TALKIN' ABOUT! IT'S FRAGGERIN' TIME!
HNNNNN!!
RRAARGH!
DESTROY THIS, KNEEL BEFORE THAT... DUDE REALLY NEEDS TO GET SOME NEW MATERIAL.

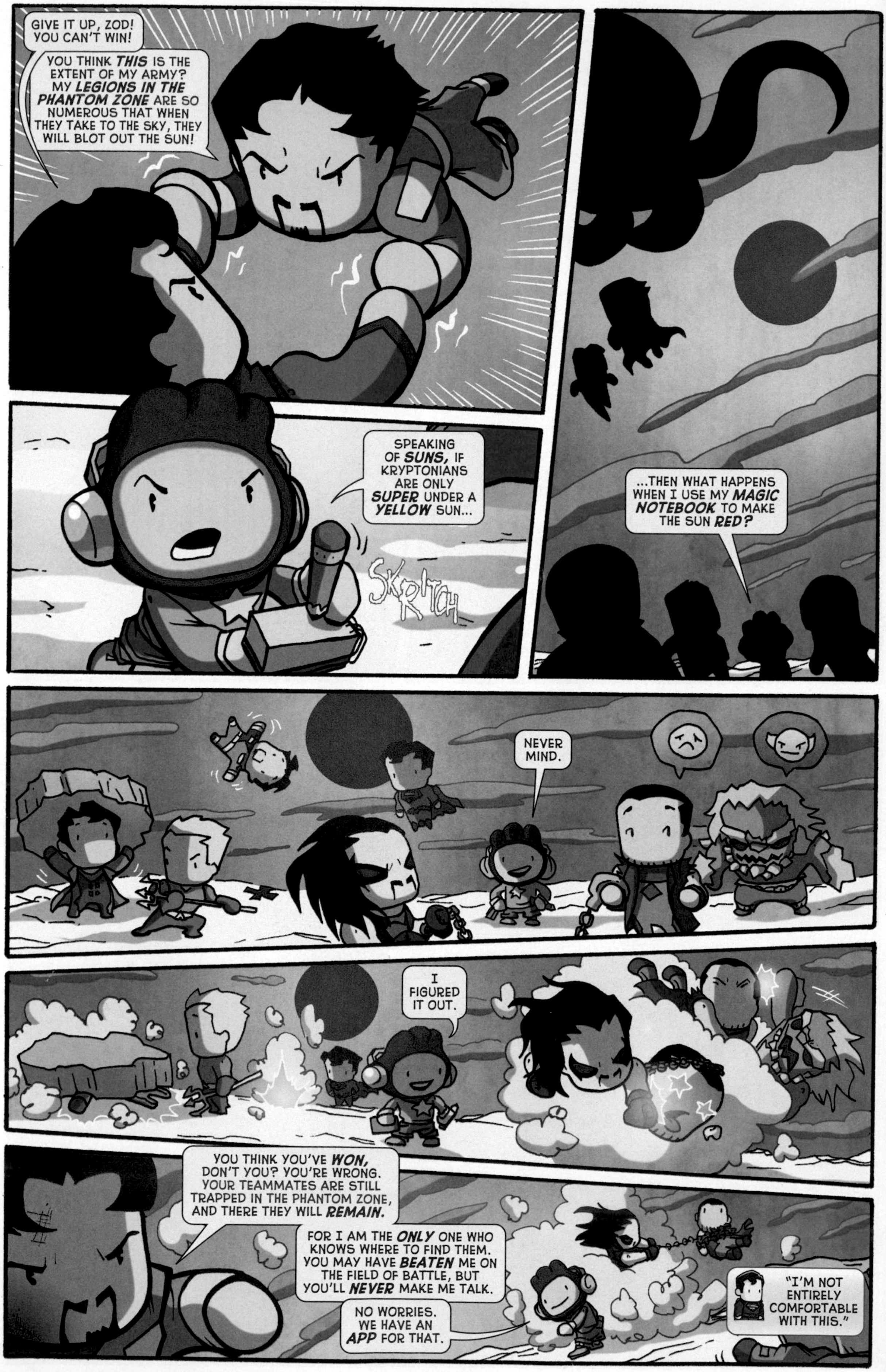
GIVE IT UP, ZOD! YOU CAN'T WIN!
YOU THINK THIS IS THE EXTENT OF MY ARMY? MY LEGIONS IN THE PHANTOM ZONE ARE SO NUMEROUS THAT WHEN THEY TAKE TO THE SKY, THEY WILL BLOT OUT THE SUN!
SPEAKING OF SUNS, IF KRYPTONIANS ARE ONLY SUPER UNDER A YELLOW SUN...
SKRITCH
...THEN WHAT HAPPENS WHEN I USE MY MAGIC NOTEBOOK TO MAKE THE SUN RED?
NEVER MIND.
I FIGURED IT OUT.
YOU THINK YOU'VE WON, DON'T YOU? YOU'RE WRONG. YOUR TEAMMATES ARE STILL TRAPPED IN THE PHANTOM ZONE, AND THERE THEY WILL REMAIN.
FOR I AM THE ONLY ONE WHO KNOWS WHERE TO FIND THEM. YOU MAY HAVE BEATEN ME ON THE FIELD OF BATTLE, BUT YOU'LL NEVER MAKE ME TALK.
NO WORRIES. WE HAVE AN APP FOR THAT.
"I'M NOT ENTIRELY COMFORTABLE WITH THIS."

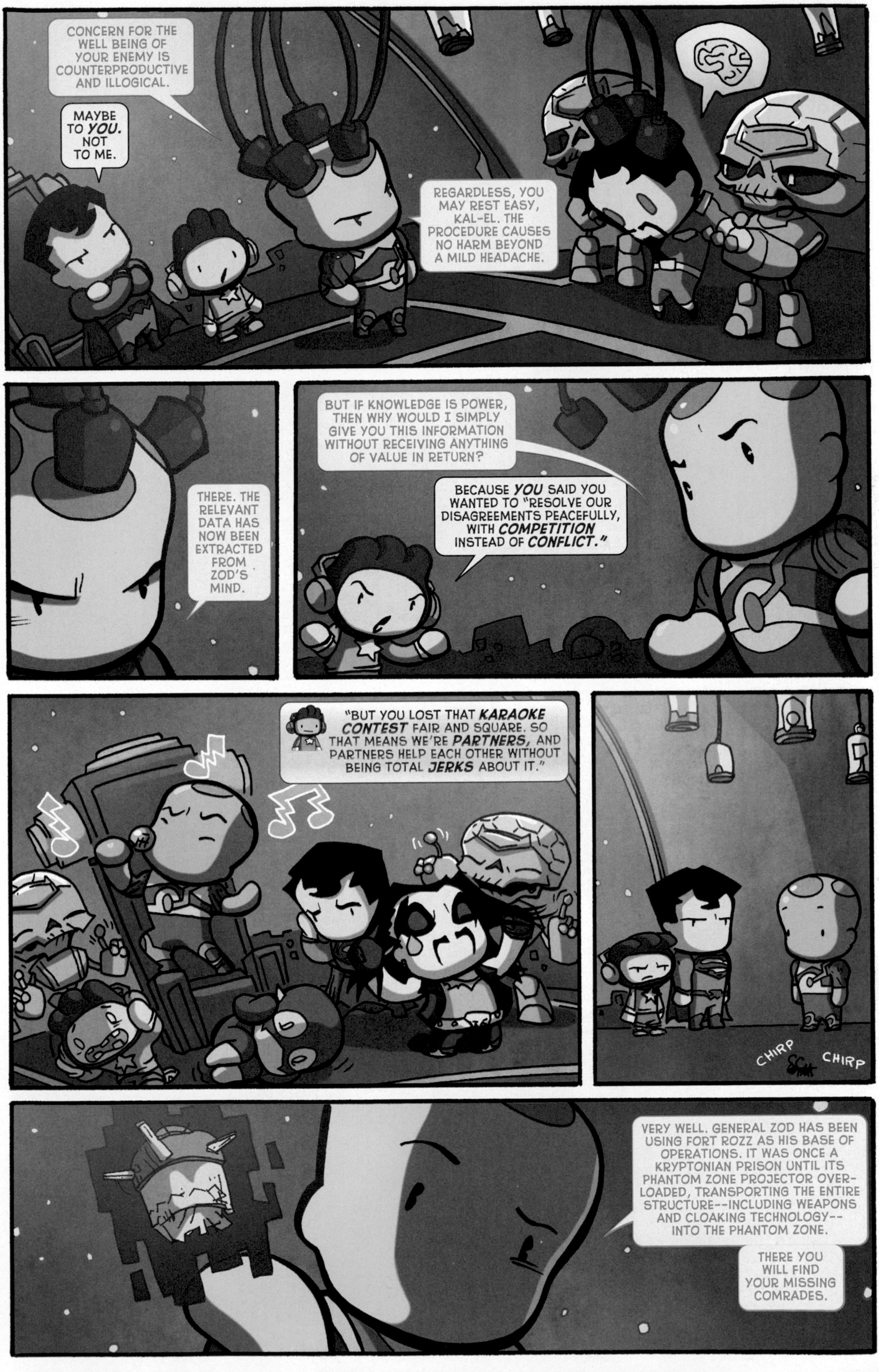
CONCERN FOR THE WELL BEING OF YOUR ENEMY IS COUNTERPRODUCTIVE AND ILLOGICAL.
MAYBE TO *YOU.* NOT TO ME.
REGARDLESS, YOU MAY REST EASY, KAL-EL. THE PROCEDURE CAUSES NO HARM BEYOND A MILD HEADACHE.
THERE. THE RELEVANT DATA HAS NOW BEEN EXTRACTED FROM ZOD'S MIND.
BUT IF KNOWLEDGE IS POWER, THEN WHY WOULD I SIMPLY GIVE YOU THIS INFORMATION WITHOUT RECEIVING ANYTHING OF VALUE IN RETURN?
BECAUSE *YOU* SAID YOU WANTED TO "RESOLVE OUR DISAGREEMENTS PEACEFULLY, WITH *COMPETITION* INSTEAD OF *CONFLICT.*"
"BUT YOU LOST THAT *KARAOKE CONTEST* FAIR AND SQUARE. SO THAT MEANS WE'RE *PARTNERS,* AND PARTNERS HELP EACH OTHER WITHOUT BEING TOTAL *JERKS* ABOUT IT."
CHIRP
CHIRP
VERY WELL. GENERAL ZOD HAS BEEN USING FORT ROZZ AS HIS BASE OF OPERATIONS. IT WAS ONCE A KRYPTONIAN PRISON UNTIL ITS PHANTOM ZONE PROJECTOR OVER-LOADED, TRANSPORTING THE ENTIRE STRUCTURE--INCLUDING WEAPONS AND CLOAKING TECHNOLOGY--INTO THE PHANTOM ZONE.
THERE YOU WILL FIND YOUR MISSING COMRADES.

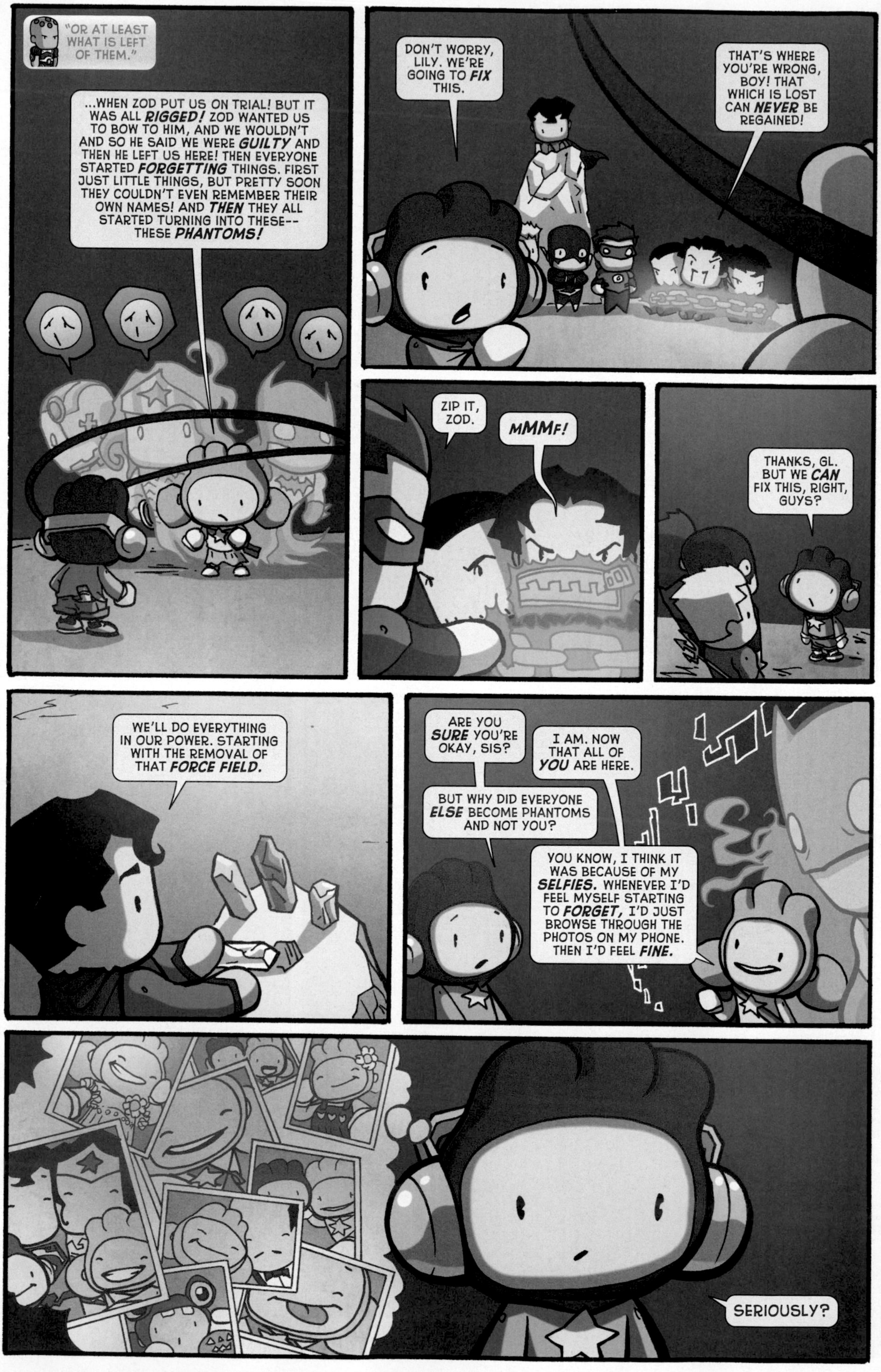
"OR AT LEAST WHAT IS LEFT OF THEM."
...WHEN ZOD PUT US ON TRIAL! BUT IT WAS ALL RIGGED! ZOD WANTED US TO BOW TO HIM, AND WE WOULDN'T AND SO HE SAID WE WERE GUILTY AND THEN HE LEFT US HERE! THEN EVERYONE STARTED FORGETTING THINGS. FIRST JUST LITTLE THINGS, BUT PRETTY SOON THEY COULDN'T EVEN REMEMBER THEIR OWN NAMES! AND THEN THEY ALL STARTED TURNING INTO THESE-- THESE PHANTOMS!
DON'T WORRY, LILY. WE'RE GOING TO FIX THIS.
THAT'S WHERE YOU'RE WRONG, BOY! THAT WHICH IS LOST CAN NEVER BE REGAINED!
ZIP IT, ZOD.
MMMF!
THANKS, GL. BUT WE CAN FIX THIS, RIGHT, GUYS?
WE'LL DO EVERYTHING IN OUR POWER. STARTING WITH THE REMOVAL OF THAT FORCE FIELD.
ARE YOU SURE YOU'RE OKAY, SIS?
I AM. NOW THAT ALL OF YOU ARE HERE.
BUT WHY DID EVERYONE ELSE BECOME PHANTOMS AND NOT YOU?
YOU KNOW, I THINK IT WAS BECAUSE OF MY SELFIES. WHENEVER I'D FEEL MYSELF STARTING TO FORGET, I'D JUST BROWSE THROUGH THE PHOTOS ON MY PHONE. THEN I'D FEEL FINE.
SERIOUSLY?

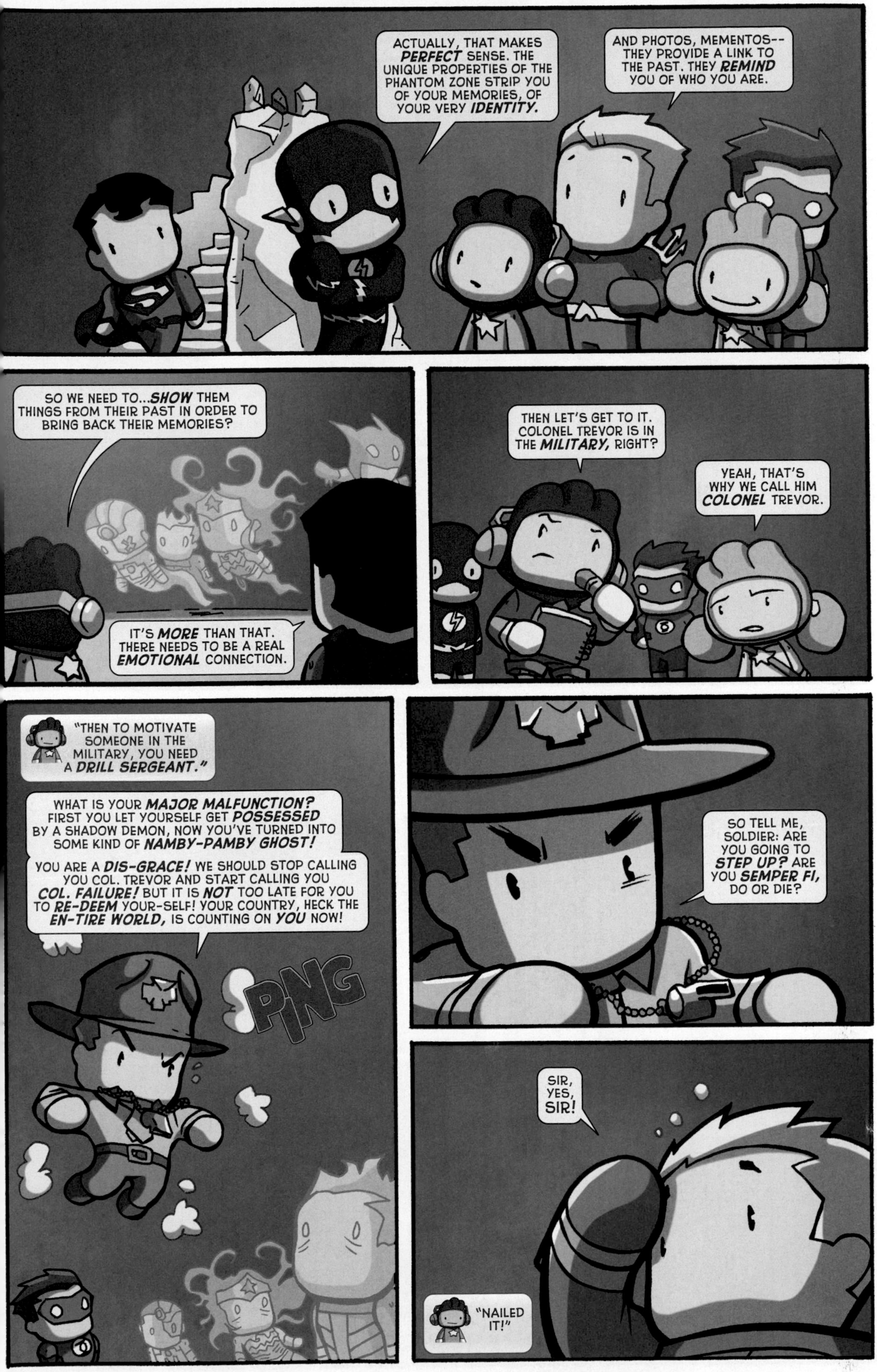
ACTUALLY, THAT MAKES PERFECT SENSE. THE UNIQUE PROPERTIES OF THE PHANTOM ZONE STRIP YOU OF YOUR MEMORIES, OF YOUR VERY IDENTITY.
AND PHOTOS, MEMENTOS-- THEY PROVIDE A LINK TO THE PAST. THEY REMIND YOU OF WHO YOU ARE.
SO WE NEED TO...SHOW THEM THINGS FROM THEIR PAST IN ORDER TO BRING BACK THEIR MEMORIES?
IT'S MORE THAN THAT. THERE NEEDS TO BE A REAL EMOTIONAL CONNECTION.
THEN LET'S GET TO IT. COLONEL TREVOR IS IN THE MILITARY, RIGHT?
YEAH, THAT'S WHY WE CALL HIM COLONEL TREVOR.
"THEN TO MOTIVATE SOMEONE IN THE MILITARY, YOU NEED A DRILL SERGEANT."
WHAT IS YOUR MAJOR MALFUNCTION? FIRST YOU LET YOURSELF GET POSSESSED BY A SHADOW DEMON, NOW YOU'VE TURNED INTO SOME KIND OF NAMBY-PAMBY GHOST!
YOU ARE A DIS-GRACE! WE SHOULD STOP CALLING YOU COL. TREVOR AND START CALLING YOU COL. FAILURE! BUT IT IS NOT TOO LATE FOR YOU TO RE-DEEM YOUR-SELF! YOUR COUNTRY, HECK THE EN-TIRE WORLD, IS COUNTING ON YOU NOW!
PING
SO TELL ME, SOLDIER: ARE YOU GOING TO STEP UP? ARE YOU SEMPER FI, DO OR DIE?
SIR, YES, SIR!
"NAILED IT!"

"OOOH, LET'S DO MR. CYBORG NEXT!"

PING

CYBORG

CYBORG     DARKSEID

"HE'S A *MUCHO* HARDCORE GAMER. I KNOW *EXACTLY* HOW TO GET HIS ATTENTION."

NEW HIGH SCORE! *BOOYAH!*

"NOW WHAT ABOUT MS. WONDER WOMAN?"

I THINK I SHOULD HANDLE *THIS* ONE, KIDS. THE *GOLDEN LARIAT* WILL COMPEL THE TRUTH FROM WHOSOEVER HOLDS IT, EVEN HERE.

WHO ARE YOU?

I AM...DIANA... OF THE AMAZONS. DAUGHTER OF... HIPPOLYTA.

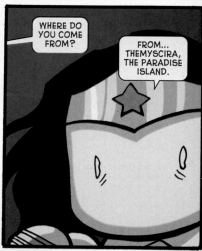

WHERE DO YOU COME FROM?

FROM... THEMYSCIRA, THE PARADISE ISLAND.

WHAT DO YOU FIGHT FOR?

I FIGHT FOR...TRUTH. FOR *FREEDOM.* I FIGHT FOR THOSE WHO CAN'T FIGHT FOR THEMSELVES.

SMOOCH

I AM *WONDER WOMAN!* HEAR ME ROAR!

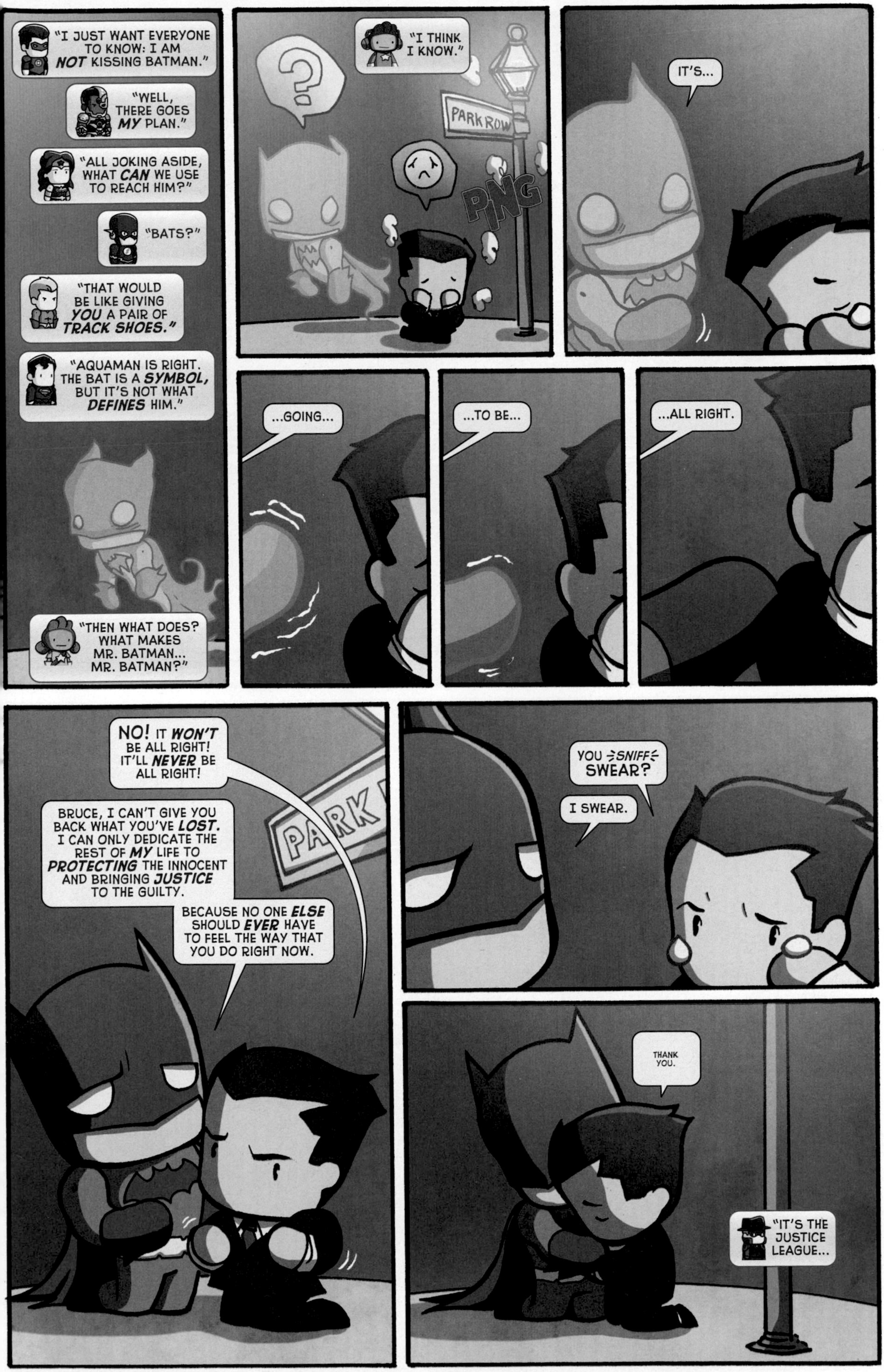
"I JUST WANT EVERYONE TO KNOW: I AM NOT KISSING BATMAN."
"WELL, THERE GOES MY PLAN."
"ALL JOKING ASIDE, WHAT CAN WE USE TO REACH HIM?"
"BATS?"
"THAT WOULD BE LIKE GIVING YOU A PAIR OF TRACK SHOES."
"AQUAMAN IS RIGHT. THE BAT IS A SYMBOL, BUT IT'S NOT WHAT DEFINES HIM."
"THEN WHAT DOES? WHAT MAKES MR. BATMAN... MR. BATMAN?"
"I THINK I KNOW."
?
PARK ROW
PING
IT'S...
...GOING...
...TO BE...
...ALL RIGHT.
NO! IT WON'T BE ALL RIGHT! IT'LL NEVER BE ALL RIGHT!
BRUCE, I CAN'T GIVE YOU BACK WHAT YOU'VE LOST. I CAN ONLY DEDICATE THE REST OF MY LIFE TO PROTECTING THE INNOCENT AND BRINGING JUSTICE TO THE GUILTY.
BECAUSE NO ONE ELSE SHOULD EVER HAVE TO FEEL THE WAY THAT YOU DO RIGHT NOW.
PARK
YOU SNIFF SWEAR?
I SWEAR.
THANK YOU.
"IT'S THE JUSTICE LEAGUE...

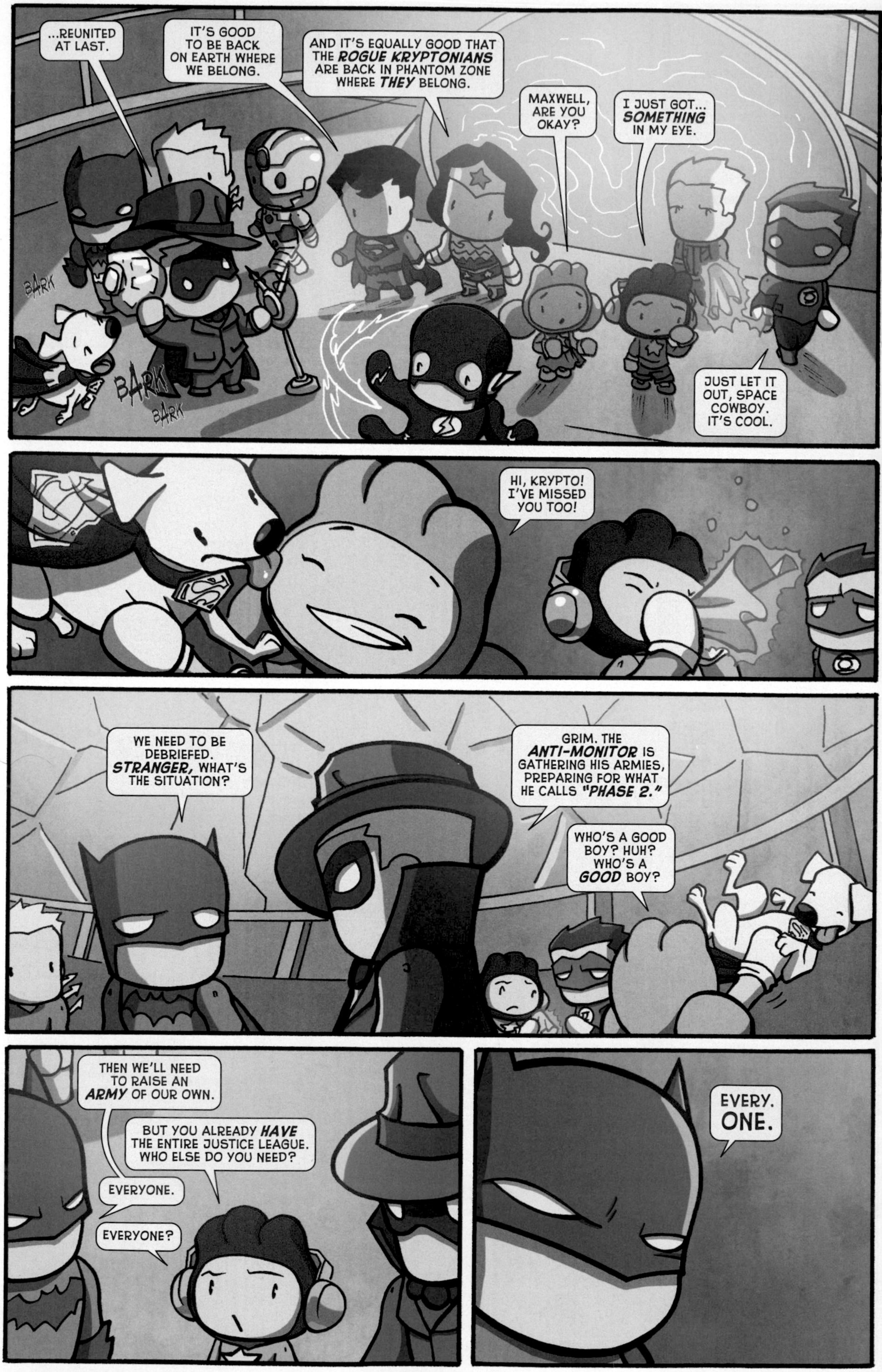

...REUNITED AT LAST.
IT'S GOOD TO BE BACK ON EARTH WHERE WE BELONG.
AND IT'S EQUALLY GOOD THAT THE ROGUE KRYPTONIANS ARE BACK IN PHANTOM ZONE WHERE THEY BELONG.
MAXWELL, ARE YOU OKAY?
I JUST GOT... SOMETHING IN MY EYE.
BARK
BARK
BARK
JUST LET IT OUT, SPACE COWBOY. IT'S COOL.
HI, KRYPTO! I'VE MISSED YOU TOO!
WE NEED TO BE DEBRIEFED. STRANGER, WHAT'S THE SITUATION?
GRIM. THE ANTI-MONITOR IS GATHERING HIS ARMIES, PREPARING FOR WHAT HE CALLS "PHASE 2."
WHO'S A GOOD BOY? HUH? WHO'S A GOOD BOY?
THEN WE'LL NEED TO RAISE AN ARMY OF OUR OWN.
BUT YOU ALREADY HAVE THE ENTIRE JUSTICE LEAGUE. WHO ELSE DO YOU NEED?
EVERYONE.
EVERYONE?
EVERY. ONE.

THE WORLD'S MIGHTIEST HEROES GATHER AT SUPERMAN'S FORTRESS TO FACE THE GREATEST THREAT ANY OF THEM HAVE EVER KNOWN.

BUT FIRST THEY HAVE TO FIND A PLACE TO PARK.

WHAT ARE YOU, BLIND?! YOU ALMOST RAN INTO THE INVISIBLE PLANE!

"I NEED YOU TO STAND STILL WITH YOUR ARMS AT YOUR SIDES DURING THE X-RAY PROCESS."

SPACE CABBY INC.
INTERSTELLAR
TRAVEL RECEIPT
DISTANCE       2.94 x
TRAVELED:      1014 miles
FEES:          $3.25/mile +
               tolls and tip

I KNOW IT'S ANNOYING, BUT THE ANTI-MONITOR'S SHADOW DEMONS CAN HIDE INSIDE OF ANYTHING--OR ANYONE--SO WE HAVE TO TAKE EVERY PRECAUTION.

MR. STEEL?

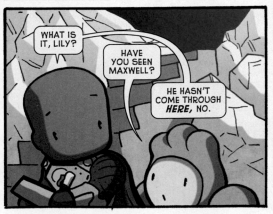

WHAT IS IT, LILY?

HAVE YOU SEEN MAXWELL?

HE HASN'T COME THROUGH HERE, NO.

I GUESS THAT MEANS HE MUST STILL BE INSIDE. I'LL GO LOOK FOR HIM THERE.

GOOD LUCK. YOU'RE GOING TO NEED IT TRYING TO FIND HIM IN THAT MADHOUSE.

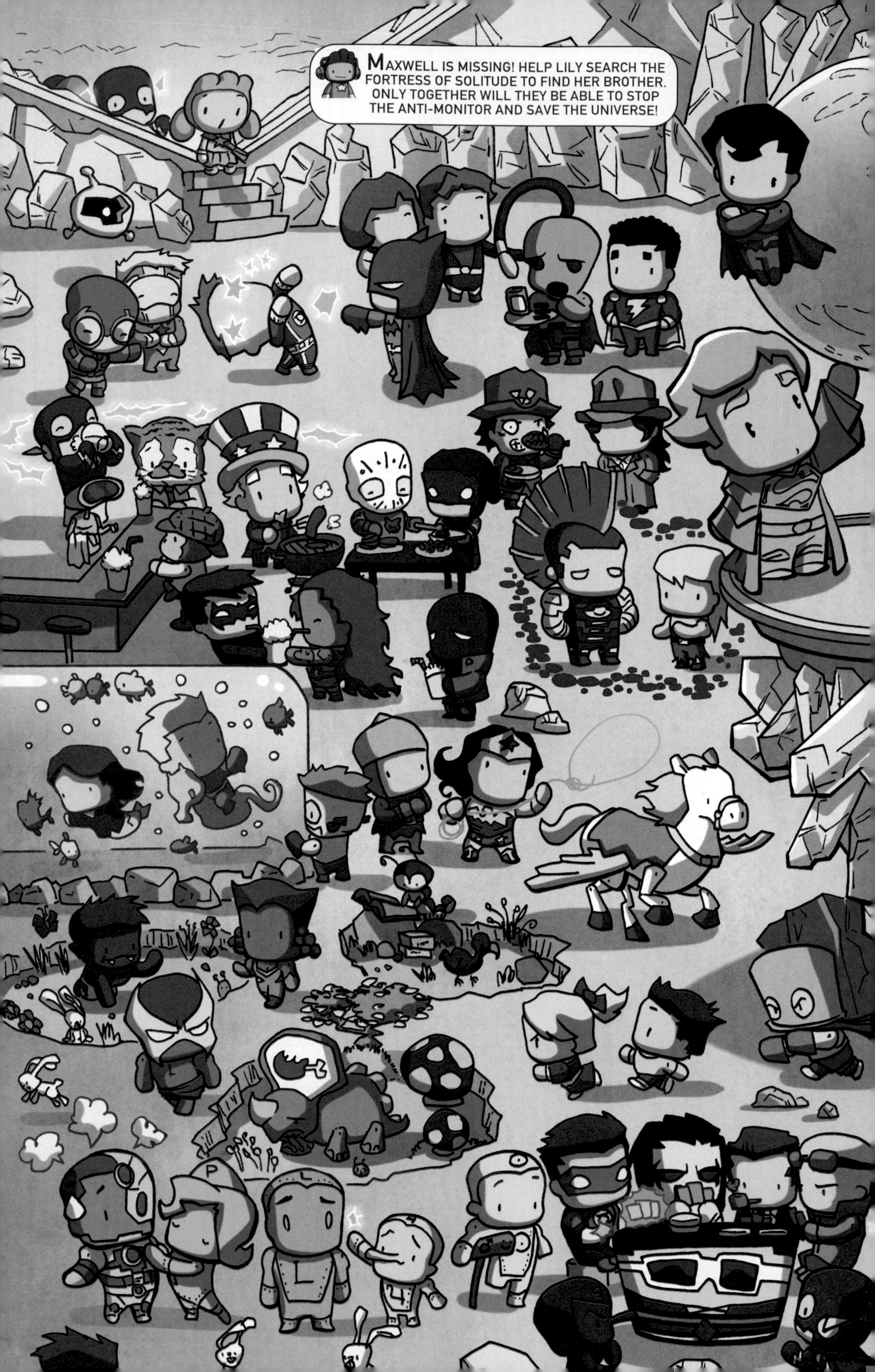
MAXWELL IS MISSING! HELP LILY SEARCH THE FORTRESS OF SOLITUDE TO FIND HER BROTHER. ONLY TOGETHER WILL THEY BE ABLE TO STOP THE ANTI-MONITOR AND SAVE THE UNIVERSE!

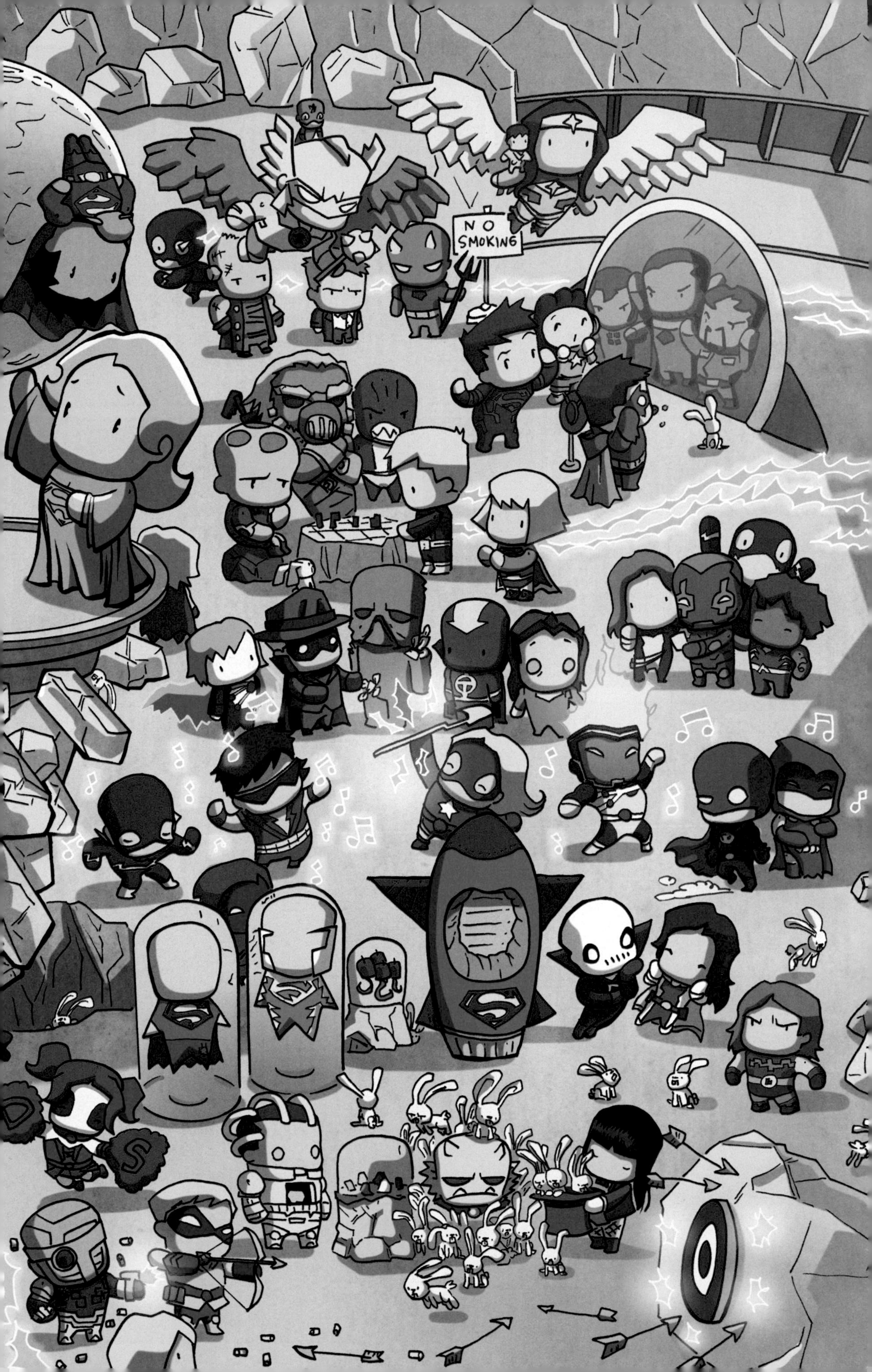
NO SMOKING

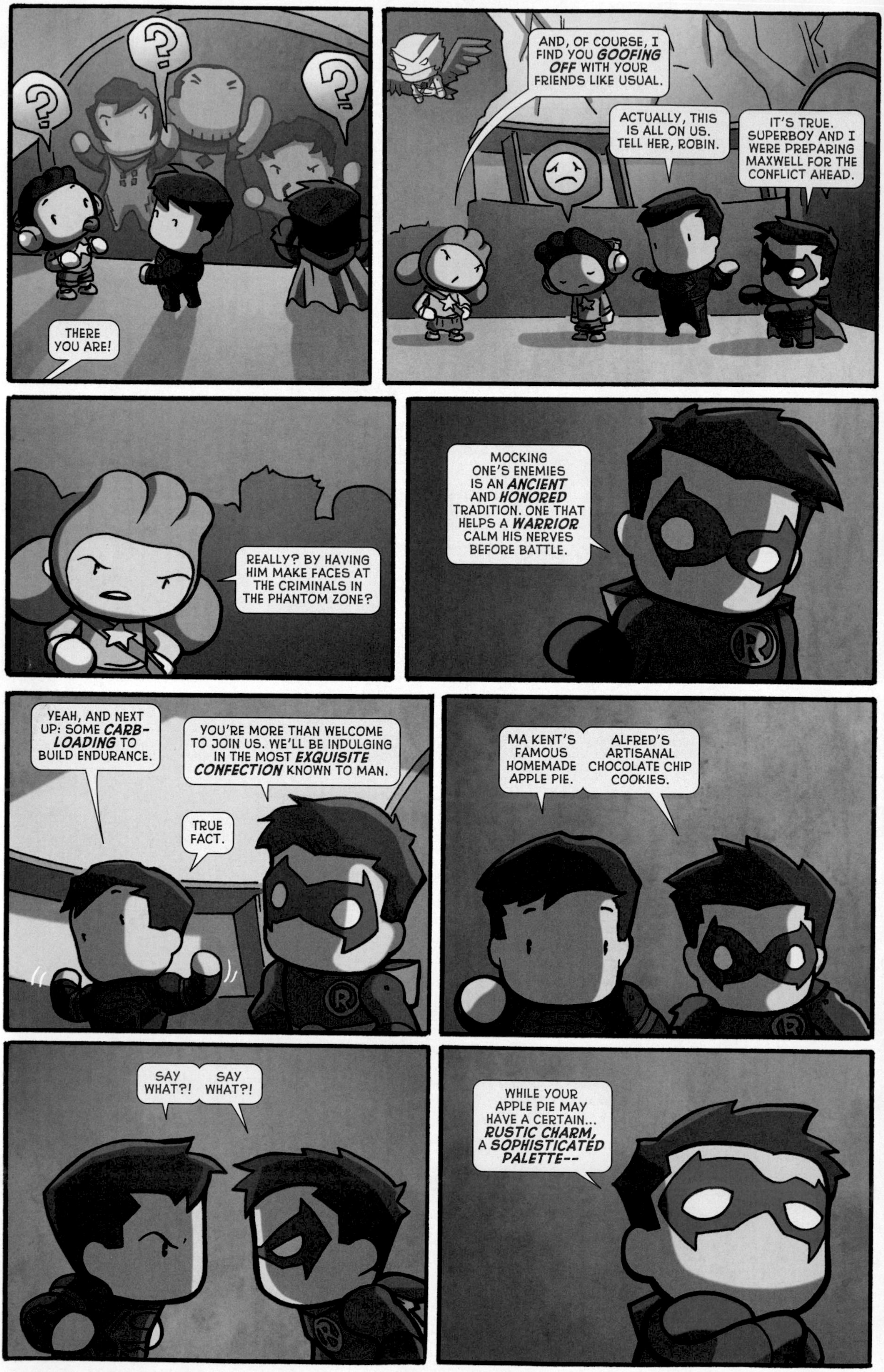
THERE YOU ARE!
AND, OF COURSE, I FIND YOU GOOFING OFF WITH YOUR FRIENDS LIKE USUAL.
ACTUALLY, THIS IS ALL ON US. TELL HER, ROBIN.
IT'S TRUE. SUPERBOY AND I WERE PREPARING MAXWELL FOR THE CONFLICT AHEAD.
REALLY? BY HAVING HIM MAKE FACES AT THE CRIMINALS IN THE PHANTOM ZONE?
MOCKING ONE'S ENEMIES IS AN ANCIENT AND HONORED TRADITION. ONE THAT HELPS A WARRIOR CALM HIS NERVES BEFORE BATTLE.
YEAH, AND NEXT UP: SOME CARB-LOADING TO BUILD ENDURANCE.
YOU'RE MORE THAN WELCOME TO JOIN US. WE'LL BE INDULGING IN THE MOST EXQUISITE CONFECTION KNOWN TO MAN.
TRUE FACT.
MA KENT'S FAMOUS HOMEMADE APPLE PIE.
ALFRED'S ARTISANAL CHOCOLATE CHIP COOKIES.
SAY WHAT?!
SAY WHAT?!
WHILE YOUR APPLE PIE MAY HAVE A CERTAIN... RUSTIC CHARM, A SOPHISTICATED PALETTE--

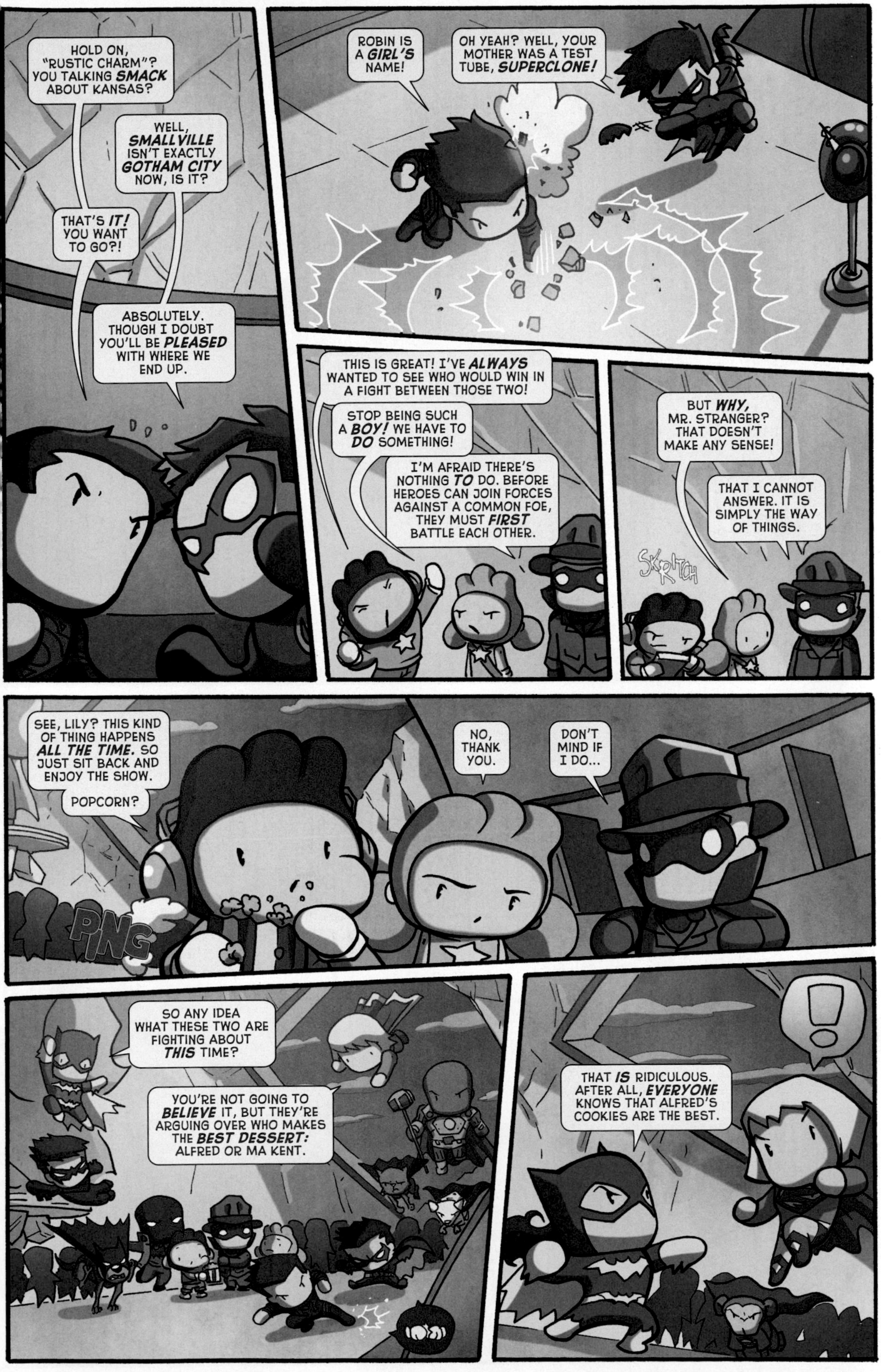
HOLD ON, "RUSTIC CHARM"? YOU TALKING SMACK ABOUT KANSAS?
WELL, SMALLVILLE ISN'T EXACTLY GOTHAM CITY NOW, IS IT?
THAT'S IT! YOU WANT TO GO?!
ABSOLUTELY. THOUGH I DOUBT YOU'LL BE PLEASED WITH WHERE WE END UP.
ROBIN IS A GIRL'S NAME!
OH YEAH? WELL, YOUR MOTHER WAS A TEST TUBE, SUPERCLONE!
THIS IS GREAT! I'VE ALWAYS WANTED TO SEE WHO WOULD WIN IN A FIGHT BETWEEN THOSE TWO!
STOP BEING SUCH A BOY! WE HAVE TO DO SOMETHING!
I'M AFRAID THERE'S NOTHING TO DO. BEFORE HEROES CAN JOIN FORCES AGAINST A COMMON FOE, THEY MUST FIRST BATTLE EACH OTHER.
BUT WHY, MR. STRANGER? THAT DOESN'T MAKE ANY SENSE!
THAT I CANNOT ANSWER. IT IS SIMPLY THE WAY OF THINGS.
SKRITCH
SEE, LILY? THIS KIND OF THING HAPPENS ALL THE TIME. SO JUST SIT BACK AND ENJOY THE SHOW.
POPCORN?
PING
NO, THANK YOU.
DON'T MIND IF I DO...
SO ANY IDEA WHAT THESE TWO ARE FIGHTING ABOUT THIS TIME?
YOU'RE NOT GOING TO BELIEVE IT, BUT THEY'RE ARGUING OVER WHO MAKES THE BEST DESSERT: ALFRED OR MA KENT.
!
THAT IS RIDICULOUS. AFTER ALL, EVERYONE KNOWS THAT ALFRED'S COOKIES ARE THE BEST.

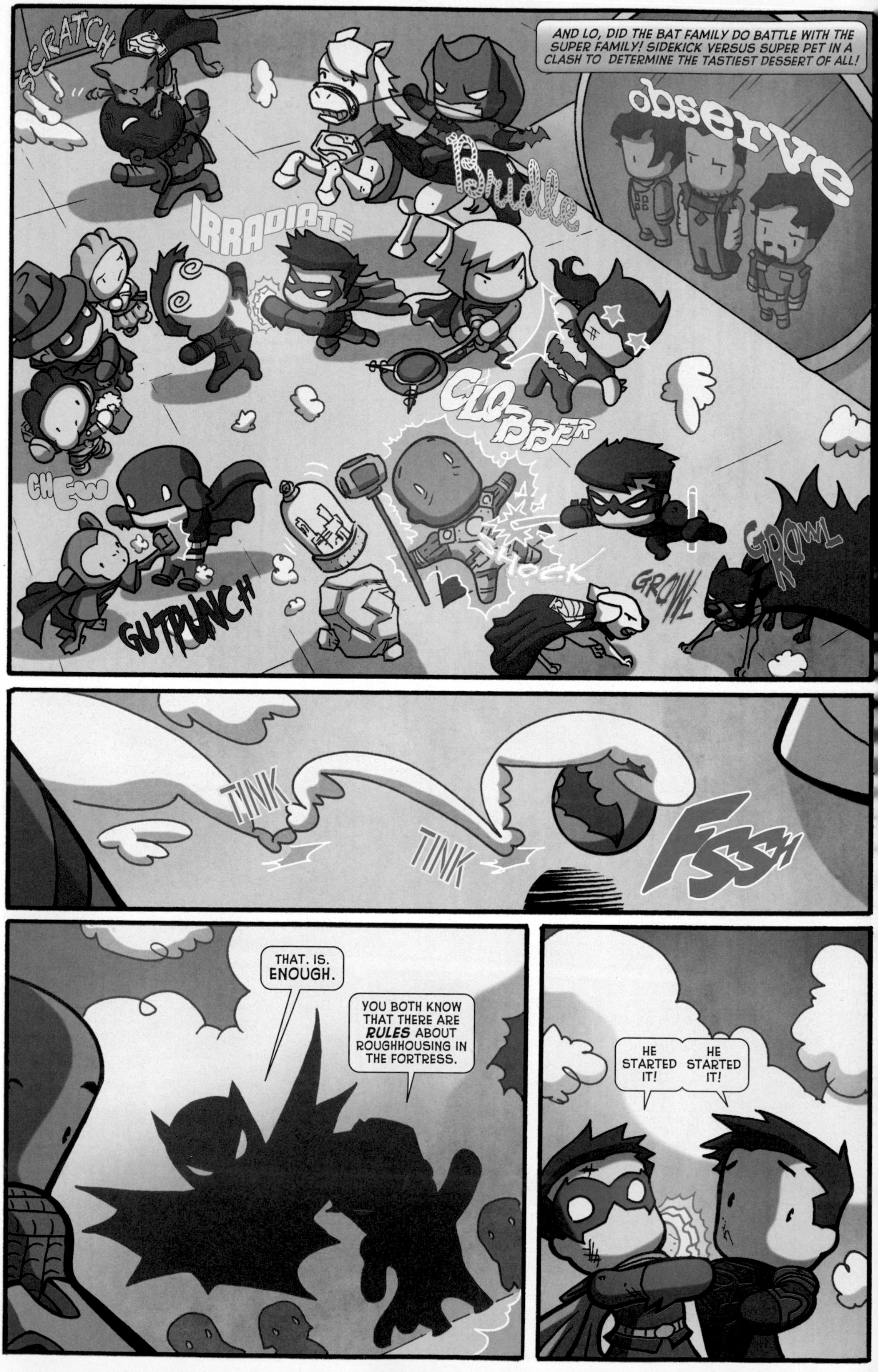
AND LO, DID THE BAT FAMILY DO BATTLE WITH THE SUPER FAMILY! SIDEKICK VERSUS SUPER PET IN A CLASH TO DETERMINE THE TASTIEST DESSERT OF ALL!
SCRATCH
observe
Bridle
IRRADIATE
CLOBBER
CHEW
SHOCK
GROWL
GROWL
GUTPUNCH
TINK
TINK
FSSH
THAT. IS. ENOUGH.
YOU BOTH KNOW THAT THERE ARE RULES ABOUT ROUGHHOUSING IN THE FORTRESS.
HE STARTED IT!
HE STARTED IT!

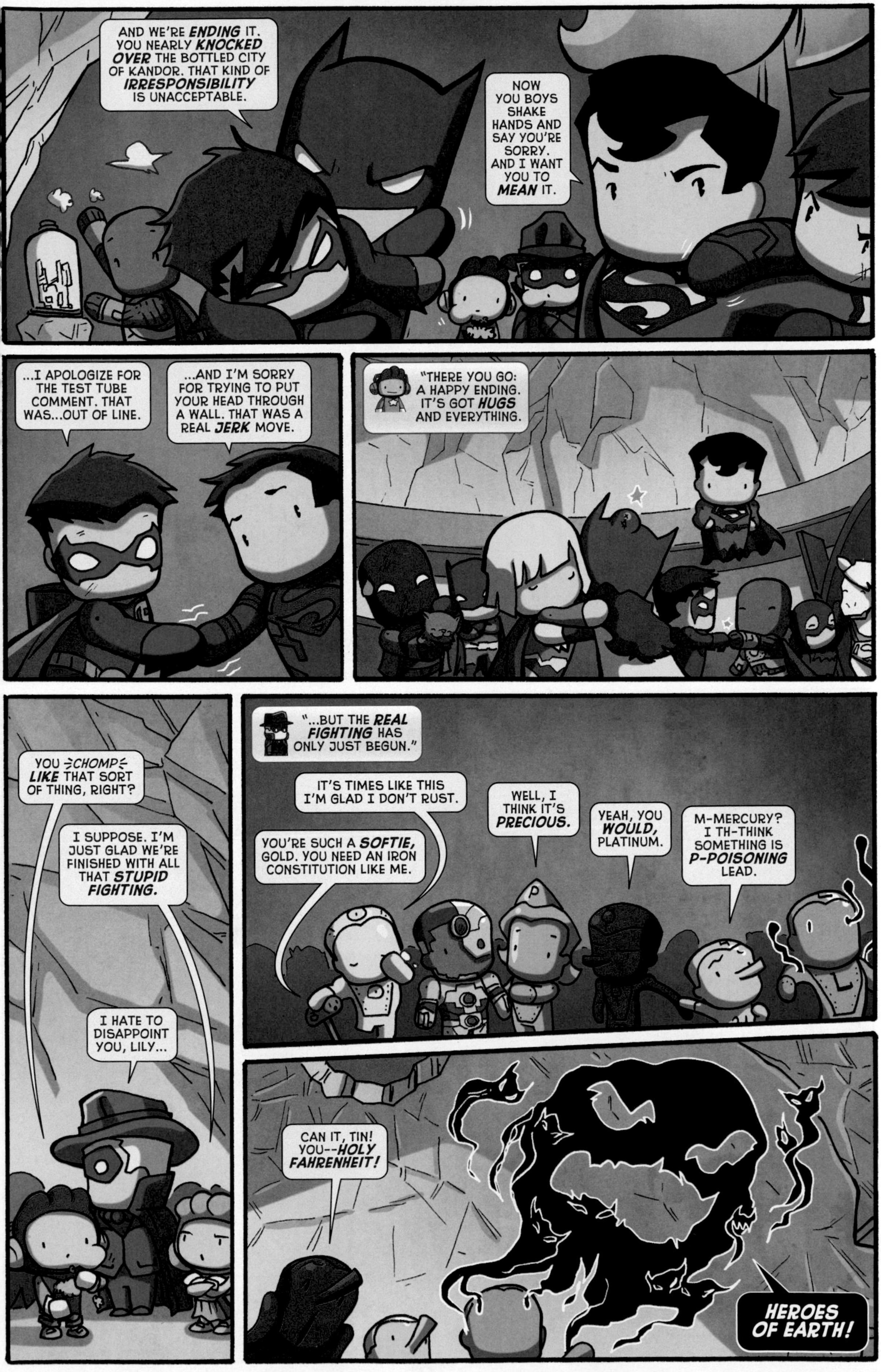
AND WE'RE ENDING IT. YOU NEARLY KNOCKED OVER THE BOTTLED CITY OF KANDOR. THAT KIND OF IRRESPONSIBILITY IS UNACCEPTABLE.
NOW YOU BOYS SHAKE HANDS AND SAY YOU'RE SORRY. AND I WANT YOU TO MEAN IT.
...I APOLOGIZE FOR THE TEST TUBE COMMENT. THAT WAS...OUT OF LINE.
...AND I'M SORRY FOR TRYING TO PUT YOUR HEAD THROUGH A WALL. THAT WAS A REAL JERK MOVE.
"THERE YOU GO: A HAPPY ENDING. IT'S GOT HUGS AND EVERYTHING.
YOU ≥CHOMP≤ LIKE THAT SORT OF THING, RIGHT?
I SUPPOSE. I'M JUST GLAD WE'RE FINISHED WITH ALL THAT STUPID FIGHTING.
I HATE TO DISAPPOINT YOU, LILY...
"...BUT THE REAL FIGHTING HAS ONLY JUST BEGUN."
IT'S TIMES LIKE THIS I'M GLAD I DON'T RUST.
YOU'RE SUCH A SOFTIE, GOLD. YOU NEED AN IRON CONSTITUTION LIKE ME.
WELL, I THINK IT'S PRECIOUS.
YEAH, YOU WOULD, PLATINUM.
M-MERCURY? I TH-THINK SOMETHING IS P-POISONING LEAD.
CAN IT, TIN! YOU--HOLY FAHRENHEIT!
HEROES OF EARTH!

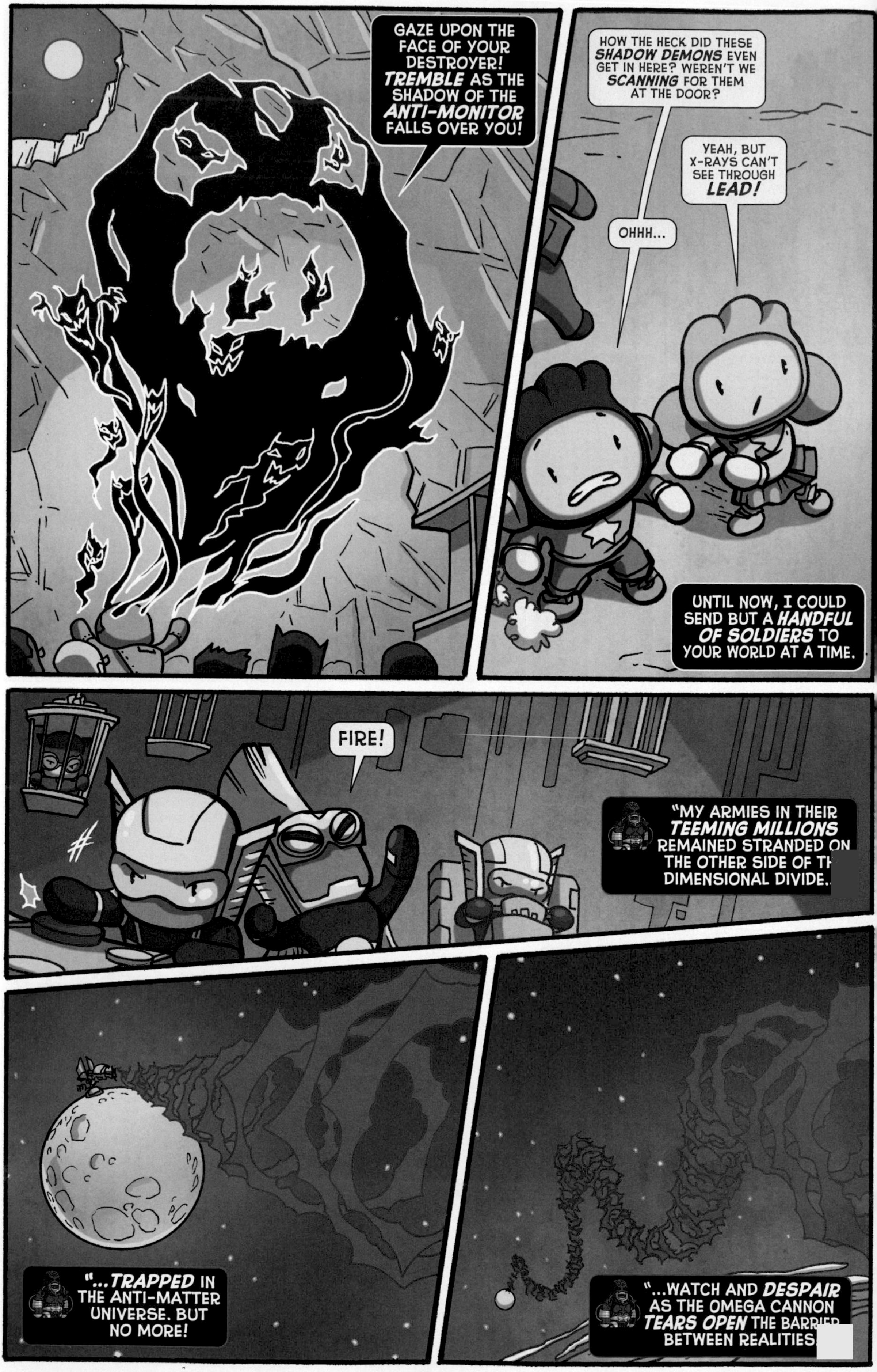
GAZE UPON THE FACE OF YOUR DESTROYER! *TREMBLE* AS THE SHADOW OF THE *ANTI-MONITOR* FALLS OVER YOU!
HOW THE HECK DID THESE *SHADOW DEMONS* EVEN GET IN HERE? WEREN'T WE *SCANNING* FOR THEM AT THE DOOR?
YEAH, BUT X-RAYS CAN'T SEE THROUGH *LEAD!*
OHHH...
UNTIL NOW, I COULD SEND BUT A *HANDFUL OF SOLDIERS* TO YOUR WORLD AT A TIME.
FIRE!
"MY ARMIES IN THEIR *TEEMING MILLIONS* REMAINED STRANDED ON THE OTHER SIDE OF TH DIMENSIONAL DIVIDE...
"...*TRAPPED* IN THE ANTI-MATTER UNIVERSE. BUT NO MORE!
"...WATCH AND *DESPAIR* AS THE OMEGA CANNON *TEARS OPEN* THE BARRIE BETWEEN REALITIES

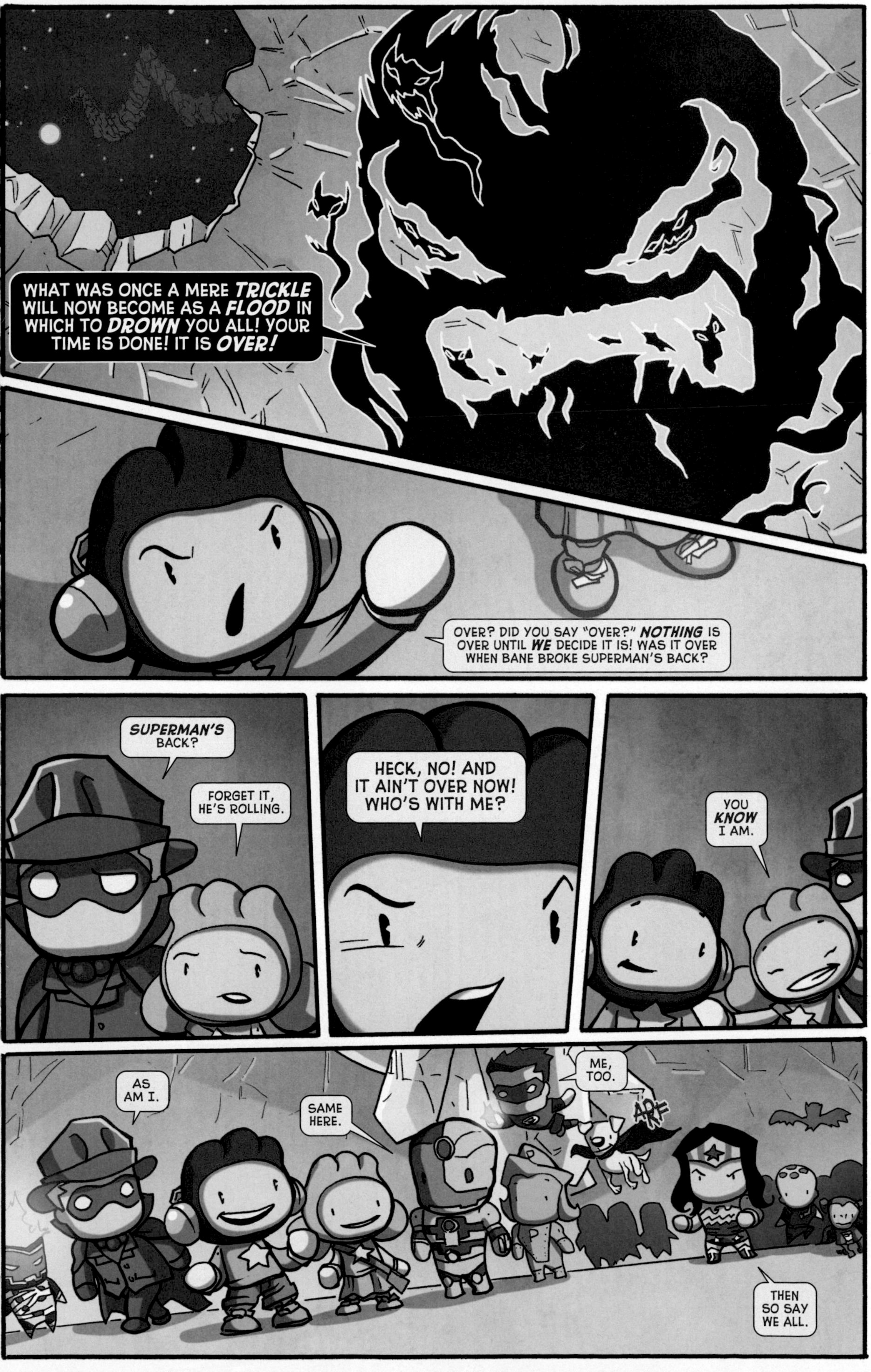
WHAT WAS ONCE A MERE TRICKLE WILL NOW BECOME AS A FLOOD IN WHICH TO DROWN YOU ALL! YOUR TIME IS DONE! IT IS OVER!
OVER? DID YOU SAY "OVER?" NOTHING IS OVER UNTIL WE DECIDE IT IS! WAS IT OVER WHEN BANE BROKE SUPERMAN'S BACK?
SUPERMAN'S BACK?
FORGET IT, HE'S ROLLING.
HECK, NO! AND IT AIN'T OVER NOW! WHO'S WITH ME?
YOU KNOW I AM.
AS AM I.
SAME HERE.
ME, TOO.
ARF
THEN SO SAY WE ALL.

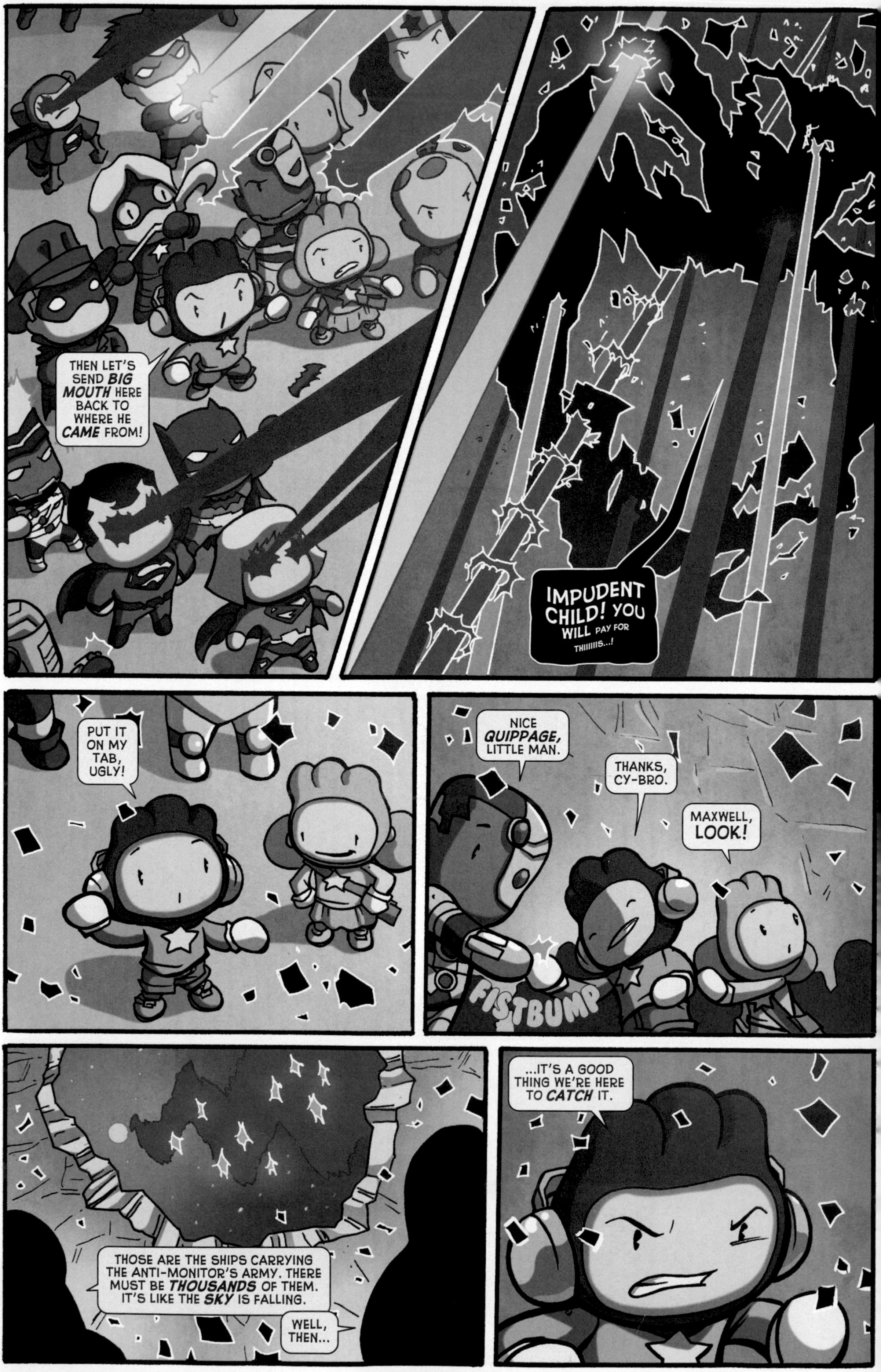
THEN LET'S SEND BIG MOUTH HERE BACK TO WHERE HE CAME FROM!
IMPUDENT CHILD! YOU WILL PAY FOR THIIIIIS...!
PUT IT ON MY TAB, UGLY!
NICE QUIPPAGE, LITTLE MAN.
THANKS, CY-BRO.
MAXWELL, LOOK!
FISTBUMP
THOSE ARE THE SHIPS CARRYING THE ANTI-MONITOR'S ARMY. THERE MUST BE THOUSANDS OF THEM. IT'S LIKE THE SKY IS FALLING.
WELL, THEN...
...IT'S A GOOD THING WE'RE HERE TO CATCH IT.

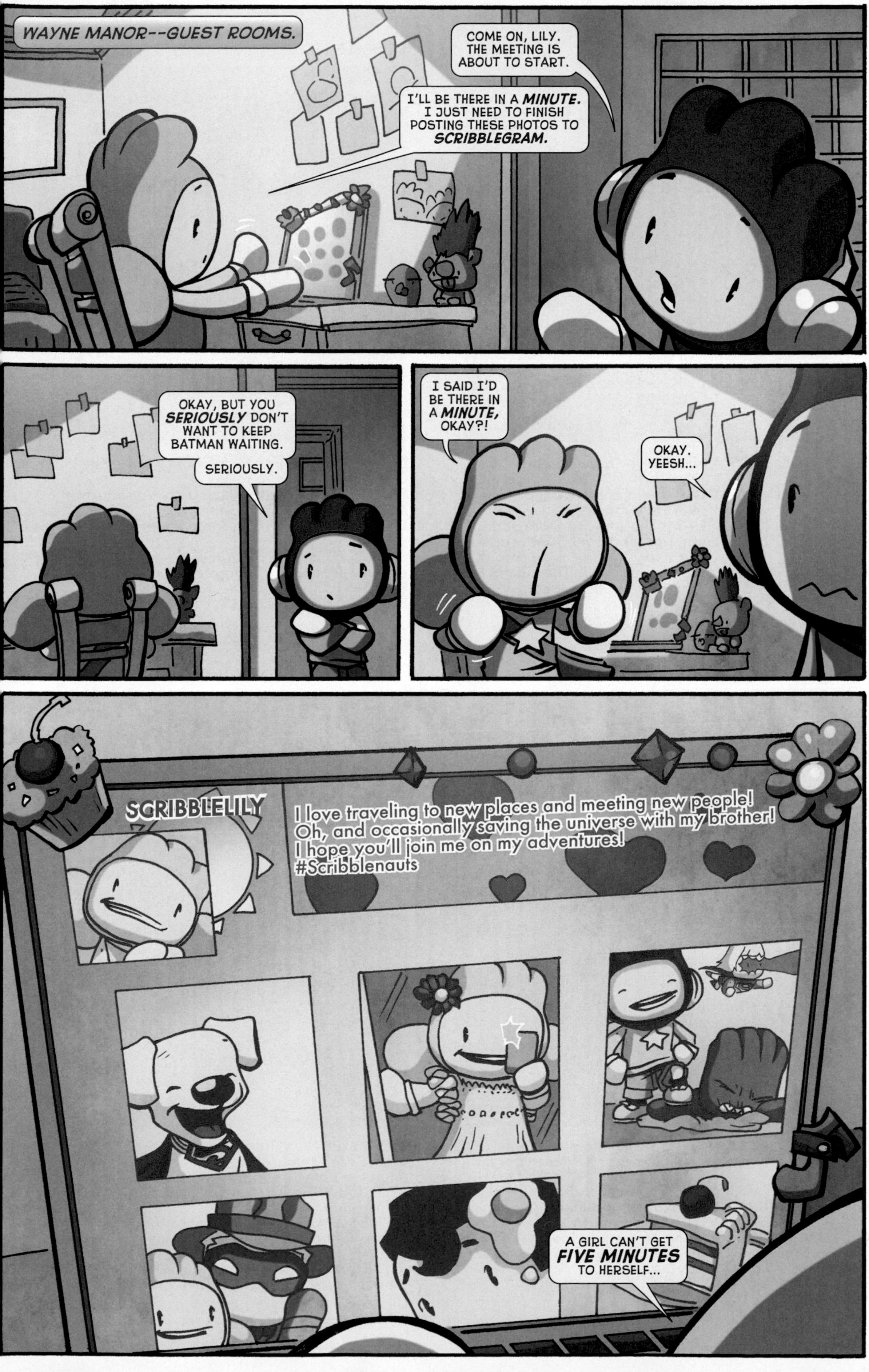

WAYNE MANOR--GUEST ROOMS.
COME ON, LILY. THE MEETING IS ABOUT TO START.
I'LL BE THERE IN A MINUTE. I JUST NEED TO FINISH POSTING THESE PHOTOS TO SCRIBBLEGRAM.
OKAY, BUT YOU SERIOUSLY DON'T WANT TO KEEP BATMAN WAITING.
SERIOUSLY.
I SAID I'D BE THERE IN A MINUTE, OKAY?!
OKAY. YEESH...
SCRIBBLELILY
I love traveling to new places and meeting new people!
Oh, and occasionally saving the universe with my brother!
I hope you'll join me on my adventures!
#Scribblenauts
A GIRL CAN'T GET FIVE MINUTES TO HERSELF...

SCRIBBLELILY 6days

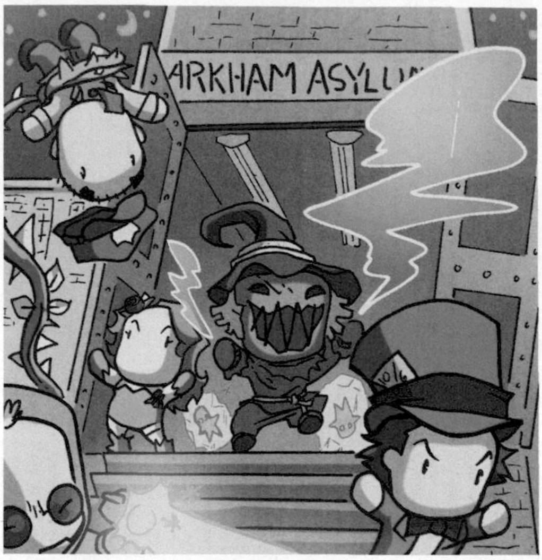

SCRIBBLELILY: World War i -- here's where it all began.
SCRIBBLEMAXWELL: A jailbreak at Arkham Asylum. Like we've never seen THAT before.
BATMANOFGOTHAM: The Anti-Monitor needed allies for his invasion, and Arkham has never had the best security.
SCRIBBLEMAXWELL: I know, right? They might as well install a revolving door on the place.

SCRIBBLELILY 6days

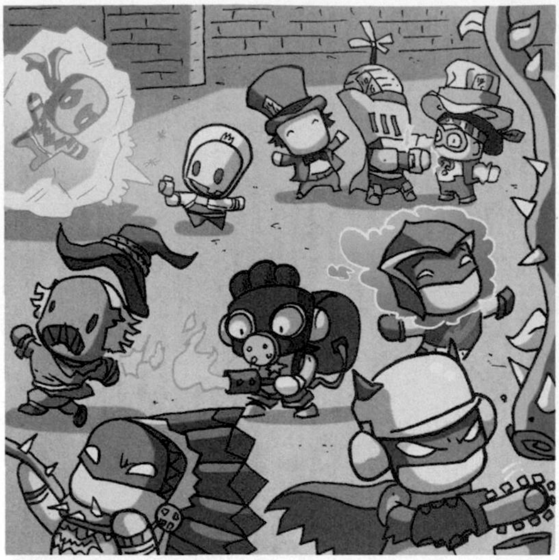

BATMANOFGOTHAM: Without Batman Inc., Gotham would have fallen.
SCRIBBLEMAXWELL: Me and my flamethrower totally had it covered, Bats.
BATMANOFGOTHAM: I told you never to call me that.
SCRIBBLELILY: Switching topics -- what does everyone think of Poison Ivy's new outfit?
BATMANOFGOTHAM: ...
SCRIBBLEMAXWELL: ...

SCRIBBLELILY 5days

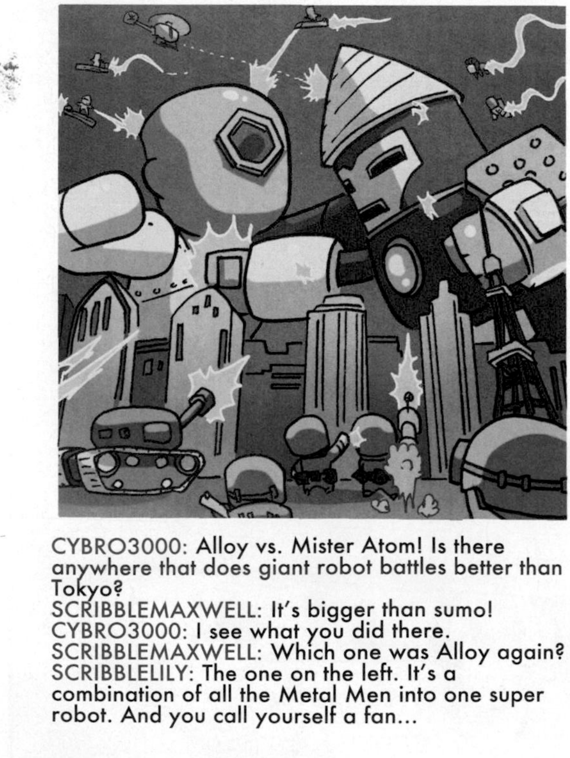

CYBRO3000: Alloy vs. Mister Atom! Is there anywhere that does giant robot battles better than Tokyo?
SCRIBBLEMAXWELL: It's bigger than sumo!
CYBRO3000: I see what you did there.
SCRIBBLEMAXWELL: Which one was Alloy again?
SCRIBBLELILY: The one on the left. It's a combination of all the Metal Men into one super robot. And you call yourself a fan...

SCRIBBLELILY 5days

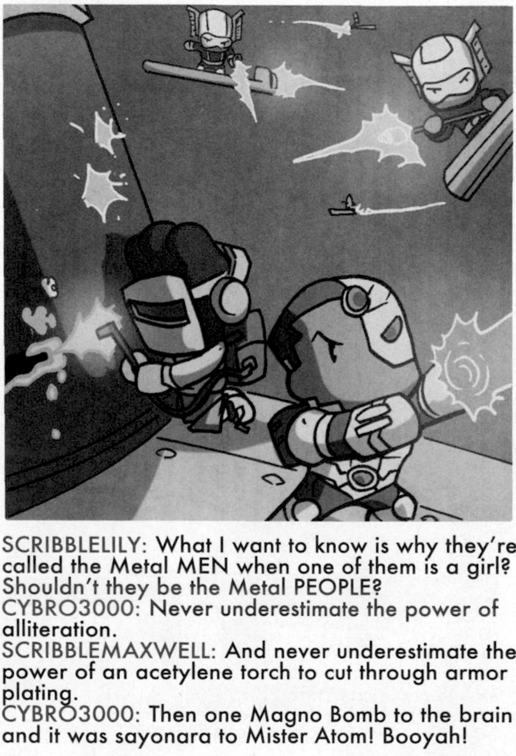

SCRIBBLELILY: What I want to know is why they're called the Metal MEN when one of them is a girl? Shouldn't they be the Metal PEOPLE?
CYBRO3000: Never underestimate the power of alliteration.
SCRIBBLEMAXWELL: And never underestimate the power of an acetylene torch to cut through armor plating.
CYBRO3000: Then one Magno Bomb to the brain and it was sayonara to Mister Atom! Booyah!

SCRIBBLELILY 4days

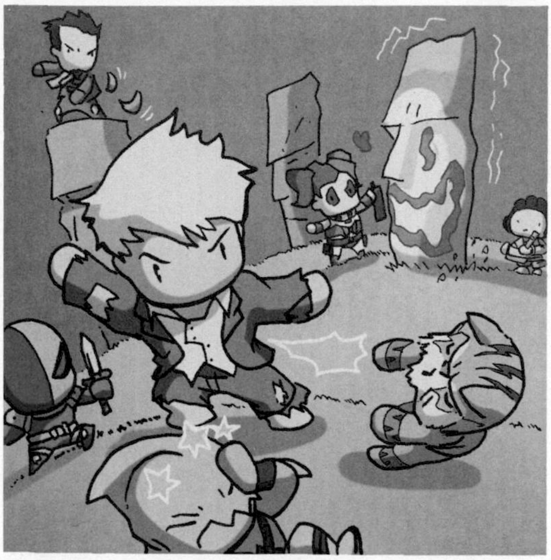

SCRIBBLELILY: Easter Island! This was my totes fave place to visit!
SCRIBBLEMAXWELL: It was okay, I guess.
SCRIBBLELILY: <Sticks out tongue at Maxwell.>
SCRIBBLEMAXWELL: <Ignores Lily.> But of all the places to invade, why here?
RUNNINGMAN: I'm no expert, but I believe it's because Easter Island sits on a major intersection of ley lines.
SCRIBBLELILY: What's a ley line, Mr. Flash?
RUNNINGMAN: They're lines of mystic power that crisscross the planet. Control them, and you control magic itself.

SCRIBBLELILY 4days

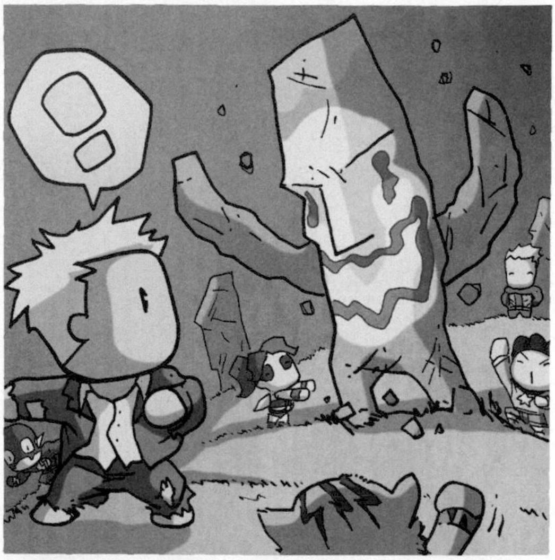

SCRIBBLEMAXWELL: Solomon Grundy absolutely WRECKED all those Task Force X guys.
RUNNINGMAN: There's no shame in that. Grundy is a virtually indestructible zombie that hits harder than Superman.
SCRIBBLEMAXWELL: That's why I have giant stone statues do my fighting for me. Definitely one of my better ideas.
SCRIBBLELILY: It was okay. I guess.

SCRIBBLELILY 3days

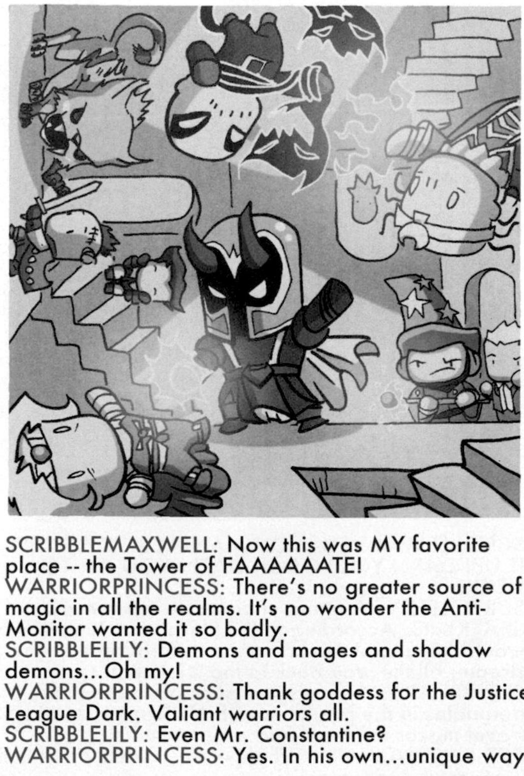

SCRIBBLEMAXWELL: Now this was MY favorite place -- the Tower of FAAAAAATE!
WARRIORPRINCESS: There's no greater source of magic in all the realms. It's no wonder the Anti-Monitor wanted it so badly.
SCRIBBLELILY: Demons and mages and shadow demons...Oh my!
WARRIORPRINCESS: Thank goddess for the Justice League Dark. Valiant warriors all.
SCRIBBLELILY: Even Mr. Constantine?
WARRIORPRINCESS: Yes. In his own...unique way.

SCRIBBLELILY 3days

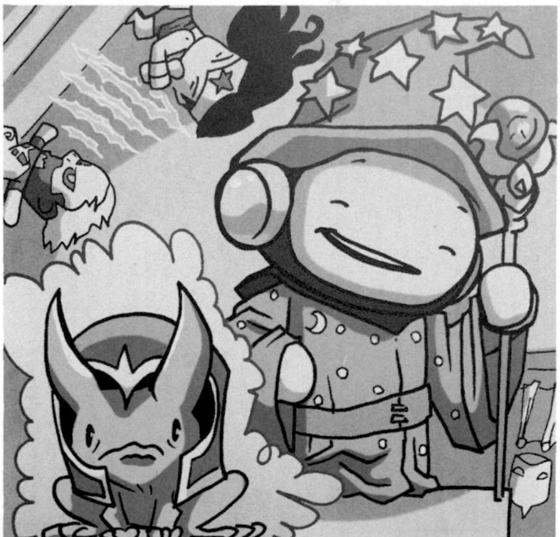

SCRIBBLEMAXWELL: I turned Satanus into a frog. A FROG! That is some CLASSIC wizarding right there.
WARRIORPRINCESS: A blow well struck, Maxwell. But remember the lesson of Icarus -- PRIDE goes ever before the fall.
SCRIBBLEMAXWELL: No worries, Double W. There's NOBODY more humble than THIS guy!
SCRIBBLELILY: <Rolls eyes.>

SCRIBBLELILY 143years

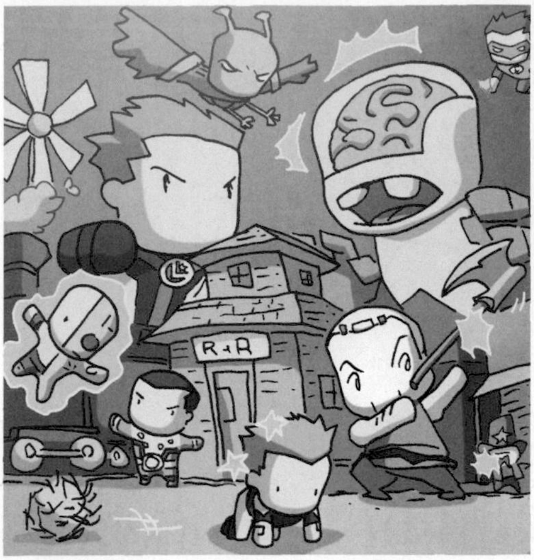

RINGSLINGER: I may have failed History, but even I know that the Fatal Five don't belong in the Old West.
SCRIBBLELILY: I'm just glad that the Legion of Superheroes came all the way back from the future to help us. They're really nice!
RINGSLINGER: We're lucky they did. If the bad guys had defeated us here, then we'd have lost the war with the Anti-Monitor before it even started.
SCRIBBLEMAXWELL: So they came from the future to the past to make sure the future never comes to pass?
RINGSLINGER: Something like that. I think. Time travel always makes my head hurt.

SCRIBBLELILY 143years

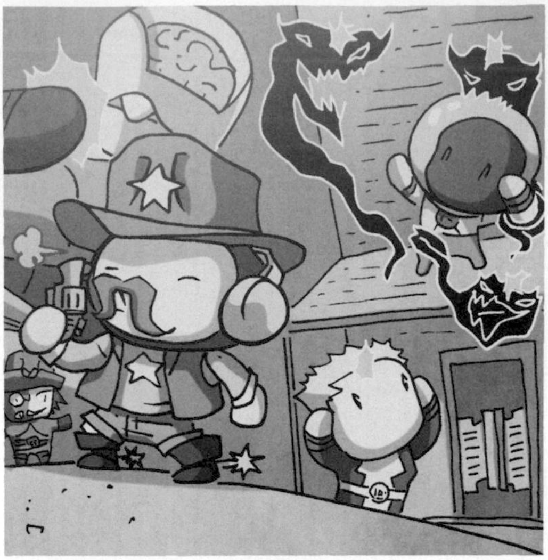

SCRIBBLEMAXWELL: Score another victory for the rootinest, tootinest, sharpshootinest cowboy in the West!
RINGSLINGER: Jonah Hex may have something to say about that.
SCRIBBLEMAXWELL: You're not going to tell him, are you? He's kind of scary...
RINGSLINGER: My lips are sealed.

SCRIBBLELILY +295years

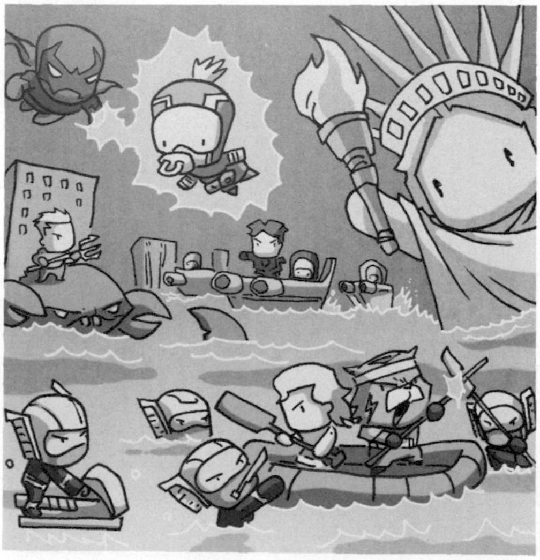

SEA_KING: So this is Earth after the Great Disaster. Actually improves New York quite a bit, IMO.
SCRIBBLELILY: I just can't get over how cute Mr. Booster Gold is as a baby.
SCRIBBLEMAXWELL: And I can't get over Kamandi and Prince Tuftan. Those dudes are HARDCORE! They fought off an entire Weaponer battalion by themselves!
SEA_KING: Indeed. Leaving me free to face Per Degaton with the help of a few mutated sea creatures.

SCRIBBLELILY +295years

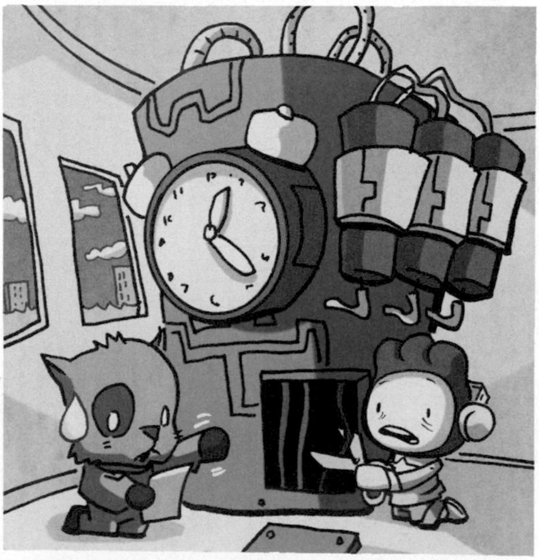

SCRIBBLEMAXWELL: YOU MANIACS! YOU BLEW IT UP! DARN YOU! GOSH DARN YOU ALL TO HECK!
SCRIBBLELILY: You and your movie references.
SEA_KING: According to the Flash, that Time Bomb would have exploded backwards through the time stream, all the way back to the 21st century.
SCRIBBLELILY: A bomb that goes off in the future but detonates in the past? I'm with Mr. Lantern -- time travel makes my head hurt.
SCRIBBLEMAXWELL: Whatevs. Dr. Canus and I had it covered. No sweat.

SCRIBBLELILY 2days

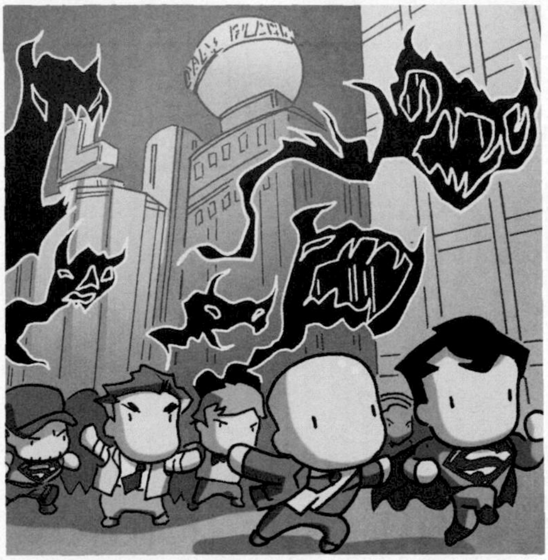

SCRIBBLELILY: I <3 Metropolis! Well, except for all the people that were trying to kill us.
MANOFSTEEL: It's not their fault. By the time the Weaponers invaded, shadow demons had already possessed over 90 percent of the city's population.
SCRIBBLEMAXWELL: Why were you running away? It's not like they could hurt you.
MANOFSTEEL: But in attacking me, they might end up hurting themselves. I couldn't let that happen.
SCRIBBLELILY: And that's why you needed that lying jerkface, Lex Luthor. So he could help you cure them all.
MANOFSTEEL: That's right. For once, he was actually using his genius for good.

SCRIBBLELILY 2days

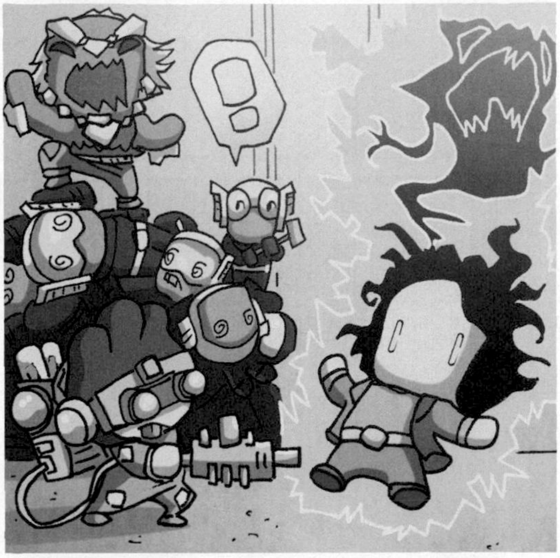

SCRIBBLEMAXWELL: I AIN'T AFRAID OF NO SHADOW DEMONS!
SCRIBBLELILY: Why worry? You were only wearing an unlicensed nuclear accelerator on your back.
SCRIBBLEMAXWELL: It got the job done. Baldy McNohair built the tools, and I had the talent!
MANOFSTEEL: After we freed Lois, we equipped her with a device of her own and then did the same for others. We may have helped, but in the end, the people of Metropolis saved themselves.

SCRIBBLELILY 1day

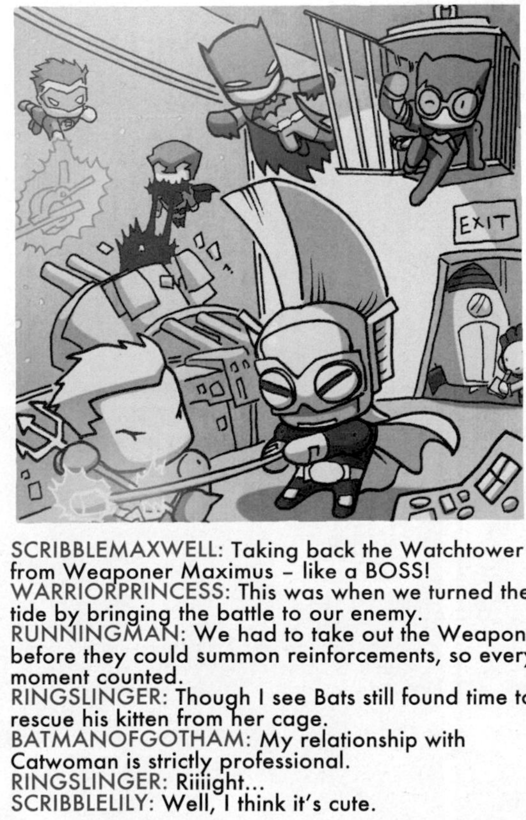
EXIT

SCRIBBLEMAXWELL: Taking back the Watchtower from Weaponer Maximus – like a BOSS!
WARRIORPRINCESS: This was when we turned the tide by bringing the battle to our enemy.
RUNNINGMAN: We had to take out the Weaponers before they could summon reinforcements, so every moment counted.
RINGSLINGER: Though I see Bats still found time to rescue his kitten from her cage.
BATMANOFGOTHAM: My relationship with Catwoman is strictly professional.
RINGSLINGER: Riiiight...
SCRIBBLELILY: Well, I think it's cute.

SCRIBBLELILY 1day

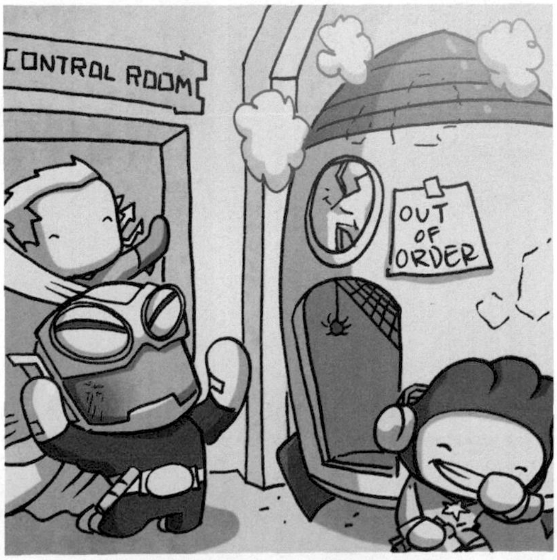
CONTROL ROOM
OUT OF ORDER

SEA_KING: I finally got my rematch with Weaponer Maximus, but the coward tried to run away. AGAIN!
MANOFSTEEL: All bullies turn tail once they finally pick on someone willing to fight back. Weaponer Maximus is no different.
SCRIBBLELILY: So how did you take out the escape pod, Maxwell?
SCRIBBLEMAXWELL: I just assigned it the adjective "busted" and *POOF* it wasn't going anywhere!
SEA_KING: The look on his face was truly a thing of beauty.

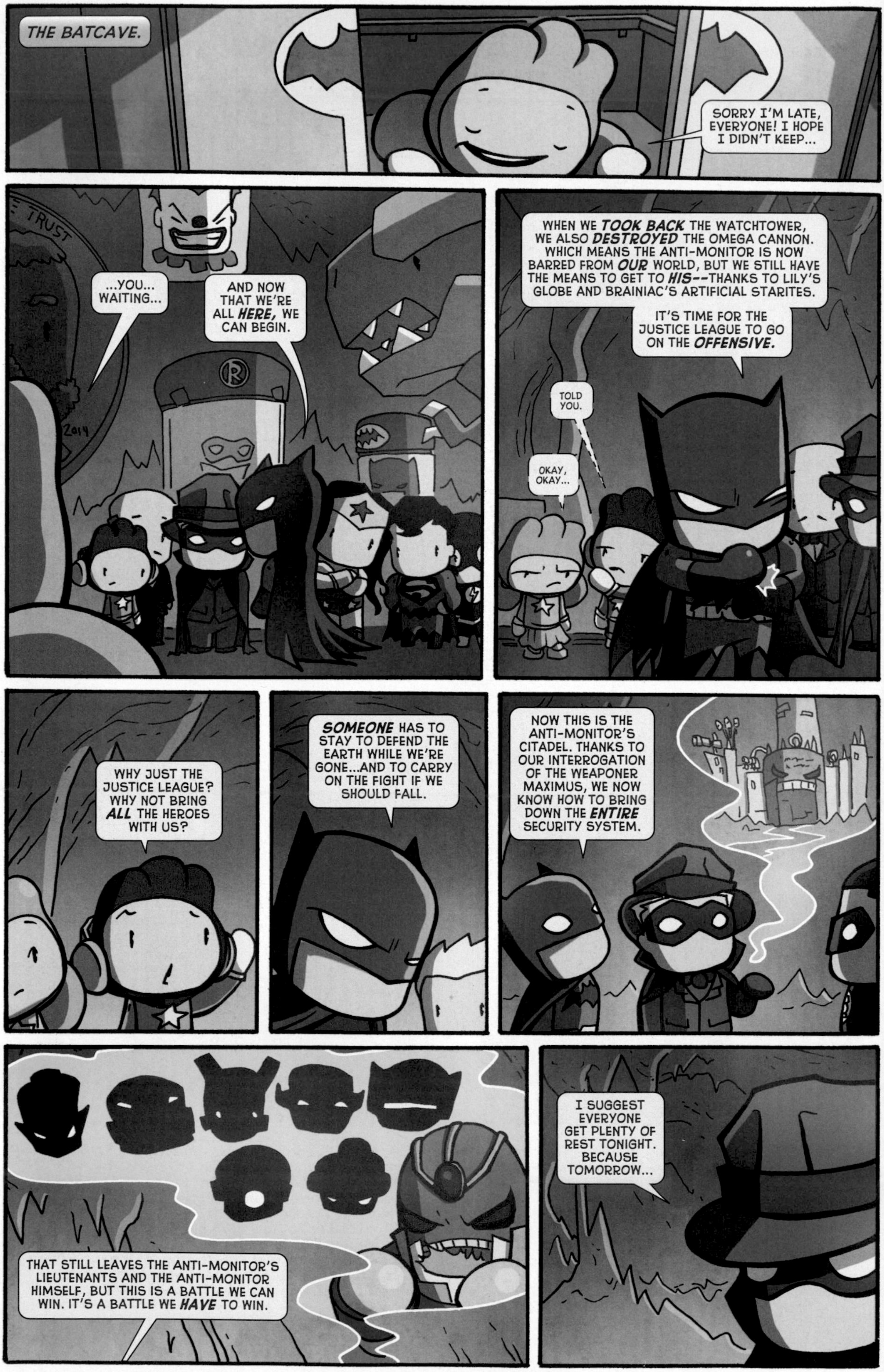
THE BATCAVE.
SORRY I'M LATE, EVERYONE! I HOPE I DIDN'T KEEP...
...YOU... WAITING...
AND NOW THAT WE'RE ALL HERE, WE CAN BEGIN.
WHEN WE TOOK BACK THE WATCHTOWER, WE ALSO DESTROYED THE OMEGA CANNON. WHICH MEANS THE ANTI-MONITOR IS NOW BARRED FROM OUR WORLD, BUT WE STILL HAVE THE MEANS TO GET TO HIS--THANKS TO LILY'S GLOBE AND BRAINIAC'S ARTIFICIAL STARITES.
IT'S TIME FOR THE JUSTICE LEAGUE TO GO ON THE OFFENSIVE.
TOLD YOU.
OKAY, OKAY...
WHY JUST THE JUSTICE LEAGUE? WHY NOT BRING ALL THE HEROES WITH US?
SOMEONE HAS TO STAY TO DEFEND THE EARTH WHILE WE'RE GONE...AND TO CARRY ON THE FIGHT IF WE SHOULD FALL.
NOW THIS IS THE ANTI-MONITOR'S CITADEL. THANKS TO OUR INTERROGATION OF THE WEAPONER MAXIMUS, WE NOW KNOW HOW TO BRING DOWN THE ENTIRE SECURITY SYSTEM.
THAT STILL LEAVES THE ANTI-MONITOR'S LIEUTENANTS AND THE ANTI-MONITOR HIMSELF, BUT THIS IS A BATTLE WE CAN WIN. IT'S A BATTLE WE HAVE TO WIN.
I SUGGEST EVERYONE GET PLENTY OF REST TONIGHT. BECAUSE TOMORROW...

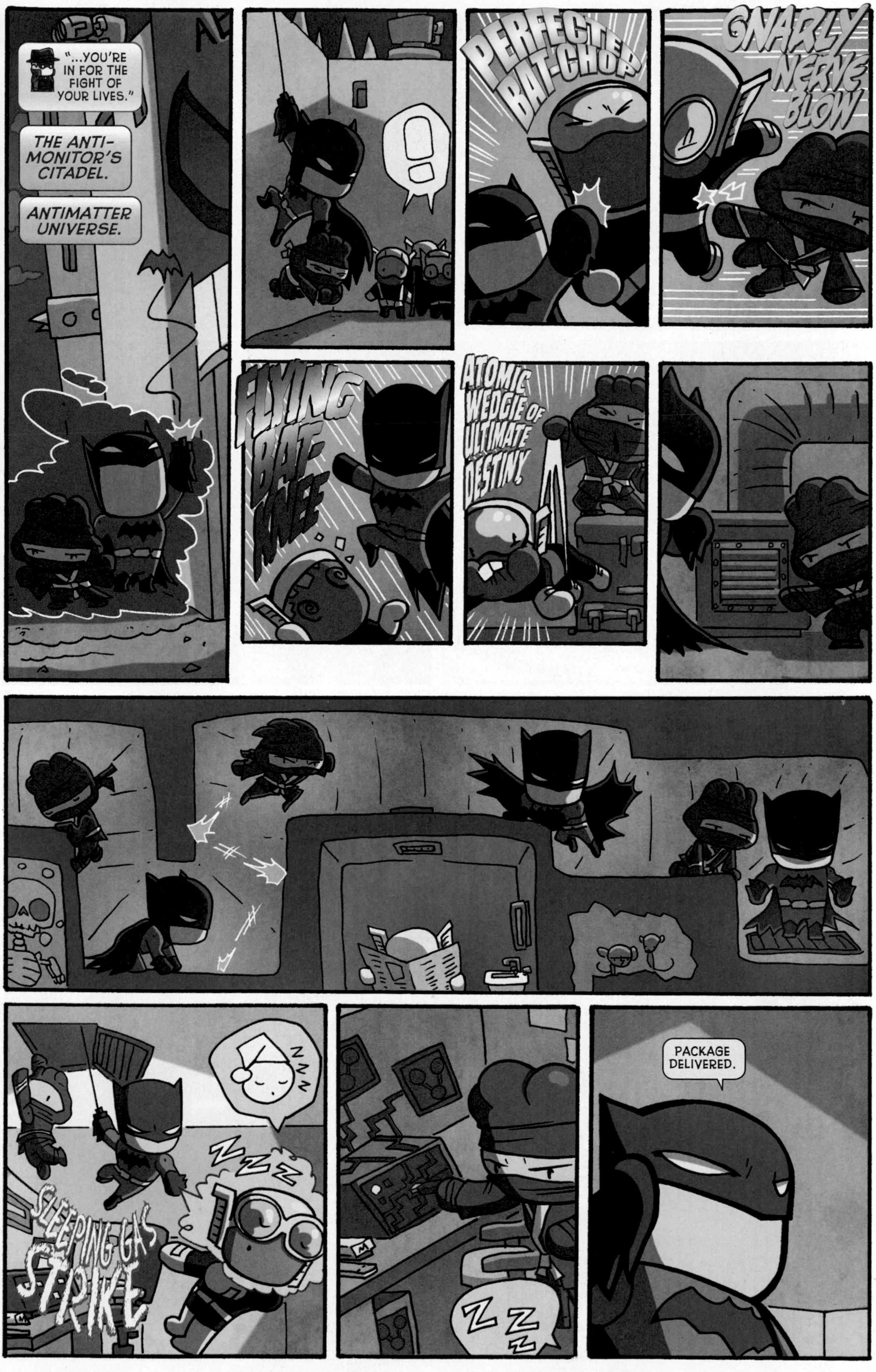
"...YOU'RE IN FOR THE FIGHT OF YOUR LIVES."
THE ANTI-MONITOR'S CITADEL.
ANTIMATTER UNIVERSE.
!
PERFECTED BAT-CHOP
GNARLY NERVE BLOW
FLYING BAT-KNEE
ATOMIC WEDGIE OF ULTIMATE DESTINY!
SLEEPING GAS STRIKE
ZZZ
PACKAGE DELIVERED.

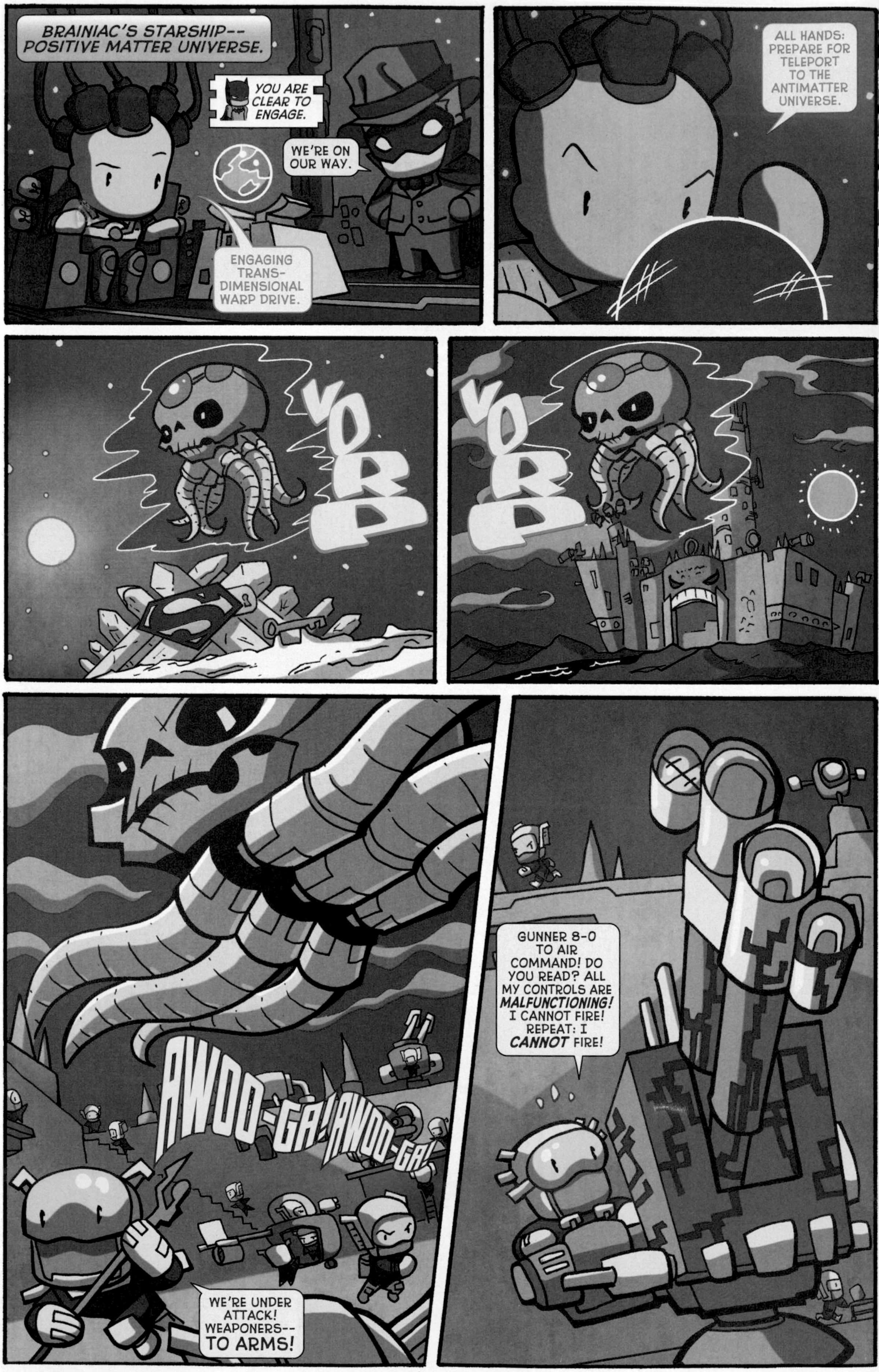
BRAINIAC'S STARSHIP--
POSITIVE MATTER UNIVERSE.
YOU ARE CLEAR TO ENGAGE.
WE'RE ON OUR WAY.
ENGAGING TRANS-DIMENSIONAL WARP DRIVE.
ALL HANDS: PREPARE FOR TELEPORT TO THE ANTIMATTER UNIVERSE.
VORP
VORP
AWOO-GA! AWOO-GA!
WE'RE UNDER ATTACK! WEAPONERS-- TO ARMS!
GUNNER 8-0 TO AIR COMMAND! DO YOU READ? ALL MY CONTROLS ARE MALFUNCTIONING! I CANNOT FIRE! REPEAT: I CANNOT FIRE!

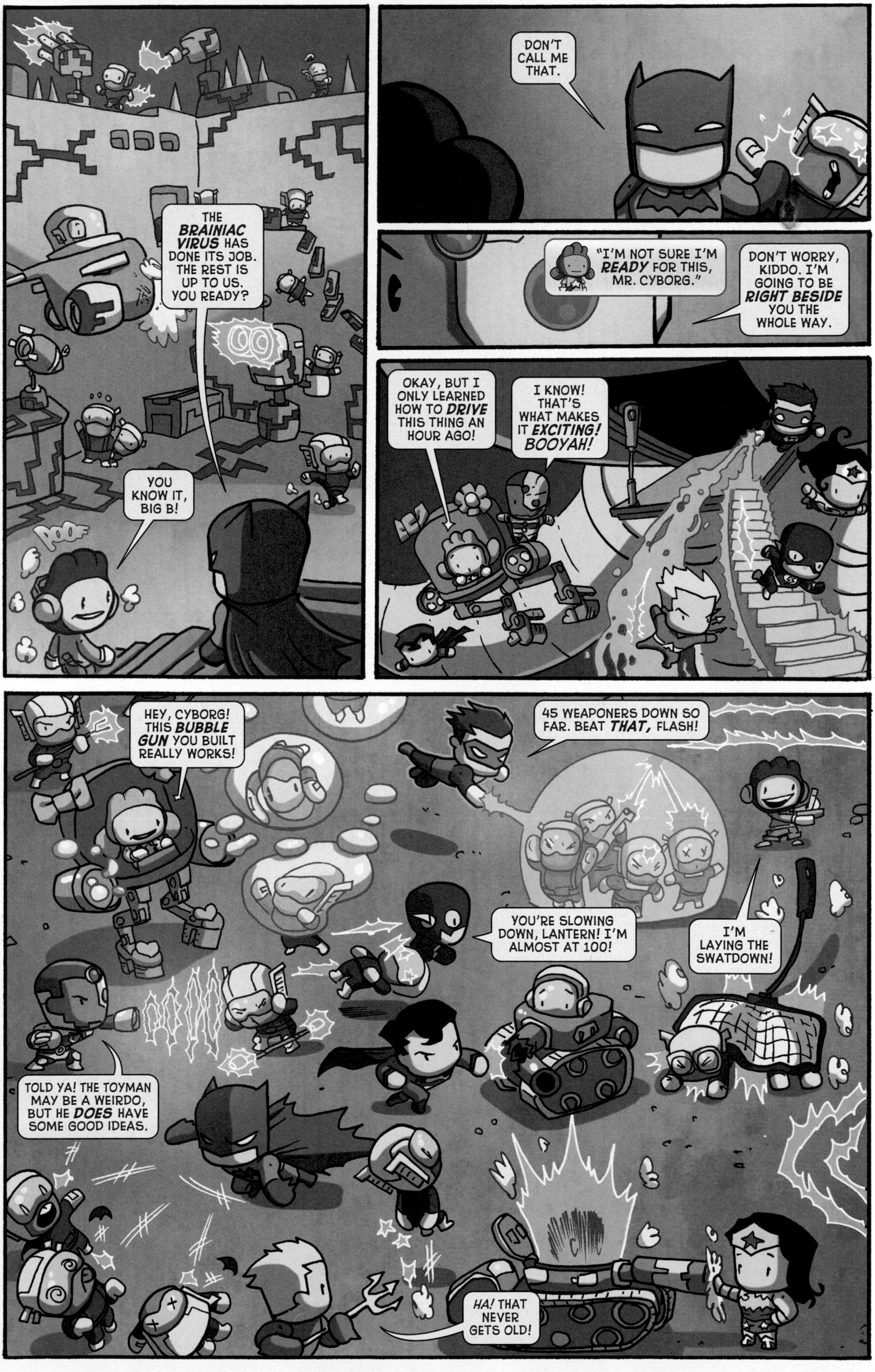
THE BRAINIAC VIRUS HAS DONE ITS JOB. THE REST IS UP TO US. YOU READY?
YOU KNOW IT, BIG B!
POOF
DON'T CALL ME THAT.
"I'M NOT SURE I'M READY FOR THIS, MR. CYBORG."
DON'T WORRY, KIDDO. I'M GOING TO BE RIGHT BESIDE YOU THE WHOLE WAY.
OKAY, BUT I ONLY LEARNED HOW TO DRIVE THIS THING AN HOUR AGO!
I KNOW! THAT'S WHAT MAKES IT EXCITING! BOOYAH!
HEY, CYBORG! THIS BUBBLE GUN YOU BUILT REALLY WORKS!
45 WEAPONERS DOWN SO FAR. BEAT THAT, FLASH!
YOU'RE SLOWING DOWN, LANTERN! I'M ALMOST AT 100!
I'M LAYING THE SWATDOWN!
TOLD YA! THE TOYMAN MAY BE A WEIRDO, BUT HE DOES HAVE SOME GOOD IDEAS.
HA! THAT NEVER GETS OLD!

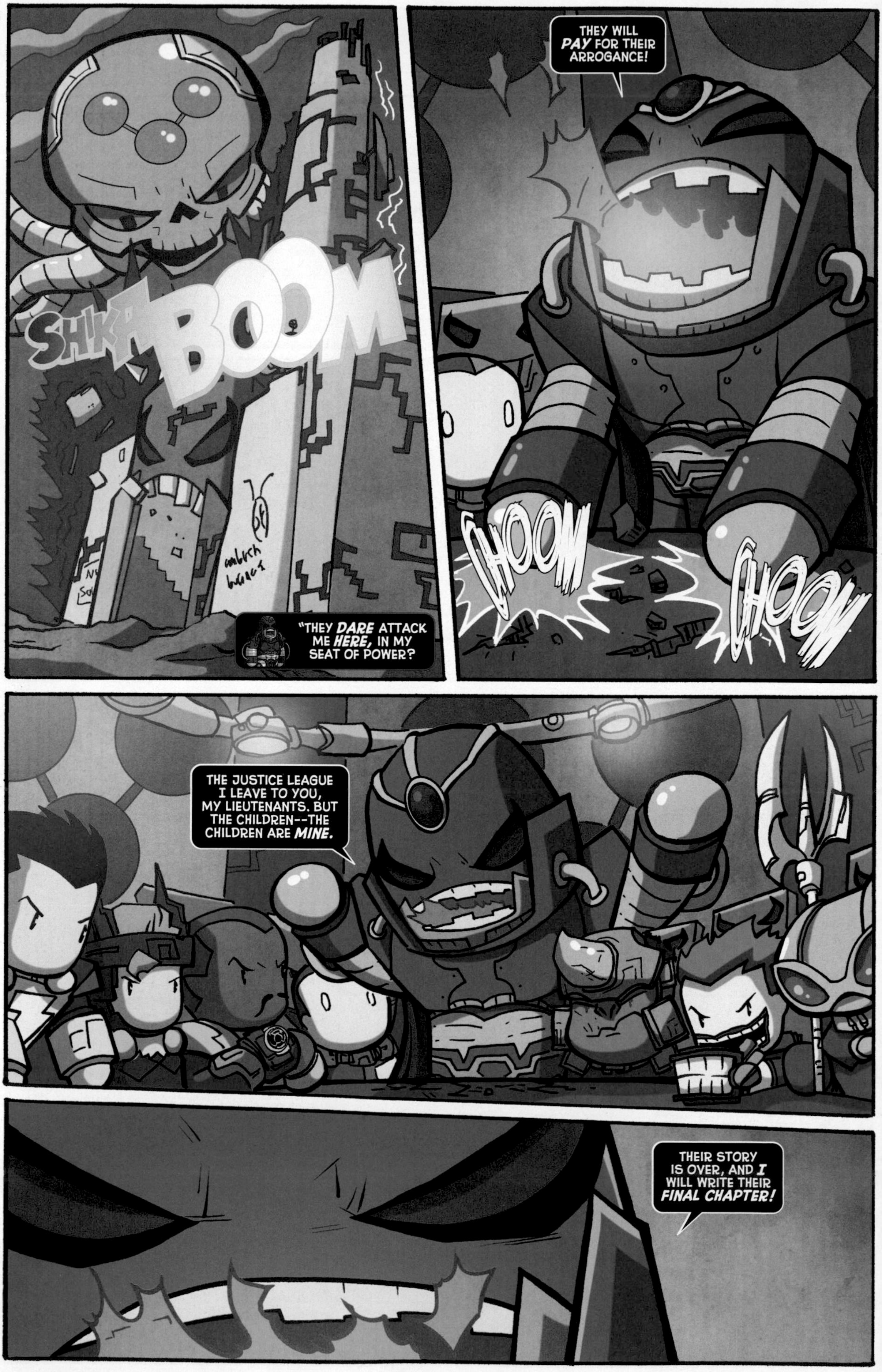
SHIKA BOOM
"THEY DARE ATTACK ME HERE, IN MY SEAT OF POWER?
THEY WILL PAY FOR THEIR ARROGANCE!
CHOOM
CHOOM
THE JUSTICE LEAGUE I LEAVE TO YOU, MY LIEUTENANTS. BUT THE CHILDREN--THE CHILDREN ARE MINE.
THEIR STORY IS OVER, AND I WILL WRITE THEIR FINAL CHAPTER!

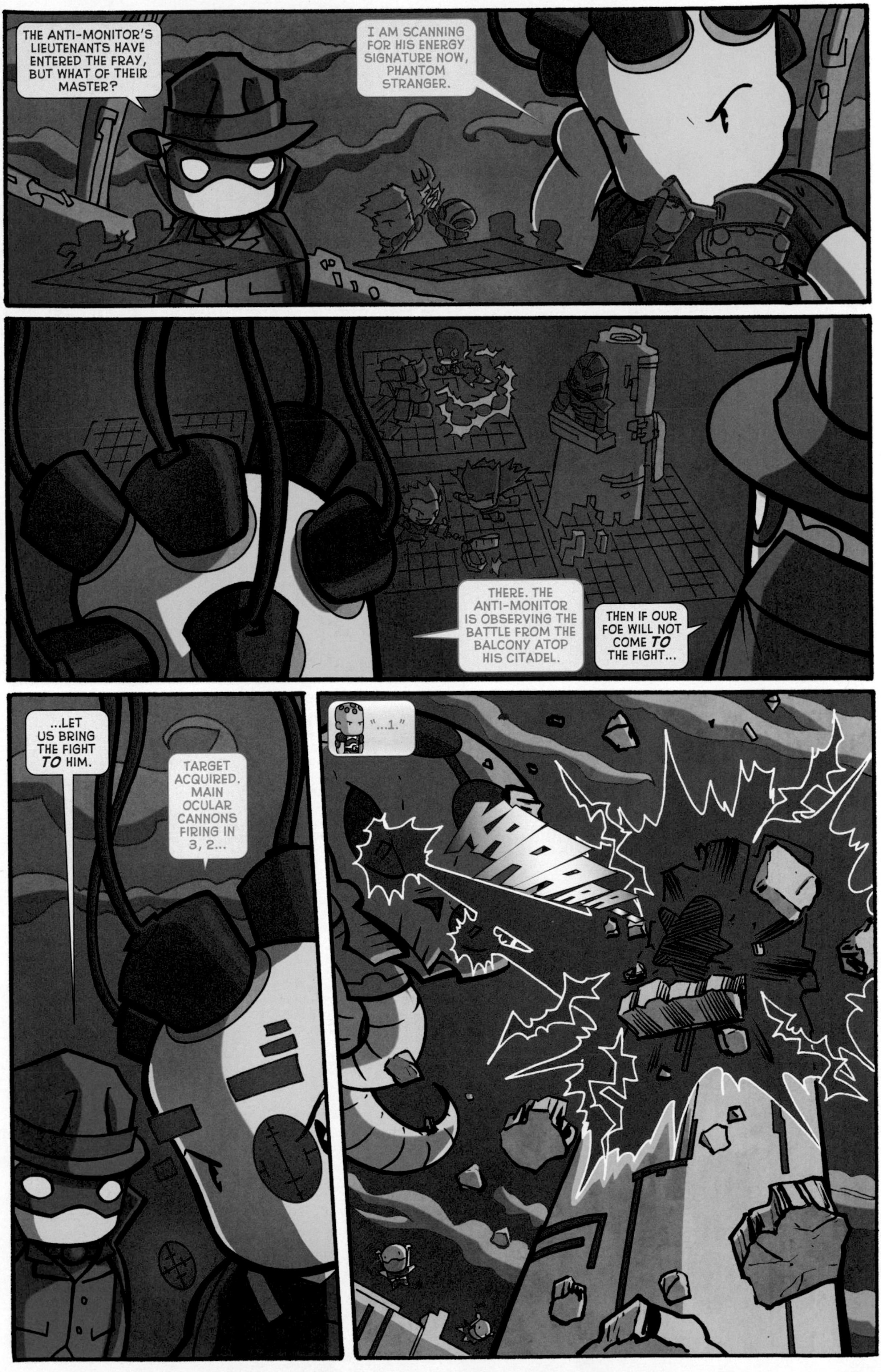
THE ANTI-MONITOR'S LIEUTENANTS HAVE ENTERED THE FRAY, BUT WHAT OF THEIR MASTER?
I AM SCANNING FOR HIS ENERGY SIGNATURE NOW, PHANTOM STRANGER.
THERE. THE ANTI-MONITOR IS OBSERVING THE BATTLE FROM THE BALCONY ATOP HIS CITADEL.
THEN IF OUR FOE WILL NOT COME TO THE FIGHT...
...LET US BRING THE FIGHT TO HIM.
TARGET ACQUIRED. MAIN OCULAR CANNONS FIRING IN 3, 2...
"...1."
KRAKAKA

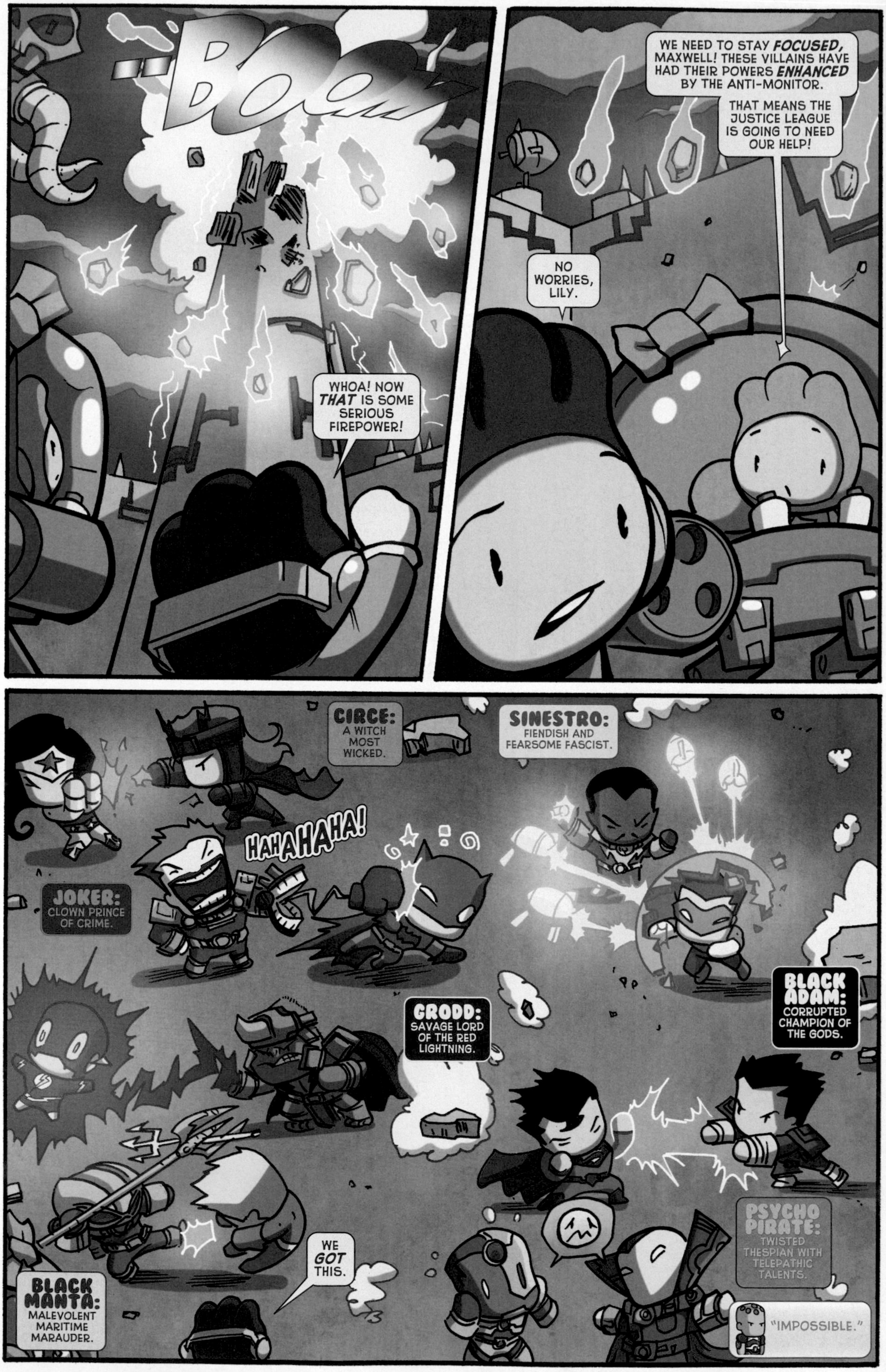
BOOM!
WHOA! NOW THAT IS SOME SERIOUS FIREPOWER!
WE NEED TO STAY FOCUSED, MAXWELL! THESE VILLAINS HAVE HAD THEIR POWERS ENHANCED BY THE ANTI-MONITOR.
THAT MEANS THE JUSTICE LEAGUE IS GOING TO NEED OUR HELP!
NO WORRIES, LILY.
CIRCE: A WITCH MOST WICKED.
SINESTRO: FIENDISH AND FEARSOME FASCIST.
HAHAHAHA!
JOKER: CLOWN PRINCE OF CRIME.
BLACK ADAM: CORRUPTED CHAMPION OF THE GODS.
GRODD: SAVAGE LORD OF THE RED LIGHTNING.
PSYCHO PIRATE: TWISTED THESPIAN WITH TELEPATHIC TALENTS.
WE GOT THIS.
BLACK MANTA: MALEVOLENT MARITIME MARAUDER.
"IMPOSSIBLE."

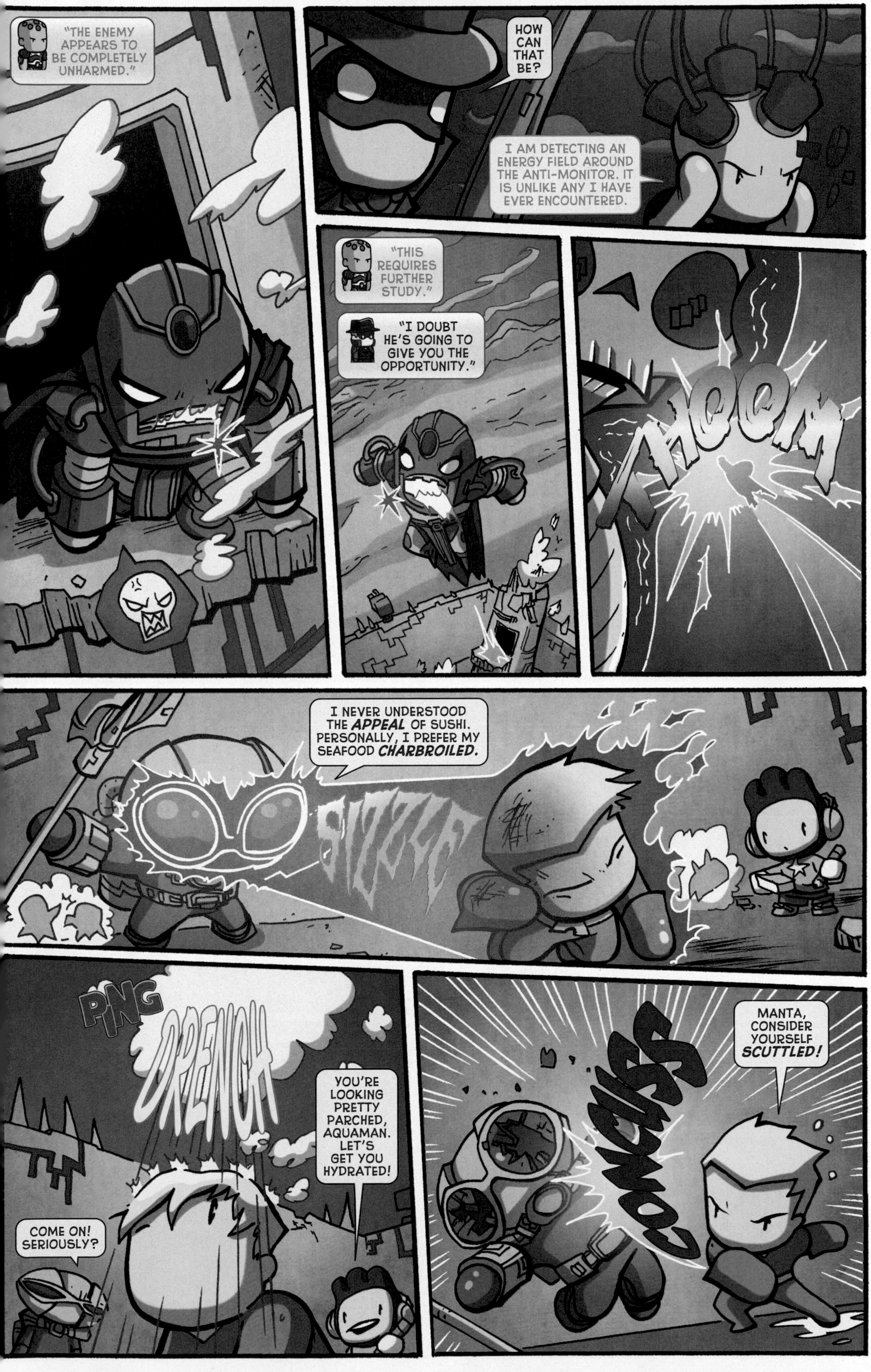
"THE ENEMY APPEARS TO BE COMPLETELY UNHARMED."
HOW CAN THAT BE?
I AM DETECTING AN ENERGY FIELD AROUND THE ANTI-MONITOR. IT IS UNLIKE ANY I HAVE EVER ENCOUNTERED.
"THIS REQUIRES FURTHER STUDY."
"I DOUBT HE'S GOING TO GIVE YOU THE OPPORTUNITY."
HOOM
I NEVER UNDERSTOOD THE APPEAL OF SUSHI. PERSONALLY, I PREFER MY SEAFOOD CHARBROILED.
SIZZLE
PING
DRENCH
YOU'RE LOOKING PRETTY PARCHED, AQUAMAN. LET'S GET YOU HYDRATED!
COME ON! SERIOUSLY?
CONCUSS
MANTA, CONSIDER YOURSELF SCUTTLED!

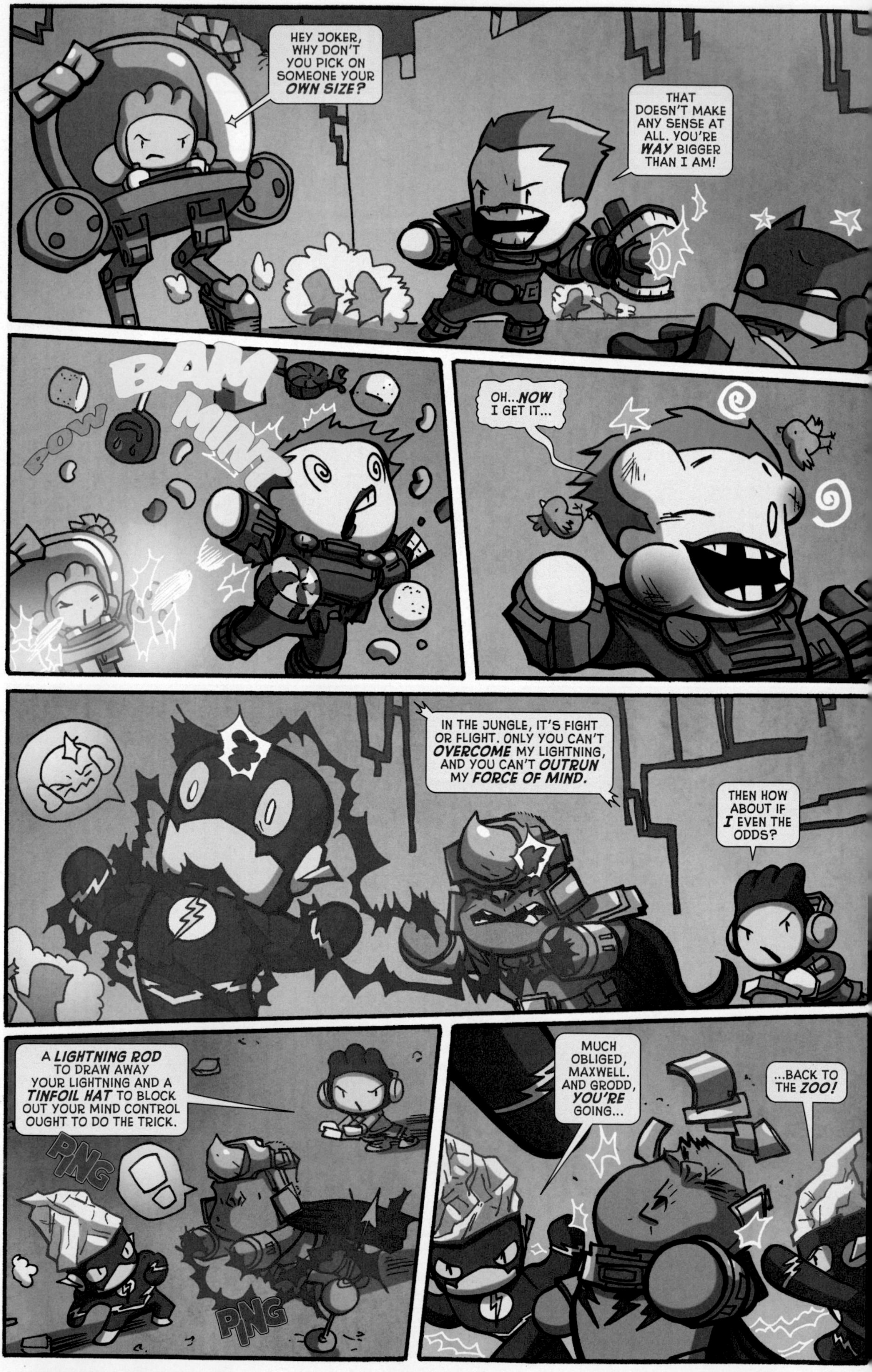
HEY JOKER, WHY DON'T YOU PICK ON SOMEONE YOUR OWN SIZE?
THAT DOESN'T MAKE ANY SENSE AT ALL. YOU'RE WAY BIGGER THAN I AM!
POW
BAM
MINT
OH...NOW I GET IT...
IN THE JUNGLE, IT'S FIGHT OR FLIGHT. ONLY YOU CAN'T OVERCOME MY LIGHTNING, AND YOU CAN'T OUTRUN MY FORCE OF MIND.
THEN HOW ABOUT IF I EVEN THE ODDS?
A LIGHTNING ROD TO DRAW AWAY YOUR LIGHTNING AND A TINFOIL HAT TO BLOCK OUT YOUR MIND CONTROL OUGHT TO DO THE TRICK.
PING
PING
MUCH OBLIGED, MAXWELL. AND GRODD, YOU'RE GOING...
...BACK TO THE ZOO!

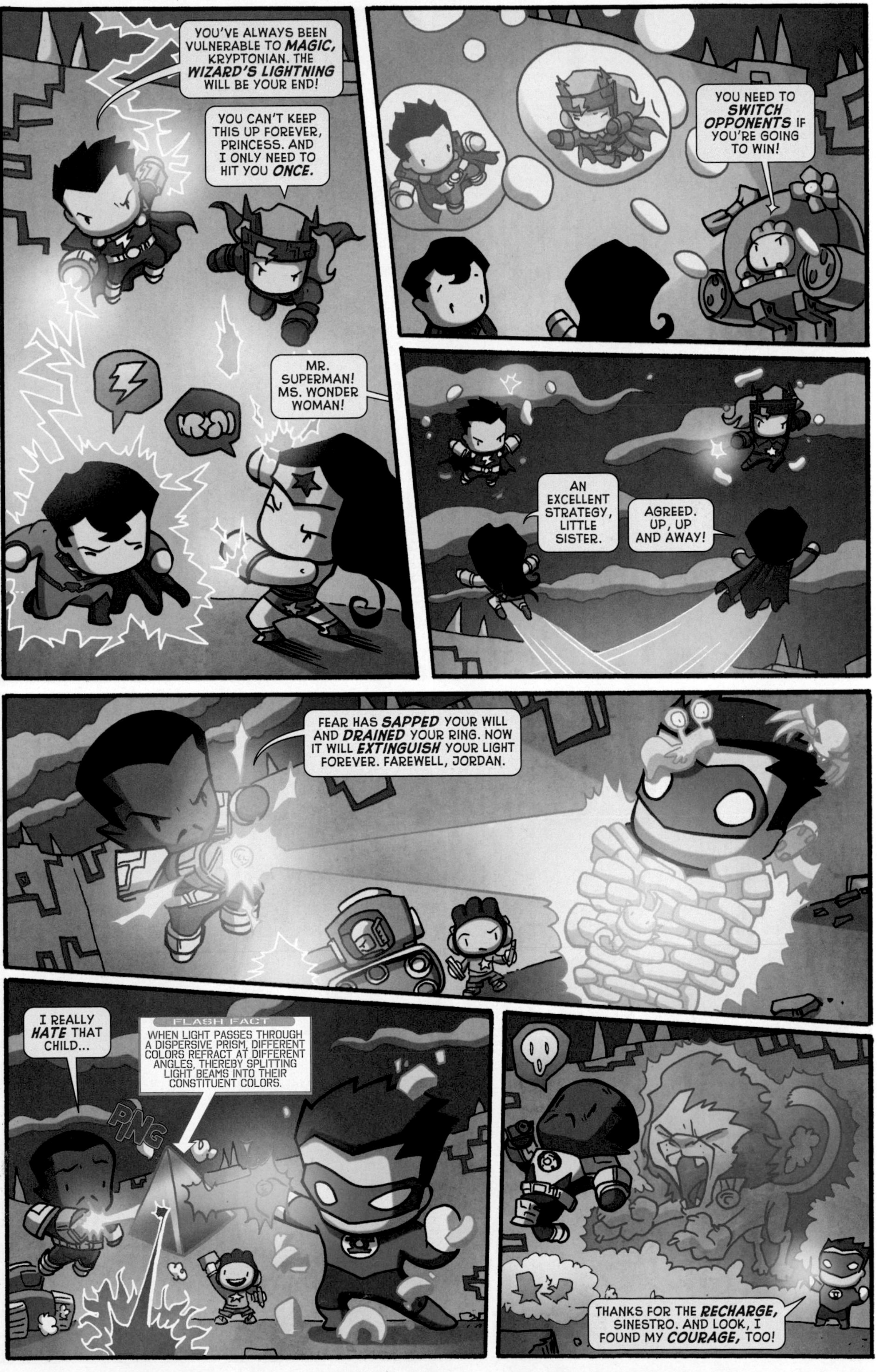

YOU'VE ALWAYS BEEN VULNERABLE TO MAGIC, KRYPTONIAN. THE WIZARD'S LIGHTNING WILL BE YOUR END!
YOU CAN'T KEEP THIS UP FOREVER, PRINCESS. AND I ONLY NEED TO HIT YOU ONCE.
MR. SUPERMAN! MS. WONDER WOMAN!
YOU NEED TO SWITCH OPPONENTS IF YOU'RE GOING TO WIN!
AN EXCELLENT STRATEGY, LITTLE SISTER.
AGREED. UP, UP AND AWAY!
FEAR HAS SAPPED YOUR WILL AND DRAINED YOUR RING. NOW IT WILL EXTINGUISH YOUR LIGHT FOREVER. FAREWELL, JORDAN.
I REALLY HATE THAT CHILD...
FLASH FACT
WHEN LIGHT PASSES THROUGH A DISPERSIVE PRISM, DIFFERENT COLORS REFRACT AT DIFFERENT ANGLES, THEREBY SPLITTING LIGHT BEAMS INTO THEIR CONSTITUENT COLORS.
PING
THANKS FOR THE RECHARGE, SINESTRO. AND LOOK, I FOUND MY COURAGE, TOO!

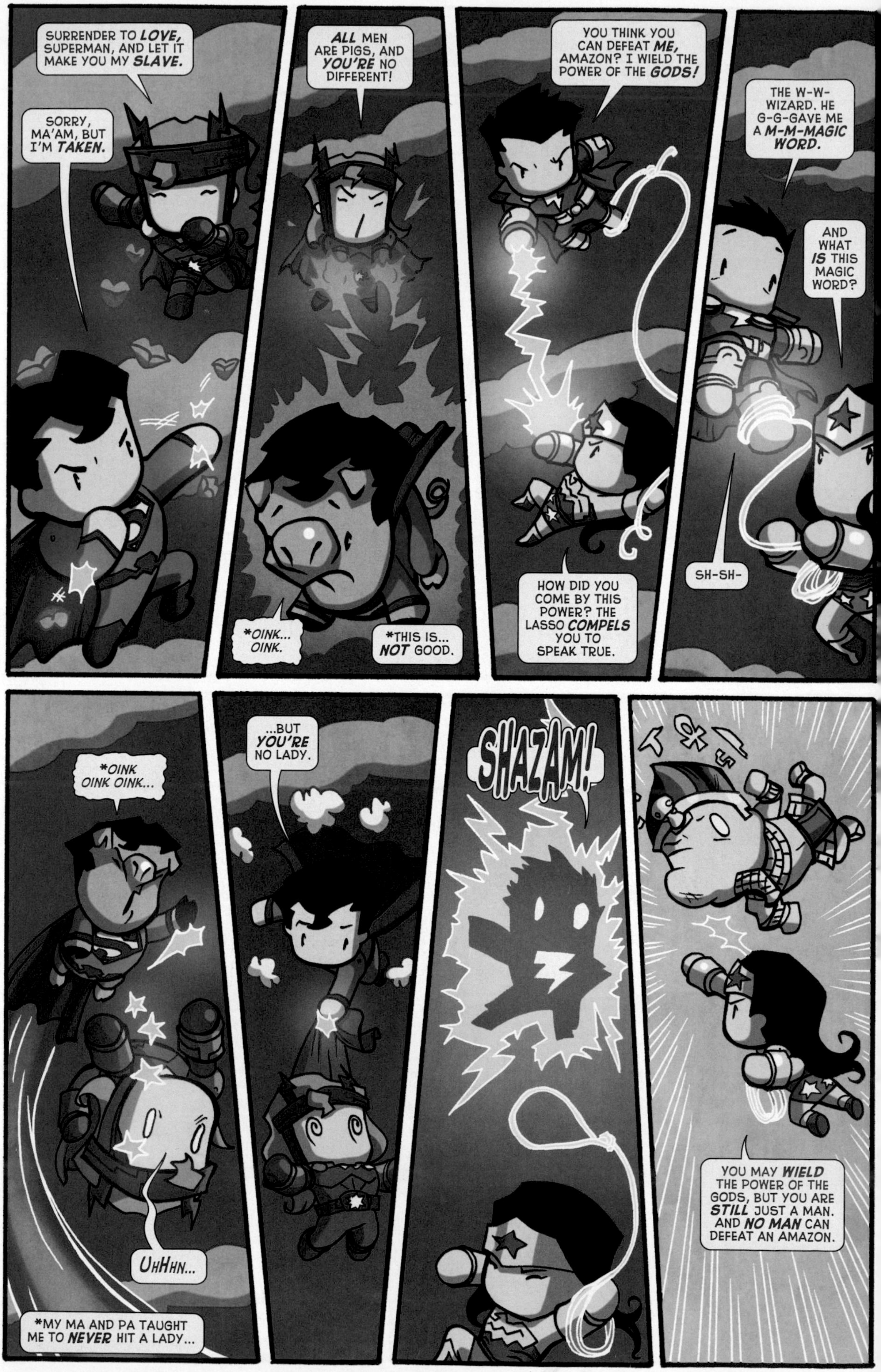

SURRENDER TO LOVE, SUPERMAN, AND LET IT MAKE YOU MY SLAVE.
SORRY, MA'AM, BUT I'M TAKEN.
ALL MEN ARE PIGS, AND YOU'RE NO DIFFERENT!
*OINK... OINK.
*THIS IS... NOT GOOD.
YOU THINK YOU CAN DEFEAT ME, AMAZON? I WIELD THE POWER OF THE GODS!
HOW DID YOU COME BY THIS POWER? THE LASSO COMPELS YOU TO SPEAK TRUE.
THE W-W-WIZARD. HE G-G-GAVE ME A M-M-MAGIC WORD.
AND WHAT IS THIS MAGIC WORD?
SH-SH-
*OINK OINK OINK...
UHHHN...
*MY MA AND PA TAUGHT ME TO NEVER HIT A LADY...
...BUT YOU'RE NO LADY.
SHAZAM!
YOU MAY WIELD THE POWER OF THE GODS, BUT YOU ARE STILL JUST A MAN. AND NO MAN CAN DEFEAT AN AMAZON.

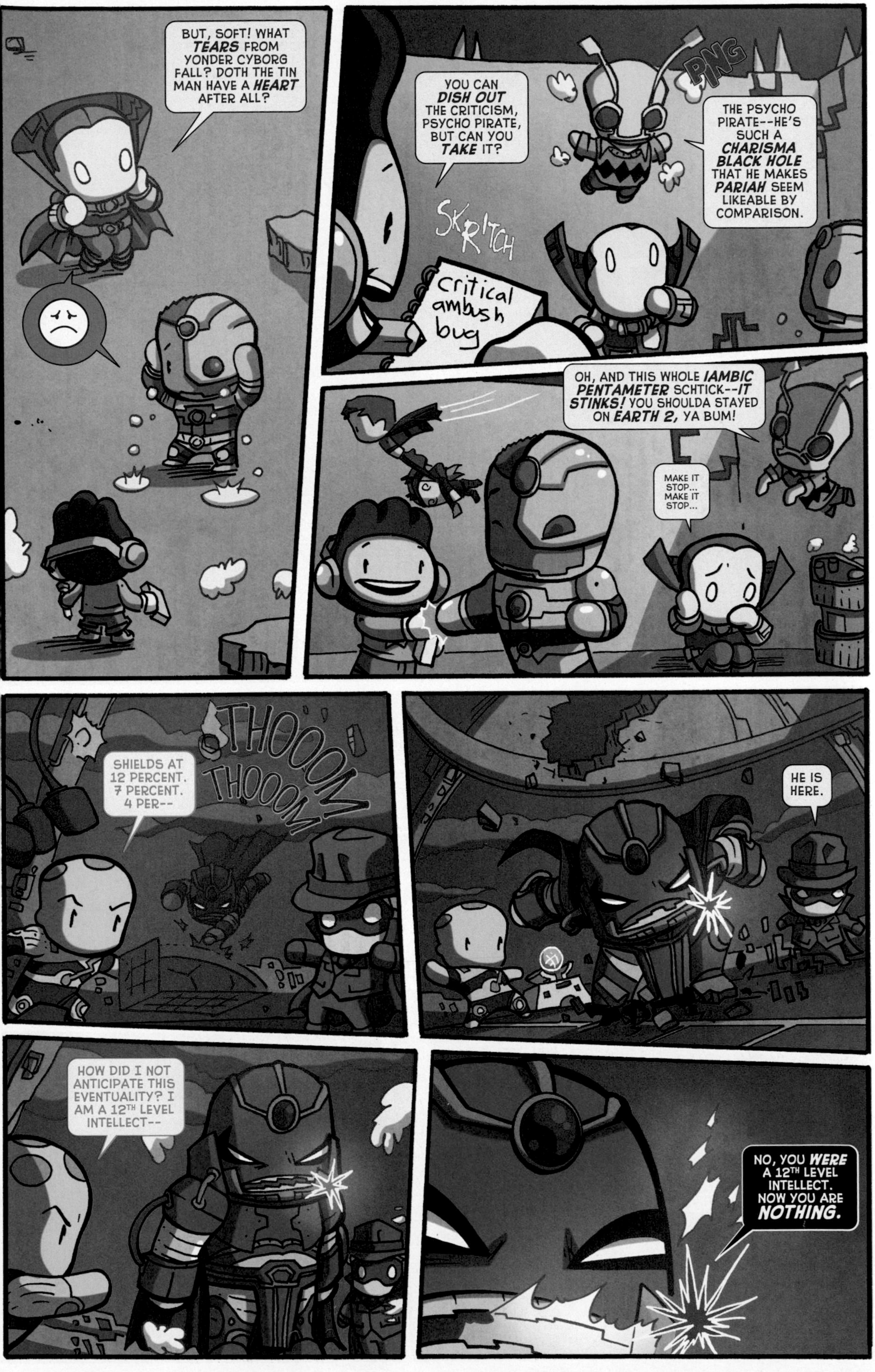
BUT, SOFT! WHAT TEARS FROM YONDER CYBORG FALL? DOTH THE TIN MAN HAVE A HEART AFTER ALL?
YOU CAN DISH OUT THE CRITICISM, PSYCHO PIRATE, BUT CAN YOU TAKE IT?
PING
THE PSYCHO PIRATE--HE'S SUCH A CHARISMA BLACK HOLE THAT HE MAKES PARIAH SEEM LIKEABLE BY COMPARISON.
SKRITCH
critical ambush bug
OH, AND THIS WHOLE IAMBIC PENTAMETER SCHTICK--IT STINKS! YOU SHOULDA STAYED ON EARTH 2, YA BUM!
MAKE IT STOP... MAKE IT STOP...
SHIELDS AT 12 PERCENT. 7 PERCENT. 4 PER--
THOOOM THOOOM
HE IS HERE.
HOW DID I NOT ANTICIPATE THIS EVENTUALITY? I AM A 12TH LEVEL INTELLECT--
NO, YOU WERE A 12TH LEVEL INTELLECT. NOW YOU ARE NOTHING.

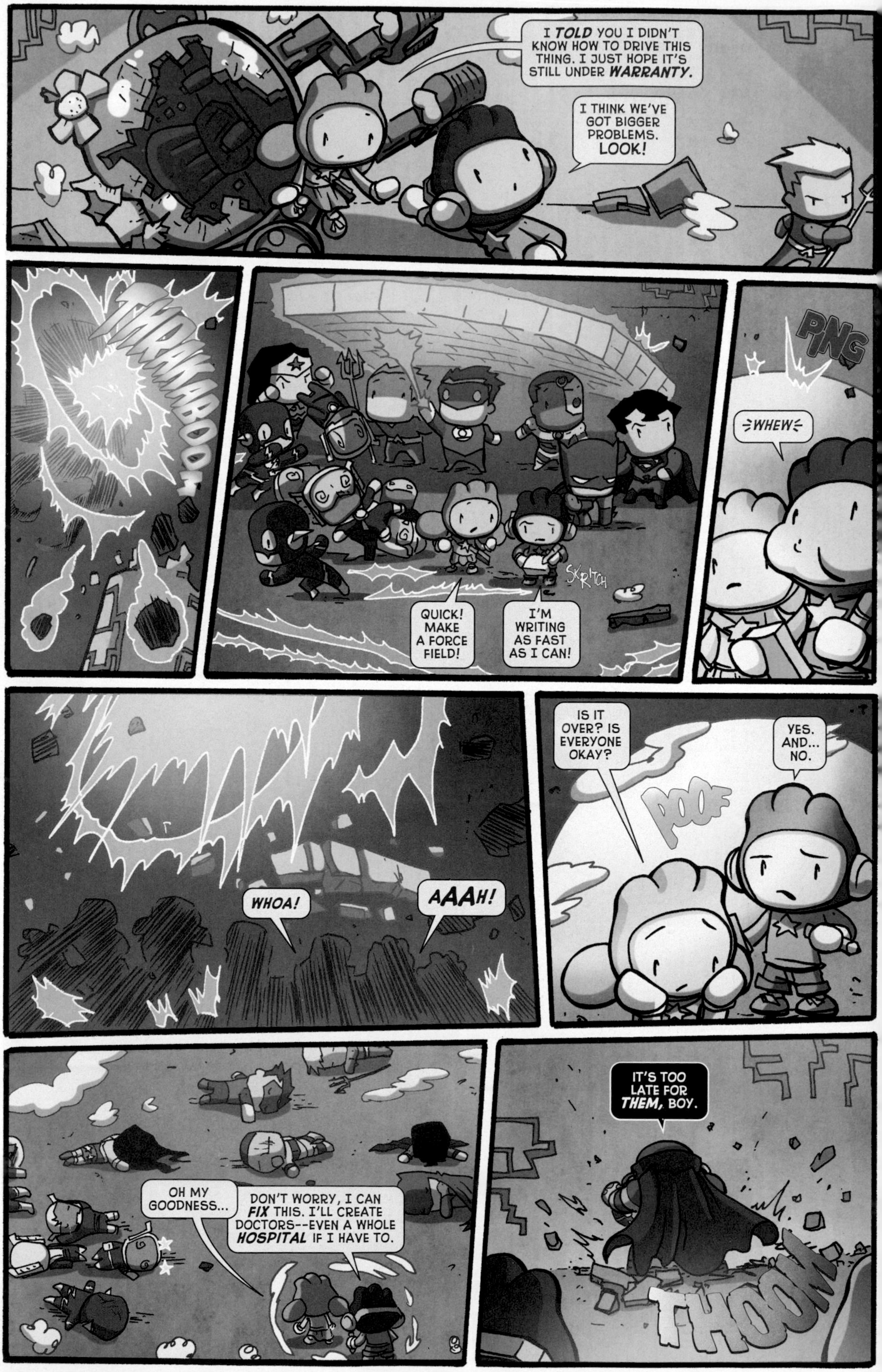

I TOLD YOU I DIDN'T KNOW HOW TO DRIVE THIS THING. I JUST HOPE IT'S STILL UNDER WARRANTY.
I THINK WE'VE GOT BIGGER PROBLEMS. LOOK!
QUICK! MAKE A FORCE FIELD!
I'M WRITING AS FAST AS I CAN!
SKRITCH
PING
WHEW
WHOA!
AAAH!
IS IT OVER? IS EVERYONE OKAY?
YES. AND... NO.
POOF
OH MY GOODNESS...
DON'T WORRY, I CAN FIX THIS. I'LL CREATE DOCTORS--EVEN A WHOLE HOSPITAL IF I HAVE TO.
IT'S TOO LATE FOR THEM, BOY.
THOOM

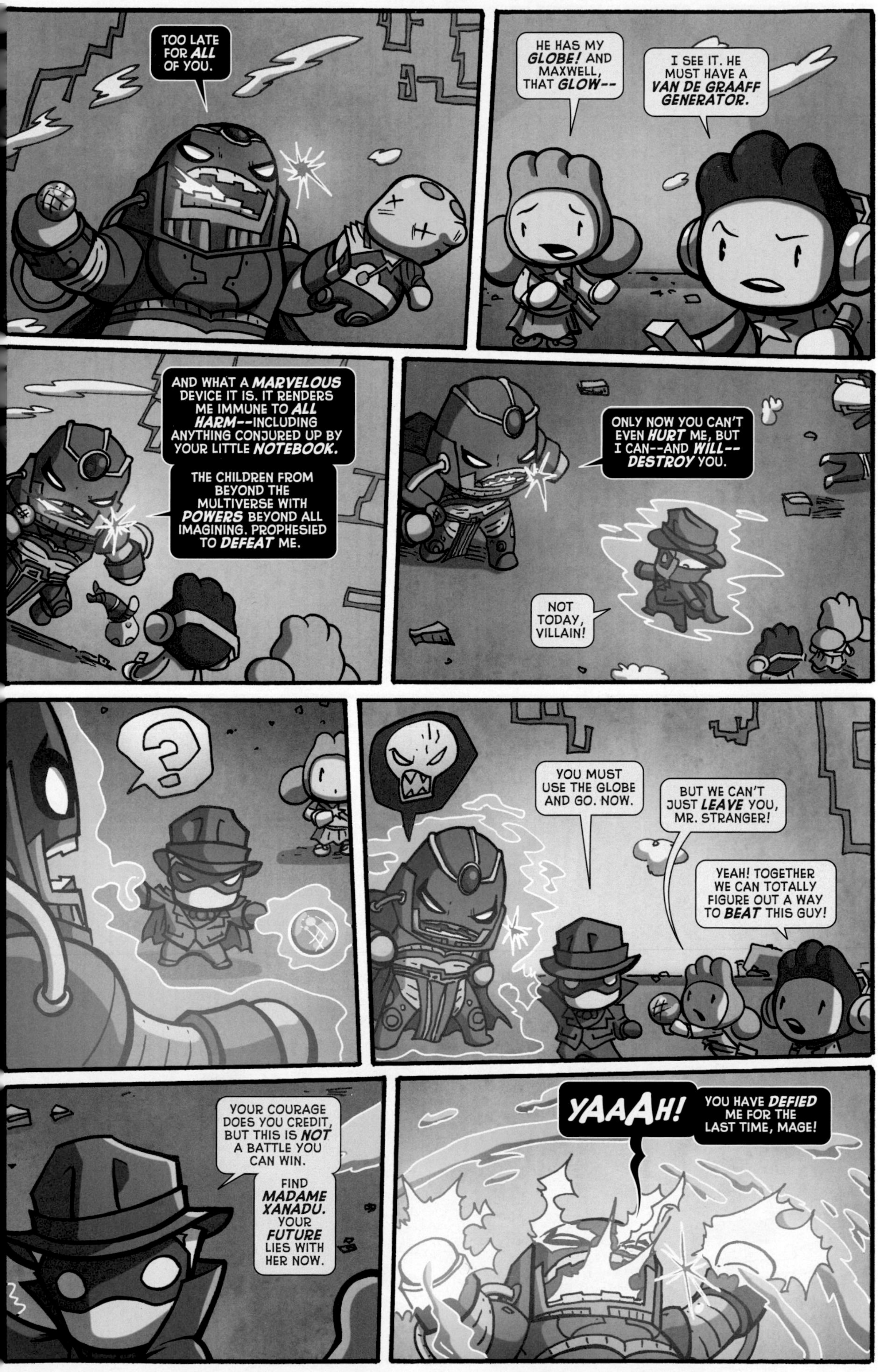
TOO LATE FOR ALL OF YOU.
HE HAS MY GLOBE! AND MAXWELL, THAT GLOW--
I SEE IT. HE MUST HAVE A VAN DE GRAAFF GENERATOR.
AND WHAT A MARVELOUS DEVICE IT IS. IT RENDERS ME IMMUNE TO ALL HARM--INCLUDING ANYTHING CONJURED UP BY YOUR LITTLE NOTEBOOK.
THE CHILDREN FROM BEYOND THE MULTIVERSE WITH POWERS BEYOND ALL IMAGINING. PROPHESIED TO DEFEAT ME.
ONLY NOW YOU CAN'T EVEN HURT ME, BUT I CAN--AND WILL--DESTROY YOU.
NOT TODAY, VILLAIN!
?
YOU MUST USE THE GLOBE AND GO. NOW.
BUT WE CAN'T JUST LEAVE YOU, MR. STRANGER!
YEAH! TOGETHER WE CAN TOTALLY FIGURE OUT A WAY TO BEAT THIS GUY!
YOUR COURAGE DOES YOU CREDIT, BUT THIS IS NOT A BATTLE YOU CAN WIN.
FIND MADAME XANADU. YOUR FUTURE LIES WITH HER NOW.
YAAAH!
YOU HAVE DEFIED ME FOR THE LAST TIME, MAGE!

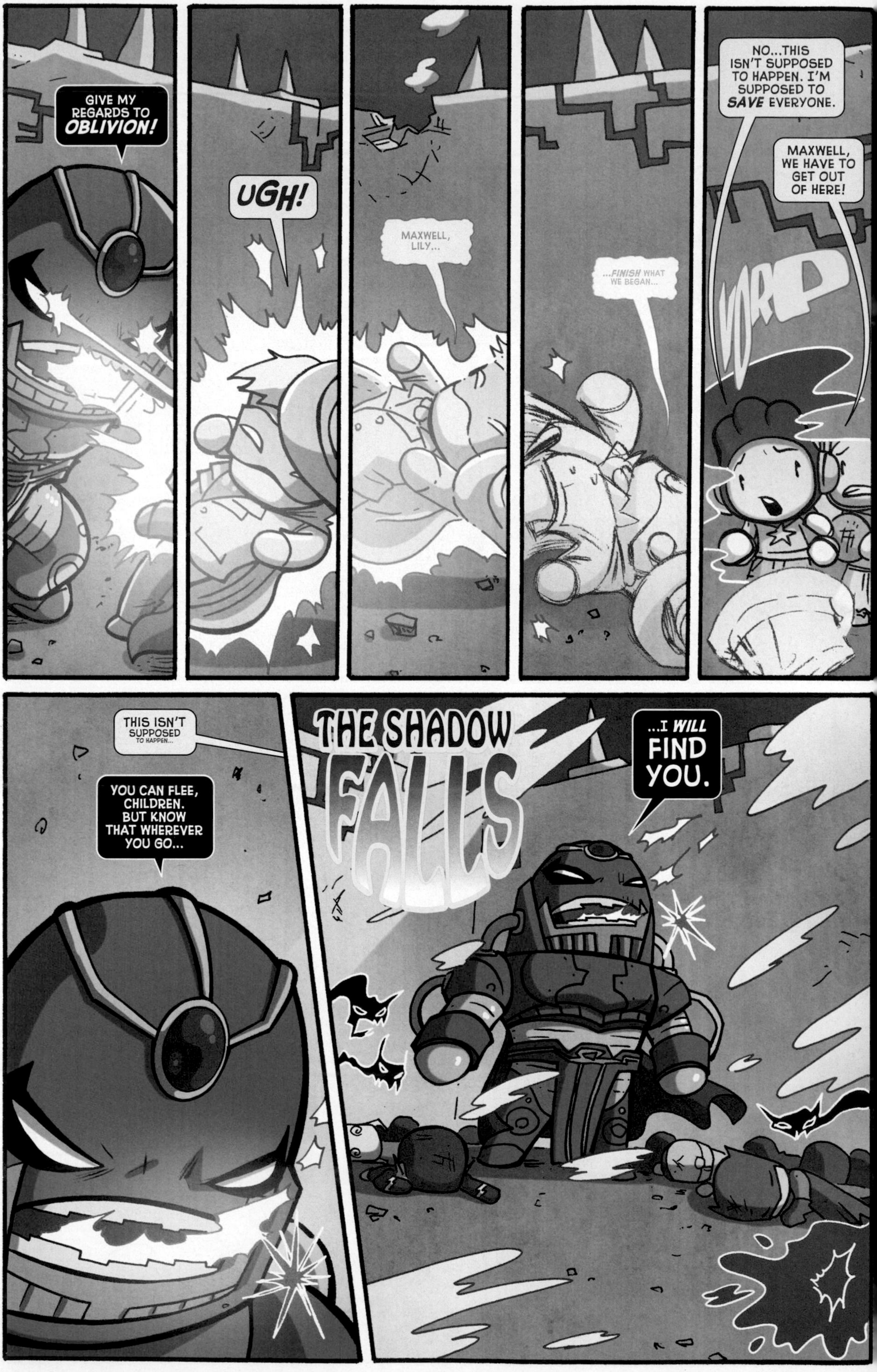

GIVE MY REGARDS TO OBLIVION!
UGH!
MAXWELL, LILY...
...FINISH WHAT WE BEGAN...
NO...THIS ISN'T SUPPOSED TO HAPPEN. I'M SUPPOSED TO SAVE EVERYONE.
MAXWELL, WE HAVE TO GET OUT OF HERE!
VORP
THIS ISN'T SUPPOSED TO HAPPEN...
YOU CAN FLEE, CHILDREN. BUT KNOW THAT WHEREVER YOU GO...
THE SHADOW FALLS
...I WILL FIND YOU.

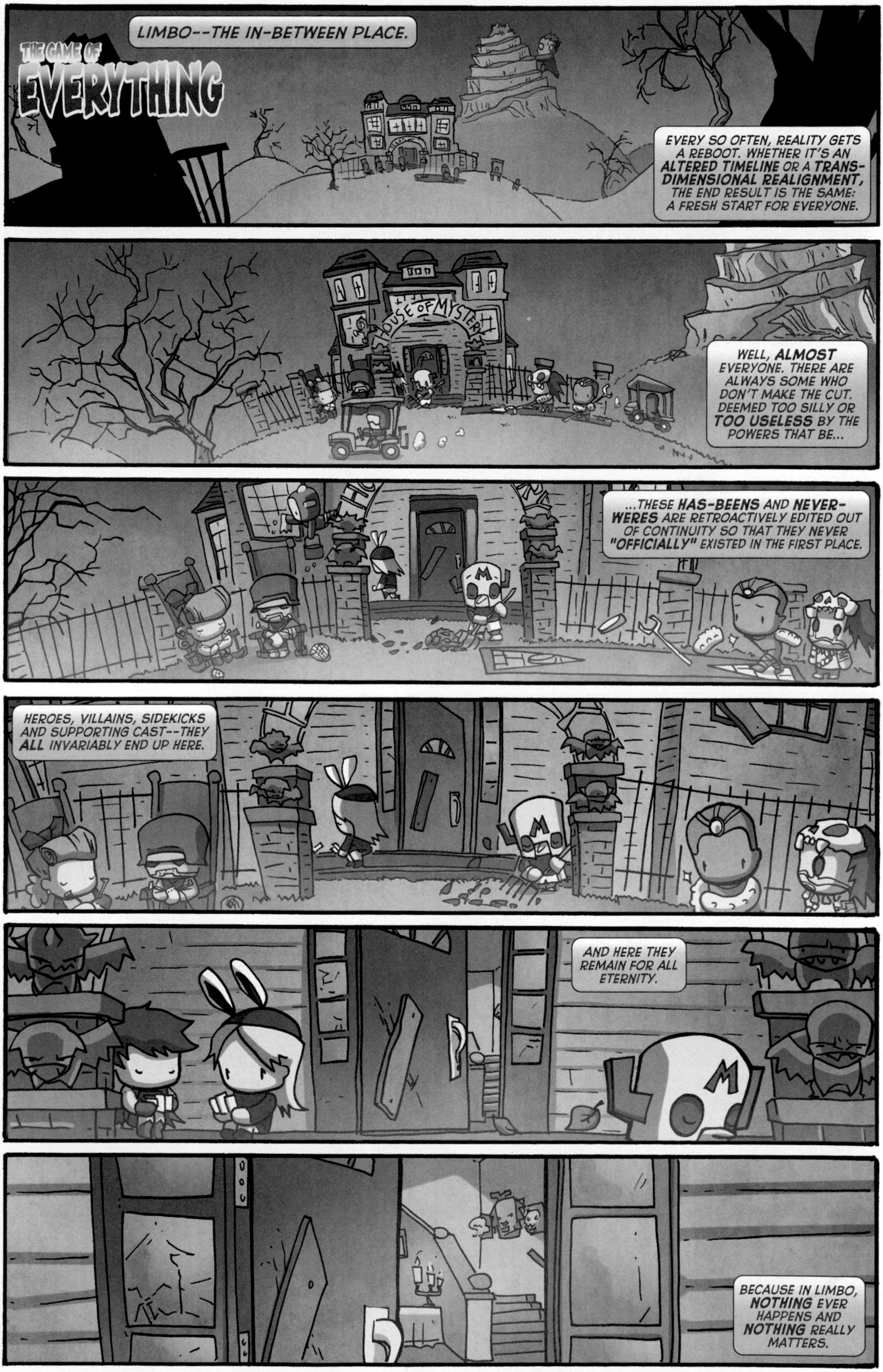
LIMBO--THE IN-BETWEEN PLACE.
THE GAME OF EVERYTHING
EVERY SO OFTEN, REALITY GETS A REBOOT. WHETHER IT'S AN ALTERED TIMELINE OR A TRANS-DIMENSIONAL REALIGNMENT, THE END RESULT IS THE SAME: A FRESH START FOR EVERYONE.
HOUSE OF MYSTERY
WELL, ALMOST EVERYONE. THERE ARE ALWAYS SOME WHO DON'T MAKE THE CUT. DEEMED TOO SILLY OR TOO USELESS BY THE POWERS THAT BE...
...THESE HAS-BEENS AND NEVER-WERES ARE RETROACTIVELY EDITED OUT OF CONTINUITY SO THAT THEY NEVER "OFFICIALLY" EXISTED IN THE FIRST PLACE.
HEROES, VILLAINS, SIDEKICKS AND SUPPORTING CAST--THEY ALL INVARIABLY END UP HERE.
AND HERE THEY REMAIN FOR ALL ETERNITY.
BECAUSE IN LIMBO, NOTHING EVER HAPPENS AND NOTHING REALLY MATTERS.

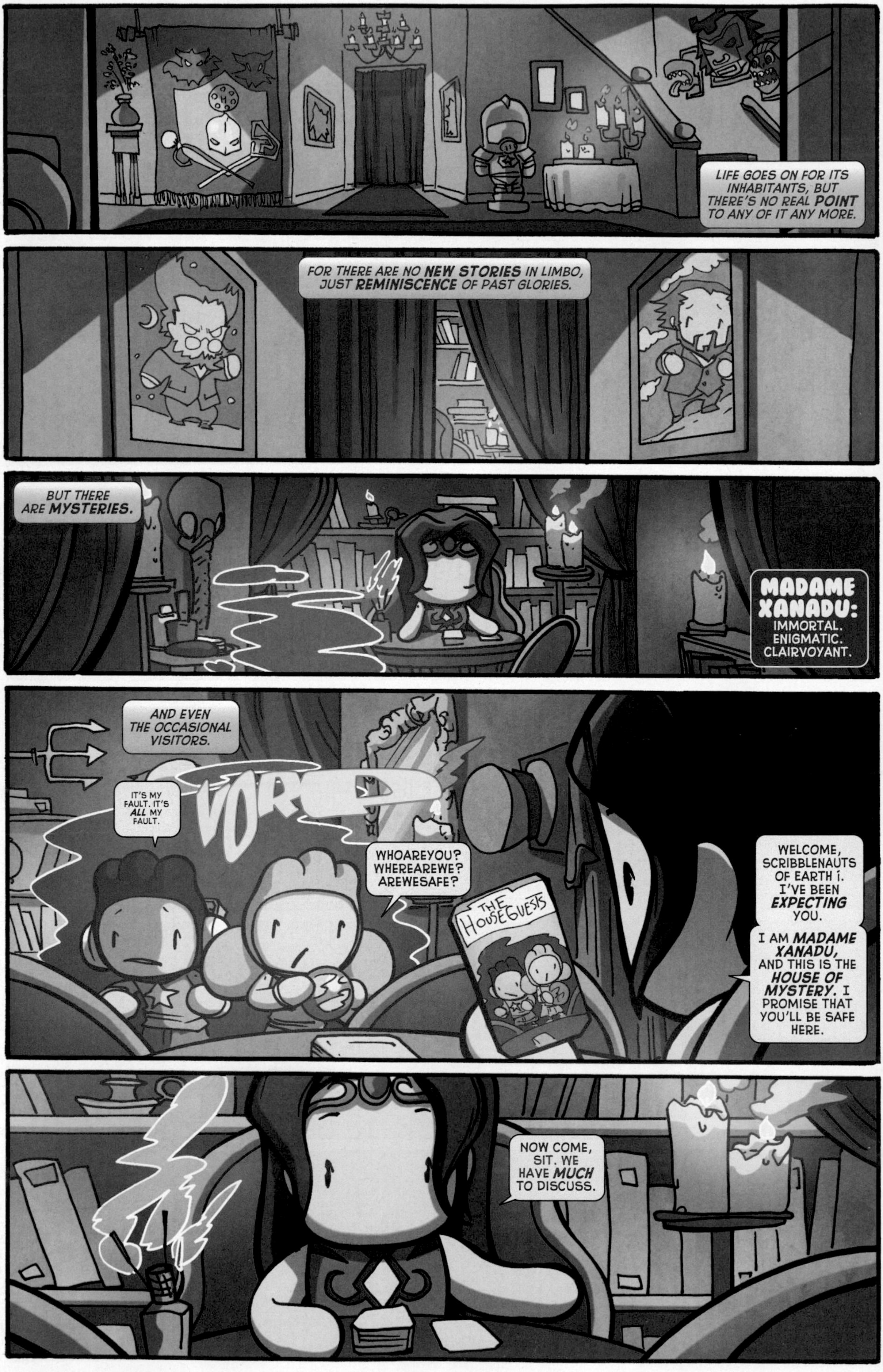
LIFE GOES ON FOR ITS INHABITANTS, BUT THERE'S NO REAL POINT TO ANY OF IT ANY MORE.
FOR THERE ARE NO NEW STORIES IN LIMBO, JUST REMINISCENCE OF PAST GLORIES.
BUT THERE ARE MYSTERIES.
MADAME XANADU: IMMORTAL. ENIGMATIC. CLAIRVOYANT.
AND EVEN THE OCCASIONAL VISITORS.
IT'S MY FAULT. IT'S ALL MY FAULT.
VORP
WHOAREYOU? WHEREAREWE? AREWESAFE?
THE HOUSE GUESTS
WELCOME, SCRIBBLENAUTS OF EARTH í. I'VE BEEN EXPECTING YOU.
I AM MADAME XANADU, AND THIS IS THE HOUSE OF MYSTERY. I PROMISE THAT YOU'LL BE SAFE HERE.
NOW COME, SIT. WE HAVE MUCH TO DISCUSS.

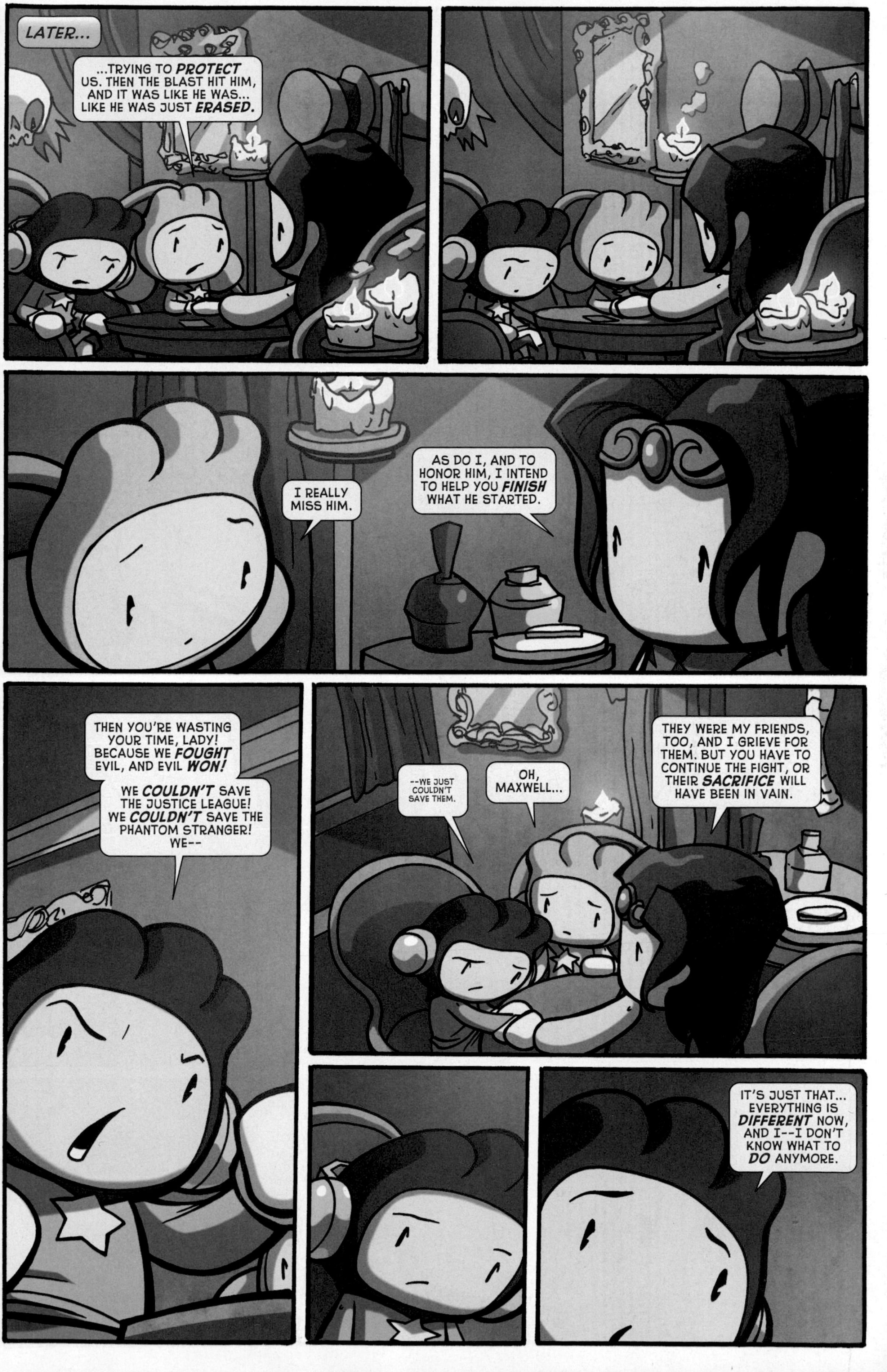
LATER...
...TRYING TO PROTECT US. THEN THE BLAST HIT HIM, AND IT WAS LIKE HE WAS... LIKE HE WAS JUST ERASED.
I REALLY MISS HIM.
AS DO I, AND TO HONOR HIM, I INTEND TO HELP YOU FINISH WHAT HE STARTED.
THEN YOU'RE WASTING YOUR TIME, LADY! BECAUSE WE FOUGHT EVIL, AND EVIL WON!
WE COULDN'T SAVE THE JUSTICE LEAGUE! WE COULDN'T SAVE THE PHANTOM STRANGER! WE--
--WE JUST COULDN'T SAVE THEM.
OH, MAXWELL...
THEY WERE MY FRIENDS, TOO, AND I GRIEVE FOR THEM. BUT YOU HAVE TO CONTINUE THE FIGHT, OR THEIR SACRIFICE WILL HAVE BEEN IN VAIN.
IT'S JUST THAT... EVERYTHING IS DIFFERENT NOW, AND I--I DON'T KNOW WHAT TO DO ANYMORE.

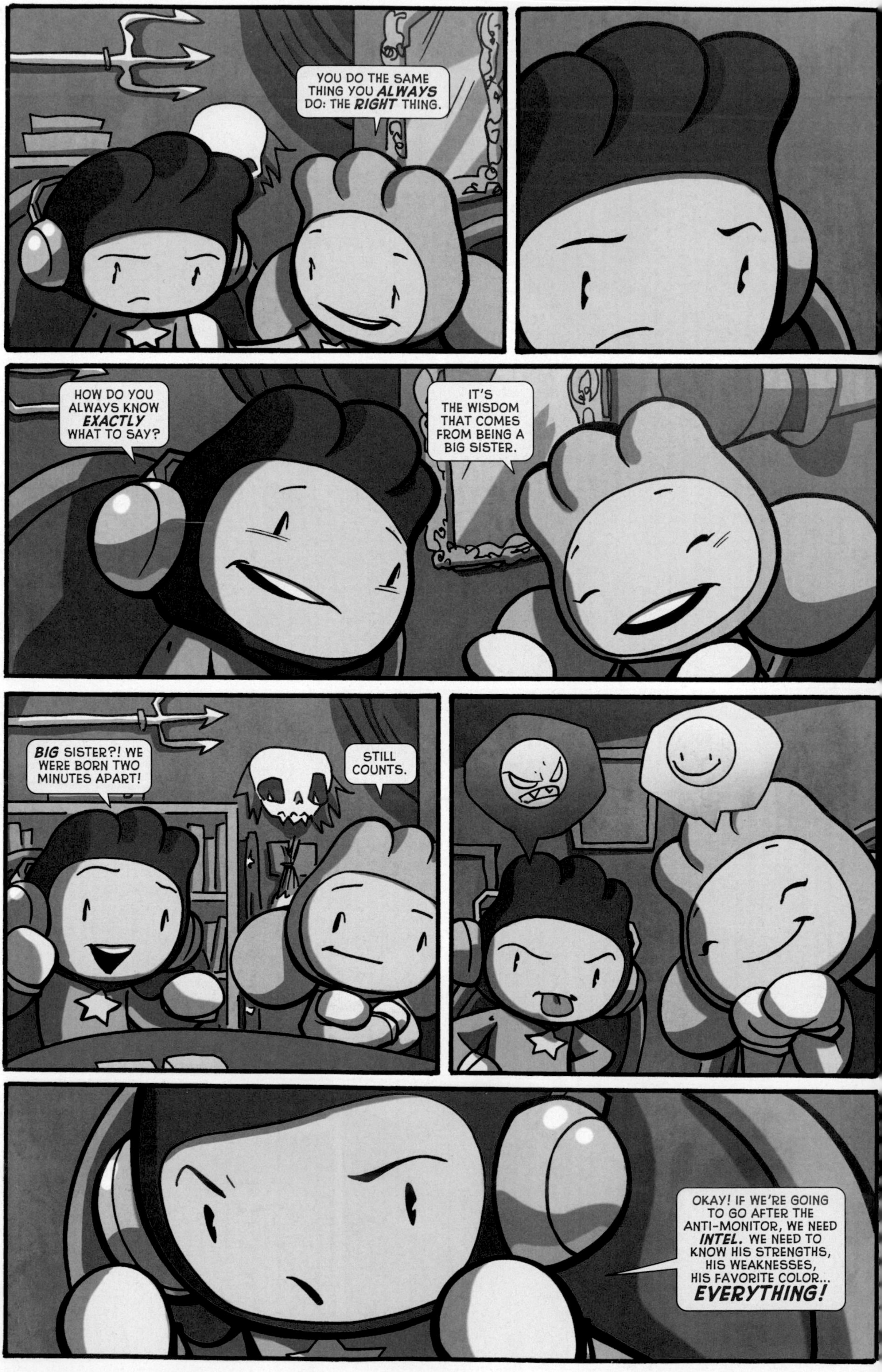
YOU DO THE SAME THING YOU ALWAYS DO: THE RIGHT THING.
HOW DO YOU ALWAYS KNOW EXACTLY WHAT TO SAY?
IT'S THE WISDOM THAT COMES FROM BEING A BIG SISTER.
BIG SISTER?! WE WERE BORN TWO MINUTES APART!
STILL COUNTS.
OKAY! IF WE'RE GOING TO GO AFTER THE ANTI-MONITOR, WE NEED INTEL. WE NEED TO KNOW HIS STRENGTHS, HIS WEAKNESSES, HIS FAVORITE COLOR... EVERYTHING!

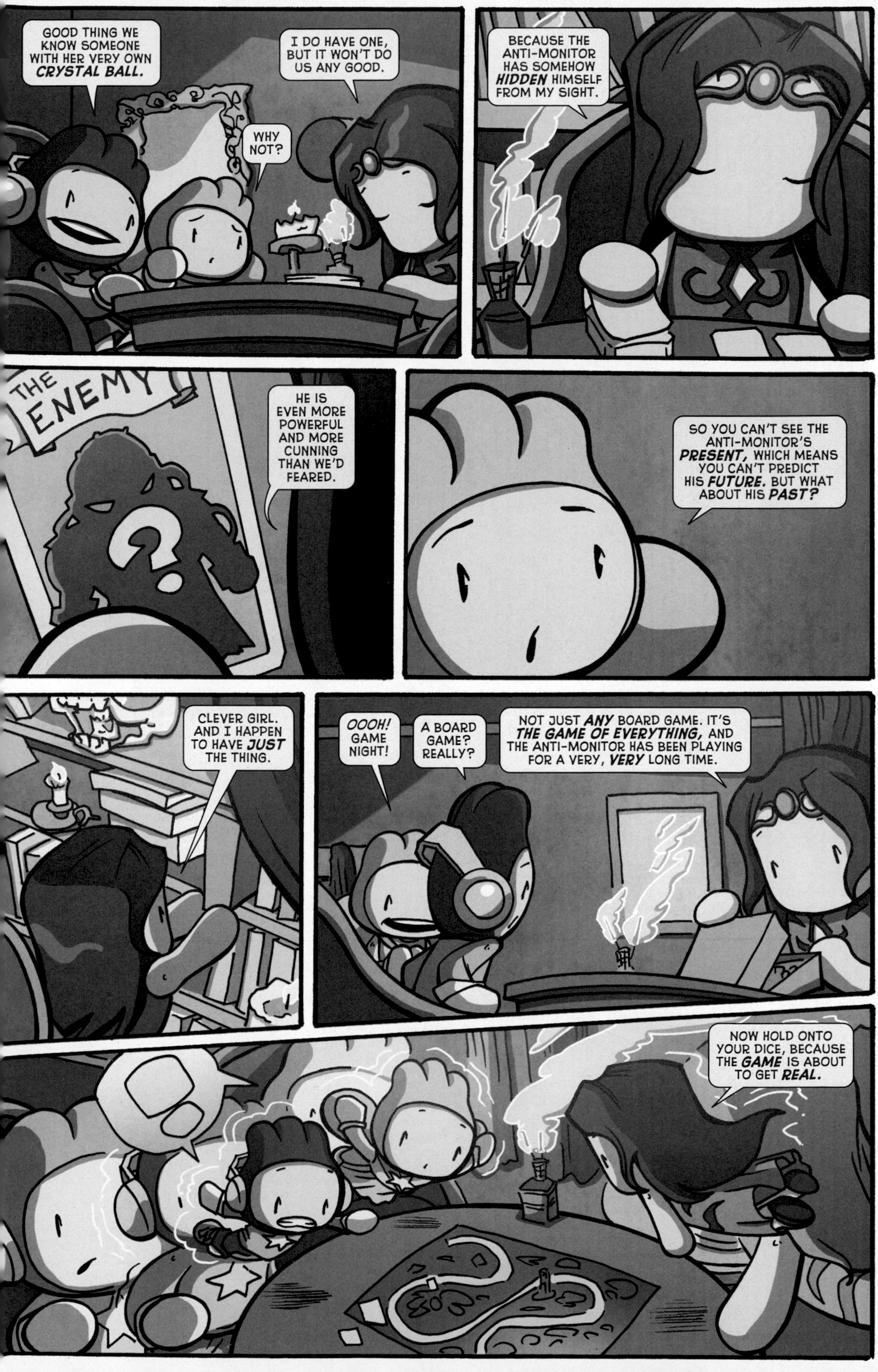
GOOD THING WE KNOW SOMEONE WITH HER VERY OWN *CRYSTAL BALL.*
I DO HAVE ONE, BUT IT WON'T DO US ANY GOOD.
WHY NOT?
BECAUSE THE ANTI-MONITOR HAS SOMEHOW *HIDDEN* HIMSELF FROM MY SIGHT.
THE ENEMY
HE IS EVEN MORE POWERFUL AND MORE CUNNING THAN WE'D FEARED.
SO YOU CAN'T SEE THE ANTI-MONITOR'S *PRESENT,* WHICH MEANS YOU CAN'T PREDICT HIS *FUTURE.* BUT WHAT ABOUT HIS *PAST?*
CLEVER GIRL. AND I HAPPEN TO HAVE *JUST* THE THING.
*OOOH!* GAME NIGHT!
A BOARD GAME? REALLY?
NOT JUST *ANY* BOARD GAME. IT'S *THE GAME OF EVERYTHING,* AND THE ANTI-MONITOR HAS BEEN PLAYING FOR A VERY, *VERY* LONG TIME.
NOW HOLD ONTO YOUR DICE, BECAUSE THE *GAME* IS ABOUT TO GET *REAL.*

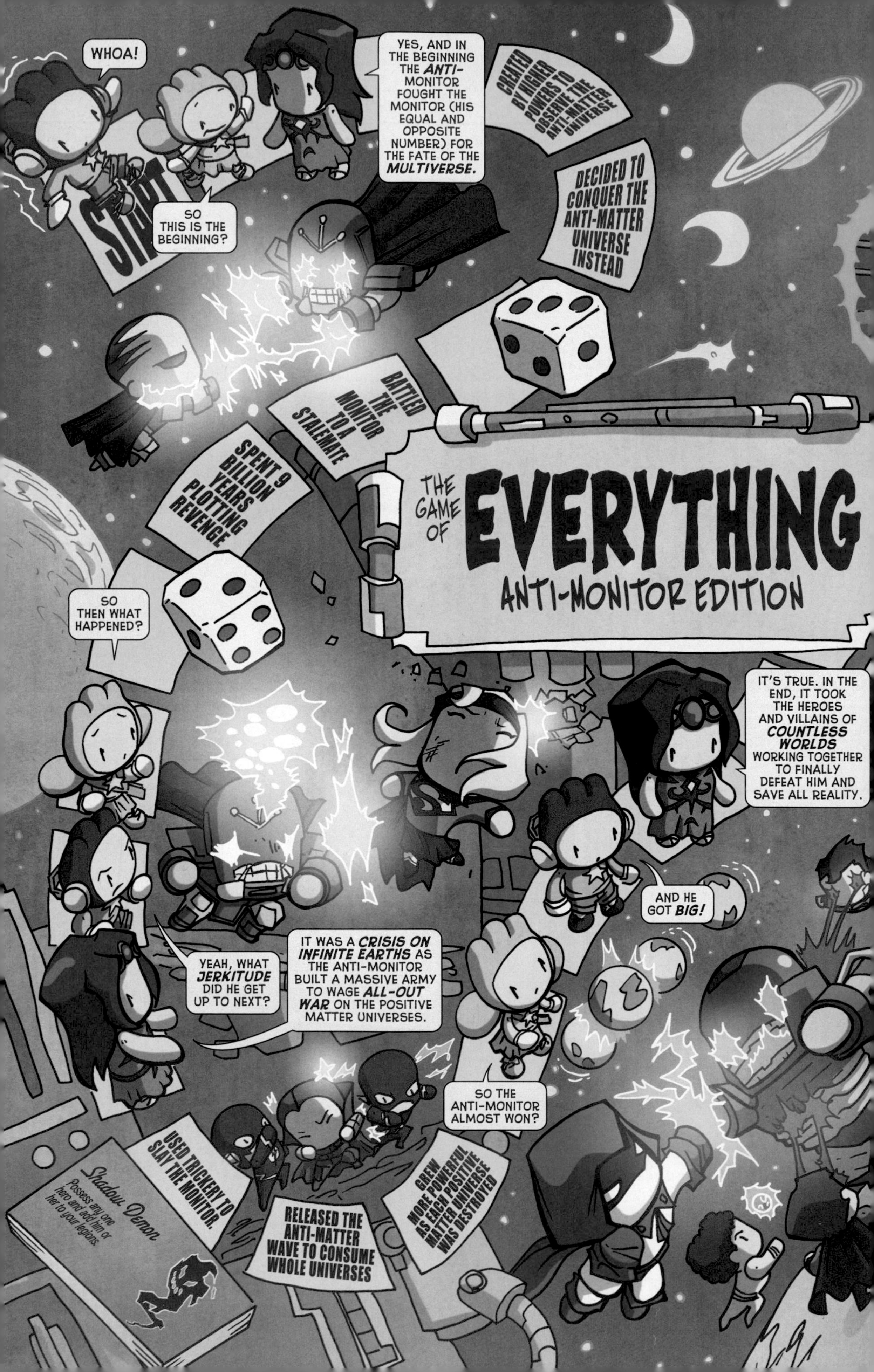

WHOA!
YES, AND IN THE BEGINNING THE ANTI-MONITOR FOUGHT THE MONITOR (HIS EQUAL AND OPPOSITE NUMBER) FOR THE FATE OF THE MULTIVERSE.
START
SO THIS IS THE BEGINNING?
CREATED BY HIGHER POWERS TO OBSERVE THE ANTI-MATTER UNIVERSE
DECIDED TO CONQUER THE ANTI-MATTER UNIVERSE INSTEAD
BATTLED THE MONITOR TO A STALEMATE
SPENT 9 BILLION YEARS PLOTTING REVENGE
THE GAME OF EVERYTHING
ANTI-MONITOR EDITION
SO THEN WHAT HAPPENED?
IT'S TRUE. IN THE END, IT TOOK THE HEROES AND VILLAINS OF COUNTLESS WORLDS WORKING TOGETHER TO FINALLY DEFEAT HIM AND SAVE ALL REALITY.
AND HE GOT BIG!
YEAH, WHAT JERKITUDE DID HE GET UP TO NEXT?
IT WAS A CRISIS ON INFINITE EARTHS AS THE ANTI-MONITOR BUILT A MASSIVE ARMY TO WAGE ALL-OUT WAR ON THE POSITIVE MATTER UNIVERSES.
SO THE ANTI-MONITOR ALMOST WON?
Shadow Demon
Possess any one hero and add him or her to your legions.
USED TRICKERY TO SLAY THE MONITOR.
RELEASED THE ANTI-MATTER WAVE TO CONSUME WHOLE UNIVERSES
GREW MORE POWERFUL AS EACH POSITIVE MATTER UNIVERSE WAS DESTROYED

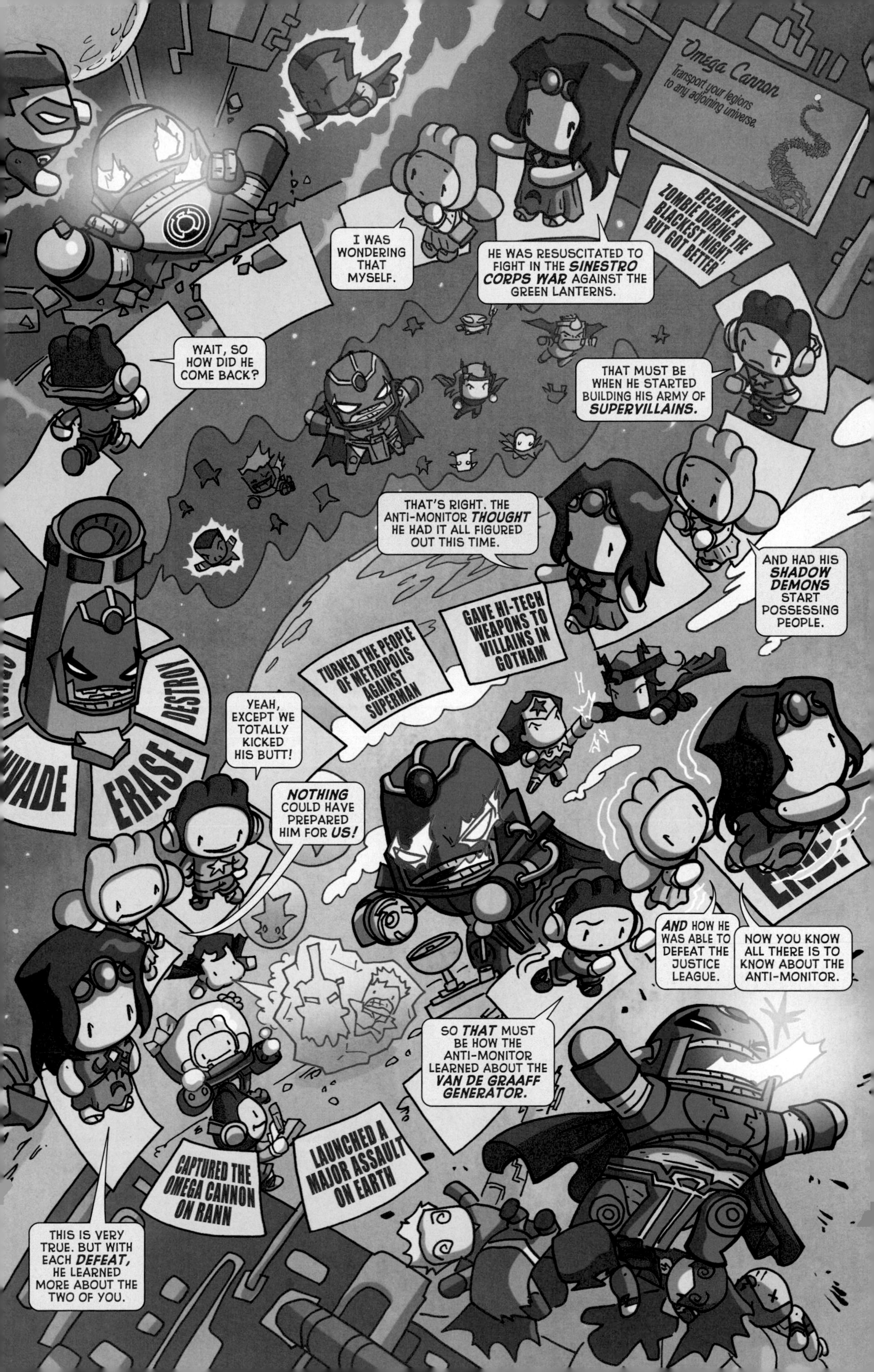

Omega Cannon
Transport your legions to any adjoining universe.
WAIT, SO HOW DID HE COME BACK?
I WAS WONDERING THAT MYSELF.
HE WAS RESUSCITATED TO FIGHT IN THE *SINESTRO CORPS WAR* AGAINST THE GREEN LANTERNS.
BECAME A ZOMBIE DURING THE BLACKEST NIGHT, BUT GOT BETTER
THAT MUST BE WHEN HE STARTED BUILDING HIS ARMY OF *SUPERVILLAINS.*
THAT'S RIGHT. THE ANTI-MONITOR *THOUGHT* HE HAD IT ALL FIGURED OUT THIS TIME.
AND HAD HIS *SHADOW DEMONS* START POSSESSING PEOPLE.
TURNED THE PEOPLE OF METROPOLIS AGAINST SUPERMAN
GAVE HI-TECH WEAPONS TO VILLAINS IN GOTHAM
DESTROY
ERASE
YEAH, EXCEPT WE TOTALLY KICKED HIS BUTT!
*NOTHING* COULD HAVE PREPARED HIM FOR *US!*
*AND* HOW HE WAS ABLE TO DEFEAT THE JUSTICE LEAGUE.
NOW YOU KNOW ALL THERE IS TO KNOW ABOUT THE ANTI-MONITOR.
SO *THAT* MUST BE HOW THE ANTI-MONITOR LEARNED ABOUT THE *VAN DE GRAAFF GENERATOR.*
CAPTURED THE OMEGA CANNON ON RANN
LAUNCHED A MAJOR ASSAULT ON EARTH
THIS IS VERY TRUE. BUT WITH EACH *DEFEAT,* HE LEARNED MORE ABOUT THE TWO OF YOU.

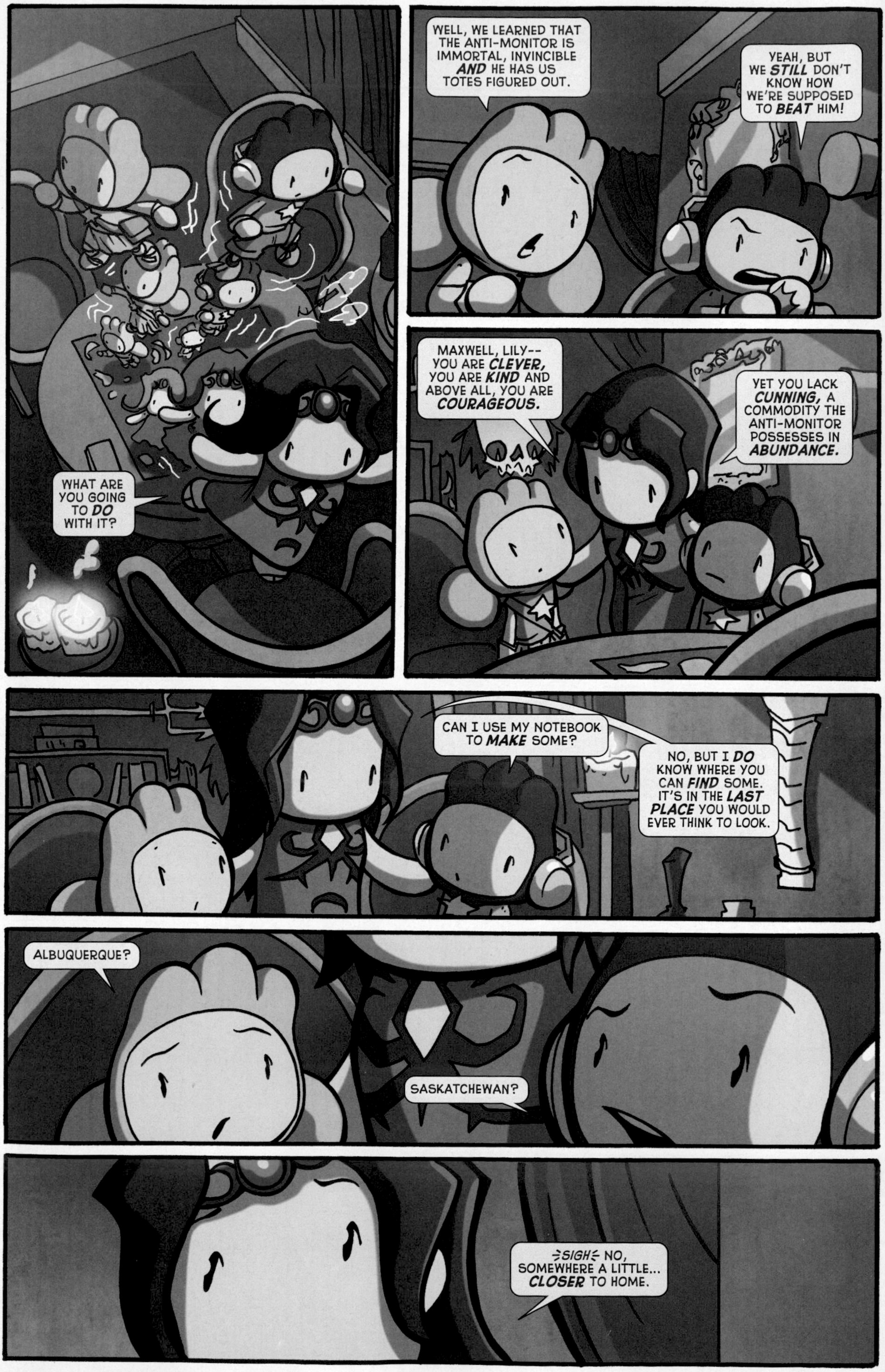
WHAT ARE YOU GOING TO DO WITH IT?
WELL, WE LEARNED THAT THE ANTI-MONITOR IS IMMORTAL, INVINCIBLE AND HE HAS US TOTES FIGURED OUT.
YEAH, BUT WE STILL DON'T KNOW HOW WE'RE SUPPOSED TO BEAT HIM!
MAXWELL, LILY-- YOU ARE CLEVER, YOU ARE KIND AND ABOVE ALL, YOU ARE COURAGEOUS.
YET YOU LACK CUNNING, A COMMODITY THE ANTI-MONITOR POSSESSES IN ABUNDANCE.
CAN I USE MY NOTEBOOK TO MAKE SOME?
NO, BUT I DO KNOW WHERE YOU CAN FIND SOME. IT'S IN THE LAST PLACE YOU WOULD EVER THINK TO LOOK.
ALBUQUERQUE?
SASKATCHEWAN?
SIGH NO, SOMEWHERE A LITTLE... CLOSER TO HOME.

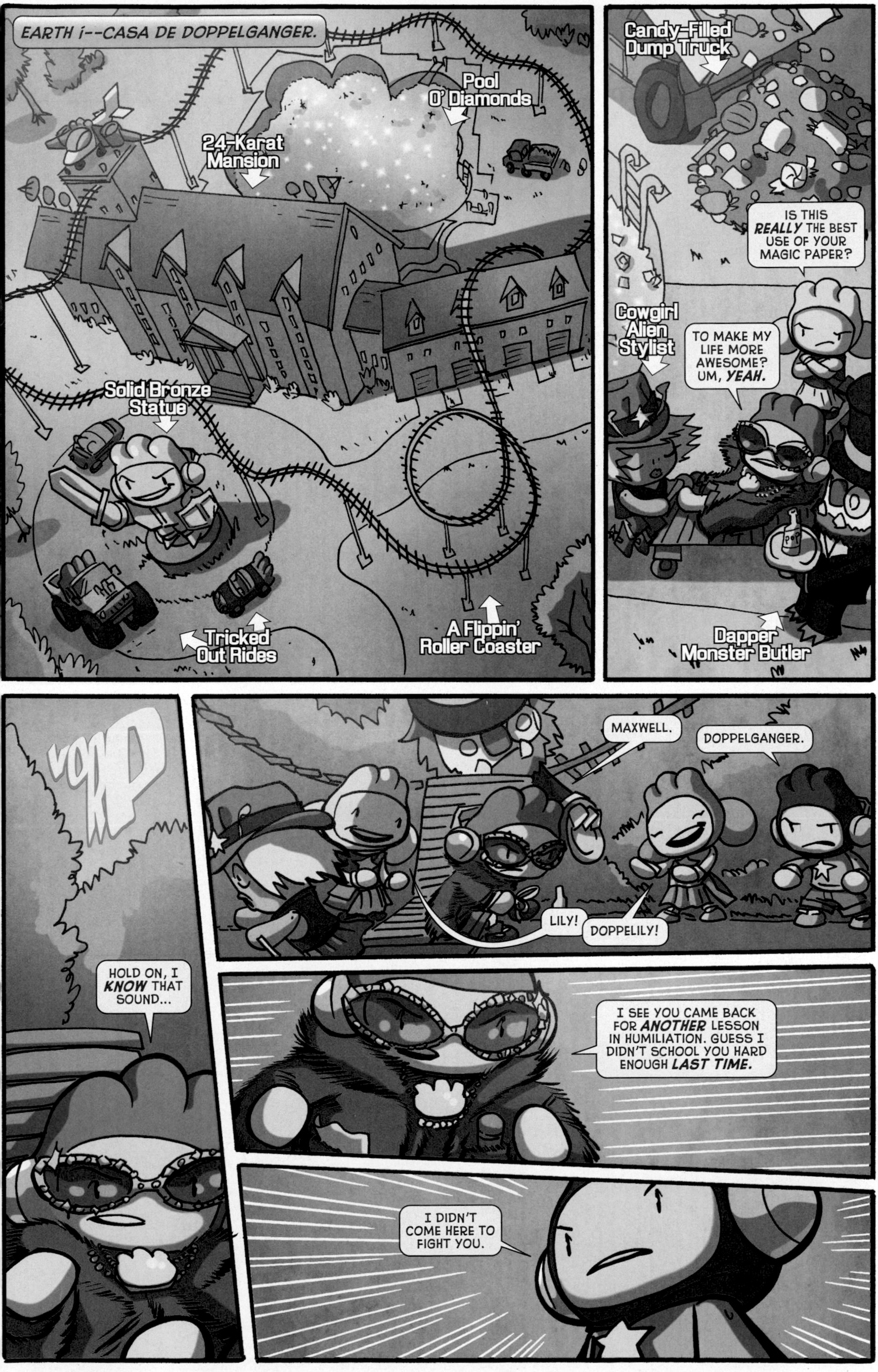
EARTH Í--CASA DE DOPPELGANGER.
24-Karat Mansion
Pool O' Diamonds
Solid Bronze Statue
Tricked Out Rides
A Flippin' Roller Coaster
Candy-Filled Dump Truck
IS THIS REALLY THE BEST USE OF YOUR MAGIC PAPER?
Cowgirl Alien Stylist
TO MAKE MY LIFE MORE AWESOME? UM, YEAH.
Dapper Monster Butler
VORP
MAXWELL.
DOPPELGANGER.
LILY!
DOPPELILY!
HOLD ON, I KNOW THAT SOUND...
I SEE YOU CAME BACK FOR ANOTHER LESSON IN HUMILIATION. GUESS I DIDN'T SCHOOL YOU HARD ENOUGH LAST TIME.
I DIDN'T COME HERE TO FIGHT YOU.

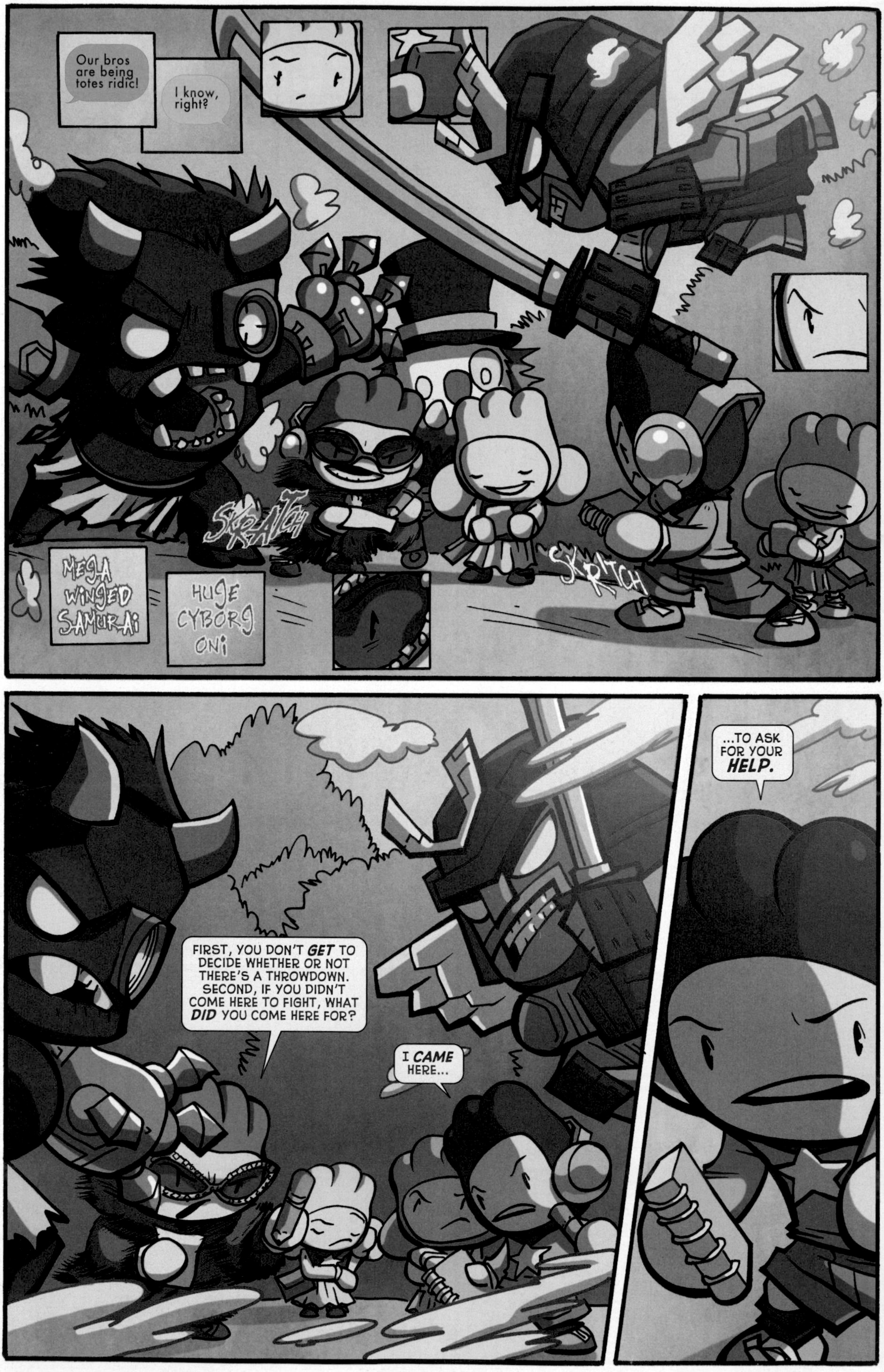

Our bros are being totes ridic!
I know, right?
SKRATCH
MEGA WINGED SAMURAI
HUGE CYBORG ONI
SKRITCH
FIRST, YOU DON'T GET TO DECIDE WHETHER OR NOT THERE'S A THROWDOWN. SECOND, IF YOU DIDN'T COME HERE TO FIGHT, WHAT DID YOU COME HERE FOR?
I CAME HERE...
...TO ASK FOR YOUR HELP.

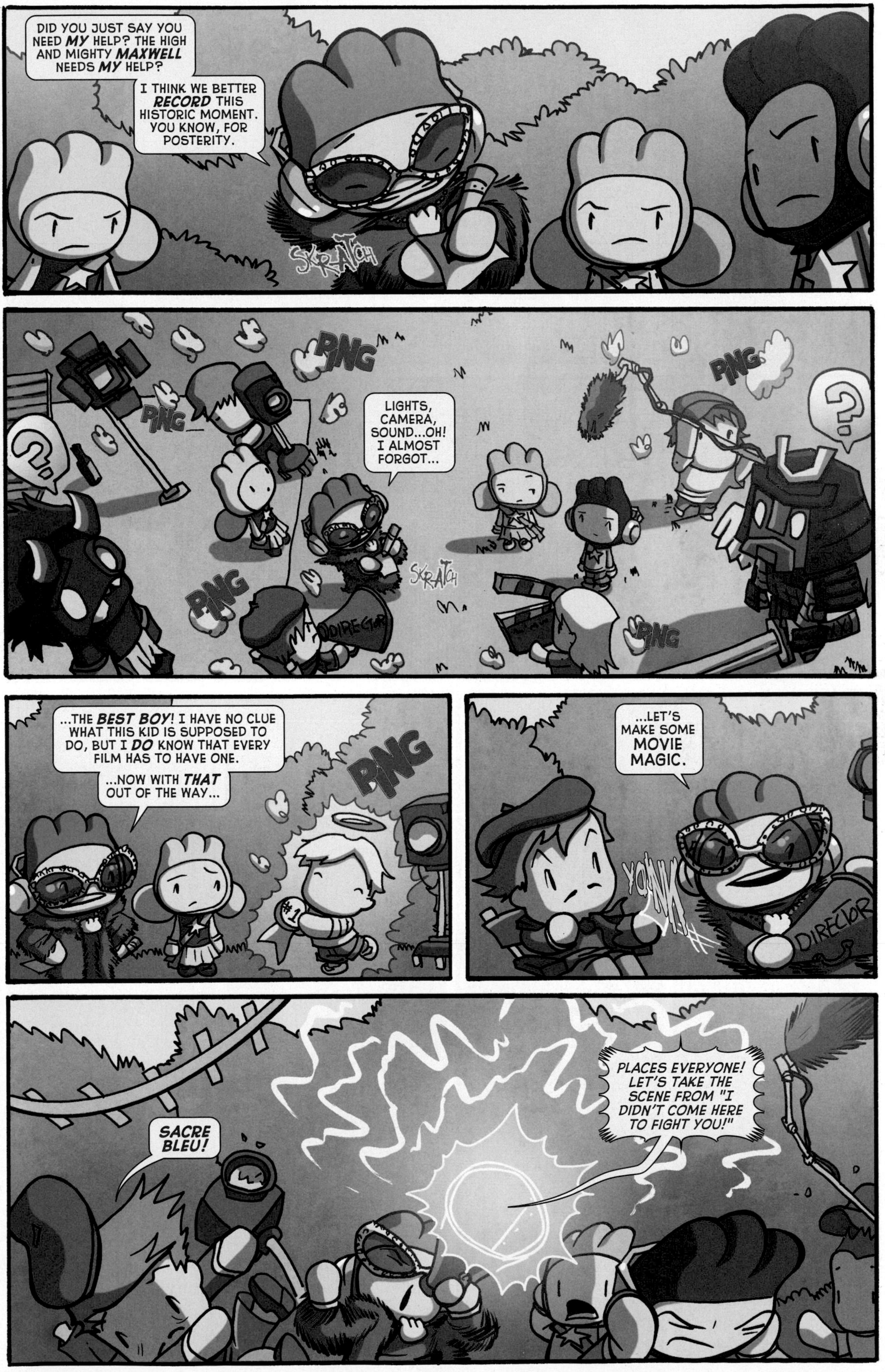
DID YOU JUST SAY YOU NEED MY HELP? THE HIGH AND MIGHTY MAXWELL NEEDS MY HELP?
I THINK WE BETTER RECORD THIS HISTORIC MOMENT. YOU KNOW, FOR POSTERITY.
SKRATCH
PING
PING
LIGHTS, CAMERA, SOUND...OH! I ALMOST FORGOT...
PING
SKRATCH
PING
DIRECTOR
PING
...THE BEST BOY! I HAVE NO CLUE WHAT THIS KID IS SUPPOSED TO DO, BUT I DO KNOW THAT EVERY FILM HAS TO HAVE ONE.
...NOW WITH THAT OUT OF THE WAY...
PING
#1
...LET'S MAKE SOME MOVIE MAGIC.
YOINK
DIRECTOR
PLACES EVERYONE! LET'S TAKE THE SCENE FROM "I DIDN'T COME HERE TO FIGHT YOU!"
SACRE BLEU!

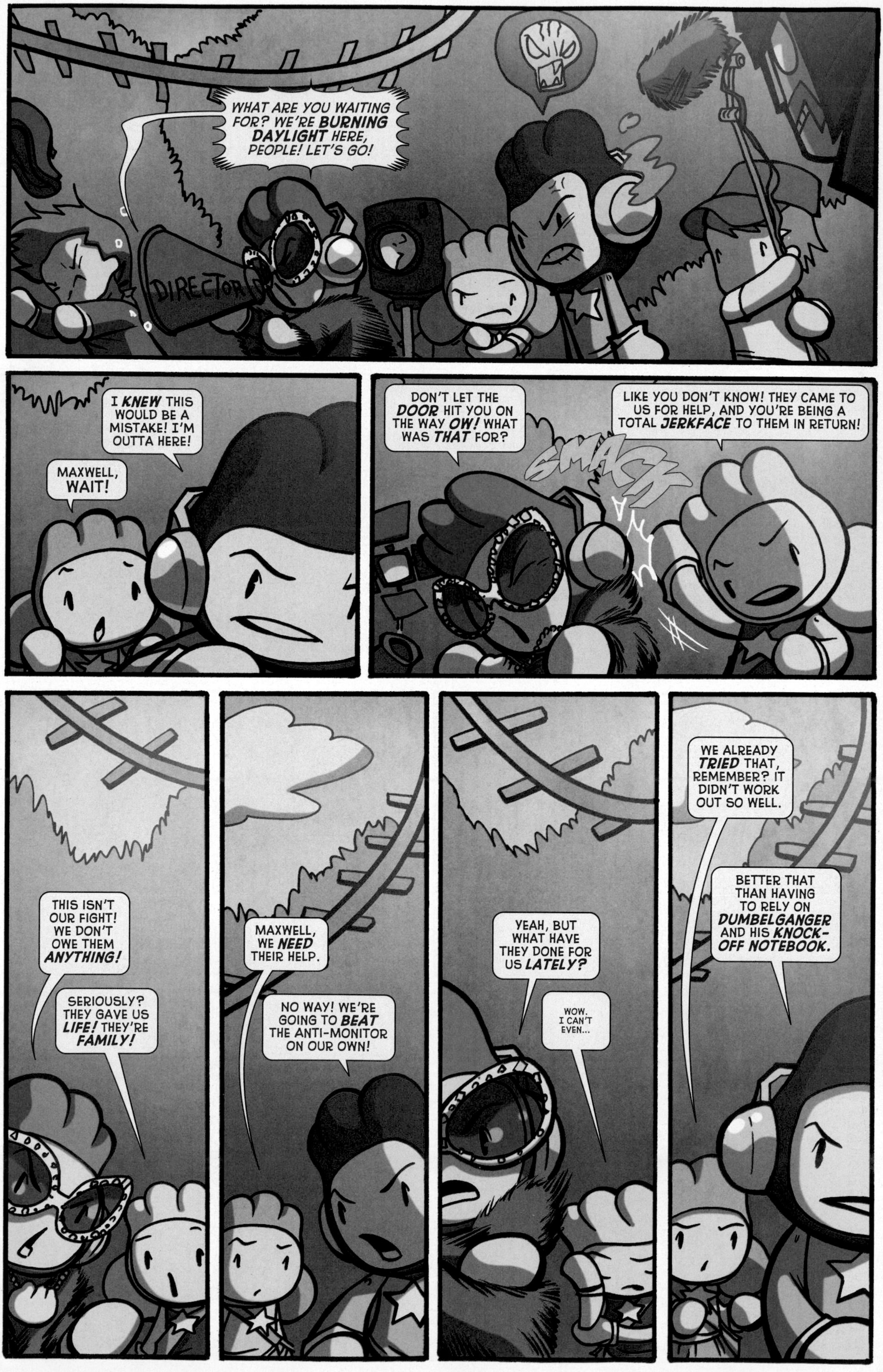
WHAT ARE YOU WAITING FOR? WE'RE BURNING DAYLIGHT HERE, PEOPLE! LET'S GO!
DIRECTOR
I KNEW THIS WOULD BE A MISTAKE! I'M OUTTA HERE!
MAXWELL, WAIT!
DON'T LET THE DOOR HIT YOU ON THE WAY OW! WHAT WAS THAT FOR?
SMACK
LIKE YOU DON'T KNOW! THEY CAME TO US FOR HELP, AND YOU'RE BEING A TOTAL JERKFACE TO THEM IN RETURN!
THIS ISN'T OUR FIGHT! WE DON'T OWE THEM ANYTHING!
SERIOUSLY? THEY GAVE US LIFE! THEY'RE FAMILY!
MAXWELL, WE NEED THEIR HELP.
NO WAY! WE'RE GOING TO BEAT THE ANTI-MONITOR ON OUR OWN!
YEAH, BUT WHAT HAVE THEY DONE FOR US LATELY?
WOW. I CAN'T EVEN...
WE ALREADY TRIED THAT, REMEMBER? IT DIDN'T WORK OUT SO WELL.
BETTER THAT THAN HAVING TO RELY ON DUMBELGANGER AND HIS KNOCK-OFF NOTEBOOK.

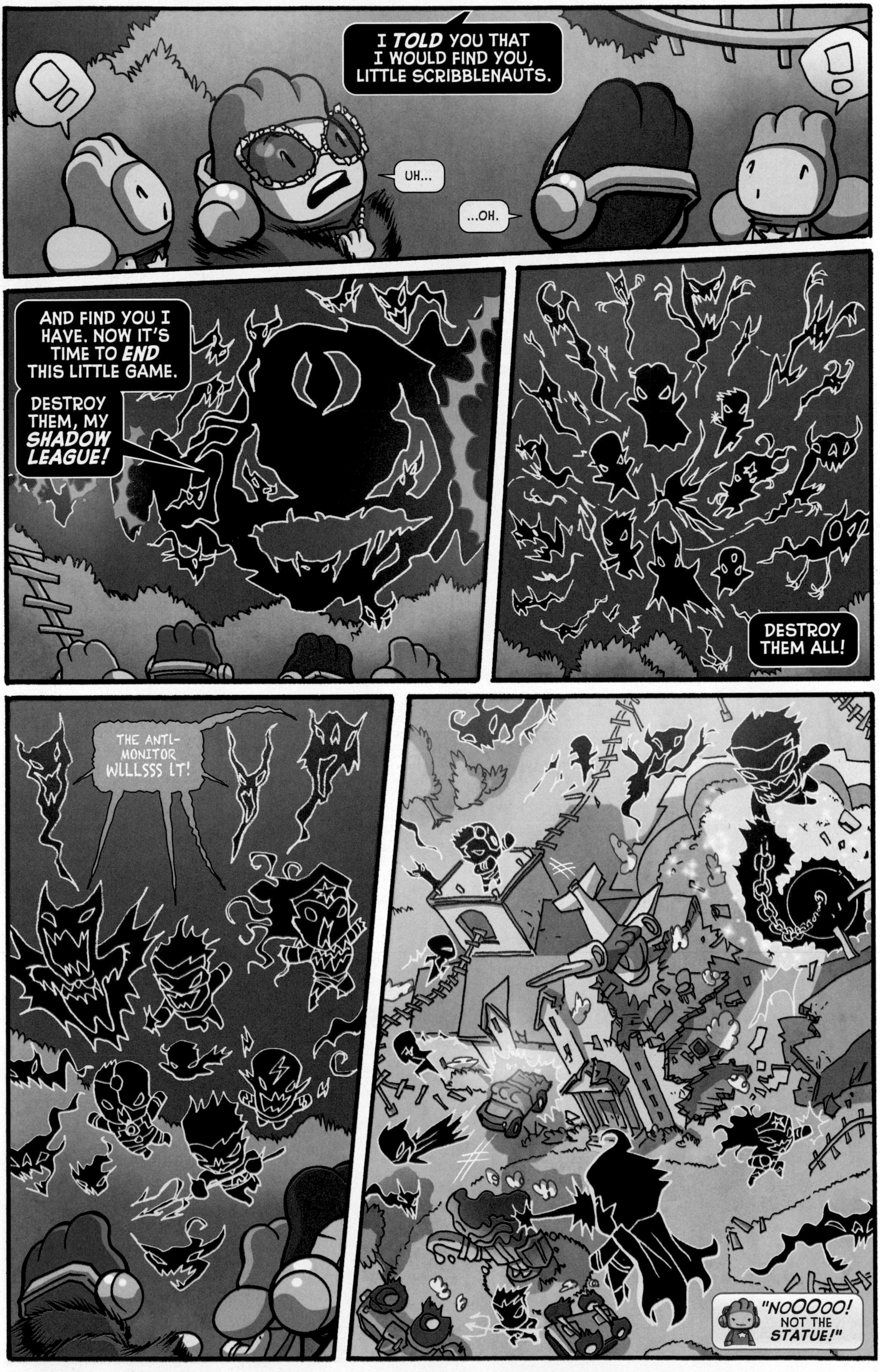
I TOLD YOU THAT I WOULD FIND YOU, LITTLE SCRIBBLENAUTS.
UH...
...OH.
AND FIND YOU I HAVE. NOW IT'S TIME TO END THIS LITTLE GAME.
DESTROY THEM, MY SHADOW LEAGUE!
DESTROY THEM ALL!
THE ANTI-MONITOR WLLLSSS LT!
"NOOOOO! NOT THE STATUE!"

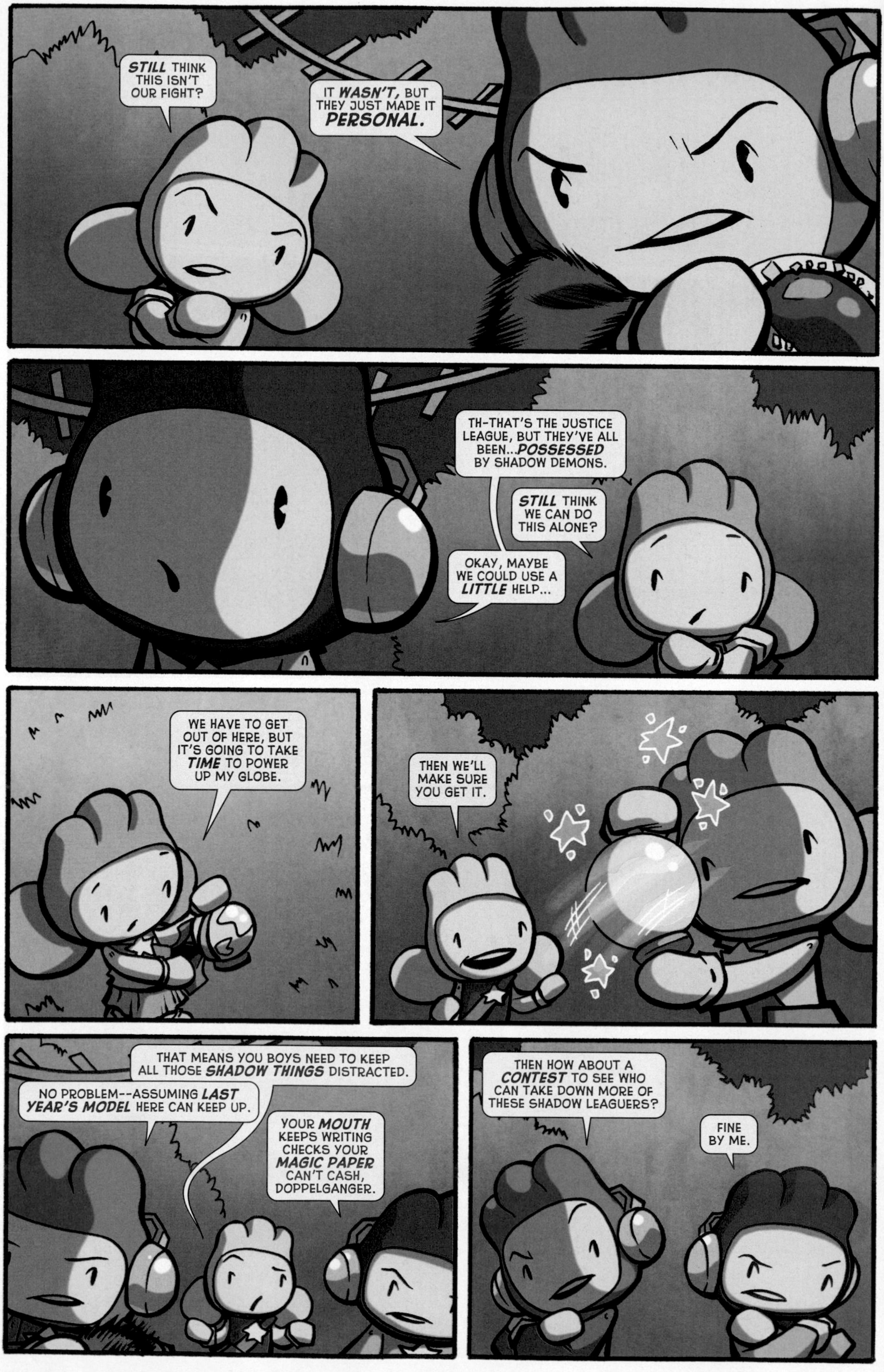
STILL THINK THIS ISN'T OUR FIGHT?
IT WASN'T, BUT THEY JUST MADE IT PERSONAL.
TH-THAT'S THE JUSTICE LEAGUE, BUT THEY'VE ALL BEEN...POSSESSED BY SHADOW DEMONS.
STILL THINK WE CAN DO THIS ALONE?
OKAY, MAYBE WE COULD USE A LITTLE HELP...
WE HAVE TO GET OUT OF HERE, BUT IT'S GOING TO TAKE TIME TO POWER UP MY GLOBE.
THEN WE'LL MAKE SURE YOU GET IT.
THAT MEANS YOU BOYS NEED TO KEEP ALL THOSE SHADOW THINGS DISTRACTED.
NO PROBLEM--ASSUMING LAST YEAR'S MODEL HERE CAN KEEP UP.
YOUR MOUTH KEEPS WRITING CHECKS YOUR MAGIC PAPER CAN'T CASH, DOPPELGANGER.
THEN HOW ABOUT A CONTEST TO SEE WHO CAN TAKE DOWN MORE OF THESE SHADOW LEAGUERS?
FINE BY ME.

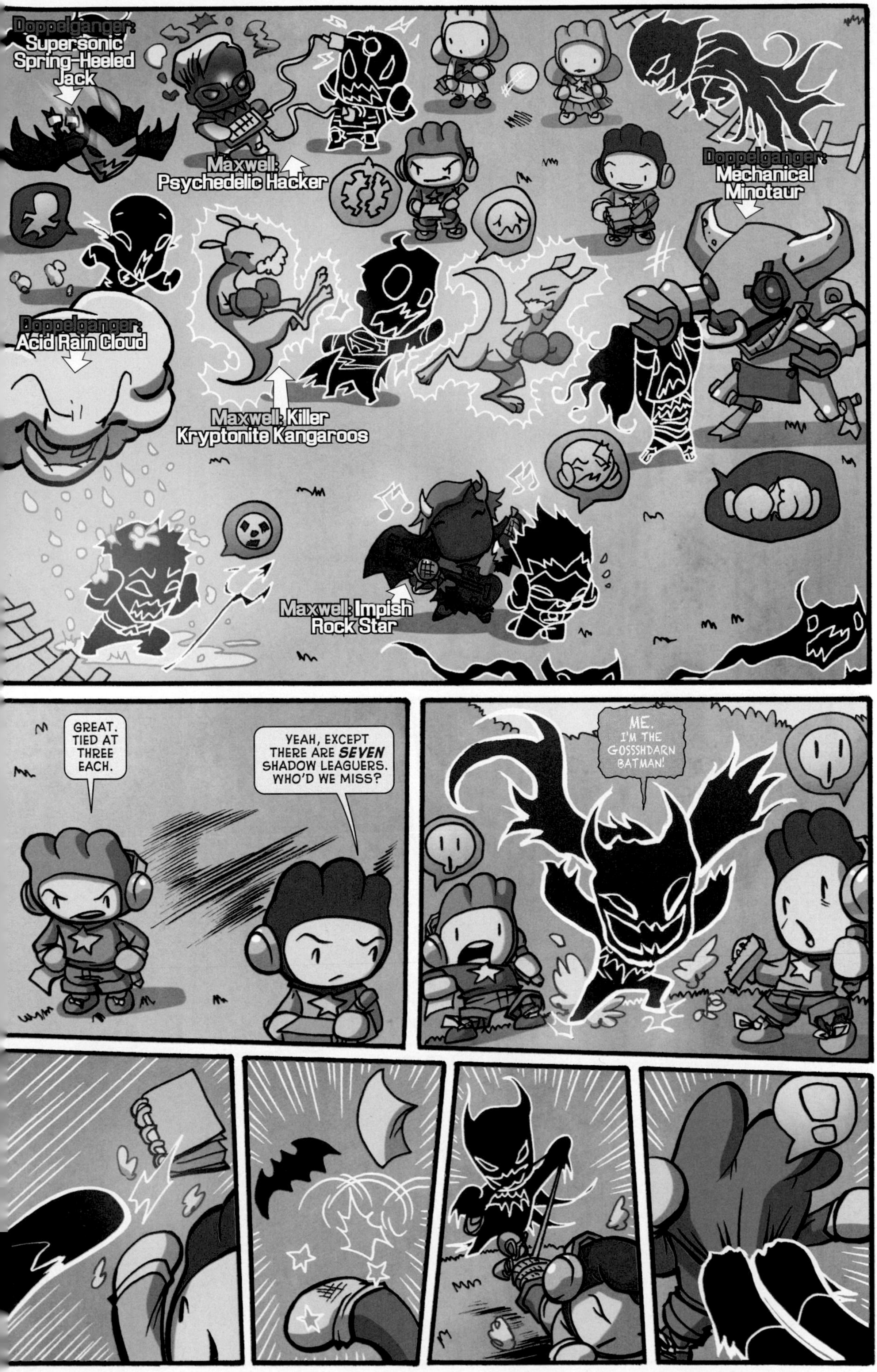
Doppelganger: Supersonic Spring-Heeled Jack
Maxwell: Psychedelic Hacker
Doppelganger: Mechanical Minotaur
Doppelganger: Acid Rain Cloud
Maxwell: Killer Kryptonite Kangaroos
Maxwell: Impish Rock Star
GREAT. TIED AT THREE EACH.
YEAH, EXCEPT THERE ARE *SEVEN* SHADOW LEAGUERS. WHO'D WE MISS?
ME. I'M THE GOSSSHDARN BATMAN!

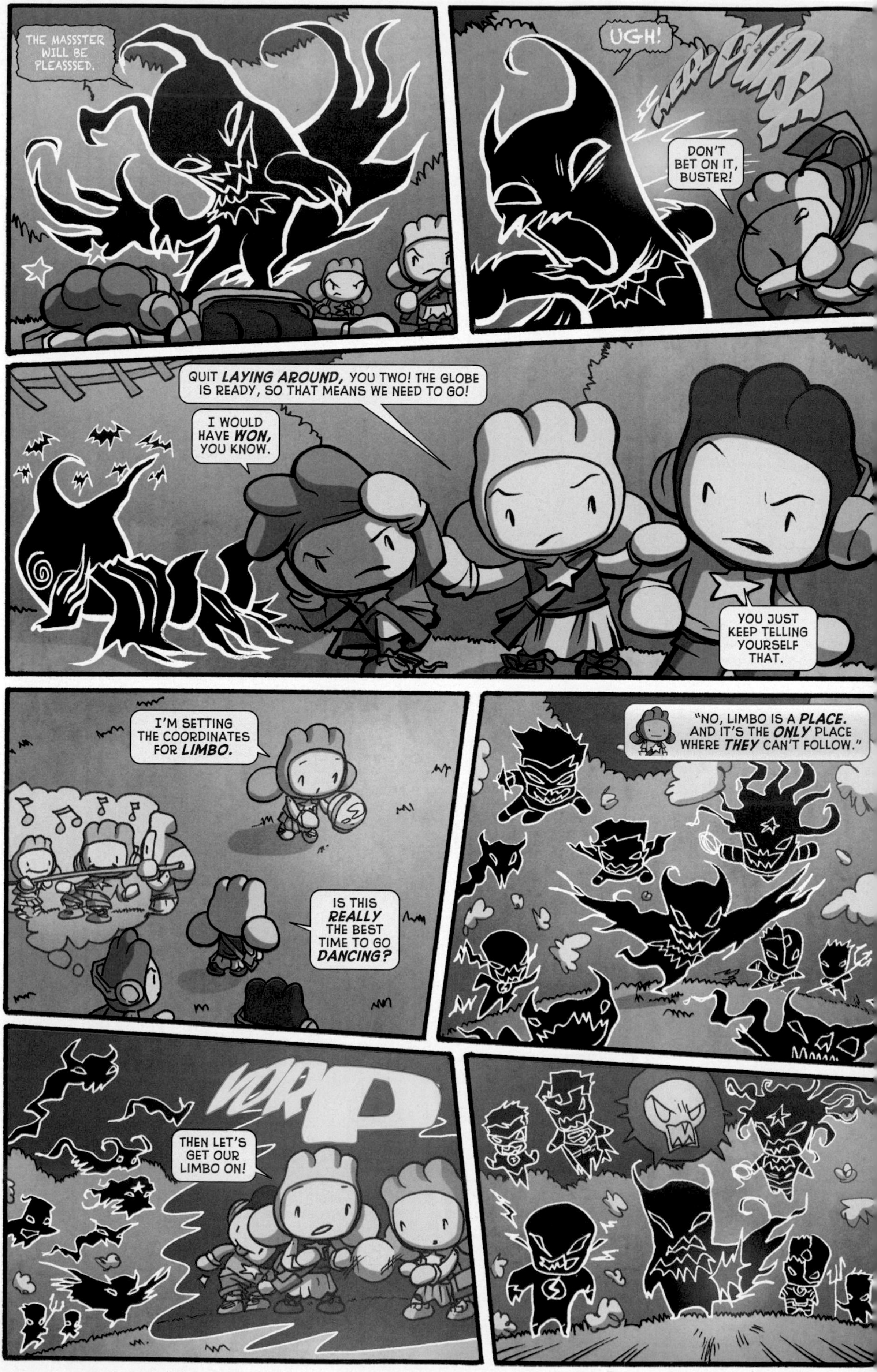

THE MASSSTER WILL BE PLEASSSED.
UGH!
KERPUNCH
DON'T BET ON IT, BUSTER!
QUIT LAYING AROUND, YOU TWO! THE GLOBE IS READY, SO THAT MEANS WE NEED TO GO!
I WOULD HAVE WON, YOU KNOW.
YOU JUST KEEP TELLING YOURSELF THAT.
I'M SETTING THE COORDINATES FOR LIMBO.
IS THIS REALLY THE BEST TIME TO GO DANCING?
"NO, LIMBO IS A PLACE. AND IT'S THE ONLY PLACE WHERE THEY CAN'T FOLLOW."
VORP
THEN LET'S GET OUR LIMBO ON!

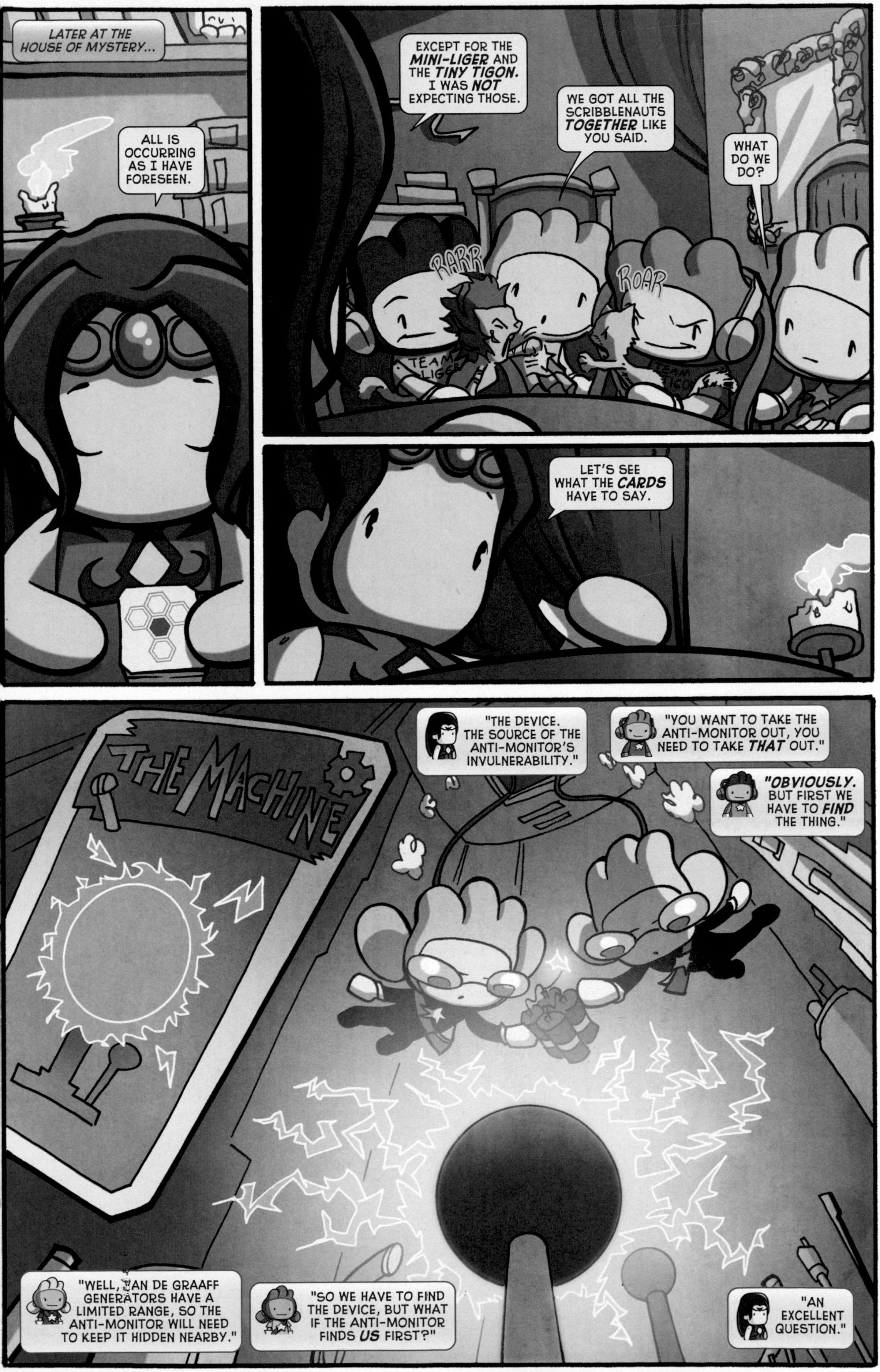
LATER AT THE HOUSE OF MYSTERY...
ALL IS OCCURRING AS I HAVE FORESEEN.
EXCEPT FOR THE MINI-LIGER AND THE TINY TIGON. I WAS NOT EXPECTING THOSE.
WE GOT ALL THE SCRIBBLENAUTS TOGETHER LIKE YOU SAID.
WHAT DO WE DO?
RARR
ROAR
TEAM LIGER
TEAM TIGON
LET'S SEE WHAT THE CARDS HAVE TO SAY.
THE MACHINE
"THE DEVICE. THE SOURCE OF THE ANTI-MONITOR'S INVULNERABILITY."
"YOU WANT TO TAKE THE ANTI-MONITOR OUT, YOU NEED TO TAKE THAT OUT."
"OBVIOUSLY. BUT FIRST WE HAVE TO FIND THE THING."
"WELL, VAN DE GRAAFF GENERATORS HAVE A LIMITED RANGE, SO THE ANTI-MONITOR WILL NEED TO KEEP IT HIDDEN NEARBY."
"SO WE HAVE TO FIND THE DEVICE, BUT WHAT IF THE ANTI-MONITOR FINDS US FIRST?"
"AN EXCELLENT QUESTION."

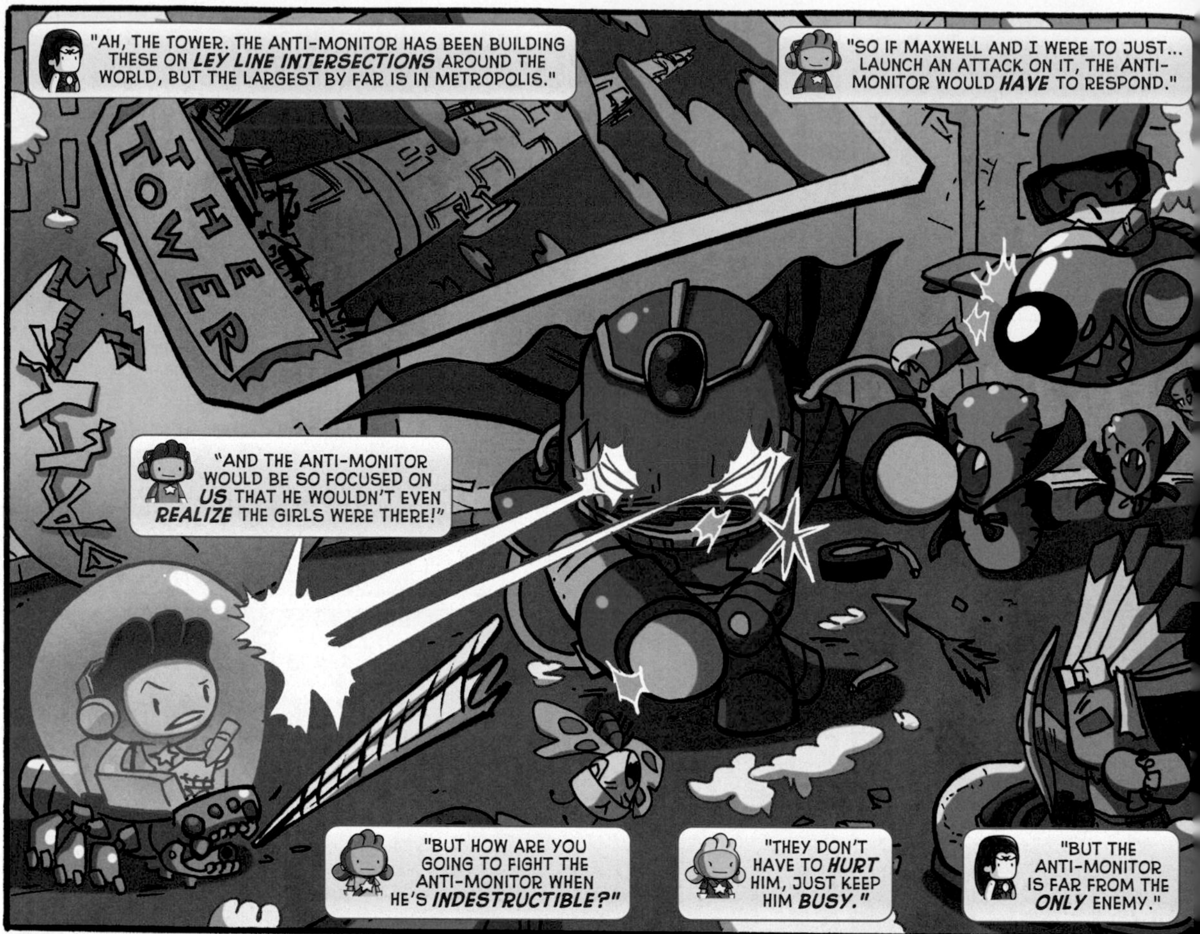
"AH, THE TOWER. THE ANTI-MONITOR HAS BEEN BUILDING THESE ON LEY LINE INTERSECTIONS AROUND THE WORLD, BUT THE LARGEST BY FAR IS IN METROPOLIS."
"SO IF MAXWELL AND I WERE TO JUST... LAUNCH AN ATTACK ON IT, THE ANTI-MONITOR WOULD HAVE TO RESPOND."
THE TOWER
"AND THE ANTI-MONITOR WOULD BE SO FOCUSED ON US THAT HE WOULDN'T EVEN REALIZE THE GIRLS WERE THERE!"
"BUT HOW ARE YOU GOING TO FIGHT THE ANTI-MONITOR WHEN HE'S INDESTRUCTIBLE?"
"THEY DON'T HAVE TO HURT HIM, JUST KEEP HIM BUSY."
"BUT THE ANTI-MONITOR IS FAR FROM THE ONLY ENEMY."

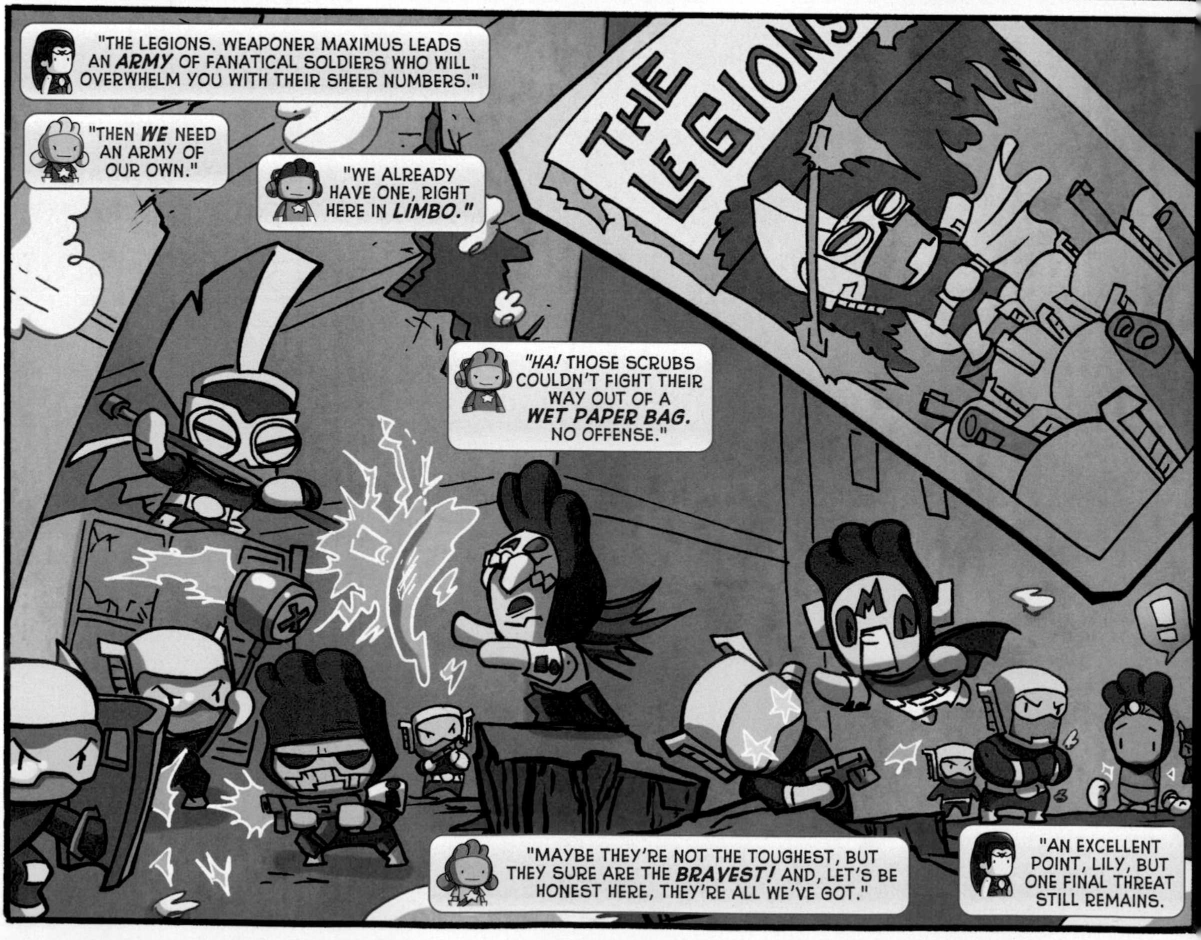
"THE LEGIONS. WEAPONER MAXIMUS LEADS AN ARMY OF FANATICAL SOLDIERS WHO WILL OVERWHELM YOU WITH THEIR SHEER NUMBERS."
THE LEGIONS
"THEN WE NEED AN ARMY OF OUR OWN."
"WE ALREADY HAVE ONE, RIGHT HERE IN LIMBO."
"HA! THOSE SCRUBS COULDN'T FIGHT THEIR WAY OUT OF A WET PAPER BAG. NO OFFENSE."
"MAYBE THEY'RE NOT THE TOUGHEST, BUT THEY SURE ARE THE BRAVEST! AND, LET'S BE HONEST HERE, THEY'RE ALL WE'VE GOT."
"AN EXCELLENT POINT, LILY, BUT ONE FINAL THREAT STILL REMAINS.

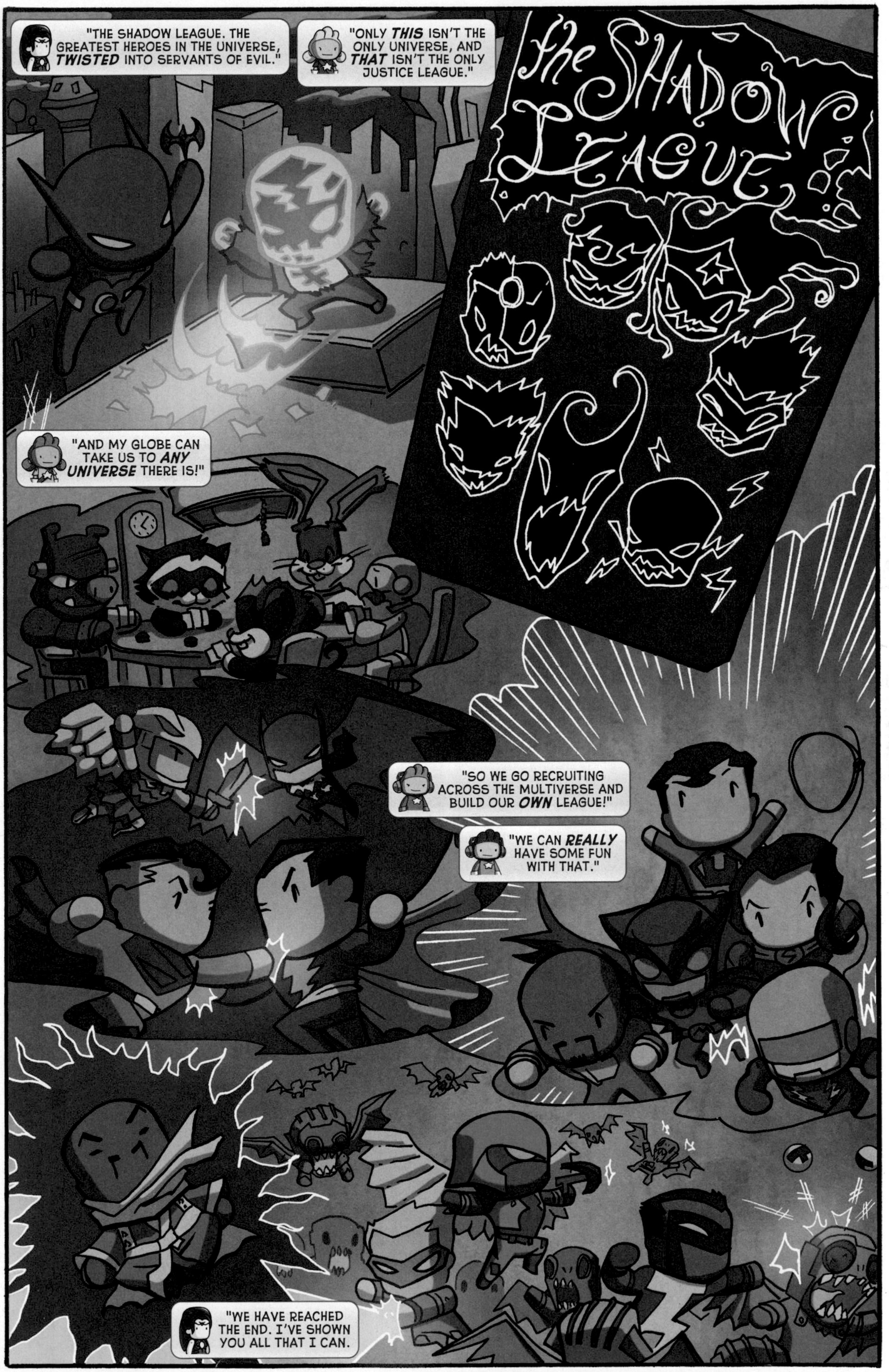
"THE SHADOW LEAGUE. THE GREATEST HEROES IN THE UNIVERSE, TWISTED INTO SERVANTS OF EVIL."
"ONLY THIS ISN'T THE ONLY UNIVERSE, AND THAT ISN'T THE ONLY JUSTICE LEAGUE."
The SHADOW LEAGUE
"AND MY GLOBE CAN TAKE US TO ANY UNIVERSE THERE IS!"
"SO WE GO RECRUITING ACROSS THE MULTIVERSE AND BUILD OUR OWN LEAGUE!"
"WE CAN REALLY HAVE SOME FUN WITH THAT."
"WE HAVE REACHED THE END. I'VE SHOWN YOU ALL THAT I CAN.

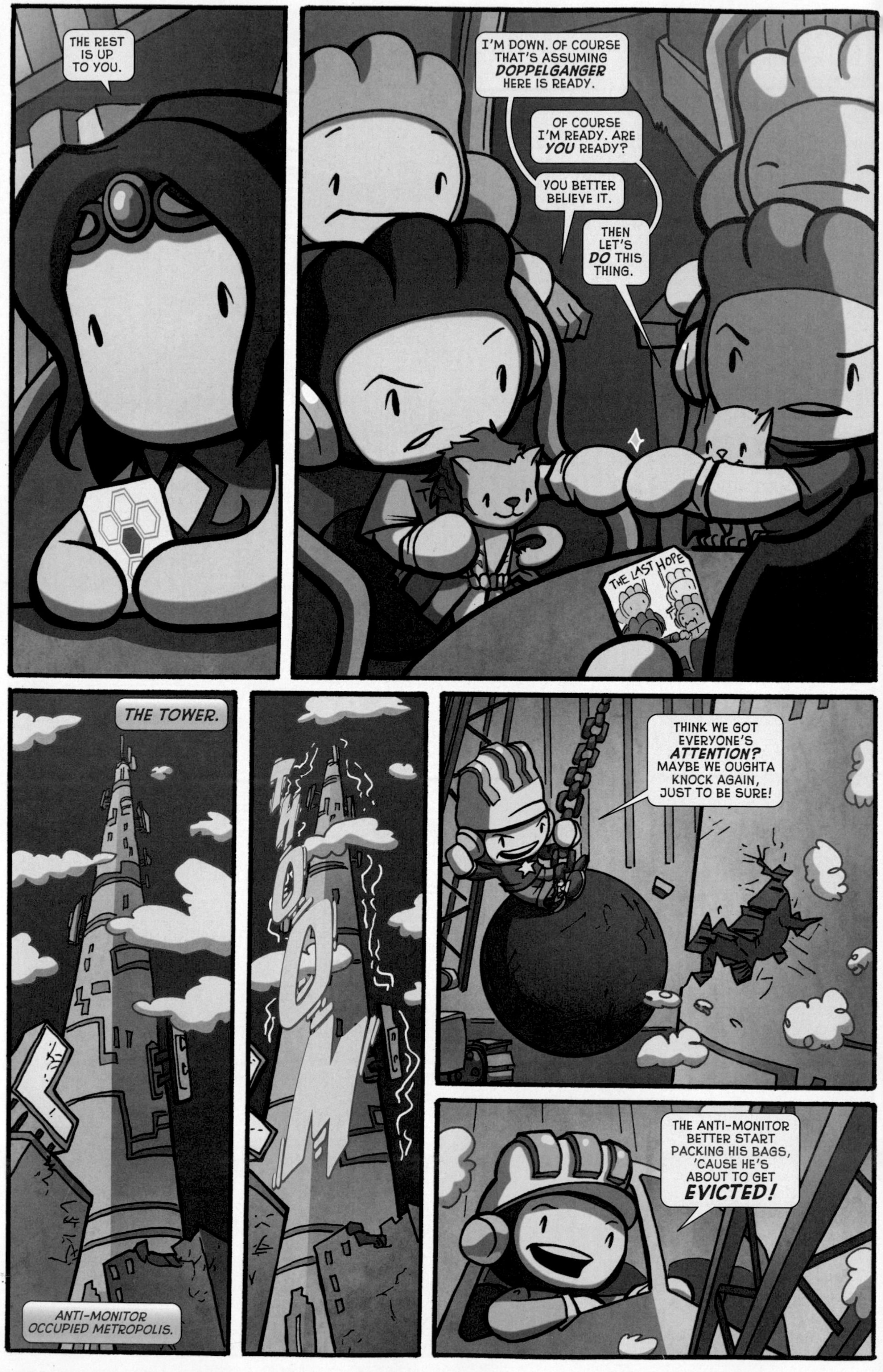
THE REST IS UP TO YOU.
I'M DOWN. OF COURSE THAT'S ASSUMING DOPPELGANGER HERE IS READY.
OF COURSE I'M READY. ARE YOU READY?
YOU BETTER BELIEVE IT.
THEN LET'S DO THIS THING.
THE LAST HOPE
THE TOWER.
ANTI-MONITOR OCCUPIED METROPOLIS.
THINK WE GOT EVERYONE'S ATTENTION? MAYBE WE OUGHTA KNOCK AGAIN, JUST TO BE SURE!
THE ANTI-MONITOR BETTER START PACKING HIS BAGS, 'CAUSE HE'S ABOUT TO GET EVICTED!

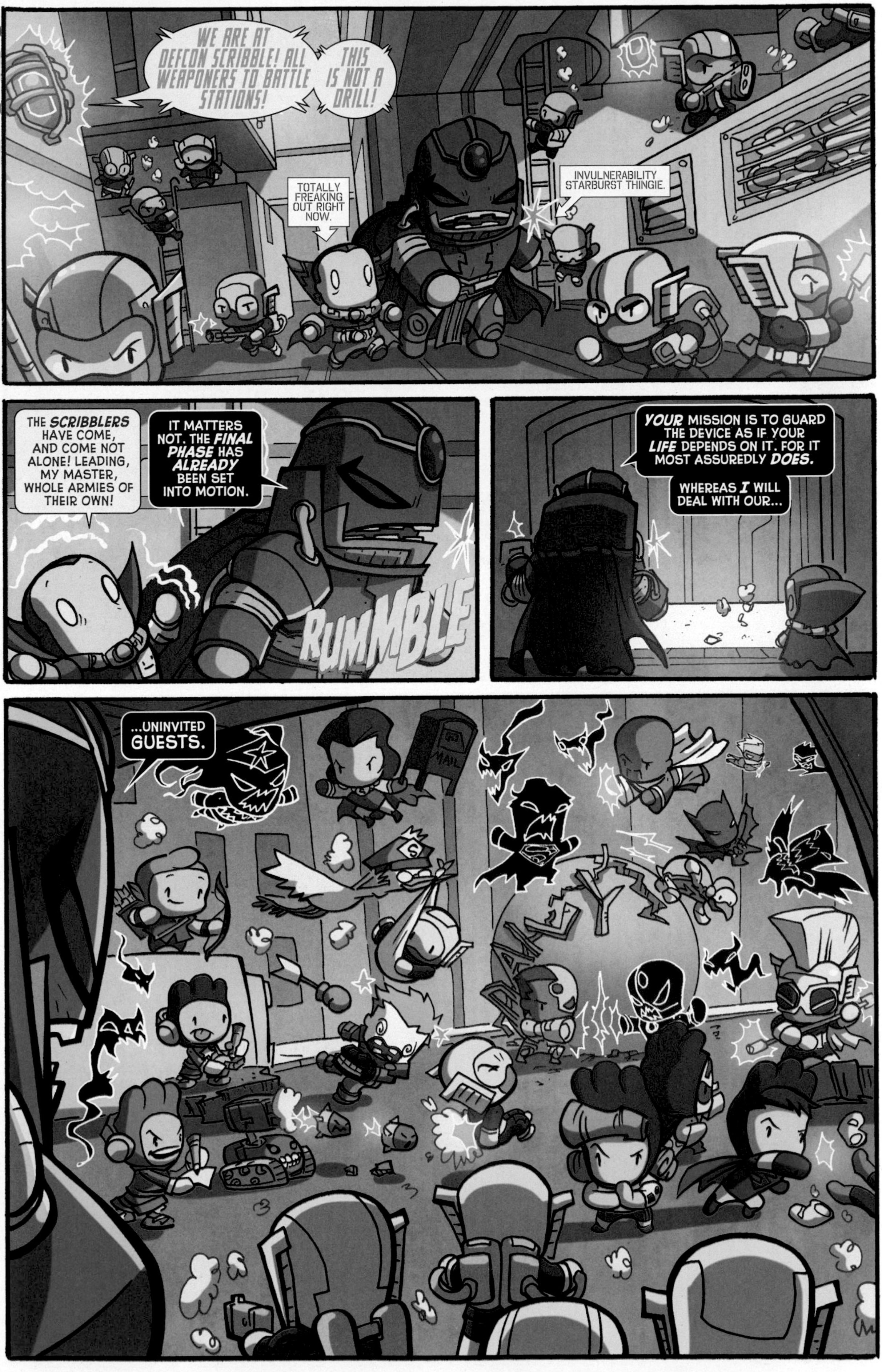
WE ARE AT DEFCON SCRIBBLE! ALL WEAPONERS TO BATTLE STATIONS!
THIS IS NOT A DRILL!
TOTALLY FREAKING OUT RIGHT NOW.
INVULNERABILITY STARBURST THINGIE.
THE SCRIBBLERS HAVE COME, AND COME NOT ALONE! LEADING, MY MASTER, WHOLE ARMIES OF THEIR OWN!
IT MATTERS NOT. THE FINAL PHASE HAS ALREADY BEEN SET INTO MOTION.
RUMMBLE
YOUR MISSION IS TO GUARD THE DEVICE AS IF YOUR LIFE DEPENDS ON IT. FOR IT MOST ASSUREDLY DOES.
WHEREAS I WILL DEAL WITH OUR...
...UNINVITED GUESTS.
MAIL

MAXWELL. I SEE YOU AND YOUR *COPY* HAVE FINALLY STOPPED *RUNNING*. GOOD. IT SAVES ME THE *TROUBLE* OF HUNTING YOU DOWN.

TELL ME HE DID *NOT* JUST USE THE *C WORD!*

KEEP YOUR COOL AND STICK TO THE PLAN, DOPPELGANGER!

I KNOW, I KNOW. WE CAN'T *BEAT* HIM.

BUT WE *CAN* KEEP HIM BUSY!

YOU WILL DO NOTHING BUT *PERISH!*

PING PING

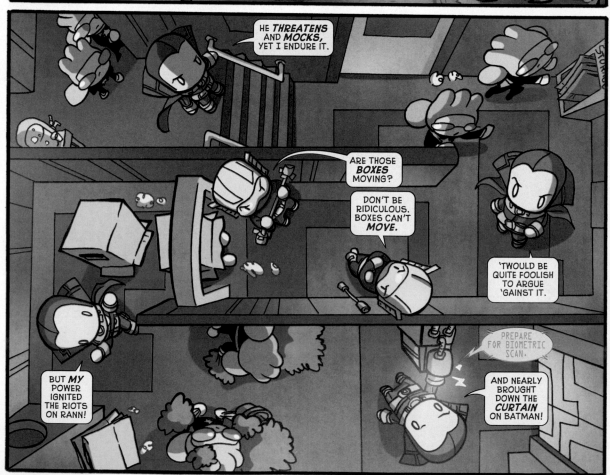

HE *THREATENS* AND *MOCKS*, YET I ENDURE IT.

ARE THOSE *BOXES* MOVING?

DON'T BE RIDICULOUS. BOXES CAN'T *MOVE*.

'TWOULD BE QUITE FOOLISH TO ARGUE 'GAINST IT.

PREPARE FOR BIOMETRIC SCAN.

BUT *MY* POWER IGNITED THE RIOTS ON RANN!

AND NEARLY BROUGHT DOWN THE *CURTAIN* ON BATMAN!

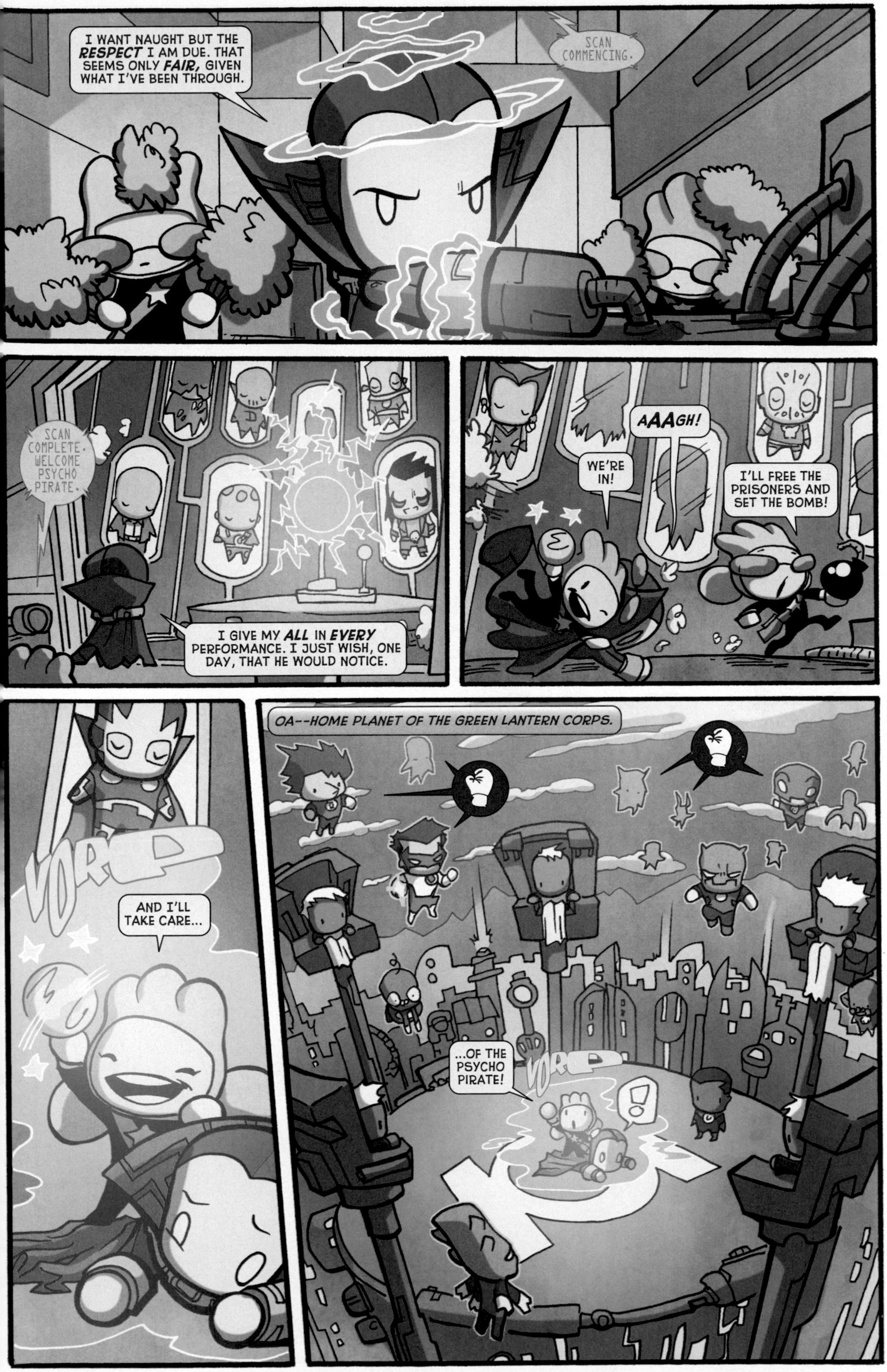
I WANT NAUGHT BUT THE RESPECT I AM DUE. THAT SEEMS ONLY FAIR, GIVEN WHAT I'VE BEEN THROUGH.
SCAN COMMENCING.
SCAN COMPLETE. WELCOME PSYCHO PIRATE.
I GIVE MY ALL IN EVERY PERFORMANCE. I JUST WISH, ONE DAY, THAT HE WOULD NOTICE.
AAAGH!
WE'RE IN!
I'LL FREE THE PRISONERS AND SET THE BOMB!
VORP
AND I'LL TAKE CARE...
OA--HOME PLANET OF THE GREEN LANTERN CORPS.
VORP
...OF THE PSYCHO PIRATE!
!

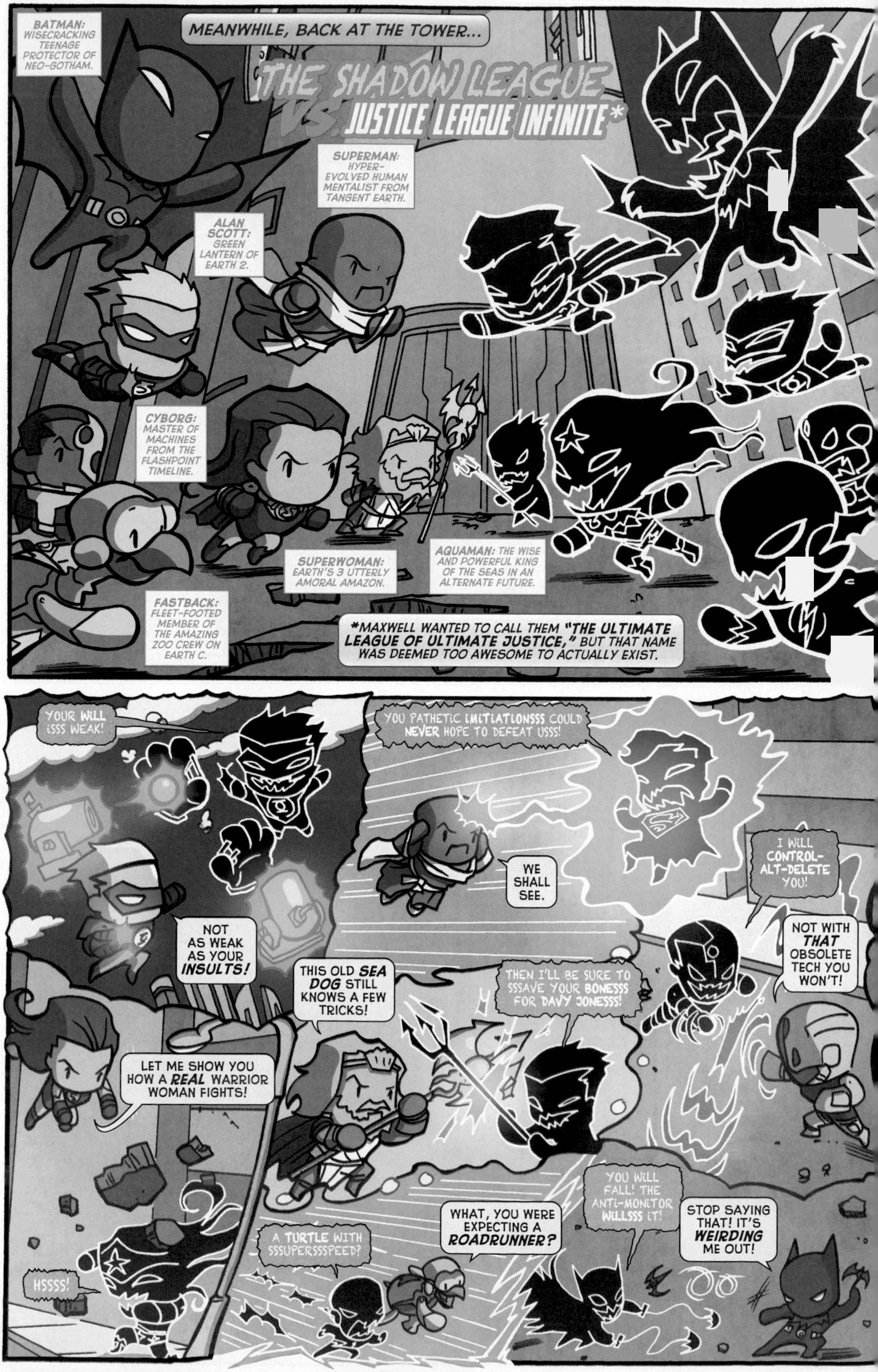
BATMAN: WISECRACKING TEENAGE PROTECTOR OF NEO-GOTHAM.
MEANWHILE, BACK AT THE TOWER...
THE SHADOW LEAGUE VS. JUSTICE LEAGUE INFINITE*
SUPERMAN: HYPER-EVOLVED HUMAN MENTALIST FROM TANGENT EARTH.
ALAN SCOTT: GREEN LANTERN OF EARTH 2.
CYBORG: MASTER OF MACHINES FROM THE FLASHPOINT TIMELINE.
SUPERWOMAN: EARTH'S 3 UTTERLY AMORAL AMAZON.
AQUAMAN: THE WISE AND POWERFUL KING OF THE SEAS IN AN ALTERNATE FUTURE.
FASTBACK: FLEET-FOOTED MEMBER OF THE AMAZING ZOO CREW ON EARTH C.
*MAXWELL WANTED TO CALL THEM "THE ULTIMATE LEAGUE OF ULTIMATE JUSTICE," BUT THAT NAME WAS DEEMED TOO AWESOME TO ACTUALLY EXIST.
YOUR WILL ISSS WEAK!
YOU PATHETIC IMITATIONSSS COULD NEVER HOPE TO DEFEAT USSS!
WE SHALL SEE.
I WILL CONTROL-ALT-DELETE YOU!
NOT AS WEAK AS YOUR INSULTS!
NOT WITH THAT OBSOLETE TECH YOU WON'T!
THIS OLD SEA DOG STILL KNOWS A FEW TRICKS!
THEN I'LL BE SURE TO SSSAVE YOUR BONESSS FOR DAVY JONESSS!
LET ME SHOW YOU HOW A REAL WARRIOR WOMAN FIGHTS!
YOU WILL FALL! THE ANTI-MONITOR WILLSSS IT!
WHAT, YOU WERE EXPECTING A ROADRUNNER?
STOP SAYING THAT! IT'S WEIRDING ME OUT!
A TURTLE WITH SSSUPERSSSPEED?
HSSSS!

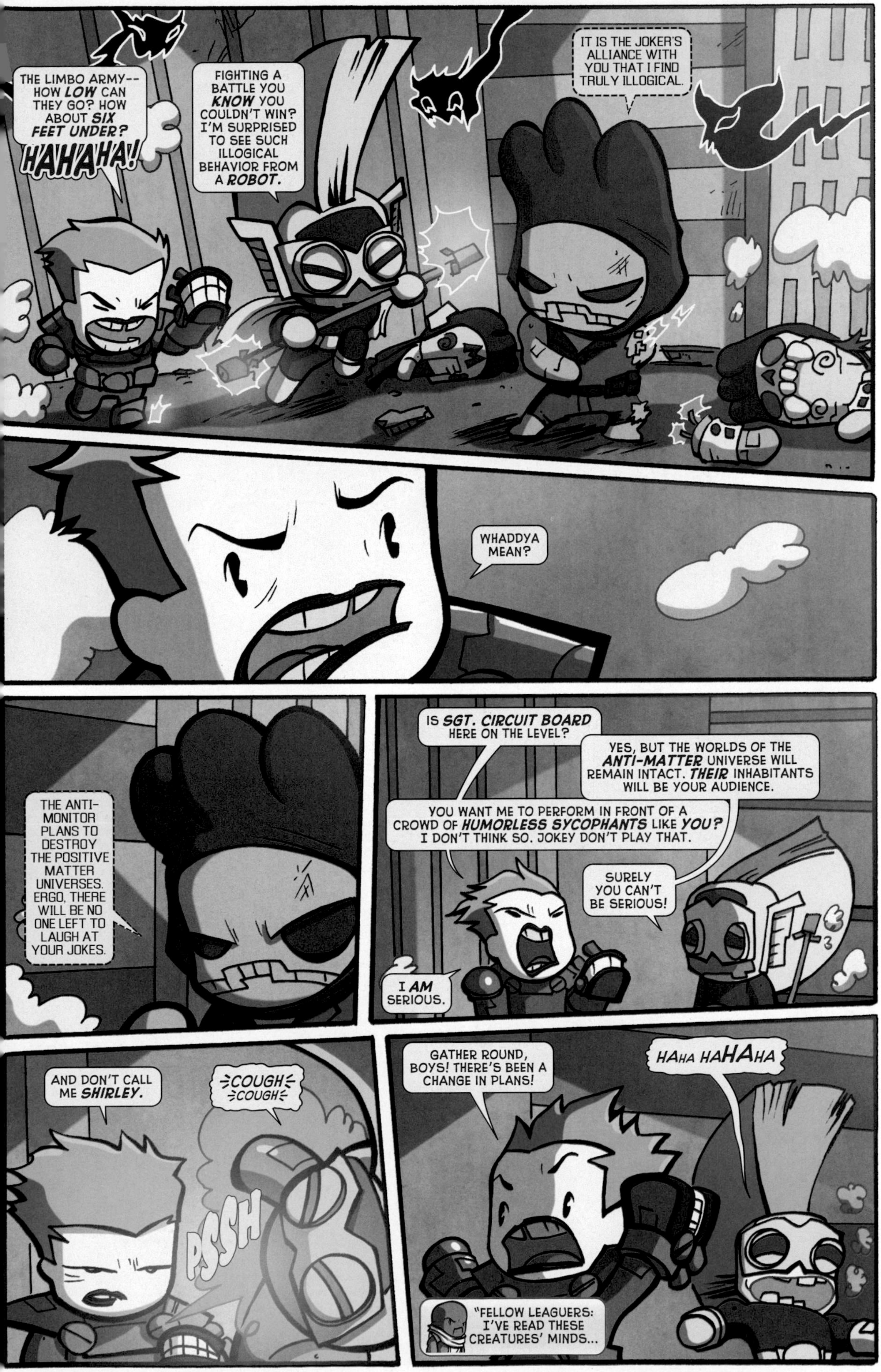
THE LIMBO ARMY-- HOW LOW CAN THEY GO? HOW ABOUT SIX FEET UNDER? HAHAHA!
FIGHTING A BATTLE YOU KNOW YOU COULDN'T WIN? I'M SURPRISED TO SEE SUCH ILLOGICAL BEHAVIOR FROM A ROBOT.
IT IS THE JOKER'S ALLIANCE WITH YOU THAT I FIND TRULY ILLOGICAL.
WHADDYA MEAN?
THE ANTI-MONITOR PLANS TO DESTROY THE POSITIVE MATTER UNIVERSES. ERGO, THERE WILL BE NO ONE LEFT TO LAUGH AT YOUR JOKES.
IS SGT. CIRCUIT BOARD HERE ON THE LEVEL?
YES, BUT THE WORLDS OF THE ANTI-MATTER UNIVERSE WILL REMAIN INTACT. THEIR INHABITANTS WILL BE YOUR AUDIENCE.
YOU WANT ME TO PERFORM IN FRONT OF A CROWD OF HUMORLESS SYCOPHANTS LIKE YOU? I DON'T THINK SO. JOKEY DON'T PLAY THAT.
SURELY YOU CAN'T BE SERIOUS!
I AM SERIOUS.
AND DON'T CALL ME SHIRLEY.
COUGH COUGH
PSSH
GATHER ROUND, BOYS! THERE'S BEEN A CHANGE IN PLANS!
HAHA HAHAHA
"FELLOW LEAGUERS: I'VE READ THESE CREATURES' MINDS...

...AND THEY'RE VULNERABLE TO *LIGHT* AND *SOUND*.

AQUAMAN, DISORIENT THEM WITH A WATERSPOUT.

AYE, AYE, MY CAPTAIN!

*FWOOSH*

FASTBACK, USE SUPERWOMAN'S LASSO OF SUBMISSION TO KEEP THEM IN PLACE.

AND BE *CAREFUL* WITH IT, OR I'LL TURN YOU INTO *TURTLE SOUP!*

OK!

I'M

IT!

ON

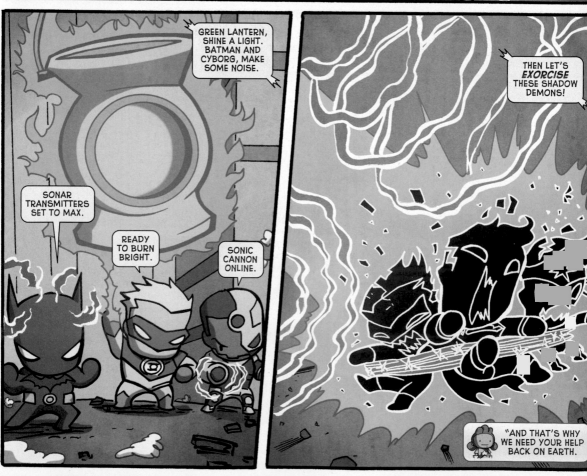

GREEN LANTERN, SHINE A LIGHT. BATMAN AND CYBORG, MAKE SOME NOISE.

SONAR TRANSMITTERS SET TO MAX.

READY TO BURN BRIGHT.

SONIC CANNON ONLINE.

THEN LET'S *EXORCISE* THESE SHADOW DEMONS!

"AND THAT'S WHY WE NEED YOUR HELP BACK ON EARTH.

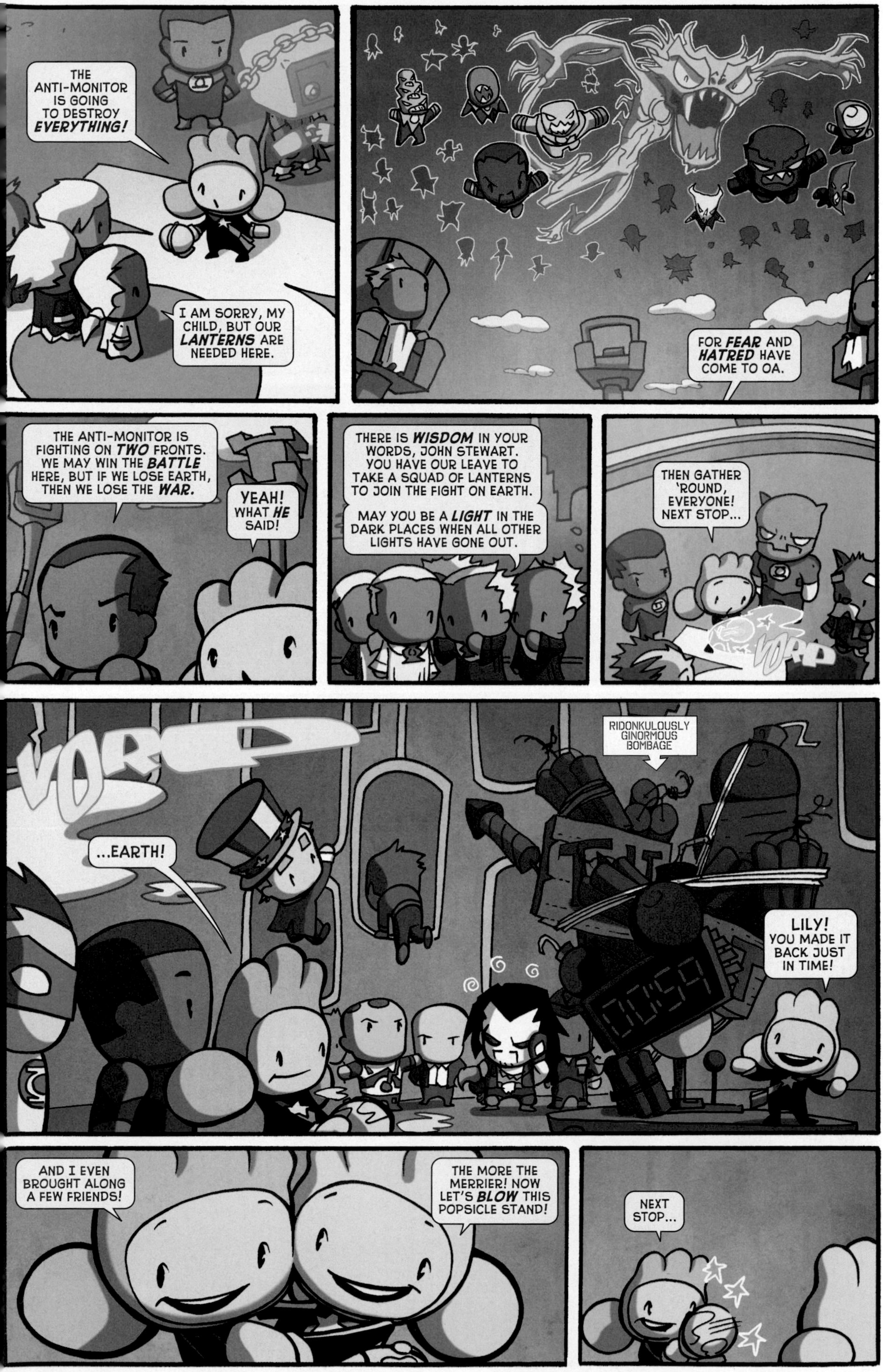
THE ANTI-MONITOR IS GOING TO DESTROY EVERYTHING!
I AM SORRY, MY CHILD, BUT OUR LANTERNS ARE NEEDED HERE.
FOR FEAR AND HATRED HAVE COME TO OA.
THE ANTI-MONITOR IS FIGHTING ON TWO FRONTS. WE MAY WIN THE BATTLE HERE, BUT IF WE LOSE EARTH, THEN WE LOSE THE WAR.
YEAH! WHAT HE SAID!
THERE IS WISDOM IN YOUR WORDS, JOHN STEWART. YOU HAVE OUR LEAVE TO TAKE A SQUAD OF LANTERNS TO JOIN THE FIGHT ON EARTH.
MAY YOU BE A LIGHT IN THE DARK PLACES WHEN ALL OTHER LIGHTS HAVE GONE OUT.
THEN GATHER 'ROUND, EVERYONE! NEXT STOP...
VORP
VORP
...EARTH!
RIDONKULOUSLY GINORMOUS BOMBAGE
LILY! YOU MADE IT BACK JUST IN TIME!
AND I EVEN BROUGHT ALONG A FEW FRIENDS!
THE MORE THE MERRIER! NOW LET'S BLOW THIS POPSICLE STAND!
NEXT STOP...

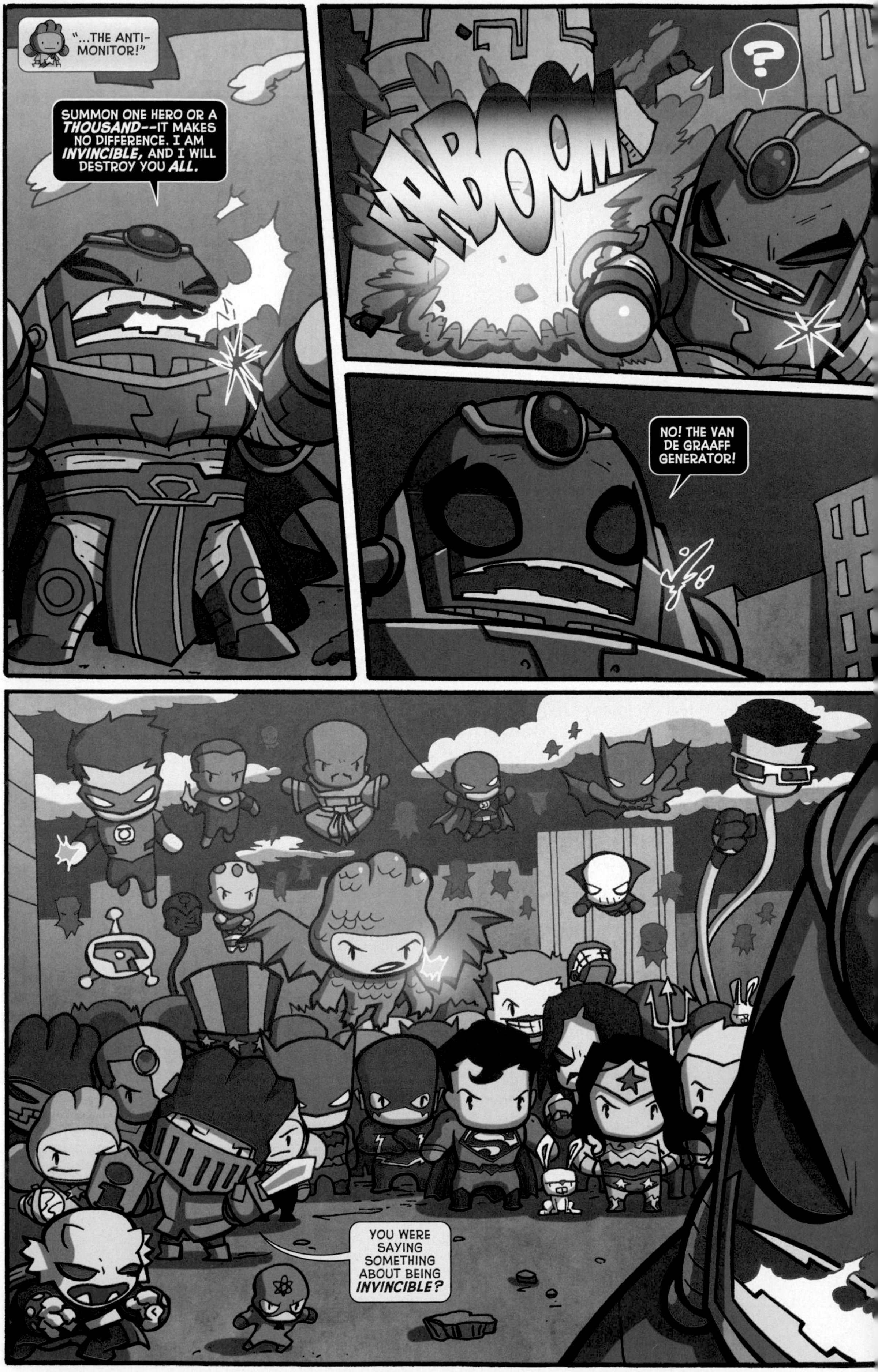
"...THE ANTI-MONITOR!"
SUMMON ONE HERO OR A THOUSAND--IT MAKES NO DIFFERENCE. I AM INVINCIBLE, AND I WILL DESTROY YOU ALL.
KABOOM!
?
NO! THE VAN DE GRAAFF GENERATOR!
YOU WERE SAYING SOMETHING ABOUT BEING INVINCIBLE?

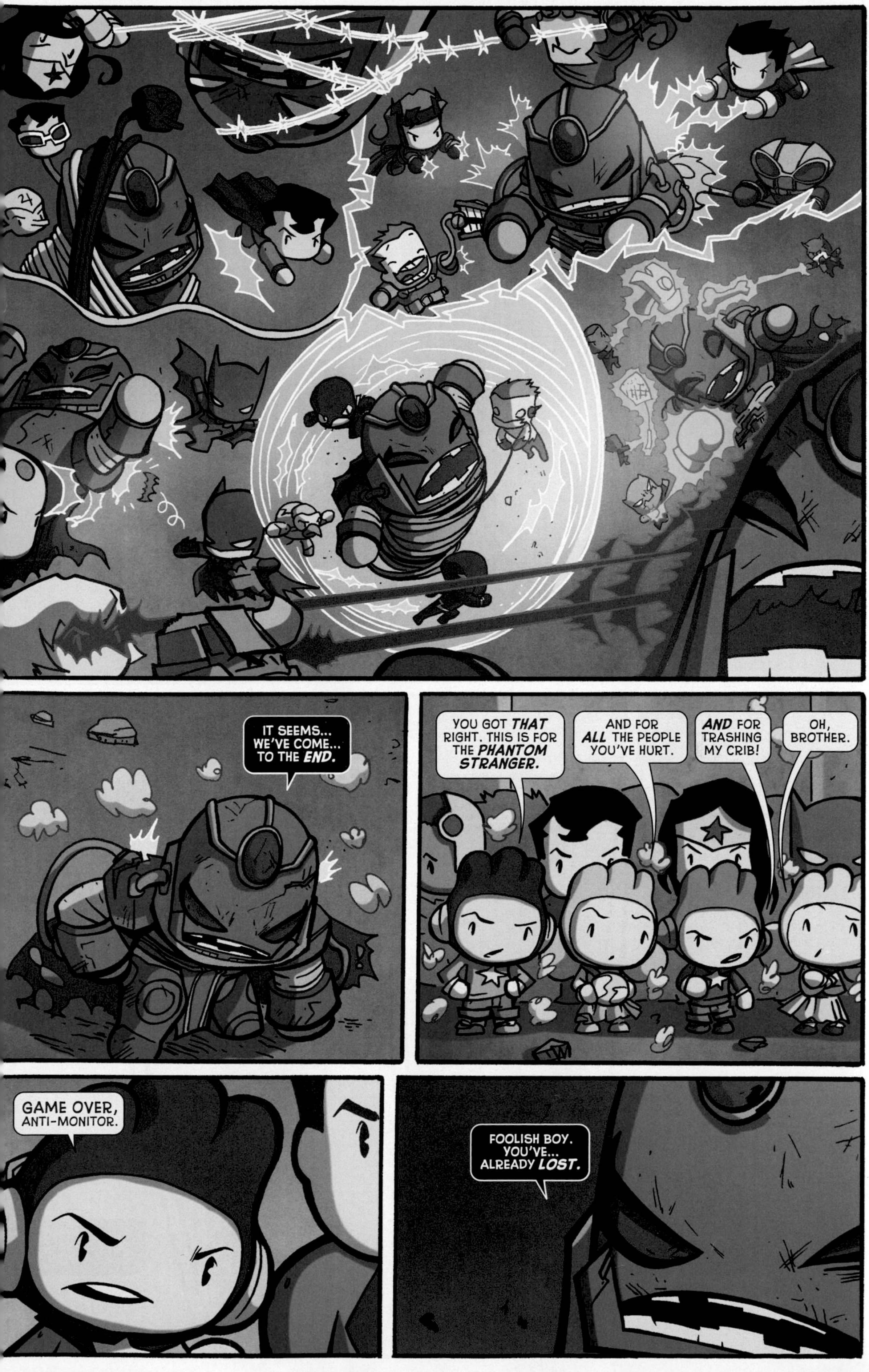
IT SEEMS... WE'VE COME... TO THE END.
YOU GOT THAT RIGHT. THIS IS FOR THE PHANTOM STRANGER.
AND FOR ALL THE PEOPLE YOU'VE HURT.
AND FOR TRASHING MY CRIB!
OH, BROTHER.
GAME OVER, ANTI-MONITOR.
FOOLISH BOY. YOU'VE... ALREADY LOST.

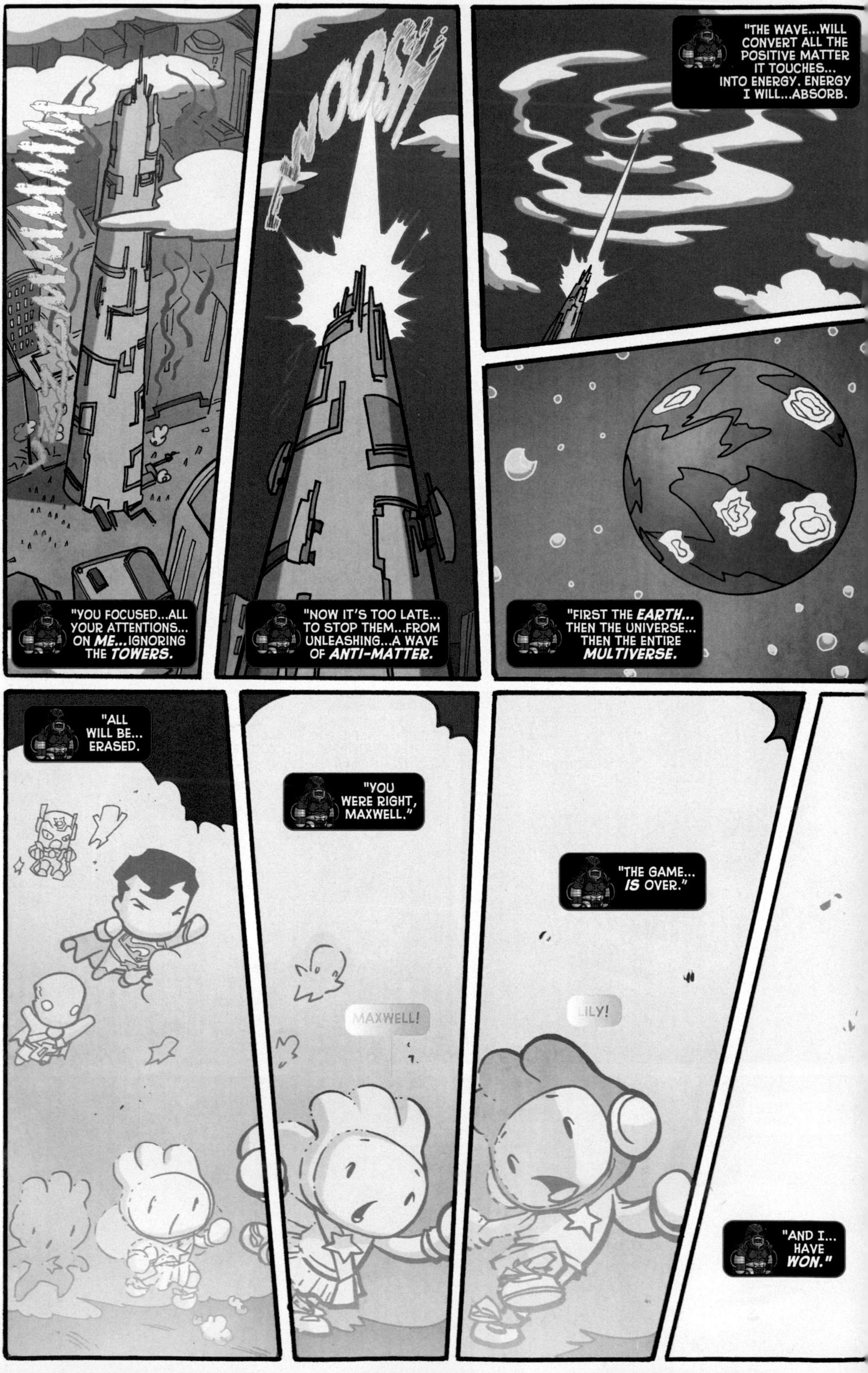

MMMMMMMMM
"YOU FOCUSED...ALL YOUR ATTENTIONS... ON *ME*...IGNORING THE *TOWERS*.
FWOOSH!
"NOW IT'S TOO LATE... TO STOP THEM...FROM UNLEASHING...A WAVE OF *ANTI-MATTER*.
"THE WAVE...WILL CONVERT ALL THE POSITIVE MATTER IT TOUCHES... INTO ENERGY. ENERGY I WILL...ABSORB.
"FIRST THE *EARTH*... THEN THE UNIVERSE... THEN THE ENTIRE *MULTIVERSE*.
"ALL WILL BE... ERASED.
"YOU WERE RIGHT, MAXWELL."
MAXWELL!
"THE GAME... *IS* OVER."
LILY!
"AND I... HAVE *WON*."

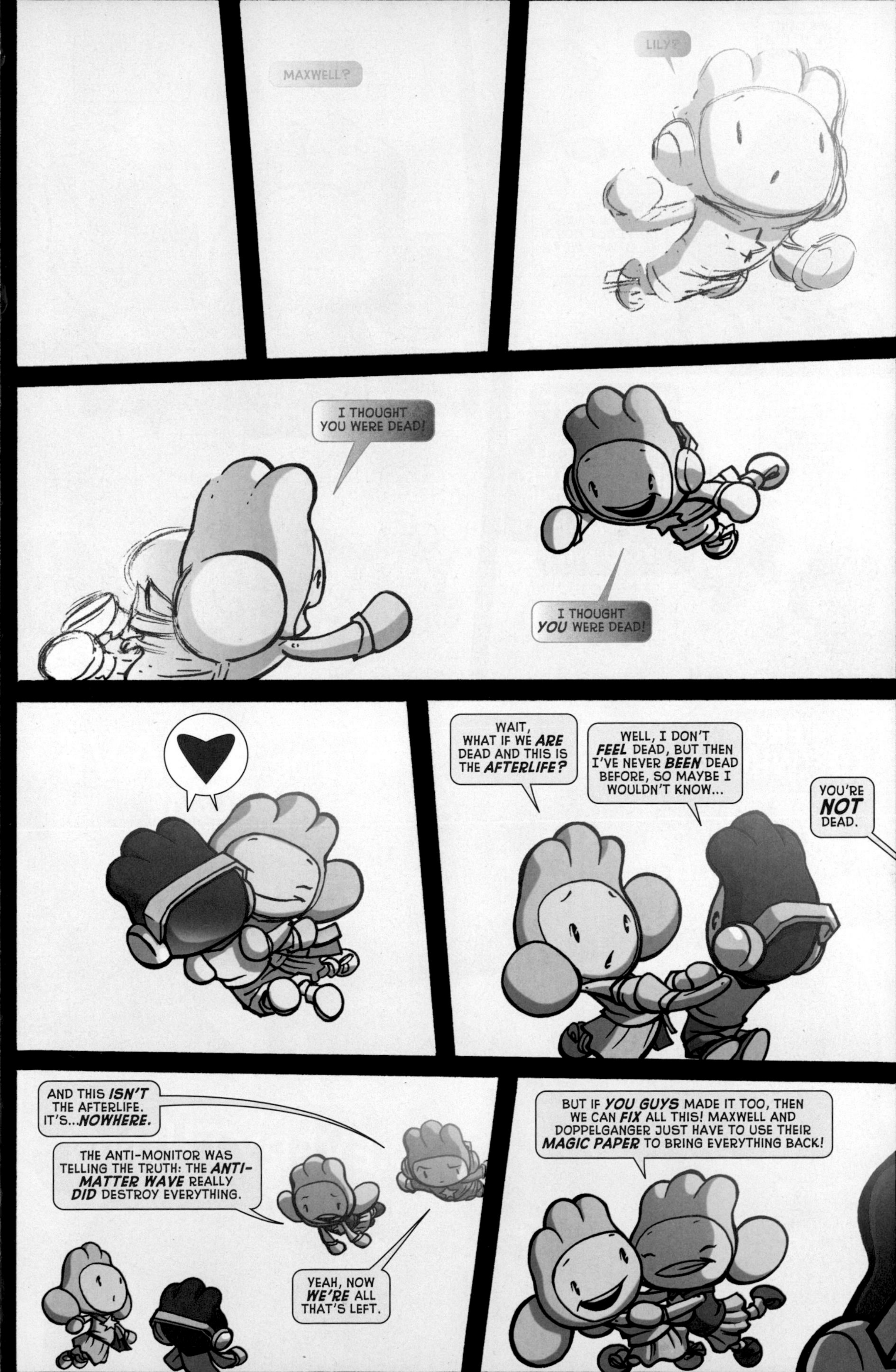
MAXWELL?
LILY?
I THOUGHT YOU WERE DEAD!
I THOUGHT YOU WERE DEAD!
WAIT, WHAT IF WE ARE DEAD AND THIS IS THE AFTERLIFE?
WELL, I DON'T FEEL DEAD, BUT THEN I'VE NEVER BEEN DEAD BEFORE, SO MAYBE I WOULDN'T KNOW...
YOU'RE NOT DEAD.
AND THIS ISN'T THE AFTERLIFE. IT'S...NOWHERE.
THE ANTI-MONITOR WAS TELLING THE TRUTH: THE ANTI-MATTER WAVE REALLY DID DESTROY EVERYTHING.
YEAH, NOW WE'RE ALL THAT'S LEFT.
BUT IF YOU GUYS MADE IT TOO, THEN WE CAN FIX ALL THIS! MAXWELL AND DOPPELGANGER JUST HAVE TO USE THEIR MAGIC PAPER TO BRING EVERYTHING BACK!

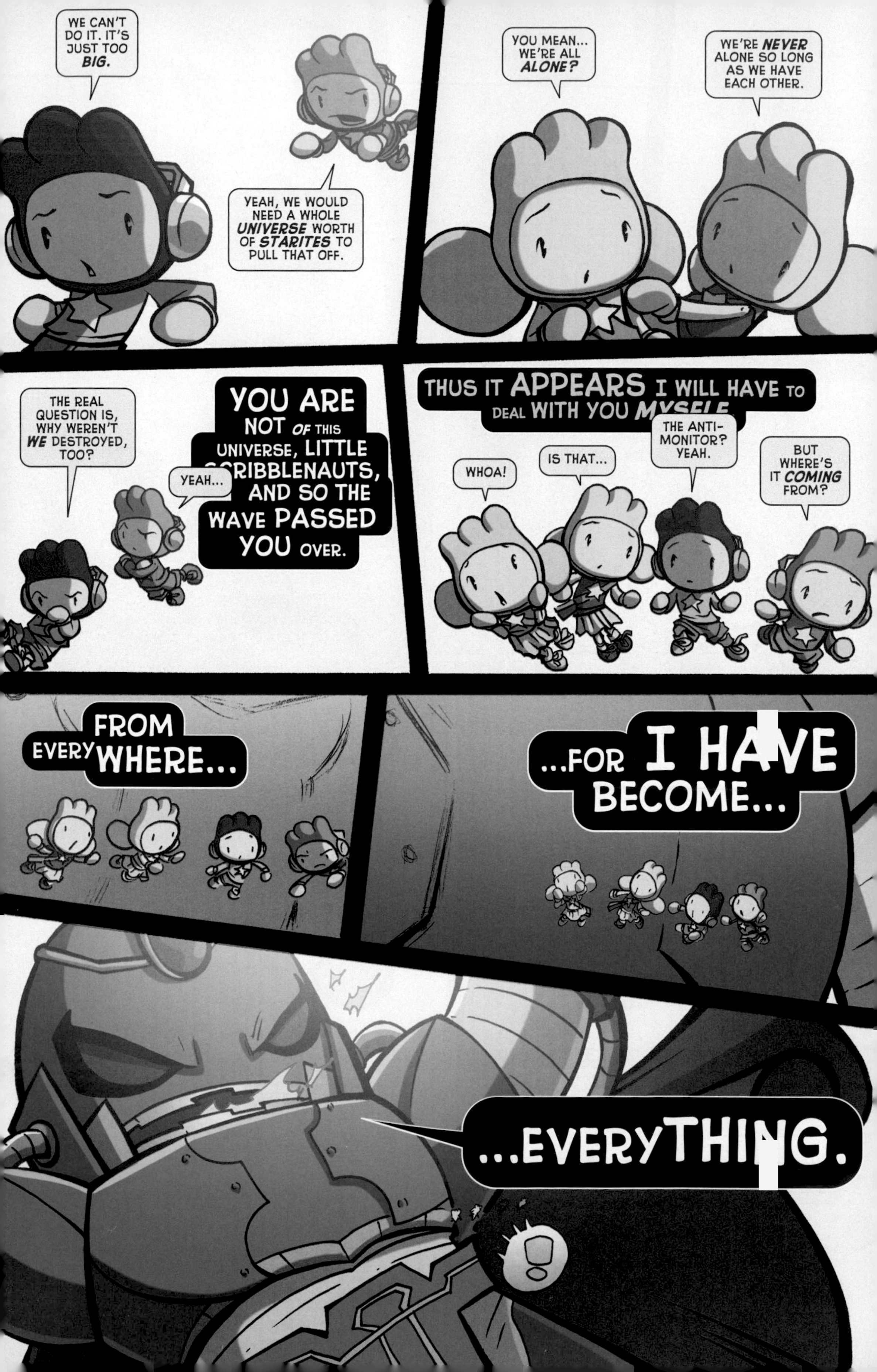
WE CAN'T DO IT. IT'S JUST TOO BIG.
YEAH, WE WOULD NEED A WHOLE UNIVERSE WORTH OF STARITES TO PULL THAT OFF.
YOU MEAN... WE'RE ALL ALONE?
WE'RE NEVER ALONE SO LONG AS WE HAVE EACH OTHER.
THE REAL QUESTION IS, WHY WEREN'T WE DESTROYED, TOO?
YEAH...
YOU ARE NOT OF THIS UNIVERSE, LITTLE SCRIBBLENAUTS, AND SO THE WAVE PASSED YOU OVER.
THUS IT APPEARS I WILL HAVE TO DEAL WITH YOU MYSELF.
WHOA!
IS THAT...
THE ANTI-MONITOR? YEAH.
BUT WHERE'S IT COMING FROM?
FROM EVERYWHERE...
...FOR I HAVE BECOME...
...EVERYTHING.

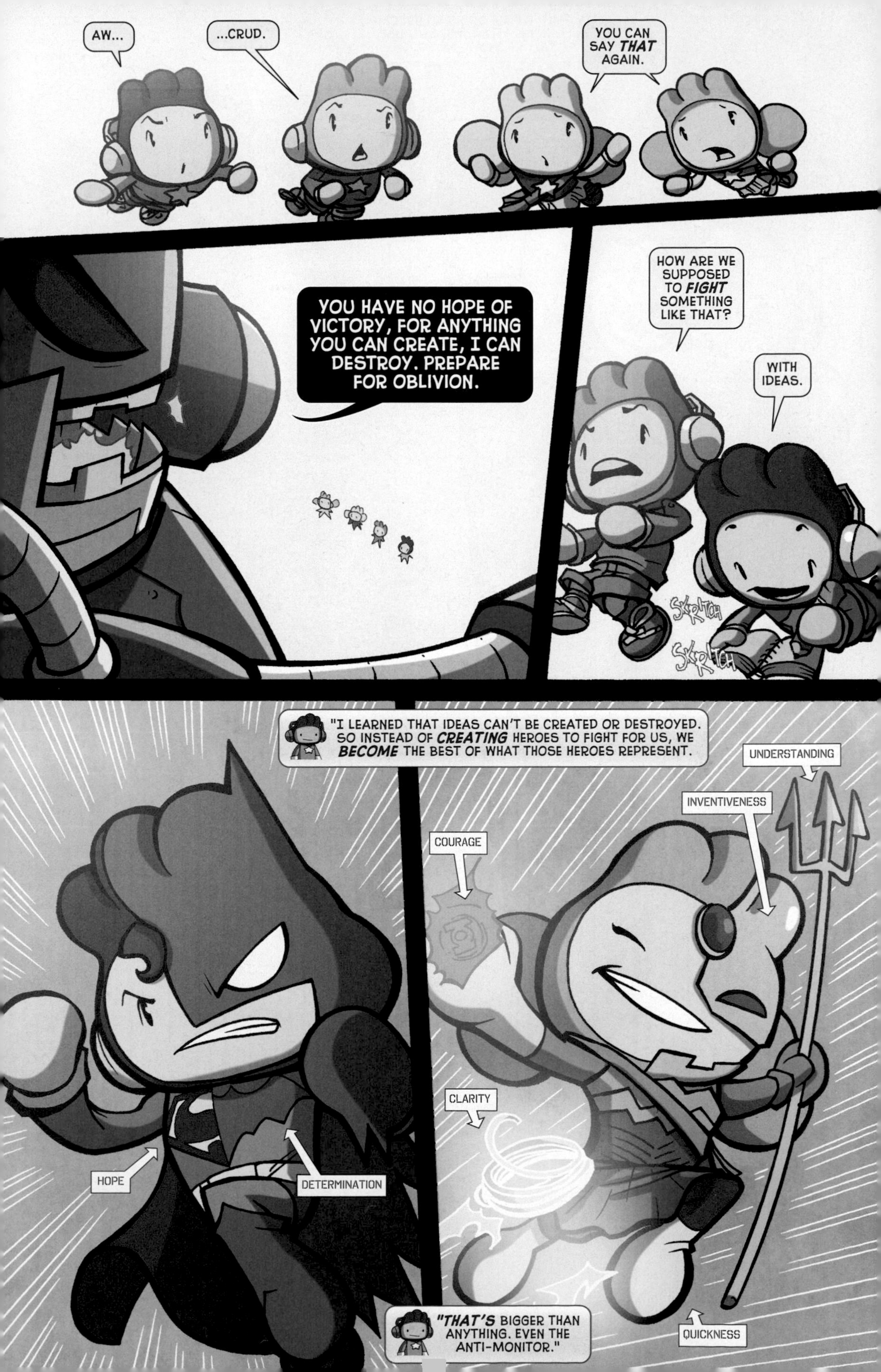
AW...
...CRUD.
YOU CAN SAY *THAT* AGAIN.
YOU HAVE NO HOPE OF VICTORY, FOR ANYTHING YOU CAN CREATE, I CAN DESTROY. PREPARE FOR OBLIVION.
HOW ARE WE SUPPOSED TO *FIGHT* SOMETHING LIKE THAT?
WITH IDEAS.
SKRITCH
SKRITCH
"I LEARNED THAT IDEAS CAN'T BE CREATED OR DESTROYED. SO INSTEAD OF *CREATING* HEROES TO FIGHT FOR US, WE *BECOME* THE BEST OF WHAT THOSE HEROES REPRESENT.
UNDERSTANDING
INVENTIVENESS
COURAGE
CLARITY
HOPE
DETERMINATION
QUICKNESS
"*THAT'S* BIGGER THAN ANYTHING. EVEN THE ANTI-MONITOR."

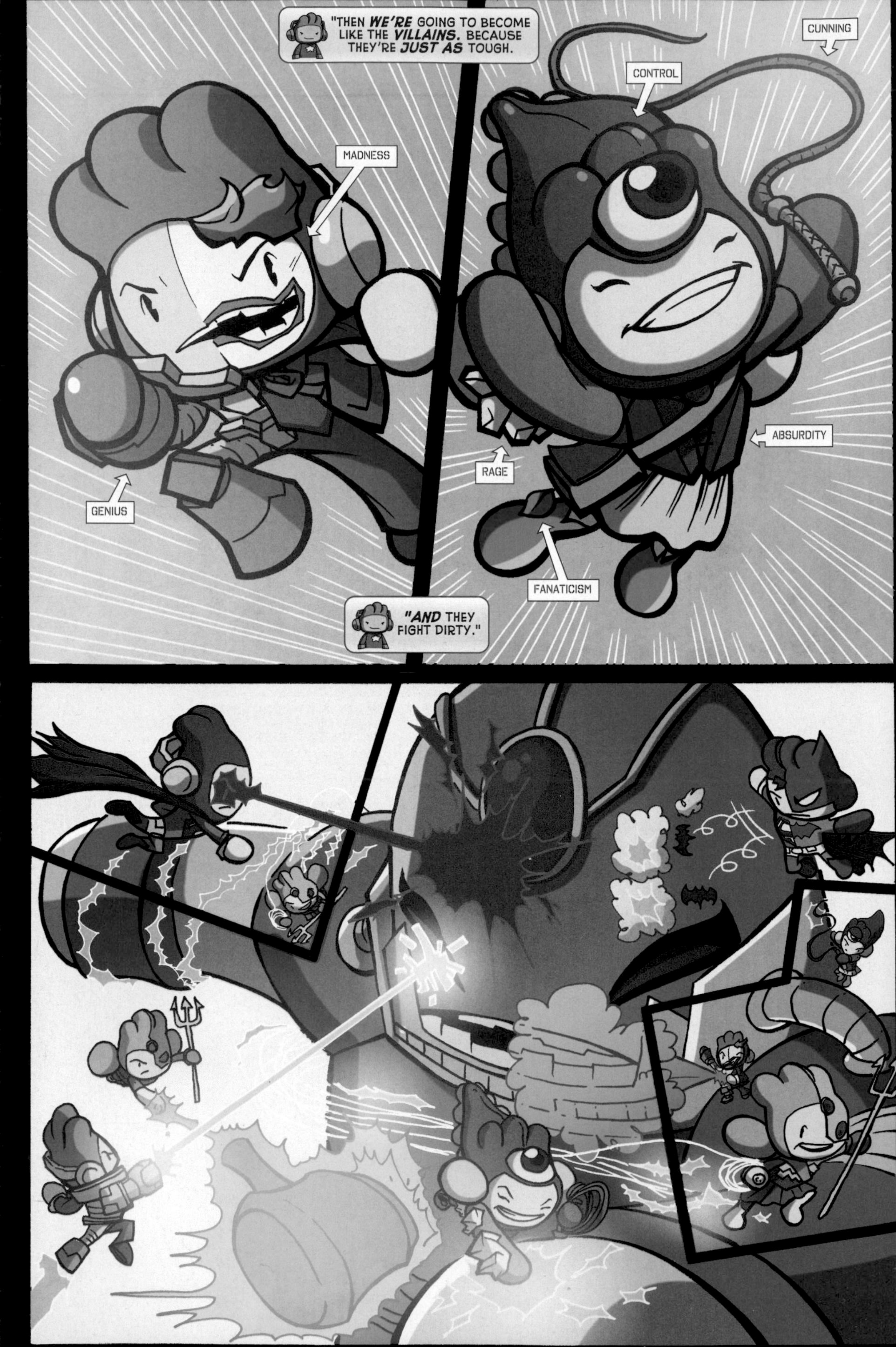
"THEN WE'RE GOING TO BECOME LIKE THE VILLAINS. BECAUSE THEY'RE JUST AS TOUGH.
MADNESS
GENIUS
CUNNING
CONTROL
ABSURDITY
RAGE
FANATICISM
"AND THEY FIGHT DIRTY."

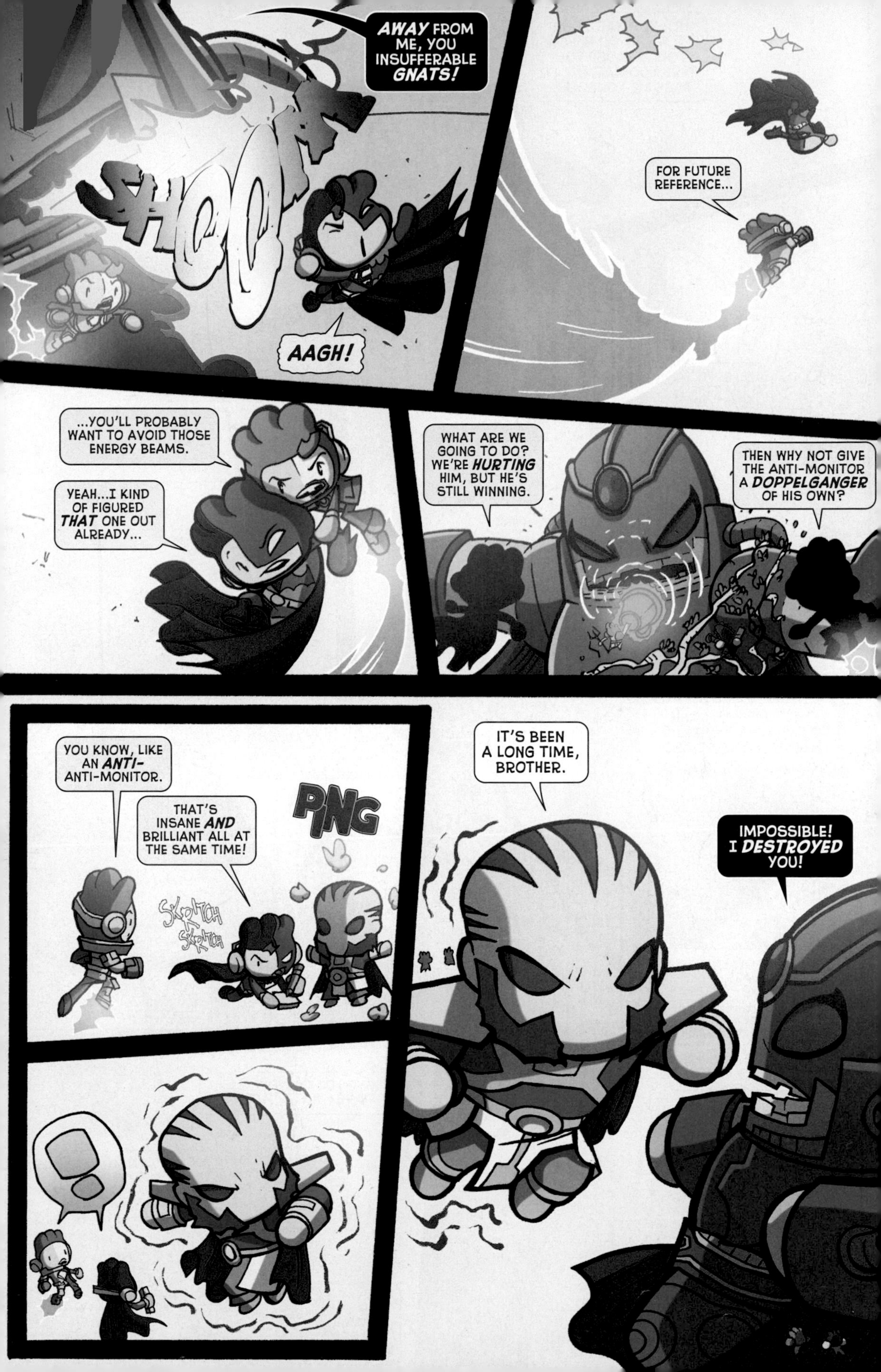
AWAY FROM ME, YOU INSUFFERABLE GNATS!
SHOOOM
AAGH!
FOR FUTURE REFERENCE...
...YOU'LL PROBABLY WANT TO AVOID THOSE ENERGY BEAMS.
YEAH...I KIND OF FIGURED THAT ONE OUT ALREADY...
WHAT ARE WE GOING TO DO? WE'RE HURTING HIM, BUT HE'S STILL WINNING.
THEN WHY NOT GIVE THE ANTI-MONITOR A DOPPELGANGER OF HIS OWN?
YOU KNOW, LIKE AN ANTI-ANTI-MONITOR.
THAT'S INSANE AND BRILLIANT ALL AT THE SAME TIME!
PING
SKRITCH SKRITCH
IT'S BEEN A LONG TIME, BROTHER.
IMPOSSIBLE! I DESTROYED YOU!

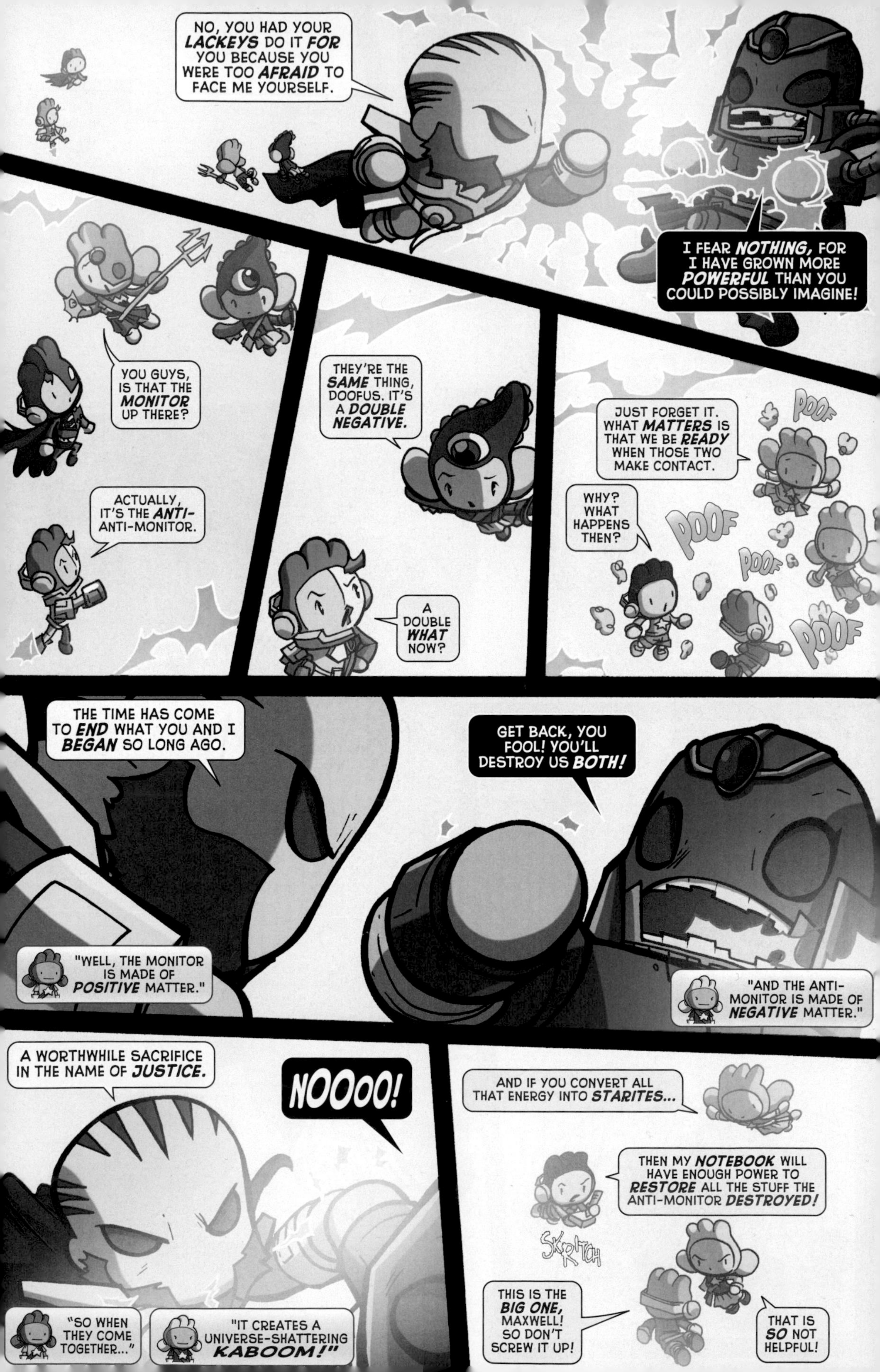

NO, YOU HAD YOUR LACKEYS DO IT FOR YOU BECAUSE YOU WERE TOO AFRAID TO FACE ME YOURSELF.
I FEAR NOTHING, FOR I HAVE GROWN MORE POWERFUL THAN YOU COULD POSSIBLY IMAGINE!
YOU GUYS, IS THAT THE MONITOR UP THERE?
ACTUALLY, IT'S THE ANTI-ANTI-MONITOR.
THEY'RE THE SAME THING, DOOFUS. IT'S A DOUBLE NEGATIVE.
A DOUBLE WHAT NOW?
JUST FORGET IT. WHAT MATTERS IS THAT WE BE READY WHEN THOSE TWO MAKE CONTACT.
POOF
WHY? WHAT HAPPENS THEN?
POOF
POOF
POOF
THE TIME HAS COME TO END WHAT YOU AND I BEGAN SO LONG AGO.
GET BACK, YOU FOOL! YOU'LL DESTROY US BOTH!
"WELL, THE MONITOR IS MADE OF POSITIVE MATTER."
"AND THE ANTI-MONITOR IS MADE OF NEGATIVE MATTER."
A WORTHWHILE SACRIFICE IN THE NAME OF JUSTICE.
NOOOO!
"SO WHEN THEY COME TOGETHER..."
"IT CREATES A UNIVERSE-SHATTERING KABOOM!"
AND IF YOU CONVERT ALL THAT ENERGY INTO STARITES...
THEN MY NOTEBOOK WILL HAVE ENOUGH POWER TO RESTORE ALL THE STUFF THE ANTI-MONITOR DESTROYED!
SKRITCH
THIS IS THE BIG ONE, MAXWELL! SO DON'T SCREW IT UP!
THAT IS SO NOT HELPFUL!

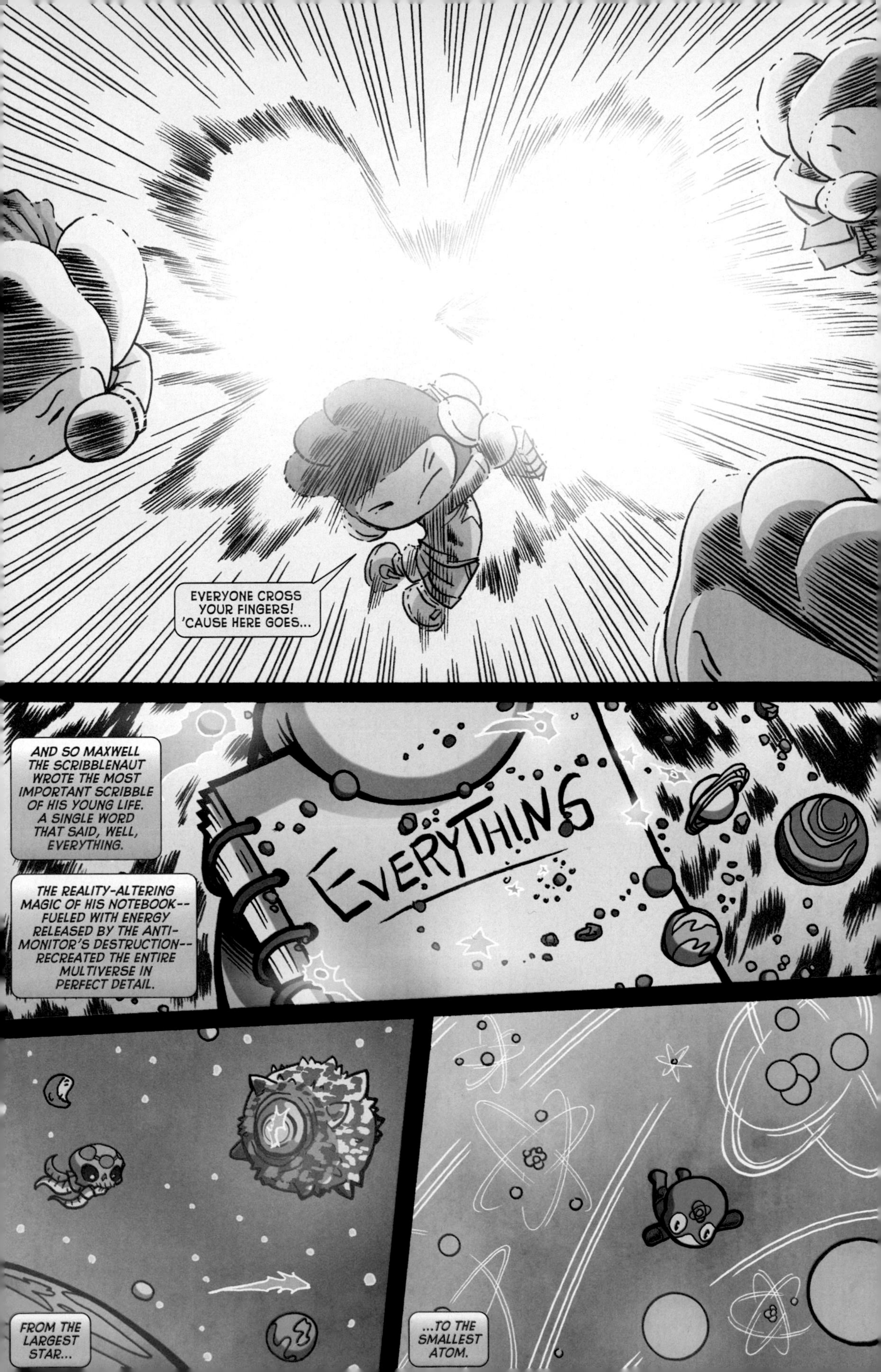
EVERYONE CROSS YOUR FINGERS! 'CAUSE HERE GOES...
AND SO MAXWELL THE SCRIBBLENAUT WROTE THE MOST IMPORTANT SCRIBBLE OF HIS YOUNG LIFE. A SINGLE WORD THAT SAID, WELL, EVERYTHING.
EVERYTHING
THE REALITY-ALTERING MAGIC OF HIS NOTEBOOK--FUELED WITH ENERGY RELEASED BY THE ANTI-MONITOR'S DESTRUCTION--RECREATED THE ENTIRE MULTIVERSE IN PERFECT DETAIL.
FROM THE LARGEST STAR...
...TO THE SMALLEST ATOM.

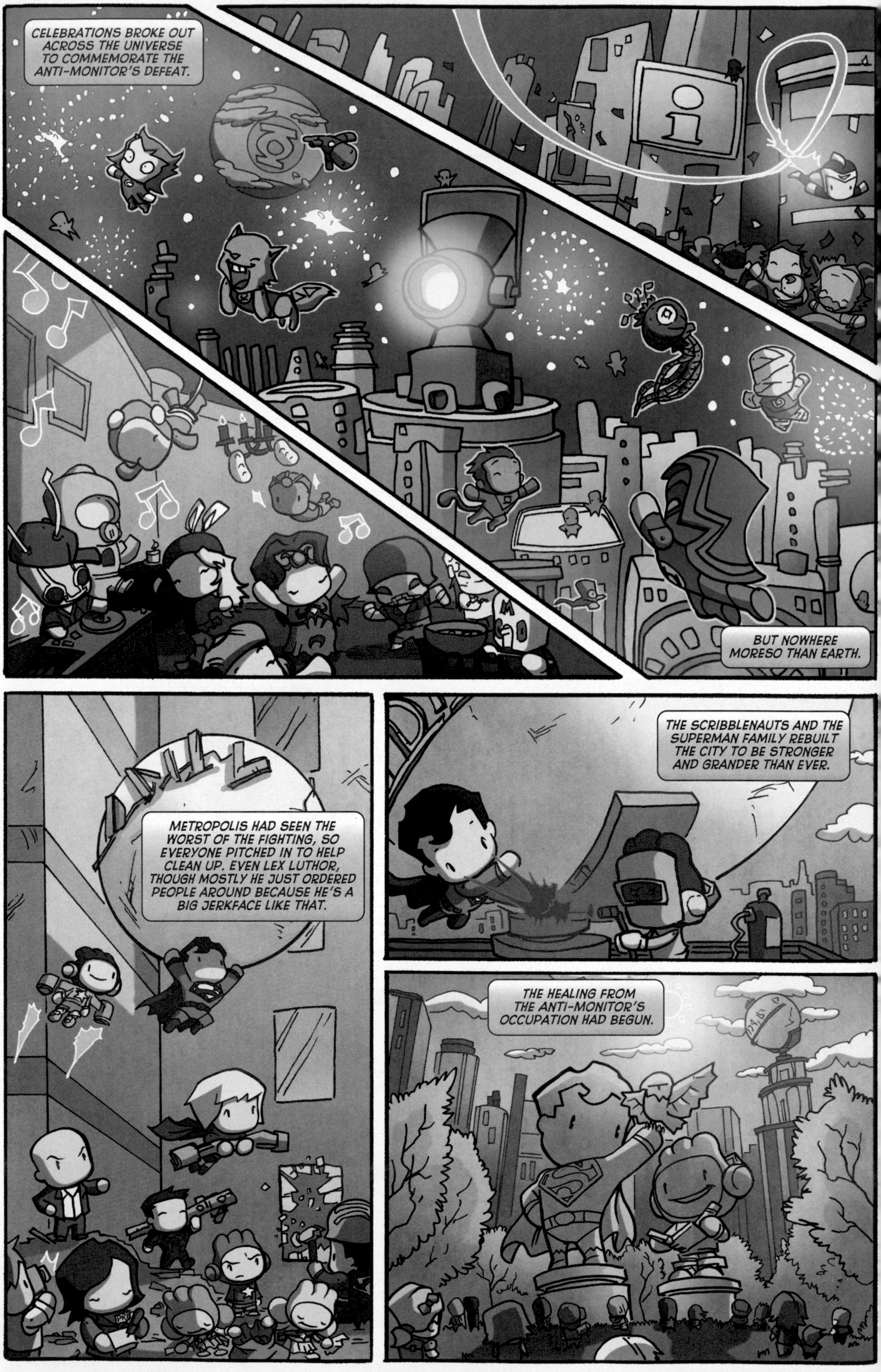
CELEBRATIONS BROKE OUT ACROSS THE UNIVERSE TO COMMEMORATE THE ANTI-MONITOR'S DEFEAT.
BUT NOWHERE MORESO THAN EARTH.
METROPOLIS HAD SEEN THE WORST OF THE FIGHTING, SO EVERYONE PITCHED IN TO HELP CLEAN UP. EVEN LEX LUTHOR, THOUGH MOSTLY HE JUST ORDERED PEOPLE AROUND BECAUSE HE'S A BIG JERKFACE LIKE THAT.
THE SCRIBBLENAUTS AND THE SUPERMAN FAMILY REBUILT THE CITY TO BE STRONGER AND GRANDER THAN EVER.
THE HEALING FROM THE ANTI-MONITOR'S OCCUPATION HAD BEGUN.

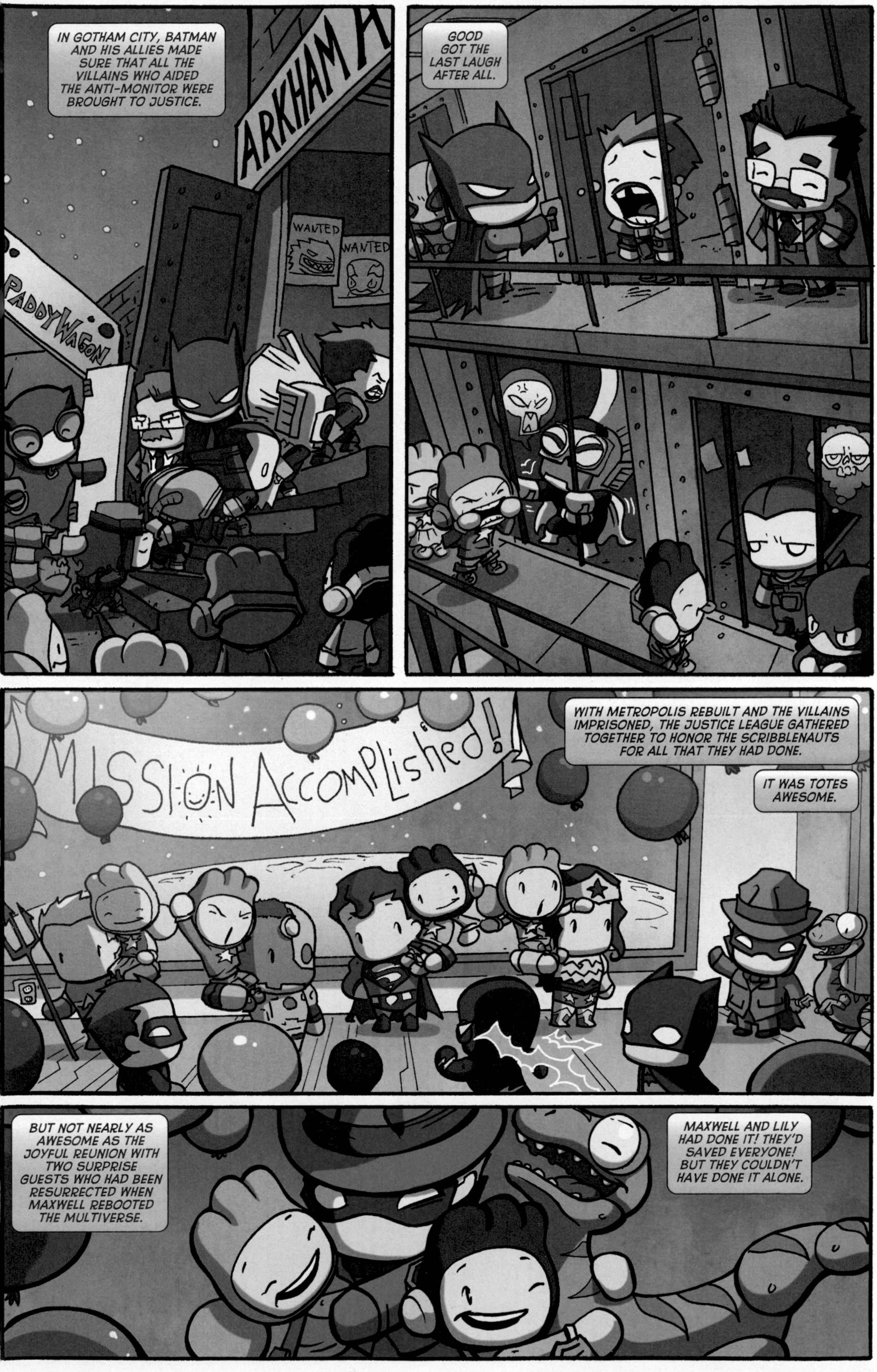
ARKHAM
WANTED
WANTED
PADDYWAGON
IN GOTHAM CITY, BATMAN AND HIS ALLIES MADE SURE THAT ALL THE VILLAINS WHO AIDED THE ANTI-MONITOR WERE BROUGHT TO JUSTICE.
GOOD GOT THE LAST LAUGH AFTER ALL.
MISSION ACCOMPLISHED!
WITH METROPOLIS REBUILT AND THE VILLAINS IMPRISONED, THE JUSTICE LEAGUE GATHERED TOGETHER TO HONOR THE SCRIBBLENAUTS FOR ALL THAT THEY HAD DONE.
IT WAS TOTES AWESOME.
BUT NOT NEARLY AS AWESOME AS THE JOYFUL REUNION WITH TWO SURPRISE GUESTS WHO HAD BEEN RESURRECTED WHEN MAXWELL REBOOTED THE MULTIVERSE.
MAXWELL AND LILY HAD DONE IT! THEY'D SAVED EVERYONE! BUT THEY COULDN'T HAVE DONE IT ALONE.

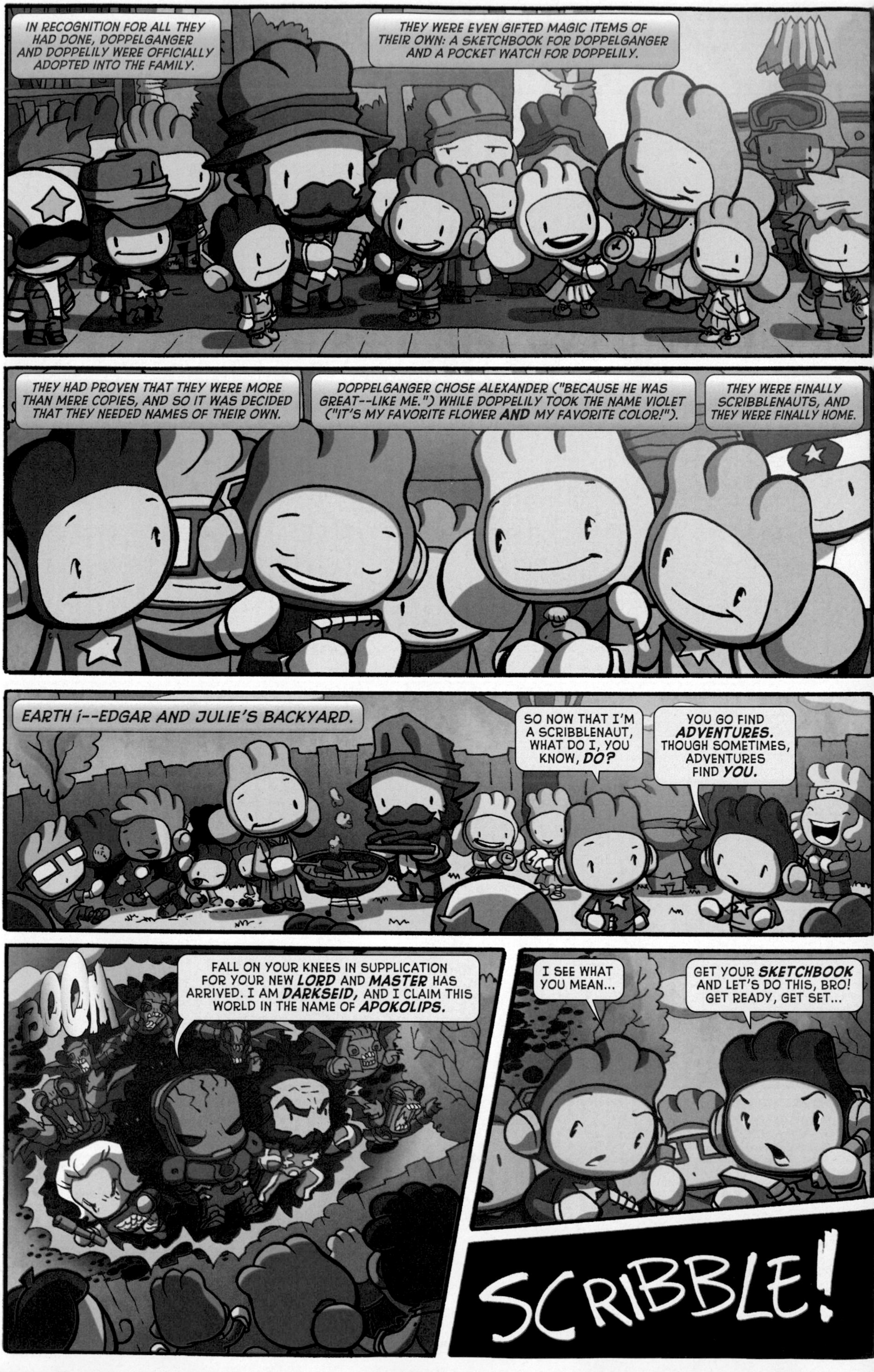
IN RECOGNITION FOR ALL THEY HAD DONE, DOPPELGANGER AND DOPPELILY WERE OFFICIALLY ADOPTED INTO THE FAMILY.
THEY WERE EVEN GIFTED MAGIC ITEMS OF THEIR OWN: A SKETCHBOOK FOR DOPPELGANGER AND A POCKET WATCH FOR DOPPELILY.
THEY HAD PROVEN THAT THEY WERE MORE THAN MERE COPIES, AND SO IT WAS DECIDED THAT THEY NEEDED NAMES OF THEIR OWN.
DOPPELGANGER CHOSE ALEXANDER ("BECAUSE HE WAS GREAT--LIKE ME.") WHILE DOPPELILY TOOK THE NAME VIOLET ("IT'S MY FAVORITE FLOWER AND MY FAVORITE COLOR!").
THEY WERE FINALLY SCRIBBLENAUTS, AND THEY WERE FINALLY HOME.
EARTH 1--EDGAR AND JULIE'S BACKYARD.
SO NOW THAT I'M A SCRIBBLENAUT, WHAT DO I, YOU KNOW, DO?
YOU GO FIND ADVENTURES. THOUGH SOMETIMES, ADVENTURES FIND YOU.
BOOM
FALL ON YOUR KNEES IN SUPPLICATION FOR YOUR NEW LORD AND MASTER HAS ARRIVED. I AM DARKSEID, AND I CLAIM THIS WORLD IN THE NAME OF APOKOLIPS.
I SEE WHAT YOU MEAN...
GET YOUR SKETCHBOOK AND LET'S DO THIS, BRO! GET READY, GET SET...
SCRIBBLE!

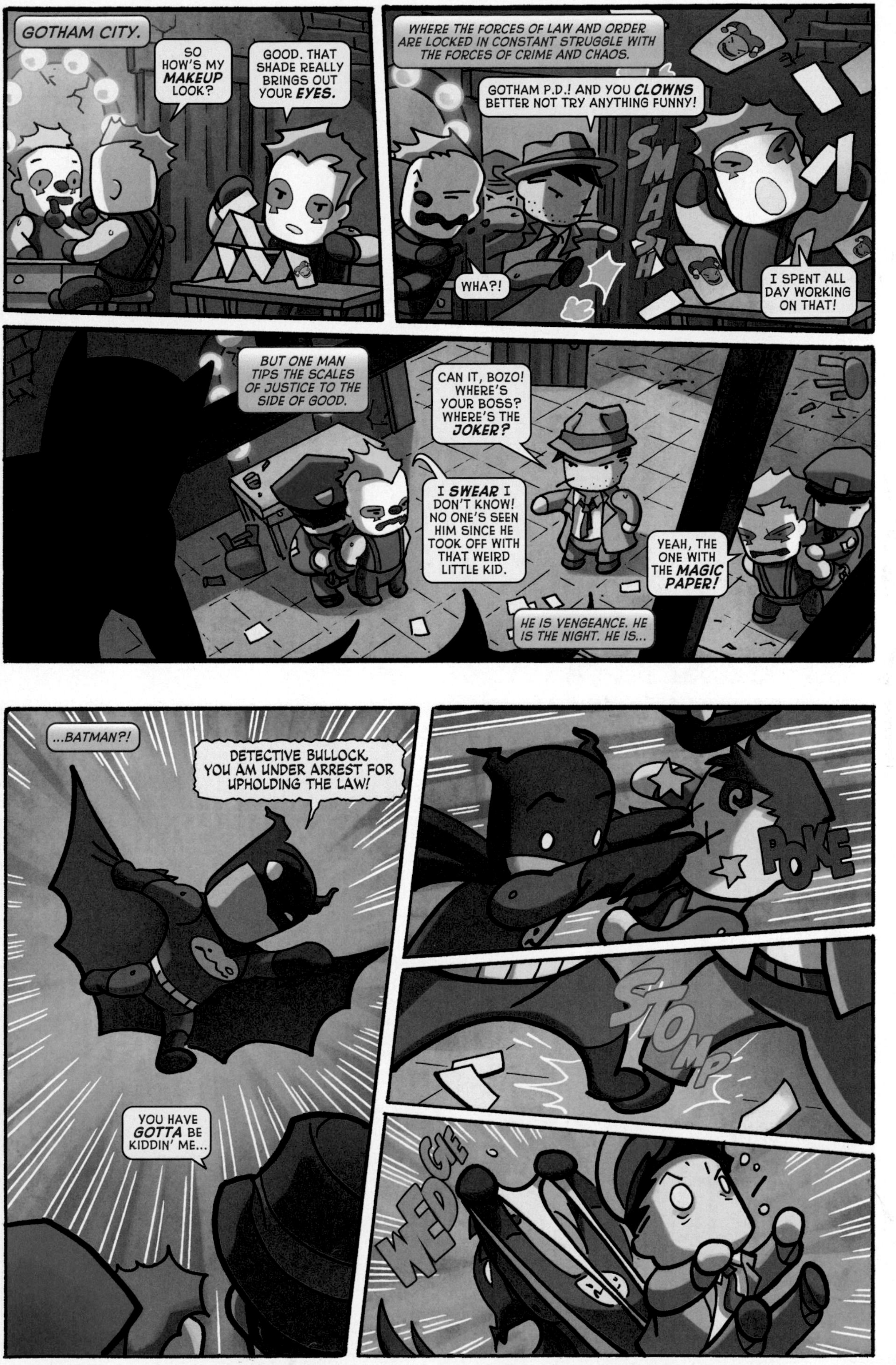

GOTHAM CITY.
SO HOW'S MY MAKEUP LOOK?
GOOD. THAT SHADE REALLY BRINGS OUT YOUR EYES.
WHERE THE FORCES OF LAW AND ORDER ARE LOCKED IN CONSTANT STRUGGLE WITH THE FORCES OF CRIME AND CHAOS.
GOTHAM P.D.! AND YOU CLOWNS BETTER NOT TRY ANYTHING FUNNY!
SMASH
WHA?!
I SPENT ALL DAY WORKING ON THAT!
BUT ONE MAN TIPS THE SCALES OF JUSTICE TO THE SIDE OF GOOD.
CAN IT, BOZO! WHERE'S YOUR BOSS? WHERE'S THE JOKER?
I SWEAR I DON'T KNOW! NO ONE'S SEEN HIM SINCE HE TOOK OFF WITH THAT WEIRD LITTLE KID.
YEAH, THE ONE WITH THE MAGIC PAPER!
HE IS VENGEANCE. HE IS THE NIGHT. HE IS...
...BATMAN?!
DETECTIVE BULLOCK, YOU AM UNDER ARREST FOR UPHOLDING THE LAW!
YOU HAVE GOTTA BE KIDDIN' ME...
POKE
STOMP
WEDGIE

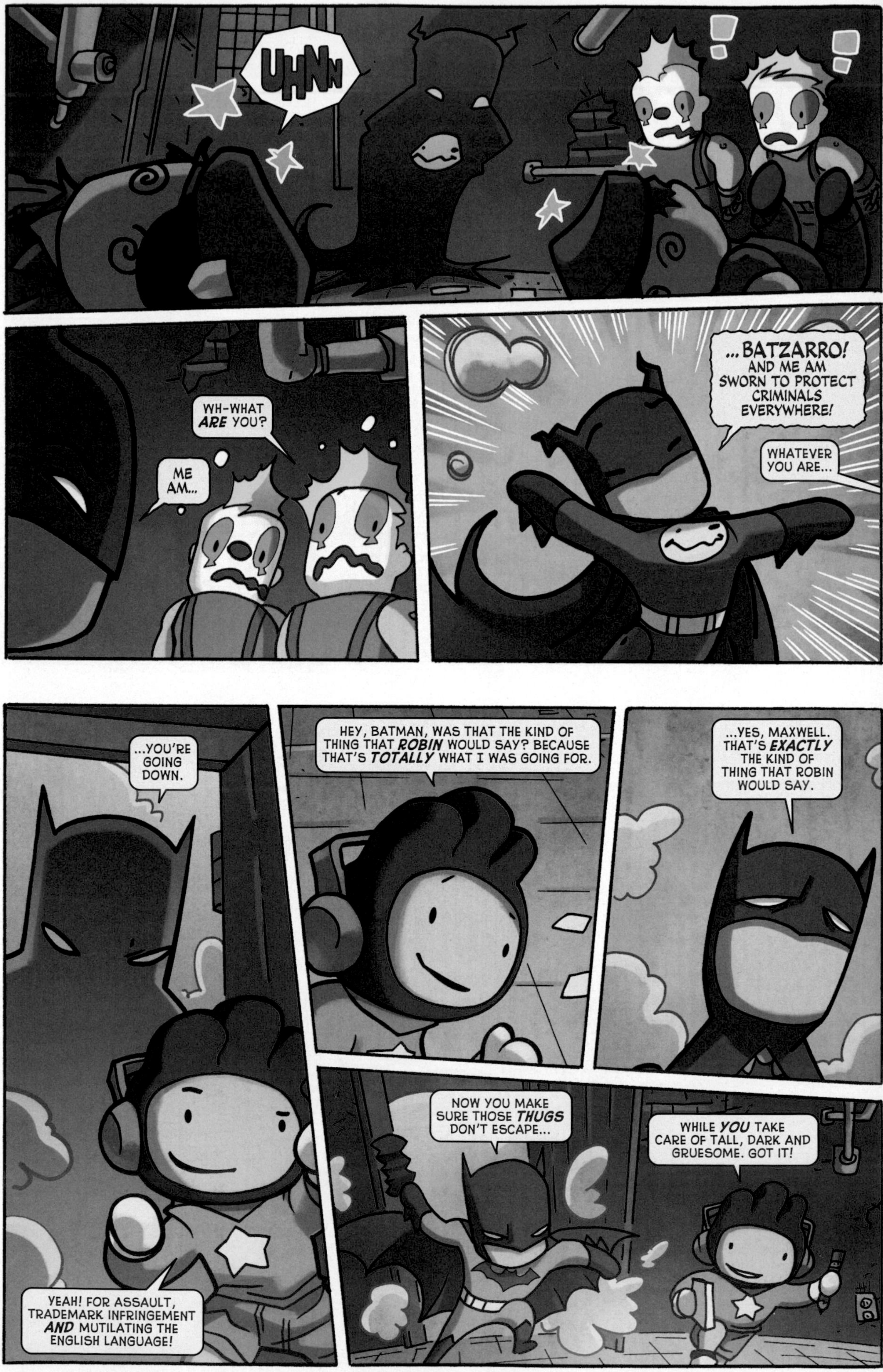
UHNN
WH-WHAT *ARE* YOU?
ME AM...
...BATZARRO! AND ME AM SWORN TO PROTECT CRIMINALS EVERYWHERE!
WHATEVER YOU ARE...
...YOU'RE GOING DOWN.
YEAH! FOR ASSAULT, TRADEMARK INFRINGEMENT *AND* MUTILATING THE ENGLISH LANGUAGE!
HEY, BATMAN, WAS THAT THE KIND OF THING THAT *ROBIN* WOULD SAY? BECAUSE THAT'S *TOTALLY* WHAT I WAS GOING FOR.
...YES, MAXWELL. THAT'S *EXACTLY* THE KIND OF THING THAT ROBIN WOULD SAY.
NOW YOU MAKE SURE THOSE *THUGS* DON'T ESCAPE...
WHILE *YOU* TAKE CARE OF TALL, DARK AND GRUESOME. GOT IT!

I'VE GOT JUST THE THING FOR YOU TWO: STOCKS AND SHACKLES!
YOU MAD, BATBRO?
ME HIT YOU UNTIL WE AM BEST FRIENDS.
REALLY? COME ON!
I KNEW I SHOULD HAVE CALLED IN SICK TODAY...
PING
PING
MAXWELL, CONTACT LILY AT THE BATCAVE.
THIS...THING CAN COUNTER ALL MY ATTACKS. I NEED A NEW STRATEGY.
PARRY
TELL HER TO CROSS-REFERENCE "BIZARRO" ON THE BATCOMPUTER.
RIPOSTE
THE BATCAVE.
HOME TO VEHICLES, CRIMEFIGHTING EQUIPMENT AND BATS. LOTS AND LOTS OF BATS.
YOU GET ALL THAT, SIS?
YEAH, AND THIS BIZARRO PROBLEM IS A LOT BIGGER THAN YOU GUYS KNOW.
MADAM LILY, WOULD YOU CARE FOR SOME MILK AND HOMEMADE CHOCOLATE CHIP COOKIES? ONE SHOULDN'T FIGHT CRIME ON AN EMPTY STOMACH, AFTER ALL.
THANKS, ALFRED! YOU'RE THE BEST!

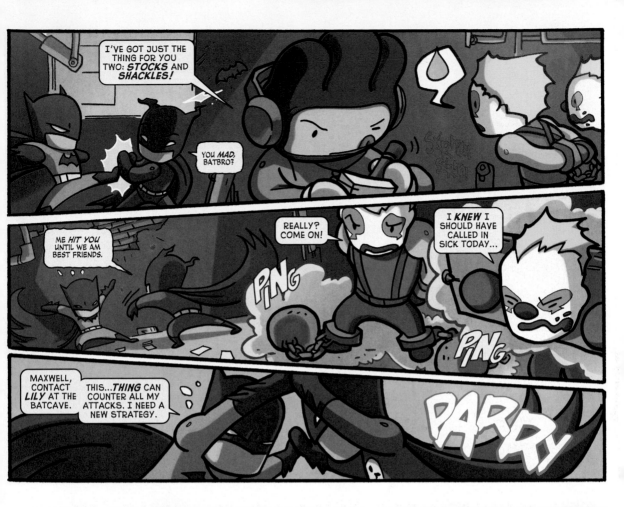

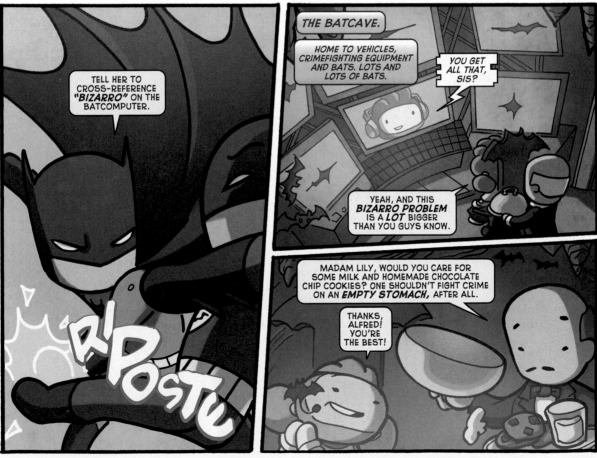

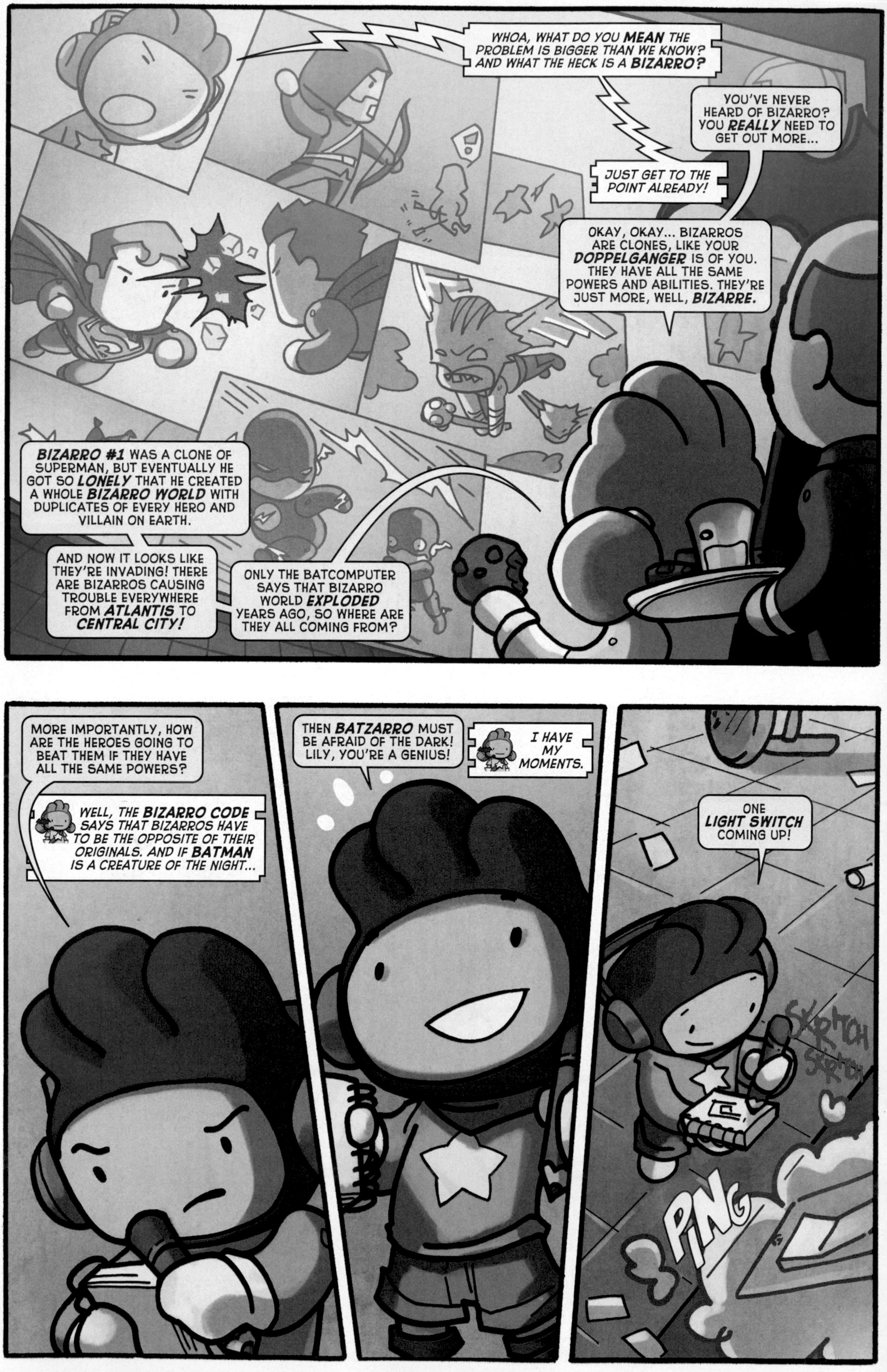

WHOA, WHAT DO YOU MEAN THE PROBLEM IS BIGGER THAN WE KNOW? AND WHAT THE HECK IS A BIZARRO?
YOU'VE NEVER HEARD OF BIZARRO? YOU REALLY NEED TO GET OUT MORE...
JUST GET TO THE POINT ALREADY!
OKAY, OKAY... BIZARROS ARE CLONES, LIKE YOUR DOPPELGANGER IS OF YOU. THEY HAVE ALL THE SAME POWERS AND ABILITIES. THEY'RE JUST MORE, WELL, BIZARRE.
BIZARRO #1 WAS A CLONE OF SUPERMAN, BUT EVENTUALLY HE GOT SO LONELY THAT HE CREATED A WHOLE BIZARRO WORLD WITH DUPLICATES OF EVERY HERO AND VILLAIN ON EARTH.
AND NOW IT LOOKS LIKE THEY'RE INVADING! THERE ARE BIZARROS CAUSING TROUBLE EVERYWHERE FROM ATLANTIS TO CENTRAL CITY!
ONLY THE BATCOMPUTER SAYS THAT BIZARRO WORLD EXPLODED YEARS AGO, SO WHERE ARE THEY ALL COMING FROM?
MORE IMPORTANTLY, HOW ARE THE HEROES GOING TO BEAT THEM IF THEY HAVE ALL THE SAME POWERS?
WELL, THE BIZARRO CODE SAYS THAT BIZARROS HAVE TO BE THE OPPOSITE OF THEIR ORIGINALS. AND IF BATMAN IS A CREATURE OF THE NIGHT...
THEN BATZARRO MUST BE AFRAID OF THE DARK! LILY, YOU'RE A GENIUS!
I HAVE MY MOMENTS.
ONE LIGHT SWITCH COMING UP!
SKRITCH
SKRITCH
PING

I'M TURNING OUT THE LIGHTS, BATMAN. THEN YOU TURN OFF HIS!
YOU ARE DEFINITELY SPENDING TOO MUCH TIME WITH ROBIN...
CLICK
EEEEEK!!! WHO TURN ON THE DARK?!
I'M GOING TO ENJOY THIS...
BIFF
POW
BAM
CLICK
ME AM...WIDE AWAKE, SO ME THINK...ME TAKE NAP...
WHOA! HE JUST DISAPPEARED! THAT MEANS--
THAT HE WASN'T A REAL BIZARRO AT ALL. HE WAS ONE OF YOUR DOPPELGANGER'S CONSTRUCTS.
WHICH MEANS YOUR DOPPELGANGER MUST BE WORKING WITH BIZARRO #1.
POOF
LILY, CAN YOU TELEPORT US TO METROPOLIS?
SORRY, MR. BATMAN, BUT I DON'T HAVE ENOUGH STARITE. MAYBE MAXWELL COULD MAKE SOMETHING REALLY FAST TO TAKE YOU THERE INSTEAD.
I'M ON IT!
MINUTES LATER...
FWOOSH
YOU'D BETTER STRAP YOURSELF IN, MAXWELL. THIS IS GOING TO BE QUITE A RIDE.

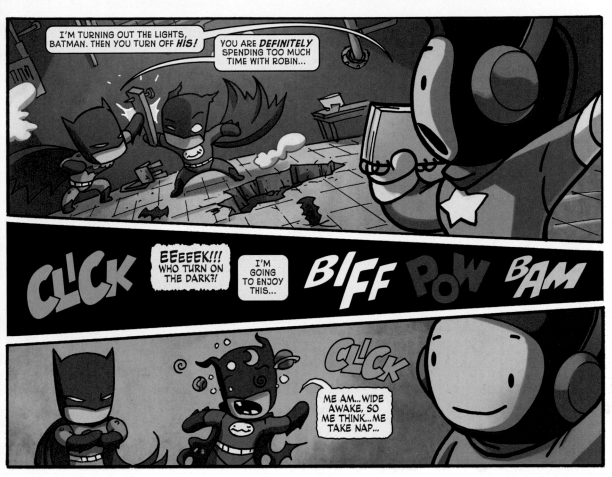

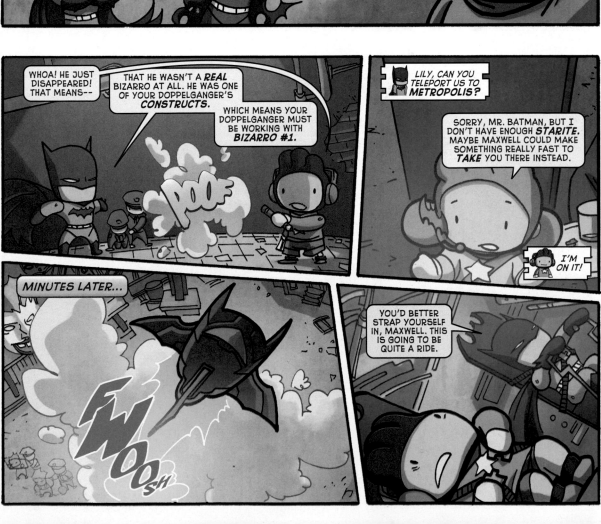

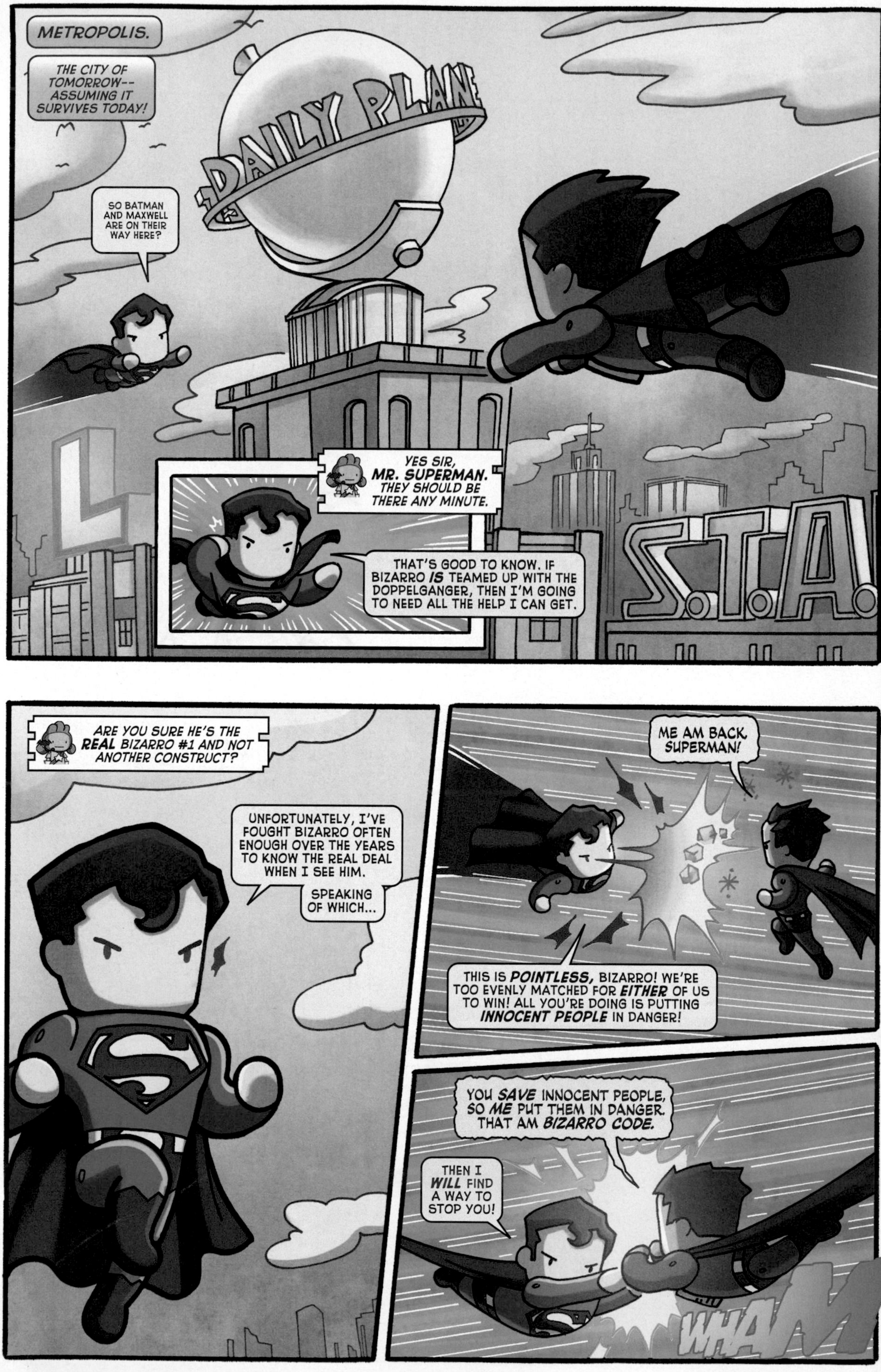
METROPOLIS.
THE CITY OF TOMORROW-- ASSUMING IT SURVIVES TODAY!
DAILY PLANE
SO BATMAN AND MAXWELL ARE ON THEIR WAY HERE?
YES SIR, MR. SUPERMAN. THEY SHOULD BE THERE ANY MINUTE.
THAT'S GOOD TO KNOW. IF BIZARRO IS TEAMED UP WITH THE DOPPELGANGER, THEN I'M GOING TO NEED ALL THE HELP I CAN GET.
S.T.A.
ARE YOU SURE HE'S THE REAL BIZARRO #1 AND NOT ANOTHER CONSTRUCT?
UNFORTUNATELY, I'VE FOUGHT BIZARRO OFTEN ENOUGH OVER THE YEARS TO KNOW THE REAL DEAL WHEN I SEE HIM.
SPEAKING OF WHICH...
ME AM BACK, SUPERMAN!
THIS IS POINTLESS, BIZARRO! WE'RE TOO EVENLY MATCHED FOR EITHER OF US TO WIN! ALL YOU'RE DOING IS PUTTING INNOCENT PEOPLE IN DANGER!
YOU SAVE INNOCENT PEOPLE, SO ME PUT THEM IN DANGER. THAT AM BIZARRO CODE.
THEN I WILL FIND A WAY TO STOP YOU!
WHAM

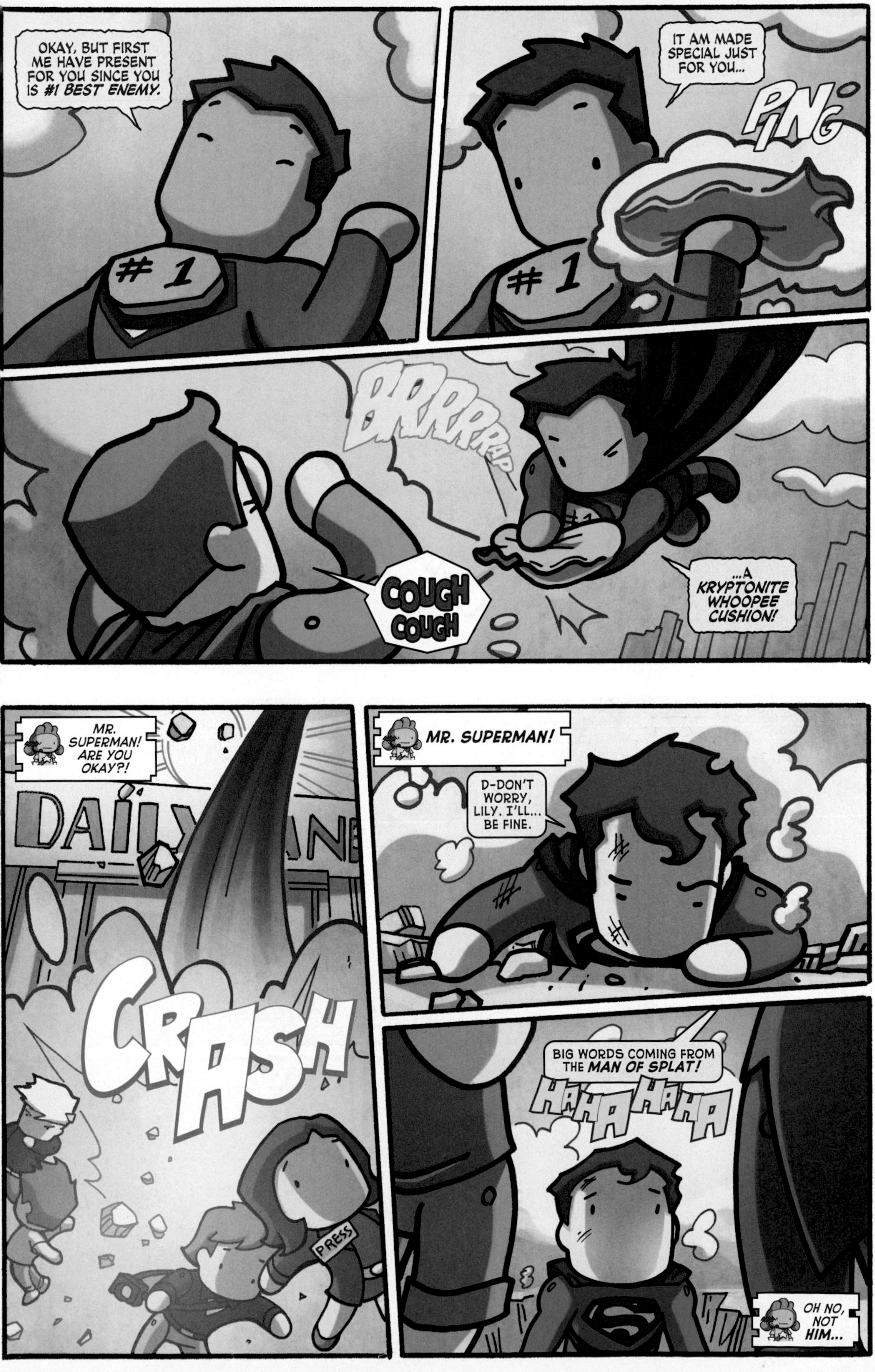
OKAY, BUT FIRST ME HAVE PRESENT FOR YOU SINCE YOU IS #1 BEST ENEMY.
#1
IT AM MADE SPECIAL JUST FOR YOU...
PING
#1
BRRRRRAP
COUGH COUGH
...A KRYPTONITE WHOOPEE CUSHION!
MR. SUPERMAN! ARE YOU OKAY?!
DAILY
CRASH
PRESS
MR. SUPERMAN!
D-DON'T WORRY, LILY. I'LL... BE FINE.
BIG WORDS COMING FROM THE MAN OF SPLAT!
HAHA HAHA
OH NO, NOT HIM...

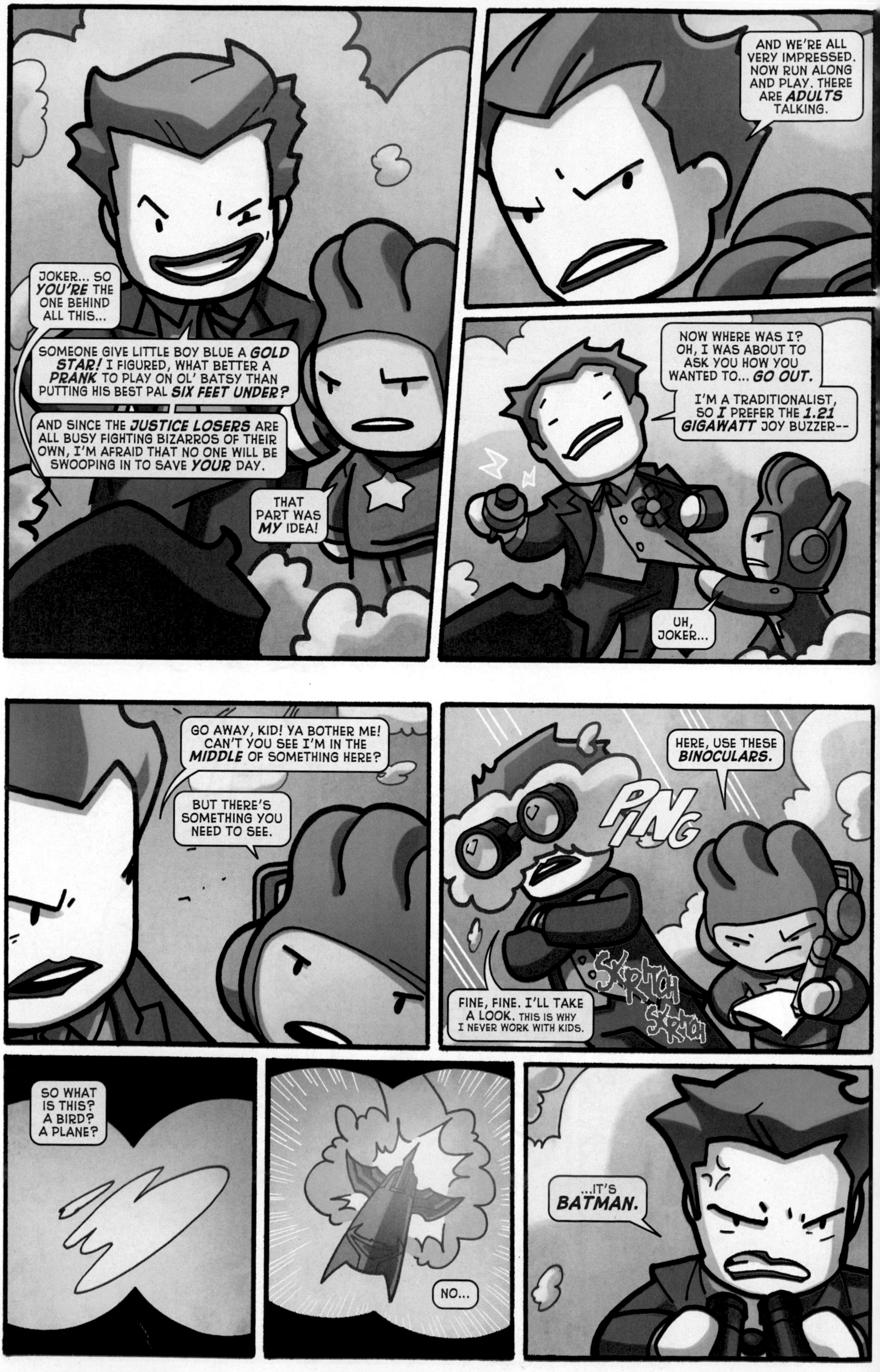

JOKER... SO YOU'RE THE ONE BEHIND ALL THIS...
SOMEONE GIVE LITTLE BOY BLUE A GOLD STAR! I FIGURED, WHAT BETTER A PRANK TO PLAY ON OL' BATSY THAN PUTTING HIS BEST PAL SIX FEET UNDER?
AND SINCE THE JUSTICE LOSERS ARE ALL BUSY FIGHTING BIZARROS OF THEIR OWN, I'M AFRAID THAT NO ONE WILL BE SWOOPING IN TO SAVE YOUR DAY.
THAT PART WAS MY IDEA!
AND WE'RE ALL VERY IMPRESSED. NOW RUN ALONG AND PLAY. THERE ARE ADULTS TALKING.
NOW WHERE WAS I? OH, I WAS ABOUT TO ASK YOU HOW YOU WANTED TO... GO OUT.
I'M A TRADITIONALIST, SO I PREFER THE 1.21 GIGAWATT JOY BUZZER--
UH, JOKER...
GO AWAY, KID! YA BOTHER ME! CAN'T YOU SEE I'M IN THE MIDDLE OF SOMETHING HERE?
BUT THERE'S SOMETHING YOU NEED TO SEE.
HERE, USE THESE BINOCULARS.
PING
FINE, FINE. I'LL TAKE A LOOK. THIS IS WHY I NEVER WORK WITH KIDS.
SKRITCH SKRITCH
SO WHAT IS THIS? A BIRD? A PLANE?
NO...
...IT'S BATMAN.

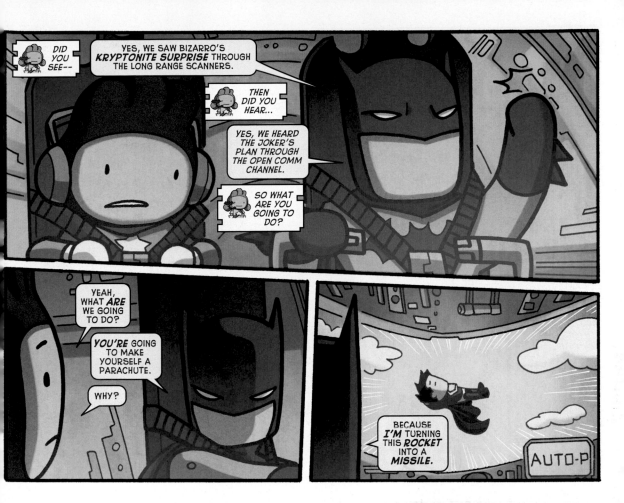

DID YOU SEE--

YES, WE SAW BIZARRO'S *KRYPTONITE SURPRISE* THROUGH THE LONG RANGE SCANNERS.

THEN DID YOU HEAR...

YES, WE HEARD THE JOKER'S PLAN THROUGH THE OPEN COMM CHANNEL.

SO WHAT ARE YOU GOING TO DO?

YEAH, WHAT *ARE* WE GOING TO DO?

*YOU'RE* GOING TO MAKE YOURSELF A PARACHUTE.

WHY?

BECAUSE *I'M* TURNING THIS *ROCKET* INTO A *MISSILE*.

AUTO-P

BIG BLACK BIRD...

...AM ON FIRE...

...GOODBYE, BIRD.

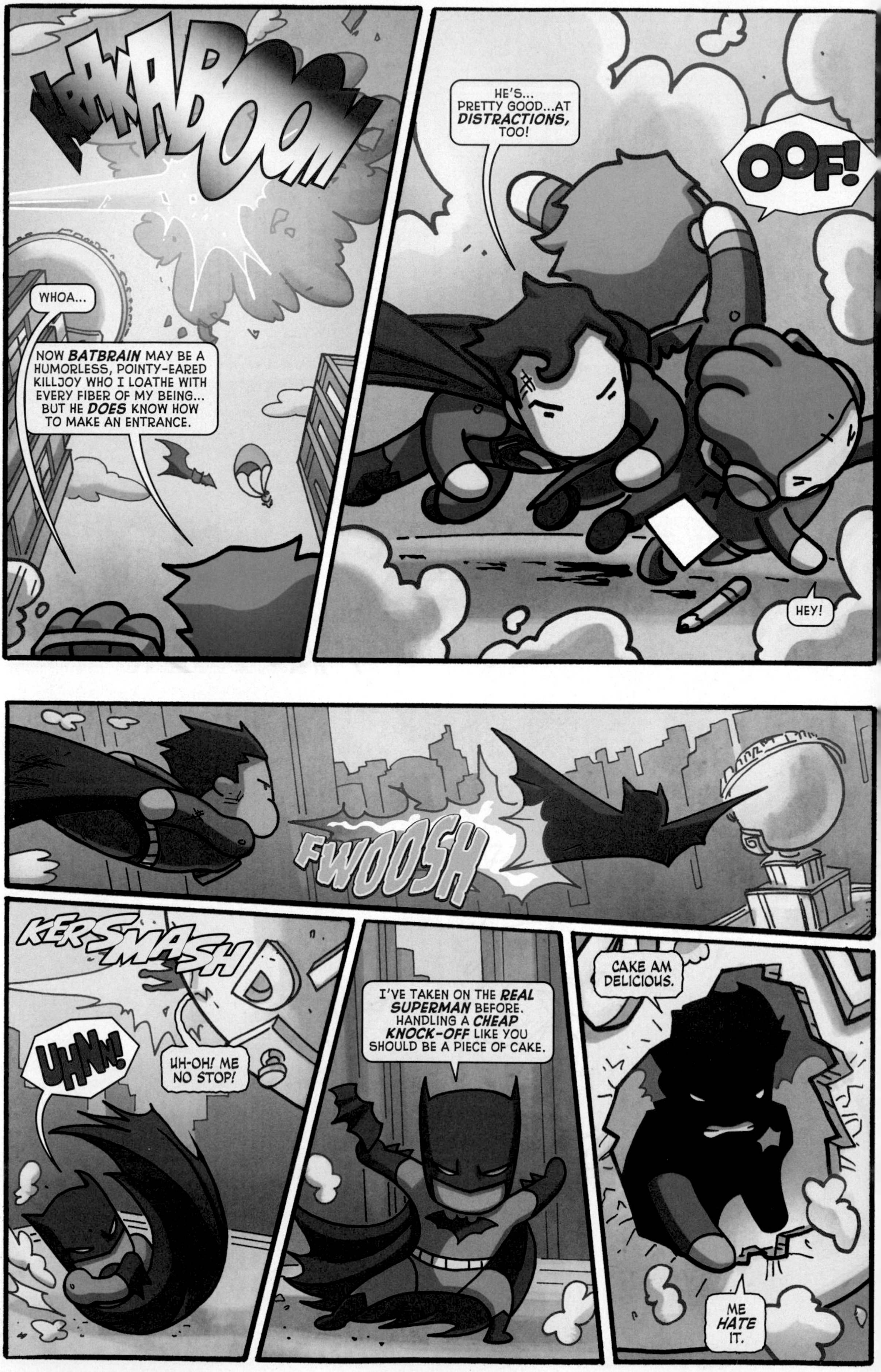
KRAKABOOM
WHOA...
NOW BATBRAIN MAY BE A HUMORLESS, POINTY-EARED KILLJOY WHO I LOATHE WITH EVERY FIBER OF MY BEING... BUT HE DOES KNOW HOW TO MAKE AN ENTRANCE.
HE'S... PRETTY GOOD...AT DISTRACTIONS, TOO!
OOF!
HEY!
FWOOSH
KERSMASH
UHNN!
UH-OH! ME NO STOP!
I'VE TAKEN ON THE REAL SUPERMAN BEFORE. HANDLING A CHEAP KNOCK-OFF LIKE YOU SHOULD BE A PIECE OF CAKE.
CAKE AM DELICIOUS.
ME HATE IT.

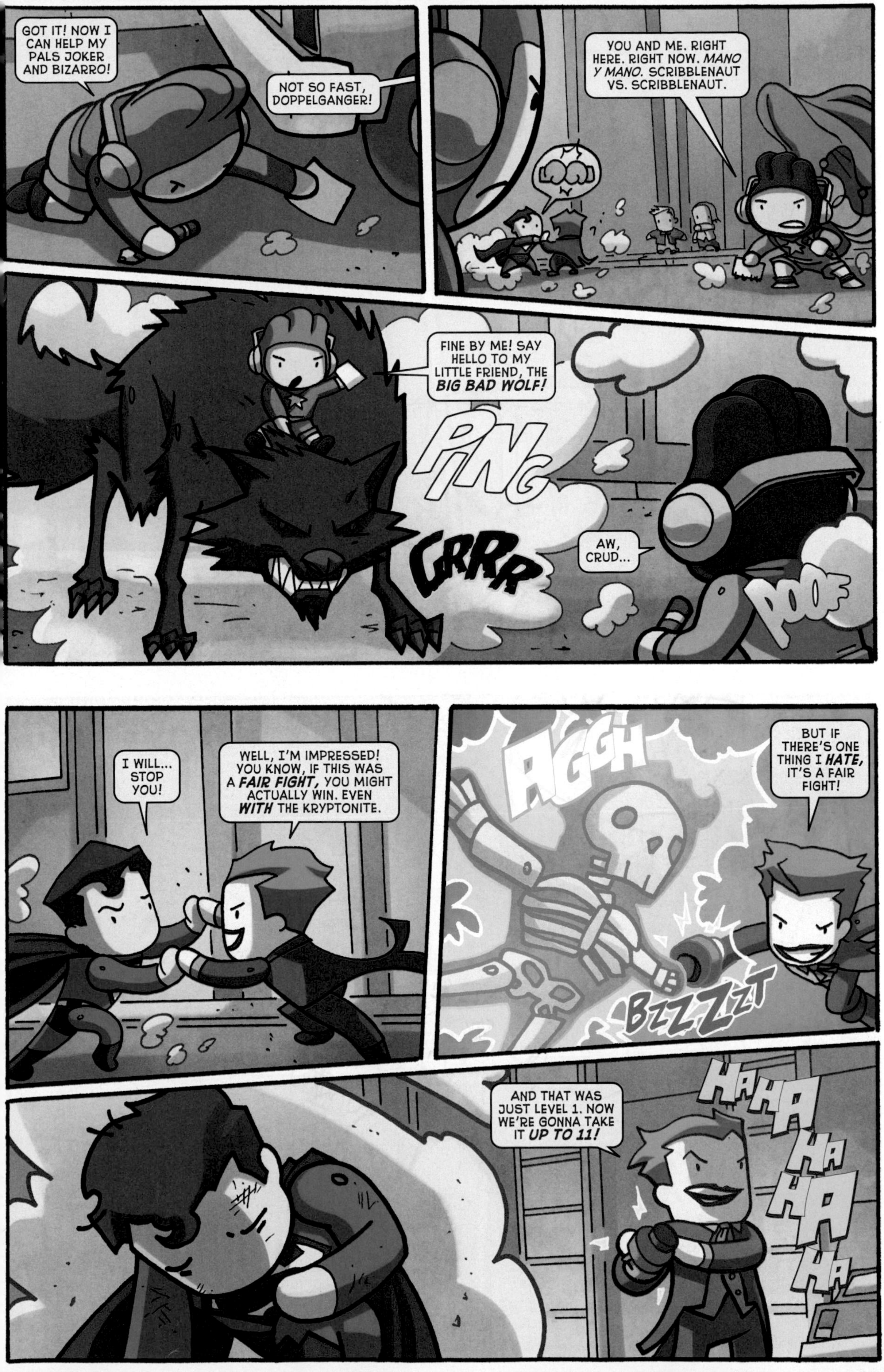
GOT IT! NOW I CAN HELP MY PALS JOKER AND BIZARRO!
NOT SO FAST, DOPPELGANGER!
YOU AND ME. RIGHT HERE. RIGHT NOW. MANO Y MANO. SCRIBBLENAUT VS. SCRIBBLENAUT.
FINE BY ME! SAY HELLO TO MY LITTLE FRIEND, THE BIG BAD WOLF!
PING
GRRR
AW, CRUD...
POOF
I WILL... STOP YOU!
WELL, I'M IMPRESSED! YOU KNOW, IF THIS WAS A FAIR FIGHT, YOU MIGHT ACTUALLY WIN. EVEN WITH THE KRYPTONITE.
AGGH
BUT IF THERE'S ONE THING I HATE, IT'S A FAIR FIGHT!
BZZZZZT
AND THAT WAS JUST LEVEL 1. NOW WE'RE GONNA TAKE IT UP TO 11!
HAHA HA HA HA

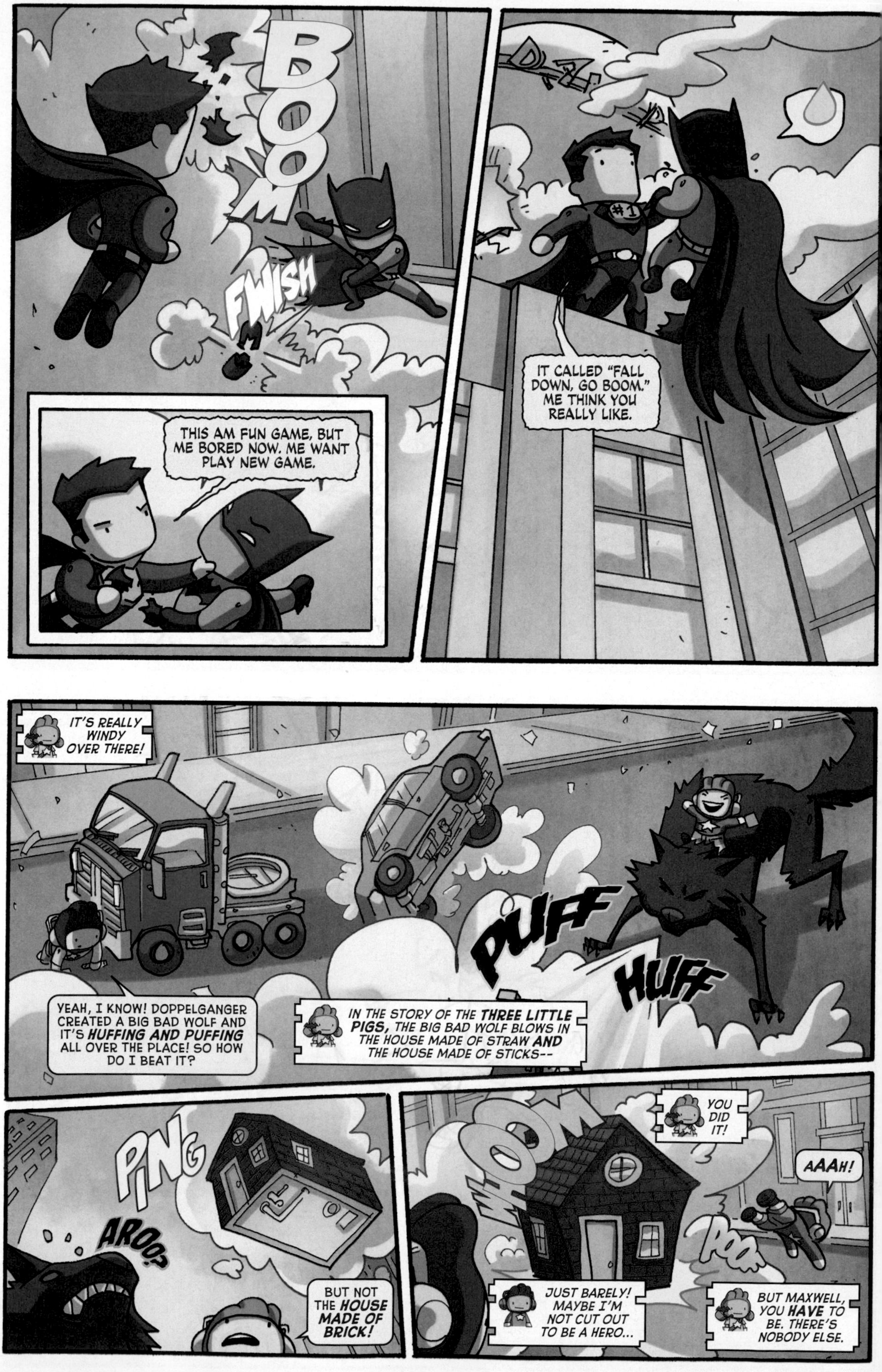
BOOM
FWISH
THIS AM FUN GAME, BUT ME BORED NOW. ME WANT PLAY NEW GAME.
IT CALLED "FALL DOWN, GO BOOM." ME THINK YOU REALLY LIKE.
IT'S REALLY WINDY OVER THERE!
YEAH, I KNOW! DOPPELGANGER CREATED A BIG BAD WOLF AND IT'S HUFFING AND PUFFING ALL OVER THE PLACE! SO HOW DO I BEAT IT?
PUFF
HUFF
IN THE STORY OF THE THREE LITTLE PIGS, THE BIG BAD WOLF BLOWS IN THE HOUSE MADE OF STRAW AND THE HOUSE MADE OF STICKS--
PING
AROO?
BUT NOT THE HOUSE MADE OF BRICK!
WHOOM
YOU DID IT!
AAAH!
POOF
JUST BARELY! MAYBE I'M NOT CUT OUT TO BE A HERO...
BUT MAXWELL, YOU HAVE TO BE. THERE'S NOBODY ELSE.

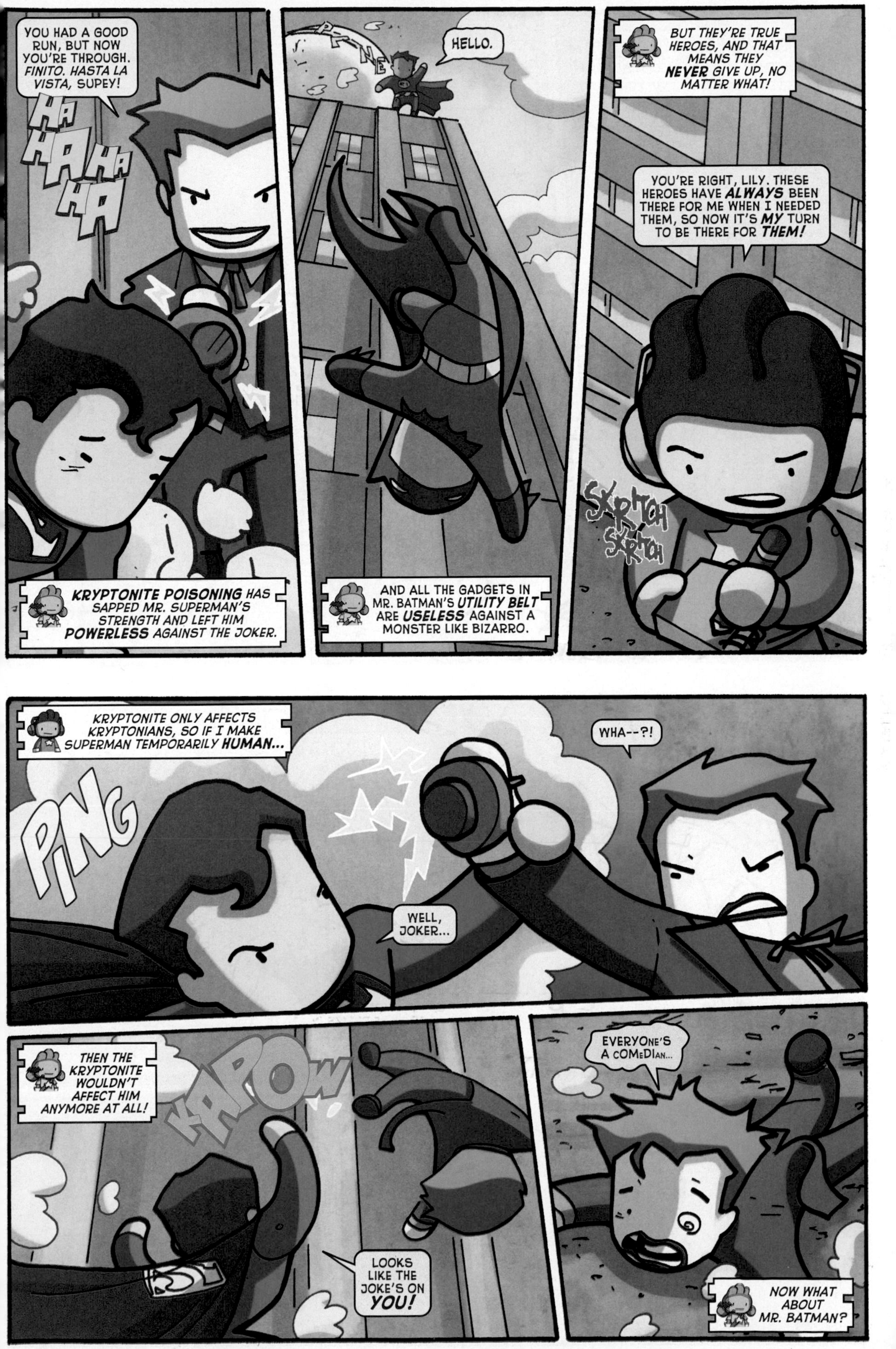
YOU HAD A GOOD RUN, BUT NOW YOU'RE THROUGH. FINITO. HASTA LA VISTA, SUPEY!
HA HA HA HA HA
KRYPTONITE POISONING HAS SAPPED MR. SUPERMAN'S STRENGTH AND LEFT HIM POWERLESS AGAINST THE JOKER.
HELLO.
AND ALL THE GADGETS IN MR. BATMAN'S UTILITY BELT ARE USELESS AGAINST A MONSTER LIKE BIZARRO.
BUT THEY'RE TRUE HEROES, AND THAT MEANS THEY NEVER GIVE UP, NO MATTER WHAT!
YOU'RE RIGHT, LILY. THESE HEROES HAVE ALWAYS BEEN THERE FOR ME WHEN I NEEDED THEM, SO NOW IT'S MY TURN TO BE THERE FOR THEM!
SKRITCH SKRITCH
KRYPTONITE ONLY AFFECTS KRYPTONIANS, SO IF I MAKE SUPERMAN TEMPORARILY HUMAN...
PING
WHA--?!
WELL, JOKER...
THEN THE KRYPTONITE WOULDN'T AFFECT HIM ANYMORE AT ALL!
KAPOW
LOOKS LIKE THE JOKE'S ON YOU!
EVERYONE'S A COMEDIAN...
NOW WHAT ABOUT MR. BATMAN?

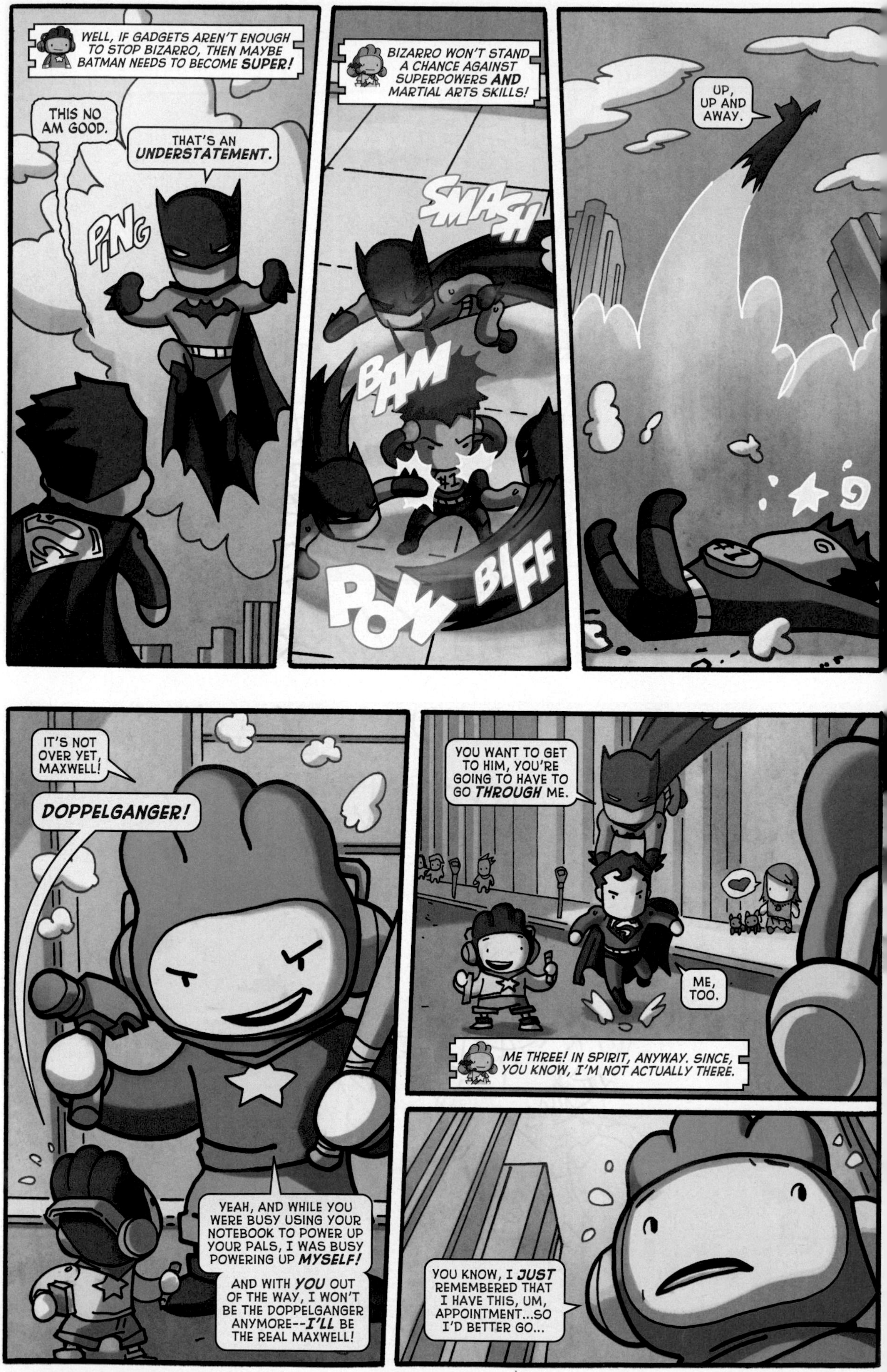
WELL, IF GADGETS AREN'T ENOUGH TO STOP BIZARRO, THEN MAYBE BATMAN NEEDS TO BECOME SUPER!
THIS NO AM GOOD.
THAT'S AN UNDERSTATEMENT.
PING
BIZARRO WON'T STAND A CHANCE AGAINST SUPERPOWERS AND MARTIAL ARTS SKILLS!
SMASH
BAM
POW
BIFF
UP, UP AND AWAY.
IT'S NOT OVER YET, MAXWELL!
DOPPELGANGER!
YEAH, AND WHILE YOU WERE BUSY USING YOUR NOTEBOOK TO POWER UP YOUR PALS, I WAS BUSY POWERING UP MYSELF!
AND WITH YOU OUT OF THE WAY, I WON'T BE THE DOPPELGANGER ANYMORE--I'LL BE THE REAL MAXWELL!
YOU WANT TO GET TO HIM, YOU'RE GOING TO HAVE TO GO THROUGH ME.
ME, TOO.
ME THREE! IN SPIRIT, ANYWAY. SINCE, YOU KNOW, I'M NOT ACTUALLY THERE.
YOU KNOW, I JUST REMEMBERED THAT I HAVE THIS, UM, APPOINTMENT...SO I'D BETTER GO...

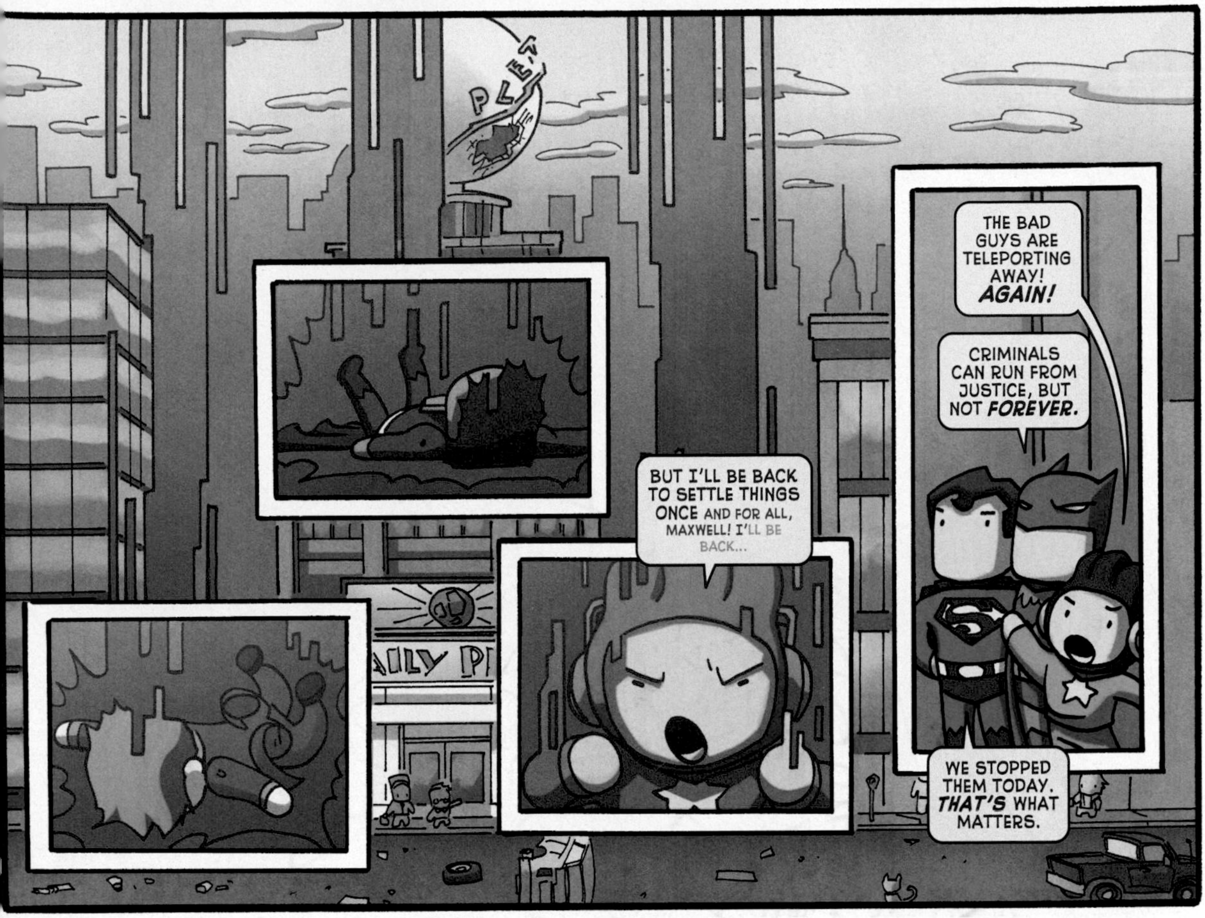
BUT I'LL BE BACK TO SETTLE THINGS ONCE AND FOR ALL, MAXWELL! I'LL BE BACK...
THE BAD GUYS ARE TELEPORTING AWAY! AGAIN!
CRIMINALS CAN RUN FROM JUSTICE, BUT NOT FOREVER.
WE STOPPED THEM TODAY. THAT'S WHAT MATTERS.

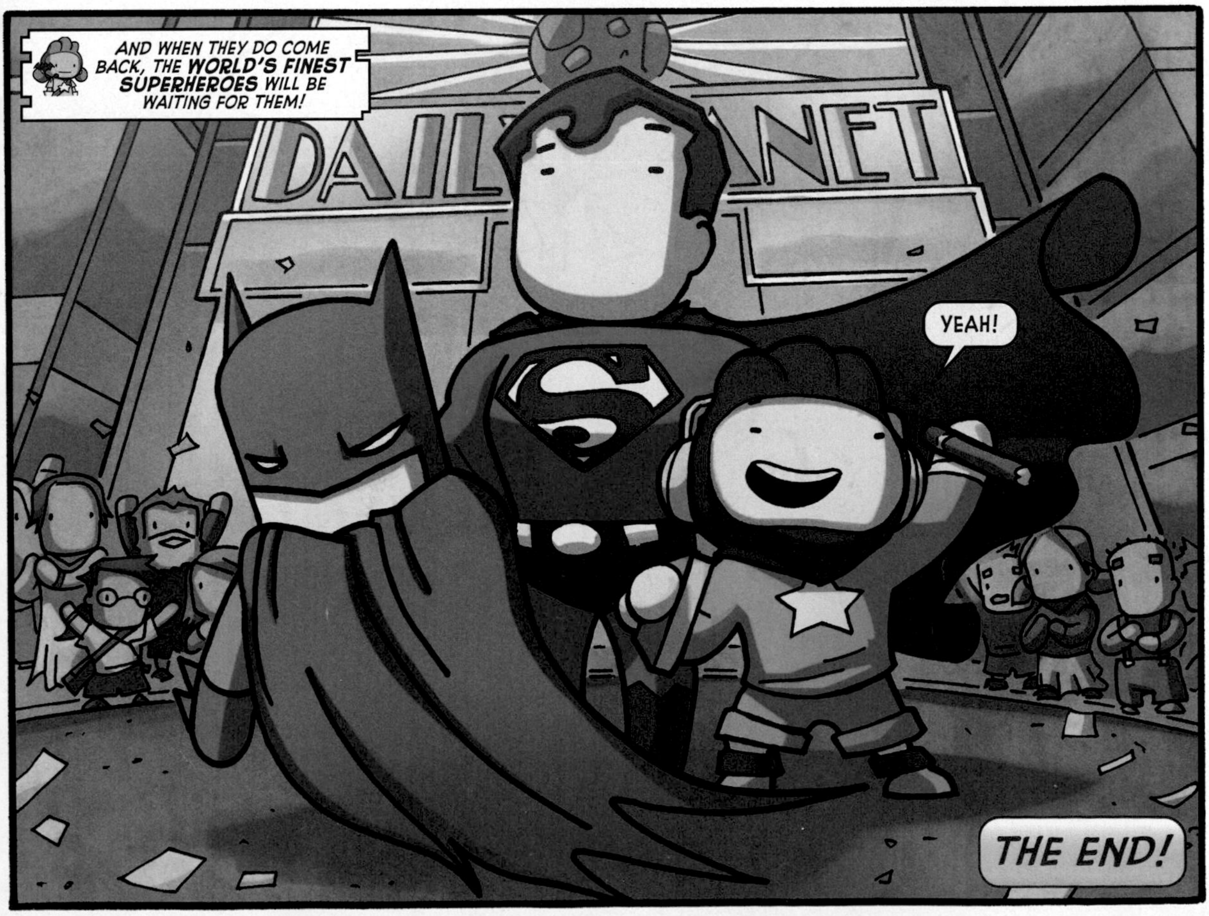
AND WHEN THEY DO COME BACK, THE WORLD'S FINEST SUPERHEROES WILL BE WAITING FOR THEM!
DAILY PLANET
YEAH!
THE END!

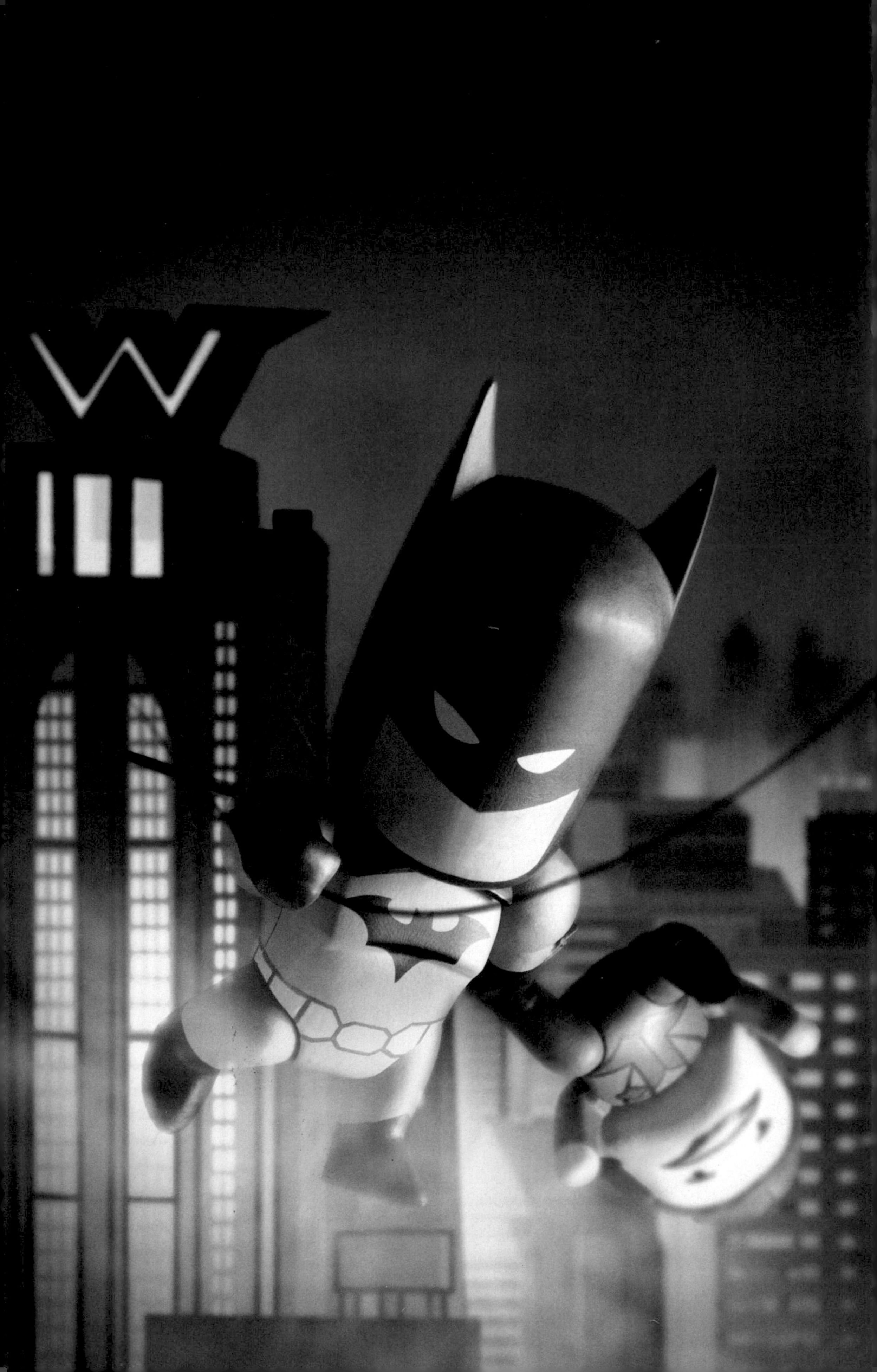

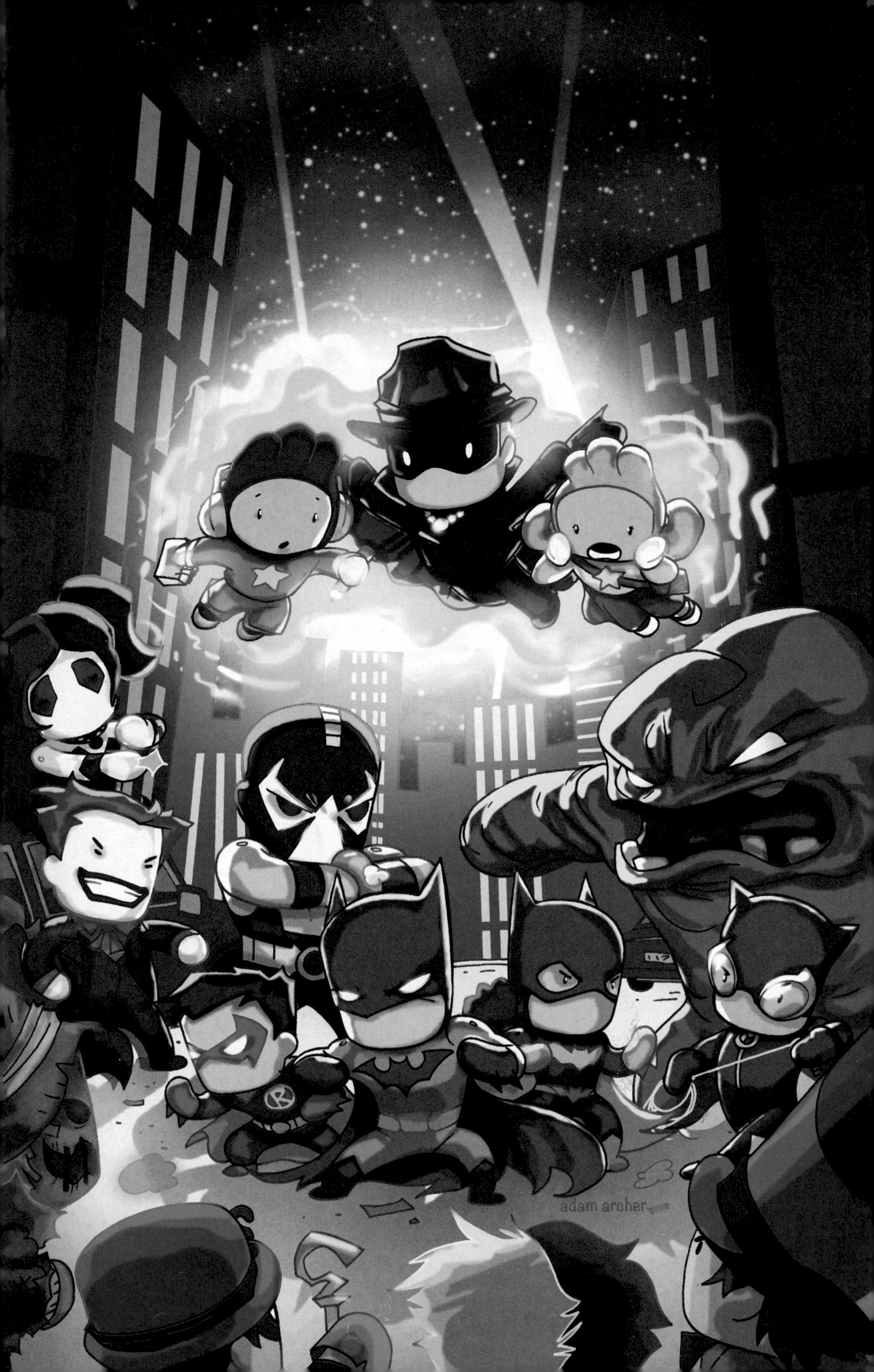
adam archer

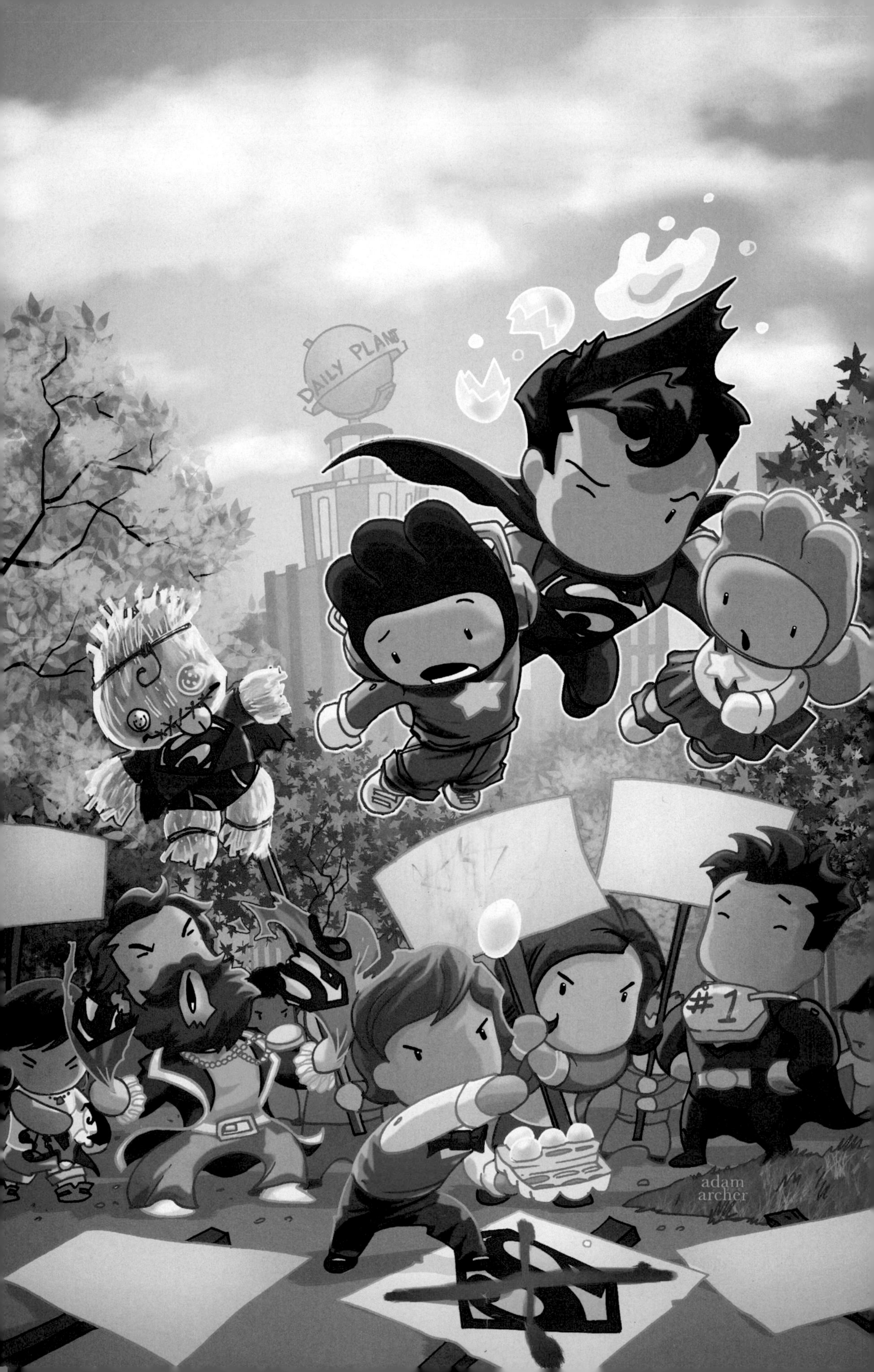
DAILY PLANET
#1
adam archer

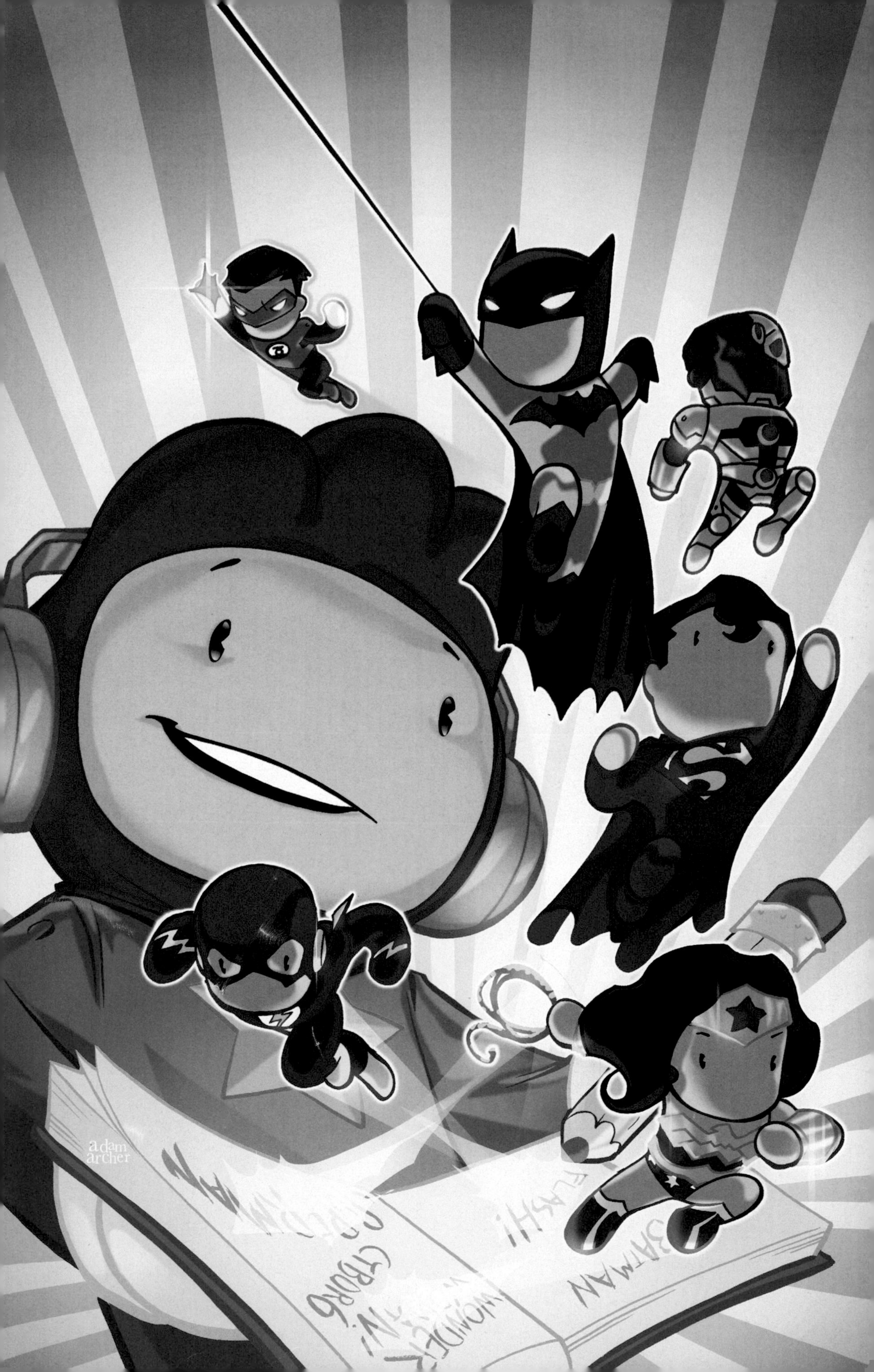
adam archer
BATMAN
FLASH!
CYBORG

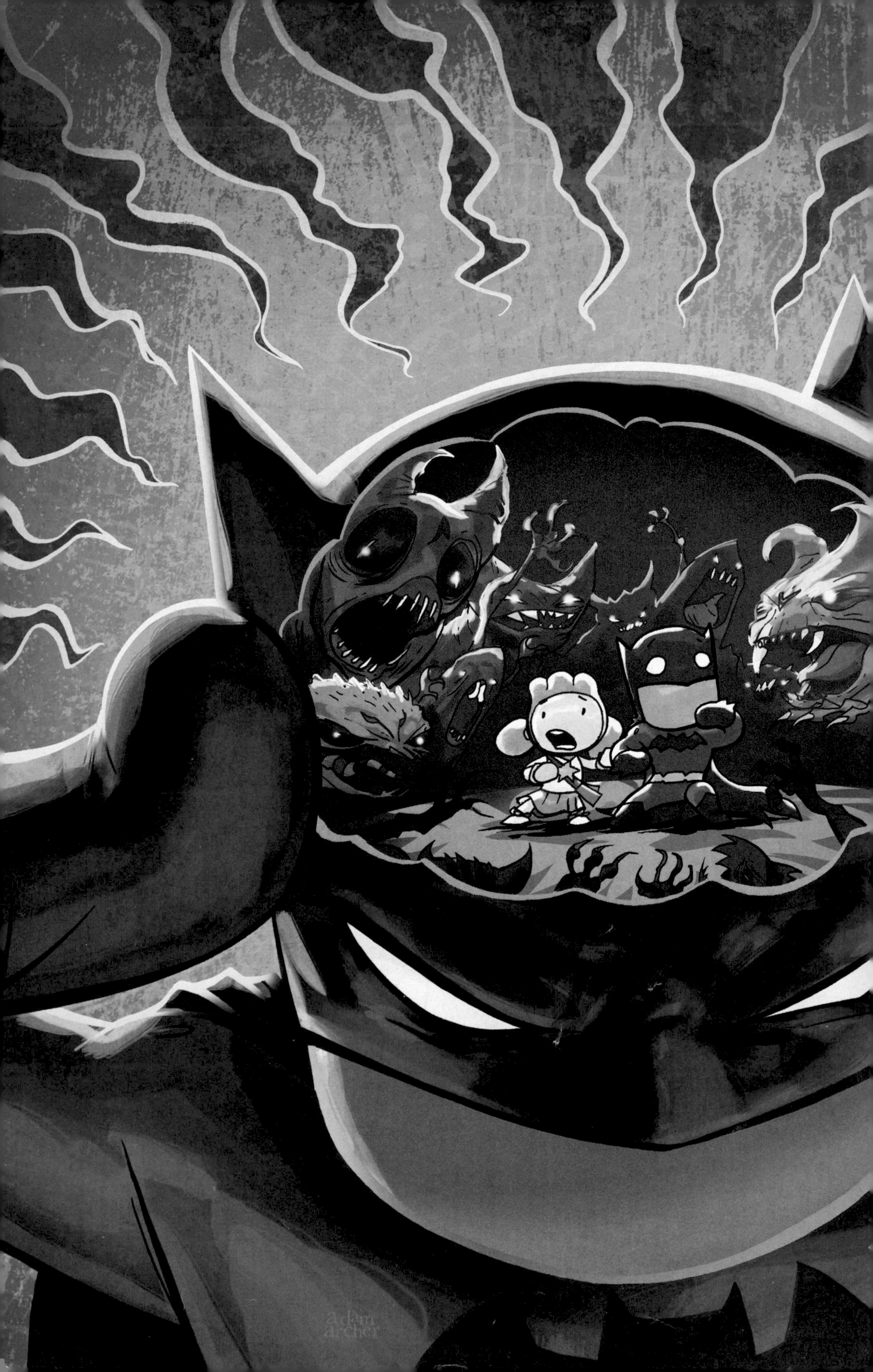
adam archer

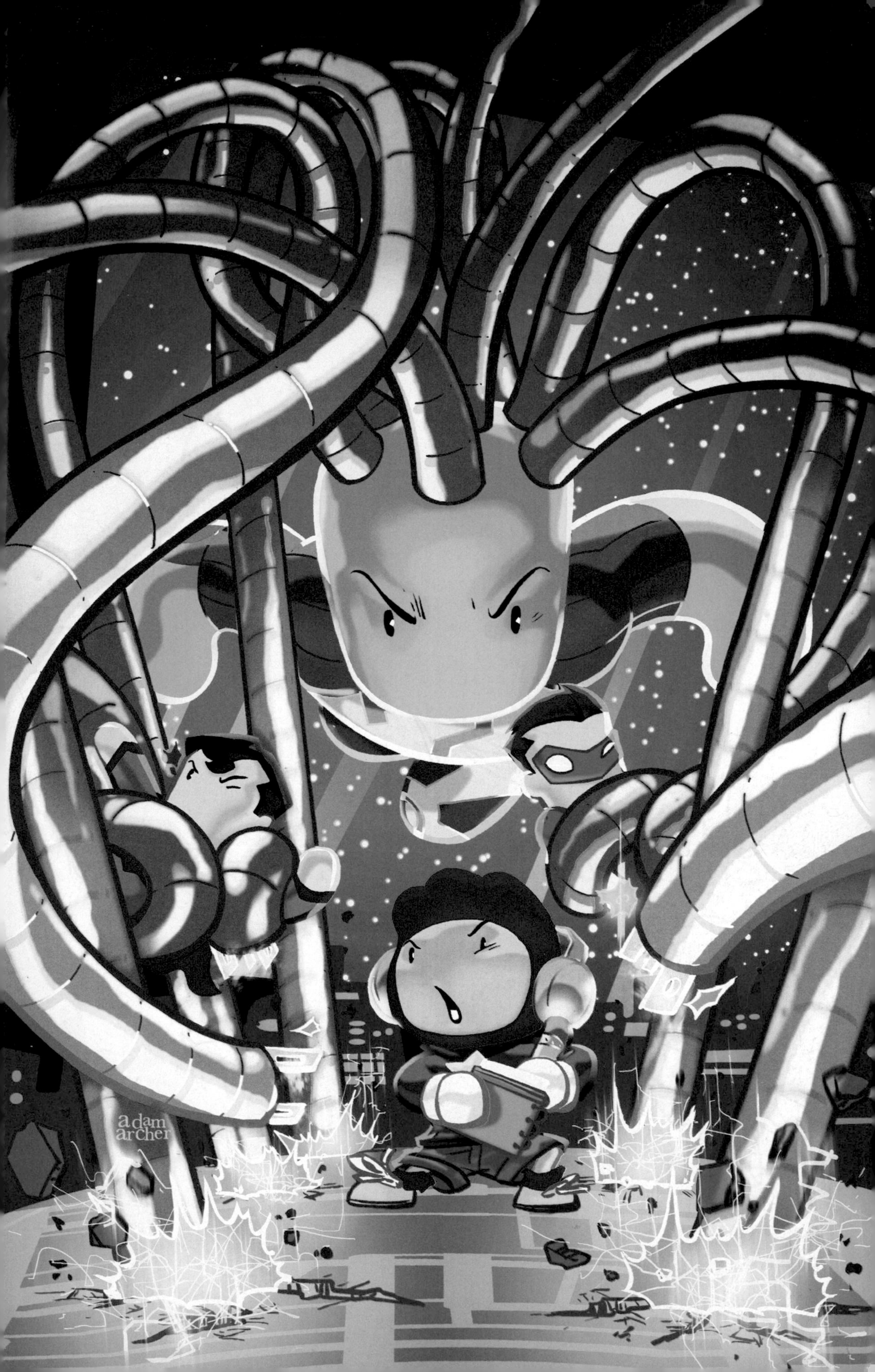
adam
archer

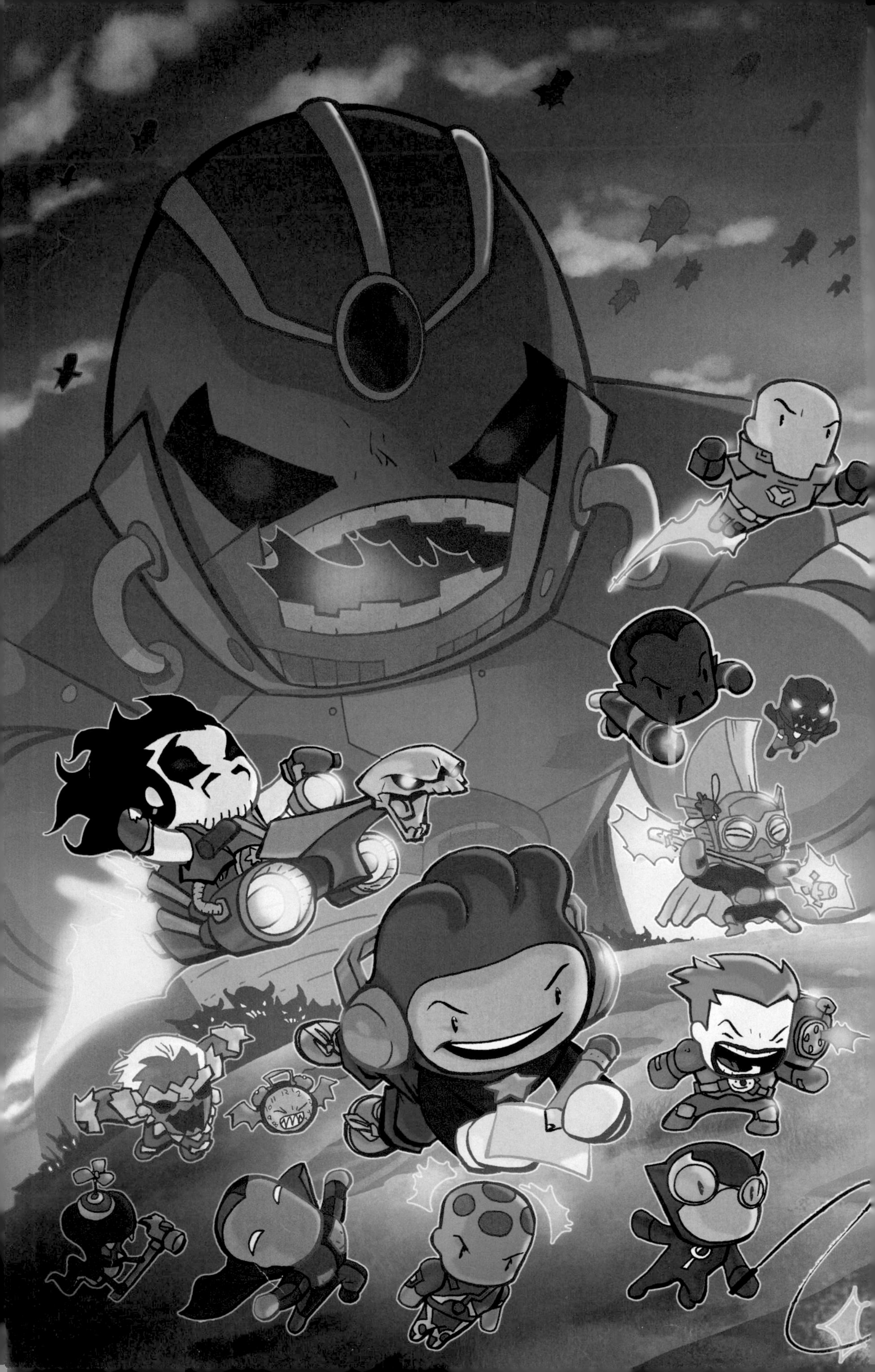

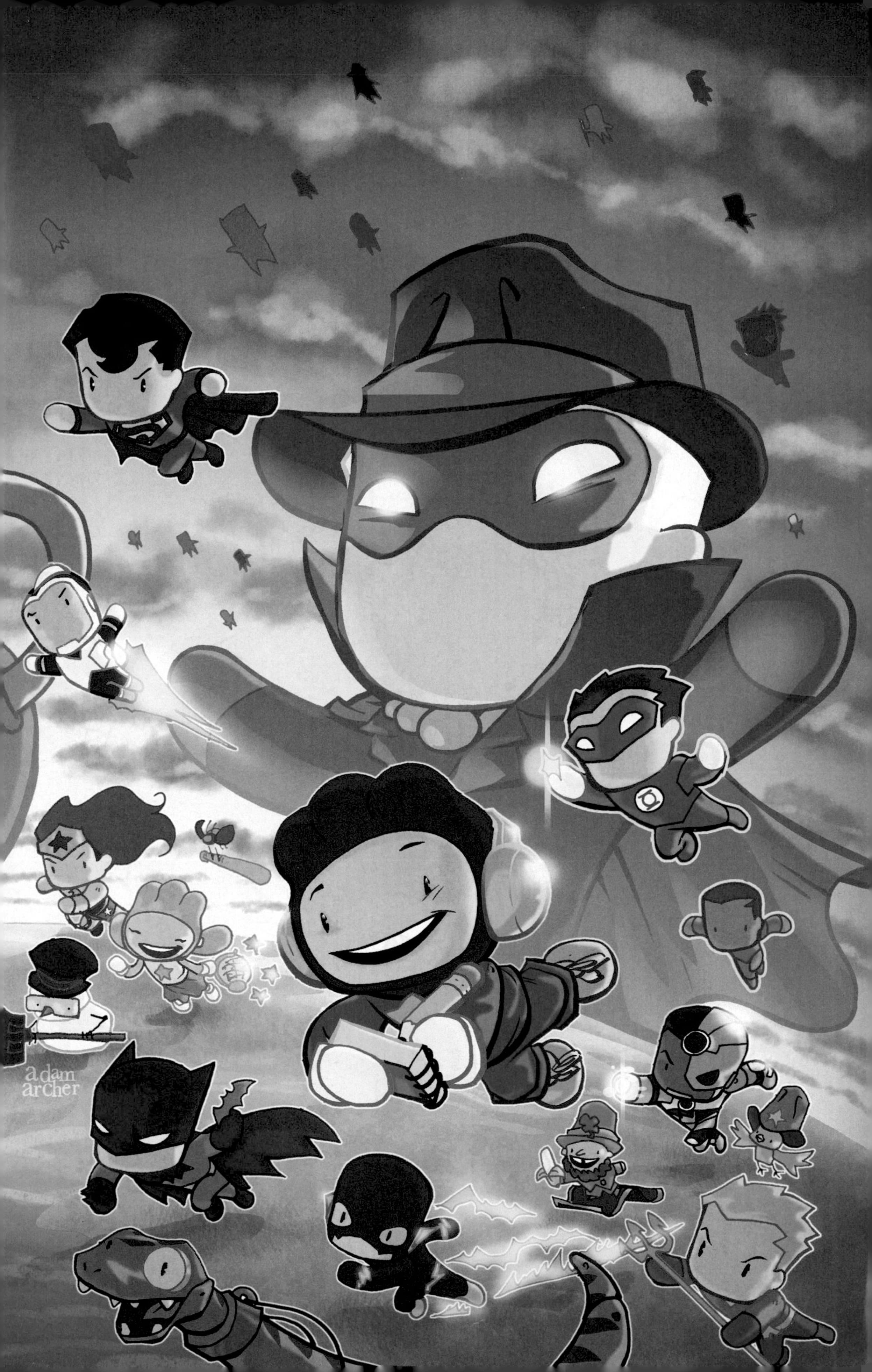
adam
archer

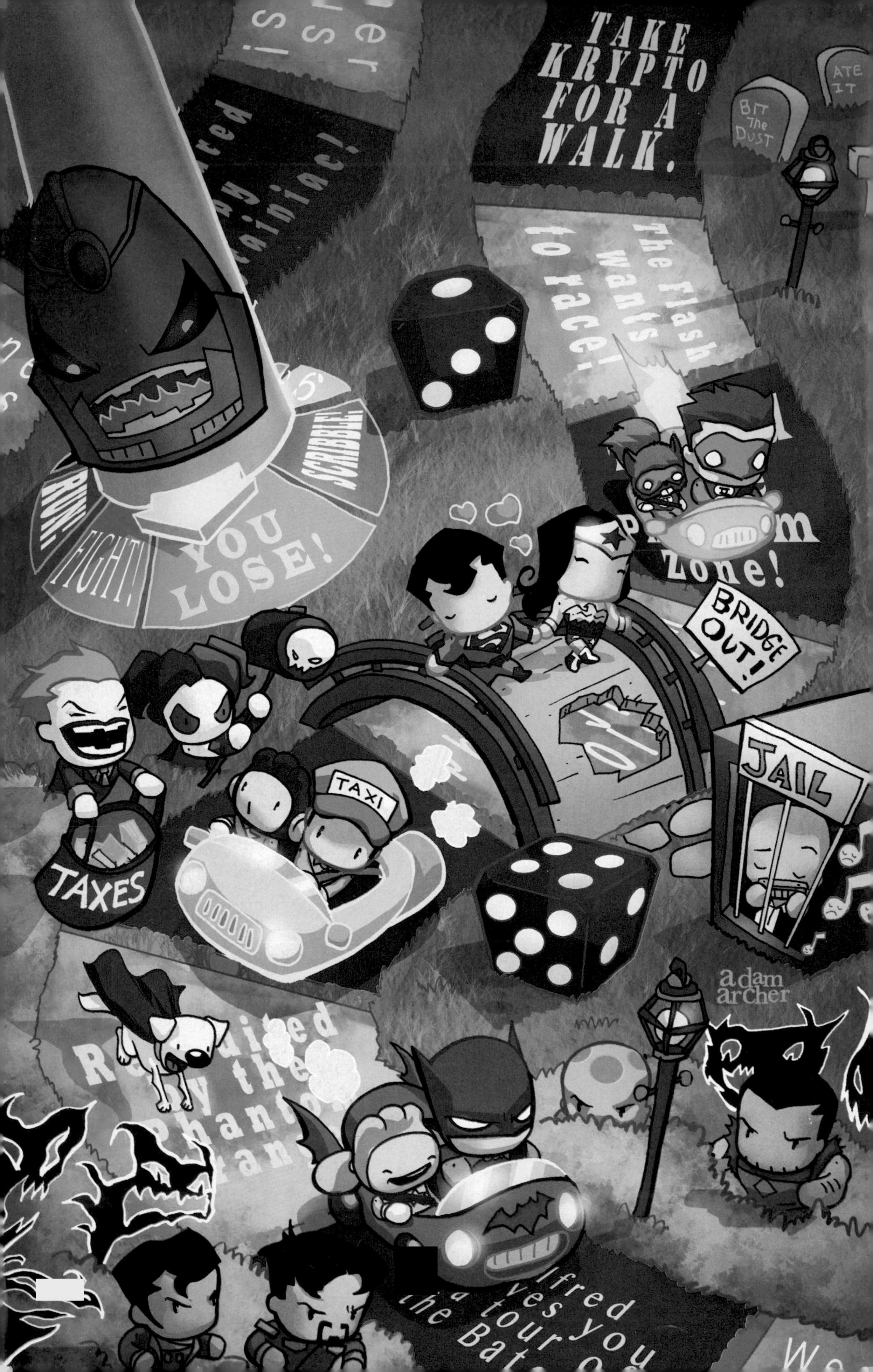
TAKE KRYPTO FOR A WALK.
ATE IT
BIT the DUST
The Flash wants to race!
SCRIBBLE!
RUN!
FIGHT!
YOU LOSE!
BRIDGE OUT!
JAIL
TAXI
TAXES
adam archer